Praise for Pete Hautman's
THE MORTAL NUTS

"Smoothly written by an expert craftsman who's created starkly memorable images that linger long after the last page has been turned. . . . *THE MORTAL NUTS* . . . is strikingly different; it's a nifty, comic thriller that reads as if it were created by Carl Hiaasen on drugs. . . . Hautman . . . makes the funny novel work with great dialogue and a convincing plot."

—Ray Walsh, *Lansing State Journal* (MI)

"You'll laugh aloud at the weird characters Hautman has invented."

—Phyllis Straughan, *West Orange Times* (FL)

"Calling *THE MORTAL NUTS* a crime novel is like dismissing a Mercedes as a passenger car. . . . *THE MORTAL NUTS* is more than a crime story. It's an incisive look at the foibles and vagaries of two generations of working-class Americans. . . . A great read. . . . Hautman has used his unerring eye for detail and ear for dialogue to create characters who will remain in our memories."

—Alan Doyle, *Valley Time* (Pleasanton, CA)

"Carl Hiaasen owns the underbelly of the Florida crime scene; now he has a Minnesota soulmate. The Minneapolis-based Hautman establishes himself as the spokesman for the local criminal wackos in this rollicking tale. . . . A crime-lover's treat."

—*People*

Praise for the Other Novels by Pete Hautman

Drawing Dead

"In this very accomplished first novel, Mr. Hautman keeps the plot moving at an exhilarating pace. The people are unexpected, the dialogue is terrific and the descriptions are laugh-out-loud funny. Bawdy, gritty and unpredictable, *Drawing Dead* is a sparkling debut."

—Tom Nolan, *The Wall Street Journal*

"The year's best American debut was this rambunctious tale of hoodlums, gamblers, con artists, real-estate hustlers, gold-digging bimbos, and crooked stockbrokers."

—*The Atlanta Journal-Constitution*

Short Money

"Exhilarating. . . . By turns funny and soulful and always unpredictable. . . . Hautman's dialogue sparkles, his plot hums, he's got a nicely complex sense of morality and he's a virtuoso when it comes to describing what it feels like to get punched."

"Hautman reminds me most of Carl Hiaasen, the Florida author who combines action, comedy and mystery in outrageous ways."

Books by Pete Hautman

The Mortal Nuts
Short Money
Drawing Dead

Published by POCKET BOOKS

PETE HAUTMAN

THE MORTAL NUTS

POCKET BOOKS

New York   London   Toronto   Sydney   Tokyo   Singapore

POCKET BOOKS, a division of Simon & Schuster Inc.
1230 Avenue of the Americas, New York, NY 10020

Copyright © 1996 by Peter Hautman

ISBN: 978-1-4767-4797-2

First Pocket Books printing October 1997

10 9 8 7 6 5 4 3 2 1

POCKET and colophon are registered trademarks of Simon & Schuster Inc.

Cover design by Tom McKeveny
Cover illustration by Ben Perini

Printed in the U.S.A.

For Tuck

ACKNOWLEDGMENTS

Becky Bohan, Marilyn Bos, Charlie Buckman-Ellis, Andy Hinderlie, Mary Logue, Tom Rucker, George Sorenson and Deborah Woodworth—I thank you for all your help and support over the past six years, and for saying nice things when I read those first tentative chapters more than six years ago. I thank Mike Hildebrand for his linguistic support, and I thank Bill Stesin, "still one of my ten best friends," for telling the tales that made this book possible.

THE
MORTAL
NUTS

CHAPTER

1

"**S**he don't seem so bad, Ax. Get 'er tuned up, maybe a new set of shocks."

"I got a hundred eighty thousand on it. They start to go at a hundred eighty thousand." Axel Speeter gripped the wheel hard, trying to suppress the shimmy that had developed thirty thousand miles before. It was a good truck, but getting old, the way things do. He looked at the speedometer. Fifty miles per, about as fast as he dared go, cars passing him on both sides, people in a hurry.

Sam O'Gara rolled down the passenger window and expelled a wad of Copenhagen. "Hell, Ax, they start to go at a hundred eighty *miles*. That don't mean you got to buy yourself a new truck every Monday morning."

"I had this one ten years. I don't want to have to worry about my truck busting down during the fair."

"You worry too much, Ax. Plus, you don't never listen to me."

Axel Speeter shrugged. He worried just the right amount, he figured, because when it came to the Minnesota State Fair, he couldn't afford to take chances. And he always listened to Sam. They'd been friends going on fifty years.

But that didn't mean he always trusted what he heard. He rested his right hand on the Folgers can on the seat beside him.

Sam said, "What you got in that can?"

Axel ignored the question. "Look, I want to buy a new truck," he said. He drifted into the right lane, pulled off the freeway onto Highway 61. "You going to help me or not?"

"I say I wouldn't help? Hell, I'm riding shotgun, ain't I?" Sam was looking at the coffee can. "You're still a goddamn peasant, ain't cha, Ax?"

"What's that supposed to mean?"

"I don't know anybody's told you, but they got these things called banks now, guaranteed by the government of the United States of America."

Axel clamped his jaw.

Sam muttered, "Goddamn peasant. Prob'ly got it all buried in your backyard."

"I don't have a backyard, Sam. I live in a motel."

"Well, there you go."

Axel thought, There he went where? Sam was always saying stuff that meant nothing and acting like it proved whatever crackpot point he was trying to make.

Axel said, "Goddamn right I do."

Sam looked at him. "Goddamn right you do what?"

They drove for a few blocks, neither man talking.

"I just want to make sure I don't get stuck with a lemon," Axel said.

"You know what they say about lemons."

West End Ford came into view on the right, a block ahead. Axel turned on his signal and started to slow down. "What do they say about lemons?" he asked.

"I don't remember," Sam said. "Something about lemonade."

King Nelson leaned a hip against the immaculate hood of a new Bronco and watched the two old men through the showroom window. The big one was kicking the tires—

2

literally kicking the left front tire of the white '94 F-150. A lot of the old farts did that, kicked the tires. What did they think, that there might not be air in them? That the wheel would fall off? King didn't know what they thought.

King remembered the big one from the day before. The old man had crept into the lot in a beat-up '78, got out, and walked straight to the row of "certified preowned" pickups.

At first, King had thought the old man wasn't serious, just a lonely old dude who had stopped in to waste his time, but after a few minutes the guy . . . what was his name? King scanned his memory. Some part of a car. Dash? Hub? Axle! . . . Axel had zeroed in on the white '94 F-150, a more modern version of the rust-speckled, creaking wreck he'd driven into the lot.

An inch or two taller than King's six one, Axel had veiny, chiseled, deeply tanned forearms and wide, sloped shoulders. He must've been a monster when he was younger, King thought. Axel's eyes were yellow at the corners, with green irises and pupils of slightly different sizes. The top of his head shone smooth pinkish brown, sprinkled with a few dark freckles, framed by two swaths of thick white wavy hair over each ear, which met in a curly little ducktail above the collar of his white short-sleeved shirt. He seemed like a nice enough guy, but kind of slow on the uptake. Yesterday King had thought he'd had the sale wrapped, but then the guy—Axel—had backed off, saying he'd have to have his mechanic check it over.

And here he was, back as promised, with his mechanic— a scrawny old dude in greasy coveralls and a quilted, visorless welder's cap—under the truck now, looking at god-knows-what, while Axel walked around kicking the other three tires and examining nearly invisible chips and dings on the truck body.

King decided to stay inside for a while, let the mechanic finish looking things over. They'd be in a more decisive mood after the sun worked on them for a while.

* * *

"Carmen's going to like it," Axel said.

Sam said, "Say what?"

"I said Carmen's going to like it. She hated that old truck of mine."

Sam wriggled out from under the truck. "Carmen the nudie fountain dancer? Thought you shipped her off someplace."

"I did. She's in Omaha." Axel did not like being reminded of Carmen's naked fountain dance. He wished he'd never told Sam about it. "She's going to medical school," he said.

"You're shittin' me. Carmen wants to be a doctor?"

"Actually, she's studying to be a medical technician. You don't need college for that. It's sort of like being a nurse."

Sam scratched his grizzled jaw. "Huh. She didn't never strike me as the nursey type."

"She's a good kid. Just got in with a bad crowd." Bad company and drugs, that was what had inspired Carmen to strip her clothes off, middle of the day, and dance nude across Loring Park. She'd been arrested, on that particular occasion, while cooling off in the Berger Fountain.

"I'm flying her back to work the fair," Axel said. "She's doing much better now, Sam."

Sam shook his head.

Axel said, "What?"

"I didn't say nothing."

"Good."

"I tell you one thing, though. I wouldn't want her changing *my* bedpan."

King waited until the two of them were standing, looking at the price sticker, arguing, then he left the cool showroom and strode confidently across the hot tarmac. The two men stopped talking and watched his approach. He was ten feet away, still bringing his smile up to full power, getting ready to offer his hand, when the mechanic, all squints and wrinkles and dirty fingernails, jabbed a forefinger at the side of the truck.

"What about these here stripes? He ain't paying extra for no dee-cals."

King stopped and opened his mouth, not sure what to say.

"I like the stripes, Sam," Axel said.

"That don't mean you got to pay for the fuckers."

"Why not? You don't think I can afford stripes on my truck?"

"Only a damn fool pays for looks."

King said, "There's no charge for the stripes."

Both men glared at him as though he had cut in on a private conversation.

"The stripes were there when we took it in on trade," King explained, wishing he'd kept his mouth shut.

Sam crossed his arms and spat, missing King's tasseled loafer by four inches. King took that as a bad omen but not a sale-killer. He started to tell them a few things about the truck, give them the canned sales pitch, directing his best lines at the big one, Axel. Axel listened, rocking back and forth on his heels, pushing out his lips now and then and licking them with a pale tongue. King tried to draw him out a little, asking him how he would use the truck, asking what he did for a living, asking how he liked the weather lately, asking what he thought about those Minnesota Twins.

"What about these here square headlights?" Sam interrupted.

King explained that the new halogen headlamps were brighter, lasted longer, and were more attractive than the old round ones.

Axel said, "I don't like 'em."

King ignored the unanswerable objection. He asked Axel how heavy a payload he would be carrying. Guys liked that word. Payload.

Axel shrugged. "Lots of tortillas," he said.

King said, "Tortillas?"

"That's right," Axel said. "Lots of tortillas. I'm gonna need a topper too."

Sam had climbed into the driver's seat. "Jesus, Ax, you get a load a this radio? I bet you gotta go to school or something to run the fucker."

As Axel looked at the radio, King told him about its automatic search function and ten available station presets, five AM and five FM.

Sam said, "FM? He don't need FM."

"I like the FM," Axel said.

"Since when did you listen to anything except 'CCO?" Sam asked.

"Carmen's going to like it," Axel said. "She hated my radio."

Sam said, "So who the hell you buying this for?"

King smiled weakly, almost wishing this Mutt and Jeff team would just up and go down the street to the Chevy dealer, buy a truck off of those assholes.

"Speedometer says twenty-five nine," Sam said. "How far'd you spin 'er back?"

"Excuse me?" As far as King knew, they hadn't spun an odometer in three years, not since the state attorney general had taken a personal interest in a truck his son was buying.

"I said, 'How far you spin it back?' It's a simple damn question."

"Those are original miles," said King.

"What the hell's that mean, 'original miles'?"

"I mean the odometer is accurate."

"I don't doubt that. What I want to know is, how far'd you spin 'er back?"

"What about this air bag?" Axel asked, reading the embossed letters on the steering wheel. "I don't want the air bag."

King was confused, but happy to be talking about something other than the mileage. "You don't want the air bag?"

Axel said, "How do I know the son-of-a-bitch won't just go off?"

"Go off?"

"I'm driving down the highway and the son-of-a-bitch just goes off."

"That won't happen," said King.

Sam had his head down under the dash. "My best guess is, the way these pedals are worn, she's got better'n fifty thou on 'er."

Axel said, "For cryin' out loud, Sam, the man says the mileage is what the mileage says it is."

"You don't want to know what I think, why'd you bring me?"

Axel grunted. "Good question."

King could feel himself starting to lose it. It was hot as hell out there. The sun felt like an iron on the yoke of his peach-colored shirt, which was turning dark around the armpits. It wasn't healthy, this work, walking from an air-conditioned showroom out into the heat, back and forth. That was why so many car salesmen had heart attacks. The two old men, who didn't seem to mind the heat, were both examining the steering wheel again.

Axel said, "What do you think, Sam?"

Sam shook his head. "Air bag ain't a bad thing to have, Ax. You run into something, you might like it."

"Yeah, and it might blow up right in my face, never know what hit me."

Sam muttered something, scratching his beard.

"What's that?" Axel asked.

"Nothing," Sam said. "Wouldn't make no difference what I said."

"Fine. So what do you think? Think you can monkey-wrench it?"

"Shit, Ax, I could monkey-wrench a gorilla."

Axel turned back to King. "You mind we take it for a spin?"

King took a deep breath, dredged up a smile, pasted it on his face, and handed Axel the keys. Ignoring his own best instincts in favor of company policy, he said, "I'll have to ride along, of course."

Sam snatched the keys and hopped into the cab. "C'mon, then. Let's have us a look at what this fucker can do."

A few minutes later, King felt his facial tic start up again. It had been months since it had bothered him, but Sam had coaxed it out. The old bastard must have kept a whole army of guardian angels busy to have lived so long. His idea of a test drive was taking it up to seventy-five on a residential street, then locking up the brakes, leaving about five dollars' worth of rubber on the tarmac.

"Brakes seem good," he commented. And that was only one of Sam's several "diagnostic tests." When they finally bounced over the curb back into the lot, missing the driveway by six feet, King had to excuse himself, go to the rest room, and sit down on the toilet for three minutes of deep-breathing exercises. It hadn't helped. His cheek was twitching every four seconds.

His only consolation was a feeling of gratitude at having survived. Axel seemed to have been equally shaken up by Sam's driving. When he rejoined the pair outside, they were heatedly arguing the truck's price. He might as well have been invisible, for all the attention they paid him.

"Wouldn't go a dime over twelve," Sam was saying.

The sticker price on the F-150 was $14,975—not a bad price, King thought, unless you considered the test drive the vehicle had just endured. That and the fact that Sam was probably right about the odometer reading. They didn't spin odometers at the dealership anymore. They mostly bought the vehicles pre-spun.

Axel shook his head. "Too low. There's no way they'd even consider that," he said.

True, King thought, happy to have Axel arguing his case.

"How about fourteen even?" King said to Sam.

Sam growled, ignoring him. "Goddamn it, Ax, even with the topper she ain't worth more'n thirteen."

"Sam, you told me it was solid."

King decided he'd do best by keeping his mouth shut. He found himself staring at the tattoo high on Axel's right wrist. A faded blue blotch. He couldn't tell what it was intended to represent.

"It's solid, but I sure as hell wouldn't go fourteen."

"You think it's worth thirteen?"

"They throw in a topper, maybe."

King Nelson's head was swinging back and forth, trying to follow the negotiation.

Axel said, "With the topper I'd definitely go thirteen five."

Sam crossed his arms. "Pay what you want for the fucker. See if I give a damn. You don't never listen to me anyways. You know I'm always right."

Axel shrugged. There was right, and there was right. He rolled his wide shoulders, then turned a yellow grin on King. "I'll pay you thirteen five, including the topper. And I'll need to pick it up tomorrow."

King closed his eyes and inhaled slowly through his nose, the way his doctor had recommended. It didn't help. His cheek was jumping like a bug on a griddle.

"Why don't we step inside," he said. "Get out of this sun, see what we can work out."

The figure they arrived at, nearly half an hour later, was $13,590. King knew he was going to get reamed by the boss on this one—the truck should have gone for at least fourteen. The difference would come straight out of his commission. He'd have to invent some story. Tell the boss he was matching an offer from one of the other Ford dealers. Or it was for his girlfriend's father. Something like that. Or maybe he'd just quit, get back into telemarketing vinyl siding. At least in that business he hadn't had to actually look at his customers. He focused on the sales contract, transcribing numbers and filling in the blanks, doing what he had to do to get the pair on their way. Axel had excused himself. King assumed he'd gone out to his truck to get his checkbook, but when he returned he was carrying a Folgers coffee can, the two-pound size.

"So you happy now?" Sam asked, firing up a Pall Mall. Axel nodded. "I think we got a good deal," he said.

"Coulda got better."

"Maybe, maybe not. I think we did good." Axel pulled out onto Highway 61, brought the old truck slowly up to forty-five. He was looking forward to driving the new one. The salesman had promised to have it ready, complete with topper, first thing in the morning.

"You're a goddamn peasant, Ax. I ever tell you that?"

"Not in twenty minutes, at least."

"You really gonna bring that Carmen gal back for the fair?"

"Sure. She's worked for me five years now. The fair is my life. I've got to have good help. Besides, she hasn't seen Sophie since Christmas."

"Thought those two didn't get along."

"They'll do okay. You know how it is, mothers and daughters. Like I said, Carmen's changed, she's matured. She'll get along with her mom just fine. She's not this wild kid anymore."

Sam rolled his eyes and expelled a cloud of brown smoke, filling the cab. "I ain't sayin' nothing."

CHAPTER

2

James Dean found her up on the balcony, sitting at one of the tiny, bolted-down tables, staring through the railing at the undulating mosh pit below, hundreds of bodies bouncing and writhing to the music. It was only ten-thirty, but the band—four guitars, an electric banjo, and a drummer—had the pit rocking to a punk salsa version of "Proud Mary." Dean stopped a few yards away, watching Carmen watch the dancers, watching her keep the beat by tapping a red polished nail on the stem of her margarita goblet. Her other hand, hanging over the railing, held a forgotten cigarette, nearly half of it turned to ash. Carmen's face looked slack and stupid, from which Dean inferred that she had been waiting for him for some time. At least three margaritas, he guessed. He smiled, running a hand over the top of his shaven head, enjoying the way the fresh stubble massaged his palm.

Carmen, by contrast, had lots of hair. Long and thick, waves that were not quite curls, black under the club lights but auburn in the sun. Dean had once told her she looked like a shampoo commercial. "I look like a *commercial?*" she'd said, rolling her chocolate eyes. Tonight she had on a

1 1

sleeveless top, some kind of thin, shiny black fabric with a lace inset above her breasts. Dean wondered whether she was wearing a bra. Sometimes she did, and sometimes she didn't. One sticky, humid afternoon he had actually seen her, at an outdoor concert, remove her bra without taking off her shirt.

Dean had never had much luck with women. Perhaps it was because he was a little strange-looking, or perhaps it was because all women were fucking gold-digging bitches. But Carmen Roman was different. Carmen liked him straight out. And tonight Dean was at his best. Two thin rings pierced his left eyebrow, hanging down so that he could see the lights glinting from the polished gold. He had on his new riding jacket, the plastic antitheft strip still anchored to the left sleeve, his thin, muscular torso naked beneath the black leather. He stepped up to the table and sat down across from her.

Carmen did not look at him. "People are animals," she said, speaking as though they had been sitting together for hours.

Dean pushed his head forward. "People are what?"

Carmen laughed as if she had been told a joke. She dragged the frosted goblet toward her mouth and leaned over it, pressing her breasts against the edge of the table, a few strands of her dark hair settling atop the crushed ice. She pursed her full lips around the thin plastic straw, wrinkled her brow, and sucked.

The mangled edition of "Proud Mary" thumped to an end; the band immediately launched into something that may once have been "Summertime Blues." Dean hunched his shoulders against the sound. He asked her again, "People are what?"

Carmen looked up from her drink, the straw still in her mouth.

"Animals," she said, letting the straw fall back into the drink. "Axel says people are animals." Carmen always found James Dean a bit startling to behold. In her head, when she thought about him and he wasn't around, she saw a black leather jacket, a shaven head, a couple of rings in his brow, and a sort of blank, ordinary face. But each time she actually *saw* him, it surprised her. Dean's head was small and well-shaped, but he had somehow got the wrong set of features. His oversize root-beer-colored eyes were the first thing that hit her, then his skin tone, a yellowish sand color. And then—she always had the same thought—where did his nose go? It was there, of course, but you had to look for it. It was almost like a baby's nose. If people were animals, she thought, James Dean would be a bald monkey. Or a hairless Pekingese.

He was blinking those doggy eyes at her right now, like he needed a treat. Carmen pushed her hair back over her shoulder. She said, "Axel's got this thing about animals. I ever tell you he's got a tattoo of a kangaroo on his arm?" She tipped her head to the side and watched blue smoke curling from the end of her cigarette. The ash had fallen off at some point, probably onto one of the moshers below. Carmen closed one eye and moved the cigarette back and forth, making zees. "He eats ketchup on everything. You ever see a guy put ketchup on a taco? Christ, I can't believe I'm going back to do the fair."

"So don't go."

"I need the money." She took a final drag on her cigarette, stabbed it into the ashtray.

"How much do you make?"

"A couple of thousand, maybe." Her mouth opened in a silent, smoky laugh. "Maybe more."

"He's paying for your school and stuff, right?"

Carmen frowned. "I'm not doing so good at school. I don't think I want to be a med tech." She reached a forefinger into her wrinkled pack of Marlboros and placed the last bent cigarette between her lips. She fumbled with her disposable lighter, turned it right side up, lit her cigarette. "Axel's gonna have a cow. Christ. What's he expect from me? It's not like he's so perfect. He's the one that lives in a Motel 6."

"Was that true, what you were telling me about him? The other night?"

"What's that?"

"About him keeping all his money in coffee cans. At the Motel 6."

Carmen drew back, squinting at him. "I told you that?"

"You said he keeps it in Folgers cans. You were pretty wasted."

Carmen regarded him for a moment, watched his nose come in and out of focus. "I think I'm a little wasted now," she said. "Speaking of which, did you bring it?"

Dean reached into his jacket and produced an amber prescription bottle. Carmen's features twitched into life. She took the bottle, held it to her ear, and shook it.

"How many?" she asked.

"About forty," Dean said. He hadn't counted, he'd just grabbed the bottle and taken off. Mickey would be pissed, but he'd just have to deal with it. Life is so ironic, he thought. He could walk down the block anytime and come back with weed, crack, dust, you name it, but try to find a few Valium, one of the most commonly prescribed drugs in the country, and he ends up having to steal it from his own sister.

Carmen said, "Thanks, Dean. You know, it's really hard to score here in Omaha."

"You just have to know the right people," Dean said.

CHAPTER

3

Sophie Roman watched Axel Speeter order the chicken-fried steak again, after all she had told him, never mind the cholesterol, the saturated fat, the calories. Axel folded the menu and pushed it away. The waitress, a blue-eyed blond girl with an outstate smile, asked him what dressing he wanted on his salad.

"Honey," he said, grinning, "I don't need no rabbit food. You just bring me that steak and a Co-Cola."

The waitress returned his smile and wrote carefully on her pad. She looked at Sophie, who was glaring at Axel. Sophie closed her menu and handed it to the waitress. "I'll have the spinach salad. And a glass of white zinfandel."

The waitress marked her pad, beamed again at Axel, and started toward the kitchen.

Axel swiveled his head to watch her walk away, then turned back, to find Sophie giving him her pinched, bloodless look.

"You are so crude," she hissed. "This is a nice place. You don't call people 'Honey' and call their salad 'rabbit food.' You don't have to go around acting all the time like a dirty old man."

1 5

Startled, Axel pushed back into the padded red vinyl. What was going on here? First Sam calling him a peasant, then Sophie telling him he was a dirty old man.

"Don't you know how to act?" Sophie continued. "Don't you care what people think about you?"

"Sophie . . ." Axel looked puzzled. "What are you talking about? That little girl likes me just fine. Besides, I am what I am."

"Calling their salad 'rabbit food.' Looking at her that way. Like you got no class. Like some dirty old man. And you should eat your salad anyway, what with your heart and all."

"Look, I got to be a dirty old man eating food I like. Tonight I like chicken-fried steak." Axel grinned.

Sophie tried to hold on to her frown. God, what a picture he made, she thought. He was wearing his usual uniform: white short-sleeved shirt, black trousers, and black suspenders. His green eyes glittered in his big red face. She tried to keep her face rigid, but Axel wouldn't stop smiling. He knew he could get her with that smile. Sophie's cheeks loosened; she gave a short laugh and looked away.

The waitress delivered their drinks and a bottle of Hunt's ketchup. Axel winked at her. The waitress smiled back.

Sophie said, "What did you just do?"

"Not a thing."

"You winked at her, didn't you? Goddamn it, Axel, that's really low-class."

Axel shrugged and sipped his Coke, avoiding Sophie's eyes. Sometimes she reminded him of her daughter, Carmen, even resembled her a little if you looked past the bleached hair, the layers of makeup, and the harsh lines framing her mouth. It wasn't something he cared to dwell upon.

"Have you talked to Carmen?" Sophie asked, as if plucking the thought from his mind.

"She's flying in tomorrow. I booked a room for her."

"You'd think she'd want to stay with her mother." Sophie lifted her wineglass by the stem, keeping her little finger well away from the others, and took a long swallow. "It would save money. Pay me the money instead of the Motel 6." She drank again from her wineglass, beginning with a delicate sip, then tipped the glass all the way, draining it.

Axel said, "Well, you know Carmen—she needs her space. It was hard enough getting her to stay at the Motel 6. She wanted me to put her up at the Holiday Inn."

Sophie shook her head, twisting the stem of the now empty wineglass between her fingers. At least Carmen had some taste; she'd taught her that much. She flagged down a passing waitress, a harried-looking woman carrying four loaded plates on her arms. "Excuse me—do you think I could get another glass of wine?"

"I'll get your waitress."

"Do you think you could just get me another glass of wine please?"

How was she supposed to keep track of who was her waitress? She had enough problems keeping track of her daughter. The waitress paused, about to say something, then shrugged and walked off to deliver her orders. Looking across the dining room in the other direction, Axel waved his hand, then pointed down at Sophie's wineglass. Fifteen seconds later, the young blond waitress appeared with a glass of wine, set it quickly at Sophie's elbow, and smiled at Axel. Sophie glared at her as she walked away.

"They'd never make it at the Taco Shop," she said.

"Who?"

"These waitresses. They have an attitude problem."

"They have a tough job."

"Why do you think Carmen won't stay with me?"

"Says your trailer's too small."

"It's a mobile home, and it's not so small."

"She's going to be spending twelve days working with you at the fair."

1 7

"Working *for* me," Sophie said. It was an important distinction. This year, Axel had made Sophie the manager of Axel's Taco Shop. This year she would be in charge.

"That's right," Axel said. "But you still have to spend twelve days working with her."

Sophie frowned and sipped at her wine. Axel had a point. Twelve days at the fair was like twelve months in the real world. The fair produced a sensory overload that stretched time to the breaking point. Twelve days serving tacos with Carmen would be more than enough.

"She's coming in tomorrow?"

"I'm picking her up tomorrow. In my new truck."

"You got a new truck?"

"I'm picking it up tomorrow."

Sophie nodded. Since Axel seemed to be in a spending mood, buying a new truck and all, this might be as good a time as any to talk condiments. She plucked a sugar packet from the bowl on the table and waggled it under his nose. "You know these little sugar and salt things?"

"Yeah?"

"Do you think you could buy them from me instead of Restaurant Supply?"

Axel's eyes narrowed. "Why?"

"I mean, if I had a bunch of condiments, would you buy them from me?"

Axel sighed. He wasn't sure what this was about, but somehow he knew it was going to cost him money.

Sophie wanted to go straight home after dinner, and that was okay with Axel. She'd been sniping at him all night. He knew it was out of nervousness. Making her the manager, maybe that had been a mistake. It had seemed like a good idea a few months ago, but now, with Carmen coming back, maybe it wasn't so good after all. He wasn't sure how Carmen would take to working under Sophie.

He dropped Sophie off at her mobile home in Landfall and got a perfunctory kiss on the cheek by way of thanks.

Axel waited for her to let herself in and turn the light on, then guided the truck out of Landfall.

At 11:45 P.M., the state fairgrounds were dark and mostly silent. Axel drove in on Dan Patch Avenue, rolled the empty streets. Lights showed in a few of the buildings, and he heard the occasional buzz of a power saw, the pounding of a hammer. Axel turned off his headlights and let his truck chug along at an idle, feeling his way around the familiar grounds. He could almost hear the crowd, smell the smells. He drove up Cooper Street to Machinery Hill, circled the silos and pole barns and tractors, then zigzagged down toward the midway. The big rides were already in place, but most of the setup would take place in a frenzied but orderly burst of activity tomorrow, the day before the fair opened. Some fairgoers, mostly the kids, thought of the midway as the heart of the fair, but Axel knew better. The midway was nothing more than a bright pimple on the west end of the fairgrounds, a lure for young people. The true heart of the fair was the livestock. Axel drove past the Swine Barn, the Cattle Barn, and the Horse Barn, each of which covered an entire block. He drove up Judson Avenue, between the Poultry Building and the Coliseum, a building shaped like a gargantuan concrete Quonset hut. These were the edifices around which the fair had erupted. Without the animals, the Minnesota State Fair would be an out-of-control street party, a beast without a soul. For half an hour, Axel slowly idled his truck around the fairgrounds, sometimes seeing what was there, sometimes seeing bits and pieces of the past thirty years. Axel ran food concessions at dozens of county fairs and special events, but none of them even came close to the Minnesota State Fair, the cornerstone of his business and of his life.

Finally, he stopped his truck on Underwood Street, at the base of the mall. White picnic tables and benches were scattered at random angles over the grassy, football-field-size expanse. Axel let his eyes rest on a small white building. Even in the dark he could read the freshly painted sign:

AXEL'S TACO SHOP. A smooth, peaceful feeling settled in his gut. Everything would be okay. He and Carmen and Sophie and the rest of the help would settle into a rhythm. His new product, the Bueno Burrito, would be a huge hit.

This would be a great fair. For the moment, he was as sure of that as he was that the gates would open, that the crowds would come, that people had to eat.

CHAPTER

4

—

"**H**ow come you want me to go?" Dean said. He was lying naked atop the rumpled bedding, watching her step into her panties, white ones printed with little pink bows, feeding his eyes on her smooth thighs, her crisp tan lines, and those incredible tits, each two-tone hemisphere bearing a dark, inviting nipple. Her body could not be better, he thought. At age twenty-one, she had achieved perfection.

"I don't want you to go. But I got to go, and you don't live here." Carmen wriggled into a pair of jeans, then sat down on the edge of the bed. Dean sat up and wrapped himself around her, grabbing one breast in each hand.

Carmen broke free and stood up. "My head hurts, James Dean."

"Call me just Dean, okay?" He liked his name, James Dean, the only thing his mother had given him that he liked, but it bugged him when people called him by it. It was like they were calling him James Dean but they were meaning somebody else.

Carmen said, "Okay. My head hurts, Just Dean. Look, I got all this stuff to do. I got to go to the laundry, and then I got to go to the institute, 'cause I'm gonna be gone for two weeks. I might be able to get them to let me do Anatomy over again or something, you know? I'll tell them I've been sick, or my mom died or something. Was I drinking margaritas last night?"

"You said you hated it, going to school."

"I do hate it. But Axel will be really pissed if I flunk out." Carmen pulled a pink-and-white Reebok onto one foot, tied it. "I hate the fair too, but I've got to work it. I'm not like you. I've got responsibilities."

"To who? A guy lives in a motel and keeps his money in coffee cans?"

"Axel's done a lot for me."

"What? He sends you to school and you hate it. He pays you a lousy two thousand bucks to work your butt off for two weeks. What's that? I thought you said this guy was rich. If he's so rich, how come he doesn't pay you more? For that matter, how come you don't just grab one of those coffee cans?"

Carmen stared at her feet. Dean was not that smart of a guy, but sometimes he took the words right out of her head. She'd been thinking a lot about Axel's coffee cans lately.

"You scared of him?"

"Axel?" She thought for a moment. "He's an old man." She put on the other Reebok, stood up, found her cigarettes on the floor, lit one.

"So maybe I oughta go with you."

Carmen did a double take, expelling an involuntary smoke ring. "You wouldn't like it." The idea of Dean coming to Minnesota struck her as bizarre. Dean was a separate thing, an Omaha thing. He had nothing to do with Axel, nothing to do with the state fair.

Dean said, "We could borrow a couple of coffee cans and head down to Puerto Penasco."

"Head where?"

"Puerto Penasco. It's in Mexico, down on the California gulf. I met a guy once lived down there. He said there were a lot of cool people down there, Americans, and you could get a villa with a cook and everything for a couple hundred bucks a month. If you have money, you can get anything down there."

"Anything? Like what?" she asked.

"Anything. And they don't have any AIDS. It hasn't gotten down there yet."

That sounded a little fishy to Carmen, who after all had not slept through *all* her classes. But the concept of being a rich gringo in Mexico did have appeal. The only problem was, first, Axel would not easily let go of his money, and, second, she would be with Dean. She liked him okay for this and that, but she didn't see him as a full-time gig.

"Look, I gotta get going, okay?" She pulled an orange Bugs Bunny T-shirt over her head; somehow got it past the cigarette in her mouth and over her ample breasts.

"So you saying you want me to leave?"

Carmen sighed. "Look. I got to go out. I got to go get some aspirin or something. My head hurts. I got to go to school, okay? I got to go to the laundry. You can stay here if you want. I don't give a shit. Okay?"

Dean sat up, swung his legs over the edge of the bed, saw himself in the mirror. He liked his body. It was thin, and not very tall, but he loved the way his muscles moved under his skin. Dean stood, watching his abs ripple. He picked up his jeans. "That's okay. I got to go anyways. I got things to do too."

Carmen scratched under her T-shirt as she watched him dress. "You shave your head every day?"

"Depends." He zipped his jeans. "Some days I just like to let it grow."

She let her shoulders drop, relaxing now, regarding him with the same regret and relief she might bestow upon an empty bottle. "You want to know something? If you let your hair grow out? You still wouldn't look like James Dean."

Forty-five minutes before her flight was due to leave from Gate 34 at the Omaha airport, Carmen tasted her Rob Roy and smiled at the nurse in the mirror. She liked what she saw. She sipped the Rob Roy again. Strange, but not bad. It had seemed like the sort of thing a nurse might order. Maybe next time she'd try a White Russian. There were so many drinks to try.

Carmen liked the feel of the white uniform. She twisted to her left, then to her right, breasts pressing hard against the stiff fabric.

She'd bought it used, from a uniform company, just for fun. Originally she'd thought of wearing it when she graduated, sort of a gift for Axel, but since graduation now looked about as likely as winning the lottery, she decided to show it off for her homecoming. What the hell—she'd bought the thing; she might as well try it out.

To her surprise, she found that she liked being in it. She liked the idea of being a nurse, white poly-cotton wrapping her like armor, smoking cigarettes and drinking a Rob Roy in an airport cocktail lounge on a Tuesday afternoon, getting a double take from every suit that stopped off for a beer. She liked that it messed with their heads, like a prizefight or a powerful new car, making their juices flow. Must be a hormonal thing, she thought. A biological process. Axel would love it. He had this thing about medical paraphernalia. Nurses and pills turned him on. But he hated doctors and machines. Carmen took a hit off her Marlboro, watching her reflection, seeing the smoke frame her face, filter through her hair. Carmen liked her hair unbound, never putting it up or tying it back no matter how impractical or uncomfortable it became. She was constantly pushing it over her shoulder, brushing it off her forehead. Sophie had once warned her that wearing her hair long and loose would make guys act crazy around her.

"A girl does with her hair like she wants for her body," Sophie had told her. "You quit messing with your hair like that and they won't be bothering you all the time."

The problem with Sophie's suggestion was that Carmen sort of liked the way men bothered her. She liked the sense of control, and of danger. Even old Axel couldn't keep his eyes off her—seventy-three years old, probably hadn't got it up in decades.

The hair was nice. Carmen wrapped a thick strand around her index finger, let it fall free. The strand remained curled for a moment, then slowly unwound. Good hair. But it wasn't the hair men looked at. It was the boobs. Axel probably wouldn't notice if she shaved her head like James Dean. God, what a strange guy *he* was. A good guy to know, always bringing her stuff, but weird-looking and sort of spooky. All he ever wanted to do was go back to her place and fuck. He seemed to think he was her boyfriend or something.

She had met Dean only a couple of months before, through his sister, Mickey, another student at Eastern Nebraska Institute of Medical Specialties. One night Carmen and Mickey and a couple of the other students had gone across the street to Bailey's Pub, and Dean had joined them. Carmen remembered her first impression: What a geek! Since then, Dean had popped up with increasing frequency, and she'd gotten used to his appearance. She thought it was interesting that he'd been to prison. Thirty months on a drug rap, he'd told her. They'd gone out dancing a few times. Dean had a peculiar style, bouncing around like a barefooted kid on a hot sidewalk. It was embarrassing. His performance in the bedroom was similar—frantic and arrhythmic. The guy didn't even have a car.

Thinking about Dean recalled the image of the blue Valium tablets in her carry-on bag. The thought sent a smooth wave rolling down her spine. A definite plus, where Dean was concerned. The Valiums would get her through the ordeal to come. The memory of the smell of the Taco Shop assaulted her: twelve days of hot grease, taco sauce, Sophie, and Axel Speeter. She shivered and dug in her purse, looking for a Tic Tac or something. It seemed unreal, almost impossible to believe that she was going back to do another season at the Minnesota State Fair. For a lousy six bucks an hour, plus whatever fell out of the till. A cash business like that, what did he expect?

There was one Tic Tac way down in the corner, covered with lint. Carmen dipped it in her drink and wiped it off with a little square napkin from the bar. She inspected the mint, popped it in her mouth, and looked up. The bartender, older and balder even than Axel, watched her. The Tic Tac was wintergreen, her favorite. She finished the Rob Roy and ordered a gin and tonic. How did Sophie stand it, having dinner with Axel every Sunday all year long? For that matter, how did Axel stand being around Sophie all that time? Carmen recalled the red mole on Axel's left eyelid, its three white hairs, and the smell of Mennen Skin Bracer. One thing about Axel, he smelled okay in spite of being seventy-three, which was in Carmen's view the next thing to having died already.

The second drink pushed Axel and Sophie to a small stage at the back of her mind. Another drink, and they would become like characters in a movie. Then, if she got really loaded, it would be like they were characters in a movie she had heard about but never seen. Her shoulder muscles relaxed, and she smiled. Carmen was good at imagining, making movies in her head. She drank some more gin and imagined herself driving, a red Corvette with the top down and the stereo turned way, way up. Where was she going? Puerto Penasco? That sounded good. Who sat in the passenger seat? James Dean. No, change that. She looked again. It was still James Dean, but not the bald one. It was the dead one, the rebel without a cause, one sneakered foot propped on the dash, squinting at the horizon. She imagined coffee cans in the trunk, filled with fat, rubber-banded rolls of money. Hundred-dollar bills. That would be the way to live. She tried to recall whose picture was on the hundred. The face that swam into view looked a lot like Axel Speeter.

CHAPTER

5

"It looks like a junkyard, Sam. I can't believe they let you do this."

"None of their business what I do, my own damn property."

"This is a nice part of town. Don't your neighbors complain?"

"Sure they do. I get letters and shit from the city telling me to get rid of 'em. I send 'em to my kid's lawyer, he takes care of it."

They were looking at Sam O'Gara's backyard in the company of eleven vehicles in various degrees of disintegration. There were two Volkswagen Beetles, a '67 Camaro, three Chevys from the early sixties, an unidentifiable car with fire-blistered paint and all its windows blown out, the front half of a hood-scooped early seventies Dodge Charger, and three trucks: a badly rusted red flatbed and a green step van, with Axel's 1978 Ford F-150 pickup truck, the newest addition to Sam's auto graveyard, tucked between them. Sam's mongrel hounds, Chester and Festus, had tired of growling and snarling at Axel and were busy christening the new truck by pissing on its tires.

"Looks to me like it'd take more than one lawyer," Axel said.

"Yeah, well, this fella, he's a good one. Tells 'em I'm an artist. These ain't cars, they're sculptures. He gives 'em a bunch of First Amendment shit, scares hell out of them. It won't be no problem, you leaving your truck here. It's got this aesthetic appeal, kinda like that Venus of Milo."

"It's still a good truck. Never know when I might need a backup."

"That's the way I figure it. You was right to hang on to her. You can't have too many vehicles."

"I don't know about that," Axel said. "You might just have done it, Sam."

"Yeah, well, one more sure as shit ain't gonna make no difference. How you like your new one?"

"It's okay. Real smooth. No rattles or anything, except ever since you disconnected the air bag there's a sort of clicking in the steering wheel every time I turn a corner."

Sam shrugged and looked away. "That ain't nothing."

"And I still haven't figured out how to work the radio." Axel looked at his watch. "I've got to get going. Got to pick Carmen up. Thanks again, Sam. We ought to get a game up someday. You and me and Tommy."

Sam said, "Yeah, we got to do that, Ax. Sometime we got to do that. Been too fucking long, the three of us."

On the way across town to the airport, Axel amused himself by trying to figure out just how long it *had* been since he'd sat down at a card table with Sam O'Gara and Tommy Fabian. It didn't seem that long ago, but the last specific game he could remember was the one in Deadwood, South Dakota. That had been in '63, he believed. Axel was sure they'd played cards on and off for a few years after that, but Deadwood was the last game he remembered clearly.

They'd been at a hotel called the Franklin, playing draw poker, he remembered. Never his best game, but one he could win at if he played his cards right. Sam was sitting on the biggest stack that night, maybe seven or eight thousand, a lot of money back in those days. Axel wasn't far behind, having just raked in a nice pot on the strength of a pair of kings. Even Tommy, who'd been hitting the sauce a little too hard, was a few hundred dollars to the good.

The other four players—a rancher named Bum, who claimed to own his own spread out near Belle Fourche, a pair of cowboys who worked for him, and a businessman who'd driven out from Rapid City—were steadily losing. The rancher and his boys had pumped about three dimes each into the game, with the businessman down only a few hundred. The way Axel recollected it, he'd had a feeling about those cowboys from the start, though he hadn't said anything to Sam or Tommy at the time.

As usual, Sam and Tommy and Axel had been exercising their three-way partner routine, signaling the strength of their hands to one another to squeeze out the maximum number of raises when one of them caught a good hand. It wasn't exactly cheating, in Axel's view, but that didn't mean it was fair, either. In any case, Tommy quickly became too drunk to signal properly, so Axel had simply been playing his own cards, playing conservative and winning.

Tommy, who could irritate a squeal out of a dead pig, insisted on calling the rancher "Bud." The rancher kept on correcting him, getting more prickly every time he had to explain his name was Bum, not Bud. Each time, Tommy would say something like, "You mean like a ho-bo?"

It had started out, Axel supposed, as a strategy to throw the rancher's game on tilt, and it had worked. But he was wishing Tommy would ease up. Bum was almost out of money anyways, so it didn't make sense to keep on needling. But that was Tommy.

At four feet eleven inches, Tommy was by far the smallest man at the table, an accident of birth that he used to justify a nasty streak all out of proportion to his size. Axel had met him back in '44, when they were both in the merchant marine, sailing supplies out of Brisbane, Australia, to support the Allied efforts in the Solomons. They had matching kangaroos tattooed on their wrists, souvenirs of a four-day weekend in Sydney. Axel couldn't remember their significance, but a lot of the guys had them. He didn't think about it much anymore. It was a long time ago.

Tommy Fabian had grown up working fairs and carnivals in the Midwest, and he had the carny's contempt for a sucker. He figured he could say just about anything, and if some sucker got upset, fuck 'em, he'd just move on to the next town.

That night in Deadwood, with most of a bottle of bourbon in him, Tommy's mean streak was glowing. By two that morning, the game was showing signs of winding down. The businessman had long since descended into a melancholic haze, without the heart to call any sort of bet at all, and the three shitkickers were on tilt, throwing what little money they had remaining after every lousy hand they got dealt. At one point Tommy was dealt trip aces before the draw. He bet, was raised by Bum, and reraised. Everybody but Bum folded. Bum called Tommy's raise, then drew two cards. Obviously, Tommy figured, the rancher was drawing to three of a kind. Which made his own three aces a very strong hand indeed. Once again, he bet heavily, was raised, reraised, and was finally called by the rancher, who, it turned out, had been drawing two cards to fill a six-high straight. It wasn't the biggest pot of the night, but Bum was delighted to have some cash flowing his way for once. Tommy, on the other hand, had been mortified by such a display of fool's luck. He would have won the money back in time, but Tommy, being Tommy, couldn't let a bad beat go without making some kind of crack.

"Guy draws two to a straight. What the fuck kinda poker's that? I was sittin' on the nuts. No way you should've called my trips."

Bum said, "I won, didn't I?"

"Well, it was a dumb play anyways. What I get, playing cards with a guy named *Bud.*"

Bum, dragging the pot toward him, looked at Tommy and said slowly, "My name is *Bum.*"

"You mean like a wi-no?" Tommy exclaimed, widening his eyes.

"As in 'bum steer,' which I got a feeling is what we're getting in this here game."

If ever there was a time to shut up and act nice, this is it, Axel thought. Naturally, Tommy did no such thing. He was too loaded to exercise anything resembling common sense, but not quite loaded enough to pass out like a civilized drunk.

"Only problem we got in this here game is you boys don't know what the fuck you're doing, *Bud,*" Tommy said.

Axel didn't remember exactly how Bum had replied. As best he recalled, they'd played a few more hands, but the air over the table had gone thick and foul, and the game broke up shortly thereafter. He remembered walking out to his car with Tommy and Sam—he had been driving a '56 Lincoln back then—the clean winter wind cutting through their jackets. Bum and his two cowboys had followed them out of the hotel, walking down the narrow, snow-dusted sidewalk about fifty feet behind them, laughing and making jokes about how broke they'd gotten. Their forced cheeriness seemed strident and out of place. When they were a block from the hotel, another block to go before they reached their car, Axel remembered saying to Sam, "Keep on walking. We get to the car, hop in fast."

He realized now that this had been his mistake. The farther from the hotel they got, the bolder and more confident the cowboys became. What he should have done, he should have forced a confrontation right outside the lobby, before the cowboys were ready, while they were still maybe undecided. Odds were, they'd have backed down. It was always best to be the instigator. You couldn't just wait for shit to happen to you, or sure as shit, shit would happen to you.

One of the cowboys yelled, "Hey, we don't even got

twenty bucks left to get our willies dipped. How 'bout you boys buy us each a lady, just for good feelings' sake, hey?"

Tommy, who was apparently even drunker than Axel had given him credit for, stopped and turned back toward the trio, unzipped his Wranglers, and unleashed a stream of urine. A cloud of steam rose from the frozen concrete.

"You can dip 'em right here, suckers!" he crowed.

At that moment, Axel abandoned any hope that they were going to make it out of Deadwood intact. The cowboys dropped their pretense of cheeriness and picked up their pace. Tommy let out a cackling howl, waved his cock at them, then took off running. He made it about twenty feet before tripping and skidding on his belly down the icy sidewalk.

Axel planted his feet and, trying to look as large and menacing as possible, waited for the cowboys to come to him. Sometimes it worked. But not that night. The two younger cowboys didn't even slow down. The first one ran straight into him, landing a glancing blow to his jaw. Axel hooked an arm around him, throwing him against a light pole, but the other one leapt onto his shoulders, slamming his fists into Axel's temples. Axel started spinning, trying to throw the cowboy. He caught a flash of Tommy being lifted by Bum, feetfirst, his tiny fists flailing without effect at the rancher's prominent abdomen. He saw Sam trying to get into the Lincoln, discovering that the car was locked. Then something hit Axel on the side of his knee, sending him sprawling. He heard something pop. His face hit the sidewalk.

The next thing he remembered was Sam breathing whiskey fumes in his face, asking him if he was all right. Axel's knee felt decidedly wrong. He tried to straighten his leg. It moved a few inches, then something caught. Tommy sat on the sidewalk in a daze, exploring a bloody mustache with his tongue.

"How come you look so fucking good?" Axel asked Sam.

"Me? Hell, once you bit the dirt, Ax, I just handed 'em the dough," Sam said. "What the fuck you expect?"

The cowboys were gone, along with most of their money. Sam still had his original poke, a few hundred dollars he'd tucked in his underwear, and Tommy had a hundred-dollar-bill in his left boot. Axel didn't have a dime.

Sam said, "You got to learn to protect your poke, Ax. You might just as well give it away. And you—" He turned his attention to Tommy. "You got to learn when to keep your yap shut. You hadn't been riding that Bum fella, this never woulda happened."

Tommy said, "Hey, you're the ones just let 'em take us. Didn't even fight back. Where the hell were you while they was shaking me upside down? Besides, you shouldn't've let me drink so damn much. I mean, don't you boys know nothing?"

Axel stood up, ignoring the spikes of pain from his knee. He limped over to Tommy and put his hands on his shoulders.

Tommy said, "What?"

Axel still felt bad about putting Tommy in the trunk, but it was a lot kinder than what Sam had suggested. They'd let him out an hour later in Rapid City, had a few drinks, and by the next night they were driving through Wyoming— Axel stretched out on the backseat with his knee wrapped in Ace bandages—looking for another game. They'd kept their partnership going for a few more months, but after the Deadwood incident Axel knew he'd lost his edge. He just didn't have the heart for it anymore. Then Tommy got into the minidonut business at the Minnesota fair, and Sam took off for Alaska to try and win a fortune off the oil jockeys— an ill-fated adventure that had lasted less than a year. Axel spent a few years in the hotel business, and a few more selling land in the Dakotas, before letting Tommy talk him into getting himself a joint at the Minnesota State Fair. He'd bought the taco concession in '69.

Now they were all a lot older, all living in the Twin Cities, still friends. They talked about getting together for a little three-man, just for old times' sake, but it never happened. They were all busy doing other things.

As the Boeing 727 settled into its final approach, Carmen thought again about the Valiums in her bag. She dug out the vial and shook out three of them, then reconsidered and put one back. She'd had four miniature Smirnoffs during the flight. She didn't want to pass out in the terminal. She swallowed the two pills dry, closed her eyes, and imagined that she was landing someplace else. Puerto Penasco.

After the plane landed she stayed in her seat and let the other passengers file past her. There was no hurry at all. Axel would wait. Once the aisle cleared, she gathered her bag and made her way carefully toward the front of the airplane. The cabin, empty now, seemed tiny and toylike. She thought she could feel her hair brushing the ceiling, and she liked it. The stewardesses waiting at the front had shrunk to four-foot-high Barbie dolls. Carmen grinned at them, mirroring their mouth-only smiles.

"Bye now," they said, their mouths moving in tandem.

Carmen laughed.

Axel was wearing a pair of red suspenders. The tufts of white hair around his ears were trimmed back, as were his nose hairs. He reeked of Mennen Skin Bracer. His dentures gleamed in the fluorescent light. Carmen, still wearing her stewardess grin, stepped into his arms, pushed herself up onto her toes, gave him a quick kiss, then stepped back and forced her eyes to focus.

She was always surprised by his size. The Axel in her memory was a medium-size old man. The Axel of the present stood three inches over six feet. She could see way up into his nostrils. And she always forgot his freckles. He had freckles like a little kid; when he grinned he sometimes looked like a balding, wrinkled, green-eyed, oversize eight-year-old.

"Well, here I am," she said, staring up at the mole on his eyelid.

Axel frowned. "You smell like liquor."

Carmen shrugged and set her bag on the floor between them. "I get tense. I hate airplanes, you know? Besides, don't I deserve a drink to celebrate my first year of school?"

"You're too young to drink hard liquor."

"I'm twenty-one now, Axel."

"Too young," he repeated stubbornly. If he had his way, the legal age for drinking would be forty-five.

Carmen changed the subject. "So how are *you* doing? How's your blood pressure?"

"All over hell. Goddamn doctor has me eating stuff you couldn't give away in Ethiopia. A guy can't live on leaves and roots, you know?" He looked at her uniform, pointed a big, speckled hand at her chest. "They let you wear that now?"

"I wore it for you. How's my mom? How's the Taco Shop? How are the chips this year? Are they rancid again? I don't want to be serving no rancid nachos this year. Come on." She moved off down the concourse. "I got a suitcase at the baggage claim."

Axel watched her move away in the white dress— wrinkled and slightly damp now from the long flight, sticking a little to the back of her thighs. He could tell by her walk, as if the floor was covered with foam rubber, that she'd had more than a couple of drinks. He picked up her bag and followed.

"That goddamn Helmut tried to give me that same shit all over again," he said. "Rancho Rauncho or whatever it is all over again, and you know they smelled the same as last year? I think he must make them in his basement, probably changes his oil about once a year. Teach me to buy Mexican from a Norwegian. I told him a guy ought to make chips a guy would want to eat. Told him to cornhole his corn chips. I'm buying from the Garcias this year."

Carmen laughed. "Good for you. Did you really say that to him? Was Sophie there? You telling Helmut to shove his corn chips. I bet she about shit."

"Where do you learn to talk like that?"

"From you," she said over her shoulder.

Axel muttered to himself as he followed Carmen toward the baggage claim, his eyes moving from her white shoes to her white cotton dress and back again. He hated it when she teased him. But he liked the uniform a lot. She looked good in it. He liked the idea of her flying in to help him. And this year he would make sure his nachos were the best. Twenty-five years in the business, he had learned you do not cut corners on product quality. People come back a year later and tell you you got shitty chips, you better have an answer for them.

It took forever for Carmen's bags to arrive. Axel tried to ask her about school, but Carmen's bubbly energy seemed to have deserted her. She replied in monosyllables, yawning repeatedly. After a few minutes, she sat down on a bench and stared at the baggage carousel, her eyelids almost closed.

On the way out to the parking lot, Axel carrying both her suitcase and her overnight bag, she stumbled twice, nearly falling.

"Are you okay?" he asked.

Carmen smiled dreamily and nodded. "Just a little tired," she explained. She didn't seem to notice that Axel had a new truck. She got in it the same way she would have climbed in his old one, didn't look around it or ask him anything, just planted her ass on the seat and waited for him to drive. He was disappointed. He had hoped to impress her with his new wheels, hoped to show her he wasn't such an old fogy after all. Wow her with the AM/FM radio and the sport wheels and the lariat stripes.

He had to laugh at himself. What difference did it make

what she thought? She was just a kid. He wished she wouldn't drink so much. A girl shouldn't grow up so fast. He pulled out onto the freeway and brought the new F-150 up to fifty miles per hour. He wanted to turn on the radio, show her how you could turn a knob and make the sound go from one speaker to another, something he'd figured out on the way over, but when he turned his head to say something she was slumped against the door, her mouth open, snoring. She looked young, her face smooth and childlike. He remembered the day she had come to work for him—a bright-eyed, elfin high schooler overflowing with girl energy. That was five years earlier, but he remembered it like yesterday.

It had been a few days before the fair. He'd been scrambling to get the restaurant ready, trying to get a crew lined up, interviewing the kids sent over by the State Fair Employment Office. He always asked them to send him all the Mexican girls, because it gave his taco stand that authentic south-of-the-border look. The employment people always gave him a bunch of shit about equal opportunity. Most years he ended up with a stand full of tall, blond, blue-eyed boys and girls.

The day he met Carmen he had been down under the counter, scraping up some congealed grease from the previous year, when he heard a voice say, "Hey, anybody named Axel in there?"

He stood up, to discover a dark-haired girl chewing gum and smoking a cigarette, shoving her burgeoning breasts up against the edge of the counter. "You Axel?" she asked.

Axel watched her blow a bubble.

"That's right. Who are you?"

The bubble popped, leaving a tiny cloud of cigarette smoke floating in front of her face. She grinned and said, "My name's Carmen. I think you're supposed to give me a job or something. How much money will I make?"

It had taken him all of five seconds to fall for her. She wasn't Mexican, but he hired her anyway.

Two days later, when he caught her pocketing a five-dollar bill, he did not love her less, though he watched her more carefully. And now? He had to be honest with himself. She wasn't a girl anymore. She was a full-blown woman, practically bursting out of her nurse's uniform, reeking of alcohol and cigarettes, snoring. Still, a wave of tenderness passed over him. She was someone he could nurture and protect, someone with whom he could share his seven decades of wisdom and experience. Like a daughter. Although it was hard not to stare at her tits sometimes.

He wished she could be trusted. He was waiting for her to change, for her grasping, childlike impulsiveness to mellow into responsibility. Maybe someday she would appreciate all he had done for her, maybe take care of him when he got old. That felt good. He liked thinking of her as a nurse, pressing a cool hand to his forehead.

The blast of a horn sent Axel back into his lane. Some kid in a Chevy, asshole kid driving too fast, swerved around him. Axel gripped the wheel and focused on his driving, his heart hammering. He wasn't used to this new truck. All the dials were in the wrong places. The steering wheel felt stiff, and you had to put on the seat belt or it would beep and flash at you. And the engine: he'd taken one look at it and closed the hood—you had to have a goddamn computer to change the spark plugs. At least Sam had taken care of the air bag situation. He drove, listening to Carmen's snores, happy not to have to worry about the thing blowing up in his face.

CHAPTER

6

Mickey Dean, dressed in her Go Big Red gym shorts and tank top, sat curled up on the upholstered rocker, reading a book, holding it between her bony knees. She didn't look up when her little brother clomped into the apartment, dragging the toes of his big black boots as he crossed the room. Her cat, Isabella, tensed up, a ridge of fur rising on her back. James shrugged out of his jacket, let it fall to the floor, and walked past Mickey into the kitchenette. She saw fingernail scratches on his back. She thought she knew whose. The cat fled into Mickey's bedroom.

Mickey heard the sound of a pop top.

"That better not be the last one," she shouted.

James shuffled back into the living room, holding a Pepsi.

"If that's the last one, you better go out and buy some more." Mickey glared at him, her oversize red-plastic-rimmed eyeglasses pushed up on top of her brittle blond hair. She was a big girl, nearly six feet tall, hard and lean, elbows and knees and shoulders sticking out everywhere, weak blue eyes, small mouth, and a beak like a roadrunner. She and her brother Jimmy looked as unlike as any two people on the planet. Even their skin color. Hers was pale, while James's skin had a dusky, almost khaki tint. Different fathers. Possibly different mothers as well—the Dean family history was somewhat muddled. Sandra Dean, their mother, looked like a seriously obese Barbra Streisand.

All Mickey knew for sure was that she'd grown up with James in the same miserable Council Bluffs rambler, watching Sandra drink herself unconscious daily. Mickey hadn't been back, hadn't seen her mom in six years, not since she took off on her seventeenth birthday and got herself a job printing T-shirts, a job she still held. A year after Mickey left home, her brother James had dropped out of school and quickly established himself in the Omaha–Council Bluffs drug trade, selling weed and acid and a few other items to former classmates. He'd lasted about five weeks before landing in the youth rehab center at Geneva, Nebraska, for six months. When he got out, Mickey found him a job with the T-shirt company, working in the warehouse. That had lasted a few months, until the warehouse manager found James asleep, again, on a stack of red 50/50 XXL raglan-sleeve sweats. James had disappeared from her life for more than a year after that. The next time she heard from him he was in jail, about to be sentenced for trying to sell three ounces of North Platte Green to an Omaha narcotics officer. That time, he was nineteen years old, and they'd sent him to the state penitentiary in Lincoln. Mickey had approved of the sentence. Maybe that would be what it took to open his eyes.

For the past ten weeks, since James had been released from Lincoln, he'd been staying with her. Sleeping on her couch. Eating her food. Being mean to her cat. Leaving the toilet seat up.

He had definitely changed. For one thing, he was shaving his head nearly every day now, leaving little hairs all over her bathroom. He had those gold rings in his eyebrow. Something else had changed too. James had never been a particularly caring or empathic young man, but after thirty months in Lincoln he didn't seem to give a shit about anything. He especially did not give a shit about his big sister, who happened to be supporting him.

Mickey said, "You're a parasite, James, you know that?"

He dropped onto the cat-shredded couch, put his boots up on the coffee table.

"You look for a job today?" she asked, staring at his boots.

"Sure. I looked all day long."

"You can't stay here forever, you know. I said you could stay for a few weeks, just till you got a job."

James Dean shrugged. "What you reading?" he asked. He tipped back the Pepsi and let a quarter ounce of cola slip into his mouth, held it there, enjoying the sensation of bubbles on his tongue.

Mickey held up the book, one of her poetry books, a big fat brown one. He leaned toward her and read the title: *The Complete Prose and Poetry of John Donne.*

"Read me something," he said. Mickey liked to think she was the smart one. It calmed her down when she could show off her education, act like she knew everything.

"Are you going to go look for work tomorrow?"

"Absolutely. C'mon, Mick. Read me something. Maybe it'll make me a better person."

Mickey frowned, trying to stay mad. Dean turned his mouth into a smile, giving her his cute big-eyed little brother look. It got her every time. She flipped through the book, looking for something. She cleared her throat and lowered her chin, just like when they were little kids and she would read to him.

"Any man's death diminishes me," she read, *"because I am involved in mankind."*

Dean interrupted. "What's that supposed to mean?" He liked to ask her what poems and things meant, see what kind of bullshit she could come up with.

"That means that we are all brothers. And sisters."

"I met a lot of guys in Lincoln weren't my brothers," Dean said.

"You just don't get it."

"Sure I do. Let me see that." He grabbed the book. "Show me where you were."

Mickey pointed at a highlighted paragraph. Dean furrowed his brow and read. "The guy can't spell for shit," he said. "'No man is an Iland.' No *s*. That's not how you spell it."

"You are so ignorant. That's the original spelling, the way they used to write."

"What he's saying," Dean said, reading further, "is that you are a part of me."

Mickey hesitated, then nodded uncertainly.

He was getting it now. "So I can do whatever I want with you. Like you are a hair on my head."

She shook her head. "No, no, no," she said. "You're missing the point, as usual."

Dean said, "Oh, I got the point, all right. The man's saying what I knew all along. You are just a part of me. I pull the string, you jerk." He faked a punch at Mickey's face; she jerked her head back.

"See? You're a part of me."

Mickey stood up. "You're worse than ignorant. You're ignorant and stupid on top of it." She snatched the book and went into the bathroom. Dean heard the toilet seat bang down.

Dean stared at the closed door, the word *stupid* stuck in his ears. He was not stupid. He was right. What the guy John Donne was saying was something Dean had only recently come to suspect: that the world and all things in it were simply extensions of himself. He thought about Carmen. Was she part of him too? He thought about her laughing, drunk and loose, letting him smother himself in her soft flesh. How many nights in Lincoln had he lain in bed dreaming of exactly that? He'd been thinking about her a lot lately. Maybe Mickey was right. Maybe it was time to move on. When Carmen returned from Minnesota, he could just move in with her.

He heard the toilet flush, then the distinctive click of the medicine cabinet opening.

Uh-oh, he thought.

Five seconds later, the bathroom door slammed open, hitting the wall, and his sister stomped out. "You shit!" She hurled the book at him. Dean ducked; the book hit the wall above him and dropped onto his lap. "You little worm!" Dean felt the fear in his belly, his body remembering all the times she'd beat him up when they were kids. Mickey would hold her long arms out to the sides, hands forming rigid claws, being the monster, and he'd have to run and hide, because if she caught him—she always caught him—she'd punch him repeatedly, over and over, in the exact same spot on his shoulder, until he started bawling and begging.

She was really mad; no telling what she'd try to do.

"You shit, you better give them back to me."

Dean said, "Take it easy, Mick. C'mon now—"

"You sold them, didn't you?" She towered over him, her shins against the low coffee table.

"I didn't sell them." He grasped the book, holding it up to have something between them. "I gave them to Carmen."

"Carmen *Roman?*" From the way Mickey's face bloomed red, Dean knew he'd made a mistake. "That *bitch?*" Mickey did not like Carmen. Carmen had that effect on most women, Dean had noticed.

"You can get more. Just call your doctor, tell him your purse was stolen or something." He knew he shouldn't be afraid. He'd faced worse in Lincoln.

Mickey lifted one long leg and stepped over the table. Her hands came down on his bare shoulders, nails digging deep. She moved her face in on him. Dean's body went rigid, every muscle quivering.

"Get out," she said.

Dean slammed the book against the side of her head.

Mickey's hands came up off his shoulders; her body straightened above him, wavered, then went backward over the coffee table. Her feet flew up, her head hit the hardwood floor. Dean winced at the sharp sound, the book still clenched in his hand. For a few seconds, she did not move. He stared at the bottoms of her Nikes—purple, white, and gray—propped up on the table. He heard a sudden intake of breath, the feet came off the table, Mickey tipped her head forward and looked up at him, her face frozen in an expression so odd that Dean almost laughed. For a moment, very brief, he thought everything would be okay. Mickey rolled to her side, got onto her hands and knees, and climbed to her feet. Without looking back, she tottered into her bedroom. The door closed. Was she all right? Dean didn't want to follow her into her room. He sat quietly on the sofa, surprised to discover that he really didn't care whether she was all right or not. It was her own damn fault. He'd only been defending himself. He looked at the book in his hand and smiled. The title stood out crisp and clear against the buff-colored cover. He could see the fibers in the paper. He explored the room with his eyes. Everything he looked at came back in hard focus, as if his vision had suddenly improved. He liked the sensation that went with that. He tried to define it but could only come up with the word *big*. He felt big inside his skin. He could feel the air pressing against his taut integument, holding him in. Opening the book, he read a few lines at random. The archaic language struck him as profound, though puzzling. *"Oh doe not die, for I shall hate / All women so, when thou art gone / That thee I shall not celebrate / When I remember, thou wast one."*

What the hell was that supposed to mean? Waste one what? One doe? Dean closed the book and set it on the coffee table. The old-fashioned spelling was really throwing him.

He decided he'd better check on Mickey. He knocked on

her door. No response. He pushed the door open and looked in. She was on her back on the bed.

"Mick?" he called out. She didn't twitch. He entered the room and took a closer look. Her eyes were both blackened. How had that happened? He could hear her breathing through her mouth. Dean backed out of the room and closed the door. Let her sleep. She could sleep all day long, for all he cared.

CHAPTER

7

Sophie Roman pressed the Play button on her pink Emerson boom box, eased a heaping teaspoonful of International Coffees orange cappuccino into her cup, watched the pale powder sink into the hot water, stirred. The sweet sound of Luciano Pavarotti's voice poured from the speakers and echoed from the paneled walls. She lifted the coffee cup, closed her eyes, and inhaled the exotic aroma of Italy. Had she ever visited Italy, she was sure, the sweet, spicy brew would have returned her to that little café in Milan—just as promised in the commercials. This would be her last morning to herself before the fair started. She wanted to make it special.

Sitting at her fold-out kitchen table, the sun warming her taupe-colored velour robe, Sophie celebrated the deal she had made with Axel. It would, she believed, go down in Sophie history as a marketing triumph. Axel had agreed to buy her collection of condiments sight unseen, for their full wholesale price. The whole lot. Sophie knew from his weary acquiescence to her demand that he had not fully appreciated the scope of her program. For the past year she had loaded her purse at every meal out, stuffing it with sugar packets and ketchup pillows, like money in the bank. Axel would probably have his next heart attack right there in her kitchen.

She had separated her booty into eleven Folgers cans, now lined up neatly on the kitchen counter of her mobile home. Domino sugar packets overflowed one can. Sweet'n Low nearly filled another. The other Folgers cans contained, in order of decreasing volume, Heinz ketchup packets, salt packets, Equal, black pepper, Taco Bell hot sauce, Burger King salt, and coffee creamer. The last two cans were filled with miscellaneous condiments such as artificial horseradish, pickle relish, and barbecue sauce. Sophie reversed the Pavarotti tape in her pink boom box, lit a Virginia Slim, and congratulated herself on her foresight, industry, and bargaining skills.

The quantities were written in eyebrow pencil on the side of each coffee can. There were 443 sugar packets. She had actually counted only 419, but her count may have been off, and besides, Axel would never take the time to recount. Sophie wasn't sure of the exact wholesale value of her hoard, but it had to be a nice chunk of cash. She thought two, maybe even three hundred dollars for everything would not be unreasonable. She turned up the volume on the boom box, sipped her cappuccino, and gazed out the window toward Tanners Lake. A strip of water showed between Laurie Armstrong's sagging pale-gray Artcraft and the Redfields' double-wide.

With the extra money she could buy a yellow metal awning for her home. She knew exactly what she wanted. She'd seen the metal awnings on other homes. They were popular at Pine Creek Village, an upscale mobile home park down in Eagan, where they got three sixty a month for a single lot. That was a lot of money. Sophie would put her money toward an awning any day. With a nice awning across the front of her home, she could have the classiest-looking home in Landfall. Not that that would take much, given the motley collection of "manufactured homes" that surrounded her, not one of which had ever been profiled in *House Beautiful*.

A tiny, incorporated village of 685 souls, Landfall clung like a barnacle to the eastern margin of Saint Paul, bordered by Tanners Lake on the north and west, I-94 roaring by on the south, and 694 squeezing against it from the east. At one time, Landfall had been a thriving community, with its own grocery store, beauty parlor, liquor store, and community center. Now the fiberglass-and-aluminum homes were disintegrating from age and neglect. The only surviving business was the Village Spirits Shop.

Sophie thought about something else then, something she'd been saving in the back of her mind. The bonus. Axel had promised her a bonus this year. If they had a good year, he'd promised to take care of her, give her a share of the profits. But he hadn't said how much. "Let's just wait and see how we do," he'd told her. Numbers flickered behind the curtain in her mind. She let herself peek. Was that a thousand? Two? Five? She could buy a new car, put a payment down on one of those Saturns, replace her aging Plymouth. Wait. She squeezed her eyes shut. She could see it. A real house. One you could walk through without the dishes rattling. A house with a basement. A place to go when the tornadoes came.

She couldn't think about it. It was too exciting, and too unreal. Instead, she looked at the watch Axel had bought for her at a fair in Iowa. That was a real, solid object. Like the condiments, it was in her possession. A classy gold ladies' watch with the cubic zirconiums that you couldn't tell from real diamonds. A house was one thing, but looking good was important too. She reached across the table and ejected the Pavarotti tape. That was enough opera for one day. It was time for Phil Donahue, then Jenny Jones. She always looked good. Then Oprah. She looked good too.

Dean woke up on the sofa with the TV still going, Phil Donahue talking to three black couples. He was in his sister's apartment. It continued to surprise him, almost every morning, to discover that he wasn't in his cell at Lincoln. Mickey's door was still closed. She hadn't come out all yesterday afternoon or evening. When he'd checked on her around midnight, she hadn't moved. He yawned and sat up. The black couples were arguing, but he couldn't figure out what about. Donahue also seemed at a loss. Dean never could figure out black people, even before his thirty months in Lincoln, where he'd actually had to share a cell with one of them, and where, first day in, he'd been accused of *being* one on account of his curly hair and dusky skin. His first night there, his cellmate, a guy named Chip, whose skin was the color of a chocolate-chip cookie including the chips—some sort of skin condition—had asked him what way he was going. At first, Dean thought it was a come-on, an invitation to bend over and hug his pillow, but Chip had quickly made it clear that he was talking politics, not sex. "You got two ways to go here, a kid like you," Chip had explained. "You hang with the brothers, or you hang with them Air-yan mothafuckas."

"I don't hang with nobody," Dean had told him.

Chip had said, "Then you fucking bait."

"Anyways, I'm white."

Chip raised an eyebrow. "An' I'm the fucking man on the moon."

"Fuck you."

Chip had laughed. "Ain't no two ways about it—your mama went and got herself some dark meat, boy."

Dean almost jumped the guy right then and there. He had held himself back only because Chip had been hitting the iron pile for years and looked like a polka-dot Mike Tyson and would probably have killed him. Also, it might have been true. Dean didn't know his father, and his mother had never been very selective about her dates. This wasn't the first time Dean had been called a nigger, but it was the first time he'd been called a nigger by a nigger.

Chip turned out to be a nice guy. Eighteen years into a

thirty-year bid, he'd learned to get along with just about everybody. He said he didn't care what way Dean decided to go. "You seem like a good kid," he'd said. "I'm just sayin', is all. You got some choices to make, boy. You go with the powers, or you wind up in Punk City. Ain't no two ways 'bout it."

The two powers, according to Chip, were the Black Muslims and the Aryan Circle. There were other affiliations as well, but those were the only ones likely to accept him. "Punk City," also known as Protective Custody, was where all the snitches and baby-fuckers and weaklings ended up. That wasn't an option, so far as Dean was concerned. He decided to go with the Circle, since they scared him only half as bad as the Muslims.

Chip recommended that Dean shave his head.

"You lose the hair, you can pass for white bread all day long, boy."

So Dean had shaved off his kinky, ginger-colored mat and done his best to fit into the Aryan Circle, most of whom, it turned out, were not bad guys, and just as scared as him.

An advertisement for bathroom cleanser, a talking brush, jerked him back to the present. He found the remote between the sofa cushions and turned off the television.

Ten weeks out of Lincoln, and so far nothing had turned up for him. He supposed he could get back into dealing, buying and selling ounces and grams. It was easy money, but chancy, likely to land his ass back in jail. That was the thing about dealing. The mathematics was for shit. Ninety-nine times out of a hundred you did the deal and that was that. The problem was, to make a decent living at it, you had to make a lot of deals, which meant you had to have a lot of customers. Sooner or later, someone was bound to fuck you over. No, to make money in the dope business you had to move the big weight, three or four deals a year and no more. The problem with that was the same as in any other business—it required an initial investment, a reputation, and connections, none of which he had. He knew plenty of people in the business, sure, but all of them were small time and most of them were in jail. Lousy way to make a living anyway, hanging out with people who were all the time fucked up and broke. He'd learned his lesson. Aside from scoring for Carmen, he'd been more or less behaving himself—hanging out, killing time, keeping his eyes open, waiting for the right situation to present itself.

The phone rang. Dean tensed up. Mickey would not sleep through a ringing phone. He watched her door. At twelve rings the caller gave up. Dean opened the bedroom door and looked in. Mickey looked the same as before, only paler. He walked to the bedside. Her eyes were open slightly. He reached down and touched her face. She was cool. He felt her neck but could detect no pulse.

A wisp of sadness came and went, leaving nothing behind. He looked at his right hand, curled it into a fist. He was stronger than he had thought. Well, shit happened. Now he had to deal with it. Obviously, he couldn't call the cops. He'd be back in Lincoln, accident or no. He packed his few articles of clothing in Mickey's gym bag, then added the John Donne book and the three hundred dollars she had stashed in her drawer. He found another forty-odd dollars in her purse, along with the keys to her Maverick.

It was another hot day in Omaha. Not even noon yet, and the seats of the Maverick scorched him right through his jeans. He drove to Ames Avenue, turned left, no destination in mind yet, letting the flow of traffic pull him from one intersection to the next, thinking. Clenching and unclenching his fist, feeling strong. Dean the killer. A guy who you did not fuck with, who could end a life with a single blow. He was surprised how good he felt. Everything he'd heard before had led him to believe that killing another person would have severe emotional consequences. No one, not even Chip, who had killed three people, had told him how easy it would be. As with any other crime, it seemed, feelings of guilt came only when you got caught.

Am I a monster? he wondered. He had always thought

that those guys who killed their relatives were nuts, but he didn't feel nuts at all. He felt clear and clean, as if he had shed a rotting old skin.

He wanted to tell someone. But of course that would undermine the feeling—others could look at him and have their own inconsequential thoughts, but only he would know what he had done. He turned onto I-80, drove east. Hours later, the sun fell behind him and the approaching headlights became balls of sparks. He felt totally alert, ready to drive all night long. As he approached Des Moines, a brown bat struck the windshield and stuck there for an instant—he could see its tiny, pointed teeth—before sliding up and over the Maverick. An omen, a sign that his life was about to get interesting. He turned north on I-35. For the first time since he'd been sentenced to the Nebraska State Penitentiary, he knew exactly where he was going.

The ringing telephone would not stop. Carmen opened her eyes. The room was dark except for two bright lines of daylight squeaking past the sides of the heavy curtain. She carefully elevated herself to a sitting position, feeling a little sick but overall not bad, considering that she didn't know where she was. She cleared her throat and stared down at the ringing telephone. The last thing she remembered was Axel meeting her at the airport. She was probably in a room at the Motel 6, or so she hoped. She picked up the handset between her thumb and forefinger, the way she might handle a dead bird.

"I'm sleeping," she reported.

"I can't get my lens in. Did I wake you up?"

It was Axel, of course, calling her from room 3. Axel had lived in room 3 ever since she had known him.

"Christ, Axel. What time is it?"

"Eight-thirty in the morning. You've been sleeping for twelve hours."

Carmen shook her head to clear it. "Oogh," she said,

sinking slowly back onto the mattress. "Big mistake." The pain in her head, she recalled from her studies, was due to dehydration of the lining of the brain. She needed some water.

"What's that?"

"Talking to myself. I feel a little sick." Carmen groped for the light switch, squeezed her eyes closed, and flipped it up. She let her eyes open slowly, taking in the light a photon at a time. Axel was still yammering on about his contact lens.

"Okay. Okay. Give me a minute, okay?" One night, and already he needed a nurse. She looked down at her uniform and grimaced. The crisp whiteness had given way to the look of a well-used flour-sack dish towel. Carmen unzipped and unbuttoned, let the dress fall to the floor, then kicked it aside. Her mouth tasted awful. She could smell herself. She needed a hot shower, bad.

"It's open!" Axel shouted.

Carmen opened the door, stepped into room 3 and was instantly transported back in time. The smell of Mennen Skin Bracer. The bed made military style. The first time Carmen had visited Axel's room, he had tried to bounce a quarter off the taut bedspread to show her how tight it was. The quarter hadn't bounced very high. Actually, it hadn't bounced at all.

"How come you make your own bed?" she'd asked.

"I don't like the maids in here messing with my stuff," Axel had replied.

Axel's big thirty-one-inch TV dominated the wall opposite the bed. It was turned on to a fishing show, the sound off. The rest of his possessions—his "stuff"—were still neatly arranged in red plastic Coca-Cola crates stacked nine across and six high against the wall. Back in the sixties, he claimed, he had been able to make do with three crates: one for shirts and underwear, one for pants and shoes, and one for miscellaneous.

Miscellaneous, Carmen knew, included ten- and twenty-dollar bills, neatly rolled, held tight with wide rubber bands, nestled together in red Folgers coffee cans.

She made it a point to avert her eyes from the crates. It felt like bad luck. She remembered the last time she had been there. One year ago, on the third day of the fair, Axel's contacts had turned on him; he needed his eyeglasses and eyedrops, and he'd sent Carmen back to the motel with the key to room 3. It was during that visit that she had discovered the rolls of bills packed in a two-pound coffee can in one of the bottom crates. Shaking with excitement, she had pulled one bill from each of the eighteen fat, solid rolls that filled the can. It had been the single most exciting moment of her life. She wished she'd had the guts to take more. There had been at least seven other Folgers cans, which she had been too excited, too scared to open.

Just thinking about it now sent her pulse climbing. Her eyes shifted toward the Coca-Cola crates; she jerked them back.

Axel sat perched on a chair in front of the dressing mirror. His right eye was red and tearing. The end table at his elbow was covered with plastic squeeze bottles of lens cleaners, lubricants, and rinses. Several different brands were represented. Axel was looking at her in the mirror.

"You took your time."

"I took a shower. Give me a break. What's your problem?"

"I got one in, but this son-of-a-bitch won't sit right." He pointed at the contact lens, tinted blue, resting on a folded piece of toilet paper.

Carmen sat on the taut bedspread, forcing him to turn and look at her directly. She was wearing jeans and an oversize white V-neck T-shirt. No bra. She leaned forward. Axel stared into her shirt, letting his teary eyes rest on the cleavage, freckled and tanned. It was impossible to focus with only one eye working. Carmen shifted her shoulders, causing her breasts to swing to the left. Axel followed the path of her large nipples across the white cotton fabric. "I can't see for shit."

She leaned back and brought her legs up. Over a year he had been putting his contacts in all by himself; now suddenly he needs help. She wrapped her arms around her shins and rocked back and forth. If he wanted her to install his contact lenses, she wasn't going to make it easy for him. She did not want this to become a daily chore.

"How come you can't get it in yourself?"

"I don't know."

"How come you don't just wear your glasses?"

"I paid good money for these lenses. Besides, once I get them in I see better. Are you going to help me or not?"

Carmen sighed. She picked up the lens and squirted it with saline solution, then knelt on the carpet before him. "Lean forward."

She separated the upper and lower eyelids, letting her breasts brush against his forearm, and planted the lens over his bright-green iris.

"There. Now you got your eyes on." She sat back and crossed her arms. "There something you wanted to look at?"

Axel sat propped against the headboard, looking at his wall of Coca-Cola crates. Carmen had gone back to her room, insisting that she needed another hour of sleep. Axel couldn't remember the last time he had been able to sleep like that. He was lucky if he got four hours at a time. One of the things that happened when you got old. Tired all the time, but can't get a good night's sleep.

He wondered why he'd had so much trouble with his contacts. Had he been acting like a kid, looking for attention? Probably.

And that Carmen, thinking she was such hot stuff. Not that she wasn't a pretty girl, but that didn't make him so mush-brained that he hadn't noticed her looking at his coffee cans. Last year, she had grabbed just a few hundred dollars, thinking he wouldn't notice. He hadn't minded that so much and had never called her on it. But this year she might want more. Carmen liked money more than anything.

The last time he counted, the coffee cans contained two hundred sixty thousand dollars, cash money, most of it undeclared income. He'd thought about putting the whole pile in the bank, but he was scared the IRS would notice, and besides, Axel had never trusted bankers, doctors, politicians, or preachers. Still, he had to do something—it was far too easy to imagine Carmen stuffing her purse with roll after roll of his hard-earned green.

Axel wished, not for the first time, that he had a backyard. If he had a backyard he could bury it. Put it about four feet down, then plant a tree over it. That would make him feel good. Axel sighed. He had been through it in his head a hundred times before, but the money was still sitting in his room, where anybody with a spare key or a crowbar could bust in and walk off with it.

He would have to do something soon, make some decisions.

But not today.

CHAPTER

This time, Carmen was awake enough to notice his new truck.

"Cool!" she said, pressing the buttons on the radio. Her extra hour of sleep, plus a jumbo coffee from Denny's, had perked her up considerably. "Hey, you got them all set for WCCO."

"I *like* 'CCO," said Axel as he steered onto the freeway entrance ramp. He did not want to tell her that he had accidentally—no idea how he'd done it—set all the buttons on the same station. Besides, it was true. He *did* like WCCO, the Good Neighbor station. It was the only station where you could get the weather report anytime you wanted, and they didn't play any of that rock and roll.

Carmen did something to the radio and found a rock station. "Listen to this, Axel. Guns n' Roses. You got the same name as their lead singer. Except he spells it different. They're really cool. Listen." She twisted the volume knob.

The shrieking that poured out from his new speakers caused Axel to cross two lanes of freeway traffic before he found the volume knob, turned it down, and regained control of the vehicle. Angry motorists passed him on either side, glaring and honking. Carmen was doubled over, laughing.

"Goddamn it, Carmen, you want to get us both killed? The fair starts tomorrow!"

"Sorry," she gasped, wiping her eyes. "It was just too funny, you and Axl Rose singing. . . ."

"Well, don't do that anymore. You'll wreck the speakers." He guided the truck onto the Snelling Avenue exit ramp and turned toward the fairgrounds.

"How come we got to go out here, anyway?"

"I have to meet the Coke guy. Also, I want to check out the restaurant and make sure we're ready. Why? You have something else you wanted to do?"

"I thought Sophie was supposed to get everything ready."

"She did. I just want to take another look."

He pulled into the fairgrounds through the six-lane blue-and-green entrance gate. The quiet, peaceful fairgrounds he had visited the night before had transformed into a human anthill of activity, cars and trucks everywhere, the grounds crawling with exhibitors, concessionaires, deliverymen, and state fair employees. It was setup day, the last day before the first day of the fair. Axel nursed his truck along Dan Patch Avenue. Groundskeepers were mowing and trimming the grassy boulevards and lawns and sweeping the wide streets. As always, he was struck by the beauty of the freshly groomed fairgrounds. The grassy aprons were a deep rich green, perfectly manicured, looking almost artificial in the bright morning sunlight. Sculpted rock and flower gardens decorated the grassy medians, brilliantly colored, every plant at its florid peak. Even the streets and curbs were spotless. The benches sported fresh coats of green and blue paint, as did the trash receptacles and recycling bins and information kiosks and lampposts. Many of the concession stands were new or had been refurbished, each one striving to be unique and more visible than its neighbor.

"That's new," said Axel, pointing at a fresh-fried-potato-chip stand. "So's that." He nodded toward a small, brightly colored stand that advertised Tropical Shaved Ice. "That'll give the sno-cone guys fits."

They turned on Underwood Avenue. Painters from Midway Sign Company were adding a fresh coat of paint to the Beer Garden signs. "I'd love a piece of that action," said Axel. The Beer Garden was the ultimate fairgrounds concession. For twelve days, twelve hours a day, dozens of strong young bartenders poured 3.2 beer as fast as it would come out of the kegs. Ten thousand gallons a day, he'd heard. "I bet they clear a million bucks."

"You should sell beer," Carmen said.

Axel shook his head. "Wish I could, but the beer concessions are all tied up." He pulled the truck to the curb opposite a wide, sloping, tree-lined grassy mall. The mall ran the length of the block and was a good two hundred feet wide. The central area was dotted with small picnic tables, benches, and trash containers. To the left side, the squat, ugly shape of the Food Building ran the entire length of the mall, an assortment of concessions—Orange Treet, Pineapple-on-a-Stick, Black Walnut Taffy—lined up against its white cinder-block wall. On the other side of the grassy expanse, blazing red and white and green in the morning sunshine, sat Axel's Taco Shop. "Here we are."

Carmen said, "Hey . . . cool. You got new signs."

Axel climbed out of the truck and strode proudly toward his concession. It was beautiful. AXEL'S TACO SHOP, the overhead sign proclaimed in big red and green outlined letters. A red-and-black zigzag border made the letters pop out. That had been the sign painter's idea. To the left of the lettering a smiling Mexican wearing a sombrero was saying, *Muy bueno! It's good!* The Mexican's plywood sombrero extended out past the edge of the sign, giving him a larger-than-life look. That had been Axel's idea. The opposite end featured a picture of a taco overflowing with meat, cheese, and lettuce. The taco, too, extended out past the border, balancing nicely with the sombrero. It looked delicious.

The rest of the twenty-five-foot-long concession sported a

new coat of bright white paint, with the corner posts painted red to match the new countertop. Axel unlocked the plywood front and swung it open. A small sign hanging from hooks above the serving window read: *Axel Speeter, Prop.* He turned to Carmen, but she had wandered off and was now standing forty feet away, smoking a cigarette, talking to a man wearing a white Stetson. The crown of the man's hat was level with the top of Carmen's head.

Tommy Fabian, the diminutive owner of Tiny Tot Donuts, looked up and waved. Axel waved back, then walked over to join them.

"Lookin' good, Ax," said Tommy. His small hand was swallowed in Axel's grip. Tommy was decked out in an embroidered western-style shirt with mother-of-pearl snap buttons, Wrangler jeans, and a pair of black lizard Tony Lamas with excessively high raked heels. His fingers glittered with an assortment of gold, including an oversize, diamond-encrusted horseshoe ring. He pointed at the taco shop. "Nice paint job."

"I thought I'd brighten it up a little this year."

"Got lots a flash. Makes me hungry just to look at it. That there taco is a beaut. And the guy in the sombrero—that you, Ax?"

"Sure it is," Axel said. "That was me in my heyday."

"Heyday? I guess I don't remember no heyday. I only known you—what—fifty years?"

"Ever since Sydney."

Tommy looked up at the Space Tower and squinted, searching in his mind for confirmation. "Forty-four," he said.

Carmen looked bored.

"Nineteen hundred and forty-four," said Tommy, with renewed certainty. "Met playin' cards on the *Henrietta*. I remember now. I won."

"We both won," said Axel.

"Yeah, but I won more."

"You always won more."

Tommy laughed and cuffed Axel on the shoulder.

Axel said, "Carmen? You want to get those boxes of napkins and cups out of the truck?"

"I s'pose," she said, walking toward the truck. She flipped her cigarette toward the sidewalk. It landed in the grass. Axel walked over to the cigarette, stepped on it, picked it up, and delivered it to a nearby trash can.

Tommy Fabian watched him, shaking his head. "I see little Carmen's still the same gal as before. I thought you sent her off to be a nurse or something."

"I flew her back for the fair."

"You're a glutton for punishment, Ax. Is the other one gonna be here again too? Her old lady?"

"Sophie. Yeah. I made Sophie my manager this year. She's pretty excited."

Tommy grinned and pulled out a short, slim cigar, licked it, held it up in the sunlight to inspect it, then set it ablaze with a battered stainless-steel Zippo.

"I oughta get the name a your sign guy," he said, sending up a cloud of blue smoke.

Axel looked down the mall at the faded Tiny Tot concession, one of three minidonut stands owned by Tommy Fabian. Tiny Tot was one of the big moneymakers at the fair. Tommy claimed he netted out at over a hundred thousand a fair. Every year, Axel watched the customers lining up for their little wax-paper bags of greasy sugared minidonuts. He figured Tommy was lowballing his net. Tommy had once boasted about the number of sacks of donut mix he'd used during the fair. Axel did some quick math and came up with numbers that made his nuts ache. One thing for sure, Tommy didn't waste any of his cash on paint—the red Tiny Tot lettering was faded, and the wooden sides of the forty-foot-long building showed through a ten-year-old layer of peeling yellow paint.

"Could use a little touch-up," Axel said.

Tommy puffed his cigar. "I'm thinking I'll throw some paint on next year. The space rental guy's been bugging me

6 1

about it. Image of the fair and all that crap. What the hell—by this time tomorrow there'll be so many people here you won't even notice." He pointed with his cigar at the pristine mall. "All that grass? You remember what it looks like at the end of the fair? And last year, you remember the mud? What the hell."

Axel had to admit there was something to that. By the time one and a half million people had trampled over the three-hundred-plus-acre fairgrounds, there would be little evidence remaining of the groundskeepers' labors. This time tomorrow, the mall would be covered with fairgoers. After a few days the grass would be pounded flat and brown, and the streets would be dark and sticky with a pungent slick of spilled beer and sno-cones. The sea of munching, gawking people would obscure any view of the concession buildings, especially the ever popular Tiny Tot Donut stands. Axel looked back at his taco stand. He didn't care if his new paint and signage paid off; it was worth the money just to see it standing out clean and proud against the lush green grass.

"You know," said Tommy, "just so's you don't come back at me later and say I didn't warn you, you're outta your mind lettin' those two broads run your operation."

"They don't run it," Axel said. "They just work for me."

Tommy raised his short, comma-shaped eyebrows and sucked hard on his cigar.

"They do," said Axel.

The Coke guy showed up on schedule, for a change. As soon as he left, Axel discovered one of the syrup hoses leaking, a sticky mess sure to draw ants and yellow jackets. Over Carmen's complaints, they drove into downtown Saint Paul to pick up a hose fitting.

"How come you don't just have the Coke guy come back out and fix it?" Carmen wanted to know.

Axel said, "I just want to get it taken care of. I don't want to have to worry whether he's gonna show up."

Carmen sulkily maintained that riding around in his

truck all day was not her job; she had thought they were just going to look at the stand and go straight back to the motel. At first, he ignored her demands because he thought he wanted her company, but by the time the guy at the parts store had located and sold them the fitting, her whining was wearing on him. He could've dropped her off at the motel, but he made her ride with him all the way back to the fairgrounds out of pure stubbornness, telling her he didn't have time to drive ten miles out of the way. That didn't stop her complaining, though. Axel set his jaw and kept on driving.

Carmen was pissed. Bad enough she'd have to sell tacos for the next couple weeks. At least she was getting paid for that. This riding around with Axel was boring. She'd rather watch TV.

They were almost back to the fairgrounds, coming up to Snelling and University, when a blue BMW passed them on the right, then cut in front of them and stopped at the light. Axel had to hit the brakes hard; Carmen, who was not wearing her seat belt, slid forward with a shout and cracked both knees on the glove compartment door. Axel slammed his palm down on the horn, giving the guy a ten-second blast. An arm appeared from the Beamer's window, a middle finger shot up.

For a brief moment, Axel held on to the wheel, his knuckles white and shiny. Then he jammed the gear selector into Park, unbuckled his seat belt, and opened the door.

"Hey," Carmen said, "I'm okay. Really."

Axel turned his head toward her for an instant. He didn't seem to see her. His face and the dome of his head had turned pink, with deeper red spots forming on his cheeks and forehead. His jaw was twitching, and the pupils of his eyes had contracted to poppy seeds. He jumped out of the truck. Carmen watched him run up to the BMW, jerk open the driver's door. She saw a hand, the same one that had flipped them the bird, reach for the door handle, trying to

6 3

pull it closed. Axel grabbed the wrist and jerked the driver, a soft-looking young man wearing a gray suit with a yellow tie, out of the car. Carmen thought he was going to hit the guy. Instead, grabbing the yellow tie in one fist and the guy's belt in the other, Axel lifted him and sat him on top of the Beamer. He then ducked into the car and came out holding a key chain. He bared his teeth, shook the keys in the man's face, then threw them across the street into a row of bushes fronting the Midway State Bank.

Axel, his face afire, returned to the truck, backed up, and drove around the Beamer. Carmen looked back. The young man still sat on top of his Beamer, staring after them with his mouth open. She released a nervous burst of laughter.

"Shut up," Axel snapped, staring straight ahead. "It's not funny."

Carmen choked off her laughter and said, "Hey, I just—"

"Just shut the fuck up."

Carmen clamped her lips together. This side of Axel, rarely seen, scared the shit out of her. He drove with his hands stiff on the wheel and didn't say a word the rest of the way back to the fairgrounds. Carmen played with her hair, winding it around her left forefinger, trying to act bored. She wished she'd brought a Valium with her. Or two.

Axel was embarrassed. He parked the truck by the taco stand and went in with the new hose fitting. Carmen sat in the truck, listening to some god-awful shrieking rock music while he replaced the fitting. He couldn't believe he'd lost it that way, right in the middle of Snelling Avenue. His back hurt from lifting the guy.

On the way back to the motel he pulled in to a Kmart. Leaving Carmen in the truck, he went in and bought a Sony Walkman with Mega Bass.

Carmen's mood leapt from sullenness to childish joy as she tore into the box. She gave Axel an enthusiastic hug and kiss. The Walkman had cost him $49.95 plus tax, plus another four bucks for the batteries. Expensive, but worth it if it made him feel less guilty for his outburst, not to mention the wear and tear it would save on his truck speakers. Carmen plugged in the headphones, installed the batteries, and cranked up the music. Axel could hear the tinny shrieking spill from the miniature headphones. Smiling, Carmen bounced up and down on the seat all the way back to the Motel 6.

Carmen gave him another hug when he parked the truck in the motel lot.

"You sure you don't want to drive over to Landfall with me later?" he asked.

"What?" She pulled the headphones away from her ears.

"You want to go see your mom? I'm going to pick her up in a couple hours and go back out to the fairgrounds. The employment office is sending me some kids to look at—supposed to meet them by the stand at three. We need to hire three more girls."

"Gimme a break, Axel. I'm going to be spending too much time already with Sophie. Besides, you had me out there all morning." She put the headphones back in her ears. "Thanks for the tunes," she said, waving the Walkman, her voice two notches louder than usual.

Axel locked the truck, watched her enter her room, then walked slowly over to his own room, keeping his back straight, hoping that a handful of Advils and a short nap would get him through the rest of the day.

He woke up with his heart pounding. That dream again. The one where the fair was starting, and he hadn't ordered any tortillas, and he hadn't hired any help, and he couldn't find his restaurant. Carmen was following him, laughing.

He eased himself off his bed. The back felt stiff but serviceable. Must've been a muscle spasm, nothing to worry about. He looked at the clock. Two-thirty. Damn. Axel's naps usually lasted about twenty minutes, but this one had gone nearly two hours. He washed his face, rinsed his mouth, splashed on an extra dose of Skin Bracer, and combed back the white remnants of his hair. He thought about calling Sophie to tell her he was going to be a few minutes late. Either way, she'd be pissed. But then, that was nothing unusual.

CHAPTER

9

"**O**kay, okay, okay," Axel said. "You can drive it. Just don't crash it, okay?"

"I'm not going to crash it," Sophie said, her voice tense.

Axel was puzzled. What was she so mad about? He'd agreed to buy all her sugar and salt and stuff at the regular wholesale price, the same price he always paid at Pillow Foods. He'd even rounded up the amount to an even twenty bucks. She'd snatched the money away from him, practically tore the twenty in half, mad as hell.

Sophie put the truck in gear and rolled out of the trailer court about twice as fast as Axel liked. "Jesus!" he said, grabbing at the armrest. "We being chased or something?"

Sophie, her jaw set tight, drove directly from the access road onto the entrance ramp, a slight tap on the brakes her only acknowledgment of the stop sign.

"I said you could drive it. I didn't know we were going to do the Indy 500." Axel did not like being a passenger in his own truck. Sophie was always talking him into doing things he didn't like. "The hell's the matter with you?"

"You know."

Axel considered. "You mad about the sugar and stuff?"

Sophie stared grimly ahead.

So that was it. "Jesus, Sophie, that stuff is cheap as hell. What am I supposed to do, pay you ten times what it usually costs me?"

"I been saving it up all year. And I saved all those coffee cans for you."

"So you made twenty bucks—what the heck's wrong with that? And I don't need any more coffee cans. Would you please slow down?"

"My purse is ruined."

"What?"

"Those sugar packs break open, you know. My purse is all sticky inside. My purse cost more than twenty dollars."

"I'll buy you a new purse," Axel said.

"I was going to buy a new awning. I need an awning."

Axel looked out the window and took a deep breath.

"You don't even appreciate it. I been saving sugar and salt for you for a year, and you just think how much cheaper you can get it from Pillow Foods." She pushed down on the accelerator pedal until the speedometer reached seventy.

Axel cleared his throat, reached into his pocket, extracted a small plastic box, and took a yellow pill.

"What's that?"

"Nothing."

"That was a heart pill, wasn't it?"

Axel shrugged. "I'll be okay."

"Then how come you had to take a pill?"

He did not reply. It had only been a vitamin tablet, but it was working beautifully. Sophie slowed the truck to fifty-five miles per hour, and they rode the rest of the way to the fairgrounds listening to the mellifluous voice of Cannon on 'CCO, Sophie giving Axel an occasional worried side glance.

Kirsten Lund wore lip gloss, a pink oxford shirt, stone-washed blue jeans, and her newest, whitest, white-on-white L.A. Gear cross-trainers for her job interview. Her mother had told her she should wear a dress, but her best friend, Sheila, who had worked last year at the Cheese-on-a-Stick stand, said to just wear blue jeans. Kirsten usually tried to please her mother, but this job was important to her. She was supposed to meet the guy at three o'clock but had been waiting since two forty-five, sitting at one of the picnic tables on the mall in front of the concession. It was almost quarter after. A couple of the other kids had gotten tired of waiting and left, but Kirsten needed this job really bad. All of her clothes from last year were totally embarrassing. She crossed her legs and looked up at the sign. AXEL'S TACO SHOP. There was this picture of a guy with a Mexican hat on. He was smiling, and he looked like a nice guy. She caught herself biting her fingernail, took a file from her purse, and repaired the rough edge she had left. The fair would last twelve days. Sheila had told her if she worked every day she could make six or seven hundred dollars. That would buy a lot of clothes. Kirsten unwrapped a stick of Freedent and folded it into her mouth.

At three-twenty, two more girls walked up to Axel's Taco Shop. They both had dark-brown hair and were wearing jeans and T-shirts. Kirsten thought they looked Mexican, which was not good. She figured that Axel, who might be the guy on the sign, would hire Mexican girls first. The two girls stood looking at the stand, pointing and talking, then sat down on the grass, in the shade provided by the stand, and lit cigarettes. A boy with long hair, wearing a Metallica T-shirt, wandered over and squatted in front of them. One of the girls gave him a cigarette and lit it. A few minutes later, two more girls, fortunately not Mexican, had arrived. Kirsten frowned at her competition. She had to get this job.

Five minutes later, a white pickup truck pulled up to the curb at the lower end of the mall. A tall, balding old man and a woman with bleached hair and sunglasses got out and approached the taco stand. The old man didn't look like the guy on the sign, but Kirsten was sure he was the one. He looked like an Axel. She closed her eyes and swallowed the wad of gum, took a deep breath, stood up, and walked to meet them.

"Hi," she said, intercepting them twenty feet away from the taco stand. She put out her right hand. "My name is Kirsten Lund, and I'm here to apply for a job."

Axel stopped, a little startled. He reached out and shook the girl's hand, then looked past her at the five kids who were sitting in the shade, watching sullenly. Kirsten Lund was tall and healthy-looking, and her shoes were white and clean. Her blond hair was teased up into a sort of halo around her forehead; the rest of it cascaded down her back in a torrent of heat-treated curls. She looked strong, her shoulders pulled back and her breasts thrust forward, and she was smiling so he could see her excellent teeth. She looked like a tennis player.

"You're hired," he said. He turned to Sophie. "Okay with you?"

Sophie frowned, crossed her arms, and examined Kirsten Lund. She wasn't sure she liked the way the girl had come right up to them and asked for the job. A girl like that would be asking for things all day long. She would be wanting to have her way.

"You have any fast-food experience?" she asked.

"Sure," said Kirsten. "I always work at the pancake breakfasts at my church."

Sophie looked at Axel. "She makes pancakes at church. You still want to hire her?"

"I'm real fast," Kirsten said.

"Can you work Friday and Saturday nights?" Axel asked.

Kirsten hesitated, then said, "Sure. I can work whenever you want. I'll take all the work you can give me."

"You're hired," said Axel. He regarded the other five applicants. "We need two more," he said to Sophie. "You go ahead and pick 'em. Ask 'em if they know the difference between a taco and a burrito." He turned back to Kirsten. "Are you a tennis player?"

Wow. Kirsten couldn't believe she had actually done it. Walked right up to him and got the job. And he said she could make $700 easy, maybe even more if she worked every day. In less than two weeks she would have all that money, more money than she had ever had at one time ever in her life. Plus, Axel was a really nice guy. He was going to give her six dollars an hour, which he said was a dollar an hour more than he was paying anybody else, because he said he knew right away she was a hard worker. He told her not to mention this to any of the other help.

Waiting for the bus that would take her back home, Kirsten began mentally to spend her earnings. By the time the bus arrived, she had gone through three hundred dollars, and she still saw herself in the sweater department at Dayton's.

CHAPTER

10

Carmen held the french fry between her thumb and forefinger, smiling at it. Sophie looked up from her salad, irritated.

"Are you going to eat it?" she asked.

Slowly, Carmen inserted the fry in her mouth, bit the tip off, and chewed.

"I don't think she's hungry," Axel said.

"I'm hungry. I just like to eat slow." She took another small bite.

Sophie fished an olive from her salad bowl, watching Carmen.

"So," Axel said. "Tomorrow's the big day. The weather's supposed to be perfect. Should be a good crowd."

Both Carmen and Sophie ignored him. Sophie's narrowed eyes were locked on her daughter; Carmen gazed dreamily back at her.

"You're acting like a zombie," Sophie said. "Why don't you sit up straight?"

Carmen giggled and slumped farther down in the vinyl booth.

"We should've let her stay in Omaha," Sophie said. "Look at her."

"She looks all right to me," Axel said. "She's just tired."

"That's right, I'm just tired."

"You're both nuts." Sophie stabbed a chunk of lettuce.

Axel, who had finished his porterhouse a few minutes before, rattled the ice in his glass. Every year, he took Sophie and Carmen out to dinner at Flannery's Steakhouse the night before the fair. Neither of them ever ordered steak, and every year they found something to argue about. It wasn't worth it. Next year he'd just give them each some flowers and let them order takeout.

Carmen was slowly dissecting her deep-fried walleye, scraping off the breading, separating the fillet, picking out the tiny black veins, every now and then placing a small piece of white flesh in her mouth. Axel could see Sophie struggling to keep her mouth shut. It wouldn't last. She was right about her daughter, of course. Carmen was acting as if she was terminally bored. Maybe this was one of those things young people did to drive old folks crazy. He'd done his share, Axel recalled. He wasn't going to worry about it. Once the fair started, she wouldn't have time to be bored. Once those customers got a load of his new menu item, the Bueno Burrito, she'd be too busy to feel anything.

"Can I watch TV in your room?" Carmen asked as she stepped down from the truck. They were stopped in front of her room, number 19.

Axel put the transmission in Park and leaned past Sophie. "Why? Don't you have a TV?"

"It's a little one. You got that big screen."

"Well, you can't watch it. I don't like people in my room when I'm not there."

Carmen pushed out her lower lip. "I just want to watch for a little while."

"Not tonight. I have to take your mother home."

Carmen slammed the truck door. Axel waited until she had let herself into her room, then he rolled out of the parking lot.

"Why wouldn't you let her watch your TV?" Sophie asked.

Axel took a minute to reply. "I don't want to get home, have my room stinking of cigarettes."

Sophie nodded. "I'm glad she wanted to be dropped off first. She was getting on my nerves."

"She's always got on your nerves."

"Not always. Only since she turned twelve."

"That's a tough age."

"So's thirty-nine."

Axel laughed. Sophie had been thirty-nine for nearly a decade.

Sophie said, "What's so funny?"

Carmen lay on her back on the bed, finding animal shapes in the ceiling tiles. So far she had found a wolf, a kangaroo, and two bunnies. The bunnies were screwing. She was glad she hadn't had to ride all the way over to Sophie's. Axel was probably pissed that she'd insisted on being dropped off first.

Actually, now that she thought about it, he had seemed sort of relieved.

She wished she had something to drink. The Valium was nice, it had kept her calm during dinner, but a drink would make it even better.

Someone knocked on the door. Carmen sat up, startled. Was Axel back already? She went to the window and peeked out around the edge of the curtain, but she couldn't see who was knocking. Axel's truck was gone. She opened the door.

"Hey, Carmen," said James Dean. He buried his index finger in her left breast. "How they hangin'?"

Axel did not think it was love. Not the kind of heart-floating, bowel-stopping love he had experienced in his younger years. He could not think of himself loving this woman, with her bleached hair and her aging body. He thought about her dark eyes, always squinting because she would never admit to needing glasses. It was not love.

Nor was it lust. There was not the hunger, the desire, or the breathlessness.

Beneath him, in the dark, Sophie was breathing through her nose. Sounds like short, sharp sighs. Axel moved his hips slowly and rhythmically, feeling himself sliding inside her, separated only by a generous layer of K-Y jelly.

There was affection, certainly. For all her pretentious snottiness and selfishness, he cared about her. There was a bond. He wanted her to be happy. But the sex had nothing to do with that.

Once every couple of months they fell into bed together. They did not talk, never discussed it before or later, never acknowledged their physical relationship in the light of day. It was something that just happened between them, almost accidentally, a kind of random bonding, like molecules colliding, briefly adhering, flying apart. No sense of dominance, or of tenderness, or of submission. They remained separate, inside themselves. She never flattered him, and she displayed no particular interest in pleasing him.

The patient rhythm of their movement flowed through the narrow bed to the shell of the mobile home; Axel could hear faint creaks as the trailer body flexed in sympathy.

If it was neither love nor lust that drew them down onto this foam mattress, then perhaps it was the need to know that it was still possible that affection could manifest itself physically. That the plumbing still worked.

Sophie's breathing was coming more rapidly now; he increased the tempo of his movement. It was good. In the dark, though he could not see it, he was sure that her face was changing. She would look more like her daughter now, younger and softer, without the hard shell of fear and mistrust. At these times he wished that he could have met Sophie in her younger years, before they had both grown their hard, dry shells. Sometimes he could even believe it was still possible, that they could both become young again.

He felt himself unlocking inside; the swirl of sensation low

7 5

in his gut would soon become an orgasm. A thought from some other part of his mind appeared: In twelve hours, they would be at the fair. The smell of hot oil. Sophie's breath had become harsh and loud. He pictured her in the taco stand, rolling a burrito. Her mouth was wide open now, and he could hear air rushing through her throat, feel it hot in his ear.

His thoughts fragmenting, Axel came.

Bill Quist, night manager of the Motel 6, stood behind the glass door in the lobby and watched room number 19. What he should've done, he should have called her and told her she had a visitor. He shouldn't've just given the kid her room number, especially a kid as weird-looking as that one, especially with the kid not even knowing her last name or anything. But he'd been watching *Rescue 911,* and it had been easier to just tell the kid what he wanted to know.

He had turned away from the TV long enough to watch the kid drive his beat-up Maverick across the parking lot to her room. Carmen, old Axel's daughter or niece or whatever the hell she was, had let the kid into her room. After *Rescue 911* was over, he noticed the kid's car was gone. A little later, he saw the kid return with a shopping bag, and she let him in again. So he figured everything must be okay.

Tired of watching, Quist replaced his greasy eyeglasses in the front pocket of his flannel shirt and returned to the comfortable chair behind the counter. He leaned back and closed his eyes and thought about what he had seen. He wondered if old Axel knew what was going on. Probably not.

Quist smiled. Mostly his job was a snore, but now and then it got sort of interesting. Shit happened. Opportunities occurred. He sat up and put on his glasses and looked again at number 19. He was pretty sure they were in there screwing. He figured she would be on top, hanging those big tits in the kid's face, bouncing them off his cheeks. None of his business, of course, but it was interesting to think about.

CHAPTER

11

Sophie made her first sale at eight fifty-five in the morning, a bean burrito and a cup of coffee to Willie the glassblower, who ran a concession at the top of the mall.

"You owe me five," Axel said to Tommy Fabian. The two men were standing on the shallow slope leading up to the Horticulture Building, a vantage point from which they could keep an eye on their respective businesses.

Tommy said, "That don't count. He's a carny. The bet was you wouldn't break ice before nine."

"So? I made a sale, didn't I?"

"Yeah, well, I don't call that breakin' ice. Carnies don't count."

Axel held out a hand, palm up.

Tommy muttered, "Fuckin' Willie." He pulled a thick roll of bills from his back pocket, peeled off a five. "Technically, I shouldn't be paying you. How 'bout we go double or naught on if it's gonna rain."

"Gonna rain when?"

Tommy looked up at the clear blue sky. "I'm saying it's gonna rain before Monday."

"Monday's four days away. I'd need some odds on that."

"It don't rain, I pay you twenty."

"Fifty. And it doesn't count if it rains between midnight and eight A.M."

"You're killing me, Ax."

"Then pay me the fin."

Tommy slapped the bill into Axel's hand. "You watch, though. See if it don't fucking pour."

"I hope to hell you're wrong. Wet people don't like to eat."

Tommy grunted, then pointed. "Look who's here," he said. "Sammy the motorhead. Come to the fair to look at the tractors, I bet."

Sam O'Gara, hands buried in the pockets of his coveralls, cigarette planted dead center in his mouth, sauntered across the mall toward them, wearing a spotless green John Deere mesh baseball cap.

"Hey, Ax," Sam said, "how do you know if a carny girl likes you?"

Tommy looked away.

"She shows you her tooth." Sam cackled.

"I don't get it," Axel said.

"That's because it's not funny," Tommy snapped. He didn't like carny jokes, unless he was the one telling them.

"Where'd you get that fancy chapeau?" Axel asked.

"I stole the motherfucker," Sam said. His cigarette bobbed up and down, losing an ash. "Where the hell you think I got it? What does it say on it? I got it from showing genuine interest in purchasing a new John Deere tractor."

"You never owned a new vehicle in your life," Tommy said.

Sam inhaled through his cigarette, then spat it onto the grass. "You should see these harvesters they got up there on Machinery Hill. Even got CD players in 'em. Like fuckin' Mercedes with six-foot tires. I shoulda been a farmer."

"You were a farmer, you'd have to work all day."

"That's true," Sam said. "So when we gonna play some cards?" He reached out and bipped the top of Tommy's

Stetson. "Ax is gonna give us a shot at his coffee can—right, Ax?"

Tommy pushed his hat back up. "You still keeping your money in coffee cans, Ax?"

Axel crossed his arms. "What do you mean, 'still'?"

"I heard you owned the First National Bank of Folgers."

"Who told you that?"

"That little gal a yours, Carmen. She told me last year. I figured she was bullshitting me, y'know? I mean, what kind of idiot would keep his money in coffee cans?"

"I don't know," Axel muttered, looking over at his taco shop. A small line had formed. Sophie was serving, and he could see Carmen in the back of the stand, draining a rack of tortillas. It's beginning, he thought. The money is starting to flow.

Carmen poured herself another cup of coffee, her sixth that morning. It wasn't helping. The morning of the first day, and already she was beat.

"Three beef tacos, one bean tostada," Sophie shouted over her shoulder.

Carmen set her coffee on the shelf above the prep table, proceeded to build three tacos. "Where's our help? I thought they were supposed to be here."

"It's only nine-fifteen. I told them to come at nine-thirty. Don't forget the tostada."

"I got it, I got it." It was all that James Dean's fault, showing up that way. It had been a long night.

"What are you doing here?" she'd asked him.

"I missed you. What's the matter, you aren't glad to see me?"

"How'd you find me?"

"There's only a couple Motel 6's. It wasn't too hard."

He had been dressed the same way she remembered: jeans, leather jacket, no shirt, heavy military boots. Only now he seemed jazzed up, talking too fast, wired from driving straight through from Omaha.

"You drove all the way up here to see me?"

"I sure did. You got anything to drink? Beer or anything? I gotta jack down. I'm thirsty."

Seeing her chance to get rid of him for a few minutes, give her some time to think, she'd suggested that he run over to the liquor store for some of those canned martinis, maybe a twelve-pack of beer too. After he left she'd considered locking the door, not letting him back inside. A guy like Dean, he could really make her life complicated. On the other hand, no one had ever driven that far just to see her before. And he was sort of cute, if you didn't look too close. By the time he knocked on her door again, she was thinking that it might be sort of fun to have him around. They'd sat up drinking martinis and talking till after two.

Carmen wrapped the tacos and the tostada, delivered them to the front counter.

"I need two Bueno Burritos and a nachos," Sophie said. "We've got a line, girl."

"Okay, okay, okay," she muttered. "Keep your shirt on." Those fucking Bueno Burritos, another one of Axel's dumb ideas, took twice as long to make. They had so much stuff in them, the tortillas kept tearing.

Some of the things Dean had been saying had been interesting. He kept talking about Puerto Penasco, about how good you could live if you had money.

"So get some money and let's go," she had said.

"I'm working on it." Dean had grinned, his teeth bright. "Maybe we'll stumble across some coffee cans or something."

At that, Carmen had felt her belly go thumpity-thump, and a shiver had crawled up her back. "That's not funny."

"Hey, I was just kidding you." Then he'd started reading poetry from this book he had, and she'd tuned him out. Really boring. And *then,* all night long, he'd tossed and turned and muttered to himself. He'd still been twitching and rolling around on the bed when she'd left the room to ride over to the fairgrounds with Axel. Would he still be around when she got back? She sort of hoped he'd just go away. On the other hand, she wanted to hear more about Puerto Penasco. It gave her something to think about while she was rolling burros. Maybe it wasn't such a crazy idea after all. She wondered how many coffee cans full of cash it would take to buy a villa on the ocean.

Axel leaned through the door at the back of the stand, smiling. "Carmen, what's up?"

"Nothing!" she said, startled.

"Those Buenos selling?"

"Yeah. I'm busy as hell. You want to give us a hand?"

"Can't. I've got some business to take care of. Those girls haven't shown up yet?"

"You see them? I don't." Carmen loaded a pair of chimichanga-size tortillas with meat, beans, lettuce, and cheese. She added a few olive slices, a spoonful of sour cream, and a glob of guacamole, which was what put the *Bueno* in the Bueno Burrito. She popped a tray of nachos into the microwave, then proceeded to roll and wrap the burros.

"Carmen?" Axel said.

"What?"

"I need you to roll me six Buenos. And I need a bag to carry them in."

"What for?"

"Some friends of mine."

"I don't have time. Roll them yourself."

Axel continued to smile. He said, "Just roll me six, would you, sweetheart?"

Dean's naked body snapped up into sitting position, pouring sweat. He was in his cell—no! He was in his sister's apartment—no! Muscles rippled and twitched, vibrating his frame. Dream images of Mickey screaming at him gave way to the tangled mess of twisted sheets and bedspread, sunlight slanting past the heavy curtains, the collection of aluminum beer cans on the nightstand. He was alone. A headache gripped the back of his neck, and his jaw hurt from gritting his teeth. He breathed out, swung his legs over the edge of the mattress, and stood up; the room tilted, righted itself. "Where the hell is she?" he muttered, moving toward the bathroom.

Dean hadn't shaved his scalp in two or three days. His hair was about an eighth of an inch long already, and starting to curl. If he didn't take care of it soon, it would start looking like a mat of tiny ginger-colored springs. He found a disposable razor on the sink, soaped up his head, and went at it. He was a little shaky, cut himself three or four times. The bright-red spots on the white Motel 6 towel made him dizzy. He wondered whether Mickey's death would have bothered him more if there had been blood involved. Say, if she'd cut her head open. Maybe he'd have called 911. Or maybe he'd have had to leave the apartment right away. She would still be dead, but he wouldn't know it.

Now that he thought about it, it was *possible* that she *wasn't* dead. It was *possible* that she was in a coma. He'd heard that people in comas were cold and that their pulse was so weak you couldn't feel it. It could be.

He thought, Do I feel better now, knowing that she might be alive? He stared at his reflection in the mirror, circles beneath his eyes, soap bubbles on his head, a jailhouse tattoo of a burning cross on his right shoulder. He felt exactly the same. She could be dead or alive; it made no difference. Weird.

Twenty minutes later, he was dressed in his jeans and one of Carmen's T-shirts, the orange Bugs Bunny shirt he'd seen her wear back in Omaha. His stomach needed food. He thought he remembered a Denny's just up the street. The image of eggs and bacon and hash brown potatoes propelled him out the door. He was just getting into his car when he saw this old guy coming out of a room at the other end of the motel. Was that him? The Coffee Can Man? He was old enough. Dean crossed his arms on the roof of the Maverick, rested his chin on his wrists, and watched the old man walking toward him, a green plastic garbage bag swinging from one hand. For a few seconds, he thought the guy might be coming over to talk to him, but it turned out he was heading for the white pickup parked on the passenger side of the Maverick. The old man opened the door and threw the bag into the cab, then noticed Dean and jerked his chin up, startled.

Dean said, "Morning."

The old man nodded, his eyes quickly checking out the interior of the Maverick, then looking to each side. "Nice day," he said. He had a big voice, but he seemed on edge, like he'd gotten caught doing something.

Dean smiled. "Yeah, it sure is." He still wasn't sure if this was the Coffee Can Man. The guy was staring at the rings in his eyebrow. Dean could always tell.

"You staying here?" the old man asked.

"Maybe. Thinking about it."

"It's a nice place." They regarded each other uncomfortably, having talked a moment too long.

Dean said, "So I hear there's some kind of big fair going on here."

The guy brightened at that, seemed to relax a little. "There sure is," he said. "The state fair. You must be from out of town."

"Nebraska."

"Well, how about that." The old man gave him a sort of wave, climbed into his truck, closed the door.

Dean said, "Hey!"

The old man rolled down his window.

"You know how to get there?" Dean asked.

"Depends on where you're going, son."

"To the state fair."

The old man leaned out the window and pointed. "You just head on up Larpenteur there, turn south on Snelling.

8 3

You can't miss it. Once you get there, stop by Axel's Taco Shop and grab yourself a free taco. Just tell 'em Axel said it was okay."

Kirsten Lund showed up for work wearing a Benetton top that matched her pink lips and nails perfectly. Her hair was bound back in a French braid, and the pimple that had erupted on her nose the day before was hardly noticeable beneath the layer of medicated makeup. She put her head into the back door of the stand and said, "Hello?"

Sophie, back at the worktable trying to build two tacos and a Bueno Burrito while a line of customers formed at the front of the stand, snapped at her. "Don't just stand there, girl. Get in here."

Kirsten stepped into the stand, looking around uncertainly. "What do you want me to do?"

Sophie rolled her eyes and shook grated cheese off her hands, scooped up the order she had assembled, and brought it to the front counter. Kirsten looked around the stand helplessly, spied an apron hanging on a hook near the door, and tied it on. Sophie took another order and rushed back to the prep table. "Watch me," she said, laying out a row of four flour tortillas like a dealer spreading a new deck of cards. Kirsten watched her fill the flour disks with blinding speed, roll them, wrap them, and deliver them to her waiting customers. Kirsten took Sophie's place at the table and, trying to remember, set out four tortillas. Sophie looked over her shoulder. "No, no, no. Now I need two tacos and a side of beans." Kirsten stepped back, helpless. Carmen stepped in through the back door.

"Where've you been?" Sophie snapped at Carmen.

Carmen ignored her. "Hi," she said to Kirsten, looking her up and down. "You got my apron on."

Kirsten said "Oh!" and reached back to untie it.

Carmen motioned for her to stop. She took a last long drag off her Marlboro and flicked it into the grass. "Relax, I don't need one." She was wearing a T-shirt that read *Axel's*

Taco Shop in red and green letters. "You must be one of the new girls, huh?"

"I just started."

Sophie interrupted. "I need two tacos and a side of beans. I've been busy as hell."

Carmen shrugged and said to Kirsten, "She show you anything yet?"

"I just got here."

"My name's Carmen."

"Kirsten Lund."

Carmen looked down at Kirsten's hands. "That polish ain't gonna last long around here."

"I don't mind," said Kirsten.

"Okay, here's how you build a taco. By tomorrow you're gonna be so good at this you can do it dead drunk."

"Really?" Kirsten had never been drunk.

"Really. It'll be like you never did anything else. First off, you get your taco shell. Here."

CHAPTER

12

The old man was right. You couldn't miss it. But getting in was another story. All the parking lots—the biggest parking lots he had ever seen—were full. Dean finally had to pay some lady in a pink sweatshirt five dollars to park his car on her front lawn. Then he had to walk a mile just to get to the fairground gates. Then stand in line behind the Fat family, Mom and Pop and three towheaded, pear-shaped kids, hulking through the revolving wooden turnstiles like hogs going to slaughter. He should've just eaten breakfast at Denny's.

Inside, the landscape teemed with pale, light-haired Minnesotans, all of them eating. The Fat family melted into the crowd, merging with their own kind. Everyone he looked at had a face full of something, even the skinny ones. And if they weren't eating, they were crowding in front of some rickety-looking shack or trailer or tent, buying something: corn dogs or minidonuts or zucchini-on-a-stick or sno-cones or foot-longs or whatever—some of the stuff they were eating didn't even look like food. People walking and eating at the same time. Dean tried to remember when he had last eaten. A bag of dill-pickle-flavored potato chips he'd bought in Iowa. Unless you counted all the beer he'd drunk last night.

He'd been on the fairgrounds only a few minutes when he lost his bearings completely. The number of people milling about was staggering—like a rock festival, only without the stage to provide direction and focus. He had never seen so many people, especially so many chunked-out people, all in motion at the same time. Where the hell was he? The crowd moved in and out of itself, groups of pedestrians twining together and separating like a confluence of molasses and oil; Dean was drawn along in the wake of passing bodies, unable to stop. Where were they all going?

They were going nowhere and everywhere. The sounds of people talking, chewing, shuffling and dragging their feet over the streets and sidewalks, some sort of aerial cable car clattering overhead, vendors shouting, an engine revving in the distance, music coming from every direction, all different tunes. It was insane. Dean had been to carnivals and fairs before, but nothing on this scale.

How was he going to find the taco place? A man carrying a five-foot-tall purple dinosaur nearly ran him down. Dean stepped aside, bumping into a pair of big-shouldered farm kids, both of them wearing caps that read *MoorMan Feeds*. One kid grinned at him and said, "Nice day, huh?"

Nice day? That was what the old man had said. He looked up at the clear blue sky, then back at the kid, whose red hat was the only part of him still visible as the crowd on the street closed. He had a bad thought then, out of nowhere. What if Carmen didn't really like him? How did he know Carmen hadn't been faking it, just using him to get her weed and her Valiums? The notion rolled uncomfortably in his gut. He forced his mind to engage the problem. Suppose she didn't like him? When he thought of her that way, she didn't seem so interesting. If she didn't like him, then she wasn't who he thought she was, and if that's what she was, then it didn't really bother him. The concepts clicked neatly into place. If she didn't really like him, that wouldn't change anything, as long as she continued to fake it. They could still go to Puerto Penasco.

Another bad thought hit him then. What if she'd lied about liking him and lied about the coffee cans full of money too? What if she'd made that up, just to get him to like her? He veered to the sidewalk, grabbed hold of a light post, and breathed slowly, filtering the greasy-smelling air through undersize nostrils. He really had to get something in his stomach.

He spotted a sign ahead, INFORMATION, and angled toward it. A smiling, cockeyed older man wearing a *Great Minnesota Get-Together* mesh cap stood in a small kiosk, scanning the crowd. Dean approached him, was about to ask him where he could find the taco place, when the man said, "Nice day, huh?"

Dean turned, thinking the man was talking to someone behind him, but no one seemed to be looking his way.

"Low eighties this afternoon," the man said. Apparently this was the type of information booth where you didn't have to ask questions. You simply passed within earshot, and information was delivered. The man continued: "They're saying we might get rained on some this weekend, but we sure did get a good one today!"

Dean regarded the man curiously, waiting for the next weather report.

"There something I can help you with, son?" the man asked.

"Yeah," Dean said. "I'm looking for this Mexican restaurant."

The man raised his gray eyebrows. "You mean like tacos and stuff?"

"That's it." What the hell did he think he meant?

"Well, there's lots of little taco stands around, only I don't know that you'd call 'em restaurants. There's one over on Judson Avenue, back the way you were coming from. And then there's a couple of them, I believe, up by the Food Building."

"I'm looking for one owned by a guy named Axel."

"Ah!" The man thrust a forefinger into the air. "Then you'd be looking for Axel's Taco Shop."

"Yeah, that's it."

"I can tell you just how to get there. But tell me something, son—how come you got those rings in your head?"

"How come you got one eye pointing the wrong way?"

"On account of I was in the war, son."

"You gonna tell me how to get where I'm going?"

"Seems to me a fellow can't help but get where he's going, but if you want to get to Axel's, you just go straight up the street here to the Food Building. Axel's is right across the mall from it."

"Thanks," Dean said.

"You betcha," the man called after him.

Dean imagined the Food Building as being this huge shrine surrounded by a sea of obesity. Maybe it was made out of food, like a gingerbread house. Or made out of corn dogs and bomb pops. He walked right past it and finally had to ask a guy who was selling plastic cowboy hats and Mylar balloons and yardstick canes where the hell was the Food Building. The guy pointed him back the way he'd come. When Dean started walking away, the guy said, "Hey, aren't you gonna buy something?" So Dean paid him three dollars for a heavy green yardstick cane with a leather loop on the end.

The Food Building turned out to be a squat, ugly, cinder-block structure, painted white, covering half a city block, surrounded by and filled with food vendors. Dean walked into the building, letting himself be pushed and jostled past the Navaho fry bread, caramel apple sundaes, giant Vietnamese egg rolls, strawberry cream puffs, deep-fried cheese curds . . . deep-fried what? He had to get out of there. The cacophony of smells was making his eyes water, exciting both his appetite and a desire to vomit. He pushed through the crowd, past the fried elephant ears and mini-Reubens and Soups-of-the-World, emerging at last onto a wide, grassy mall covered with picnic tables and surrounded by more food concessions. Frozfruit bars, Orange Treet, Black Walnut Taffy, Rainbow Cones, chocolate-chip cookies, fried chicken, sno-cones, Pronto Pups, French-Fried Ice Cream, Tiny Tot Donuts . . . Where was the Mexican restaurant? This had to be the place. When he finally spotted Axel's Taco Shop, the bright red-and-green sign jumping out at him, he felt as if his Mexican dinner had turned into a taco chip.

Dean stood staring at Axel's Taco Shop. This was no restaurant. This was a little wooden shack. A crummy little shack, no larger than most living rooms, about the size of three cells at Lincoln, if that, with the front wide open like a big window and a sign up above, a picture of a taco and a guy in a sombrero.

The lower part of the stand was also covered with signs. Dean squinted but couldn't read them. Probably menus. A blond woman stood at the counter. Behind her, he spotted Carmen. At least he was in the right place.

A man wearing overalls stopped and ordered something. The blond woman took his money and handed him what looked like a burrito. The man walked away, pushing the paper-wrapped burrito into his mouth. Dean thought, Another—what—dollar fifty? Great. He tried to imagine that burrito multiplying into a coffee can fortune. He shook his head. This was bullshit. No way this guy was rich, selling burritos to farmers in overalls and baseball caps. He was going to have to have a talk with Carmen. All the way from Omaha for burrito money.

CHAPTER

13

Sophie was used to seeing a lot of strange people at the fair, so when the bald kid with the rings in his eyebrow approached, she thought nothing of it. In fact, she would likely have forgotten him within seconds if he had not drawn attention to himself by demanding a free taco.

"Excuse me?" she said.

The kid smiled. He had small, neat teeth, very white. He looked past her.

"Hey, Carmen!" he said in a loud voice.

Carmen approached the counter. "Dean?"

"I can't have you giving away food to your friends," Sophie said. "It'll come out of your pay." It was best to put a stop to it now, before it got out of hand.

"Do I look like I'm giving away food?" Carmen said.

Sophie set her jaw. "I'm just saying."

"I can't believe you actually came out here. I mean to the fair," Carmen said.

A couple wearing matching black cowboy hats and Garth Brooks T-shirts stopped a few feet away from the stand and read the menu signs.

Sophie said, "You want to step to the side, uh, Gene. I have some customers here."

"His name's *Dean*," Carmen said.

"Yeah, and I'm a customer too. I talked to your boss, Axel, and he told me to stop by for a free taco. So here I am."

"You talked to *Axel?*" Carmen said.

Sophie said, "Look, let's not tie up the counter here, okay?"

Carmen motioned with her head. "Come on around the back."

Dean circled the stand. Carmen handed him a taco through the back door. "You talked to *Axel?*" she repeated in a low voice.

Dean nodded, biting into the taco. He chewed as he spoke. "Saw him at the motel. In the parking lot."

Carmen stepped out the door. "What was he doing there?"

Dean shrugged. "He had a garbage bag full of something."

"You tell him you knew me?"

"Hey, do I look stupid?" he asked, his mouth full of taco. A glob of salsa dropped onto Carmen's orange Bugs Bunny T-shirt.

Carmen thought it best not to answer his question.

"You got my T-shirt on," she said.

Dean said, "How about you take a break, show me around a little?"

Sophie appeared in the doorway, grabbed Carmen's apron strap. "No way, José," she said, dragging her daughter back into the stand.

Dean finished his taco, watching the women work. A few seconds later, Carmen poked her head out. "Stick around," she whispered. "I'll be out of here in no time."

"So what do you think?"

"I don't think your mom likes me."

"I mean the cheese curds."

Dean chewed the deep-fried cheese curd, searching for flavor. He examined the remaining batter-fried nodules in the paper tray. He brought the tray up to his face and sniffed, then picked out another curd, bit into it, chewed for a few moments, and swallowed. He looked at Carmen, bewildered.

"So what do you think?" she asked.

"I don't get it."

"People love them. Axel told me they take in twenty thousand a day out of this one stand."

"Dollars? What is it? It's got no taste. Needs salsa or mustard or something."

"You know when they make cheese? What Axel says is, this is the stuff they used to just throw it away. You can deep-fry anything here and sell it. Deep-fried ice cream— they even got that."

They were walking up the hill past a concession stand made in the shape of a giant baked potato. Dean shook his head and tossed the remaining cheese curds toward an overflowing trash can, missing it by three feet. "Do you take in twenty grand a day at the taco shop?"

"You kidding? We're lucky to break five on a good day."

"That much?" It wasn't twenty grand a day, but he was impressed. Maybe there was something to those coffee cans after all. "I thought you told me this guy Axel had a restaurant."

"Axel calls it a restaurant. He says if a building stays up all year, it's a restaurant. If you knock it down and move it after every fair, it's a stick joint. If you can pull it behind a car, it's a trailer."

"I was expecting something bigger. You were telling me about all this money he makes, I thought there would at least be tables people could sit down at."

"Axel says you don't want them to sit down. You want them to keep moving."

"I gotta sit down. I had to park, I don't know where. I feel like I walked ten miles." Dean veered off the sidewalk and sat down on an empty bench. Carmen stood in front of him and lit a cigarette.

Dean said, "So he makes, like—what—fifty thousand in twelve days?"

"I guess."

"So he won't miss a few thousand, right?"

Carmen crossed her arms and looked away. "What do you mean?" she said.

"Well, it's just sitting there, isn't it? Sit down." He patted the bench.

Carmen sat down beside him, puffing on her cigarette. The conversation was making her uncomfortable. She liked the idea of getting her hands on some of Axel's money, but Dean was moving too fast for her. She said, "Maybe we ought to think about it."

"That's what I've been doing," Dean said. He laid his yardstick on her thigh, rolled it back and forth. "All that money. What's he gonna do with it, anyways? He lives in a Motel 6, f'Chrissakes."

Carmen stood up, knocking the yardstick aside. She needed time to think.

"Listen, you want to see a real money machine? Come here." She turned her back and started walking. Dean watched until she was nearly out of sight, then got up and followed her across the street and back toward the mall. He caught up with her in front of a large, rickety concession, a bank of glass-fronted mechanisms surrounded by a crowd of people five deep. There were fourteen machines, each operating with relentless precision. A batter-filled hopper plopped tiny rings of sweet, sticky dough into a moat of bubbling oil. The rings floated single file around the oil-filled trough, were flipped by a clever metal arm at the halfway point, and finally fell into a basket to drain, briefly, before being rolled in sugar and scooped into wax-paper bags.

"Little donuts," Dean said. "I've seen those before."

"Check out the guy with the hat."

Dean looked past the machines and saw a short, stocky man with a deeply tanned and wrinkled face sitting on an elevated stool. He wore an enormous black cowboy hat.

"That's Tommy. He owns Tiny Tot. He's a millionaire. Axel says he takes in more money in a day than we do the whole fair. Takes a bag of cash down to the bank two, three times a day. Axel says he's got the hottest concession at the fair, except for the Beer Garden. I bet Tommy's got ten times as much money as Axel, and he lives in a trailer!"

Dean squinted at the stocky little man. "He looks pissed."

"He always looks like that. Me and Tommy are buddies." She waved over the crowd, but Tommy didn't see her.

Dean shook his head slowly. "The guy is miniature. Like his donuts."

Carmen grabbed his arm. "Shit! There's Axel. He better not see us together."

Dean looked but could not pick Axel out of the crowd. "What's the problem?"

"You don't know Axel. He gets really weird around my boyfriends. I'll see you later, okay?"

Dean said, "Wait a minute . . ." But she was already out of sight. Boyfriend? Was that what he was? He watched the donut machines for a few minutes, trying to think of himself as Carmen's boyfriend but soon becoming fascinated by the little guy in the cowboy hat. He couldn't get over how small the guy was, almost like a midget. A midget millionaire. It was something to think about.

CHAPTER

14

Kirsten Lund stared with open fascination at the daughter, Carmen, telling the mother, Sophie, to go fuck herself.

Carmen in her food-stained T-shirt, breasts moving up and down behind the Axel's Taco Shop logo, shaking as she thrust her middle finger at Sophie and stamped her feet on the painted plywood floor of the stand. Kirsten wondered what it would be like to have breasts like that, to have them hanging out there twenty-four hours a day.

The mother and daughter were different but the same. Sophie was taller, thinner, and paler than her daughter. She looked like a version of Carmen that had been leeched, milked, stretched, and bleached. Kirsten waited for Sophie to slap Carmen, or start crying, or throw something, but all she did was yell back, calling her daughter a spoiled little bitch. Kirsten, gripping her apron, pressed her back against the cooler, giving them plenty of room. Carmen was on a roll now. "I take a five-minute break, you'd think the fucking world ended," she shouted as she slapped a tortilla onto the prep table. "Look at me! I'm fucking working! I'm putting the fucking beans on." She slammed a scoop of crushed pink beans across the tortilla. "I'm putting the fucking cheese on." She slapped a handful of bright-orange cheese down on top of the beans. "The fucking lettuce. Fold the fucker up—here, stick it up your fucking ass you don't like it." She threw the taco on the floor and stomped out of the stand.

Kirsten tried to imagine talking to her mother that way. The thought made her heart accelerate. Screw you, Mom, she imagined herself saying. Put it in your butt.

Sophie, her face having gone from pink to red to white, let her breath out and turned back to the serving window. A plump, gray-haired woman with a determined smile was waiting there, holding her purse on the counter with two hands. Behind her, an old man in a misshapen felt hat, the man old enough to be her father or even her grandfather, was crouched over a cane.

The woman said, "Could we buy some beans from you? Just a cup of beans?"

"It'll be a dollar," Sophie said. "Thank you for waiting." Her hands were shaking.

"That's all right. I could see you were busy. I have a daughter too." The woman dug in her purse, found a wallet, and extracted a dollar bill. "We'll take one cup." The old man behind her was shaking visibly, holding himself up by gripping the handle of his cane with both hands. Sophie deposited the money in the steel cash box under the counter. Kirsten filled a small Styrofoam container with beans. She set a spoon and a napkin alongside it, aware of Sophie's eyes on her. The gray-haired woman led the old man to a nearby bench, sat him down, and presented him with the cup of beans.

"When you get old," Sophie said, twisting her hands together, "they make you eat beans all the time. My dad had to eat beans every day. He liked those green ones. Lima beans."

"I like lima beans," said Kirsten.

Axel stepped in through the back door. "What's going on? Where's Carmen?"

"She took a break," Sophie said. "It's about time you showed up. Where've you been?"

Axel shrugged.

Sophie said, "Can you give us a hand here? I need three Buenos."

Axel looked at Kirsten and raised his eyebrows.

"She doesn't know how to make them," Sophie explained. "Juanita won't be here for another hour, and I need three Buenos."

Axel smiled at Kirsten. "Never rolled a burro, eh?"

Kirsten shook her head. "But I made some tacos. Carmen showed me how to do the tacos and tostadas and nachos."

"Waiting for three Buenos," Sophie said.

"The secret of a Bueno," Axel said to Kirsten, "is getting the right proportion of ingredients on the tortilla. You always start with the beans. Not too much, though. Come over here where you can see. A little closer. Now watch how I do this."

James Dean found a bench where he could eat his bag of donuts while keeping an eye on the guy, Lord of the Donuts, perched on this stool that was high enough so he could sit down and still be taller than the kids working for him. Sit and yell at them. What was the guy's name? He couldn't remember what Carmen had told him, so he thought of him as Tiny Tot, Lord of the Donuts. Dean sat and waited until Tiny Tot got down off his stool and left the stand, passing so close Dean could have reached out his yardstick cane and tripped him. When he was almost lost from sight in the crowd, Dean abandoned the bench and followed him. As it turned out, he was visiting the rest rooms. Dean went in and stood down from him at the long steel trough, pretending to piss. Tiny Tot stood about five two in his pointy cowboy boots, a good five inches shorter than Dean. Tiny Tot pissed quickly, rattling the stainless with angry bursts of urine, then returned to the donut stand. Dean followed, swinging his cane.

The next time Tiny Tot climbed down off his stool, he took a plaid canvas shoulder bag and filled it with cash from the metal drawers under the donut machines. Dean followed him again, this time to a second donut stand, near the Beer Garden. While Dean bought a third bag of donuts, thinking of the dollar fifty as money in the bank, Tiny Tot collected the cash and left off several rolls of coins, then walked away in another direction. Dean, stuffing his cheeks full of greasy little donuts, stayed ten yards behind, enjoying the idea of so much money being carried by such a small man. He was not planning to actually do anything, of course. This was a simple reconnaissance. Later he could think about what to do with his knowledge. Right now it was just a game.

The third donut stand was tucked in under the grandstand. Tiny Tot collected the cash, then got into a discussion with two of his employees, which ended with him angrily hanging an out-of-order sign on one of the seven machines. Dean sat on a grassy spot across the street, tapping his stick on the curb and watching. When Tiny Tot finally left, redfaced, biting down hard on one of his little cigars, Dean closed the gap between them to less than twenty feet. The guy had no idea he was there. Totally oblivious. Dean might as well have been invisible.

Tiny Tot crossed Carnes Avenue, fat shoulder bag swinging, jamming his feet into the toes of his cowboy boots with each short, angry step. He cut across a large grassy area dotted with groups of fairgoers, past an exhibit promising a look at a Real, Live Albino Whale, $10,000 Reward If Not Alive, then turned up a wide alley behind a row of food concessions. Where was he going? Dean tucked his yardstick under his arm and stepped up his pace. Tiny Tot rounded a corner; Dean followed and almost collided with him. They stood frozen for a moment, their eyes locked.

"How are you doing?" Dean said, waggling his yardstick cane back and forth between them.

Tiny Tot grasped the cane with his right hand, smiled

around his cigar, then slowly reached his left hand toward Dean's face. For a moment, Dean thought the little old man was going to caress him. Instead, Tiny Tot hooked his fingers through Dean's eyebrow rings. Dean lowered his head, following the sudden pain in his brow, to a place beneath the brim of the black cowboy hat, down to the level of Tiny Tot's bright blue eyes.

"I'm doing fine," Tiny Tot said. "How are you doing?"

Dean felt as if his brow was separating from his skull.

Tiny Tot growled, "You better let go that stick."

Dean released his grip on the cane, thinking he'd have his shot later, as soon as the son-of-a-bitch let go of his rings. "Okay," he said.

Tiny Tot blinked. The smoldering tip of his cigar was an inch from Dean's nose.

"I let go," Dean pointed out.

Tiny Tot grinned and exhaled a cloud of smoke. Dean felt him tense, then heard the whoosh of the cane, felt it whip up between his legs and crash into his testicles. He jerked back, felt a tearing sensation in his forehead, and dropped to the ground, globules of pain bubbling up through his abdomen, his eyes pulsing with black flashes.

"I can't hardly stand to work with her," Carmen said.

Axel pulled out of the lot onto Como Avenue. It was nearly midnight, and he was feeling old. The first day of the fair was always a killer. The body needed time to adapt.

"I mean, we're in there for a couple hours, and she's all over me. Like I can't do anything right. Like I don't know my job. The bitch." Carmen lit a cigarette.

"Crack the window, would you?"

Carmen rolled her window down.

"We have eleven days to go, Carmen."

"Christ, tell me something good."

"I need you two working together. Can't you humor her?"

"That's what I did all night. Me and Juanita just made

food and let her and that Kirsten girl serve. Juanita's all right. Sophie doesn't bother her."

"How did Kirsten do?"

Carmen shrugged. "She was okay. She sure is clean. I don't know how she stays so clean. It's like food doesn't stick to her."

Axel smiled, thinking that Carmen was right. Kirsten Lund could walk through a shit storm and come out looking like she'd just had a bubble bath. "We did good today," he said.

"Oh, yeah?" Carmen looked at Axel. "How good?"

Axel patted the canvas bank bag on the seat beside him. "About thirty-five hundred and change. That's a good first day. Maybe once you get some sleep it'll be easier to work with her."

"I don't know about that." Carmen could now feel the two Valiums she had swallowed while they were cleaning up the stand. They helped. Eleven more days working with Sophie. She told herself it would be the last time, ever. Puerto Penasco was looking better than ever. Rich and free in Mexico. Flicking her cigarette out the window, she closed her eyes and imagined herself on the beach, dipping into a coffee can to pay for her rum punch. She let her mind drift.

"Here we are."

Carmen opened her eyes as they turned into the Motel 6 parking lot. "Want to drop me at the lobby? I need some cigarettes."

Axel swung the truck over to the brightly lit lobby and let Carmen out. "See you in the morning," he said. Carmen walked into the lobby, digging in her purse for change. Cigarettes were up to two fifty. She dropped ten quarters into the slot and pressed the Marlboro button.

"Back again, eh?"

Carmen turned away from the cigarette machine to look at the man sitting behind the counter. He was holding a copy of *Penthouse,* looking at her over the top of it.

"You talking to me?" she asked.

The man lowered his magazine. His eyes were small, gray, and moist.

"You stayed here last year," he said. "I remember you. You work with Mr. Speeter. Out at the fair, right?"

Carmen picked up the fresh pack of Marlboros. "That's right," she said. "Good night." She took a step toward the door.

"I hear you're gonna be a nurse now," the man said.

Carmen stopped. "Axel tells you stuff, huh?"

"Now and again. He's my best customer, you know. He's stayed in number three since before I even worked here. We're like neighbors; we talk." Quist looked back down at his magazine. "I see you got a roomie now." He turned a page.

Carmen lifted a cigarette out of the pack, placed it directly in the center of her mouth, then rested both elbows on the counter between the rack of postcards and the American Express applications. She waited. After fourteen hours at the fair, she was too beat to figure out what was going on. She waited for him to explain it to her.

"He's in there now," Bill said, keeping his eyes glued to the magazine. "Your skinhead boyfriend. I saw him go in your room a couple of hours ago."

"So? Hey, you got a light?"

Bill dug in his shirt pocket and extracted a book of matches. He looked at the matchbook cover. "'Call 1-900 QUICKIE,'" he read, then tossed them to her. Watching her light the cigarette, he continued: "You know, I'm supposed to get more for double occupancy. Since the old man's footing the bill, you think I should maybe ask him for the money?"

Carmen shrugged, blew out a long stream of blue smoke, examined her fingernails. They were yellow and orange from handling processed cheese.

"Or maybe I shouldn't bother him. What do you think?"

"I wouldn't bother him with it. You know how it is."

"So how am I going to get paid?"

"I'll see what I can do. How much do you want?"

"Twenty cash ought to do it. Twenty a night."

"I'll have to get back to you on that. In the meantime, let's just keep it between you and me."

"Gotcha, babe. You and me."

Carmen crossed the parking lot, let herself into room 19, dropped her purse on the near bed. One day at the fair, and already she was exhausted. She took a canned martini from the cooler by the nightstand and popped it open. The Valiums were stroking the base of her neck. She sipped at the martini and felt the tension roll away, felt her shoulders dropping, felt her legs growing longer. The clock read 12:24. In eight hours she would be back at the fair, spreading beans over fried tortillas.

Dean lay on his side on the other bed. He was wearing his underwear and holding a wet towel against the left side of his head. His brown eyes followed her.

Carmen took another sip of martini. She said, "I got blackmailed about five minutes ago." Dean did not reply. "So what happened to you?" she asked.

After several seconds, Dean replied, "I don't want to talk about it."

Carmen shook a cigarette loose and lit it. She would be asleep soon; she could feel it gathering. But at the moment, she was staying up on a few untamed shreds of anxiety. She traced a design on Dean's muscular belly with her forefinger.

"You want to fuck around?" she asked.

This time, he took even longer to reply. In fact, he never did. Well, what the hell. She didn't care. It was just an idea to kill some time. She was all but asleep when he got up to go to the bathroom, walking funny, keeping his legs apart, almost like a chimpanzee. Carmen fell asleep thinking of him as James Dean, the naked ape.

CHAPTER

15

Near the back of the south parking lot, deep in the RV ghetto, Tommy Fabian emerged from his sun-bleached Winnebago at six-thirty in the morning. It was a nice day, the second day of the fair, still cool from the night but with plenty of sunshine promising a warm afternoon. He crossed the parking lot, his short legs pumping, and paid his way into the fairgrounds. He bought a cup of coffee from a grab joint in the Coliseum, added plenty of sugar and coffee creamer, then walked up to Tiny Tot #1 and sat on a folding stool to watch the early-morning action. Fairgrounds employees and concessionaires were moving about, carrying things, opening stands, and unloading supply trucks. A street sweeper passed by, its enormous rotary brushes hissing over the asphalt. A man wearing a Minnesota State Fair windbreaker was handing out copies of the *State Fair Daily News* to anyone who looked as though he might be in charge of something. Tommy accepted a copy without looking at it. Years ago he had read things like that, but lately it seemed to be too much trouble.

At seven o'clock he visited the doniker behind the deep-fried-zucchini joint. They were actually clean, this time of day, and plenty of toilet paper available. A few more hours, you wouldn't want your bare ass anywhere near those toilet seats. Tommy snapped off a loaf, then walked back up to the Jaycees' and bought another cup of coffee. He returned to his seat outside his donut joint, sat, and sipped slowly.

A few farmers were straggling onto the fairgrounds now, wearing their clean overalls and go-to-town feed caps. The farmers were always the first suckers to arrive. Then the families. The couples and the teenagers wouldn't show up until much later, an hour or two before dark. Tommy lit one of his small cigars, his first of the day.

At seven-thirty, he saw Axel's manager, Sophie, pass by, carrying a grocery bag. Holding the paper bag in one arm, she tried to unlock the back door of Axel's Taco Shop. The bag started to slide from her grasp. She grabbed at it, and the bag tore open, spilling several plastic pouches of flour tortillas onto the ground. Tommy watched as she picked them up, let herself into the stand.

Duane, the kid who managed Tiny Tot #1 for him, showed up at seven-forty, five minutes early. Tommy unlocked the stand, fired up four of the machines, then picked his new yardstick cane from its hook on the wall and, swinging it jauntily, strolled off toward the grandstand to get his next joint up and running. By eight o'clock sharp, he expected to sell his first bag of donuts.

The second time, Carmen woke up to the sound of Axel's fist beating on the door. She sat up, looked at the clock.

"Shit!"

Dean, who was sitting up, reading, watched her scramble out of bed, naked except for the cellophane wrapper from a pack of cigarettes stuck to her ass.

"Shit, I'm late. How come you didn't get me up?" Vaguely, she remembered waking the first time, grabbing the ringing phone, talking to Axel, hanging up. She must've gone back to sleep.

Axel's muffled voice came through the door. "Carmen! Let's go!"

She looked helplessly around the room, still too sleepy to know what to do next.

Dean said, "Why don't you tell him you're not ready. I'll drive you over later."

Axel beat his fist on the door.

Carmen took a deep breath, opened the chained door a crack.

"Axel? I fell back asleep. I'm sorry."

"How long will it take you to get your butt out here?"

"I gotta take a shower."

"Christ, Carmen. We're going to be late!"

"Why don't you go ahead. I'll catch a cab or something, okay?"

Axel threw up his arms and marched back to his idling truck.

Carmen closed the door. "He's pretty pissed," she reported.

Dean touched his brow lightly, looked at his finger.

"It's still sort of puffy," Carmen said.

Dean's jaw twitched. "Listen to this. . . ." He had his poetry book open.

"Isn't it sort of early for that?" She pulled the curtain aside, letting more light into the room.

"Listen: *This Soule, now free from prison, and passion, hath yet a little indignation.*"

"So?"

"So what do you think?"

"I think maybe some of your brains leaked out."

Dean closed the book and swung his legs over the edge of the bed. He said, "Life is too short to let an opportunity slide—you know what I mean?"

Carmen didn't. "All I know is Axel's gonna be really pissed if he gets stuck in the stand rolling burritos all day."

"So what? What I'm thinking is we just go to Puerto Penasco. What do you say?"

Carmen stared at the scab on his eyebrow. "What do you mean?"

"I mean, let's take a look in the old man's room. See what we find."

"We can't do that."

"Why not?"

"He'll know who did it."

"So?"

"So . . . I don't know." She felt her belly tingling, like she was coming on to some good acid, or like she was standing at the edge of a high cliff, looking down. The same reckless, scary feeling she got when she climbed into bed with a new guy, or lifted a twenty from the Taco Shop till, only more intense. "I don't have a key," she said.

Dean shrugged. "My guess, from what you told me about that guy in the office, that won't be a problem."

Tommy Fabian was taller than a lot of guys. His cowboy boots, which he wore because they were comfortable, brought him up to an even sixty-two inches. Lots of guys weren't that tall. The Stetson added a few more inches to his stature and, he felt, made it clear to all just who was in charge at Tiny Tot Donuts.

Tommy stood beside the rock garden on the mall, keeping an eye on Tiny Tot #1, his flagship location. The day had started off with a bang. He'd had twelve machines going before ten, and he'd made his daily nut by eleven. The rest of the day, the next twelve hours, that was gravy.

It was almost noon, and the lines were lengthening. Lines were good for business, if they weren't too long. One of the things he told his kids over and over was to work slow when there were only a few customers. Shut off a few of the machines if you have to, because you got to have a line to get a line. Then you got to kick ass when you get busy, keep them from getting too long. People would wait only a minute or so before they decided to go instead for some cotton candy, or a caramel apple, or a paper cup full of

1 0 7

french fries. It was just like his days with the carnival. You wanted to make any money, you had to know how to work the tip. That was what made this fair great. Most of the joints were run by amateurs, didn't know what the hell they were doing. A guy like Tommy, who'd grown up in the carnival, could make a small fortune.

They were starting to get hungry now; the donut lines were growing. He could see people eyeing the crowd in front of his stand, looking to see what they were missing. Tommy willed Duane, his assistant, to open up the last two machines. As he watched, Duane did exactly that.

He was a good kid.

"Hey, Tommy." Axel Speeter came up the slope and stood beside him. Tiny Tot Donuts was two spaces down and across the mall from Axel's Taco Shop. This was their usual observation point, the only place on the mall where both stands could be comfortably observed. This was their place for exchanging gossip and speculating about the weather. They were the old pros.

Tommy nodded and waved his cigar. They stood for a few moments in silence, surveying the crowd.

"Look at that pair," Axel said.

The two girls were walking, laughing, eating Pronto Pups and drinking Orange Treets. Both were wearing jeans that had been carefully ripped, shredded, and safety-pinned to dramatic effect. They were wearing thin tank tops, one pink and the other yellow. The one in yellow was wearing a Minnesota Twins baseball cap with a fuzzy green plastic butterfly pinned to the front.

"Easter eggs," said Tommy.

"What?"

"Like four Easter eggs. That's why all the old cooch shows folded up. Who needs 'em, you got that young stuff struttin' around for free?"

Axel licked his upper lip and nodded. "I wonder how they get past their mothers that way. I wouldn't let my kid go out like that."

"You ain't got a kid."

Axel raised his eyebrows. "Now, how the hell do you know that? I might have one someplace."

Tommy shrugged. "You know what she's wearing today?"

Axel frowned. The thought was doubly disturbing: that he might have a daughter and that she might be half dressed in public. He shook it off. Sophie and Kirsten were starting to get busy. If Carmen didn't show up soon, he would have to get in there and help them.

"How's your help this year?" Tommy ashed his cigar.

"Not bad. Only one major battle so far."

"Yeah, I saw that one. Heard it from way over here." Tommy chewed his cigar, spat, then said, "You know the blonde is H.O.'ing on you."

Axel looked down at Tommy, his cheeks slack.

"I seen her show up this morning with a sack of grocery store tortillas," Tommy elaborated.

Axel said, "So? What makes you think she's holding out?"

Tommy rolled his cigar in his mouth. "I know when I'm getting ripped on account of I keep a count of the donut bags. I know how many bags I got at the start of the day and how many I got at the end, and I just match up the cash and the bags, and if it don't come out I know I'm getting ripped. Now, I'm guessin' you do something like that with tortillas, right?"

"It's only approximate."

"But it gives you an idea, right? You have 'em give you a tortilla count so you know about how much money you're supposed to have, right? So I'm wondering, this morning I see the old broad—"

"Her name's Sophie."

"Yeah, Sophie. I ask myself, why's she bringing in grocery store tortillas?"

Axel nodded sadly. He didn't want to know this stuff. He trusted Sophie. Carmen, he'd have believed anything. But not Sophie. Maybe she was H.O.'ing. Maybe not. Either way, he was inclined to ignore the situation, as long as she didn't take too much.

As if reading his thoughts, Tommy said, "Look, you want to let her cop a piece, that's your business. I'm just telling you."

"Okay, you told me."

"Also," Tommy continued, "long as I'm telling you stuff you don't want to know, that little Carmen has a boyfriend she probably don't want you to know about."

"What?" This was new. Carmen had a boyfriend? The thought made his stomach drop an inch.

"Yeah. A punk kid, followed me on my cash run yesterday like I'm some jerk don't know any better than to get rolled, like I ain't been doing this my whole goddamn life." Tommy sucked furiously at his cigar, his cheeks flaming with the memory. "I'm making my run, and I noticed this bald-headed kid following me—walking right behind me like I'm deaf, dumb, and blind. I'm taking my usual shortcut." He drew a line in the air with his cigar. "I got about six thousand bucks with me and this weird-lookin' kid on my ass. So I stop, and he waves one a them yardsticks in my face and says, 'How you doing?'" Tommy dropped his cigar and ground it into the grass with the tip of a cowboy boot. "So I grab the stick and I give the son-of-a-bitch a little nut massage."

"Just like that?" Axel was impressed.

"Went down like a sack a mix. I got his stick hanging over in my joint there. One a those canes they sell, you know, got markings on it like a yardstick."

"What did he do?"

"He just laid right down."

"I mean, what did he do that you hit him for?"

"He was up to no good. I could tell, the way he was watching me. Watching me pull the money out of the tills. And I seen him with Carmen, sitting with her."

"Jesus, you just hit him? Did you think about . . . what if

he was just going to ask you where's the bathroom or something?"

Tommy grinned. "Probably that's exactly what he was going to do. He wasn't actually going to try to roll me, not in the middle of the day like that. But he was thinking about it, thinking how he could do it later on. I figured I could save us both some trouble. You shoulda seen him go down. Now there's one more son-of-a-bitch knows not to mess with Tommy Fabian."

Axel blew out his cheeks and pushed back a thin strand of hair. "You say he's bald?"

"Like he shaves his head. Creepy-looking."

"You saw him with Carmen?"

"Hand on her ass and everything. You watch yourself, Ax. Those two are cookin' up somethin', and it don't smell like frijoles."

"What does the kid look like?"

"Like a bald monkey. He's got this flat face. Used to have these rings in his eyebrow. I even got myself a little souvenir." He held up his right hand, showing off the two gold rings rattling loose on his middle finger.

Axel said, "Oh." He felt sick.

CHAPTER

16

Carmen set two twenty-dollar bills on the counter, hit the bell with her fist, then went to the coffeemaker and filled two paper cups with "complimentary coffee." Bill Quist, yawning, near the end of his shift, came out from the office, saw the money, then saw Carmen, then smiled broadly.

"Why, thank you, darling. I was starting to wonder about you."

Carmen added three packets of sugar to each of the coffees. "I told you I was gonna pay you," she said.

"That you did."

Carmen started toward the door, stopped, and turned back to Quist. "I almost forgot. Axel just called and asked me to bring him his eyedrops. He said you had a key to his room I could use."

Quist tipped his head to the side like a robin listening for a worm. "Say what?"

"I need a key to get in Axel's room."

"Mr. S. didn't say nothing to me about that."

Carmen set the coffees back on the counter, reached in her pocket, and pulled out a handful of bills. She counted out three more twenties. "He also said I should pay you a few days in advance. Also, I'm gonna need another key for my room."

"I could get in big trouble."

Carmen sipped one of her coffees, waiting.

"You just gonna go in and get something for Mr. S.?"

Carmen nodded.

Quist swallowed, looking at the money. "I think I need a little more deposit." He cleared his throat. "I mean, if you don't want me to bother Mr. S. about it."

Carmen said, "I'll see what I can do. But I need the keys right now. Axel doesn't get his eyedrops, we're both gonna be in deep shit."

The Coca-Cola crates were stacked against the wall just like she had described. Dean lifted one down from the top row and looked inside. It was full of boxer shorts. He grinned and looked at Carmen, who was standing in the doorway watching the parking lot. She looked scared.

"What are you worried about?"

"You don't know Axel," she said. "You never seen him get pissed. He finds out we were in his stuff, he's gonna be pretty mad."

"Relax, Carmen. You never seen me get mad, either." Dean thought about Mickey, something he hadn't done for more than twenty-four hours. He couldn't remember what she had done to make him mad. The memory, three days old, had grown fuzzy. He brought another crate down and set it on the bed. It contained several pressed and folded white shirts. This guy is strange, he thought.

"Why don't you just look through the sides of them," Carmen said. "He keeps the ones with the coffee cans on the bottom row. You can look through the sides of the crates and see the coffee cans."

Dean got down on his hands and knees and examined the bottom row of crates. Two of them, the two on the end, contained red coffee cans. Dean could feel his heart start up. He stood and lifted another crate off the top.

1 1 3

"He's gonna know we were here. He'll know his crates are all mixed up."

Dean ignored her and continued to dismantle the wall of red plastic crates. When he reached the bottom layer, he lifted one of the red cans. There were ten of them. He dug his nails under the edge of the plastic lid and lifted it away.

The can was jammed full of black fabric. He grabbed a fold and pulled, extracting a pair of black nylon calf-length men's stockings. He shook the contents of the can out onto the bed. The can was full of identical pairs of stockings. Dean looked at Carmen, puzzled. Carmen gaped at the stockings with an expression of utter incomprehension. Dean grabbed another can and opened it. It too was filled with black nylon calf-length men's stockings. They were held together with the original plastic hanger and still had the size and fiber content stickers: 100% nylon, fits sizes 10–13.

"Those are the kind of socks he likes," she said. "He must've found a sale."

The other coffee cans were different. They contained, in order of discovery, nine three-packs of cheap ballpoint pens, several dozen Hav-a-Hank handkerchiefs, and six new decks of Bicycle brand poker-size playing cards. Three of the cans contained fourteen pairs of new white cotton boxer shorts. One held a dried-out and yellowed set of dentures, and strangest of all, the last can was half full of ground coffee.

By the time he discovered the coffee, Dean had grown a grim little smile. He walked around the bed, stood in front of Carmen, circled her neck with his hands, and gently massaged her throat with his thumbs. She didn't look so attractive to him now. She looked like any other stupid bitch. "Carmen," he said, "I am beyond shock."

"It was there," Carmen said, her face gone white.

"Sure it was."

She shook her head. "I have to get to work. We have to put everything back like we found it."

"Tell me something—do you like me?"

Carmen nodded, feeling his thumbs on either side of her Adam's apple.

Dean held her for another five seconds, then let go and began repacking and closing the coffee cans. "You think he put it in a bank?"

"Axel doesn't like banks. But I don't know. I never know what Axel will do." She took the prescription bottle from her purse, tapped out three blue Valiums, swallowed them dry, then watched Dean reassemble the wall of Coke crates. "What are you gonna do?" she asked.

"I don't know yet."

"You just came here to get Axel's money, didn't you?"

Dean paused and stared back at her. He hadn't thought that was why he came, but now he wasn't sure. He said, "If I'd a known that you were lying to me about the money, I might not've liked you enough to drive all the way up here to see you."

Carmen thought about that. "I wasn't lying," she said.

Dean said, "Hey . . ." He pulled a grease-spotted, khaki-colored canvas bag out of one of the crates and tugged open the drawstring top. Reaching into the sack, he grinned and pulled out something wrapped in an oily rag, unwrapped it to reveal a .45-caliber pistol and a loaded clip. He popped the clip into the handle and pointed the old army weapon at Carmen's face.

"Bang," he said.

Carmen rolled her eyes and waited for the Valiums to kick in.

After helping the girls with the lunch rush, Axel poured himself a Coke and left the stand, telling them he'd be gone for a while. He wandered down Carnes Avenue, heading toward the midway. He needed the anonymity that came with the clatter and flash of the rides and games. He kept thinking about Tommy and the bald kid, imagining the scene again and again in his mind, remembering the kid he'd met at the Motel 6. It had to be the same one, the bald monkey with the rings in his head.

He would not be Carmen's first boyfriend, nor, probably, her last. He knew he would have to get used to it, and he knew he never would. Like it or not, he was beset by a father's protective fears and a lover's jealous rage. Carmen would have men, and they would have her. This one, though, this one was bad news. Even if he could not trust his own instincts in these matters, he could certainly trust Tommy's.

Axel sipped his Coke and stared up at the Ferris wheel—what Tommy would call a "chump heister"—rising above the entrance to the midway. The worm turns, he thought. Perhaps this bald monkey was a manifestation of his wicked thoughts. He imagined what Sam O'Gara would say to that, and he laughed.

Axel liked to walk the midway, a clattering, roaring, flashing, spinning quarter mile of rides, games, and sideshows that dominated the west end of the fairgrounds. He liked the noise and the action, and he liked to stand and watch the carnies work the tip, proving again and again that beneath the tight-lipped, practical exterior of the typical Minnesotan there lies yet another compulsive fool. This year, the suckers were being lured into tossing rings, basketballs, and coins by four-foot-tall Bart Simpson dolls, Inflatable Power Rangers, and Nirvana posters. Axel stopped to watch a clean, athletic-looking young man trying to win a Pink Panther doll for his girlfriend by throwing a highly inflated basketball through an undersize hoop that was farther away than it looked. He watched the kid spend twenty dollars before giving up, shaking his head, embarrassed more by his lack of skill than at his lack of good sense.

Axel walked to the end of the midway, where *Serpentina, the Snake Woman* was doing a teaser routine with a reticulated python on a small stage in front of the freak show. The freak show had evolved over the years—now it was called the Cavalcade of Human Oddities. *Three-Legged Lonna*, the *Siamese Twins from Darkest Africa*, and *Bigfoot, Monster or Mutant?* were no longer featured acts. The "freaks" were now performance artists. Serpentina could be any of three women, depending on what time of day it was. The one up there now was wearing thick eyeglasses, her thighs spilling past the edges of her faux-snakeskin leotard. Two of the women who played Serpentina also did duty as *Tortura, the Puncture-Proof Girl*. The third woman, a gaunt, hollow-eyed blonde, was occasionally featured as *Electra, Mistress of the Megawatt*. Axel preferred this modern approach. It seemed kinder than the ogling of physical deformities that had gone on a decade or two earlier. Down in the South—Mississippi, Alabama, Louisiana—the freak shows were still popular, but up here the fascination with birth defects had given way to other perversions. He had to admit, though, that watching a sword swallower, a contortionist, or a woman who could stand on an electrified plate that made her hair stand on end was not as powerfully evocative as staring at the man with feet swollen to the size of watermelons, or the young girl with an extra leg jutting from her inner thigh.

He paused at the Dump Bozo joint, watched a trio of small-town football heroes spend ten dollars for the privilege of trying to dump the obnoxious "Bozo" into a tank of water. The carny playing Bozo hurled taunts and insults at the players, driving them into a frenzy. When one of the players hit the target and dropped Bozo into the tank, Bozo would be back on his seat in seconds, spitting water and imprecations back at the ball throwers. It looked like a tough job, making people hate you so much they'd pay to get you wet. Tommy would have been good at it.

Axel was feeling fine. The buzz and clatter of the midway made him feel sane and normal. And he felt good about what he'd done with his money. He felt he could relax a little now, not be worrying about it all the time. Carmen always had been a little too interested in his money. Dipping into his coffee cans last year, thinking he wouldn't notice. He'd meant to talk to her about that but had kept putting it off, thinking about things he had done when he was her age, half a century ago, thinking she would change as she got older.

Change into what?

Yesterday, when he'd learned that she'd been blabbing it around, mentioning it to Tommy and who knew who else, he'd finally moved it all to a new, safer location. Now the entire $260,000 rested three feet underground, wrapped in two layers of Hefty bags, beneath his old pickup truck in Sam O'Gara's backyard. Axel smiled, remembering the way Sam's supposedly vicious guard hounds, Chester and Festus, had quickly lowered their hackles when presented with a half-dozen Bueno Burritos. The Bueno was a great product—even the dogs knew it. They'd wolfed the burros, then lain in the shade and watched contentedly as Axel dug the hole, dropped in the money, covered it up, and returned the old pickup to its original position. Except for the fact that the dogs were a little fatter, there was no evidence that he'd ever been there. Only he and the hounds would know. The money was safe, for now.

Axel stared sightlessly across the sea of bobbing faces moving in and out of the midway, drifting comfortably on the familiar current.

A few minutes after 4:00 P.M., Carmen stepped into the back of the taco stand. She put her purse under the counter but did not remove the mirrored sunglasses she was wearing. Sophie stood at the front counter, waiting for a customer. If she noticed Carmen's arrival, she gave no sign.

"You guys been busy?" Carmen asked.

Sophie jerked her head to the side, like she was shaking a fly off her nose.

"Sorry I'm late," Carmen offered after a moment. "Axel didn't wake me up. I overslept."

"Eight hours," Sophie said.

"Where's Axel?"

"He didn't say," Sophie said.

"Axel's weird," said Carmen. "Probably went to sit in his truck and space out."

Sophie arched an eyebrow and regarded her daughter. "He's not so weird."

"Yes he is. He's one of the weirdest guys I ever knew."

"You think he's as weird as your friend that was here yesterday?"

"Who, Dean? Dean's weird too. How come it's so dark out? It's not that late, is it?"

Kirsten and Sophie looked at Carmen, seeing themselves reflected in mirrored lenses.

"Take off your sunglasses," Sophie said.

Carmen said, "Oh!" She reached up and touched the glasses, pushing them up on her nose, but didn't remove them. Sophie shook her head, muttering, and turned back to the counter to wait for customers. She had not noticed the purple bruise that showed just past the edge of the right lens, but Kirsten did. "Did somebody punch you?" she asked in a whisper.

Carmen shook her head. It had not been a punch, exactly. More like a slap. "I ran into something I didn't know was there," she said.

After putting Axel's room back in order that morning, Carmen and Dean had walked down the street to Denny's to get something to eat. Dean had Axel's .45 stuck in his belt, under his motorcycle jacket. He asked the waitress to bring him steak and eggs, Canadian bacon, sausage links, and two glasses of apple juice. Carmen ordered pigs-in-a-blanket, her favorite breakfast when she'd been a little girl. While they waited for their food to arrive, she had asked him what he planned to do next.

119

"Next?"

"Yeah. You going back to Omaha?"

Dean shook his head. "Can't do that."

"How come?"

Dean stroked her kneecap with the barrel of the .45. That was when he'd told her about Mickey. Carmen was glad she'd had the foresight to eat the three Valiums.

"It's all your fault, you know," Dean said. "If you hadn't wanted those Valiums, it never would've happened."

"Wait a second," Carmen said. "I didn't do anything."

"And if you hadn't wanted to go to Puerto Penasco, I wouldn't even be here. Now it turns out you were lying to me about the coffee can thing."

"The money used to be there," Carmen said. "He must've done something with it." She didn't like how calm he was acting.

"What? What did he do with it, Carmy?"

Carmen shrugged. She didn't like being called "Carmy," either. Their breakfasts arrived. She watched Dean eat his meat. He held on to the plate, lowered his face, and forked the food in quickly. He ate the steak, then the bacon, then the sausage, then the eggs. Carmen unrolled her pancake-wrapped sausages and ate a few pieces of pancake, wondering in a distant sort of way what was going to happen next. Even filtered through the Valium, Dean was making her nervous as a mouse in a cage with a sleeping cat.

She pushed her plate aside. "What are you gonna do now?" she asked.

Dean drank his second glass of apple juice. "What would you do?"

"I don't know."

"Maybe I'll rob a bank. What do you think?" He lifted the .45 and set it on the table beside the remnants of his breakfast.

"You better put that away before somebody sees it."

"Don't tell me what to do, Carmy." He stared at her,

unblinking. After a few seconds, he picked up the gun and put it in his belt. "I just can't believe you got me all the way up here for nothing."

"I didn't ask you to come," she heard herself say, knowing before the sentence was finished that she'd made a mistake. She saw his left hand close, then drift toward her across the table. The fist looked large, soft, and inflated. It floated toward her, growing larger until she could see nothing else. Her head snapped back and hit the plastic booth divider. She gasped and slid down in the vinyl seat. Dean stood and walked calmly out of the restaurant. Carmen felt no pain. She touched her eyebrow, saw blood on her hand. She dipped her napkin in her ice water, dabbed at her brow. None of the other customers seemed to have noticed anything. The waitress stepped up to the table and delivered the check, raising an eyebrow but making no comment about the blood-spotted napkin Carmen held against her brow.

Carmen paid the check and walked back to the motel. Dean's car was gone. His bag was gone too, but he'd left his poetry book behind. She lay back on the unmade bed and stared up at the thousands of tiny black holes in the ceiling tiles.

A few hours later, she had awakened, put on her sunglasses, picked up a bus on Larpenteur, and gone to work. It was better than waiting, not knowing whether or when he would come back.

Now, standing in front of the prep table, her hands greasy from the ground beef and spattering oil, reliving the morning in her mind, she was surprised to discover that it was making her slightly aroused. She could still feel the warm gun barrel touching her knee. The sensation ran up the inside of her thigh into her belly. He could have shot her. He had considered it—she had seen it in his eyes—but he had chosen not to. His fist had cut her, given her a black eye, but it had felt solid and real, and compared to what he might have done, what might have happened to her, the blow had felt like a caress.

Dean might be dangerous, but he wasn't boring. He really did like her. He'd killed his own sister, but the way he told it, it wasn't exactly his fault. A part of Carmen hoped he would disappear from her life, but another part wanted to see him again. And somehow she knew she would.

CHAPTER

17

After Dean paid his five bucks and pushed through the turnstile, he bought a Harley-Davidson painter cap and a pair of cheap, dark sunglasses from one of the souvenir kiosks. It was late, ten o'clock at night, and everybody else was moving the other way, out the exits and into the parking lots to search for their cars. Dean moved against the flow of bodies, toward the center of the fairgrounds. His new sunglasses blurred the details of the late-night fairground action. A bank of low clouds had moved in over the city; the air was warm and moist. At the corner of Carnes and Nelson, he bought a foot-long hot dog, piled high with onions, and ate it while he watched the flickering, wheeling lights from the midway reflect off the clouds. When he had finished, he strolled up Carnes to the mall, where he bought a blue-raspberry sno-cone and found a comfortable bench where he could suck on the flavored ice and watch the donut guy.

Tiny Tot Donuts was surrounded by people picking up their final snack of the night. Through occasional breaks in the crowd, Dean could see the black cowboy hat bobbing up and down. It didn't look like the stand would be closing anytime soon. Dean finished sucking the blue juice out of his sno-cone and dropped its flavorless remains on the trampled grass. The trash bins were overflowing anyway, nearly invisible beneath mounds of greasy paper. Two hundred thousand people had come to eat and spread their refuse over the three hundred acres. Dean strolled farther up the mall toward Axel's Taco Shop. He watched Carmen serving a small group of hungry customers. He waited a few minutes for a break in the action, then walked right up to Carmen with his new cap and shades and ordered a bean tostada.

Carmen took his order without recognizing him.

"Hey," he said. "How late you think that donut place'll stay open?"

"What?" she asked. She looked tired. A long strand of hair was pasted down one cheek. The blond girl brought his tostada and set it on the counter.

Carmen's mom had her head in the sink, cleaning it or something. Dean leaned in over the counter and said in Carmen's ear, "Wake up, Carmy. It's me."

Carmen jumped back, bumping into the blond girl.

"Hey!"

Dean laughed.

Carmen said, "Dean?" She looked quickly back over her shoulder at her mother.

"I just need to know how late the donut guy stays open."

"Probably eleven-thirty or so. Why?"

"What time is it?"

"Quarter to. Why? What are you gonna do?"

"See you later." He turned and walked away.

Kirsten Lund, still holding her arm where Carmen's elbow had hit her, yelled, "Hey! Don't you want your tostada?"

Dean kept walking. Sophie turned away from the sink and asked, "What happened?"

Carmen picked up the tostada and put it back on the prep table. "Some guy didn't want his food."

Sophie looked at the rejected tostada. "Something wrong with it?"

"No. He was just some weirdo. He decided to have some donuts instead."

"Did he pay for it?"

Carmen shook her head.

Sophie frowned. "Anybody hungry?" she asked. Carmen and Kirsten shook their heads and watched Sophie regretfully push the tostada over the edge of the table into the trash can. "Another one wasted," she sighed. She looked tired, and sad.

One of the things Axel always said was, "You got to leave a little for the next guy."

Not too many years ago, he had stayed open until the last customer had left the fairgrounds, sometimes until after midnight, unable to bear the thought of a missed sale. To let even one customer walk away hungry was an opportunity forever gone, or so he had believed. In those days he had been younger, able to function on three or four hours of sleep. And he had been hungrier, more desperate for the green.

Age had mellowed him in many ways. He could now close his restaurant before eleven, sometimes before ten-thirty. When the weather was bad he could close it earlier yet. The toll demanded by the late, long hours he had once worked was not commensurate with the few paltry dollars they had generated. He could leave that business for the other, younger concessionaires. Or for the next day, or the next year.

He could see, as he approached the restaurant, that his girls were beat, moving slow, their faces lacking animation. He stepped in through the back door. Sophie gave him a look but didn't say anything. She hated it when he disappeared. She sent Kirsten home, then the three of them proceeded with their evening wrap-up, packing the perishables into the cooler, sweeping, making everything ready for the next day. Carmen wore sunglasses. Axel wondered why, but chose not to ask. He went outside and hooked up his hose and started spraying down the grass and cement around the taco shop, sending bits of tortilla, lettuce, and miscellaneous jetsam flowing into the gutter. Axel enjoyed this part of the cleanup ritual, seeking out invading bits of cheese curd, cigarette butts, and candy wrappers, sending them on their journey into the sewer system. A pair of large, round young men stopped and tried to order a couple of burritos. Axel smiled and held out his hands helplessly.

"Sorry," he said. "We're closed."

Dean watched from a bench at the other side of the mall. The blond girl left the stand and walked toward the east exit, giving Dean a cautious look as she passed him. Stuck-up suburban bitch. He could tell she didn't like him. He returned his gaze to Axel and his women, watched them closing up. The old guy had a thing going with his hose, like he was taking the world's longest piss. The longer Dean watched him, the more he became convinced that Carmen's story about the coffee cans had been a fabrication.

Funny how that had changed the way he felt about Carmen. He still liked her, but now it was more like John Donne had said, like she was an extension of his self.

It took Axel, Sophie, and Carmen twenty minutes to close up. None of them noticed Dean. He watched them walk away, then turned all his attention toward Tiny Tot. The black cowboy hat was moving around the machines, bobbing up and down. Now and then he could hear Tiny Tot shouting at his employees. Dean reclined on his bench, crossed his arms, and watched through dark lenses, waiting patiently as the donut machines shut down one by one.

CHAPTER

18

Tommy Fabian claimed to be the hardest-working guy in the concession business, and he never got any argument. He opened his three Tiny Tot stands every morning at a quarter to eight, worked them all day long, and stayed until closing every night. During the Minnesota State Fair, he figured he got maybe four or five hours of sleep a night. He would hit the sack sometime south of midnight, then be up with the poultry for his first cup of sugar-saturated coffee.

The first two days were always tough. By the third day, Saturday, he would find his groove. Pacing was the secret. Plenty of coffee in the morning, sip a little JD starting around ten, and make sure to keep sipping all day long—but keep it low key. Two or three half pints was about right. A sip here and a sip there, just enough to keep the earth level, the gears meshed, and the engine humming. He never got stumbling drunk, although by the end of the day his motions became noticeably deliberate, and while he always remembered having locked his stands, he rarely recalled the long nightly walk back to his Winnebago.

Back in the old days, he'd actually slept in his donut stand. That was how it had been when he was growing up, working the county fairs with his old man, running alibi joints. Six Cats, Cover the Spot, String Game—they'd run them all. Whatever the game, they'd always slept with it. It was the carny way. But the last few years, as his limbs stiffened and his digestive system began to assert itself, Tommy had compromised by spending nights in his Winnie, which had all the comforts of home—a soft bed, a shower, and, most important, a toilet. Much as he hated to leave his stands, it was worth it.

The thirty-foot RV was parked way out at the end of the southern lot, back in the middle of the horse trailer ghetto. This year he was sandwiched between a Peterbilt semi-tractor and an old silver Airstream occupied by the Mexican candlemaker and his harelipped daughter. The Peterbilt had a high red wind deflector that was easy to spot from a distance, even late at night. After closing up, he could point himself at the Peterbilt, and the next thing he knew, he would be asleep in the Winnebago. His legs carried him home like a good horse.

On this night, only the second day of the fair, Tommy felt that something was not right. After locking up, swinging shut the plywood front, and fastening it with a Yale padlock the size of a hockey puck, he stood beneath the wooden eaves and watched the late-night action.

Most of the people still on the grounds were late-closing concessionaires and the state fair cleanup crews. With all the grab joints closed, there was no food available, and the few fairgoers still wandering around the grounds were finding little to entertain them. The late-summer air cooled quickly, the greasy, beery fairground odor purged by breezes sweeping across the grounds from the north. The garbage trucks were out in full force now; every few seconds he could hear the groan of a dumpster being upended, the wet crunching of paper and uneaten food being crushed by powerful hydraulics. The gutters ran with greasy water: someone up the hill was hosing down the picnic tables. He

watched a waxed cardboard carton float by, carrying frag-
ments of cheese curds.

Everything looked perfectly normal.

Tommy reached into his hip pocket and extracted the last
half pint of the day. He unscrewed the plastic cap and took
his usual moderate sip, then said the hell with it and had a
good belt. He still felt funny. The carpetbag slung over his
shoulder held nearly three thousand dollars in bills and
change. Most of the day's receipts were already in the bank;
the cash in his bag was from the last few hours of operation.
It was too late to make another deposit. A couple of
swallows remained in his bottle. He finished it on his way to
the gate, tossed the bottle into a trash can, and pushed out
through the wooden turnstile. The Peterbilt was easy to
spot, even from two hundred yards away. Tommy sighted on
it and launched himself out across the desolate parking lot,
trying to ignore the bad feeling, hoping for another forgetta-
ble walk home.

Dean could not believe how long it was taking the little
son-of-a-bitch. First he stands around like a stunned go-
pher, doing nothing, then he decides to have a couple. When
he finally gets moving, he's walking like the earth is made of
Jell-O, holding his arms away from his body like an ape on a
tightrope. Dean stayed well behind him, invisible in his
black hat and sunglasses. This time, he would make sure he
was not spotted.

He followed Tiny Tot out through the turnstile and across
Como Avenue. There were only a few cars dotting the main
parking lot. He could see the trucks and trailers parked at
the back of the lot, four football fields away. Tiny Tot
seemed drawn toward a big red-and-chrome semi. Dean
stayed fifty yards back and to the side. Tommy disappeared
behind the semi and did not emerge from the other side.
Backtracking, Dean circled the semi until he could see what
had not been visible to him before—an old Winnebago

motor home tucked in between the semi and a big silver trailer. As he watched, a light came on in the Winnebago. A shadow began moving about inside.

After a few minutes, the light went out. Dean turned away and began the long walk to his car. He'd hoped for a chance at the little bastard tonight, but it hadn't worked out. He let his mind explore the details of his future, feeling himself take things one step at a time, being smart. He watched the fairground lights grow crisp and brilliant in the cooling night air.

Axel stopped the truck outside the door to number 19, put his hand on Carmen's shoulder, and gave it a gentle shake. Her head came up slowly and turned toward him; she blinked and licked her lips. "We here?" she asked.

"We're here." He watched Carmen fumble for the door latch, then step out onto the Motel 6 parking lot. She moved sleepily, like a little kid awakened from a nap. She wouldn't remember this in the morning. He waited until she let herself into her room, watching to make sure she got home okay. When she was safely inside, he drove around the building to his own room.

He kept thinking about her boyfriend. He didn't see the green Maverick in the lot. That was good. But he couldn't escape the feeling that he was losing her. Anger and sorrow flickered in random bursts—he was too tired to edit his emotions.

Axel unlocked his door and flipped on the light, wanting nothing more at that moment than to turn on his television and let the networks do his thinking until he could fall into sleep. He dropped the canvas money bag on the bed, sat down on the wooden side chair, bent forward, and untied his shoes. Lately, it seemed, his feet were farther away than he remembered. He pulled off each shoe after untying it, set it beside the bed, toes pointing out, then sat back and shrugged out of his suspenders.

That always felt good.

Digging in his pockets, he came out with a handful of loose change and reached over to drop it into the ashtray on his bedside table, but he did not complete the motion.

The ashtray was empty. That was wrong. He was sure he had left a small collection of coins there. Not much, a few dollars' worth, maybe, but it had definitely been there the last time he'd left his room.

He stood up, feeling naked, a trickle of cold inching down his neck. Someone had been in his room. His eyes went to his crates. They looked different, not in the right order. Someone had been messing with his stuff. He checked the bathroom. Whoever it had been was gone. Feeling none of his earlier weariness, Axel dropped to his hands and knees and reached under the bed, feeling for the slit in the muslin bottom of the box spring. There. He reached through the opening, pulled out a waxed-tissue-wrapped bundle that had been wedged in a spring. He unwrapped it, sat and stared at yesterday's receipts, about thirty-five hundred, most of it in twenties and tens. The chill of fear warmed, coagulating into anger. Axel forced it back, forced himself to stand up, breathing deeply. This wasn't an emergency. Nothing bad had happened. His money was safe in Sam's backyard. They hadn't gotten anything. He needed to take time, to think.

The alarm clock beside the bed read 12:17. He thought, I can deal with this tomorrow. Images of the bald monkey rooting through his crates. With Carmen? He couldn't be sure. Had he had anything in those crates that they'd take?

Crate by crate, he went through a mental inventory of his possessions.

A few minutes later, he started dismantling his wall of Coke crates. He found what he was looking for on the third row from the bottom: a khaki-colored canvas sack. He lifted it out of the crate. The weight was gone. Loosening the drawstring top, he looked inside, to discover three pairs of his black nylon socks.

* * *

Bill Quist thought that Chuck Woolery, the leering host of *Love Connection,* had one of the best jobs on TV. He'd read someplace that all the women who appeared on the show had to give Chuck a private audition. Or maybe he'd made that up in his head. Quist was very good at making things up. He thought he should have been a writer. Write those miniseries, get to meet the actresses. One of the women on *Love Connection* looked like a red-haired Heather Locklear. Now, there was an actress he would like to meet.

The redheaded Heather recrossed her legs. Quist thought he could hear the sound of nyloned thighs rubbing together. Or maybe that was the hydraulic closer on the lobby door, hissing air.

The chrome bell on the counter dinged.

"Okay, okay," Quist said, spinning his chair around. It was Axel Speeter. "Mr. S., how you doing?"

"Can't complain, Bill. How about you?"

"Just fine, just fine. What can I do for you?"

Axel rested his forearms on the counter and leaned into it. "I was wondering," he said, "if you know anything about this kid, this bald kid I've seen hanging around. Kid about yea high, with no hair and a little tiny nose?" He pointed a thick finger at his eyebrow. "Used to have these rings in his head."

Quist contorted his brow to show he was thinking, looking away from Axel's asymmetric green eyes. Inside, he was panicking. Never should've given the bitch the key. Damn, damn, damn! He didn't know what to say now. Didn't know if he should lie or just half lie.

"Wears army boots?" Axel prompted.

Quist nodded slowly. If he told Mr. S. that he'd never seen the kid, it would look like he hadn't been doing his job. It couldn't hurt to just have seen him. What did that have to do with anything? Nothing. It was safe. True, but safe. "Uh-huh," he said, nodding faster. "Uh-huh, I think so. A couple times, I'm pretty sure. Last couple of days. What about him?"

"He staying here?"

"Well . . . he's not a registered guest, if that's what you mean. What I saw was, I saw him a couple times. I figured he was just passing by, you know?"

"You sure he isn't staying here?"

"Like I say, Mr. S., he's not a registered guest. But he might be staying with somebody else. I mean, I'd have no way of knowing." Quist waited, his eyes on Axel's chest, hoping that the interview was over. Laughter from the TV made him turn his head, but as soon as he had the screen in view, Axel asked him something about a key.

"What? What's that?"

"I asked you, 'Who else has a key to my room?'"

Quist shook his head rapidly. "No one! Nobody goes in your room, Mr. S. Not even the maid, just the way you want it."

Axel raised his eyebrows, as if he was waiting for more. Quist didn't know what else to say.

Axel said, "Okay then, Bill, if you say so. But I'm having the lock changed tomorrow."

Quist said, "I don't know about that, Mr. S. I'd have to talk to the office on that."

"That's fine, Bill. You talk to them. Tell them how somebody's been going in and out of my room. Somebody with a key. In the meantime, I'm getting myself a lock." He turned and left.

Quist watched Axel's broad back receding. That was easy, he thought, returning his attention to Chuck Woolery. The redheaded Heather Locklear had been replaced by a guy with a ponytail. Quist changed the channel, hoping to stumble across a late-night rerun of *Baywatch*, something good like that.

James Dean pulled into the Motel 6 parking lot and backed the Maverick into the parking space opposite room 3. He was about to shut down the engine, when he saw Axel coming out of the motel office, walking funny, his chest pushed out like a marching soldier's. Dean stayed in his car, waiting for him to pass, but the old man looked up, saw the green Maverick, and stopped, not twenty feet away from the front bumper, looking right at him.

Dean thought, I could just step on the gas.

Axel stood with his feet apart, staring at him through the windshield. Dean remained expressionless and motionless, trying to think what to do. If he ran over him, someone would see. The guy in the office, or somebody passing by.

After a few seconds, Axel started walking toward him.

Dean thought, Shit, he knows we were in his room. He dropped the car in gear and hit the gas pedal. The old man didn't move. Dean cranked the wheel, missing him by a few feet, and sped out of the parking lot. Once on the street, he let the air rush out of his lungs. He felt weak and shaky, as though he had just survived an accident. Something about the old man scared him. He was two blocks away when he remembered that he had the .45 under his front seat, remembered that he had nothing to fear.

The Tonight Show was just ending. One thing that Axel missed these days was Johnny Carson. Axel didn't care for the new guy, but things changed and there wasn't a damn thing you could do about it. He sat on the edge of his carefully made bed and clicked through the cable channels. He watched a few minutes of a war movie, identified it as *Pork Chop Hill,* which he had seen already. That was okay; he didn't like the war movies anymore. What had once looked like heroic men fighting and dying now looked to him like children fighting and dying. He switched to channel 2, where he found a show about Australia. Herds of kangaroos bounding across the outback. Axel untied his shoes and placed them at the foot of the bed. He propped the pillows up against the headboard and settled back to watch the kangaroos. Axel liked animal shows, especially the ones about Australia. Maybe this would calm him down.

That little prick. He was the one who'd been in his room, all right. The way he'd driven off proved it. He might've slipped the lock somehow, but more likely that sleazy clerk had something to do with it. Should bounce his face on the counter a few times, make him own up. Feeling his rage mount, Axel forced himself to jack down and watch the show. He didn't like himself when he got mad.

He liked kangaroos. Most people didn't realize how tough they were, how hard it was to be a kangaroo. Two males—boomers, the narrator called them—were clinched like boxers, kicking at each other with their big hind feet. Then the boomers broke apart and started making these flying kicks at one another, ripping at each other's abdomens with kangaroo claws. The big red boomer with the torn ear, according to the narrator, was the alpha male, the aging ruler and protector of a group of fliers, or female kangaroos, and their joeys. The fliers could be seen watching the battle from a shady eucalyptus grove a few yards away, waiting to see who would lead them. The challenger, a smaller but much quicker boomer, mounted a relentless attack, leaping again and again without pause, pounding the alpha male backward, shaking off return blows without apparent effect. Axel, no longer smiling, rooted silently for the alpha male, willing him to repel the smaller boomer's assault. The narrator noted that for the aging alpha male this was a fight to the death, that if he lost he would be forced out of the group, weakened and bleeding, forced out to die alone in the desert.

As Axel watched, the alpha male, looking as if he had just remembered another appointment, turned away from his challenger and loped weakly out of the grove onto the arid Australian plain, pursued for a few hundred yards by the kicking, biting challenger: the new alpha male.

He could have won, Axel thought, upset. The big 'roo could have stuck it out, used his greater size and experience to defeat the invader.

You could learn a lot from watching animals.

The scene shifted to a group of wallabies. The wallabies were smaller than the kangaroos, and they were grazing peacefully. Axel shut off the television, undressed, and got under the covers. He turned off the light. It seemed like a long time before sleep came for him. He couldn't stop thinking about the goddamn kangaroos.

CHAPTER

19

Dean pumped another quarter into the DeathMek machine in Tony's East Side Lounge. The machine was against the wall at the back of the bar, directly between the doors marked GALS and GENTS. Dean played the game automatically, his mind wandering as he destroyed one attacker after another, keeping his cyborg alive.

He was thinking about what to do next. Except for Carmen, he didn't know anybody in this town. All he had was about twenty dollars—the last of the money he'd got from Mickey. It wasn't enough to rent a room, and he wouldn't be able to get his donut money until the next night. What lousy luck, the taco guy seeing him. He'd been looking forward to telling Carmen about his plans for the donut guy. He should've just run the taco guy over.

He supposed he could use the gun to get some money, knock off a gas station or something, but he'd never done anything like that before. Walking into a lighted business and robbing it, that was not his style. Basically, he was a nonviolent person. Besides, robbing a gas station for fifty or a hundred bucks contradicted his new philosophy: the fewer transactions, the better one's chances of getting away with it. Only the big scores were worth the risk. What he'd do, he'd play it smart, sleep in his car tonight. One more quarter in the machine, then he'd head out to the Maverick and crash. He wished he had some speed. He should've picked some up before he left Omaha. A few leapers, and he wouldn't need to sleep at all.

Dean had just disintegrated another mechanical dinosaur, when he felt someone breathing on his neck, watching him play the machine. He put up with it for about five seconds, then faked like he was giving the machine a little body English and brought his heel down hard on somebody's toe.

"Ow. Motherfucking ow!" The voice was whiny and nasal.

Dean looked over his shoulder. A narrow head, as hairless as his own.

"You stepped on my fucking foot," the skinhead said. He was young, no more than seventeen, and blade thin. Pimply hatchet face, pale-blue eyes, a faded and shredded T-shirt over a sunken chest. Beltless gray jeans, slung low on his narrow hips, puddled over a pair of disintegrating snakeskin cowboy boots. One of the boots was held together with a wrapping of silver duct tape.

Dean let himself relax. This skinhead cowboy was no threat. Just another punk kid. Reminded him of himself a few years earlier. He was about to come back at the punk with some really nasty crack, when he noticed another nearly hairless head coming toward them from the bar, carrying two bottles of beer.

The second skinhead was older and larger by about two hundred pounds. His eyes were set a few inches back inside his skull, little pig eyes, and he was wearing a black leather jacket that must have used up three cows and still looked a little tight around the shoulders. Dean, wishing he hadn't left the .45 in the car, grinned and held out his hands. "Sorry about your foot, man," he said. "You want I should buy you a beer or something?"

The kid stared at Dean, taking his time, letting the giant arrive with his beer.

"Where you from, man?" he finally asked.

"Chicago," said Dean. It was better to be from Chicago than from Omaha. People knew where it was. "Name's Dean," he added.

The kid said, "They call me Tigger, man." He reached out and gave Dean a complicated handshake, a sort of wrist-grabbing routine that reminded him of a biker handshake. Dean faked it. Tigger seemed satisfied.

"This here's Sweety." Tigger jerked his head toward the giant. "We're from here in Frogtown, man. Whole bunch of us."

Frogtown? He thought he was in Saint Paul. Dean looked around the bar. There were some factory-worker types, all white with small eyes, and a few horsey-looking women to match, but not other skins. Tigger sucked at his beer like he hadn't had a drink in days. Sweety stared down at Dean, looking at him as if he were a bug.

Dean said, "How's it going, Sweety?"

Sweety shrugged and looked away. The bottle of beer almost disappeared in his massive fist.

"So what the fuck you doing in Saint Paul?" Tigger asked.

"I thought I was in Frogtown," Dean said.

"Frogtown's in Saint Paul," Tigger said.

Dean scratched his chin. Three guys in a bar, drawn together by their mutual hairlessness. But these two were not your typical skinheads—not the Aryan Circle type, banded together to protect themselves from the other minorities, nor your garden-variety neo-Nazi skins with an unemployed-working-class hard-on—and that was fine with him. Dean had never cared for political agendas, with or without hair. Guys like these, they wouldn't even be looking for jobs. They had to have something going. They'd paid for two beers, and the money had come from somewhere. Maybe they knew where he could find some uppers. If nothing else, he might get a free place to crash.

Tigger waited for him to say something. Dean still wasn't entirely sure whether he'd found a friend or a fight. He pointed at Tigger's empty bottle. "How about I buy you another one?" he said.

A dull blue light flickered in Tigger's eyes. "I could see that," he said.

Dean said, "How about you, big guy?"

Sweety was out there someplace, not listening, glaring at the wall. Dean had seen guys like Sweety in Lincoln. You either got real close to them or stayed the hell away.

Tigger said, "You better get him one."

Dean bought the next round too. One more, and he'd be out of money. They were sitting in one of the booths near the back. Sweety, on the opposite side of the booth, was digging into the tabletop with a short, spade-shaped blade that he'd pulled out of his belt buckle, concentrating hard, his forehead red with effort, carving letters into the Formica surface. Tigger was bragging about some friend who had a Harley.

"So what's this guy do?" Dean asked. He couldn't figure out why Tigger was talking about him.

"Do? He don't do nothing. He deals."

"Deals what?"

"Whatever the fuck you want. Pork's connected, man."

Sweety said, "Fuckin' Pork." Dean tried to read what Sweety was carving.

"You want to score, I can get it for you. Pork and me, we're like this." Tigger crossed his fingers.

Dean shrugged. He didn't have any money left. "Maybe tomorrow," he said. "Can this guy get any speed?"

"You kidding me? Pork's got this crank, man, you wouldn't believe. Crystal meth, man. He knows a guy fuckin' makes the shit in his bathtub. Like I was telling you, he's connected."

Dean had never tried crystal meth before. In Omaha, it was not common on the street. Omaha was a weed and acid town, although lately it was becoming a crack town too. "Is it any good?" he asked, thinking if the price was right, he could maybe buy some weight, haul it over to Sioux Falls, and sell it to a guy he knew there. Double his money; maybe even triple it. The real question was, were these guys for real? The kid with the taped-up cowboy boot was a punk, showing off and trying to act tough. And the big one, the cyborg, looked like he had the walnut-size brain of a tyrannosaurus.

"It's fucking dynamite," Tigger was saying. "Right, Sweety?"

"Huh?"

"Pork's crank."

"Fuckin' Pork," said Sweety.

CHAPTER

20

Axel seemed different the next morning. Even through her morning fog, Carmen could sense the difference. He was acting sort of crisp and nasty, and he took off the second she got in the pickup.

"Whoa," she said, slamming the truck door closed.

Axel pulled out of the parking lot onto Larpenteur Avenue without stopping, prompting a horn blast from a passing Honda.

"What's going on?" Carmen asked, wide awake now.

"You have a good night's sleep?" Axel asked. He hunched forward over the steering wheel, like a little kid trying to make his car go faster.

"I slept okay," said Carmen cautiously.

"Have a little trouble waking up?"

Carmen considered her answer. "No." It was safest, when the correct answer did not suggest itself, to lie.

"I was sitting out there almost five minutes."

Was he mad because she'd made him wait? Carmen was confused. She had made him wait plenty of times before. Suddenly she was afraid. Maybe he'd noticed someone had been in his room.

"Are you sure you're okay?" she asked.

Axel pushed back from the wheel. "I'm fine," he said, not looking at her. "I just wish you'd be a little more responsible."

Carmen settled into her seat. If he didn't want to talk about it, that was fine with her. The first Saturday of the fair was going to be a long, hard day. The sky was bright blue, and the air was warming quickly. In most ways she dreaded the long hours ahead, but a part of her was looking forward to the energy and focus the day would bring. Responsible? The word had a strange flavor. Did he think he was her dad, or what?

The *Daily News,* official newsletter of the Minnesota State Fair, predicted a new attendance record that Saturday. As many as a quarter of a million people were expected. The weather looked like a perfect eighty-degree high, the sky appeared cloudless for two hundred miles in every direction, and Garth Brooks was scheduled to play the grandstand.

As usual, Sophie already had the front of the Taco Shop open and the deep-fryers heating by the time Axel and Carmen arrived. Ever since Axel had given her the title "manager" and promised her a bonus, Sophie had been putting in heroic hours. It was hard for him to believe that she was stealing from him. Nevertheless, as soon as she left the stand to visit the rest rooms, Axel took a careful look at the tortillas in the cooler. The flour tortillas came from Garcia's in plastic bags of one hundred, and the smaller corn tortillas in pouches of six dozen. He moved some of the bags aside and found eight ten-count pouches of Zapata tortillas, a grocery store brand, tucked in behind the regular stock.

So Tommy was right. Sophie was H.O.'ing. It was the only possible explanation. Eighty extra tortillas, assuming they were made into Bueno Burritos, would translate into over two hundred dollars. Over the course of the fair, that would add up to $2,400. Axel replaced the tortillas. So much for the five-hundred-dollar bonus he'd planned to give her. He would have to do something about it. But not today, not with a record crowd pouring through the gates. When Sophie got back from the john, it would be business as usual.

They had a line by ten that morning, and in the rush and bustle of business, Axel quickly purged his mind of Sophie's tortillas, the bald kid in the Maverick, and his missing .45. The day flew by without the usual midafternoon slump. Sophie, Carmen, Juanita, Kirsten, and Janice, the weekend girl, hardly stopped moving all day. By early evening they'd run out of cups, and Axel had to go begging from other concessionaires, none of whom were eager to dip into their supplies to help a competitor. He finally coaxed half a case out of the Orange Treet guy by promising to give him free tacos for the rest of the fair. At seven o'clock, Sophie told Carmen to start skimping on the cheese. At seven-thirty, they ran out of corn tortillas; and shortly after nine o'clock, they ran out of flour.

Twenty years in the business, and Axel had never run out of tortillas. Elated by record sales but distraught over the business he was losing, Axel ran to each of the three other Mexican food concessions on the fairgrounds and tried unsuccessfully to buy more tortillas. He thought about making the run to Cub Foods, but by the time he got back with them it would be too late to do any good. Garcia's truck would show up the next morning with Sunday's supply of fresh tortillas, and they could start all over again. He returned to the stand empty-handed but feeling better knowing that he had at least tried.

An exhausted Sophie stood proudly at the serving window, offering refried beans to each new customer. Axel stopped and watched as she actually sold some. A bubble of pride expanded in his chest; the woman really and honestly cared about his business. He had planned to talk to Sophie about the grocery-store tortillas that night, but he didn't have the heart to hit her with it after such a killer day. He told her to go home, told her he and Carmen would close up the stand. Wearily, Sophie agreed. Axel watched her walk off toward the parking lot, thinking she was worth every penny he paid her. Maybe even worth every penny she stole.

Carmen and Kirsten, with little to do in the way of food preparation, sat on folding chairs by the side of the stand, smoking cigarettes. Kirsten was just getting started with her first pack of Virginia Slims. She watched Carmen carefully, trying to emulate her stylish smoking technique. Carmen had a way of taking the smoke into her mouth, then letting it stream out over her upper lip into her nose. She called it a French inhale. When Kirsten tried to do it, she sneezed and started coughing.

"First you got to learn to inhale regular," Carmen said. "You got to start a little at a time."

Kirsten nodded, her eyes watering, and took a tiny puff from her Virginia Slim.

Juanita was perched on a cheese carton, chewing on a fingernail. Carmen offered her a cigarette.

"No, thank you," Juanita said.

Carmen said to Kirsten, "Juanita is very polite."

That cracked them up, all three of them. It had been a long day.

James Dean stood between the railroad tracks at the back of the forty-acre parking lot, tossing stones up in the air and trying to hit them with an old broom handle. He was a lefty. Because it was dark, he could only connect with about one out of every four or five swings, and most of those he drove straight into the ground. Now and then, though, he got a good piece of one, and the rock would go sailing out into the parking lot. He caught this one rock perfect, listened, heard the sharp crack of stone on safety glass.

Last night, he'd closed up the bar with Tigger and Sweety.

They'd been on the sidewalk, just leaving, when Tigger had suggested that Dean stay with them at "Headquarters."

That had sounded good to Dean. Tigger had an aging, oil-burning Cadillac Fleetwood, about a '76, rust-spotted black, with tinted windows and a peeling black vinyl roof. Dean got in his Maverick and followed the smoke through a tangled neighborhood, parked on the street, then accompanied his new friends down an alley, over a fence, and through the broken basement window of a dark, boarded-up house. The air smelled of spray paint, mildew, piss, and cigarette butts.

Tigger lit a candle, then said he had to go grab the juice. At first, Dean thought he was going for a bottle, but Tigger crawled back out through the window trailing a long orange extension cord. A minute later, the work lamp at the end of the extension cord blinked on.

"Headquarters" contained two mattresses on the floor, a torn vinyl beanbag chair, a few hundred beer bottles, an old TV. Empty spray cans were scattered among the beer bottles. Spray-painted slogans and drawings covered the walls. *Heil Hitler. White Power. Fuck Off and Die.* A few scattered swastikas, crosses, and skulls. One wall bore an enormous stylized vagina, fluorescent pink labia stretching from floor to ceiling. A pile of well-thumbed magazines— *Soldier of Fortune, High Times,* assorted skin mags—sat atop an upended cardboard box.

"This is, like, our meeting place," Tigger explained as he climbed back in through the window. "A bunch of us hang here."

"What's the deal with the light?" Dean asked.

"The guy next door has an outside outlet. We just plug ourselves in. He don't miss it."

Dean nodded. A real four-star operation, this. He'd have been better off sleeping in his car. "There a bathroom here?"

"Yeah. What they used to call the furnace room. The toilet paper's on top of the water heater."

Despite all that, he'd slept pretty good. The mattress wasn't bad, and nothing ran over him or bit him during the night, although he had heard some scurrying.

Tonight things would be different. Tonight he'd get himself a real room, and tomorrow, if Tigger could be believed, he'd be scoring himself a chunk of very pure, very cheap, very marketable methedrine.

Dean tossed a rock into the air, swung the broom handle as hard as he could. He hit the rock low. It went up in the air, came down a few feet away.

Enough. He decided to quit before he dropped a rock on his head, or before some guy with a busted windshield came looking for him.

Axel bought Carmen a bomb pop on the way to the truck. Carmen liked bomb pops. She liked to bite away the ridges, feeling the red, white, and blue ice cold on her front teeth. Twelve hours of action had left her numb; she sucked the bomb pop and listened to Axel chatter about what a great day they'd had. The day's receipts were inside his burlap shoulder bag. Axel patted the side of the bag affectionately.

"A great day," he said. "You did a great job, Carmen. You're a great kid."

"Uh-huh."

"If the rest of the fair is good—hell, even if it's not good—I'm going to be giving you a nice bonus. Buy yourself some new clothes."

Carmen bit the tip off her bomb pop and looked at the money bag.

"That would be great."

"You worked hard. You deserve it."

"I sure do."

Axel gave her a sharp look. He unlocked the passenger door and opened it, then circled the truck and let himself in the other door.

"You stick with me, Carmen, and you'll do all right."

"Uh-huh."

"I'm not kidding you. Hang in there with me, Carmen. I'll take care of you. I really will. We're a team."

Carmen pulled the bomb pop out of her mouth and looked at Axel. He was staring at her, looking right into her eyes. He looked like he was going to cry.

"Okay," she said, looking away. She hated it when Axel got maudlin. She thought about the six-pack of canned martinis waiting in her room, wondering whether they would still be cool from the night before. Not that it mattered. They went down just as fast warm.

Two hundred yards away, James Dean sat against the back of Tommy Fabian's Winnebago, playing with Axel's .45, feeling the checkered wooden handle, smelling the tangy odor of gun oil. He had never fired a pistol. Cocking the hammer, he sighted along the top of the barrel. The gun was heavy. He uncocked it carefully, set it in his lap. The long wait had diminished much of his excitement. He was getting hungry. To pass the time, he played the scene out again in his mind, seeing Tiny Tot's face when he showed him the gun. He wasn't sure what he would do after that, but whatever it was, Tiny Tot wouldn't like it.

He gripped the gun and listened. He could hear footsteps. The footsteps passed. It was still too early.

He let his head fall back on the rear bumper of the RV and watched the moon, not quite full. A faint ringing sound wound its way through the RV camp—someone's mobile phone, perhaps. Dean thought, It tolls for thee, Tiny Tot.

What he would have to do, he had decided, was show him the gun about two seconds after he got to the door. Take charge of the situation before Tiny Tot could figure out which key to use. Come around the side of the Winnebago fast.

Nearby, someone in one of the RVs turned on a radio. Some old disco music from the seventies, before his time. Dean closed his eyes and listened, breathing deeply.

Something jarred him awake, a movement of the Winnebago's bumper against his head. He jumped up, heard the gun flip off his lap, hit the ground. Shit! He looked around the corner of the motor home.

Shit! The donut guy was there, already standing on the fucking step, turning the key. Where had the gun fallen?

No time. Tiny Tot had the door open. He was stepping inside. His plan forgotten, Dean ran straight at him, caught the door just before it closed, tore it open. He saw Tiny Tot turn toward him, mouth open, then twist away, reaching for something. Dean grabbed him by the ankles, jerked. Tiny Tot went down hard, the RV shaking, then twisted around with something in his hand, bringing it down on Dean's shoulder. Galvanized by a shock of pain, Dean threw himself backward out the door, dragging Tiny Tot with him, hurling the little man hard against the wheel of the Peterbilt. A baseball bat flew from Tiny Tot's hands, thudded to the gravel a few yards away. His cowboy hat fell forward onto his lap. He sagged against the big tire of the semi, his eyes bugging out, gasping for breath. Dean ran for the bat, scooped it up as Tiny Tot drew a loud breath, started to rise, saw Dean coming at him with the bat, and raised his arms.

Dean swung the bat, a downward chopping motion, hitting the donut man's forearm. Tiny Tot howled and fell back against the tire. Dean struck again, the bat glancing off Tiny Tot's skull. The little man's face went slack, his eyes pointing in two different directions, blood curtaining over his right ear. The sight of blood made the earth tilt; Dean dropped to his knees and closed his eyes. His ears filled with a rushing sound. He swallowed. The sound in his ears abruptly ceased. Voices. He heard someone shouting something. He pushed aside the dizziness, dropped the bat, and jumped up into the Winnebago, searching frantically for Tiny Tot's money bag. Everything was so bright, so in focus, it was hard to see, like a television with the contrast set too high. There, on the floor. He scooped up the bag in one hand, jumped out. The donut guy was moving, crawling away. Dean kicked him twice in the ribs till he curled up, his hands over his bloody head, fingers glittering. A flashing horseshoe snapped into hard focus. Dean kicked again, and again, until Tiny Tot's arms flopped away from his head. He ripped the horseshoe ring from Tiny Tot's slack fingers.

Someone yelled, "Hey! What's going on back there?"

There was a watch too, glittering in the faint light. Dean tore it from Tiny Tot's wrist. The band broke. He threw the watch away and started to run, then remembered his gun. He found it immediately, right where he'd dropped it at the back of the RV. His senses were totally keyed; he was seeing like a fucking owl.

"Hey!" A figure appeared from the other side of the Peterbilt. "What the hell's going on here?"

Dean pointed the .45 at the figure, a tall, burly man with a dark beard. He could see every detail of the man's face, every wrinkle, every pore. He was too out of breath to reply, so he just waited for the man to get close enough to see the gun.

CHAPTER

21

The cute one that worked in the donut place, the one that reminded Kirsten of Luke Perry, showed up at the taco stand before they even had the fryer up to temperature. Kirsten leaned over the counter.

"Morning," she said.

He smiled at her.

"How's it going?" Kirsten asked. "You hungry already?" God, did that ever sound lame. She wished she knew his name, but since they had been trading tacos and donuts back and forth for three days now, it seemed like it would be rude to ask him. He didn't know her name, either, but he called her Blondie, which she liked. So she just thought of him as Luke. She loved that name: Luke.

"Mr. Speeter around?" he asked.

Kirsten shook her head. "Huh-uh."

The kid, Luke, frowned and looked up and down the mall. "You seen Mr. Fabian?" he asked.

"Who?"

"My boss?"

"Huh-uh." Thinking, God, do I sound like a dork, or what?

He looked past Kirsten into the stand, where Sophie was shredding lettuce.

"We're supposed to be open now, only he never showed up this morning."

Sophie came up to the counter, wiping her hands on her apron. "Tommy hasn't shown up?"

"He's like two hours late already. What do you think we should do?" He pointed at the locked-up donut stand, where eight girls in Tiny Tot T-shirts were standing under the eaves, watching him. "They're talking about going home."

Now that Luke was talking to Sophie, Kirsten could look at him real close. She liked the way his upper lip sort of folded back when he smiled, and she was hoping he would smile now while she could get a good look. He had a few pimples, but she let her eyes slide away from them, and anyway, they weren't permanent. His eyes, though, his eyes were the best thing of all. When I have my kids, Kirsten thought, I want all nine of them to have eyes that same bright sparkly blue.

Sophie pointed up the mall, her arm blocking Kirsten's view. "Here comes Axel now."

The kid intercepted Axel several yards away, talking and pointing at the Tiny Tot stand. Sophie went back to shredding lettuce. Kirsten watched Axel hand Luke a ring of keys, clap him on the shoulder, and point at the donut stand. Luke, a determined look on his TV-star face, nodded several times, then trotted toward the bored octet of Tiny Tot girls, holding the keys in the air and waving them.

"Where's Carmen?" Sophie asked as Axel stuck his head through the back door.

"She'll be taking the bus in this morning. I had to leave early. Tom Fabian called me from the hospital at six o'clock this morning."

Sophie scraped shredded lettuce into a stainless-steel bin and pressed it down with the lid. "He have a heart attack?"

she asked, tearing open a five-pound plastic bag filled with grated cheese.

"He got jumped. Somebody beat him up. He looks pretty ugly. He can hardly talk."

Kirsten said, "Wow!"

"I had to pick up the keys from him. It was either that or he was going to crawl out of the hospital on his hands and knees and open the stands himself. The doctor made him call me."

He looked across the mall at the Tiny Tot concession, where the nine teenagers in their Tiny Tot T-shirts were moving around with an excess of confused energy.

"Look at that," Sophie said. "They don't know what they're doing. Tommy should have a manager. I mean a real manager, not some high school kid."

"I don't know," Axel said. "Looks to me like they're doing okay. In any case, Sam's going to come out later. Tommy asked him to run things while he was laid up."

"Sam *O'Gara?*" Sophie let her mouth drop open.

Axel smiled, almost laughing. "Hey, he'll do fine. All he's got to do is sit on the stool and eat donuts. Those kids know what they're doing. Look at them. They already got the front of the stand open. Another ten minutes they'll be frying and bagging. Look, I've got to go get his other two stands up and running."

Sophie pushed out her chin. "What about *our* stand?"

"What about it? You can't run things without me?"

Sophie crushed her lips together.

"I'll be right back," Axel said. "Listen, if Sam shows up, take him over and introduce him to Duane, would you?"

"Who's Duane?" Sophie asked.

Axel pointed toward the Tiny Tot stand, at the Luke Perry clone. A look that fell somewhere between horror and nausea crossed Kirsten Lund's face. *"Duane?"* she said.

Carmen drifted into work around ten, still wearing her sunglasses even though the day was overcast, getting darker, thunder rumbling in the distance. She'd tried covering up her black eye with makeup, but it hadn't worked.

She had dreamed that night about James Dean, the original one. Dreamed she was on this beach . . . Puerto Penasco? Maybe. A nice beach, and James Dean comes up on a motorcycle and gives her a breakfast sausage, then roars off. She was getting all her Deans mixed up. Anyway, she was glad he was gone. It had been a bad zigzag in her life, but now it was over. He'd probably driven back to Omaha. Left his stupid poetry book and booked. And that was okay with her, because she could damn well take care of herself. Maybe she'd go to Puerto Penasco herself. Maybe she could get Axel to send her. Maybe they had a nursing school down there. Maybe she could just take the money, few hundred dollars a day, just slip it in her pocket.

She was thinking about that as she stepped into the Taco Shop, trying to figure out how much she could take before he noticed. Axel grabbed her wrist. "Come here, Carmen." He pulled her out of the stand, jerking her arm.

Carmen flashed that she was being arrested, as if he'd been reading her thoughts. He led her out onto the mall, to an empty picnic table, sat her down, sat beside her. He leaned forward and turned his head so that his face was only a few inches from hers. He said, "Talk to me, Carmen. Tell me about your friend."

Carmen leaned back. "Friend?" She pulled her purse onto her lap and dug for her cigarettes.

Axel dropped his hand to her wrist. "Don't bullshit me, Carmen. You know who I'm talking about. Your friend beat up Tommy last night. Hurt him real bad. Robbed him. I want to know who he is and where I can find him."

"Oh!" So he'd gone and done it. A nervous laugh bubbled out of her.

"You think that's funny? He coulda been killed. If Mack hadn't shown up, he probably would've been."

"Mack?"

"Big Mack, the guy runs the high-striker. He says the kid

had a gun. Pointed it right at him. Could've got himself shot."

Carmen shook her head. She could almost see it, like in a movie. Big Mack, who could ring the high-striker with a one-handed sledgehammer blow, against Dean. Dean with Axel's gun. Like a showdown.

Axel's hand closed on her wrist. "Talk to me, Carmen. You know who I'm talking about."

Carmen said, "That hurts."

Axel let go.

"I don't really know him," she said. "He's just this guy."

"What's his name?"

"Dean. James Dean."

Axel snorted.

"That's what he says it is. Look, I just met him, you know? I met him in Omaha, and then he followed me up here. I had no idea he was coming."

"You let him stay with you."

Carmen shrugged, put a cigarette in her mouth. "Yeah, well, he's gone now." She spoke around the unlit cigarette as she searched for her lighter. Axel reached up and plucked her sunglasses from her face.

"He hit you, didn't he?"

Carmen shrugged.

"You're lucky he didn't shoot you."

"Why would he do that?"

"Maybe just to try out my gun. He's got my gun, doesn't he?"

Carmen's eyes slid away. "I told him not to take it. It wasn't like I had any choice, you know."

"You always have a choice."

"Yeah, right." Carmen found her lighter, lit her cigarette, blew smoke. "I could live or I could get myself killed. Some choice." She fixed her eyes on Axel's shoes. They were planted solidly on the tarmac, pointing right at her. His hand appeared in front of her face, cupped her chin, and gently lifted her head.

155

"You should get that eye looked at."

"Axel, you're talking to a nurse, almost. I'm gonna be okay. I just don't want people staring at it is all." She twisted her head away, snatched her sunglasses from his other hand, and backed away from him.

Axel did not move. He stood with his hand still out where her chin had been, his face stiff and hard like one of those old-fashioned photographs where the men all have beards. A drop of rain hit her face. A curtain of gray moved across the fairgrounds from the east. Another large drop hit her knee. Suddenly it was raining hard, sending people running toward the buildings.

Axel said, "Where is he, Carmen?"

She turned her hand, shielding her cigarette from the rain. "I swear to God, Axel, I haven't got a clue." Then, unable to stop herself, she asked, "How much money did he get?"

Axel sat on a stool at the Beef Hut, watching a Styrofoam cup of coffee cool. The creamer he had added produced an oil slick, which shimmered prismatically under the fluorescent lights. All those colors in his cup, yet when he looked up he saw only gray sheets of cold rain. He felt ill.

Not sick in his body or in his head. He felt sick in his life. His carefully nurtured and controlled life was coming apart like an overfilled burrito. His friend had been put in the hospital by some skinhead freak. That same bald monkey—Axel couldn't bear to think of him as "James Dean"—had beat up his . . . Carmen. The rain was killing his business on what should have been a big day. And Sophie—what was going on with Sophie? Bringing in her own tortillas—he knew that for sure—but the money, the money was good. If anything, it was too good. The last two nights, he'd matched up his cash receipts with the tortilla count, and both times he'd come out two to three hundred dollars rich, almost as if she was doing some sort of reverse rip-off. At first, he'd thought that the Bueno Burrito was throwing off his estimates, but even taking the new product into account, the money was coming out too damn good. Axel didn't like it. It would bug the shit out of him until he figured out what was going on.

He looked out at the flooded street, its slick black surface churning with raindrops. Maybe he *was* sick in his head. Maybe the tortilla thing could be explained. Maybe he had simply misplaced his .45. Maybe Carmen had run into a door. Maybe Tommy had gotten too drunk and fallen down twenty or thirty times. Maybe it wasn't raining.

CHAPTER

22

Of all the things Axel Speeter did not like, hospitals rated number one. Axel did not like the way they looked or the way they smelled, and he especially did not like the doctors who worked there. He hated their phony smiles, their dry hands, and the way they used all the buttons on their prissy white coats. Most of them wouldn't have made it through one busy Saturday at the Taco Shop.

He did, however, enjoy watching the nurses.

Tommy Fabian had a room on the fourth floor of Midway Hospital. Axel set the brown paper bag on the bedside table and sat down on the molded plastic chair. Tommy had his head turned away, staring out the window at the gray sky. A plastic bag filled with clear fluid drained into his left arm.

"I told you it was gonna rain," Tommy said, his voice a hoarse whisper. "Cost us both."

Axel shrugged. "Yesterday was good."

"Yeah. First part anyways." Tommy pressed a button, and the bed slowly contorted, bringing him to a sitting position. The left side of his face was undamaged. Tommy turned toward Axel. The other side was mottled maroon, with deep-purple patches. His right ear was completely covered with gauze, and portions of his scalp had been shaved, stitched, and taped over. The pale-blue iris of his right eye floated on a sea of cherry red.

"You're looking good," Axel said.

"Fuck you," whispered Tommy.

"Okay," Axel said. "You look like dog shit."

"Thank you. How my joints doing? Sam burned any of 'em down yet?"

"Sam's doing okay," Axel said. He thought for a moment, wondering whether he should say more.

Tommy asked, "Okay, what happened? He bust one a my machines?"

"No. Everything's fine. He did try to fire one of your help."

"Which one? There's a couple of 'em maybe need firing."

"It was Duane. The kid told him he couldn't smoke in the stand."

Tommy sat halfway up. "Goddamn right he can't! The health heat'll shut the joint down, they see him smoking in there." An agonized look flooded his face, and he fell back against the pillow.

Axel said, "Relax, Tom, it's all straightened out."

"I sure as fuck hope so. Fucking Sam. I told him to just sit there and fucking watch. I shoulda known better."

"Well, that's what he's doing. I told him he should go outside, he wants a smoke."

"I suppose he's sitting in there chewing that fucking snoose."

"Yeah, well, I told Duane to make sure he wasn't spitting it in the batter." Axel held up a paper bag. "I brought you some donuts."

Tommy tried to lift his left arm toward the bag, winced, let it fall back. His forearm was bound in a plastic splint.

"Here," Axel said, opening the bag and extracting a sugar-coated minidonut. "You want me to stick it in your mouth?"

"Screw you," he said. "You know I don't eat the fucking things anyways."

"Oh. Screw me." Axel ate the donut, watching Tommy's red eye watching him back. He finished chewing, swallowed, then looked in the bag. His eyes widened, and he said, "Now what's this, do you suppose?" He pulled out a half pint of Jack Daniel's, the black label speckled with sugar from the donuts. Tommy reached across his abdomen with his right arm. Axel brushed the sugar off the bottle, opened it, and placed it in Tommy's hand.

"Thank you," Tommy said.

"You're welcome." Axel watched Tommy empty a quarter of the bottle. "So, you tell the cops who hit you?"

Tommy said, "I don't tell the heat nothing, Ax. You know that. I take care of myself."

"Looks like you take care of yourself real good."

"That fucking Bald Monkey blindsided me. Got six grand off me."

"This is the guy you said was never gonna mess with Tommy Fabian again? Doesn't sound to me like he stayed scared for long."

"He'll be plenty scared, I ever see him again."

"They found a baseball bat by your Winnie."

"My own fucking bat."

"Doctor says you're gonna be here at least a week. You got blood clots." He pointed at the fluid dripping into Tommy's arm. "They have to get you thinned out."

"I ain't being here no week." He took another pull at the Jack Daniel's. "It'll thin out faster with Jack."

"You know what his name is?" Axel asked.

"Who?"

"Bald Monkey. He says his name is James Dean."

Tommy blinked. "What, you mean like the sausage guy?"

When Axel got back to the fair, the three girls—Carmen, Kirsten, and Juanita—were huddled in the stand, looking out at the nearly deserted mall. It was raining, getting dark, and the only people outside were crouching under umbrellas or running from one building to another, shielding their heads with plastic bags or newspapers.

He'd be lucky to clear a thousand bucks. The day was a bust. None of the concessionaires would do well, not even the joints inside the buildings, where the crowds clustered in stagnant, sodden masses. A rainy day was bad for everybody. Even Tiny Tot Donuts, possibly the most weatherproof concession at the fair, looked dead. They had only two machines going. Sam O'Gara's green feed cap showed above the top of the machines, moving from one end of the stand to the other, then back. He still had eight kids working; all of them standing at one end of the stand, talking.

Axel changed course, veering away from the Taco Shop, heading for Tiny Tot.

"Hey, Sam."

Sam looked up, met Axel at the side door. "What the hell do you call this?" He made a gesture that included the entire universe outside the stand.

"I call it rain, Sam."

"So what are they sayin', Ax? They saying the fucker's gonna let up?"

"Won't make any difference at this point, Sam. It's after eight. Won't be anybody more coming to the fair this day. Maybe you ought to send some of your help home. What do you think?"

Sam regarded the group of teenagers at the other end of the stand. "I don't know," he said. "What if it gets busy?"

"It's not going to get busy."

"I mean, what the fuck do I know about donuts? I never sold a fucking one of 'em before this morning, Ax. Swear to Christ, that fucking Tommy—even when he gets the crap beat out of him he's making trouble for me. You remember that time in Deadwood?"

Axel nodded.

"Fucking Tommy-the-Mouth fucking Fabian. Probably how he got his ass kicked last night, mouthin' off."

"You know, you don't have to do this, Sam. I can keep an eye on things, you got something else you got to be doing."

Sam rolled his shoulders. "Fuck it. He wants me to run his business, I got no problem with that. How is the little shit anyway?"

"He's hurting. But he's got all the nurses pissed at him, so I'd say the prognosis is good. They'll have him out of there as soon as they can."

"I sure as fuck hope so. I got this Camaro I'm working on. Got a guy wants to buy it if I can get the fucker running." He tugged his cap down low over his eyes. "So you think I got too much help?"

"Send half of them home. The other two stands too. Waste of money. Besides, they'll just be thinking too much, getting into trouble."

Sam nodded uncertainly, wiping his mouth with the back of a hand. Axel enjoyed seeing him out of his element. He was such a cocky son-of-a-bitch, it was good to see him floundering for once.

Sophie had gone home at seven, according to Carmen.

"She said she wasn't feeling good. I dunno."

"She was sick?" Axel asked.

"I don't think so. More like she was pissed off about the weather. You couldn't hardly talk to her. Bite your head off. Maybe she was having her hot flashes again. She said she'd be opening in the morning."

That Sunday night, the grandstand featured something called a Christian Rock Festival. The rumor was that advance ticket sales had come in at a record low, and the rain had reduced attendance even further. Axel closed the Taco Shop at nine-thirty and sent the help home. He didn't even have the heart to wait for the small rush of business that would come after the show. He just couldn't see a bunch of wet Jesus rockers getting excited about his Bueno Burrito. He lowered the front of the stand and performed the end-of-day cleaning and counting rituals.

Once again, the numbers didn't make any sense. He'd started the day with 1,500 flour tortillas and 764 corn tortillas, more than enough for a busy Sunday. But the day had been a bust. He'd taken in $1,407, roughly a break-even day. But based on his tortilla count, he had sold only 260 burritos and 126 tacos and tostadas. Again, he was three hundred dollars long. In other words, he thought, about what he'd expect if someone was adding a hundred tortillas to his stock.

Somewhere in all this, there had to be a scam. But for the life of him, Axel couldn't figure it. It just didn't make any sense.

Something Axel had told her that she couldn't get out of her head: "A bad day is a bad day. You can't unlive it. You try to get it back, you go nuts."

Sophie thought she knew what he meant, but it didn't help. She took the rain personally. She felt herself responsible. Saturday had been such a great day. Record sales. Axel had been elated. Then they get rained out the very next day. It killed her to have to pay those girls to stand there watching it rain. She wished now she'd sent one of them home. But she'd been thinking all day that it might clear up, the people might come.

Pouring herself a second glass of white zinfandel, Sophie listened to the sound of steady rain filtered through the mosquito screen. Landfall could be a noisy community—some summer nights, the parties and fights went on till dawn—but on this wet Sunday the only sounds were those of rain on aluminum and the hissing of traffic from Interstate 94.

She wished Axel were with her.

As soon as the desire reached her conscious mind, Sophie recoiled from it. He was busy. Too busy. And anyway, why should she care? All the things she did for him, did he ever say thank you? Actually, he did. But there were a lot of things she did that he didn't know about. Like coming in early. Like taking responsibility for the shrinkage—how many managers would do that? Sophie set her jaw, the quickly dissipating but heady joy of martyrdom flowing through her. One way or another, she would make this the Taco Shop's best year ever. She would show him what a good manager could accomplish. They still had a shot at setting a record gross, if next weekend was good. And even if the gross was off, she'd show Axel a net like he'd never seen before—she would cut back the help, eliminate shrinkage, and push every sale like a pro. Sell those nachos, those extra-large Cokes. She'd show him. When he saw what she could do, he'd come up with one beluga of a bonus. How could he not?

CHAPTER

23

The week started out cool, in the sixties but mostly clear, with just a few cirrus clouds off to the south. The *State Fair Daily News* predicted attendance at 110,000—a solid week-day showing that would provide steady, profitable business for most of the concessionaires. By eleven o'clock, sales at Axel's Taco Shop had already matched Sunday's totals. Axel could count the number of times that had happened on one hand and have five fingers left over. The first Monday was usually for shit.

Sam O'Gara, heading into his second day at the donut stand, was feeling his oats.

"Maybe I'll get into it," he said. "Get myself a joint like this, sell deep-fried lutefisk on a stick or some goddamn thing. Get myself rich like you and Tommy."

"I'm not rich," Axel said, a bit nettled. "And besides, it's not that easy." He had worked hard to build his business. His first years at the fair had been tough, and not very profitable. Axel hated it when people looked at his opera-tion as if it were a cash cow gifted to him by the state. It was a business, like any other, only maybe tougher. And the money wasn't nearly what people thought. The Taco Shop might net thirty in a good year, and if he was lucky he could make another twenty doing special events and county fairs, but it wasn't as if he was rolling in it. There were guys spinning nuts in factories making better money.

Tommy, on the other hand, *was* rolling in it—a fact that had not escaped Sam.

"What do you figure they cost, a little bag of donuts?" Sam asked.

Axel shrugged. They were standing in the same spot on the mall where Axel usually stood with Tommy. Every now and then, Axel would realize with a jolt that the man standing beside him was not Tommy.

"I figure about a dime," Sam said. "So he makes a dollar forty a bag. You know how many of them bags we sold today? Man, I could get into that. Now, I'm just talkin' out loud here, but it seems to me it'd be one hell of a lot easier'n fixing cars, that's for sure. Seems to me a guy could just kick back and let the green roll in, just like findin' buried treasure."

"You think it's so goddamn easy, I hope you take a run at it, Sam. I like the idea of lutefisk on a stick. I think you should go for it."

"You bein' a little sarky on me, Ax?"

Axel said, "Ninety percent of new concessions, they're history in six months. Of course, those guys went broke, they didn't have the lutefisk-on-a-stick idea."

Sam scratched his neck. "Better odds'n a inside straight, and I won plenty of times with those. Besides, how hard could it be, a peasant like you doin' so good, a guy what keeps his money in freakin' coffee cans."

"I don't keep my money in coffee cans," Axel said.

"Oh, yeah? What'd you do with it, then? Put it in T-bills?"

"It's none of your goddamn business what I do with my money, Sam."

Sam bobbled his eyebrows. "That a fact?"

"That's right. I can take care of myself. I don't need your financial advice."

"Well, la-di-fucking-da," Sam said, fitting a Pall Mall between his lips. "You wanna be a peasant, that's your own damn problem. Jus' don't come cryin' to me if that bald-headed kid decides to hit you next."

"Since when did I ever come crying to you?"

"Sheeit, I pulled you outta so many scrapes I lost count."

"Well, you can just relax, on account of I don't need you looking after me. You understand?"

Sam said, "Hey, Ax?" He thrust up his middle finger. "Fuck you."

"I'll see you later," Axel said. He'd had his morning dose of Sam O'Gara.

"I don't like leaving her in charge," Sophie said. "She's like a zombie lately. I caught her giving out two burritos and only charging for one. And forgetting the cheese, twice! Better we should have left that Kirsten in charge. Or even Juanita."

"Carmen will be okay," Axel said. "She was having a problem with her boyfriend, but they broke up."

They were walking down Carnes Avenue, going to the Waffle Shop for breakfast.

"Sometimes I think she's on dope, the way she acts. I don't know how she does so well at school. Or anyway she says she does. What boyfriend?"

"A punk with no hair on his head."

Sophie said, "Oh, yeah, I met him. He was hanging around the stand the other day."

"He's the one beat up Tommy, you know."

"Oh?"

"Yeah. And Carmen too. You see what he did to her eye?"

"That how come she's wearing those glasses? She was probably asking for it. Are we going to eat breakfast or just stand around?"

Axel unclenched his fists and let his shoulders sag. "What the hell," he said. "He's probably a hundred miles away by now. Let's go get some waffles."

Sophie sipped her black coffee and watched Axel arrange five pats of butter on his waffle. He moved the pats around with his fork, getting a measure of molten butter into each waffle pit. When the butter was distributed to his satisfaction, he picked up the strawberry syrup, guiding the thin stream up and down the rows of square waffle pits.

The Waffle Shop was one of the older concessions at the fair. You could still get a full breakfast there, but most of their business these days was in oversize, hand-formed waffle cones with your choice of ice cream flavors.

Sophie felt jittery. Axel had never before asked her to have breakfast with him. Something was going on. "You shouldn't eat that," she said.

Axel cut into the waffle with the side of his fork, speared a large wedge, and pushed it into his mouth. When he had swallowed it, he said, "I've been wondering about something."

"You should wonder about what you eat." She didn't know why she ragged on him that way. She watched herself do it again and again, always with the invisible, internal wince, expecting to be hit. With her husband—ex-husband—that was how it had worked. Made remarks, poked at him until he hit her. Poked at him some more. He'd been so dense, if she said something subtle he never got it. Just asked her what the hell she was talking about. She could see his stupid face, hear herself berating him.

"I think about it all the time."

"You didn't eat that stuff, you'd still have all your teeth." Difference was, Axel got it all, but he never hit her. That made her mad too. If she couldn't get under his skin, how much could he like her?

"Sophie, my teeth are gone whether I eat this or not. I'm not worrying about my teeth today. What I'm worrying about is, how come I've got so many tortillas at the end of the day?"

"It's not just your teeth," she said. Then she replayed, in her mind, what Axel had just said, and this time she heard it. She felt the heat building in her cheeks, feeling his green eyes. Axel had told her he used to be a professional poker player. She had always thought that was just a story, but seeing him now, seeing his intense, utterly unreadable expression, she believed it. "It's your heart," she said weakly.

"See, what I don't understand is, if you're going to all that trouble to set me up with the tortillas, how come you don't take the money?"

Back in the 1960s, when she was in her twenties, before she met her jerk-off ex-husband and got pregnant and had Carmen, Sophie had spent a few months living with a bunch of pseudointellectual dropouts down on the West Bank. They'd taken over a trio of roomy apartments above the Triangle Bar and formed a commune loosely bonded by a lack of money, a taste for cheap wine, and a tolerance for the seismic event that occurred each night from nine till one in the morning, when the blues bands cranked up their Peaveys and started the walls shaking. She'd been with this guy back then, a protohippie they called Mr. Natural, Natch for short, an occasional bass player with Skogie and the Flaming Pachucos, who had thumbed his way out to San Francisco and returned in a VW bug with a cigar box full of discolored sugar cubes. Sophie had stirred one into her jasmine tea one morning and, shortly thereafter, noticed that the walls were breathing and that a microscopic receiver in her left ear was playing the theme to *I Dream of Jeannie* over and over again.

Which was much the same way she felt right now, only it was the table breathing and the theme to *Jeopardy*.

Axel said, "Are you okay?"

Sophie shook her head, meaning yes. She'd had moments like this before. Like when she got pulled over for speeding, or the time Carmen, at age eight, had come home from school unexpectedly and found Sophie on the bed astride a neighbor's undressed body. Her embarrassing moments always brought with them this sense of unreality.

"Did you hear what I asked you?"

Sophie cleared her throat but was unable to reply. The thing was, what did she have to be embarrassed about? Axel was the one who benefited. What right did he have to accuse her of anything?

Axel said, "Aren't you going to eat your muffin?"

Sophie regarded the untouched bran muffin on her plate. Of course, if you looked at it another way, he wasn't really accusing her of anything. "I'll eat it later," she said.

Axel nodded and ate a large bite of waffle, watching Sophie. She noticed that one of his eyes was tending to drift these days. It would wander off on its own, then snap back a second later.

Axel set his fork on his tray and said, "Look, I'm not accusing you of anything, Sophie—I swear I'm not. I mean, even if you were holding out a few bucks, which I'm not saying you are, I wouldn't mind it. I mean, you work harder than anybody. But it's driving me nuts, trying to figure out why you've been sneaking in those extra tortillas."

Sophie crossed her arms. "Those Bueno Burritos, the girls ruin a lot of tortillas when they make them. Too much filling."

"So?"

"You told me part of my job was to reduce the shrinkage. You told me if I got the net up, you'd pay me a bonus." She pushed her chin forward and stared back at him, watched his face changing, saw his lips part, then curve into a loose smile, saw his left eye drift up and away. For a long time, he said nothing at all.

The kid, Duane, intercepted them as they were walking back to the donut stand. Axel let his arm fall from Sophie's shoulder, feeling sheepish, as if he'd been caught kissing on school grounds.

"Mr. Speeter? Can I talk to you a minute?" The kid seemed upset.

"Sure." Axel let his hand brush Sophie's arm. "I'll catch up with you," he said.

The kid was shifting nervously from one foot to the other, like he had to pee.

"What's the problem?" Axel asked.

"You know Mr. Sam?"

Axel nodded.

"I mean, he's a nice guy and everything, but I don't think Mr. Fabian would like it, you know?"

Axel said, "No. I don't. What are you trying to tell me, son?"

"Well, it's, like, he's changing the mix."

Axel wasn't sure he'd heard that right. He cocked his head and waited for more.

"I mean, he thinks the donuts need more salt, you know? So he's changing the mix."

"He's changing the *donut* mix?"

"They're tasting sort of weird now, you know?"

Axel had to say it again. "He's changing the *donut* mix?"

"I mean, they're not bad, but I don't think Mr. Fabian would like it. Can you talk to him, you think?"

CHAPTER

24

"**I** could get arrested for this," Axel said.

"You could get arrested for blocking traffic, f'Chrissakes. This is a freeway, not a cow path. You're driving like an old man." Tommy Fabian had one of his little cigars going, his first in three days. "Damn, this tastes good!"

"It smells like your bandages caught fire." Axel edged the truck up to fifty-five miles per hour and moved into the left lane. "Just don't let it kill you while you're in my truck. I don't want to go to jail. I don't know how the hell I let you talk me into this. I shouldn't have said anything."

"I got a reputation," Tommy said. "My donuts, they gotta be right every fucking time. Fucking Sam. Salt, f'Chrissakes!"

"I made him go back to the standard mix, Tom. We had a little talk. He's pretty pissed at me, but everything's okay now. You got some damn good kids running it for you. That kid Duane is humpin' like a camel. I think he runs it better than you do. Three days without you, and it's running smoother than ever, despite the fact you got Sam in there."

"Don't tell me that shit. All the more reason I gotta get back. These kids figure out they can make it without you,

172

and the next thing you know, you tell 'em to do something and you might as well be pissin' at the moon."

"Maybe you oughta relax, quit yelling at them. I've been thinking lately that we try to do too much ourselves. Besides, you got bunged up pretty bad there. I don't like doctors either, but when they say you gotta stay in the hospital you ought to at least think about taking it easy. Let Sam and the kids run the stand a couple more days. I mean, you can't do it all yourself, right?"

"Speak for yourself. Anyway, those doctors haven't got no sense of priorities. All they worry about is if somebody's gonna sue them. Once I get back in the saddle, I'll heal up faster anyway. By the way, you seen our bald friend hanging around anyplace?"

Axel hesitated. "He's gone," he said.

"What?"

"He was staying with Carmen, like you said. But he's gone now. Got in his car and took off. We probably won't see him again."

"Shit. I was looking forward to jumping up and down on his face. You think he's really gone?"

Axel guided the truck up the Snelling Avenue exit ramp. "Yeah," he said, "I do." It felt like a lie.

"Son-of-a-bitch."

Axel drove down Snelling at twenty-five miles per hour. He turned west at Como Avenue. While they were sitting in line, waiting to get into the parking lot, Axel said, "Hey, Tommy, you know kangaroos?"

"Kangaroos?" Tommy blinked and looked at Axel, who was staring vacantly out the windshield. "What about 'em?"

"You ever see how they fight? They tear each other up. They got these big kangaroo feet and claws, and they just take turns jumping on each other and tearing each other's bellies open until one of them goes off in the desert and dies."

"Yeah? What are they fighting about?"

"Lady roos, what else?"

173

"Lots of stuff. They could be fighting about who gets the kids, or about politics, or about money." Tommy flicked away his cigar.

Axel looked at his bruised and bandaged friend. "Don't be stupid," he said. "Roos don't care about that kind of stuff."

"I gotta sit down." Tommy Fabian veered to the right and collapsed on a bench.

"You okay?" Axel sat down beside him. They were on the fairgrounds just north of the Coliseum, halfway between Tommy's Winnebago, where he had changed his clothes, and the main Tiny Tot stand on the mall. "You don't look so good. Maybe you ought to go back, take a little nap."

"I just gotta rest a minute. I get to the stand, I can sit down, relax."

"Let's go back to your Winnie. You can take a nap."

Tommy shook his head. The two men sat in silence and watched the flow of people passing before them. It was a beautiful day, warm but not too warm, the sky a clear, distant blue. A mild, changing breeze kept the fairground odors moving and shifting, and even here, at the periphery of the grounds, Axel could pick out the hot, greasy smell of frying corn dogs, the tangy raw-onion scent from the foot-long stand half a block away, and the sour reek of spilled beer. Underlying the food odors were earthy animal aromas from the hogs, horses, cattle, sheep, goats, chickens, geese, turkeys, rabbits, and other blue-ribbon contenders contained in the barns and exhibition halls that dominated the southern quarter of the fairgrounds. Thinking about it that way made the odors overwhelming; Axel shifted to breathing through his mouth.

"I got a feeling he's still around someplace," Tommy said.

"Who?"

"Bald Monkey."

"He's not staying with Carmen anymore, I can tell you that."

"You wondering how come he went after me instead of you?"

"I think he was thinking about both of us. He got in my room and went through my stuff," Axel said. He was about to mention the missing .45 auto but decided it could keep until later. He didn't want to get Tommy thinking about guns. Until a few years back, Tommy had carried a little nickel-plated .32 in his belt. Then he'd gotten into an argument with the fried-zucchini guy, pulled out his piece, and started waving it under the other vendor's nose. The zucchini guy made a big stink and got the cops and the fair administration involved, and there had been a bunch of meetings that added up to Tommy retiring his pistol and—worst of all, according to Tommy—having to apologize to the fried-zucchini guy. "After all, it wasn't like I shot the son-of-a-bitch," Tommy had complained. Axel thought it just as well, the way Tommy could blow his cork over nothing, that he didn't carry his gun around anymore. "He didn't get anything," Axel continued. "And my guess is he's left town. Carmen says he's from Omaha. Maybe he went back."

"Didn't get into your coffee cans, huh?"

"I got rid of the cans."

"You put it in a bank like a normal person?"

"Something like that."

Tommy took a breath, then pushed himself up off the bench. As Axel watched Tommy walking away, he thought, Maybe I drive like an old man, but *he's* the one that's *walking* like an old man. Is that how I'll be walking soon? Like the world is made of Jell-O? Axel remembered something then.

He remembered being in a duck blind with old Andy, his dad, on a rainy but unseasonably warm November day in 1940, waiting for the ducks to come, his last hunt before signing up for the Merchant Marine, the father and son wearing nothing but cotton dungarees, hip boots, flannel shirts, and light raincoats; standing in the wet cattails with seventeen cork decoys floating on Long Lake, searching the horizon for the black specks that would become mallards, bluebills, canvasbacks, teal. The sky was close and gray and wet. Old Andy's faded canvas hat rested on top of his ears, flaring them at the tips. Axel remembered standing on the trampled cattails that made up the floor of the blind, watching his dad, wondering how the old man could see with his eyes squinted down into little wrinkled slits. Andy had pointed across the lake and said, "Lookie dere, Ax."

Axel looked, expecting to see an approaching flock, but what he saw was a disturbance of the lake's surface. The water on the far side of the lake was leaping and chattering, yet the water directly in front of the blind was perfectly calm. As they watched, the disturbance raced toward them, and then the wind hit the cattails and bent them back, and Andy's hat went up into the air and disappeared. The temperature dropped twenty degrees. Axel looked at Andy then and saw the fear in his father's face as the weather struck.

The temperature continued to fall as the wind whipped their faces with stinging sheets of ice and snow. It was over a mile to where they had parked the '36 Ford. They trudged along the dirt road, heads down, slogging through the freezing mud and gathering snowdrifts, moving their hands from their armpits to their ears. Axel remembered looking at Andy, thinking: He's an old man. He's not gonna make it.

But they had survived. Andy had lived another twenty-two years. Now, watching Tommy Fabian's painful gait, he counted back and realized with some sadness that on that day in 1940 old Andy had been only sixty-two years old, younger by eleven years than Axel was today.

Axel caught up with Tommy. "You ever feel old?" he asked.

Tommy shook his head. "Just a little sore sometimes."

"You ever think about taking a partner on? Somebody to help you when you get old? I mean, older?"

Tommy said, "No way."

"I've been thinking about my future," Axel said. "I get sick or something, I don't want to have to close up shop, you know?"

Tommy Fabian wasn't listening. They had reached the mall, and he was staring at Tiny Tot #1. The lines were good, and most of the machines were cooking. Tommy watched the stand as though he could not quite believe it could run without him. His employees, most of whom had cooked their first donut only a week before, were cranking the little rings out like they owned the place. Sam sat atop Tommy's stool, an unlit cigarette in his mouth.

Tommy turned to Axel, shaking his head in wonder. "Just stay with it and don't get old. The best thing you can do about it is don't get old."

Axel said, "I don't know, Tom. I can't say I much like the other choice."

Kirsten sat on the folding chair behind the stand, smoking a cigarette, blowing smoke out through her nose like Madonna. She was halfway through her second pack ever of Virginia Slims. It was her first break practically all day, and now it was starting to rain again. And wouldn't you know, Sophie shows up with her evil eye and says, "Can't you find anything to do?" She never showed up when Carmen was taking a nap behind the stand, no way. Kirsten wanted to stomp her feet and say, "You can have your stupid job, you smelly old . . . witch!"

Instead, she dropped her Virginia Slim and followed Sophie into the stand.

Carmen, moving as if the air were syrup, was making a Bueno Burrito for a rosy-cheeked, alert young man wearing a mesh Wayne Feeds cap.

Sophie glared. "For Christ's sake, Carmen. What did you do, take a slow pill today?"

Carmen said, "Hi, Sophie." She folded the burrito, giving it a final delicate pat, and presented it to her customer. "Thank you," she said, turning away, ignoring the five-dollar bill in his hand.

"Don't you want my money?" he asked Carmen, who seemed not to hear him.

Sophie stepped forward, snatched the bill out of his hand, and gave him his change. She grabbed Carmen by the arm and spun her around. "What is *wrong* with you?"

"Oh, I don't know. Why do you ask?"

For a second, Kirsten thought Sophie might rip the sunglasses off and claw Carmen's eyes out. A group of kids approached the stand. Sophie took Carmen by her shoulders and shook her; Carmen's head flopped back and forth. The group of kids stopped and watched for a moment, then left. Seeing this, Sophie let go and told Carmen to go sit behind the stand.

Carmen said, as though nothing had happened, "We need change."

Sophie checked the cash box. They were out of ones and quarters.

"Well, then, go tell Axel. He's over at Tiny Tot, talking with Tommy."

Carmen nodded, hung her purse over her shoulder, and drifted across the mall toward Tiny Tot Donuts.

Axel and Tommy, sitting on a pair of canvas chairs behind Tiny Tot, watched the light rain darken the street. People were moving into the buildings, some of them holding plastic bags over their heads.

Axel said, "You were a little hard on Sam there, Tom. I mean, he deserved it and all, but it's not like he was one of your employees."

"Son-of-a-bitch smoking in my stand."

"He was just trying to help you out while you were laid up."

"I ain't laid up anymore. Changing my mix, f'Chrissakes."

"Sometimes you got to let people help you the way they know how."

Tommy shrugged and lit a fresh cigar, his hand shaking.

"You feeling okay?" Axel asked.

"I feel great. How the fuck are you feeling?"

Axel took the question seriously. "I'm feeling alone," he said. "That's why I decided about Sophie, you know?"

"I still think you're nuts," Tommy said. "The broad's rippin' you off every day, and you want her for a partner? That's nuts."

"I told you, she's not ripping me off. She was just trying to make herself look good."

"You believe that, you oughta be down on the midway, trying to win yourself some plush."

"I'm tired of doing it all myself."

"What the hell? It looks to me like you got a bunch a broads in there doing it for you."

"You know what I mean. You ought to, anyways—I mean, look at you. You got a head all covered up with bandages, and every time you stand up you get dizzy—"

"That was earlier. I feel fine now."

"Whatever. The point is, if you had a partner you wouldn't even have to be here."

"A few hours ago you were telling me I didn't have to be here anyway."

"You wouldn't even want to be here. Besides, we're talking about me, and I'm tired of running the show all by myself. Sophie works her ass off. Sometimes I think she cares more about that stand than I do."

"She's so great, how come you don't marry her?"

"Too old."

"Seventy-three's not so old."

"I mean her."

Tommy, who had been drawing on his cigar, broke into a coughing fit. He leaned forward in his chair, and Axel thumped him on the back. When he got his breath back, he said, "Chrissakes, Ax, she's young enough to be your daughter."

"She's almost *fifty*," Axel said.

Tommy's eyes were still watering. "Pretty goddamn selective for an old cocker, you ask me."

"I'm gonna take her over to this lawyer tomorrow," Axel said. "Get it all set up. Why wait?"

"Christ, Ax, why don't you wait till the fair's over, at least. Give yourself a chance to think on it."

"I think on it, I might not do it, and I want to do it, Tom. If I wait till the fair's over, I'll forget what it's like to be alone in this business."

Tommy said, "You're always alone in this business. Well, look what we got here—speak of the devil's daughter. How you doing, Carmen?"

"Hi, Tommy," said Carmen. "I'm doing okay."

"How's the eye?" Tommy asked her. "I hear you got a heck of a shiner under those shades."

Carmen shrugged and turned toward Axel. "Sophie says for me to go get some change," she said.

Axel dug in his pocket and pulled out a set of keys. He handed them to Carmen. "You know where the truck is? Along the far row, way over on the other side of the lot. About ten cars in from the back. The change is in the back; you have to use the round key."

"Thanks." Carmen floated off.

"You're lucky he didn't use a baseball bat," Tommy called after her. Carmen gave no sign she had heard. "She looks sort of out of it," he said to Axel. "If she worked for the railroad they'd have her pissin' in a cup."

"She's just sleepy," Axel said.

"Yeah, right. Prob'ly been up all night banging Bald Monkey."

"He's gone, I told you. He's been gone almost three days."

"You mean you ain't seen him in three days. Guys like that don't go away until you make 'em. It's like trying to get rid of a hungry dog. They just lie in the weeds and wait." He looked up and pointed at the thirty-story-tall, blue-and-white Space Tower, with its rotating elevator. "He's probably sitting up there looking down at us right now."

CHAPTER

25

Carmen arrived at the truck, it seemed to her, only moments after she left Axel and Tommy at the Tiny Tot stand. Her hair was wet. She didn't remember the walk at all. She let herself into the cab and, resting her hands on the wheel, let her mind wander, hoping to remember what she was doing there. It started raining harder; she watched through the windshield as the world went out of focus. Dean had been gone going on three days now. She might never see him again. She knew she should be glad he was gone. It was no fun getting punched in the eye; it was hard to see in the rain, looking through mirrored sunglasses. Now, though, she found herself bored into a near-catatonic state. The days and nights of her future appeared endless and gray and smelled of frying tortillas. She almost wished some guy would come along and blacken her other eye.

After a time, more than a minute but less than half an hour, she remembered why she was there. She was supposed to get change. Sophie was out of change.

The back of the truck was as precisely organized as Axel's room at the Motel 6. Cartons of cups and napkins and plastic forks were laid out along the left wall; condiments, chips, and other nonperishables were arranged on the opposite side. Carmen stood at the back of the truck, looking in through the open tailgate, feeling the rain on her bare arms. Where would he keep the change? She was supposed to know this. The bed of the truck was covered with a green packing pad. Carmen climbed inside. At the far end, against the cab, the packing pad stepped up and over a boxlike shape. Carmen pulled the pad back and discovered an oblong wooden box with an open top. The box contained a row of coffee cans. She felt excitement struggling to penetrate the Valium haze as she pried the top off one of the coffee cans.

It was filled with packets of sugar.

The second can was full of salt packets. She opened the rest of the cans. Taco sauce. Horseradish. Horseradish? More sugar. Equal. She replaced the covers and drew the pad back up over the box, wondering in a mild Valium sort of way why Axel was saving coffee cans full of condiments. Where was the change? She had done this before, last year, and she was supposed to remember. Axel kept the change in a special place, but where? She took inventory of the items surrounding her. Cups, napkins, paper servers, forks, canned chilies, chips, taco sauce . . . Wait. Back up. Cups. She opened the top of the carton and reached inside. There it was, the canvas bank bag. She opened it, emptied the contents out onto the packing pad, took five rolls of quarters, a roll of dimes, and three fifty-dollar bundles of one-dollar bills, and stuffed it all in her purse. That left three rolls of pennies, a roll of dimes, two fifty-dollar bundles, and two rolls of fives, tens, and twenties, held together with thick blue rubber bands. Carmen took a twenty from each roll, folded the two into a small square, and slid it into her back pocket.

Wandering back toward the Taco Shop, she wondered what Axel had done with his coffee can money. One thing she was pretty sure about—it had to be somewhere. Cheap as Axel was, there was no way he could have spent it. It occurred to her that he might have put it in a bank, which was what any normal person would have done a long time ago. But Axel hated banks. He said you could not trust them. He even hated going into a bank to buy change, always counting it twice, right there in front of the teller. It was embarrassing. Carmen experienced a moment of disorientation. She stopped and let her brain spin free for a moment, enjoying the floating sensation.

Her mind returned to the physical task at hand. Her hair was heavy with water. The rain was lighter now, but steady, and the parking lot had become a maze of puddles, the larger of which Carmen walked around. She paid no attention to the smaller puddles; there were just too goddamn many of them.

James Dean sat in the torn and stained beanbag chair and watched Tigger tattooing Sweety's forehead.

"Sweety's even got muscles on his forehead," Tigger said, pausing to wipe away the blood and excess ink. Sweety turned toward Dean and contorted his brow, which writhed impressively. The words FUCK ME were carefully outlined in black. Sweety himself had conceived the message. Dean had helped draw the letters with a felt-tip pen, and Tigger was working now on filling them in, using a pushpin to open the skin and a red Sanford marker for color.

"You know, it's not going to last," Dean said. "You want it to last, you should use ashes from Styrofoam. That's how we did it in Lincoln."

Tigger said, "Yeah, well, we ain't in Lincoln, and we don't have any Styrofoam."

"When's the guy going to be here?" Dean asked.

"He'll be here. Pork always does what he says he's gonna."

"That's what you said yesterday."

"Yesterday he was in Wisconsin. He didn't get my message."

"Fuckin' Pork," Sweety said, gritting his teeth as Tigger performed a series of pricks on the letter *C*.

"Hold still," Tigger said. "You want this to look good, don't you?"

He worked in silence for a few minutes.

Dean was bored. He figured he'd give Pork another hour, then take his money and leave. The more time he spent with Tigger and Sweety, the less he was inclined to trust their choice of drug dealers.

For the past two nights he'd had a room at the Golden Steer out on I-94, watching MTV, counting and recounting his money, and waiting for Tigger to arrange an introduction with "Pork," the supposed connection, the guy with the meth. His idea was to parlay most of the six thousand seven hundred dollars into a half kilo of crystal methedrine—an incredible price, if it was any good—then double his money by selling it to a guy he'd met in Lincoln named Stinger, who, if all went as planned, had got out of prison on schedule, had returned to Sioux Falls, had got back into the drug business, and had as much cash as he'd claimed to have. And even if Stinger didn't work out—a distinct possibility—there were always people looking to get high.

He hadn't minded waiting at first. The Golden Steer wasn't a bad place, but late last night he'd heard a crash outside his room and looked out to see that some drunk in a Cadillac had crushed his Maverick, driven right up onto the trunk. The guy was staggering around, muttering to himself, every few seconds giving the Cadillac a kick in the side.

Dean's first reaction was to go out and beat the hell out of the guy, but then he started thinking about how the cops would be showing up pretty soon. At first, they'd be interested in the Cadillac guy, but sooner or later they'd be looking at those Nebraska license plates on the Maverick, and if they ran the plates, well, that couldn't be good. He threw his stuff into his bag, walked down the hill to Concord Avenue, and called a cab. Since then, he'd been staying with Tigger and Sweety.

A scraping sound came from the window.

"There he is." Tigger set the pushpin on the table. "That you, Pork?" he called.

A pair of black lace-up motorcycle boots entered through the basement window, followed by a blocky man with a stubble of dark hair covering his scalp and jaw. His eyes were black and alert.

"This here's Pork," Tigger said.

Pork was wearing a camouflage-pattern sweatshirt and a pair of baggy olive-drab pants with cargo pockets. Though he was about Dean's height, he carried another forty pounds. His fingers were thick and short, and he held his arms a few inches out from his body, letting everybody know that he'd put in his hours on the bench. The guys Dean knew with bodies like that, they'd spent at least five calendars in Lincoln.

Pork grinned, his mouth forming a wide, pointed vee. "This place reeks," he said. He looked at Sweety. "What did you do to your head, Sweety?"

"I'm giving him a tattoo," Tigger said. "It was his idea."

Pork took a closer look. "Hope you don't land in jail with that on your head, my man."

"They can fucking try," Sweety growled.

Pork shrugged. "Believe me, they do." He looked at Dean. "You the guy?"

Dean, half buried in the beanbag chair, gave a slight nod.

"How good you know this guy, Tig?"

"He's cool," Tigger said.

Pork put his hands in his back pockets, raised his eyebrows, and looked at the ceiling, still smiling, shaking his head like he couldn't believe it. Dean didn't blame him. Tigger was not the kind of guy you would believe anything he said. But Pork looked like a guy you could do business with. A guy who'd paid some dues, learned how it's done.

"Look," Dean said, "you don't know me; I don't know you. That's cool. You don't want to talk, I can take my business someplace else."

"Relax," said Pork. He was looking at Dean, his alert eyes probing. Noticing the antitheft strip on Dean's jacket sleeve, he said, "How come you don't cut that thing off there?"

Dean looked at the plastic strip anchored to his jacket sleeve. "I kind of like it," he said.

"So you walk down the street and everybody knows you're a bad guy?"

Dean shrugged. "They can think what they want."

Pork shook his head, but the stolen jacket seemed to make him more comfortable. What kind of cop would go around wearing something like that?

"What you looking for?"

Dean said, "What do you got?"

"Tigger said you were asking about some crank."

Dean shrugged.

"I can get it."

"Good."

"How much you looking for?"

"I was thinking a half key, if the price is what Tigger said."

"The price is good. I suppose you'll want to sample the merch."

"You got it with you?"

Pork laughed. "You got your money with *you?*"

Dean, who did in fact have the money stuffed in his jacket pockets, shook his head.

Pork said, "Let's take this one step at a time, then. How about we get together tomorrow night for a little taste. You got someplace we can meet? I mean someplace besides this pisshole?"

CHAPTER

26

At ten-thirty Thursday morning, Frank Knox greeted Axel and Sophie at the front door of his aging two-story South Minneapolis Tudor. The house smelled like Lysol and something that Sophie could not identify. The attorney nodded to Axel, then smiled at Sophie and said, "You must be Sophia Roman." He did not offer his hand but rather backed away from her, then he turned and led them through a cluttered hallway and up the wooden stairs, which were half covered with stuffed manila folders, notebooks, and loose stacks of paper. Knox moved through his possessions with a kind of sinuous grace, like a cat, keeping his hands close to his sides and touching nothing.

His office may have once been the master bedroom. Sophie halted at the door, fearful of entering. The far wall was braced by a collection of four-, five-, and six-drawer file cabinets, all different heights, widths, makes, and colors, all featuring no fewer than two open drawers, and all capped by piles of folders and papers that could only be the result of years of careful stacking. The floor of the office also supported a mass of paperwork, mostly piled along the walls and, except for one teetering stack, limited to a height of four feet. Everything seemed to lean in toward the center of the room, drawn in by the mountainous jumble of books and files that dominated the space and served to mark the location of Knox's desk. Sophie was afraid it was all going to come crashing in on her.

Axel put his hand on Sophie's back and coaxed her into the room. Knox moved two piles of documents from a pair of wooden side chairs, then wiped his hands on the shiny lapels of his black twill suit. Axel directed Sophie to one of the chairs and sat beside her.

Knox sat behind his desk and smiled at them, his chin barely clearing the stacked documents. Frank Knox was an ashen, wispy-haired man. The hands he folded in front of his chin had a gray, powdery aspect, the nails stark yellow in contrast to the surrounding flesh. Large-lensed, black-rimmed bifocals made his face seem insubstantial, as though he were made of dust and the shiny suit was all that contained him. Sophie thought he looked like a ghost.

"I guess I should congratulate you," he said to Sophie, sliding his glasses up his long nose with a gray forefinger.

Sophie folded her arms over her breasts and nodded, her expression serious. The air in the room was suffused with a familiar chemical smell. What was it?

Knox looked at Axel and raised his eyebrows.

Axel said, "Frank has put together a contract for us, Sophie. Frank? You want to explain to her how we're going to do this?"

Knox nodded, causing his glasses to slide down his nose. He cleared his throat and began to talk.

By the time he had finished his explanation, Sophie's lips had become a thin line, her face was pink, and her breasts hurt from the pressure of her tightly crossed arms.

"You said you were going to make me your partner," she said, not looking at Axel.

Axel, as relaxed as Sophie was tense, smiled broadly and said, "That's what we're trying to do. But we have to do these things right."

"What's he talking about, ten percent?"

"Excuse me," Knox said. "I'll be right back." He left the room.

"He's going to wash his hands," Axel whispered. "Kill the germs."

"What's that smell?"

"Rubbing alcohol. That's what he washes his hands with."

"What's this about ten percent? You said we were going to be full partners."

"It's ten percent a year," Axel said. "Every year you get another ten percent, and in five years you own half of Axel's Taco Shop. Fifty percent. We have to do it that way because of taxes."

Sophie shook her head.

"I can't just give you half the business all at once," Axel said. "It doesn't work that way. We're valuing the business at one hundred thousand dollars, even though it's worth twice that, and you'd never be able to pay the taxes on fifty grand. If I just up and gave it to you, you'd be stuck with a twenty-thousand-dollar tax bill."

Sophie said, "Five years? What if . . ."

Axel waited a moment, but she did not finish her sentence. "You want to know what if I die," he said for her.

Sophie nodded.

"Then you'll have to negotiate with your new partner. My share of the business will go to my heir."

"Your heir?"

"Yeah. Alice."

She looked at Axel. "Alice from California? You're leaving it to Alice?"

"Yup." Axel grinned. Alice Zimmerman was his sister, a bad-tempered, disapproving, formidable matron who, contrary to the usual aging sequence, had grown taller, louder, and stronger in her advancing years. Axel had seen her only once in the last decade—two years ago she had flown out from San Diego for an unannounced seven-day visit, a week that left Axel with a bad stomach and a lifetime's worth of unsolicited advice. Alice had never approved of Axel or his friends, particularly his women friends.

"You don't even like her. You told me you never wanted to see her again as long as you lived."

"That's right, I don't. And I won't have to."

"Alice hates me."

Axel shook his head sympathetically. "Yeah, that could be a problem. But you don't have to worry about it now. I've decided I'm not gonna die till later."

On the ride back to the fairgrounds, Axel kept the conversation going by telling Sophie how great it would be to be partners. Sophie watched the traffic, gripping the armrest and pushing her right foot against the floor, trying to make the truck go faster. She didn't like being a passenger.

"I'll stop by Midway Sign and get a guy out to paint your name on the stand. *Axel and Sophie Speeter, Proprietors.*"

Sophie gave Axel a sharp look. "Sophie *Roman,*" she said. Axel turned red.

"You're blushing!" Sophie said, her face breaking up into laughter.

"Anyway, I'll get the guy out to paint it."

They rode along in silence. Axel rested his hand on her back. It felt good. She had never seen Axel blush before.

"It's going to be great," he said again. "We'll make one hell of a team."

Sophie was starting to believe it. She reached up and put her hand over his, held it there against the back of her neck.

Axel's Taco Shop was still standing when they returned. Carmen and Kirsten had handled a few minor emergencies, and failed to deal with a few others, but people were still lining up and pushing their money across the counter. That was what counted. Sophie tied on an apron and dove into the fray. Axel went for a walk, heading down Carnes Avenue with no destination in mind.

The idea of making Sophie his partner had grown quickly, like the idea of buying a new truck, or the decision to pay for Carmen's schooling. He was glad he'd acted while the idea was still fresh and clean and free from doubts and overanalytical thinking. This streak of impulsiveness had been with him all his life. It didn't hit him as often now, but when it did, he embraced it as a sign that the young man still resided within him.

He no longer had to wonder whether he wanted Sophie in his life. It was done. They were partners now, for better or worse. He'd felt this way after committing himself to a big poker hand, after buying the Taco Shop, after burying his money in Sam's backyard.

A sudden movement from above caught his eye. He looked up, to see a round metal cage fly straight up into the air, reach a height of about one hundred feet, then tumble earthward. Two screaming figures were locked into the cage. The Ejection Seat, one of the fair's newest attractions, was a cross between a giant slingshot and a bungee cord. Sixty bucks a ride, and they had a constant line of thrill-seekers waiting to get strapped in and shot skyward. Axel grinned and watched the cage bounce up and down between the sixty-foot-high towers. He understood how they felt, and why they paid the money. The thrill was in the decision to go for it, the idea of being strapped in, the moment before the slingshot was triggered.

CHAPTER

27

Axel snapped the padlock closed and took one last walk around the outside of the restaurant. Everything seemed to be in order. Most of the concessions on the mall were closed, or closing. Sophie had gone home. Carmen slumped on a bench, smoking a cigarette. Axel wished, as he often did, that he still smoked. The end of the day was a good time for a cigarette. He missed the break, and the morsel of warmth that came with a good cigarette.

Tiny Tot Donuts remained open, feeding the last of the grandstand crowd. Tommy Fabian sat on his stool, looking as though he might fall off at any moment.

It took fifteen minutes for Axel to talk Tommy into closing. By the time the kids had shut down the machines and finished cleaning, it was nearly midnight. Axel helped Tommy lock down the stand.

Carmen had fallen asleep on her bench. Axel gave her a gentle shake.

"Let's hit the road, kiddo."

They walked to the truck in silence. Both Carmen and Tommy looked like they were going to pass out. Tommy walked with one hand inside his shirt, like his gut hurt.

They were almost to the Winnebago when it occurred to Axel that Tommy might be holding on to something besides himself.

Axel gave Tommy's elbow a nudge. "What you got there, Tom?"

Tommy glared up at him. "I don't want to hear it, Ax."

"Administration sees you packing a gun again, you could lose your spots."

"I run into that Bald Monkey again, it'll be worth it."

In the truck, as they pulled into the motel parking lot, Carmen roused herself to ask, "What's Sophie so hyper about, anyway?"

Axel said, "Sophie? What do you mean, hyper?"

"All day she was all over my case. All of a sudden she's worried about I might put too much meat in somebody's taco. You'd think I was giving away money, the way she's been acting."

Axel forced his face to assume a serious expression. "Really?"

"Yeah. She's turned into a real bitch all of a sudden. I don't get it."

Axel could hardly contain himself. This partnership was going to work out great. Grinning, he asked, "So how much meat are we talking about here?"

Carmen opened the passenger door and said, "You're just as weird as she is."

"Get some sleep," Axel said. "You'll feel better tomorrow. Try to get in before the lunch rush, okay?"

Carmen closed the truck door and waved him away. Her head hurt. She was tired and she was bored.

She could hear Dean's voice before she opened the door.

He was sitting on the writing table, his booted feet resting on the chair, reading from his poetry book. He looked up briefly as Carmen entered, then continued reading. On the bed directly in front of him sat a young giant with arms the circumference of her waist. He wore an olive-drab tank top,

1 9 3

khaki-colored cotton duck pants, and a pair of boots like Dean's, only bigger. His head was shaved, and most of his forehead was covered by a swollen, scabby bruise. He didn't look up at Carmen but kept his eyes fixed on Dean, his arms rigid and flexed, his jaw pulsing every few seconds.

"No man hath affliction enough, that is not matured and ripened by it, and made fit for God by that affliction . . . ," Dean read.

Behind the giant, who took up most of the bed, a boy of perhaps seventeen, also bald, lay gazing up at the ceiling tiles, hands laced behind his head. He wore shredded black denim jeans and a pair of snakeskin cowboy boots held together with silver duct tape. Carmen closed the door and leaned against it.

"How'd you get in?" she asked Dean.

The boy with the cowboy boots turned his head. "Pork just fuckin' picked it," he said, showing her his collection of mottled gray teeth.

"Pork?"

Dean read, *"This Soule, now free from prison, and passion, hath yet a little indignation."*

This, Carmen thought, is too weird. She walked quickly between Dean and the giant, heading for the bathroom, hoping to give herself a minute to think. She found another intruder, bent over the back of the toilet tank, using a razor blade to chop chunks of dry white matter into powder.

"What you got there?" Carmen asked, forgetting her confusion. "Coke?"

The man turned his head and leered at her while he continued chopping the lumps into powder with short, rapid strokes. He was the most feral-looking of the group, possibly due to the furry patch that served to connect his eyebrows with his long, meaty nose. Also, he had neglected to shave for some time, and his head and face were covered with short, dense dark hairs.

"We don't do yuppie dope," he said.

Carmen looked curiously at the lines he was now making on the white porcelain. "What is it?" she asked.

"Crank. You're Carmen, I bet. I'm Pork."

"Pork? Crank?" Carmen was looking at the lines. "Is it any good?" she asked.

Pork grinned. "Pure crystal meth. You could drive all the way to L.A. on a quarter gram." He rolled a five-dollar bill into a tube the diameter of a pencil and handed it to her. "Want a little wake-up?"

A few minutes later, Pork followed Carmen out of the bathroom, carrying the top to the toilet tank. Carmen's nose throbbed agonizingly, but it was getting better. She could feel the amphetamine flooding her system.

Dean was explaining something to the kid in the shredded denim, who was now sitting up on the bed, next to the giant. They were both leaning forward intently, listening. The words spilled from Dean's mouth, tumbling over one another. "It's not you, Tigger. That's the whole point. It's everybody. So it's like you are part of the nigger, and part of the yuppie, and part of the whore, and like they are part of you."

"Bullshit," said Tigger.

"Look," said Dean. "What do you do when you got a big zit, big old whitehead, hanging off the end of your nose. You squeeze it off, right? And you got a right and an obligation to do that, right? On account of you don't want people to get sick from looking at you, right? And what do you do when your little sister, who is a part of you—"

"I ain't got a sister."

"Well, suppose you did, and she's like a part of you, which she would be, and she starts hooking, doing coke and smack, and hanging out with the niggers. What's the righteous thing to do?"

"Me an' Sweety fuckin' kick ass on her and the niggers both."

"Exactly. What I'm saying is, it's on account of *you got to* because they are a part of you. Which is what my man Donne is on about. When the fucking bell fucking tolls, you better fucking listen, on account of it means somebody needs to get their fuckin' head kicked."

The giant, who had been nodding energetically, curled a meaty arm around Tigger's head and started rapping his knuckles against his skull. "Lemme soften his head up. He don't listen."

Tigger twisted loose. "Fuck you, Sweety."

"'Fuck you, Sweety,'" Sweety parroted, pitching his voice as high as he could get it.

"Hey," said Pork, still holding the ceramic toilet tank top. "I gotta set this down someplace."

Dean slid off the writing desk. "Right here," he said. He looked at the lines, six neat parallel slashes of white on white.

"Me and Carmen here, we already got our consciousnesses raised. This is for you guys. You ready for seconds, Deano?"

"You better go first," Sweety said to Tigger. "Your conscious got more climbing to do."

Tigger said, "Fuck you," but he took the rolled-up bill from Pork and did his two lines quickly, one up each nostril, and threw himself back on the bed, holding his hands over his nose.

Pork laughed. "Stings, don't it? That's how you know it's good."

Pork and Carmen watched Sweety and Dean do their lines, then Carmen opened the cooler and distributed warm canned martinis.

"Awright," said Sweety. "We gonna have a party."

"Where'd you guys come from?" Carmen asked.

"Headquarters," Tigger said.

"Drove over here in Tigger's Caddy," Dean said. "Man, that is one big ugly car you got there, Tigger."

Tigger grinned. "The Black Beauty."

"It's a fuckin' tank."

"Got a big old five-hundred-cubie V-8."

"So we drove on over here, sitting around reading John Donne, working on Sweety's head, man. These guys never heard of Donne before. Sitting around waiting all day for the Porker to show—"

"I got hung up," said Pork.

"It was worth it," said Dean, pinching his nose. "This is great shit. I want it. I want it all. So anyway, we sit around here waiting, but at least Tigger got done with Sweety's tattoo, man. What do you think?"

Carmen, enjoying the buzz but with no idea what was going on, asked, "Are you guys from Omaha?" She pulled a cigarette out of her pack.

"Gimme one of them," Sweety said. "Gimme two." Carmen handed him two cigarettes.

"We're from Frogtown, man," Tigger said.

"I found 'em," Dean said.

"Bullshit," Sweety said. "We found you. You didn't know where the fuck you were." He had both cigarettes in his mouth. Carmen lit them.

Dean said to Carmen, "Went into this bar, place full of factory creeps, and Tigger comes up."

"Stepped on my fucking toe," Tigger said.

"So we start bullshittin'."

"Skins hang together," Sweety said, sucking hard on his cigarettes.

"So I asked these guys if they knew where I could get some speed."

Carmen's head was waggling back and forth as she tried to follow the conversation, retaining almost none of it. Her eyes settled on Sweety's forehead. "What happened to your head?"

Sweety grinned, contorting his brow.

"It's a tattoo," Dean said.

Carmen looked at it for several seconds before distinguishing the words FUCK ME.

"Fuck you?"

"You got it, bitch. Fuck me fuck me fuck me." He stood up and moved toward Carmen, his arms held out before him.

Dean pulled Axel's .45 out of his jacket, pointed it at Sweety, and said, "Bang."

Sweety clapped his hands over his chest and fell back on the bed. "Arrrgh. You got me. I'm fucking dead."

Tigger was giggling.

Dean blew imaginary smoke from the muzzle and slid the pistol back into his jacket pocket. "You got to watch these guys every minute," he said to Carmen. "They're a buncha fuckin' animals."

An hour or so later, even as he was talking—telling Carmen and the skins about how he'd avenged himself on Tiny Tot, telling them how much cash he'd scored, telling them about how easy it was—a little man behind his left eyeball was telling Dean to shut up, to be discreet, to not trust this bunch with every thought that ran through his head. But that small portion of his consciousness could not withstand the tongue-loosening power of the methedrine. He was gabbing away like a speed freak!

Dean barked out a laugh, interrupting himself.

"What's so funny?" Tigger asked.

"I'm talking like a fucking speed freak!"

That turned out to be the funniest thing anybody'd heard all night. Dean basked in their admiration, feeling his chest expand. He decided to read them some more passages from John Donne, but when Pork saw him reaching for the book, he turned to Carmen.

"I hear the guy you work for is really rich," he said.

"He keeps his money in coffee cans," she said.

"Bull*shit!*" Dean said. "We checked his damn coffee cans and didn't find shit."

"Well, it was there. I saw it. It's not my fault he moved it."

"Yeah, well, anyways, the donut guy is the one with all the money."

"He's back at work, you know," Carmen said.

Dean said, "No shit?" He was surprised. He thought he'd killed him.

"Maybe you ought to score off him again," Pork suggested.

Dean laughed. "Not a bad idea."

"I don't know," Carmen said, getting into the spirit of it. "Him and Axel, they walk back to his place together now."

"So hit 'em both," said Pork.

Tigger jumped in. "Fuck, why don't we hit the fuckin' gate? Man, would that be cool, or what? Get, like, a million bucks or something!"

Pork said, "Tigger, I ever tell you what a fucking idiot you are?"

Sweety made a rumbling sound in his chest.

"I ain't talking about you, Sweety," Pork said. "You're one of the smartest Aryan motherfuckers I know. And big too." He pulled a folded paper from his pocket. "What do you say we do a little booster?"

Sweety grinned, using his entire face. Dean could hear his scabbed brow crackle.

Sweety's stomach started growling a few minutes into the 6:00 A.M. edition of *Sesame Street*.

"He's hungry," Tigger explained. "We got to go get something to eat."

"I'm hungry too," said Dean. "Hey, Pork. You hungry?"

Pork nodded. Dean looked at Carmen, who was curled up on the floor. "You hungry, Carmen?"

Carmen did not answer. Two hours earlier, she had swallowed a few Valiums, and she was now on the floor, wrapped in the bedspread, snoring.

They took Tigger's car to a Perkins. Sweety ordered a breakfast steak and six eggs, scrambled. Tigger explained to the nervous waitress how to prepare them.

"He likes 'em just barely cooked. You go tell them to just stir the eggs up and dump 'em in a pan and then dump 'em right out again on a plate. Hardly cook 'em at all. He likes 'em real soupy like. And get him some extra toast too, so's he can sop it up. Okay?"

The waitress said, "Steak and eggs with a side order of six eggs, scrambled, very loose."

"Yeah, only you know how loose you think he wants 'em?"

The waitress nodded.

"He likes 'em even looser than that."

Pork was talking to Dean. "I can get it for you. But not till tonight."

"That's cool."

"I'd have brought it last night, but I didn't know for sure you wanted it. Besides, I don't like carrying weight."

"No problem. I can have the money for you whenever." Dean could feel the money pressing against his ribs, two thick bundles stuffed in the inside pockets of his jacket.

"So what do you guys want to do today?" Tigger asked. "You guys want to do something?"

Pork scratched his chin with a fork. "I was thinking I'd go someplace and crash."

"Fuck that," rumbled Sweety.

"Yeah," said Tigger. "Fuck that. Let's go do something. What do you guys want to do?"

Dean said, "You guys ever go to the state fair?"

They all looked at him.

"I mean, I was thinking we could go over there and get some donuts or something. Go look at the freaks."

CHAPTER

28

Shortly before Friday noon, Midges Flores, the maid, knocked lightly on the door to room 19, hoping that no one was there. She put her ear to the door and listened, then knocked again, louder this time. Midges did not like the girl who was staying there, and she liked the bald man even less. But he hadn't been around since last weekend, when he had sat and watched her make the bed, cleaning his teeth with a fingernail and not saying a word. And the girl, she was a slob. Midges knocked again. No response. She relaxed, inserted her passkey into the doorknob, and opened the door.

What a mess; this was the worst yet. The bed all undone, and it stank of cigarettes, sweat, and alcohol. Midges had pushed her cleaning cart all the way into the room before she noticed the girl lying on the floor.

"Oh! Excuse me!" Midges said.

The girl on the floor didn't move. Midges started to back her cart out of the room, then stopped. The girl was very still.

"Hey, are you okay?" Midges licked her lips and felt her heart accelerating. Was she dead? In the past, Midges had found money, drugs, children, clothing, interesting Polaroid photographs, and even someone's eight-foot-long pet boa constrictor . . . but never a corpse. She approached the girl, who was lying flat on her back, fully dressed but with only one button holding the front of her shirt together, and bent over her. She sure did look dead. Midges froze. What if she had been murdered? What if the murderer was still in the room? He could be in the bathroom. He could be under the bed. The bald man. Midges' hand was only inches from the girl's neck. She would just check, very quietly, for a pulse. Keeping her eyes on the bathroom door, she pressed her fingers against the girl's throat. The girl's eyes popped open. Midges jerked her hand away, took two steps backward, and screamed as she collided with her cleaning cart.

Carmen sat up, blinking. "What's going on?" she asked. "Where did everybody go?"

Sophie hated to admit it, even to herself, but Kirsten and Juanita were a hell of a lot faster, pleasanter, and more reliable than her daughter the sleepwalker. They both did their jobs, complained only a little, and never ever told her to shove a burrito up her ass. Sophie liked that. Also, she liked the idea of having a real Mexican girl like Juanita rolling burros and frying ground beef and every now and then waiting on customers. Business was brisk going into the last weekend of the fair. The rainy midweek had kept many of the fairgoers at home; now they were out in force for this final weekend of cheese curds and corn dogs, skyrides and giant slides, Machinery Hill and the twelve-hundred-pound prize hog, and, of course, Axel's Taco Shop. It was eleven-forty in the morning, and they'd had a steady stream of customers since ten.

The system that seemed to be working best was to keep Kirsten up front serving customers, Juanita building tacos, burros, and tostadas in back, and Sophie running the orders back and forth and doing the soft drinks and making sure Juanita was stocked and running the fryer and taking care of whatever else came up. Juanita wanted to take her break now, and she mentioned it every time she pushed an order across the stainless-steel table.

She said, "I gotta go to the ladies'."

"Wait till Carmen gets here," Sophie said, grabbing a pair of Buenos. "Anytime now."

When Sophie came back for an order of beans, Juanita said, "I got my period. I gotta go to the ladies'."

"You had your period last weekend," Sophie said. "Are you a rabbit, or what?"

"That Carmen, you know, she might never come, and I gotta go to the ladies'."

"Just wait." Sophie grabbed the beans and delivered them to the front counter. When she turned back, Juanita was gone. "Damn." She stepped around the food table and spread out three tortillas and spooned a layer of beans across each of them.

"Hey," Kirsten said, looking back. "How come she gets to take a break? I need two more tacos and a side of beans."

Sophie folded the burritos, snatched a pair of taco shells from the arms of the deep fryer, loaded them, wrapped them, and motioned Kirsten to come get them. "She'll be right back," she said.

"I was here first thing this morning. It's not fair. I came in early, and she gets to take a break."

Juanita was gone for over twenty minutes. "You got to wait in line," she said in response to the look Sophie gave her. Sophie scowled, knowing that it was probably true—the lines were longer at the women's rest rooms than they were at the cheese curd concession. A line had formed in front of the taco stand now, six hungry people staring in at the painted menu board. Sophie moved into high gear, loving the sense of crisis, seeing each customer now as another buck in her pocket.

Carmen showed up at twenty after twelve.

"Well, look who's here," Sophie said. "We thought you'd got lost."

"Can I go on break now?" Kirsten asked, untying her apron. Sophie nodded and took her place at the front counter.

Carmen looked at the people lined up waiting to be served, then at Juanita, who was trying to do about six things at once. "What do you want me to do?" Carmen asked her.

"Need more taco shells, cheese, beans, and roll two deluxe for the guy with the red hat."

Carmen thought about leaving, about just walking out and losing herself in the crowd. Walk right off the fair-grounds and onto the street and stick her thumb out and get picked up by some guy in a Mercedes, go have a few drinks.

"You want to get your lazy butt moving?" Sophie said.

Carmen tore into a bag of corn tortillas and loaded the fryer. She'd stay for a while, maybe leave later. If she felt like it. She still had some crystal folded into a square of paper tucked down deep in the front pocket of her jeans. Last night, Pork had looked through a magazine to find a good picture and finally found one of Nancy Reagan, tore it out, spooned some crystal meth over Nancy's nose, folded her up into a neat square with the corners tucked in, and handed it to Carmen. "This is for letting us use your room. What do you say?" he asked her.

She had said, "Thank you." Pork had laughed and told her she was supposed to "Just say no." Carmen didn't get it.

She laid out a row of six flour tortillas and started rolling burros, and by the time the sixth burrito was rolled and wrapped, she was caught up in the rhythm of the Taco Shop and almost enjoying herself. Carmen was capable of moving quickly and precisely, especially when she began the day with a nose full of methamphetamine.

The nearest rest rooms, located in the shadow of the Giant Slide, had grown a thirty-foot-long tail of females—about a ten-minute wait, by Kirsten's estimate. She took her place in line and watched enviously as men walked easily in and out of their side of the building. She had to pee too bad to let herself get mad, but it bugged her how slow most women were. Some of her friends complained that rest rooms were designed by men, that women *needed* more time, so they should have more toilets available. Kirsten did not agree. She could take care of business as fast as any guy, maybe faster. Unless she had her period, of course, but even then she wouldn't just sit there staring down between her legs like some of these women.

God, did she have to *go!*

The trick was to let your butt touch the toilet seat lightly, or not at all—at these rest rooms, she went for not at all—and just pee, wipe, and get out. Make room for the next person, who maybe had to go *really* bad.

Kirsten shifted her weight from one flexed leg to the other. She fantasized squatting down right where she was and letting loose. No, thinking about it that way didn't help at all. Maybe she was keeping her muscles *too* tense. She tried relaxing her belly. She imagined a hollow space inside her abdomen. All the room in the world. An empty lakebed. As her eyes danced over the heads of the people passing by, she wished she were one of them: people who did not have to pee. A dome of flesh caught her attention. One, two, three. Four. Four of them, standing over by the Pronto Pup stand. One of them, the one in the orange T-shirt, looked familiar.

Sweety was able to fit the entire Pronto Pup into his mouth without swallowing. He held it there, cheeks distended, and stared at the girl who had sold it to him. She wouldn't meet his eyes. He grinned, his lips parting to show her the floury, meaty, mustard-yellowed mass that strained at his teeth.

Tigger said, "C'mon, let's go do some rides, man."

Sweety forced his lips over the corn dog and began to work his jaw back and forth as he fell in behind Tigger. Pork gave Dean a look, shrugged, and followed.

Dean thought, This is like being the bionic man, the terminator. He was sweating like a pig, but that was okay. He'd left his jacket back in Tigger's car, and that helped.

With just the T-shirt on, he could stay cool. He liked the way the .45 felt in his waistband, and the bulge it made in the T-shirt. He would be cool and bionic, cruising the fair with his bionic pards. He could feel his joints as he walked: snick, snick, snick. He could hear his engine humming.

Carmen admired the face she had created. The pinto beans formed a smooth layer over the tortilla disk. Two black olives made eyes. A green olive nose. A white sour-cream smile. Shredded lettuce hair. Who did it look like? She pulled off the lettuce. James Dean! No. It wasn't quite right. She moved the olives farther apart.

"I'm out of lettuce," Juanita said.

"Need three deluxe and two bean," Sophie called back. "Carmen! Let's get a move on. What are you doing back there?"

"She's making faces again," Juanita said.

Sophie shouted, "Carmen!"

Carmen's feet flexed, popping her a couple of inches into the air.

"I told you not to do that. Quit acting silly and do your job, girl!"

Regretfully, Carmen folded the tortilla face into a burrito, wrapped it, began again.

Axel was strolling up the mall toward the Taco Shop when Kirsten ran up to him, breathless.

"Mr. Speeter! I saw that guy."

Axel cupped her shoulders in his hands. "What guy?"

"That guy they say beat up Mr. Fabian. That skinhead guy."

"Where?"

Kirsten pointed down Carnes Avenue. "Down by the Giant Slide. He was with some other guys, some other skinhead guys."

Axel dropped his hands and started back down the mall, his jaw clamped so tight he could feel his bridge flexing.

CHAPTER

29

"That Fuckin' Tigger," Pork said. "He does this shit all the time." He reached in his pocket and came out with his fist wrapped in brass. "You can't take the little shit anywhere without him pissin' somebody off."

A pair of cowboy-hatted young studs had Tigger up against the side of the Headless Woman trailer, one of them holding Tigger's arms, the other slapping him in the face. After each blow he shouted at Tigger, "What did you say?"

Tigger kept replying, "Fuck you." They all seemed to be having a good time.

Sweety charged with his fist held straight out and hit the first cowboy on the side of his neck. The cowboy bounced off the aluminum side of the trailer and slid to the ground. Dean, not sure what was going on, followed Pork, who jumped on the other cowboy's back and pounded him several times on the temple with his metal-sheathed fist. The cowboy was spinning around, trying to throw him, when Sweety came in with his big fists locked together and brought them both up under the cowboy's jaw. The sound of that made Dean's stomach roll. The cowboy went down hard. Tigger, bleeding from his nose, was kicking the other one, who was too dazed to resist. Pork grabbed Tigger and pulled him away. Several people had stopped to watch.

"Let's get the fuck out of here," Pork said. They moved out through the crowd, Pork looking pissed off, brushing dirt from his shoulders, Sweety with his arm locked around Tigger's neck, giving him knuckle raps on his hairless skull, Tigger going, "Ow, ow, ow . . ."

"What was that all about?" Dean asked.

"Our Tigger has trouble relating to people," Pork said over his shoulder. "Can't say three words in a row without somebody wanting to jump up and down on his ugly little face."

Dean's breathing slowed. Sweety had released Tigger and caught up with Dean and Pork. Tigger's face was flushed, and he was wearing a big gray grin.

Dean said, "Wipe your nose, would you?"

Tigger laughed and wiped the blood on his sleeve. "Man, those fuckers never fuckin' knew what hit 'em!" he said, kicking the air. "Fuckin' Sweety, man, pow! Like a fuckin' tank, man. Damn!"

"You're gonna get us killed one of these days," Pork said. "Go mouthing off to some guy, and it turns out he's got six friends."

"That would be okay," said Sweety.

Pork made a sour face. "I don't know about you guys, but I could use a blast."

With over a hundred thousand people milling about the fairgrounds, it was tough finding a private place where four guys could sit down and do a little crank. Tigger thought he knew a spot over near the grandstand where they could squeeze in between an egg roll joint and the back wall of a mechanical horse race game, but when they got there it was full of high school kids passing a joint. Tigger wanted to kick them out, but Pork said what do you want to do, fight or get high? "I mean, let's get our priorities straight here. We already had one fight, right?"

Sweety finally said, after they had wandered around for twenty minutes or so, "We just sit down someplace and fuckin' do it."

"Too many cops around," Pork said.

"I don't see no cops."

"Yeah," said Tigger. "Let's just do it. What do you say, Dean?"

Dean shrugged, going with the flow.

"You guys ain't on probation," Pork complained. "You guys get cracked, it's no big deal. I fucking go back to Stillwater for another three years."

Dean agreed with that.

"You guys don't got to do it with us," Tigger said.

"It's my shit!"

Tigger said, "You guys can each go in the can. Me and Sweety, we'll just do it here. Fuck 'em." He pointed at a patch of flattened brown grass between the curb and the sidewalk.

Pork didn't like it, but he didn't have an argument ready, so he handed the paper to Tigger. Dean and Pork crossed the street and watched Sweety and Tigger sit right there in front of a hundred thousand people and snort crystal, scooping it from the paper with a Popsicle stick, staring down anyone who gave them a double look. Pork frowned as he watched Sweety treat himself to an extra blast before refolding the paper. Sweety grinned and waved.

Dean couldn't get the hang of the dodgem cars. Sweety and Tigger had him pinned down; every time he got moving, one or the other of them would slam into him from the side. He was glad when it was over. Pork, who had been watching, laughed and punched him on the shoulder. "Now you know why I don't do dodgem cars," he said.

Dean rubbed his shoulder. "Let's go see if Carmen showed up yet. I'm getting hungry."

"Go ahead," Sweety said. "We'll be around someplace. I want to go see the freaks."

"Maybe we could get some free burritos or something. I bet she'd feed us." Dean didn't want to be alone. He had a good buzz going with the meth, and he was getting off on the skinhead energy. "Come on, we can stop at the Beer Garden. I'll buy you guys a beer."

"C'mon, Sweety," said Pork. "Let's go see Dean's bitch. We can do the freaks later."

Sweety was clicking his teeth together, swinging his head back and forth, looking like a big lizard on the prowl. Dean started to say something, then noticed Pork shaking his head. Pork gestured in the direction of the Beer Garden, and he and Dean started walking. "He gets real pumped sometimes, and you got to be careful," said Pork. Dean looked back over his shoulder. Sweety was following them, trailed by Tigger. "He'll follow us, but you can't argue with him when he gets this way. I seen him once throw this guy. Just picked him right up and threw him about ten feet like he was a shot put."

"What did the guy do?"

"You mean to get tossed? He was wearing a baseball cap. Sweety don't like baseball caps. That might've been it. With Sweety you never know. This was downtown, right in the middle of the day on Hennepin Avenue. The guy landed and just up and started running, so no harm done, but this other time he went after this cop, and the next thing you know there was three cops beating on him with their sticks, and Sweety, he don't even care, he's just beating on them right back. They were hitting him on the head with their sticks and everything, and it took the three of them it seemed like hours to knock him down. Cops all had nosebleeds and shit. Sweety, blood all over his head, was just having a good old time. Point is, he's got no judgment and he's about as strong as the Incredible Hulk. We used to call him that, but he likes Sweety better."

"So what are you telling me?"

"Just that when he's like this he doesn't care what happens. You just got to be real easy around him, he gets this way. Couple beers might calm him down some. He likes beer. It makes him happy, usually."

Dean bought a round of watery Leinenkugels at the Beer Garden, then he bought another round. Sweety was making him nervous, staring at people and sticking his tongue out about a yard, with that FUCK ME scrawled across his forehead. Dean didn't like the way he was making his jaw muscle twitch. He said, "You guys want a hot dog or something?" Nobody did, so they had another beer. Except for worrying about Sweety, Dean still felt great, had a nice buzz running up and down the back of his neck, eyes getting sharper all the time. Crystal clear. Hanging with these guys, looking dangerous, cruising on the meth, the good stuff, made in America, makes you faster and stronger and smarter and improves the eyesight too. That was something he really liked, how good it made him see. Not like coke, which was for niggers and yuppies, or like weed, which was for punks and hippies. Yeah, it was a good feeling. Not like Carmen and her Valiums, falling asleep all the time. Dean liked the wound-up, tight-jawed power he got from the meth, and he liked the smooth-rolling easy confidence that came from being with his new friends. He liked the feeling of the .45 stuck in the waistband of his jeans, the barrel just touching the tip of his dick, the grip barely concealed by Carmen's Bugs Bunny T-shirt. If you knew what to look for, you could see the shape pushing through the thin orange cotton. He liked the way it felt when he walked. He wasn't so sure, though, about Sweety, who was now sitting in this big room full of guys, half of them wearing baseball caps, Sweety all wound up, his eyes fixed forward, his head swinging back and forth, jaw working, neck muscles bulging, blinking now and again. He made Dean think of a double-barreled sawed-off he'd seen back in Omaha. Some guy had cut it off right across the chamber, letting most of the shell stick out past the end of the barrel; it was about as close as you could get to a hand grenade—pull the trigger and who knows? Nobody'd ever had the nerve to shoot the thing. Sweety looked like that, like his eyes were those two red plastic twelve-gauge shells full of shot sticking out an inch and a half, hanging out there looking for some excuse to explode.

Sweety finished his third jumbo beer, and Pork, who kept giving Dean this raised-eyebrow look, filled Sweety's plastic cup from his own. Tigger was cutting into the tabletop with the key to his Caddy, writing the word FUCK, checking Sweety's forehead to make sure he was spelling it right. Pork spoke in a low voice to Sweety, who seemed not to hear him. A group of college-student types, all wearing baseball caps with college logos, sat down at the next table with their tall plastic cups full of beer. Sweety rotated his head and fixed his eyes on them. Dean thought, Here it comes.

Pork was on his feet now, tugging at Sweety's arm, then dropping it and walking toward the exit. Dean stood and followed, not looking back.

"He might just follow us out," Pork said. "He's mean as hell, but he's just a big old dog. He don't like to be alone."

They were out on the street, blinking in the afternoon sunlight, when Sweety and Tigger caught up with them. Pork said to Dean, "See?"

"Where we goin'?" Tigger asked.

Pork shrugged and looked up at Sweety. "How you doing?"

Sweety said, "Those fuckers."

"Who?" Tigger asked.

"Fuck you," Sweety said. "This place sucks. What the fuck are we doing here?"

"You want to go home?" Pork asked. "You want to go someplace else?"

"You want a taco?" Dean asked.

Sweety swung his head toward Dean. "Yeah," he said. "That's it. A fuckin' taco."

"Then let's go get us some tacos."

Dean got his good feeling back then; they were all back on track, back on the taco track. They were moving together, moving through the crowd with Dean on point. Behind him, sticking up a head above the rest, came Sweety, then Pork and Tigger hanging back, the four of them giving off that dangerous vibe that made people slide their eyes off and away.

Dean said, "All these guys are rich out here, every one."

Pork had his own buzz going, bopping his head back and forth to some tune buried deep in his head. Dean didn't think anybody was listening, but he kept talking anyway.

"All that cash money, man. We oughta just set up a business, score off a new one every day. That's what John Donne would do. All these guys with their money, man. Make 'em share the wealth." Dean searched his mind to see how it would be. The master plan would appear before him at any moment now, logical and complete. He would lay it out for Pork, Tigger, and Sweety. Show them how smart he was. He imagined the respectful look he would get from Pork, like he really knew his shit. Read them some more John Donne. He imagined himself talking to the old man, Axel, asking him questions. He reached a hand under his T-shirt and felt the warm wooden grip of the .45, imagined working the steel barrel between the old man's teeth. That would definitely be part of the plan, get the taco man sucking his own gun.

Except for one thing. It was probably all a figment of Carmen's stoned-out imagination. He had no reason to think the old man had that kind of money. It sure as hell wasn't sitting in his motel room. Reluctantly, Dean let the fantasy slide away. He would have to settle for some free tacos and just do the drug deal with his Tiny Tot money. That would be cool. He could turn the six K into twelve K when he got to Sioux Falls, and from there who knew? Set himself up as a distributor. The world was looking sharp, clear, and full of opportunities. They rounded the corner of the Food Building, slicing through a crowd of people in front of a busy french fry stand, and moved up the mall toward Axel's Taco Shop.

Pork said, "You say this guy has a million bucks in cash?"

"That's what Carmen says," Dean said. "Only she's probably full of shit."

They were passing Tiny Tot Donuts. Dean looked inside and stopped. Sweety ran into him and asked him what the fuck he was doing. Dean pointed into the donut stand. "See that guy with the bandage on his head? The little guy with the hat? I don't believe it. The guy, the guy is up and walking? I must be losing my touch."

As Dean spoke, the guy, Tiny Tot, looked up from his work and saw him and dropped the bag of sugar he was holding and disappeared out the back of the stand. Dean laughed. "Guy's scared shitless. You see him take off?" He turned back to Pork and Tigger.

Pork was grinning. Then his face closed and he said, "He don't look scared to me." He started walking backward. Dean turned and saw Tiny Tot, limping, coming around the side of the donut stand, red-faced, coming right at him with something in his hand.

Dean said, "Shit." He backed away, bumped into Sweety, moved sideways away from the donut guy. The kids in the donut stand were leaning out over the counter, watching, and the crowd of customers was now turning to see what was happening. Dean turned and ran twenty yards up the mall, then stopped and looked back. He didn't see the guy at first, then he did. What was he holding in his hand? Tiny Tot was limping, not moving fast but moving steady. Dean relaxed, knowing now that he could outrun the little man. He waited for him to get closer. When he was less than twenty feet away, Dean recognized the object in his hand. It was a bright, shiny revolver. Dean backed away, holding one hand out palm forward like a shield and reaching with the other hand for the .45 in his belt. He lost sight of Tiny Tot behind a cluster of people, then saw him again, still coming. Dean had the gun out now, trying to keep it pointed at Tiny Tot as the guy raised his own gun, holding it with both hands, pointing it at Dean's chest. Dean pulled on the trigger, but the .45 did not fire. Shit, what was wrong? Was the safety on? He looked down at the gun and tripped, falling backward, seeing as he went down Sweety's broad leather-clad back eclipse the image of the donut guy, and he heard a loud snap, then another, not so loud, then screams.

CHAPTER

30

Sophie was on her knees, trying to change a tank of Coca-Cola premix, when she heard Kirsten say, "What's going on? Oh my God!" The urgency in Kirsten's voice brought Sophie quickly to her feet, and she cracked her head on the edge of the counter. Holding a hand to her head, she looked out across the mall. At first, she couldn't tell what she was seeing. Then she saw Carmen's bald friend, James Dean, stumbling backward through the crowd, crashing into people, spilling a little boy's sno-cone, the kid's mother shouting through a mouthful of cheese curd. The expression on James Dean's face was so wide-eyed and openmouthed that Sophie started to laugh. What was he doing? Then Kirsten screamed "Oh my God!" again, only louder and right in her ear.

Carmen pushed between them. "What?"

Sophie saw Tommy Fabian limping toward Dean, pointing with one hand, bringing up his other hand, holding something shiny. A huge bald man in a black leather jacket appeared, seeming to sprout up between the two, and dove at Tommy—Sophie was seeing it in slow motion now—and as the pistol flashed and bucked in Tommy's hands, Sophie saw it for what it was, heard the sharp explosion echo off the white brick sides of the Food Building as Tommy disappeared beneath the big man, then she heard another muted pop. The two men rolled, spilling a blue recycling can, white plastic cups exploding across the trampled grass mall. Those within a few yards of the tumbling pair fled, others rushed forward for a better view. The big man regained his feet and came up with one of Tommy's hands and a foot locked in his grip. Sophie heard a high-pitched keening. Tommy was screaming, and so were several people in the crowd. The big man swung his shoulders and his arms, and Tommy came up off the ground. Spinning like a shot-putter, the big man swung Tommy around in an airplane ride, a couple of complete orbits, then let go and sent the little man cartwheeling through the air. Tommy hit the lamppost hard, with an audible crack.

A man in a white shirt and black suspenders appeared from the crowd. Sophie recognized Axel the way she might suddenly recognize an actor in an unfamiliar role. Where had he come from? Sophie leaned out past the edge of the counter and shouted a warning, but her voice was devoured by the buzzing crowd.

Axel had been feeling a little silly. He had walked up and down Carnes Avenue twice, from the Giant Slide to the midway, doing a double take at every bald head in the crowd. No Bald Monkey.

What did he think he was going to do if he found the kid? Lecture him? Beat him up? Make a citizen's arrest? He shook his head, smiling at himself. Just another old fool rushing off half-cocked, too mad to think straight. Besides, the girl was probably mistaken. These teenage girls, always looking for drama.

He was only a few yards from the Taco Shop when he heard Kirsten scream "Oh my God!" His first thought was that Carmen had put her hand in the deep fryer. He ran to the back of the stand, saw that they were all, Sophie and

Kirsten and Carmen, staring at something outside, on the mall. Someone is having a heart attack, was his next thought, then he heard the unmistakable sound of a gun firing once—loud and sharp—then again, muffled. He was afraid he knew whose gun. He rushed around to the front of the stand in time to see Tommy Fabian's cartwheeling flight, arms and legs spread out like a sky diver's. Axel's senses grew suddenly, painfully acute. Everything stopped for an instant, formed a tableau: the big black-jacketed man, frozen in mid-stagger, Tommy striking the lamppost, and, a few feet away, sitting on his butt on the grass, Bald Monkey, holding his arm out toward the place where Tommy had been, one hand gripping a .45, the other hand fumbling with the trigger guard. Axel broke loose and ran, forcing his body through air gone thick as sand. He heard a strange howl, felt his throat shuddering, and realized that he was screaming. Bald Monkey's head swiveled, his eyes widened, he rose to his feet, and his arm came around with the gun. Axel saw the kid's thumb find the hammer, draw it back, saw the end of the barrel fix on his chest. He stopped, an arm's length away, eyes on the hole in the end of the barrel. The kid's hands were shaking. A glitter caught Axel's eye, and he saw a familiar horseshoe-shaped diamond ring on the kid's finger.

The sight of Tommy's ring shattered Axel's instinct for self-preservation. He threw himself forward, slapped his right hand down hard on the .45, a sharp pain lancing his finger. His palm wrapped warm steel. He hit the ground with his shoulder, rolled, came up with the .45 in his hand, swung it, giving it everything he had, slapping the steel slide hard against the kid's bald skull. He felt the shock travel up his arm, causing intense explosions of pain in his elbow and shoulder. He expected Bald Monkey to go down and stay down, but instead the kid jumped to his feet and took off like a startled rabbit, legs churning, his shiny head quickly melting into the crowd.

Axel pulled the hammer back, released his trapped and

torn finger, and locked the safety. His right hand had gone numb.

The big skinhead had fallen to his hands and knees. Axel circled him and ran to Tommy, whose head had flopped sideways at an impossible angle. He tried to push Tommy's head back where it belonged, thinking that if he straightened it out quickly enough he might be able to undo what had happened. There was no response, no complaint, no sign of life. He looked up in time to see the big man crawling toward him.

"What did you do?" Axel shouted, the words rolling out deep and slow, as if shouted through molasses.

"I don't feel good," the big man said. A peculiar-looking bruise covered most of his forehead, blood pulsed from his chest. "I gotta lie down." He listed to his left, then relaxed and let himself fall onto his side on the grass.

Axel struggled to put it together, to make sense of things. The crowd had drawn back, forming a circle about thirty feet across, with Axel in the center. He looked down at the bleeding man, then back at Tommy. He didn't understand. The crowd was moving in on him, needing to be nearer the blood. He heard a siren. Axel stood. He could see two cops pushing through the crowd. He eased back through the crowd toward the taco stand, slipping the .45 into his pants pocket. There was nothing more he could do.

The fence at the north end of the fairgrounds finally stopped him. James Dean fell against the galvanized steel, pressed his face against the mesh, gasping for breath. He remembered his flight as a series of frozen, garish images. The back of his head radiated bright tendrils of pain. Had he been shot? He could not bring himself to touch it, afraid he might find a soft, pulpy mass of erupted brain tissue. Unlacing his fingers from the steel mesh, he turned his back to the fence, let himself slide down onto the grass, drew his knees up to his chest, wrapped his arms around his shins.

His heart was beating too fast. How old did you have to be to have a heart attack?

The donut guy coming at him with a gun. Unbelievable. He could have been killed! And he'd lost his gun. How could he lose the gun? One moment he'd had it, then a glimpse of the old man, then Wham, something had hit him in the head, and suddenly he was running faster than he'd ever run before.

Curiosity overcame fear. Dean reached back and delicately probed his skull. It was swollen and tender, but not bleeding. The knowledge that his brain was still inside his skull helped him regain his feet. He had to get out of there. He had to get to Tigger's car. That was the most important thing.

It took him twenty minutes to cross the fairgrounds. He pushed through the turnstile in time to see Tigger's rusted Cadillac pulling out of the parking lot onto Como Avenue. Dean ran into the street, shouting at them to wait. He could see Pork's face through the tinted glass, looking right at him. The car turned away and accelerated, leaving behind an oily blue cloud. A blast from the horn of a Ford station wagon sent Dean hopping back to the curb. He couldn't believe it. Pork had been looking right at him. They left him there on purpose. A wave of dizziness, then of nausea, forced him to sit down on the curb. He closed his eyes, squeezed them until he saw flashes of light, remembering with a thud that he'd left his leather jacket in Tigger's back seat, its pockets solid with cash.

If someone had asked Axel how he was feeling, he would have said that he was feeling very, very old. And very sore. He would have said that his mind was hurting from too many fresh memories, and that his right arm was throbbing painfully, and that his finger was bleeding where he had caught it under the hammer. He would have said that it is the things you have to remember that kill you. Like it was the things that Tommy remembered that killed him. Memories and his friend Axel Speeter, who had busted him out of the hospital so he could keep his appointment with death.

If someone had asked Axel how he was feeling, he might have said something like that. Or he might have simply said that he felt lousy.

But nobody was asking.

He could hear the honking and short siren blasts of an ambulance working its way through the crowd. It pulled up onto the pounded grass mall, and two paramedics rushed toward Tommy and the bald giant. After a brief examination the paramedics relaxed, their movements becoming slower and more deliberate.

None of the police officers—there were five of them now—asked him how he was feeling. One of them, yellow-haired, still with a trace of his grandfather's Swedish in his voice, asked Axel if he had seen what happened. "Not a thing," Axel said. "When I got here, it was all over." The officer took his name and address anyway, then turned to Sophie.

Axel wrapped a few scoops of ice in a towel and held it against his elbow.

Sophie said she had been under the counter, changing the Coke canister. She hadn't seen a thing, either. Carmen, sitting on the grass behind the stand, hugging her knees to her chest, claimed she had been busy making a Bueno Burrito. The police officer wrote their full names and addresses on his clipboard. He had better luck with Kirsten Lund, who was anxious to share her experience. She related the events in detail, pointing to places on the mall, acting out the way Tommy had waved his gun, describing with her hands the way he had sailed through the air; her face was flushed and bright. Axel had never seen her so animated, her Nordic reserve forgotten in the thrill of violent events.

Making careful notes, the yellow-haired cop asked her to go over several points again. Axel listened carefully as Kirsten related the events of twenty minutes earlier.

So Tommy had been the shooter, just like he had thought,

and it was the big man who had broken Tommy's neck. And Bald Monkey was mixed up in it somehow. Tommy chasing the monkey with his six-gun, that made sense. Tommy would do something like that, probably thinking he was going to make a citizen's arrest. Or maybe he was just going to shoot the kid. Either way, it hadn't worked.

The ambulance backed off the mall out onto Carnes Avenue and moved slowly through the crowd. The cop was asking Kirsten to tell him again, was the man from the Tiny Tot stand firing the gun before the big man tried to stop him? Or was he just waving it about in a threatening manner? What the hell difference does it make, Axel wondered, with both of them dead? Kirsten went over her story again, adding some detail about the wild look on Mr. Fabian's face. She described how Axel had run to help Mr. Fabian and how the big man had fallen almost on top of them. The cop frowned at Axel, who smiled grimly and nodded, relieved that Kirsten had not noticed or had at the least failed to mention that there were two guns and that one of them was at this moment distending the lining of Axel's right-hand pants pocket.

Axel put his hand on the gun, discovering a prideful place inside himself. He'd disarmed the little shit, just like that. And given him one hell of a headache to boot. Bald Monkey must have a thick skull to take a hit like that and then go running off. He'd think twice before messing with Axel Speeter again. Axel inhaled deeply, taking in the smells of the restaurant—the hot oil, the tangy aroma of fresh salsa, the heady mix of scents from Sophie, Kirsten, and Carmen. He could even smell himself, the old boomer, reeking a little after defending his fliers. Axel shifted the ice pack to a new spot on his elbow and smiled, seeing himself as this grizzled old kangaroo. Then it hit him again, low and hard. Tommy Fabian was dead. He closed his eyes, shutting out the color and heat of the fair, letting the cold truth settle deep in his gut.

CHAPTER

31

James Dean sat on the curb outside the fairground fence, waiting for the numbness to pass. He needed an idea, an impulse, a reason to move. It could have been anything at all. A pang of hunger, an itch that needed scratching, a question demanding an answer. He kept seeing Pork's face in the car window. The donut guy pointing the silver gun. Sweety's broad, black-jacketed back. Tigger nailing him with the dodgem car, pinning him against the rail, not letting him move, laughing. He could not move now. How could he stand up? He had nothing left, no place to go.

A horse stopped in front of him, nearly crushing his foot. He looked up and saw a helmeted cop sitting on the beast, leaning over, asking him if he was okay.

Dean said he was fine. He said he was waiting for somebody to pick him up.

The cop gave him the look, waited for him to stand up, then clopped off down the fenceline, his horse leaving behind a pile of steaming manure. Dean tried to remember a line from Donne, something he had read weeks before. Something like if you cut off part of your body, you save what is left, but it's better to cut off part of a dead man.

Something like that. He wished he had the book, but he had left it back in Carmen's room. He started walking along the curb, placing one foot after the other.

Everything seemed complicated and uninteresting; he needed one clear idea, something to get him going. Or maybe what he needed was some more crank. He thought about some other things he wanted, listed them in his mind.

His book. At the motel.

Carmen? Did he want Carmen? He wasn't exactly aching for her, but it was nice to have company.

His money. Shit. What was he thinking of, leaving his jacket in Tigger's car? Stupid, stupid. He had forgotten to be smart. He didn't even know their real names—he sure as hell wasn't going to find a Tigger or a Pork in the phone book.

He stopped walking. Would Tigger and Pork be dumb enough to return to that basement after ripping him off? It didn't seem possible. On the other hand, he had nothing to lose by going there and waiting for them. He dug in his pockets, coming out with two twenties, a five, and a few ones. Whatever else, he would need some money, and soon.

A block ahead of him, an ambulance pulled out of the fairgrounds, lights dead, and drove up Como Avenue. First thing he had to do, he had to get out of there. Maybe just get on one of the buses and figure out where he was going later. He had just turned back toward the bus stand when he saw the old man, Axel, not fifty feet in front of him, crossing the street toward the parking lot, moving slow, looking like he was about two hundred years old. Dean froze. The old man didn't see him. Dean felt his face grow warm with anger and dread. He watched until Axel faded into the parking lot. As soon as the old man was out of sight, the heat in Dean's face flowed right down into his balls.

It felt good. Suddenly he felt his perspective shift, as if he had stepped around a dark corner and found himself in full sunlight. He had been thinking that everything was fucked up, but what if it wasn't? If you looked at it another way, he was the luckiest guy in the world to come through all that with just a bump on the head. He *could* have been shot, like Sweety, or had his neck broke like Tiny Tot. As it was, he still had his moves to make, and nobody to stop him. The old man had given him his best shot. Next time, next time he'd be ready, he'd be the man in charge.

It was all about attitude. You had to be smart, and you had to have the right attitude. You couldn't afford to feel sorry for yourself. It was the same thing as doing time. You had to be cool and smart, and you couldn't afford to get all emotional.

He recalled another line from the book. Mostly, reading John Donne had been a show-off thing, a way to prove to Mickey that he wasn't the illiterate she took him for, a way to fuck with Carmen's head, a way to impress Tigger and Sweety and Pork. But there were a few times when he'd sat by himself and tried to make sense of the words. It was nothing like reading a newspaper or magazine. Everything was spelled weird. He could pick his way through a few pages, but the type would quickly fuzz into a gray, meaningless mass.

But then some stuff would jump out at him. This one thing was coming back to him. Shit, he wished he hadn't left the book in Carmen's room. But he remembered the one line, word for word: *This Soule, now free from prison, and passion, hath yet a little indignation. . . .*

Carmen remembered a thing she used to do. When she was a little girl and she and Sophie were living in the projects up north of University, she had learned to turn the world into a cartoon. Sometimes she could force it, other times it would just happen on its own. Colors would brighten and flatten, and people would form black outlines and move in little jerks, like Yogi Bear. In the cartoon world, she would get her own black outline, and she could make her arms and legs stretch or shrink or get heavy or change color or disappear. Usually she would do this at

Pete Hautman

night in her bed, closing her eyes and watching it happen, but sometimes she could make it happen outside in the daylight. Carmen had not turned the world into a cartoon or even thought about it for many years until now, watching Sweety get shot and Tommy Fabian flying through the air and Axel bending over him and Dean standing there and then running and the cops asking her questions, and all of a sudden the outlines came back and the colors were cranked way up. Carmen looked at her hand and made her fingers stretch.

"What are you doing?" Sophie asked.

The cartoon version of Sophie was pretty, Carmen thought. Prettier than the regular Sophie. She looked a lot like Wilma Flintstone. No wrinkles. "I'm looking at my hand," she said.

"I can see that. We've got a business to run, don't forget. People don't stop eating just because somebody gets killed."

Carmen looked toward the front of the stand. "We don't have any customers," she said. "What do you want me to do?"

"I don't know. Clean something. Never mind. Take your break. Be back here in a half hour, okay? Kirsten and I will handle things. You get out of here—you're dangerous. You and your friend."

Carmen said, "Friend?"

"Your friend with the gun. Just because I didn't tell the police, don't think I didn't see him."

"You mean Dean? It was Tommy shot the gun."

"Your friend had a gun too. I saw it in his hand. Now get out of here, take a break."

Carmen shrugged and left the stand. Who knew *what* Dean was doing? Him and his cranked-up hairless friends. She was glad she and Dean hadn't found the money in Axel's room. That was crazy, the idea of going to Mexico with Dean. A sense of release rolled up her body; she did a little dance step, causing a few people to veer aside, giving her room. An image appeared in her mind of a Mexican village on the sea, a thick packet of U.S. dollars in her purse, an icy pitcher of margaritas, and a man. Not James Dean, but a new man, with hair. Curly hair on his head and on his chest, and buried in it a nice gold necklace. Tropical sun beating down on them, a nice breeze coming in over the surf . . .

Without warning, the image faded and she became suddenly aware of herself as alone, without substantial funds, standing in the midst of a hundred thousand corn-dog-eating yokels. She was nobody, nothing, going nowhere. The realization nearly caused her knees to buckle. She felt it in her stomach, and in a band of pressure against the nape of her neck. She stumbled toward an empty bench a few yards away. Carmen knew what was happening. She was crashing, coming down off the meth. She'd come down off Dexedrine before, and coke, but never crank. This was different, more intense. She sat on the bench and squeezed her eyes shut and forced her thoughts away from herself, back to the image of a wad of money. Thinking about money was good. That was the trick to crashing—you had to keep grabbing onto the good thoughts. If you let the bad thoughts in, it would get bad. She summoned up the image of Axel's coffee cans.

Cans and cans and cans. She felt her chest swell, her breasts rise. The thought of the money stroked her body like a plunge into warm water. She could see herself walking along the ocean toward her Mexican beach house. She could see a shelf in her bedroom lined with a row of Folgers cans, cans full of green corn cash tamales.

Axel's nylon socks. Like a slow-motion punch to the stomach, the thought brought her crashing down again. How could she think about the money when she didn't know where the money had gone? She tried to think of places he might have hidden it, but she couldn't think while she was crashing. She squeezed her teeth together until the pain in her jaw shattered her thoughts, focusing her senses on the outside world. A few yards away, a cartoon Indian was selling cartoon fry bread to cartoon fairgoers. The outlines were there, but the colors seemed muted. She watched him until his movements began to recycle.

Carmen lit a cigarette and sat back and closed her eyes. She was getting a new buzz now, not unpleasant, a sort of smooth, rolling vibration. She imagined herself floating over the fairgrounds. She thought about the places the money might be. In Axel's room. In Axel's truck. Her imagination stopped there. In his room or in his truck. What did he do with the money every night? He put it in his burlap shoulder bag. They walked to his truck. He dropped her off at her room. In the morning they drove back to the fair. Was the bag empty in the morning? She thought that it was. Her mind drifted back to an imagined Mexico.

When she opened her eyes, the cartoon show had ended. Objects had become dull and three-dimensional. How long had she been sitting there? Had she been sleeping? Carmen wasn't sure. When she stood up, she knew from the way her legs felt that she'd been there for quite a while.

Everything felt and looked different. The day crowd had begun to thin out. There was a general movement toward the fairground exits, eaters of cheese curds and Pronto Pups and Tiny Tot donuts and sno-cones moving slowly and uncomfortably toward the turnstiles, parents herding flocks of exhausted kids, ignoring their automatic whining about having to leave so soon.

It was still daylight, but the crowd was changing. The after-work crowd had begun to arrive: the teenagers and the beer drinkers, adults in groups of two and four, people coming to see the show at the grandstand or to ride the Ferris wheel in the dark or to stroll up and down the clattering, blinking chaos of the midway, trying to win a four-foot-tall Barney. There were fewer farmers, fewer children, and fewer old folks. The people looked fresher, not yet bagged out from massive infusions of sugar and lard.

Before returning to the taco stand, Carmen went to one of the rest rooms and unfolded the square of paper Pork had given her. She licked the last traces of crystal from Nancy Reagan's smiling face, then flushed her image down the toilet.

Sophie was loading the fryer with tortillas when Carmen entered the stand.

"Sorry I took so long," Carmen said.

Sophie said, "You're fired."

Axel fiddled with the truck radio until he stumbled across a classical music station. He was thinking that it would make him feel better to listen to a wordless yet coherent progression of sounds. It wasn't working; the sounds were too complex and insistent. He turned off the radio and sat in silence, giving in to the flickering memories of Tommy alive, Tommy dead. Trying not to think about the Bald Monkey, struggling to find a tolerable balance between anger and grief. He would feel the tears mounting his lower eyelids, will them to come to wash it all away, then his jaw would clench and anger would squeeze his eyes dry. It was too soon to grieve. He sat and let his mind turn this way and that, like a driver lost in a strange city.

Carmen rapped on the window, startling him. He touched a dry eye with the back of his hand and rolled down the window. "What's the problem?" he asked, his voice ragged. He cleared his throat.

Carmen was smoking a cigarette, kicking the packed dirt with her pink-and-white Reeboks.

"What's the problem?" he asked again, forcing concern into his voice.

She flicked her cigarette straight down and ground it out with her toe, crossed her arms, and looked up at Axel. "Can Sophie fire me?"

"Why would she want to do that?"

"You got me. She says I'm fired."

"What did you do?"

"Nothing. I took a break, and when I got back she says, 'You're fired.'"

Axel waited.

"Maybe I was a few minutes late getting back. I don't know. Can she fire me? I mean, am I working for Sophie or am I working for you?" She had her arms crossed, squeezing her breasts in her Axel's Taco Shop T-shirt. Her eyes half scared and half angry, she waited for Axel to pronounce his judgment.

Axel said, "Carmen, what do you want me to do? Sophie's running the stand; I can't just tell her to hire you back."

"So fire *her!*"

Axel said, "Why?"

"I can run the stand better than Sophie any day. She's so cheap she's got us counting olives. I put four olive slices on a tostada, and she's all over me. People like lots of olives."

"I can't do that, Carmen. Your mother's my partner now, you know."

"She's what?"

"I took her on as a partner, and part of the deal is she runs the stand the way she wants. Maybe if you go back and talk to her . . ." He shrugged. Carmen was lighting another cigarette.

"No way. You don't know my mom."

She's right, Axel thought. Both of them are right. Sophie was probably right to fire Carmen, and Carmen was right— no way would Sophie change her mind so easily. She would stay mad for at least a day, maybe longer. If he told her to hire Carmen back, she would fight him on it through the last day of the fair. He sighed and wondered how he was going to keep his family together.

Carmen paced a circle on the packed dirt. The sun was near the horizon. She moved in and out of the shadow of the truck, smoking her cigarette with rapid, jerking motions. My family, Axel thought. He had never before thought of it that way. Or maybe he had, but without using the word out loud in his mind. What did that make Carmen—his daughter? Something like that, he decided. Or something else. In any case, he knew what he should do. He should let the women deal with each other, keep his nose out of it.

But he knew he wouldn't.

"Tell you what," he said. "Let me talk to Sophie. You stay out of her way tonight, and we'll see about tomorrow."

"What am I supposed to do till then? Can I take the truck back to the motel? I'll come back tonight and pick you up."

Axel hesitated, imagining himself standing in the empty parking lot at one o'clock in the morning, his shoulder bag full of money, waiting for Carmen to show up, thinking about her flat on her back at the Motel 6, snoring at the television.

"I have a better idea," he said. "How about if you take the bus?"

The sky glittered with the nightly fireworks show as Axel returned to the Taco Shop. Sophie was frying a final batch of taco shells, getting ready for the small rush of business that would come after the grandstand show let out. She looked at Axel, her jaw set, saying nothing. Kirsten was gone, her shift over at nine o'clock. Sonya, one of the part-time girls, leaned out over the counter, chewing on a plastic straw and watching the groups of people drift slowly toward the exits. Axel decided to let Sophie break the news to him right away.

"Where's Carmen?" he asked.

"I fired her," Sophie said.

"Oh. Well, she probably deserved it." He decided to leave it at that for now. "How did we do today?"

Sophie hesitated. "She took a three-hour break. I don't have to put up with that from any of my girls."

"It's your show, Sophie. So how did we do today?" He pointed at the cash box under the counter.

"I'd guess close to six thousand. Maybe more. And no help from Carmen."

"You must've been busy. Who do you have for to-morrow?"

"Juanita starts at eight, Kirsten comes in at twelve. Sonya won't be here."

Axel nodded. "It's gonna be busy. Supposed to be a nice day, and they got Kenny Rogers in the grandstand. You want me to find you another girl?"

"We only have three days to go. I don't want to be training somebody new right now."

"I don't blame you."

Sonya said, "I need two tacos and a Bueno and one nachos." Axel watched Sophie prepare the order. He could see she was tired; her movements had the needful precision of one whose energy reserves are dangerously low.

"You know," Axel said as he watched her loading the pair of tacos, "it might be smart to keep Carmen on tap, just in case you need her. Get her in here for the lunch rush, so you can take a break."

Sophie, focused on making the tacos, did not reply. Axel waited, letting her process his words.

"What makes you think she'd even show up?" Sophie said after handing the order to Sonya.

"Maybe she won't, but we'd be no worse off than before, would we?"

"I fired her."

"That's right, you did. I was just thinking that we might want to keep our options open."

"You can keep your options open. I have a stand to manage. I can't afford to count on her."

"You're right," Axel said. "You can't count on her."

"She's completely unreliable."

"I suppose if she did show up, though, and we were really busy, you might find some use for her."

Sophie considered. "We don't need her."

"I know that. But maybe we can use her."

Sophie shrugged. "She's fired as far as I'm concerned. She

shows up here, she's working for you. It comes out of your share."

"I'll talk to her," Axel said.

Timothy Alan Skeller, aka Tigger, lowered himself feet first through the basement window, the pointed toes of his duct-taped boots scrabbling against the cinder-block wall. He dropped the last ten inches to the concrete floor, then felt around in the dark for the end of the extension cord, muttering to himself. "Where's the, shit, fuckin' thing—" A beer can crackled under his boot. "Fuckin' fuck shit, fuckin' shit." He dug in his pockets. "Goddamn, goddamn son-of-a-bitch." Two coins fell from his pocket and clacked on the concrete. "Fuck! Shit!" He found the matchbook in his hip pocket, fumbled loose a match, made three attempts to light it before it flared up, casting a weak orange glow.

The extension cord was not where he had dropped it. Tigger had perhaps a half second to wonder where it had gone, then had his question answered when a length of thick orange electrical cord dropped past his face and tightened over his Adam's apple.

CHAPTER

32

Axel untied his shoes, placed them at the foot of his bed, set the .45 on the nightstand, then carefully arranged himself on top of the spread and stared up at the ceiling, arms crossed over his chest. He knew he wouldn't be able to sleep. Too much bouncing around inside his head. Closing his eyes, he tried to find a comforting thought. After a few minutes, he reached down and unsnapped the front clips of his suspenders. The bands of pressure on his shoulders disappeared, but his arm still throbbed, his finger burned, and the money hidden in his bed—over twenty thousand dollars now—produced a dull ache in the center of his back. He wasn't sure he could actually *feel* the money. It was tucked down in the box spring. In theory, it should have been undetectable to anyone lying on the mattress. But it didn't matter whether the sensation was a physical thing, since it was undeniably there, pressing up at him.

They'd been in his room once. He couldn't count on a simple dead bolt to keep them from coming back, and maybe next time they'd look a little harder. Carmen had to figure that he was stashing the money in his room. Was she still hooked up with that kid, that Bald Monkey? Axel took a deep breath. Carmen was driven by forces he could not understand. Why had she gotten involved with a punk like that in the first place? He could see it if the kid was good-looking or had something going for him. Maybe she was just going through a delayed adolescent thing, trying to drive her parents crazy— Shit! He was doing it again, thinking of her like she was his daughter. He shifted the position of his legs. The fight with the kid had really taken it out of him—he must have used every muscle in his body. He could already feel his limbs stiffening. His right elbow felt like a throbbing ball of concrete. It would be a rough morning.

He wondered how Bald Monkey was feeling. Did he have a little headache? Axel hoped so. He hoped he had a huge one. He hoped his head hurt so bad he'd go back to wherever the hell he came from. That was what he hoped, but what he feared was that the kid wasn't finished. He had a feeling about Bald Monkey, the same way he'd had a feeling about those guys in Deadwood, three decades ago.

One thing he had to do for sure, he had to do something about this cash. He couldn't just leave it in his room. He had to move it, put it with the rest of his money. Unfortunately, when he had entombed the bulk of his fortune, he hadn't thought about how difficult it would be to make deposits.

The thought of digging made his elbow throb even harder.

What Sam O'Gara hated most about middle-of-the-night phone calls was that when the fucker went off, goddamn Chester started howling. And when Chester howled, then Festus, he'd jump up on the bed and start licking for all he was worth. It was like a goddamn air raid siren going off in his bedroom, then getting drowned in dog spit.

He sat up, throwing Festus and his blankets off the bed in one motion. "All right, goddamn your tongue— Chester! You shut up 'fore I have your balls lopped!" He swung his legs off the bed and staggered toward the kitchen, where his vintage Princess dial phone was giving forth another insistent ring, followed immediately by another howl from

Chester. "Goddamn it, I'm coming!" He snatched the phone off its base and shouted into the receiver, "If this is a wrong number, I'm gonna find you and shove this fucker right up your misdialing ass, you sorry son-of-a-bitch!"

"Hi, Sam, it's me."

"Jesus fucking Christ, Ax. You know what happens in this house when the phone goes off?"

"Let me guess. You use a lot of bad words, then you answer it."

"You don't know the fucking half of it." Chester and Festus sat in front of him, panting happily now that they'd done their job.

"Sam, I've got to tell you something."

Sam shook his head, suddenly wishing he hadn't picked up the phone. Festus whined nervously. Chester slumped to the floor and rested his chin on his paws.

"Sam, I can't believe I didn't call you before. I must've been all messed up in my head. I just thought to call you now."

"Jesus Christ, Ax." Sam's voice came out soft and ragged. "You're gonna tell me somebody's dead, ain't you?"

"Tommy."

"Aw, f'Chrissakes."

That was the other thing he hated about middle-of-the-night phone calls. It was always some goddamn awful thing he didn't want to know about.

Tigger drove with one hand on the wheel, touching his neck gently with the other. "I swear to God, man, it wasn't my idea to leave you there, man." His voice sounded hoarse. "It was that fuckin' Pork, man." He swallowed, winced.

"You were driving the car," Dean said.

"He told me if I stopped he'd fucking kill me."

"And he took my jacket."

"What was I supposed to do? You seen the guy. I mean, Sweety was big, but Pork, man, the dude's kinda scary, y'know?"

"Scarier than me?" Dean asked.

Tigger shifted his eyes to Dean, then looked back at the road. "Not right now he ain't," he said.

"Where is this place?"

"We're almost there, man."

"You think he's still gonna be there?"

"He'll close the fucker up."

"Good."

"Here it is." Tigger turned into a small parking lot crowded with pickup trucks, Chevy Camaros, and Harley-Davidsons. A flickering red neon sign read: THE RECOVERY ROOM.

Dean said, "How come you aren't still in there drinking?"

Tigger pulled his car into one of the few open spaces. "I got eighty-sixed, those fuckers."

"Show me which one's his bike."

Tigger pointed at a black-and-silver Harley. "The one with the rebel flag on the tank, okay? Can I go home now?"

"No." Dean pulled the keys from the ignition. "We're partners now, asshole. Partners stick together."

Tigger drew his head back, squinting at Dean. The speed and the lack of sleep made Tigger look much older, like maybe twenty-three. "Whaddya mean?"

"You want to make some money, don't you?"

"Well . . . sure."

"Good. Then we're partners."

"You mean, like, half and half?"

"We'll work something out," Dean said as he opened the door. "I need something out of your trunk."

"What? There ain't nothing in there."

"Nothing? You got a spare tire, right?"

"Sure. Only it's flat."

"That all? You don't have anything to go with it?"

Tigger struggled to understand. "What, you mean like a jack?"

"I was thinking more like a tire iron. You got one of those, don't you, partner?"

Tigger shook his head. "Nope." He brightened. "But I do got a crowbar."

* * *

Pork was feeling hard and tight and fast. His new jacket squeezed his shoulders, constricting his movements. It made him move different, made him swing his upper body with each step, giving him a don't-fuck-with-me walk like a weight lifter's, only much more dangerous-looking. He liked the way that felt. He especially liked the feel of all that money hanging against his sides. Who would've thought it would be so easy? That punk Dean, thinking he was some kind of gangster. What an idiot! He couldn't believe it when he'd stuck his hands in the jacket pocket and come out with a fistful of twenties.

With that kind of money, Pork could have made a lot of friends at The Recovery Room, but that wasn't his style. Anybody could make friends. What Pork wanted was respect. He went for the lone biker image, parked himself at a table in the back of the bar, flashed some cash, got himself a whole bottle of Jack Daniel's, then lay back and watched the scene, seeing himself as a modern-day Mafia boss. Guys that knew him would swing by, nod, then fade. That was cool. One of the bitches sat down with him for a while, grabbed his hand, and put it on her tit. He gave her a vicious squeeze, which got rid of her in a damn hurry. He didn't need any of her biker cooties, nor anybody else's. The kind of money he had now, he could afford the good stuff. Right now he just wanted to relax and moderate his amphetamine buzz with a few shots of Jack.

By the time the bar closed, Pork was ready to hop on his Harley and take a ride out in the country, letting the night air scour him clean. He sat and watched everybody else file out of the club. It was best to be the last to leave. That was the cool way to do it. Let everybody know he was in no hurry. He let the bartender give him a few looks, then got to his feet and did the don't-fuck-with-me walk over to the bar, slapped down a pair of twenties, headed for the door.

The first thing he saw—unbelievable!—some asshole sitting on his bike. More curious than angry, he walked across the dirt parking lot toward his Harley. The light from the flickering neon sign made it hard to see. He was only a few feet away when he recognized the figure on his bike as Tigger.

Pork said, "Man, what the fuck are you doing back here?" He saw Tigger's eyes shift, look past him. Pork had seen that look before. It was the look you saw in the prison yard when somebody was about to get a shank between the ribs. Instinctively, he ducked and twisted, bringing up an arm to protect his face. Something hit him hard on the elbow. He caught a snapshot of Dean's face, expressionless, then a blur of movement and an explosion of intense pain as the backswing caught him on the side of his neck. He fell, crashing into the Harley, hearing Tigger shout something, hearing the bike crash to the asphalt, feeling the footrest jab into his kidney. The three ravaged points—elbow, neck, kidney—joined in a triangle of agony, and for a moment, as his vision filled with black bubbles, he thought he was passing out. He squeezed his eyes and rolled to the side, felt the gritty surface of the parking lot beneath his palms. He took a breath, heard the sound of air rushing into his body, tasted dust, opened his eyes. There was the packed dirt, the earth, right there in front of him, real and solid.

The worst of it is over, he thought. He knows he hurt me, knows he can have what he wants. Now we talk.

He turned his head, slowly. This was no time to play the tough guy. Again, Dean's face appeared in his eyes, looking as slack and dead as any mug shot. It was not a talking face, or even a fighting face. It was a killing face. Pork saw the hooked end of the crowbar silhouetted against the red neon. He tried to roll away, got one hand in front of his face just as the steel bar came chopping down. The force of the blow audibly snapped his fingers, slammed his hand into his cheekbone, his head into the packed dirt. He felt a scream in his throat, smelled the earth rising up to swallow him, heard the dull slapping sound of steel striking leather and flesh. He heard it again, then heard nothing at all.

CHAPTER

33

The morning started out cool and moist, with a dew point in the middle sixties. During the night, the picnic tables and benches on the mall had gathered an oily slick of moisture that remained until after eight o'clock, when the sun rose high and hot enough to steam it away.

Axel sat on his folding metal chair behind the Taco Shop, holding an ice-filled towel against his elbow, listening to Sophie and Juanita setting up for the day. Sophie gave her orders in a quiet voice, not her usual snapping tones. Fairgoers filtered slowly onto the grounds. All three Tiny Tot Donut stands were closed. A TV news team rolled in and shot some film of the dead stand on the mall, probably planning a follow-up report on violence at the state fair. People who had been coming to the fair for thirty years for their bag of minidonuts would walk right up to the plywood window covers and try to see in, unable to believe that they were to be denied their ritual. Often they would then come up to Axel's Taco Shop, not to buy tacos but to ask about Tiny Tot Donuts.

If they asked Sophie where they could get some donuts, she would direct them to the Tom Thumb Donut stand down on the midway, or to the Mini-Loops stand on Judson Avenue. If they asked Axel, he would simply respond by saying that the owner had passed away and deny all other knowledge. He could not bring himself to send customers to one of Tommy Fabian's competitors. Even if Tommy no longer cared, Axel did. He was in no mood to be reminded every five minutes that his oldest and best friend was gone. It was just as well. It would have killed Tommy to see all those customers walk away without their donuts.

Every now and then, one of Tommy's carny friends would walk up from the midway to pay his respects by standing silently in front of the Tiny Tot stand, smoking a cigarette. A few of them drifted farther up the mall to exchange a few words with Axel. They all seemed to take Tommy's death philosophically. One, Froggy Sims, the aging, chain-smoking mike man for Wee Wanda, the World's Smallest Woman, didn't want to leave.

"Tommy, he was a good un. Real old-time carny, him." Froggy put his cigarette in his crumpled mouth, made a pair of fists, clacked his rings together. The first time Axel had seen him do that, he'd wondered whether it was some obscure carny thing. He'd asked Tommy about it, and Tommy had said it was just Froggy's way of making sure you noticed his jewelry. Tommy hadn't cared much for old Froggy, but he'd always given him free donuts.

Axel shifted the ice pack to a new spot on his elbow. He resented this guy hanging around, making out like he'd been Tommy's best friend. He figured Froggy was mostly sad about losing his donut connection. The guy had about five thousand bucks in gold on him, not counting what was on his teeth, but he'd walk a half mile across the fairgrounds for free food.

"Use to run an alibi joint, me and him. Those were the days, I got to tell you."

"I bet they were," Axel said. "Listen, Froggy, you want a taco or something?" Maybe that would get rid of him.

Froggy made a face like he was surprised. "Jeez, Ax, that's white a you."

Axel smiled with his mouth and told Juanita to get Froggy a taco and a Coke.

Froggy said, "You don't got no Pepsi?"

By nine-thirty the outside temperature had risen to eighty-four degrees. It was going to be a hot one, a late-summer Minnesota sauna. Every third person in the state would say, at some point, "It's not the heat; it's the humidity."

The ice helped. Axel flexed his arm. The swelling had gone. It felt almost normal. He stared across the mall at the dead hulk of the Tiny Tot stand. Tommy's ghost was hovering over the mall, staring down at the boarded-up remnant of his life. Axel didn't want to know what that felt like, ever.

A familiar figure stopped in front of the Tiny Tot concession, then walked slowly up to Axel.

"Hey, Ax," said Sam.

Axel looked up. "What are you doing here?"

Sam lit a cigarette. "I'm not sure," he said. "I couldn't get no work done, thinking about Tom."

Axel nodded. He understood. Another of Tommy's friends, paying his respects.

"I didn't think he'd be the first one of us, Ax."

"Yeah? Who'd you think it would be?"

Sam spat out a fragment of tobacco, looked critically at his cigarette, then grinned at Axel. "Fact is, I thought it'd be you."

"Thanks a lot." Axel was not amused.

Carmen, still wearing yesterday's clothes, woke up with a headache. It wasn't a bad headache. In fact, it was the mildest one so far that week.

Someone was pounding on the door. She had the sense that it had been going on for some time.

"Just a minute!" She looked at the clock: ten-fourteen. "Who is it?"

"Management!"

Carmen opened the door. Bill Quist stood in the doorway and looked past her, smiling.

"Where's your friend?"

"What do you want?"

"I haven't heard from you lately. Is your friend still staying here?"

"No. He's gone."

"Oh. Mr. Speeter called. He says you're supposed to go in to work."

"I was fired."

Quist shrugged. "I don't know about that. I just know he called and asked me to wake you up and tell you."

"He could've just called my room."

"He's been trying all morning." He pointed. "Your phone's off the hook."

Carmen remembered dreaming about this incessant ringing noise, then making it stop.

"Did that key I loaned you work out?" Quist asked.

"What key?"

Quist laughed. "That's what I say: 'What key?' You were going to give me some money, remember?"

"No. Did Axel say anything else?"

"Just that you're supposed to go to work. How about you give me twenty bucks now and the rest later?"

Carmen slammed the door.

Quist blinked at the closed door, still smiling, then shrugged and walked back across the parking lot to his office. It was always worth asking. You never knew.

"You're leaving?"

"I called Carmen. She'll be here anytime now." Axel found a paper bag and started filling it with burritos.

"But—" Sophie looked at the line forming in front of the restaurant, shook her head like she couldn't believe it. "You're leaving *now?* Just me and Juanita?"

"Kirsten and Carmen should be here soon."

Juanita shouted over her shoulder. "I maybe need some help right now, you know."

"I'll be right there," Sophie said. She gave Axel a dark look. "Kirsten's an hour late, and you know Carmen."

Axel said, "I'll be back in an hour. Look, I've asked Sam to help out. He needs to be doing something. He'll be right back—he just went to the john."

"Sam O'Gara? I don't want him anywhere near here. I heard what he did to Tommy's donut mix."

"It's up to you. I gotta go, Sophie. Back in a couple hours, okay?" He added the paper sack of Bueno Burritos to his burlap bag, slung it over his shoulder, and walked across the mall. He heard her shout that it was goddamn well not okay, but he kept moving.

"Now where's he going?"

"How the fuck do I know?"

"He's got that bag with him."

"The money's in the bag?"

"Some of it is, I bet. C'mon, podna, let's get a move on." Dean stood up, his straw cowboy hat riding low on his forehead. He felt ridiculous. He wore a light-blue western-style shirt and a red paisley bandanna around his neck. The shirt was made of polyester or something, hot as hell, sticking to him like a sheet of glue. All three items had been purchased at a western-wear stand in the Coliseum. The only good thing was, next to Tigger he looked great.

Tigger had selected a colorful shirt with *Let's Rodeo* embroidered in rope letters, front and back. His hat was white felt with an outrageously high crown. It had cost fifty-nine bucks, but Dean figured it was worth it if it made the kid happy. He needed him, for now. But he'd drawn the line at new boots. They didn't have time. He planned to keep an eye on the old man every minute. This was serious business, and there would be no mistakes.

Somehow, Pork had managed to spend or lose over four

thousand dollars during the few hours he'd had Dean's jacket. When Dean had discovered how little money was remaining, he'd told Tigger to drive back to The Recovery Room's parking lot and drive over him a couple times, just in case the beating hadn't killed him. Tigger had not responded well to that suggestion, so he'd let it go. He realized now that it wouldn't have been the smart thing to do. From now on, he was going to do only smart things. The plastic bag Pork had left in the chest pocket of Dean's jacket helped. It contained several grams of powdered methamphetamine. A few fat lines, and he'd got so smart it was like he could predict the future.

"Don't get too close," Dean said. One bad thing about wearing disguises on a day like this: He was sweating buckets. The speed made his sweat smell like chicken soup. Chicken soup running down his cheeks and trickling along his ribs. He smelled like a high school cafeteria.

"He ain't looking," Tigger said. "He's heading out through the gate."

"Going out to his truck."

"What're we gonna do?"

"Just stay cool, podna. We get in your car and follow him, see where he goes."

Kirsten Lund was late, and it wasn't her fault. It was her mom's fault. Kirsten had made a big mistake, a huge mistake, a mondo mistake, when she'd told her mom about the fight at the fair.

"Young lady, if you think I am going to let you go back to that horrible taco shack, you have got another think coming."

Wow. Kirsten never thought her mom would get so twisted about it. It wasn't like people got shot at the fair every day. In fact, it was probably the only time ever in history. Not go back to work? Not possible, she explained, but her mom was being a real load.

"You don't need the money that bad, dear. Most of your school clothes from last year still fit you fine."

Kirsten was horrified. "Jesus, Mom, what are you trying to do to me?"

That was another mistake.

"I won't have language like that in my house! You are not going back to that awful place, and that, young lady, is final!"

Big, huge, mondo mistake. She'd had to wait for her mom to leave for work, then rush to the bus stop. Her mom would kill her if she found out, but that was better than going back to school wearing last year's clothes. And Sophie was going to be mad too. Everybody was going to be mad at her. She might even get fired, like Carmen.

"What's he doing? Can you see?"

"He's got a little, like, stepladder. He's setting it up next to the fence."

"Has he got his bag with him?"

"Yeah. Now he's got a shovel. He's throwing it over the fence. He's up on the ladder now. He's taking something out of the bag."

"Can he see us?"

"He's not looking this way."

"I hear dogs barking."

"Now he's throwing some stuff over. It looks like food."

"Food?"

"Yeah. It looks like tacos or something. . . . He's climbing over now. He's climbed over. I can't see him anymore."

"Shit. Okay, let's go see what he's doing." Dean jumped out of the car and trotted down the sidewalk, Tigger close behind. The fence, in violation of city ordinance, was seven feet high. "Okay. Boost me up so I can see," Dean said in a low voice.

Tigger crouched beside the privacy fence and let Dean straddle his shoulders. He tried to rise, groaned.

"Come on!" Dean said, grabbing the top of the wooden fence.

Tigger straightened his legs, gasped, and fell over, sending both of them sprawling onto the sidewalk. "I can't," he gasped.

Dean climbed to his feet, rubbing his elbow. "What a fucking wuss. C'mere, I'll lift you up. Tell me what the fuck he's doing in there." They exchanged positions, Tigger on Dean's shoulders.

"Can you see?"

"Yeah."

"Well?"

"It's some kind of junkyard. A bunch of cars. Shit. There's a couple big motherfucking dogs in there, man. Looks like they're having lunch."

"What about the guy?"

"I can't see him. Wait a minute. He's in one of them. He's in this old pickup truck, trying to get it started. He's backing it up now. Okay. He's getting out. There's—he's—he's standing there looking at this hole, man. Like a big hole somebody dug up, you know? He's just looking at it. . . . He don't look happy, man. He looks pissed. His fuckin' face, man, he looks like he's gonna blow. Shit! Shit, lemme down, man! Lemme down!" Tigger pushed away from the fence, sending Dean staggering backward just as something heavy hit the fence from the other side and dual howls shattered the quiet neighborhood.

The dogs.

The goddamn dogs. Now they were barking, howling at something on the other side of the fence. First they ruin his life, then they bark about it.

Axel stared down into the shallow pit at the fluttering remnants of a dark-green Hefty bag. He thought, If I ever have a heart attack, please, God, let it be now. He looked up at Sam's dogs jumping against the wooden fence and amended his wish. First, God, give me time to kill the dogs. He reached into his bag, pulled out the .45, cocked it, and pointed it toward the bellowing mutts.

He held it on them for several seconds, knowing there was

no way he could do it. It wasn't the dogs' fault. A week back, he'd invaded their territory carrying two bags, one filled with Bueno Burritos, the other filled with cash money. He'd given one to the dogs, then buried the other right before their hungry canine eyes. Axel uncocked the pistol and put it back in his bag.

The dogs had started digging at the back bumper. He could almost see it, the two dogs working together, or maybe in shifts, sending a steady spray of loose dirt flying out from under the truck. Yeah, he knew a dog-dug hole when he saw one.

But where was the money? He stepped into the pit, lifted the torn Hefty bag. Nothing. He kicked aside some dirt, thinking for a moment that perhaps this was some other doubled-up garbage bag and that the one with the money still lay beneath his feet. A corner of gray-green caught his eye. He bent down and tugged a twenty-dollar bill from the earth. Falling to his hands and knees, Axel shoveled aside handfuls of dirt, throwing some at the dogs, who had sauntered over to watch him.

The twenty was all he found. He stood up, distastefully regarding his dirt-caked fingernails. He hated that. Dirt under his nails.

One loose twenty. Where had it all gone? Had high wind passed through the neighborhood and blown it all away? Not likely. He threaded his way among the derelict vehicles, trying to follow the perimeter of the fence, keeping his eyes on the ground. After five minutes of searching, he found another twenty, stuck in the grille of the Dodge Charger. At the base of the fence, between the two VW Beetles, he discovered an entire roll, still held together with its rubber band, the bills slightly chewed but still spendable. The dogs? The dogs wouldn't be able to eat an entire quarter-million dollars, even if it did smell like Mexican food.

No, he knew who had his money. He just wasn't sure what he should do about it.

CHAPTER

34

The walk from the bus stop to the mall would normally take about three minutes. Carmen stretched it out to forty. She did not want to go to work. The tactile memory of the texture of a flour tortilla gave her the shudders.

Also, it had kind of bothered her, being fired by Sophie. Fired by her own mom.

It was getting so she couldn't count on anybody.

She stopped to watch a yellow Skyride capsule pass overhead. All day long, the Skyride ferried people, two to a capsule, from the Horticulture Building, at the head of the mall, to Heritage Square, at the far corner of the fairgrounds. Carmen had worked under the cable for five seasons and had yet to ride it herself. She didn't like the idea of being locked in a bobbing capsule, riding along an unchangeable route.

She couldn't count on any of them. Not Sophie, not Axel, and certainly not James Dean. Now that *he* was gone—gone for sure this time, she thought—she really needed to firm up her position with Axel. If he wanted her to work with Sophie, then that's what she'd have to do. At least for now. She opened her purse and took two more Valiums from the prescription bottle, swallowed them, and lit a cigarette. The two she had taken back at the motel didn't seem to be working. She decided to wait for these to kick in before giving herself up to the Taco Shop.

Carmen noticed that the Tiny Tot stand was boarded up, then remembered that Tommy Fabian had been killed. She'd forgotten all about it. She couldn't count on him, either. Next thing she knew, Axel would go and die on her too.

"How's this?" Sam O'Gara held up his latest effort at rolling a Bueno Burrito.

Sophie groaned. "Would you eat that?" she asked.

Sam frowned at the lumpy, leaking wad in his hand, shrugged, and tossed it into the trash. "I never claimed to be a goddamn cook," he said. "Besides, those tortillas are like wet toilet paper. Don't take nothing to rip 'em."

"Try again, only take your time with it. And be gentle. You're not changing a tire; you're making someone's dinner."

"If you wasn't so goddamn picky, I'd be doing fine." Sam was in an ugly mood. This was turning into one of the worst weeks of the first half, or two thirds, or fifteen sixteenths, or whatever the hell fraction of his life it was that he'd lived so far. First thing, Axel waking him up, then finding out that Tommy had finally got hisself killed, then the damned dogs dig up the yard and make the worst goddamn mess he'd ever seen. It had taken him near an hour to clean it up. And then his Chevy wouldn't start. Nor his truck. All those vehicles, and every last one of them a junker. What a guy ought to do, a guy ought to go buy himself a horse. He'd had to take the bus to get to the fairgrounds. Axel was going to owe him big for this one. Make no mistake, Axel would pay big time for this.

"I'm not picky," Sophie said. "It's just that we have certain quality standards here. Kirsten doesn't seem to have any problems with it. At least not when she decides to show up for work."

Kirsten wrinkled her brow. "I said I was sorry."

"Sorry doesn't make up for lost business."

"Now ladies," Sam said. "Bitchin' ain't gonna get the people fed."

Sophie threw up her hands. "Fine. Fine. Kirsten, will you please give Mr. O'Gara a lesson?"

Kirsten smiled at Sam. "It just takes practice is all." She rapidly put together four Buenos, had them folded and wrapped within seconds. "I can do them as fast as Carmen now."

"Faster," Sophie amended.

Sam snorted, a flapping sound that made both women jump. He had to get out of there, and the only way he was going to do it would be to find himself a replacement. He pointed across the mall.

"What about the little princess? You gonna leave her stand there all day?"

Carmen, wearing her sunglasses, stood a hundred feet away, leaning against the white cinder-block wall of the Food Building, facing them, smoking a cigarette. "She's been holding up that wall half an hour now. And what about that little Mex gal was here? Where'd she take off to?"

Sophie said, "If you mean Juanita, she was only scheduled for the morning shift. As for my daughter—if she wants to work, all she has to do is ask."

"Yeah? Well, maybe she's just sitting over there waiting for *you* to ask *her*."

"Well, I do not intend to do any such thing."

"You want me to go get her?" Anything to escape.

Sophie considered. "I suppose. Even Carmen is an improvement on you, Sam."

"Thanks a hell of a lot." Sam untied his apron, let it fall to the floor, and stalked out of the stand.

* * *

Carmen watched Sam O'Gara walking toward her. His gait was smooth and rolling, almost as though he were on a ship. Other people on the mall, she noticed, were also walking that way.

She figured she was coming on to the Valiums.

Suddenly he was there, in his bib overalls and V-neck T-shirt and green cap. "Hot one, isn't it?"

"Hi, Sam. Is it hot? I guess I didn't notice."

"Well, actually it ain't the heat so much. It's the humidity. You want to work? Your mama could use you."

Carmen looked past him at the taco stand, nine or ten people in line, Sophie and Kirsten moving around inside at dangerous velocities.

"You sure she wants me?"

"Sure she does. She told me to come and get you. She said you're the best burrito roller she's ever seen."

"Really?" Carmen agreed with that, but she didn't think Sophie had ever noticed.

"Yeah. You help your mama out now, okay?"

Carmen nodded. Sam gave her a grin, buried his hands in his overalls, and turned away.

Carmen said, "Hey! Aren't you gonna be there?"

Sam looked over his shoulder. "Who, me? I'm gonna go eyeball the animules, honey. I hear they got a hog runs twelve hunnert pounds this year."

Carmen said, "Yuck."

Sam muttered, "Besides, another minute in that stand with your mom, I'm a goddamn basket case."

Carmen laughed. "You just got to ignore her," she said.

Five minutes later, she was finding Sophie impossible to ignore. She'd seen her mom in foul moods before, but never like this.

"Dammit, Carmen, did you forget everything you ever knew, girl? First I lose that fumble-fingered Sam O'Gara, then I get you. What do you call this?"

"That," Carmen said, "is a beef tostada."

"I asked for a beef *taco!*"

"Sorry! Jesus!" Carmen couldn't seem to do anything right. She tried not to let it bother her, relying on the Valium to buffer Sophie's flak. That worked for a while, until Kirsten had to make an emergency run to the restroom. As soon as she was out of the stand, Sophie turned up the volume on her complaints.

"Kirsten would never do that," Sophie said. "When I ask for 'two bean,' I mean tacos, not burritos."

"How am I s'posed to know that? Do I look like a mind reader?" Carmen said.

"We've been doing it that way for five years now. What's wrong with you, girl?"

"Jesus, Sophie, would you just jack down?"

"Jack down? I have a business to run here. I need two bean tacos, pronto. Try to get it right this time, would you please?"

Carmen got it right that time, almost. Sophie yelled at her again for being too generous with the cheese. Carmen didn't understand why she was being so hyper. What Sophie needed, she thought, was a Valium. This idea took root in her mind and grew on its own for several minutes. The more she thought about it, the more Carmen liked the idea of a calm, benevolent Sophie Roman. She considered simply offering her a Valium—or maybe two—but rejected the idea. Sophie would never agree to take a pill from a prescription bottle without her name on it.

There was another possibility, however. Sophie kept a six-pack of Canada Dry seltzer under the front counter. She always had an open can going, from which she would sip at frequent intervals. All Carmen had to do to mellow her out was to drop a few Valiums in Sophie's seltzer. It made all kinds of sense. Everyone would benefit, even Sophie.

Carmen couldn't believe she'd never thought of this before. She only needed an opportunity, a few seconds when Sophie wasn't paying attention.

* * *

Axel remembered driving his old pickup back over the hole, shutting it down, and climbing the fence again. He remembered being in his new truck. He did not remember driving back across town, but he must have done so, because here he was, clutching his burlap shoulder bag, following a line of people through the gates into the fairgrounds.

Must have gone on autopilot, Axel thought. His mind on his missing money, trying to imagine what Sam would do if he came home to find his backyard full of cash. Would he guess where it had come from? Would he want to know? Or would he just squirrel it away. Just stash it and wait to see if anybody came looking.

Axel's biggest question was, why hadn't Sam mentioned it to him? They'd been friends going on forty years now. If a guy finds a quarter-million dollars cash in his backyard, wouldn't you think he'd want to tell his friends about it? A guy might, but what about Sam O'Gara?

Either someone else had found the money—could be anybody who'd had the good fortune to peek over the fence at the right moment—or Sam didn't want Axel to know he'd found it. Yet if Sam had wanted to conceal the fact that he'd found the money, you'd think he would have filled in the hole, made it look like nothing had happened.

Axel didn't know *what* Sam would do. He had always been like that, especially at the card table. Sam was harder to predict than Minnesota weather. He was a human randomizer, which was what had made him a great cardplayer. As far as Axel knew, Sam could have spent the money, burned it, given it to charity, or tossed it in a closet. Any, all, or none of the above seemed equally possible.

But the money was Axel's. Sam had to know that. It was under Axel's truck.

Thinking back over his friendship with Sam O'Gara, examining it in a way he never had before, Axel searched for chinks, flaws, misunderstandings, hidden resentments. They argued all the time, sure, but wasn't there an underlying trust between them? When it came right down to the nuts, couldn't he count on Sam? Of course he could.

On the other hand—how many hands was he up to now?—Sam had been pretty pissed at him the other day. What had that been about? Money. Sam had been telling him what to do with his money, and Axel had told Sam where to put his advice. He remembered telling Sam that he didn't need his interference, that he could take care of himself.

Well, shit, that had just been talk. They'd been arguing like that for forty years. They were still friends.

Axel caressed the rough exterior of his shoulder bag, felt the rolls of money pressing against the burlap. At least he still had this year's money. He reached into the bag and let his hand rest on the .45. He was passing a Pronto Pup joint. The concessionaire caught his eye, recognized him, gave a nod. Axel's grip tightened on the gun as he nodded back.

He tried to think of what to say when he saw Sam. He tried to simplify it, to reduce the problem to manageable proportions. He might say, "Suppose you lost, say, twenty bucks. Suppose you lost it in your friend's house and your friend finds it. Later you tell him you lost a twenty. He would say, 'I found your twenty. Here it is!'"

Even though you couldn't prove the twenty was yours, he would give it back to you because, for one thing, twenty bucks isn't worth losing a friend over. And he wouldn't have to ask, because you would just give it to him.

Now, make that twenty dollars a larger amount—say a quarter million. Axel put himself in Sam's place. What would he do if he found that much cash buried on his property and, the next day, Sam O'Gara showed up and claimed it was his? How good a friend would he have to be to believe him?

"You wanna know what really pisses me off?"
"No."

"What pisses me off is they made us pay to get back in. Don't that piss you off?"

"No, it doesn't," Dean said.

"I mean, we already paid to get in once. You'd think that'd be enough."

Dean lifted his cowboy hat and scratched the top of his head. His scalp felt odd, as if it were shrinking. Shrinking and itching. Before following Axel back into the fairgrounds, he and Tigger had done another line of Pork's crystal. It had seemed like a good idea at the time, but now he was wondering whether they'd done one line too many. Every time he blinked, the world shifted about a quarter inch up and to the left.

Tigger said, "We shoulda just sneaked in. Just climbed over the fence is what we shoulda done."

"You know what you should do?" Dean said. "You should shut the fuck up."

"I'm just sayin'," Tigger said.

"Well, don't. Just keep an eye on the guy, okay? That four bucks you paid won't add up to nothing. Think of it like an investment. That's what you gotta do."

"It just pisses me off is all."

"Okay, it pisses you off. Hey. Where'd he go?"

"He's still there. He's talking to Carmen."

When Axel stepped into the Taco Shop, Sophie grabbed him by the arm and pulled him back outside.

"She's acting awfully weird, Axel. I think you should take her back to the motel."

"What? Who?" He didn't need this right now. He had more important stuff on his mind. "Where's Sam?" he demanded.

Sophie, not about to be derailed, squeezed his arm and shook it, as if trying to wake him up. "Not Sam! Carmen! She told me I was a cartoon."

"Really?" Axel looked through the door at Carmen. She was making burritos. "She looks okay to me." He pulled his arm away from Sophie. "Where's Sam? Wasn't he helping you out here?"

"If you can call it help. Listen to me, I'm trying to tell you something. There's something wrong with her. I think she's on drugs or something. Just watch her for a few minutes, okay? You'll see what I mean."

"I have to find Sam," Axel said.

"Just wait a goddamn minute. And watch her." Sophie stepped back into the stand and took an order from a customer.

Axel washed his hands and put on an apron. "Was Sam here helping out?" he asked Kirsten.

Kirsten nodded. "He left about twenty minutes ago."

"He said he was gonna take a walk," Carmen said.

"He's gone, thank God," Sophie said. "I need four tacos and one Bueno."

"I need shells," Kirsten said.

Axel loaded the deep fryer and rotated a batch of tortillas into the hot oil. He watched Carmen moving around the stand, building tacos and burritos. She was moving slow, but maybe she was just tired. Maybe Carmen was right, maybe Sophie was too hyper. Axel relaxed, forcing his mind off his missing money, and let himself swing into the rhythm of Axel's Taco Shop, keeping the tortillas cooking, the meat frying, and the burritos rolling. There were four of them in the stand—Axel, Sophie, Carmen, and Kirsten— all working as one. The customers were stacked up out front, food was flying out the window, and money was flowing into the cash box. Axel thought it a bit strange when Carmen called him "Fred," but he didn't worry about it. The restaurant was humming, and for the moment all was right with the world.

He had known it wouldn't last, but he was stunned by how quickly things fell apart. He was lifting the batch of tortillas out of the oil when there was a thump, a squeal, and Sophie shrieking. Axel dropped the rack back into the oil and whirled in time to see Sophie shaking Carmen, holding

257

her by the neck, slamming her back against the cooler. Kirsten was pressed against the counter, her eyes open wide.

"Is it poison? What are you trying to do to me?" Sophie shouted.

Carmen's face was turning red. She was trying to say something. Axel stepped between them, grabbing Sophie's arms and pulling her hands away from Carmen's neck. A small, appreciative crowd had gathered in front of the stand. Axel pushed the two women out the back door.

"What's going on?" he demanded.

Carmen was rubbing her neck. "She choked me," she said.

"She tried to poison me. I caught her putting something in my water."

"Your water? What water?" Axel asked.

"My Canada Dry. She was putting pills in my Canada Dry."

"Is that true?"

Carmen shrugged. "Did you know you look like Fred Flintstone?"

"She's insane. She tried to poison me," Sophie said. "She thinks we're the Flintstones."

"Wait a minute. Back up," Axel said, as much to himself as to them. "Carmen, did you put something in Sophie's water?"

Carmen pushed out her lower lip. "I was just giving her a couple Valiums."

"Dope?" Sophie shrieked. "You were trying to give me *dope?*"

"Just to calm you down a little," said Carmen reasonably.

"You were slipping your mother a mickey?" Axel asked, struggling with the concept.

"Just a couple Valiums." Carmen held up the prescription bottle.

Sophie pointed. "Look. She has them in her hand."

"Let's see," Axel said, reaching for the bottle.

Carmen backed away. "I don't have to. You're a cartoon."

"My God, she's on dope. My daughter's a drug addict."

"Give them to me, Carmen."

Carmen was walking backward. She pushed the bottle into her pocket, turned, and ran away through the crowded mall. Axel and Sophie watched her until she rounded the corner of the Food Building.

"I told you," Sophie said. "We should've just left her fired."

Axel shrugged. "She'll be okay," he said doubtfully.

"Are you kidding? She's on dope. An addict. I'm lucky she hasn't murdered me in my bed and stolen my VCR."

"Don't be silly," Axel said. "Carmen wouldn't hurt a bug."

"Hey, you guys," Kirsten called from the stand. "Are you just going to leave me in here alone?"

CHAPTER

35

It was too bad she hadn't got her mom to take the Valium, and really too bad that Sophie and Axel had busted her. At least they hadn't gotten the pills. Carmen shook the plastic bottle, held it up to the light. Only a few left. Maybe that was okay, seeing as she would probably get fired for real this time. She wouldn't have to work with Sophie anymore, so maybe she wouldn't need the Valium. At the moment, it wasn't something she wanted to worry about. She'd figure something out. Why not relax and enjoy the cartoons? They were the best ever. It was almost like being on acid, only smoother and not so scary. Everything had an outline. Some people became familiar characters. Axel and Sophie as Fred and Wilma Flintstone had been hilarious. Carmen wondered whether she would run into Barney and Betty Rubble. She knew people weren't cartoons, not really, but at the same time, they really *were*. The illusion was at least as convincing as the images on a TV set, and as a bonus, she could make her arms and legs stretch like Plastic Man. She could even float, though not more than a few inches off the ground. It was like wearing antigravity skates. Carmen moved down Carnes Avenue, letting herself drift toward the midway on the crowded, littered street. She was thinking about how it might be fun to go on a few rides, when a figure appeared before her wearing a straw cowboy hat, mirrored sunglasses, and a red paisley bandanna. He put out a hand, palm forward, and she ran into it with her left tit.

The glasses slid down and caught on the tip of his nose, revealing a pair of big brown cartoon eyes.

"Hey there, Carmy," said a familiar voice.

She tried to make him into Elmer Fudd. It didn't work. It was James Dean.

Carmen said, "Guess what?"

"What?"

Nothing occurred to her. "Just a minute." She squeezed her eyes down to slits, blurring his image. She heard another voice.

"What's she doing?"

"She's fucked up on something. Hey, Carmen, snap out of it. I gotta talk to you."

Carmen said, "What do you want?" She had an idea. "You want to go on the Tilt-A-Whirl?" They were on both sides of her now, James Dean and his friend with the big white hat—what was his name? Trigger, like Roy Rogers's horse. Carmen asked him, "Is that a ten-gallon hat?"

"I don't know," he said.

"I gotta go to the bathroom." She started walking again. They fell in on either side of her. "Then I wanna go on the Tilt-A-Whirl."

Dean said, "I do not want to go on the fucking Tilt-A-Whirl."

She ducked her head below the brim of Trigger's white hat and said, "How about you? You want to go on the Tilt-A-Whirl?"

"Those things make me puke. Hey, Dean, what about the guy?"

Dean grabbed Carmen's wrist, jerking her to a halt.

"Hey! I gotta pee, y'know."

"You want I should go back and watch him?"

"Yeah, you do that, and I'll take her to the can."

"Then we go on the Tilt-A-Whirl, okay?"

He squeezed her wrist, really hard. "Fuck the Tilt-A-Whirl, Carmy. Let's go. Talk to me about the man. What happened back there?"

"Sophie got mad." She pulled away, but her wrist was stuck in his hand. They were walking again.

"That bag he's got. You know what's in it?"

"Who?"

"Your taco guy."

"Axel?"

"Yeah. What's he got in the bag?"

"You want me to look?"

He seemed surprised. "You think you could?"

"Sure I could. Only I really gotta go to the bathroom, okay?"

The restrooms by the Giant Slide were in a long wooden structure, with entrances at both ends of the building. A line of women waited at the south entrance.

"I'll be just a minute."

He released her, and she squeezed past the women in line and pushed her way into the building, oblivious to the stares and comments from women who had been waiting for twenty minutes. She walked past the row of toilets, past the sinks, and out the opposite end of the building, where she turned toward the midway. She wanted to immerse herself in the flashing and the shouting and the overamped rock and roll. She needed to get back to cartoon land as soon as possible. Those skinhead cowboys, they were no fun. If she wanted to answer a bunch of questions, she'd have stayed at the Taco Shop.

Dean lifted his hat by its crown and fanned himself with it. "This fucking sun," he remarked to no one. He moved toward the shade of the Giant Slide, found a light pole to lean against, and examined his surroundings. His senses had become so acute that each blade of trampled grass stood out against its neighbors. An old guy in bib overalls and a green baseball cap stood a few yards away, hands buried in his pockets, looking at him. The old man nodded when he caught Dean's eye.

"Hot one, ain't she?" he called out in a cracked voice.

Dean gave the guy a cold stare, then returned his attention to the restroom entrance. What the hell was Carmen doing in there? He amused himself by fixing his gaze on a teenage girl waiting in line outside the restroom. If he focused, he felt, he could make her turn toward him. Lock eyes with her. He felt a presence behind him, turned his head. The guy with the green hat, inches away, an unlit cigarette in his mouth.

"You got a light, Mac?" The hair on his jaw was about the same length as the hair on Dean's head. They both needed a shave.

Dean said, "Get lost."

"What, you don't got a light?"

Dean took a quick look at the restrooms. No Carmen.

The old man said, "You waitin' on your gal?"

Dean stabbed a forefinger at the old man's chest. "What did I just tell you?"

The old man laughed.

"You think that's funny?" Dean said. He squeezed his right hand into a fist, thinking about letting the guy have it—bam!—right in the nose.

The old man widened his eyes and puffed out his ~~wer~~ lip, causing the unlit cigarette to point straight up ~~s left~~ eye. He scratched the underside of his chin. "G~~, y'know.~~ he said. "Women is funny. Use to have one ~~ntermelons.~~ Built like a fuckin' Cadillac, bazooms li~~cheek and a~~ Had a tattoo of an M-1 rifle on her l~~le was Tricksy.~~ birthmark the shape of Texas on t'oth~~in think of 'cept~~ Gal was fast as lightning every w~~just to take a leak.~~ for one. Used to take her twenty~~er lip moving up and~~ Fuckin' women. You go figur~~

Dean stared at the old m~~

down as he absorbed what he was hearing. The guy had eyes about six different colors, and more wrinkles than a ton of raisins. As Dean watched, the cigarette migrated from one side of his mouth to the other, bobbing up and down like a snake charmer's flute.

Axel had once seen a TV show about people who exploded. It had been one of those shows where they tell about UFOs and werewolves and people who can bend nails with their minds. Stuff he didn't really believe. But the segment about people who exploded—not *exploded*, really, just sort of burst into flames—had sounded very scientific and convincing. They even had a scientific name for it, he remembered: spontaneous human combustion.

At the time, Axel had wondered what those people who exploded felt like just before it happened. Now he thought he knew. They felt like this.

His nest egg, all the money he'd managed to accumulate over the past twenty-five years, had been dug up by a couple of dogs, and the only person who *might* be able to return it to him, Sam O'Gara, had also disappeared. And *Sophie*— he'd never seen her like this before. She was raging, muttering under her breath, slamming things around the restaurant. Kirsten was so shook up she was screwing up every order, making tacos into tostadas, nachos into burros, and giving people Sprite when they'd ordered iced tea. Carmen was wandering the fairgrounds with a pocketful of dope. He wanted to run after Carmen and lock her in her room, where he'd be safe. He wanted to find Sam, find him and grab him by the ankles and shake loose his money. He wanted. But a thousand miles away from Sophie and her anger. But line in from wouldn't have any of that, because there was a needed—But the restaurant, people who wanted—who had made for burritos. He was trapped inside a cage he afraid he would and if something didn't give, he was fied crowd of fair leaving behind nothing but a horri- a charred spot on the restaurant floor. They would write about it in the *Enquirer*, and only fools like him would believe it to be true. But it would be.

"You're crazy," Axel muttered as he started building a row of six Buenos.

Sophie said, "What?" Hands like claws, ready to pounce on him.

"I was talking to myself," he said. Jesus Christ, he'd better be careful. He wasn't the only one ready to blow. One wrong word, a single bad burrito, a fly landing on the wrong person's nose at the wrong time—it was the goddamn Middle East, all packed inside a hundred eighty square feet. He felt the weight of the .45 in his pocket, tugging down on his right suspender. Every time he moved, it rubbed the outside of his thigh. Looking up from his work, he rolled his neck and let his eyes play across the crowded mall. He picked his way from face to face. Even after twenty-five years, they still looked like individuals to him. Then he saw a green cap making its bobbing progress in the direction of the Taco Shop, and for a moment he felt it, an intense burning sensation, just above his belly, hot enough to ignite human flesh.

Sophie had always wanted one of those *Shit Happens* bumper stickers. She saw them all the time, but she didn't know where to buy one. It was so true, especially now. It came in waves, like the weather. When had it started? She tried to think back. Even as she smiled at her customers, took their money, pushed their food across the counter, and shouted instructions at Kirsten and Axel, a part of her, hen was reviewing the last few days, trying to remember, rmen this latest shit storm had rolled in. Was it when it when arrived from Omaha? When the fair started? Cd feelings Axel made her a partner? She was having an? And in about that. Ten percent a year. What did ork. In years the meantime, she was doing most the Taco Shop, past, Axel had spent most of ever · · · This year, doing whatever needed doing. P every time she turned around he was going somewhere, or gone, or just standing out back, doing nothing at all. Like he thought now he had a partner he didn't have to hold up his end anymore. Well, if he didn't care enough about the business to do his share, then the hell with him. Telling her she was crazy, when he was the one acting like a jerk. There was this other bumper sticker she liked: *Don't like my driving? Call 1-800-EAT-SHIT.* As long as she was the one running this restaurant, he was going to have to help out, and not just for a few minutes here and there. Sophie turned around, thinking to share her thoughts with Axel whether he liked it or not. But Axel was gone, his apron hanging by the door, still moving.

CHAPTER

36

There was only one thing Sam could have said that would have prevented Axel from asking about his missing money, and he said it.

"Hey, Ax, I think I just met up with that guy you was telling me about. Your Bald Monkey fella. Just talked to him. Doggin' that little gal a yours, all dressed up like Roy Rogers."

"You—you *what* him?" Axel shook his head, trying to make sense of what he was hearing. "You mean, he's here?"

"I'd a grabbed 'im, only I wasn't a hundred percent sure I was dealing with the right asshole."

"Got his head shaved, right?"

"Yeah, only he's wearing one a them cheap cowboy hats."

"Got a cut on his eyebrow?"

"Couldn't see. He's wearing his Foster Grants. Your little gal, she gave 'im the slip. C'mon." Sam turned and started walking away.

Axel blinked back his confusion and followed, his eyes on the sagging seat of Sam's overalls. The crotch hung low, about eight inches north of his knees. Sam walked with a hip-swinging gait, each movement of his legs forming a shallow arc, as if he was trying to avoid chafing. Or like a toddler carrying a load in his diaper.

Axel hurried forward and came up alongside Sam, who had settled into a brisk waddle.

"What do you mean, she gave him the slip? Was he chasing her?" Confusion was becoming anger; he put a hand in his pocket and gripped the .45 to keep it from abrading his thigh.

"Don't think so."

"Where are we going? You know where they went?"

"Once he realized she'd got away, he asked me where was the Tilt-A-Whirl, then headed off toward the midway."

"You're sure it was the same guy?"

Sam shrugged.

"So it might not be him."

"Might not be. Only how many bald-headed friends can Carmen have?"

Axel did not reply. He really didn't know. The Ferris wheel, at the entrance to the midway, loomed above them. Beyond lay a quarter-mile-long, U-shaped gauntlet of rides and games, and a milling crowd of cash-carrying suckers being willingly harvested by an organized gang of carnies.

"There must be ten thousand people here," Axel said.

"Just look for a straw cowboy hat," Sam said.

"Maybe we ought to split up."

Sam grabbed Axel by the elbow. "Hold on, Ax. Talk to me here. What are you plannin' on doin' once we find 'im?"

Axel caressed the slide of the .45, slick with sweat and gun oil.

"I just want to make sure Carmen's okay. Get her back to the stand."

"What about the guy?"

Axel said, "You go down the right side. I'll go this way." He entered the midway, moving quickly, not looking back at Sam. As soon as he had passed through the gate, the decibel level climbed. Every ride hammered the crowd with rock and roll—overamped tape loops of heavy-metal electric guitar clawed at his ears. Axel didn't know any of the songs. To his ears it was noise, the same jarring, discordant crap Carmen liked. He tried to ignore the music and concentrate on looking at every face under a cowboy hat. There were a lot of them. Cowboy hats were big this year. Every one he saw produced another surge of adrenaline. He concentrated on keeping his cool. Tommy was dead, and he couldn't change that. Tommy had already killed his killer. Axel's priority had to be Carmen. If she was on dope, she needed his help, whether she was with Bald Monkey or not.

Cowboy hat, dead ahead.

Axel picked up his pace, came up beside the cowboy-hatted figure, caught a look at his profile.

Another blank, blond and bearded. He relaxed his grip on the gun.

As he was walking past a wheel game, a horn-shaped speaker blasted in his ear. "Every playah a winnah!" Axel veered away from the game. "Only way to lose is to not play the game," the mike man called after him.

He decided to continue down the length of the midway and meet up with Sam. If they hadn't found Carmen by then, then he'd say the hell with it and get back to the stand. He was passing the Headless Woman joint when something caused him to stop and look behind him.

White cowboy hat, a few paces behind him. Axel took three quick steps and snatched the oversize hat. The kid let out a yell and jumped back. The front of his shirt read: *Let's Rodeo*. His head was shaved like a new recruit, but it was the wrong kid. This one had a pointy nose and tiny, startled eyes. Axel let his breath hiss out.

"Sorry," he mumbled.

The kid grabbed his hat. His small eyes narrowed. "Crazy old fucker," he said in a nasal whine. He smashed the hat back onto his head and backed up a few steps.

"I thought you were somebody else," Axel said.

"You been eatin' too many tacos, old man." The kid took a few steps to the side, then continued up the midway, looking back over his shoulder every few steps.

Axel felt ridiculous. He was suddenly sure that that was the bald kid Sam had spotted. How many cowboy-hatted skinheads could there be? He shook his head and forced himself to smile. Wild-goose chase. He pulled his gun hand from his pocket and rolled his shoulders, willing the tension from his body, watching the white hat bob and disappear up ahead. The clamoring rock and roll, the clanking of the rides, the hammering of the generators, the voices and shouts and happy screams, all blended together. Carmen, he decided, had probably gone back to the Motel 6. It was time for him to return to the stand, time to take care of business.

He was thinking about how many tortillas he would need to get through the last weekend, when an unwelcome thought wriggled into his conscious mind. Something that kid had said. Something about eating too many tacos.

Dean found Carmen standing in line, waiting to board the Tilt-A-Whirl. An old AC/DC tune blasted from the speakers mounted on both sides of the ride. He cut in, draping an arm over her shoulder. She rolled her sleepy eyes toward him and said, "Where'd you go?"

"Didn't go anywhere, Carmy. Where'd *you* go?" He flexed his arm, pulling her face into his chest, giving her head a gentle squeeze. She felt loose, like wet clay.

She said, "You want to go with me on the Tilt-A-Whirl?"

"Sure, why not?" Maybe it would wake her up a little.

The more Axel thought about it, the more it bothered him. Why would the kid say anything about tacos if he didn't know Axel was in the taco business? And how would he know that Axel was in the taco business? Axel picked up his pace, weaving through the crowd, trying to relocate the white hat. He was nearing the end of the midway, where he'd have to turn and go back up the other side.

There. He broke into a run. The .45 slapped against his thigh. He felt something rip, stopped, reached in his pocket. The thin fabric had given way; the barrel of the gun now poked through a hole at the bottom of the pocket, hanging down to his knee. Axel looked around, saw no one watching, and pulled out the gun, turning his pocket liner inside out. He wedged the gun into his waistband, tugged loose his shirttails to cover the protruding grip.

The cowboy hat was no longer visible. Axel decided to cut across the center island, between the Gravitron and the Tilt-A-Whirl, and head the kid off as he came up the other side. He ducked through a yellow bally-cloth divider. The area between the rides was a jungle of snakelike electrical cables. Above him to his right, the Gravitron, an enormous saucer-shaped device covered with flashing yellow, red, and green lights, was picking up speed. Axel wasn't sure what happened to the people who entered the ride, but they always looked a little sick when they exited. The Tilt-A-Whirl, to his left, seemed tame by comparison.

Axel picked his way over the cables, reached the other side, and climbed the low fence. Before him, the canvas front of the Cavalcade of Human Oddities stretched for fifty feet in either direction. Each performer was depicted in a series of crude but exciting painted banners. The Pretzel Girl, shown with her limbs tied in pretzel-like knots. Tortura, the Puncture-Proof Girl. The Human Blast Furnace. Serpentina, the Snake Woman. Axel had met Serpentina, an old friend of Tommy's. She was also playing Electra, Mistress of the Megawatt, this year. Behind him, the Tilt-A-Whirl clanked into life. The kid could be anywhere. He might've gone into the Hard Rock Funhouse or one of the other attractions, or ducked between the rides as Axel had, or simply taken off his hat and melted into the crowd. The rattling and clattering of the Tilt-A-Whirl became louder. Axel moved away from the noise, throwing a glance back at the undulating, whirling platform. Something caught his eye. A cowboy hat, in one of the Tilt-A-Whirl's spinning tubs. It was there, then it was gone. He squinted, trying to track the spinning cupola. The hat appeared again, and then he saw Carmen, screaming, her eyes wide. The tub whirled, and they were gone.

The effect, when the ride was operating, was both elegant and bewildering. The tub swept by again, but this time facing the other way. Axel couldn't see them. On the third sweep they appeared again. He stepped to the side, followed their tub with his eyes through its looping course up and around. Carmen was screaming. She looked terrified. What was the kid doing to her? He was grabbing her, holding on to her, shouting at her.

"Let go!" Dean pried Carmen's hands away from his body, held them. His ear was ringing from her screams. Crazy bitch.

"Eeee!" she shrieked, her mouth a distended grin.

Dean closed his eyes, willing the ride to end, hoping he wouldn't ralph all over himself. He had business to take care of, and here he was on the Tilt-A-Whirl, having his guts scrambled.

Carmen shrieked again, sending a needle of sound tunneling into his right ear. He turned his head away and opened his eyes to a blurry, striped world of garish, rushing color. He clamped his jaw tight and shut his eyes again. He couldn't decide which was worse. Just when he thought he wasn't going to make it, the spinning slowed and the Tilt-A-Whirl slowed. The blurred horizon took form. The tub rocked to a complete stop. He tried to get out, but the safety bar remained locked across the top of his thighs.

Carmen said, "You got to wait for the guy to come let us out."

Dean had about had it with her. He said, "I oughta fuckin' smack you for getting me on this thing."

"You better not."

"Oh?" Did she *want* to get hit?

Carmen pointed. He followed her finger, at first seeing

nothing, then, standing at the exit gate, the old man, staring up at him, less than thirty feet away. He was holding the pistol in both hands, not even attempting to conceal it. Dean twisted, trying to get his legs out from under the lap restraint.

"Ow! What are you doing?" Carmen said.

"I got to get out of here."

He had one leg out from under the bar.

Carmen waved. "Hey, Axel!"

"Move the fuck over!" Dean shouted.

"He's not gonna shoot you," Carmen said. "At least I don't think he is."

Axel had time to think while he was keeping his sights on Bald Monkey, but he was trying not to. The hot, animal flush felt too good. He fantasized pulling the trigger again and again. For Tommy. For Carmen. For the hell of it. Could he make the shot? Forty years ago he could have, but now he would be as likely to hit Carmen—or somebody else—as he was to hit his target. He thought about this and other technical aspects of shooting. He didn't let himself think about the consequences of a successful shot other than to imagine the monkey falling through the air, crumpled like a well-shot canvasback.

Carmen smiled and waved. The scene had become unreal to Axel; he felt as if he was watching himself go through motions. He had felt this way when Tommy got shot—like he wasn't really there. Like someone else was making his decisions.

The feeling of unreality intensified when the monkey got loose, dashed across the metal surface of the Tilt-A-Whirl, toward the edge. He had him now; nothing in his sights but bald monkey and blue sky. He was squeezing the trigger when something hit him hard under the elbow. The .45 boomed and kicked and sent a round up into the air. Someone behind him. Axel brought his elbow back, hit something, heard a grunt, then felt his leg give way. He was falling before the pain in his knee reached his brain. The instant his butt hit the asphalt, two hands scooped under his armpits, lifting him back onto his feet, pushing him forward.

"Let's go, Ax. You can walk, can'cha?"

"Sam?" Axel took a step, nearly fell again. "He was there, Sam, I saw him!" He pointed at the Tilt-A-Whirl, where Carmen, still locked into her seat, sat staring at them, her mouth hanging loose.

Sam wrapped Axel's right arm over his shoulder. "C'mon, buddy. Let's get moving." He started forward, half dragging Axel.

"What the hell happened?" Axel said. "I had him, I had the little bastard in my sights. Somebody ran into me. Wait." He stopped. "My gun. Somebody grabbed it."

"That was me, you dumb fuck." Sam slapped the front pocket of his overalls. "You can have it back later."

"I—you did that? Ow, not so fast. My knee!"

"You were gonna shoot him! Right there in front of everybody. Christ, Ax, my dogs've got more sense than that. You want to go to jail?"

Axel tested his leg, transferring weight to it, leaning forward, quickly bringing the other foot around. He could walk on it. Sort of. If he hung tight to Sam.

"What about Carmen?"

"Just keep moving. She'll be fine. We've got to get you out of here."

"I had him," Axel said.

"Yeah, well, you're damn lucky you didn't get him."

The ride boy was confused. "What was that all about?" he asked.

Carmen ignored him, stepped out of the cupola shakily, and walked down the ramp. Where had they gone? She had seen Axel, and then Sam had knocked him over, and Dean had jumped off the Tilt-A-Whirl, then she was all alone. It was too confusing to think about. She guessed that if not for the Valium, she would be pretty upset right about now. As it was, she was just miffed that they had both left without her.

The midway felt too hot and too close. The people were no longer cartoons; they were sweaty, ugly animals. She felt greasy and gritty, and her T-shirt was chafing under her arms. She continued up the midway past the Cavalcade of Human Oddities. The sword swallower was doing his teaser routine, giving the gawkers something to look at as the mike man described the collection of bizarre humanity waiting inside the tent, willing to reveal all for the price of a ticket. Carmen watched the sword swallower insert the blade deep into his body, then pull it out shiny with olive oil and saliva. Her T-shirt was really bothering her. She tried pulling her arms in. Struggling, she was able to get her right arm back through the sleeve hole, but then her arm was stuck inside the T-shirt, pressed against her body, and she could not figure out how to get it back out through the sleeve. She turned around in a circle, twice, but found the situation unchanged. One hand was sticking out the bottom of the shirt. It occurred to her then that she was going to a lot of trouble for nothing, so she pulled the bottom of the shirt up over her head.

That felt much better. Carmen draped the T-shirt over her shoulder. People were looking at her. Even the sword swallower, who had lost his audience, was staring. Carmen shrugged and walked away. People were weird. The air felt soft on her breasts, just like when she'd been a little kid, wading in Tanners Lake.

CHAPTER

37

For a second there, Tigger thought the guy had fuckin' shot James Dean. He imagined himself telling it. The guy's pointin' this gun, and then this other old dude, like, hits him! Fuckin' gun goes off: *Ka-boom!* Deano goes flying right off the fuckin' Tilt-A-Whirl, man, and it's like he got shot, but then I see Dean running like a fuckin' deer, man. And these old guys, they're limpin' the fuck off, like maybe one of 'em got shot in the fuckin' foot.

It was a good story, only Tigger couldn't think who he'd tell it to, what with Sweety and Pork gone. And Dean—if he ever caught up to him—Dean probably wouldn't think it was funny. Oh, well. He knew some other guys he could tell it to. Only now he had to make a decision—should he keep following the taco guy, like Dean said, or should he go after Dean, get the hell out of there?

Since he'd lost sight of Dean, he decided to go with the taco guy.

The first thing Sophie thought—seeing them like that, Axel hanging on Sam, staggering up the mall—was that they'd gone off and gotten drunk. Middle of the day, busy as hell, and they'd gone off and split a bottle. Sophie could feel the red blooming on her cheeks. She knew what she looked like when she got mad, but it wasn't as if she could stop it, and anyways, she'd got to where she didn't even want to stop it. This entire fair had been a disaster from the get-go. People getting killed, her worthless daughter trying to poison her, Sam O'Gara mangling tortillas by the dozen, and—worst of all—Axel spending practically no time in the stand, helping out. If this was what it was like being a partner, she didn't want any part of it. Turning her back to the approaching pair, Sophie regarded the cramped food preparation area, where Kirsten was frantically assembling an order. She lowered her eyes to the floor. Small particles of food peppered the brick-patterned linoleum surface: bits of orange cheese, sliced green and black olive, shredded lettuce, congealing crumbs of fatty ground beef. About five tacos' worth of filling. Soon it would be up to their ankles.

I could quit, she thought. The concept shivered her spine with orgasmic intensity. She could just walk away. That was it. When Axel walked in through that door, she'd drape her apron over his drunken skull and walk away. Go find a real job, something in an air-conditioned office where men wore suits and paychecks arrived every Friday at 4:30 P.M. and the floor wasn't covered with organic matter.

Kirsten said, "You okay?"

Sophie jerked herself back to the present. "I'm fine," she snapped.

"What's wrong with Mr. Speeter?"

Sophie followed Kirsten's pointing finger. At first, she didn't see him. "Where'd he go?"

"On that bench," Kirsten said.

There he was, sitting with his leg stretched out along the length of the bench.

"Hey, Soph!" It was Sam, standing behind her, in the doorway. Without Axel draped over his shoulder, he didn't look so drunk anymore.

"Don't call me that," Sophie said.

277

Sam bumped up his eyebrows, drew a malformed Pall Mall from somewhere inside his overalls, and fitted it to his mouth. "What you want I should call you? Her Holiness Madame Priss-Butt?"

Sophie's teeth clacked together. That was it. She was out of there, right now. She reached back to untie her apron.

Sam said, "Listen, before you go all lady-of-the-fucking-manor on me, how about you make up an ice pack for your partner out there. He's got himself a knee that's gonna be the size of a cantaloupe, he don't get some chill on it."

Sophie felt her anger begin to crumble. "He . . . what happened?"

"We ran into Carmen and her little no-hair friend, and old Ax, he had hisself an accident."

Kirsten was already filling a towel with crushed ice. It was just like making burritos—you got better with practice.

The younger cop, the tall one, was enjoying himself, but the older cop looked angry, embarrassed, and unhappy.

"Put your shirt on," he said, keeping his eyes averted.

"Okay," Carmen said. "Keep *your* shirt on." She laughed.

The younger cop, staring at her tits, laughed too. His partner glared at him. Carmen shook out her T-shirt and looked at it. It was inside out.

"It's inside out," she said. They were standing near the head of the midway, surrounded by gaping fairgoers. Carmen grinned at her audience and waved the shirt back and forth over her head.

"Just put the shirt on, honey."

"Are you going to take me to jail?"

"We just want you to put your shirt on."

"You should take it easy," said Carmen, pulling the shirt over her head. "You want something to calm you down? You look really unhappy."

"Are you going to keep your shirt on?" the older cop asked.

Carmen shrugged. "Is he always so uptight?" she asked the younger cop.

The cop smiled and looked away. His partner scowled at him, then looked back at Carmen, who was scratching her left breast through the T-shirt. He turned to his partner. "What do you think?"

The small crowd was dispersing.

"We'd have to walk her all the way back up there." He pointed. "I say forget it. It's not worth it." He turned to Carmen, put his hands on her shoulders, and spoke directly into her smiling face. "How about it, lady—are you going to keep your shirt on?" he asked Carmen. "Will you promise us that?"

Carmen was trying to get something out of her jeans pocket.

"We asked you a question," said the older cop.

Carmen got the bottle from her pocket, opened it, and shook two Valiums onto her palm. She offered them to the older cop. "Here," she said, "eat these. You'll feel better. You really will."

One time Tigger had gone to work for a temp agency, and they had sent him to this factory where all day long he loaded little white cardboard boxes into big brown cardboard boxes. He earned thirty-eight dollars for eight hours, then spent it all that same night at The Recovery Room, trying to wipe out the memory. It hadn't worked. He still had nightmares about that day, the white-into-brown-cardboard-box day, the most boring day of his life.

Sitting watching the taco guy was almost as bad. All the guy did was sit in his chair, holding a towel on his leg. Tigger, sitting on the grass up near the top of the sloped mall, could see the guy's foot. He had been looking at that foot for almost an hour. It hadn't moved an inch. And the other old guy, he was in the taco stand, working. That was boring too. Tigger really wanted to leave, since it was obvious the guy wasn't going anywhere, but he kept thinking how pissed Dean would be if he left. He didn't think he'd ever forget the sound of the steel crowbar hitting Pork's skull. Tigger had been in lots of fights and stuff, but he'd never heard anything like that before and he hoped he never did again. He kept remembering it, the sound, and thinking it was like the sound when you hold on to an ice cream cone too tight. When it shatters and you get ice cream all over yourself. That wasn't exactly the sound, but it was as close as he could come.

No, he didn't want to get Dean pissed off at him.

But Dean had run. The guy had shot at him and he had run. Did that mean Tigger was supposed to run too? He didn't know. But he did know that watching a guy's foot was cardboard-box boring. After a time—Tigger didn't know how long it had been or what had finally inspired him to move—he stood up and headed for the gate. The farther he got from the taco guy, the better he felt. This whole deal was getting too weird, what with people getting shot and everything. Maybe it was time to move back in with his dad again, see if the old son-of-a-bitch had mellowed out in the past six months. By the time he got to his car, he'd almost decided to do it. Just show up at his dad's house on Selby, walk right in, see what happened.

As he was unlocking the car door he decided. That was what he would do. If Dean wanted to take off the taco guy, then he could do it without Timothy Alan Skeller. Tigger opened the car door and slid in behind the wheel. He was all the way in before he realized that he was not alone.

Dean, slumped in the back seat, said, "Where the fuck *you* been?"

Tigger jumped, whacking his thighs on the steering wheel. "How'd you get in here?" he asked. Then he noticed the glass on the passenger seat, and the missing window. "You broke my window, man."

"Don't worry about your window. Taco Man's gonna buy you a whole new car."

"I don't want a new car, man. Besides, the dude's got a fuckin' *gun,* man. And he ain't afraid to use it. He *shot* at you, man. I fuckin' saw it."

"Yeah, well, he missed me, didn't he."

"He missed you on account of the other old guy *made* him miss."

Dean sat up and leaned over the seat back. "Reason he missed me," he said, "is on account of I got the fuck out of the way." He took the cowboy hat from Tigger's head and sailed it out the window. "Now start the car."

"Why? Where we going?"

"Just start the fucking car. I'll tell you where to go."

Tigger said, "I don't think I wanna."

"Yes you do."

After seven-plus decades of living, Axel had thought that he had experienced all the emotions his body was capable of producing. He had plumbed the dark, bottomless depths of terror, sailed the heights of pleasure and joy, waded through swamps of anger and disgust, and baked in the desert of despair. But he'd never felt like this before, as if the reins had been severed, as if the brake lines had ruptured, as if he was watching himself flail at life without purpose or effect. When things were going badly, Axel's thoughts took a literary turn. If life was a metaphor, perhaps he had the power to change it.

What if he had shot the kid? What if he'd killed him? Cold radiated up his leg from the ice pack on his knee. He would have gone to jail. The thought shivered his spine. Other thoughts, perhaps even worse, threatened to surface.

Feeling eyes on him, he tipped his head back and found Sophie standing in the doorway to the Taco Shop.

"How are you feeling?" she asked.

"I'm fine," he said.

Sophie shook her head. "She's a big girl, Axel. There's only so much we can do."

Axel felt his eyes heat up; he turned his face away from Sophie and blinked rapidly. She thought he was worried about Carmen. Hell, he hadn't even been *thinking* about Carmen. He'd been thinking about himself. Poor Carmen, wandering around out there by herself or—even worse—not by herself. What an all-time shitty day. He felt Sophie step back into the restaurant, heard her say something to Sam.

Damn.

Sam.

The other thing he was trying not to think about. The hole in Sam's backyard. Axel drew a deep breath, waiting for the fear and anger to hit him but feeling nothing beyond a sort of dull, distant thudding, the sound of a flaccid heart herding blood through a network of aging vessels. Not long ago that heart had been hammering, powered by the need for vengeance, driving a rage that had nearly caused him to commit murder. Now such emotion seemed unreal and impossible. He felt nothing other than weariness and the unpleasant pulsing from his swollen knee. The fact that his entire fortune had disappeared seemed meaningless. He knew he had to ask Sam about it, but he was afraid of what he might hear. Better, for the moment, not to know. Either Sam had the money and he would give it back, or he had it and he wouldn't, or the dogs had eaten it, or someone else had taken it. It didn't matter. What mattered was the fact that he did not seem to care. He'd lost his edge.

"I think we should take him to see a doctor," Sophie whispered.

"He don't want no doctor," Sam said. "Leave him be."

"He's just sitting out there staring. Did he get hit on the head or something?"

"He'll be okay. He's just noodlin'." Sam finished folding a lumpy Bueno Burrito. A glob of guacamole oozed out from a tear in the tortilla. A few hours earlier, Sophie wouldn't have dreamed of serving such an abortion to one of her customers, but now she simply watched as Sam wrapped it and handed it to a waiting Kirsten.

"What about his leg? He can hardly walk."

Sam said, "It'll get better or it'll get worser. Leave him be."

"I think he's worried about Carmen."

"Maybe he is, maybe he ain't. Maybe he's just pooped."

Sophie thought, Axel's worrying about my daughter, and I'm worrying about Axel, and Sam doesn't seem worried about anything. Thank God Kirsten is just doing her job, or this business would fall apart. She returned her thoughts to the restaurant. There was a small line in front of the window. One at a time, she said to herself wearily. Just keep on serving, and in time everyone will get fed. It had gotten to where all the customers' faces had morphed into a single identity-free blob. A couple of hours ago, when she had almost decided to quit the Taco Shop, much of the state fair energy had leaked out of her. But Axel's getting hurt, that had changed everything. She couldn't leave him hurt, couldn't let the business collapse. She wished, though, she could get that energy back.

She wanted Axel on his feet again. Seeing him sit on his folding chair with his leg out, his face sagging, his eyes staring across the mall toward the boarded-up Tiny Tot Donuts stand—it was hard to take.

"Can I help you?" she asked the next face in line.

The customer did not reply. Sophie forced herself to focus, to see the person more clearly. A woman. As her features came into focus, Sophie had a startled moment when she thought it was her mother, who had died nearly ten years before. The face displayed the same pinched nose, cold blue eyes, and determined, jutting jaw. But this woman was taller and had a large supply of gray-blond hair piled atop her head. A red spot burned high on each pale cheek.

Sophie smiled at her and repeated, "Can I help you?"

The woman's eyes were fixed on something behind her. Sophie turned her head and saw Kirsten pressed back against the stainless-steel cooler, staring wide-eyed at the angry customer.

Kirsten licked her lips. "Hi, Mom," she said in a small voice.

CHAPTER

38

By seven-thirty, Bill Quist had checked in his last guest. He turned on the NO VACANCY sign, used the vending machine keys to score himself three cans of Coke and a handful of candy bars, and settled in to watch a rerun of the *X-Files* episode where the guy with the pointy nose discovers that webbing has appeared between his toes. Quist liked *The X-Files*. In particular, he liked the guy with the pointy nose's partner, what's-her-name, the one with the bazooms. He liked her lower lip, the way it hung there almost quivering. And he liked how big her head was, too. The guy with the pointy nose, he had this little head, but the partner, she had this huge head. Quist imagined her as eight feet tall, acting the part on her knees.

He really liked *The X-Files*.

So he was sort of pissed when the bell on the lobby door dinged—just when the pointy-nose guy was showing his webbing to his partner. Probably some guy with a stupid question, or needing change, or some jerk who didn't believe the NO VACANCY sign. He kept his eyes glued to the TV, refusing to look away for a simple door ding. Maybe it was just somebody come in to use the vending machines. Maybe they'd just go away.

Then he heard the most irritating sound in the entire universe. The goddamn bell on the counter. Usually he hid the damn thing during his shift, but he'd forgotten and now they were dinging it. Not just once, but over and over: *Ding. Ding. Ding. Ding. Ding.*

He said, still not turning around, "I hear you. Just hold on." Big-head was touching the toe webbing. Man, did that send a tingle up his thigh!

Ding. Ding. Ding.

Quist spun around in his chair and looked up over the counter. "I said hold on!"

Ding.

It took maybe half a second for his eyes to go from the bell to the hand to the face. Shit, it was that punk kid hung out with that Carmen, old Axel's girlfriend or daughter or whatever the hell she was.

Ding. Standing there with his shaved head and his shitty little smile, hand suspended over the chrome bell.

Ding.

There was another one too, a scrawny, pimply kid, sitting in one of the chairs, scratching his neck.

Ding.

Quist stood up and approached the counter, picked up the bell, and put it in a drawer.

"I need a key," the kid said.

Quist shook his head. "No can do," he said. "You're eighty-sixed. Mr. Speeter told me so." He was of two minds. One mind was telling him that was that, the kid stays out of the guests' rooms. The other mind was wondering how much cash the kid might be able to come up with if he really wanted access.

Turned out the kid was of a third mind. Quist tried to step back, but the end of a crowbar snagged his neck like a stage hook and jerked him toward the counter.

* * *

With Kirsten gone, the Taco Shop was in serious trouble. Sophie put it to Axel this way: "If you can stand, you can help. If you can't, we might as well just close up."

Axel said, "It's only eight o'clock. We never close at eight."

"We need your help."

Sam's voice came from inside the Taco Shop. "Hold your horses there, young fella. I only got so goddamn many hands, y'know. You sure you wouldn't rather have a taco?"

Axel sighed and tried to stand up. His knee had a solid, heavy feel to it, as if packed with cement. He eased some weight onto it. For a moment, it felt all right, then a sharp pain lanced from the joint right up his thigh. He grabbed the edge of the doorway.

"I need a cane or something," he said.

Sam appeared in the doorway. "Hey, you two. I got my hands full up to my elbows here."

"He needs a cane, he says," said Sophie.

Sam stepped out of the stand. "You hang on there, Ax. I'll be back in a jiff." He set off toward the Tiny Tot Donut stand. Sophie ducked back inside, leaving Axel clinging to the doorway.

Sam returned in less than a minute, swinging the green yardstick cane that Tommy had taken away from Bald Monkey. He handed it to Axel, then helped him into the restaurant, propped him up against the prep table.

"Waiting on one tostada, two bean, one Bueno," Sophie said.

Axel began to assemble the order, slowly at first, then picking up speed as his body rediscovered familiar rhythms.

"What you want me to do?" Sam asked him.

"I don't care."

Sam scratched his three-day-old beard. "Maybe I shoulda let you shoot the monkey," he said.

Axel stopped moving his arms and gave Sam a nothing

look. "You could fry up some shells," he said. Within minutes, they had developed a sort of system, and the production line began to shuffle along.

Tigger wanted to say, Man, I don't hardly know you no more. Only thing was, he didn't really know the dude in the first place anyways, so why should it surprise him the guy turns out to be this psycho nut. Tearing the room apart, snarling and muttering about coffee cans full of money. Sure, there were plenty of coffee cans, but forget about money. All they found was socks and underwear and a bunch of other junk, which was now scattered all over the floor. He was starting to think the money was just a figment somehow got stuck in Dean's head. James Dean the psycho nut, now sitting on the bed with a crowbar on his lap, reading fucking poetry. Tigger shivered and tried to listen to what Dean was saying. Not that it made any sense.

Dean read, *"Unvirtuous weeds might long unvexed have stood . . ."* He paused. "What do you think, Tig?"

Tigger said, "What's unvexed?"

"Like the motel guy. He's unvexed at us."

"It means, like, pissed off?"

"Right. And I'm unvexed too. And I'm gonna stay unvexed until I get my hands on that taco man's money. Listen. *But he's short liv'd, that with his death can doe most good."*

Tigger did his damnedest to look as if he agreed, even though he was afraid that what Dean was saying was that somebody else was going to get killed pretty soon. He'd gotten to the point where the money seemed unreal. All he wanted now was to get out of this deal alive. The money didn't matter.

Dean asked, "So what are you going to do, Tig, you get a couple hundred thousand bucks in cash? You gonna buy yourself a new car?"

Tigger thought for a moment. He kind of liked the idea of one of those big black Dodge pickups with the big engine and the big wheels and the lights up top. Maybe the money mattered some after all.

"I was thinking maybe this truck I seen," he said.

Axel stood outside the restaurant and watched Sophie closing the food bins and fitting the perishables into the cooler. She looked exhausted. He wanted to say something to her, but he couldn't think what it was. Using his yardstick cane, he limped around to the front. His good leg, the one doing all the work, was giving him trouble now. His burlap bag, with the day's receipts added to it, hung like a one-sided yoke from his shoulder. Axel moved a few feet to a picnic bench and lowered himself onto it, keeping his bad knee straight. He lifted the bag onto the bench and watched Sam lower the plywood over the service window, snap a combination lock into the hasp.

He said, "So, Sam." He was hurting, but he felt better than he had. Work helped.

Sam lit a cigarette and sat down beside Axel.

"I got to tell you Ax, you got yourself one tough way to make a living."

"Beats fixing cars."

Sam puffed vigorously on his Pall Mall. The air was warm, moist, and still; a ghostly column of smoke gathered above his head. They sat in silence for a few moments, listening to the murmur of closing concessions, the grinding and whining of the sanitation trucks. "No it don't," he said.

Axel could feel a question boiling in his throat, getting itself ready. He said, "So, Sam. Let me ask you something. Suppose a guy found something that, say, was the property of this other individual, this friend of his. What would you think he should do about that?"

Sam rolled his cigarette between his thumb and his forefinger, examining it closely. "You find something, Ax?"

Axel shook his head. "Not me. But if I did—like, say, if you were to drop your wallet in my restaurant and I was to, say, find it—what I'd do then is I'd give it back."

Sam said, "I keep my wallet on a chain."

"Yeah, but hypothetically. Hypothetically, I'd give it back."

Sam snorted and took a huge drag off his cigarette, flicked it out onto the grass. Axel watched it land, suppressed an urge to hobble over and pick it up. There were a thousand other butts on the mall. One more wouldn't make any difference.

"Hypothetically," Sam said, "if a guy's dogs dig something up in his own backyard, then a guy ought to be entitled to keep whatever it is they dig up."

"I don't think you understand," Axel said.

"I mean, the whole point a private property is finders keepers."

"That doesn't make sense to me."

Sam shrugged. "You want to talk about who's making sense, I ain't the one was shooting off a forty-five on the midway a few hours back."

"Speaking of which, you gonna give me back my gun?"

"What for? So you can go get yourself killed like Tommy?"

"No, so I can get some answers from you."

Sam cackled and fired up another cigarette. "I might maybe be a horseshit burrito-roller, Ax, but I ain't a fucking idiot."

Sam turned his head away and stared at the Tiny Tot Donuts stand. Axel suppressed an urge to whap him with his cane. He wasn't sure what kind of twisted passageways were contained in Sam O'Gara's compact skull, but he figured it wouldn't do any good at this point to piss him off. He decided to open up the other subject they'd been avoiding, just to see what popped out.

"It's like he's not really dead, isn't it?"

Sam's head bobbed slightly; a cloud of smoke materialized and slowly dissipated. "I got this feeling we're not too far behind him, Ax. Tommy, he's down there getting warmed up, dealing hands with that leather-ass Satan."

"Telling him how to play," Axel said.

"Losing every hand too, I bet. Satan, he don't bet without he's sitting on the mortal nuts." Sam expelled a burst of smoke through his nose, laughed, then started sneezing. "And I bet you he gets 'em every time, Ax. Every fucking time."

"We never got together for that game, the three of us."

"No," Sam said. "We never did."

"I think Sophie's ready to go." Axel got his good leg under him, braced himself with his cane, and rose painfully to his feet. He started toward Sophie, who was locking the back door to the restaurant.

"Look at you," she said.

"Look at me what?"

"You can hardly walk. You should see a doctor."

"No way. Look what happened to Tommy. He went in the hospital, now he's dead."

"That's ridiculous."

"Well, I'm not going to any hospital. We've got two more days till the end of the fair. I'm not spending them on my back."

"Fine. How are you going to drive yourself home?"

"I don't think I can," Axel admitted. "I don't think I can bend my leg."

"I suppose I'll have to take you," she said.

"I don't think I can get in that little car of yours."

"We'll take your truck."

Sam said, "Y'know, I could use a ride home too. I took the bus over here, y'know. Cost me a buck and a quarter."

Sophie sighed, shaking her head as if disgusted, but a part of her was clearly enjoying her role. "What would you two do without me?"

CHAPTER

39

"You sure you can make it?" Sam asked.

Axel stepped carefully down from the cab. "It's only a few steps to my damn door, Sam." He transferred some weight to his yardstick cane, took a quick step, testing his bad knee. It had stiffened some more, but at least it didn't hurt worse.

Sophie, sitting behind the steering wheel, said, "Don't just sit there. Give him a hand, Sam."

Sam made a move to climb down.

Axel lifted the cane and waved its tip in Sam's face. "I can do it myself, goddamn it."

"He says he don't want no help," Sam said.

Sophie said, "Yeah. Like he didn't need any help walking to the truck."

"That was a quarter mile," Axel said, taking another painful step. "This is ten feet."

"I never seen anything so pitiful," Sam said. "Soph is right. You oughta be in the hospital."

"It's just a sprain." Axel took two quick steps, reached the door. "You know, you don't have to sit there gawking at me. Go on. I'll see you in the morning, okay?"

"I'll be here," Sophie said.

Axel inserted his key in his door and stood there watching as Sophie and Sam drove off. He turned the key, twisted the knob, pushed the door open. His hand had just hit the light switch when something crashed into his mouth, knocking his dentures back into his throat. His knee collapsed, and he fell to the floor, choking.

"That was easy," said Dean, kicking the door closed. It was always easy. Pork had been easy. And with Mickey, he hadn't even been trying.

"He's, like, having a fit or something," Tigger said.

Axel lay on the floor, holding his neck with one hand, digging the fingers of his other hand into his mouth. Dean tossed the crowbar on the bed, bent over Axel, and quickly felt under his arms and around his waist, looking for the heavy, solid shape of the .45. Axel writhed under his hands, red-faced, eyes bugged out, making wheezing, gagging noises.

"He don't have it," Dean said. "Unless it's in here." He grabbed the shoulder bag, pulled it away. Axel's body convulsed, he gave a loud cough, and something jettisoned from his mouth and bounced across the carpet toward Tigger.

Tigger jumped back. "Fuck, it's his fucking teeth!"

Dean laughed, stepping back. Nothing fazed him now. He had finally hit a plateau with the crystal, a perfectly level place where all things came easily under his control. His body had adapted to the high levels of amphetamine; he had the buzz under control. He was a machine now, turbocharged and running at peak capacity. He could see with perfect clarity. He unzipped the bag and dumped its contents onto the bed. Things fell out in slow motion. A pair of dirty socks. A bottle of aspirin. A heavy bank bag, obviously full of coins. And five white paper bags held closed with rubber bands. Dean ripped open one of the bags and found a thick bundle of paper money. He thumbed the bills, then tossed the packet to Tigger. "What did I tell you?"

"He's been carrying it with him?"

Dean shook his head. "This is just a taste. Carmen says he has coffee cans full of the stuff." He watched the old man pull himself up onto one hip, a rope of pink drool reaching from his mouth to the carpet, breathing heavily, still trying to catch his wind. "We just got to get him to tell us where."

Axel heard the kid's voice. "That's right, ain't it? You got more?"

He wiped his mouth, looked at the blood on his hand. The kid took a step toward him. "You hear me, old man?"

"I shoulda shot you." The missing dentures distorted his voice. He coughed, leaned to the side, spat a glob of spit and blood on the carpet.

"So talk to me. Where've you got those coffee cans stashed? All you got to do is tell me, and we leave you alone. Nobody gets hurt."

Axel shook his head. "Too late," he said. "I'm already hurt." His mouth tasted of blood, and his knee was pulsing unpleasantly, but oddly enough, he felt stronger, felt a kernel of anger where moments before there had been only empty spaces.

"And you don't want to get hurt more, right?"

Axel said, "That depends." This anger, it was not like the fury that had driven him that afternoon. This was a cooler, harder-edged emotion. Before, it had been his imagination driving him, but this time he could see it, right in front of him. He set his jaw, trying not to let what he was feeling show in his face.

"Depends on what?" the kid asked with a smirk.

Axel did not reply, thinking that he wouldn't mind getting hurt some more if it would get him a shot at this punk kid, this kid who'd been in his stuff, messing up his room. That would be worth getting hurt for. He had a sudden memory of the kangaroos he'd seen on television. The old boomer had run away, had survived the battle only to die alone out in the Australian desert. That wasn't for him. One way or another, he had to play this hand to the end. The only problem he could see was that there were two of them, and he was lying on the floor with a bad leg and no teeth. He couldn't kick. He couldn't even bite the son-of-a-bitch.

He said, "You're James Dean."

Dean shrugged. He didn't seem to care that his name was known.

Axel said, "He was a punk too. You see *East of Eden?*"

James Dean rested his weight on one hip, cocked his head. "The one where he got to be this rich guy," he said.

"The one where he started out a punk and then turned into a creep."

"Least he got the money. Only he didn't keep it in coffee cans."

Axel said, "You know what Tommy called you?"

Dean said, "Who the fuck's Tommy?"

Axel ran his tongue over his upper gum. "He called you the Bald Little Monkey," he said, adding the "Little" just to give it more punch.

The skinny kid laughed abruptly, shut it down when Dean snapped a look at him.

"Well, maybe I'll pay this Tommy a visit too," Dean growled.

"Maybe sooner than you think," Axel said.

Realization touched Dean's features. "Oh!" He laughed, then explained to Tigger. "He's talking about the donut guy, Tig. He's, like, *threatening* us!"

The thing to do, Axel decided, was to think of it like a game. The one with the muscles, James Dean, he was the one to beat. The skinny, slack-mouthed kid, the one called "Tig," wouldn't be much of a problem. He said, directing his words at Tig, "When it happens, you'd best run." The kid's mouth fell open another half inch. Axel figured that might just do it. Plant the idea, let it grow. Everything about the kid, his body language, said he didn't want to play this hand.

Dean said, "He's a tough guy. Look how tough he is, Tig. No teeth."

"Where's Carmen?" Axel demanded, shifting gears again.

Dean appeared genuinely confused. "How the fuck should I know?"

"You tell me where she is, maybe I'll tell you about the coffee cans."

Dean lifted the crowbar. "Maybe you'll tell me about the coffee cans anyways."

Axel watched the crowbar turning in Dean's hands. He had to say something. "It's in the safe," he said. Get out of the room, he was thinking, get outside. "I put it all in the motel safe."

Dean raised his eyebrows, then looked over his shoulder toward the bathroom.

"Hey, Motel 6! How come you didn't tell me about this?" he shouted.

"It's a lie!" came Bill Quist's frightened voice.

Axel said, "Bill? That you in there?"

"He's lying," Quist shouted.

Axel shook his head. "You in with these guys, Bill?"

No reply.

Dean said, "He says you're lying."

"What's he doing in the bathroom?"

"Let's talk coffee cans," Dean said.

"It's like I told you. I put the money in the safe. I did it when the other guy was on duty. Bill doesn't even know about it. You don't believe me, we can go look."

Sophie drifted toward the curb, then pulled a quick U-turn on Larpenteur Avenue, throwing Sam against the door.

He said, "Whoa! Hey! Hold on there, what you doing?"

"I don't care what he says," Sophie muttered.

"What? Who?"

"You saw him. The man can hardly walk."

"He don't need to walk to sleep."

"I can't leave him like that, all by himself. Somebody has to take care of him."

"Well, he ain't going to like it."

"I don't care what he likes. He needs me."

The parade moved slowly across the parking lot, Axel supported by a frightened-looking Bill Quist, with Dean and Tigger walking a few steps behind them. Axel, a glazed look in his eyes, had departed the present. As his body limped across the dimly lit parking lot, one arm hanging on Bill Quist's shoulder, his mind traveled into the past. He saw himself in Deadwood, about to get the shit beat out of him by a trio of drunken cowboys. His mistake back then had been to wait too long. He had let the cowboys confront him in their own time and place. Now, he was thinking, he'd made the same damn mistake all over again. He should have dealt with this James Dean a long time ago, the first time he'd met him. Instead, he had offered the kid a free taco.

Was it too late? Axel expelled a mental sigh and returned to the present.

"I'm sorry about this, Bill," he said.

Quist said, "This isn't fair. I just work here." His hands were tied together in front with a pair of Axel's knee-high black nylon socks. A large bruise had formed on the side of his neck.

"You seen Carmen today?" Axel asked.

"She called. She wants you to go get her."

"Get her where?"

"Ramsey County detox."

"Oh." Detox? At least she was safe. One less thing to think about. They were almost to the lobby. Well, he decided, as well this time as another, and he let his good knee collapse and fell to the tarmac. Quist tried to hold him up, but Axel slipped his arm loose, groaning piteously. Behind them, Dean and Tigger stopped.

"Get him up," Dean commanded Quist.

Quist tugged at Axel's arm, but the only effect was to make him moan.

"My knee," Axel said, coughing.

Dean said, "You better get up, or we'll just drag you."

"Why don't we just leave him?" Tigger asked. "We don't need him, right?"

"If the money's not there, we need him." Dean pointed the crowbar at Quist, who had dropped Axel's arm, edged a half step back, and was rocking slightly on his feet. "Don't you even think about it."

Quist's shoulders sagged. Dean returned his attention to Axel.

"Time to get up, old man." He gave him a vicious poke in the ribs with the crowbar.

The crowbar stuck. Dean tugged at the steel, thinking for a moment that he had actually shoved it into the old man's body and gotten it stuck between two ribs, but in the quarter second it took for him to realize that Axel had grabbed the bar, the old man twisted and yanked, tearing the bar from Dean's grasp, coming back at him with a one-handed swing. With a shout, Dean jumped back. The crowbar missed his knee, but he felt it flutter the denim of his jeans. The amphetamine plateau had shifted; things were coming at him too fast now. From the corner of his eye, he saw the motel clerk moving, stumbling back, turning, running. Tigger somewhere behind him, saying, "Hey . . . hey . . ." A car stopped on the roadway opposite the parking lot, headlights glaring. Confusing shadows. His heart made his ribs vibrate. The old man rising from the parking lot, using the crowbar like a cane. Too much, all at the same time. Dean backed away, trying to focus his thoughts. He heard himself shout something to Tigger, but Tigger wasn't there. He looked back, saw Tigger running. The old man was standing now, hopping toward him on one leg, holding the crowbar like a baseball bat, his shoe slapping loudly on the asphalt with each hop.

There was a moment when Dean almost ran, but then the scene snapped into focus again and he saw that he was still in control, still on that plateau. The guy was old, he was tired, and he was hopping along on one leg. Everything had slowed down again. The old man's hops were shorter. He was getting tired. Every time he made another little jump, Dean took a step back, keeping about eight feet between them. Let the guy wear himself out, then take him.

Hop.

Dean took another step back. He could deal with Tigger later.

The old man stopped, balancing on one leg. He lowered the bar. Dean smiled, took a step forward.

"You done now?"

The old man glared, breathing loudly.

"How about you give me the bar." Dean reached out a hand. He saw the end of the bar start to move, started to jerk his hand back. The old man fell toward him, bringing the bar up over his head, chopping down with it. Dean saw it all in slow motion, plenty of time to get out of the way, but his body refused to match the speed of his mind. The hook end of the bar crashed into his sternum, driving the air from his lungs, raked down his belly, and snagged in the waistband of his jeans. He went down, his chest in spasms, and the old man was on him.

Axel wanted to split James Dean's head wide open. He managed to bang it on the pavement a couple of times, but it was like trying to hold on to an oily bowling ball. No hair to grab. Then the kid caught his breath, howled, and snapped his body into a reverse arch, sending Axel up and off. Axel's bad knee hit the pavement. A bright flash of light hit his eyes, a moment of blindness. He heard a roar. The kid rose up before him, silhouetted against a pair of headlights coming right at him. Axel picked a direction and rolled.

* * *

"Go!" shouted Sam. "Go-go-go-go-go!" He reached over with one foot and tromped on the accelerator. The truck lurched forward, hopped the curb, and headed down the grassy embankment toward the Motel 6 parking lot, spitting sod from its rear wheels. Sophie screamed, her hands white on the steering wheel. The truck hit the parking lot, bounced, a shiny, bloody head appeared above the hood, they felt a thud, and Sophie hit the brake, still screaming, her eyes closed. The truck skidded toward the motel office, hit one of the two overhang supports, and crashed through the plate-glass doorway into the lobby.

Axel didn't see the truck strike James Dean, but he saw his body airborne, saw him rotate in the air and land flat, facedown on the parking lot, the sound of his impact covered by the louder sound of the truck crashing into the lobby.

For a moment, everything stopped. Axel gave himself three seconds, then climbed to his feet and hopped slowly toward the office. The overhang, deprived of one support, sagged dangerously. Axel squeezed between the remains of the doorway and the back end of his pickup truck. He heard a grinding, whining noise coming from beneath the hood, the sound of the starter trying to crank a frozen engine. He hopped up to the driver's door, opened it, and saw Sophie twisting the ignition key, probably so that she could back over the kid in the parking lot. Axel opened the door. Sophie stared at him fiercely, cranking the starter, pumping the gas pedal. Her eyes were squeezed down to slits, her face and shoulders covered with white powder. Axel frowned at the steering wheel, at the limp white bag dangling from its center.

He reached out and gently removed her hand from the starter. He held her face. "Are you okay?"

Sophie nodded shakily. "Something went bang," she said.

Axel looked at Sam, who sat blinking stupidly out

through the shattered windshield, a rivulet of blood running from his nose down his chin.

"You—son—of—a—bitch." Axel felt a smile flutter onto his face.

Sam wiped his sleeve across his chin, smearing blood. "What?"

"You never unhooked the goddamn air bag."

CHAPTER

40

"I raise," said Sophie. She looked across the table at Axel. "Can I do that?"

Axel frowned at his cards. "You don't want to," he said. His new dentures clicked when he talked. They didn't fit right with the stitches the doctor had taken in his gum.

They were sitting, the three of them, in Sam O'Gara's kitchen. Axel took up two chairs, one for his body and the other for his leg, now confined to a plastic cast. The refrigerator, an ancient Philco, emitted a low rumble. Chester and Festus were sacked out under the table, Festus giving Sophie an occasional interesting moment by licking her ankle. The first time, she'd squealed and jumped out of her chair, but she was getting used to it.

Sam fished a can of Copenhagen from his pocket. "Don't listen to 'im, Soph. Anyways, I fold." He pushed his cards away and shifted his chair closer to Sophie. "What you got there, sweetheart?"

Sophie pulled her cards against her breasts.

Sam said, "Don't worry, I'm out of this hand. Just show me your cards, I'll tell you if you wanna be raisin' ol' Ax. He's a tricky sumbitch. C'mon, I'm on your side."

Sophie hesitated, then tipped her cards toward Sam. He leaned closer. "Not bad," he said.

Axel snorted. "She's showing you her cards, Sam, not her boobs."

"I's talking about both."

Sophie shot out an elbow, forcing Sam to jerk his head back out of range, but she couldn't completely conceal a smile. "What should I do?" she asked.

Sam thrust a thumb in the air. "Raise it up!" he said. "Make 'im pay to see those babies." He twisted the top off the Copenhagen can, pinched up an enormous wad of the black tobacco, and packed his lower lip.

Axel groaned and watched as Sophie pushed four quarters into the pot.

He said, "What can you have?"

Sophie advanced her chin and fixed her eyes on Axel's stack.

Axel looked again at his cards. It wasn't a bad hand for five-card draw. He had a flush, jack high. Almost certainly a winner—unless Sophie's cards were better. That was the thing about poker. Any hand was a winner until it got beat.

Which seemed to happen a lot.

He fiddled with his pile of coins, found four quarters and five dimes, tossed them on the pot. "Let's see 'em," he said.

Sophie looked at Sam. "Do I have to?"

"If you want to win you do, sweetheart."

"Can I raise again?"

"You're called," Axel snapped.

Sophie carefully set her cards on the table, faceup. A full house, queens over fives. Axel rolled his eyes and threw away his hand.

"You have to show too!" Sophie said.

Axel said, "Why? You won."

Sam grabbed Axel's discarded hand and flipped it up.

Sophie said, "What's that? You didn't even have a pair."

"That's a flusher," said Sam. "A flusher and a loser. My deal." He swept the cards together.

"I win?" Sophie asked guardedly.

Axel snapped, "Yes, goddamn it, you win."

Sophie's mouth softened and spread into a wide smile as she scooped up the pot. For a moment, Axel saw her as a happy little kid on Christmas morning. What a strange woman this is, he thought. I give her half of my business, my life, and she's all frowns and doubts and suspicions, almost as if I'd given her nothing but trouble. Last night, when they'd paid off the help and counted their remaining take from the fair, her ten percent had come to over four thousand dollars. You'd think that would've made her happy, but all she could talk about was how much more they'd have made if it hadn't been for losing Kirsten and having Carmen flake out on them and Axel's being in such rough shape that he'd had to spend the last two days of the fair propped up on a stool, making burritos at half speed. Axel was glad to have made it through the weekend, period. But not Sophie. Four thousand dollars in her pocket, and all she could think about was how it should have been five. Now, a few hours later, she wins one lousy three-dollar pot, and she's all smiles and joy.

He never knew what she was going to do. Three nights ago, in the emergency room at St. Joseph's, she had surprised him then too. Throughout the entire ordeal—the scene in the parking lot, the cops, the questions, the long wait in the emergency room at St. Joseph's—she'd kept it together. He'd expected her to be hysterical, but she'd been like a rock. And then, after the doctor had finished with him, when they'd pushed him out of the examination room in that wheelchair, feeling about as bad as he ever remembered feeling, she looked at him and her face collapsed. They'd wheeled him out into the waiting room, and she'd looked at him and just lost it, started crying like a baby. He'd never seen her do that before. And then when Carmen had shown up at the stand on the last day of the fair, not wanting to work, just wanting to get paid . . . Axel had expected Sophie to lose it then. But all that happened was that she had wearily counted out Carmen's money, too tired or numb to argue. "I don't get a bonus this year?" Carmen had whined. Even then, Sophie hadn't said a word.

The blond girl, Kirsten, stopped by at the same time, all apologies and embarrassment over being hauled off by her mother in the middle of the day, but mostly wanting to collect her pay. Axel paid her off. She didn't ask for a bonus. A few minutes later, he had seen Carmen and Kirsten sitting out on the mall, smoking cigarettes and laughing. All Sophie had said was, "They don't know what's important."

Axel remembered thinking that she looked . . . not old, but mature. He thought she looked good.

She looked good now. Winning that pot had put some color in her face.

"Where's Carmen gone off to today?" Axel asked.

"She went shopping with that Kirsten." Sophie finished stacking her coins. "They went to the Mall of America. Can you imagine? What on earth could those two have in common anyway?"

Sam laughed.

"What's so funny?"

Sam squared up the deck of cards and riffled them. "They both got trouble with their mamas," he said.

Sophie made a face. "Excuse me." She left the kitchen. Sam and Axel listened to her footsteps climbing the stairs, the sound of the bathroom door closing.

Sam said, "She's got the touch, Ax. Maybe me and you and her ought to hit the road. Odds are, we'd do better, the three of us, than we ever did with old Tommy."

Axel smiled and shook his head. "Maybe we wouldn't get in so damn many fights."

"You got that right. And if we did, she'd just run 'em over."

"You know what it's going to cost to get my new truck fixed? About four dimes."

"Well, your old one's out back, ready to roll. I even gave 'er a little tune-up."

"I'm going to need what was under it too."

Sam raised his eyebrows. "Now, Ax, you say that money ol' Festus and Chester dug up was yours. Now explain to me again how come I'm s'posed to think that." He leaned back in his chair, shifted the wad of tobacco with his tongue.

"It was under my truck. I put it there."

"I said you could park your truck here, I didn't think I was including mineral rights. Besides, I don't see how come a smart fella like you would go burying his money like a goddamn dog in somebody's backyard not even his own."

Axel took a deep breath. Sam had been hanging him out there for the past two days, not admitting that the money was Axel's but not coming right out and saying he wasn't going to give it back, either. Axel was about eighty percent sure that Sam was just playing with him. He trusted Sam. Maybe not a hundred percent, but a solid ninety.

Sam said, "Even if you did find your money someplace, I don't know what the hell good it'd do you. You don't spend it. You'd probably go bury it in the goddamn park, leave it for the squirrels."

Axel did not reply.

"Suppose you did get it back," Sam went on. "What would you do with it?"

Axel looked at his old friend hopefully but saw nothing in Sam's face to encourage him. "Is this a test, or are you just trying to make me miserable?"

Sam shrugged and riffled the deck of cards with his thumb. "Just wondering."

"Maybe I'd invest it in something," Axel said.

Sam cocked an eyebrow.

"Maybe I'd put it in a bank," Axel growled. "Hell, I don't know. Does it matter?"

Sophie's footsteps sounded on the stairs.

"Don't matter to me," Sam said.

Axel muttered, "I suppose I should be glad you're letting me have my truck back." A click from his dentures took the edge off the sarcasm.

"The truck is yours."

"So's the cash."

Sam picked up the deck and shuffled. "You're a goddamn peasant, Ax. I ever tell you that?"

"I tell him that all the time," Sophie said.

Axel said, "You ready to go?" He didn't want to talk about the money in front of Sophie. He didn't want her to know. It was embarrassing.

"Where are we going?" she asked.

"The hell away from here." Axel got his good leg braced, squeezed his lips tight together, and stood up. "C'mon. We've got to go over to the fairgrounds. I want to get the rest of the stuff out of the cooler, get the restaurant closed up for the year."

Gripping his yardstick cane, Axel stood up and hobbled out the back door. Goddamn Sam O'Gara. You think you know a guy. The first few steps were tough, but once he got into the rhythm, walking wasn't all that bad. He jerked open the passenger door and climbed clumsily into the cab of his old pickup. His foot caught on something, a plastic bag on the floor. He grabbed the bag, tried to move it out of the way, then stopped. He felt through the black plastic. Rolls, like tight little burritos. He could feel them. He wanted to rip the bag open, to plunge his arms into it, but Sophie opened the other door and hopped in.

"What's going on with you two?" she asked.

Axel sat up straight. "Nothing," he said.

Sophie dropped her eyes to the bag. "What's that?"

"Just some stuff Sam was keeping for me." He rolled down the window and looked back at the house. Sam stood in the doorway, smoking a cigarette. One of the hounds poked its head out between his bowed legs.

Axel shouted, "You son-of-a-bitch! You just left it here? Where anybody coulda come and grabbed it?"

Sam just grinned.

Sophie said, "I swear to God, Axel, I don't know who'd want to steal this old pickup."

The aging Ford started right up, to Axel's surprise. She didn't have to pump the gas and grind away with the starter like before—just turned the key and they were in business. He liked the way the engine sounded. Sam must've worked some kind of magic. And once they got out onto the road, it even seemed to roll better. The shimmy had disappeared. Or maybe it was the plastic bag between his feet, maybe that was what made the ride so smooth.

Axel said, "You know that bank on Snelling? You mind stopping off there for a few minutes? I want to make a deposit."

Sophie looked at him in surprise. "You? Since when do you use a bank?"

"Things change," he said. He wouldn't put it all in. Maybe just a few thousand dollars; give himself time to get used to the idea.

"You want to know something?" Sophie asked.

"What?"

"Carmen was right. You're weird."

"You're weird too," Axel said.

Sophie shrugged. "Carmen would agree with you."

They rode down University Avenue without speaking, turned north on Snelling, Axel enjoying the comfortable silence. She was driving real nice for once, smooth and slow. As they turned into the fairgrounds, Axel was thinking that he wouldn't even get that new truck fixed, because he'd heard that once a vehicle got in an accident, it would never ride quite right again, and anyways, he'd never really gotten friendly with it. Never trusted the damn thing. He was thinking he'd sell it, or maybe give it to Sam, since, after all, the old one seemed to be working just fine.

CPSIA information can be obtained
at www.ICGtesting.com
Printed in the USA
LVOW01s2123170516
488747LV00012B/85/P

NOT ALL STORMS ARE BAD

These verses present one of the greatest descriptions of a storm found in the Bible. It is a graphic picture of the way God works when He comes to the aid of His children. David was saying in these verses that God the Creator, God the Deliverer, used everything in nature to come to his aid. The earth shook, down to its foundations. Smoke came up, and fire came out. Coals were kindled. The heavens bowed down. The wind began to blow, for God was coming on the wings of the wind. We see darkness, dark waters, thick clouds, even hailstones and coals of fire. Thunder, lightning—the very breath of God was blowing across the fields.

When the child of God is in His will, all of nature works for him. When the child of God is out of His will, everything works against him. Remember Jonah? He ran away from God in disobedience, and what happened? A storm appeared. The wind and waves were violent. That little boat went up and down on the ocean like a cork. Even the mariners were worried. Jonah disobeyed God, and everything in nature worked against him. David obeyed God, and everything in nature worked for him.

♦   ♦   ♦

God can use the storms of life to fulfill His will. Is the wind blowing? He is flying on the wings of the wind. Are the clouds thick? He will bring showers of blessing out of them. Don't be afraid of the storm. Storms can come from the hand of God and be the means of blessing.

COME OUT OF CONFINEMENT

For several years David had been forced to live in confined places while he fled from Saul. More than once he fled to a cave to save his life. Then God brought him out of the caves and out of confinement and into a large place. "He also brought me out into a broad place; He delivered me because He delighted in me" (v. 19). David was a man after God's own heart, and God delighted in him, just as He delighted in our Lord Jesus. God said of Him, "This is My beloved Son, in whom I am well pleased" (Matt. 3:17).

We often talk about our delighting in the Lord. "Delight yourself also in the Lord, and He shall give you the desires of your heart" (Ps. 37:4). That's important to do. But what about God's delighting in us? As parents and grandparents, we enjoy delighting in our children and grandchildren. In a similar way God wants to delight in us.

Because God delights in us, He delivers us. And He uses the difficult experiences of life to make us bigger. "He also brought me out into a broad place" (v. 19). Verse 36 of this chapter says, "You enlarged my path under me." When God puts us into a large place, He has to give us larger feet. But don't stop there. In Psalm 4:1 David said, "You have relieved me." God delivers us so that He can put us into a larger place, so that He can enable us to take giant steps of faith for His glory. David had gone through several years of confinement, difficulty, persecution and sorrow. But when it was over, he was a bigger man.

Let the trials of life make you a giant, not a midget. Let God put you into a large place, where you can take giant steps of faith for His glory.

♦　　♦　　♦

Life's trials are not easy. But in God's will, each has a purpose. Often He uses them to enlarge you. Are you feeling confined? Be encouraged that God delights in delivering you from confinement. Difficult times build your faith, if you let Him use them for His glory.

How Clean
Are Your Hands?

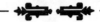

No matter how difficult our trials are, if we have clean hands, God will fill them with blessing. "The Lord rewarded me according to my righteousness; according to the cleanness of my hands He has recompensed me" (v. 20). "Therefore the Lord has recompensed me according to my righteousness, according to the cleanness of my hands in His sight" (v. 24). David's hands were clean. His enemies were lying about him—those people in Saul's court who wanted Saul's attention and affection. They lied about David. They said, "Saul, David said this," but he never said it. "David is doing this to you," but he never did that. David's hands were clean. When our hands are clean and we are keeping the ways of the Lord, God will work for us. He will give us what we need, protect us and see us through.

God responds to us as we respond to Him. "With the merciful You will show Yourself merciful; with a blameless man You will show Yourself blameless; with the pure You will show Yourself pure; and with the devious You will show Yourself shrewd [opposed]" (vv. 25,26). We decide how close God will be, how much affection He will be able to show us. "He delivered me because He delighted in me" (v. 19). The Lord delights in children with clean hands and a pure heart. *Integrity* is the key word. David was a man of integrity. Saul was a man of duplicity. He was double-minded, looking in two directions at once. But David kept his eyes on the Lord.

When our hands are clean, no matter how difficult life may be, God will see us through. He will take us through any trial and enable us to bring glory to His name when it's all over.

♦   ♦   ♦

God rewards us according to our righteousness. Are you keeping the ways of the Lord? If so, you may depend on His protection and strength. When your hands are clean, He sees you through your difficult trials and circumstances.

DELIGHTING IN GOD

God wants to have a personal relationship with each of us. He is the God of the individual believer through Jesus Christ, and He delights in us just as we delight in those we love. The highest and holiest experience we can have is the worshipful delight of the Lord.

This passage gives us insight into how we can delight in God and how He delights in us. First, *how does one delight God?* By one's character. David had integrity (v. 20). He was not free from sin, but his heart was devoted to God. *Righteous* means "obedient." David was obedient (vv. 21,22). He had the Word of God in his heart. God delights in us when we do what He wants us to do the way He wants us to do it (Matt. 3:17). What counts is that He delights in what we do, not what our neighbors think about us.

Second, *how does God deal with those in whom He delights?* He treats us the way we treat Him (vv. 25-27). We are as close to God as we want to be. David was wholly devoted to Him, so God was able to bless him. David was merciful to those who wronged him; God was merciful to him (v. 25). David was loyal; God was loyal to him (v. 25). David was pure, submissive and humble.

In contrast, Saul was devious. *Shrewd* means "to wrestle." God wrestles with us (as He did with Jacob) when we are perverse and devious. Parents often wrestle with their children when it comes to discipline. God wrestles with us to bring us where He wants us to be; then He can delight in us.

Third, *how can we increase our delight in God and His delight in us?* Believe that He wants you to be happy; happiness and holiness go together. Submit to and enjoy God's will, but not grudgingly. He will give us the best. When we delight in Him and He delights in us, life becomes delightful, and we bring glory to our Father's name.

◆　　◆　　◆

Delighting in God is an expression of your personal relationship with Him. His delight in you is an expression of His love for you. Be the kind of person who delights God. Walk with integrity and obey His Word. He will bless you and use you to bring glory to Himself.

Giving Us Hind's Feet

Life is 10 percent how you take it and 90 percent what you make it. Notice the repetition of the word *make* in verses 30-36: "It is God who arms me with strength, and makes my way perfect" (v. 32). I like verse 35: "You have also given me the shield of Your salvation; Your right hand has held me up, Your gentleness has made me great." Why does God permit difficulties to come to our lives? Sometimes He has to break us before He can make us. Sometimes He has to reveal to us what we're really like before He can make us into what He wants us to be.

David went through some difficulties. As a young man he was anointed by God as His chosen servant. He won great victories and was destined to be God's next king on the throne. And what happens to him? He becomes a fugitive. He's chased from place to place by a godless man. He's persecuted by people who lie about him. What in the world is God doing? God is making him. He is taking David's life and making him all he ought to be.

Verse 33 says, "He makes my feet like the feet of deer, and sets me on my high places." God wants to make our feet ready for His way and make us more like Jesus Christ. God wanted David to go higher. He wanted David to have feet like hind's feet that could bound over the mountains and rocks. He didn't want David to sit still, complain and pout as Elijah did later.

God gently deals with us (v. 35). It didn't look like gentleness at the time, but when David later reflected over all those years of persecution, he said, "I see the gentle hand of God in all of this." God wants you to go higher and farther. Let Him make you.

◆　　◆　　◆

The path of your walk with God is lined with both trials and blessings. When the way becomes rough and difficult, He promises sure footing to get over the obstacles. Are you traveling a rough path today? Perhaps God is using this time to make you more like Jesus Christ. Let His gentle hand make you.

REVEALING WHAT'S INSIDE

We must remember that David's enemies were God's enemies and that he was fighting the Lord's battles. As Christians, we are taught to pray for our enemies and to do good to those who despitefully use us (Matt. 5:44). David did that. He prayed for Saul, and on at least two occasions, he could have killed him but didn't. David had the right attitude toward Saul, but Saul did not have the right attitude toward David. As we read verses 37-45, we need to remember that David was not carrying out a personal vendetta. When he talked about his enemies, he was talking about God's enemies. He was the instrument God used to accomplish His purposes against those who opposed Him.

We find an interesting point in verse 42: "Then I beat them as fine as the dust before the wind." David had grown spiritually (Ps. 19,36). When God enlarged him, his perspective changed. His enemies became as small as the dust. You see, circumstances reveal character. People say, "A man is made by a crisis." No, a crisis does not make a person. It reveals what that person is made of. When the crisis came, Saul and his crowd grew smaller and smaller as their true nature was revealed. But David grew bigger and bigger. He was also established (v. 36), while his enemies became like the dust that the wind blows away.

♦   ♦   ♦

Are your circumstances making you smaller or bigger? Are they enabling you to overcome, or are they overcoming you? David rejoiced that God had given him victory in spite of his enemies and circumstances. The victory is the Lord's. Let your circumstances make you bigger and greater for Him.

DAVID'S
DOXOLOGY

David closed this long psalm of triumph and victory with a doxology. "The Lord lives! Blessed be my Rock! Let the God of my salvation be exalted" (v. 46). David had been a fugitive. He had been waiting for the day when he could ascend the throne. Now the day had come. How did he respond? He glorified God.

I suppose some of us would have said, "Well, my enemies are gone. Now I can do what I please. My battles are over. I've been put into a large place. Therefore, watch out everybody, here I come!" But David didn't have that attitude at all. He gave glory to God. He ended his song with a hymn of praise to the One who had delivered him. "Therefore I will give thanks to You, O Lord, among the Gentiles, and sing praises to Your name" (v. 49). Here was David, a Jew, saying, "I want these Gentiles to know how great my God is." Are you concerned about letting the nations know how great God is? Are you burdened to tell the Gospel to other people? If the Lord has saved you and delivered you, then you should be telling others what He has done for you.

David closed his song of victory by blessing the Lord. "The Lord lives!" (v. 46). Isn't it good to know that we trust in the living God? Some people may worship a dead god, but we don't. We are the children of the living God. David said, "God is alive, and He is my rock and my salvation. I want Him to be exalted." And he concluded, "Great deliverance He gives to His king" (v. 50).

✦   ✦   ✦

How do you respond after a victory? So often Christians fail to exalt the Lord. You trust in a living God, who protects you and delivers you. He deserves your worship and praise. Have you given God the glory for your victories?

SEEING GOD

Psalm 19 is so familiar to us. The first six verses talk about the glory of God seen in creation. Verses 7-11 talk about the glory and grace of God revealed in the Word, and verses 12-14 talk about God speaking to our hearts. He is revealed in the skies, in the Scriptures and in our own hearts and souls.

Even though creation is in travail because of sin (Rom. 8:22), God's glory is revealed there. Someone has said that if the stars came out only once every thousand years, we'd stay up all night and look at them in awe and wonder.

David gives us two pictures of facing each day. The first is like a bridegroom coming out to meet his bride with wonderful hope and love and joy. The second is like a strong man running a race. David tells us to live a day at a time and to start each day with glory and grace and a goal to be reached.

Unfortunately, some people know only the God of creation. They admire the God of wisdom, power and providence, who made everything. But it's not enough to know only the Creator. We must know God as the Savior. This is why Psalm 19 talks about His revelation in the Word. The Bible is flawless. We can trust it, test it and taste it (vv. 9,10). We need to have this Word in our hearts, and then we can have God living in our hearts as our Savior.

This reminds me of the Wise Men who came to see Jesus. They saw the message up in the heavens. Then they followed the star, and that led them to the Scriptures. The priests told them from the prophetical books where the Messiah would be born. Then they went and worshiped Him.

◆   ◆   ◆

God reveals His glory in several ways. It's easy to admire God the Creator. But have you trusted His Word? Have you tested and proved it in the furnaces of life? Have you tasted it to find out how sweet it really is? Don't worship only the God of creation or the God of revelation. Let Him be the God of salvation in your heart.

THE
PERFECT WORD

The revelation of God in nature prepares us for His revelation in the Scriptures. Ultimately, Jesus Christ reveals Himself as Savior. This was the experience of the Magi (Matt. 2). The light of nature led them to the light of the Word, which led them to the Light of the World.

The Bible meets the needs of the human heart. No other book is like it. It is God's testimony. Its name is the *Law of the Lord*. The sun is to creation what the Law is to God's people, bringing light, warmth, life and growth.

The Bible's nature is *perfect and pure*. The Bible is called the fear of the Lord because we need a reverential, holy, awesome fear of God (v. 9). We teach God's Word because it enlightens (v. 8). We trust it because it is true and righteous (v. 9). We treasure it because it is more desired than gold (v. 10). We may even "taste" the Word and test it.

The Bible *satisfies every need*. It converts the soul. It warns us. There is great reward in keeping the Law. It's a wonder that with God's revelation in nature and Scripture so many people are blind.

The Bible is the *book of our heart*. Every time we read a book, watch TV or listen to a speaker, something is being written on our hearts. Let God write His Word on your heart. The heart sees what it loves. When we love the Lord with our hearts, we see Him in creation and in the Scriptures.

If God is your Redeemer, He can be your Strength. Live acceptably in His sight, allowing the meditation of your heart to please Him. Then your life will be what He wants it to be.

♦　　♦　　♦

God is more than the God of creation and the Scriptures; He is the God of redemption. If your heart is filled with Him and yielded to Him, you can have victory over sin. Don't simply worship the God of nature. Get into the Word of God and let God get into you.

WHAT ARE YOU TRUSTING?

David wrote, "Some trust in chariots, and some in horses; but we will remember the name of the Lord our God" (v. 7). The big question is, What are you trusting today? Everybody trusts in or believes in something. Some people trust in their money or credit cards. Some trust in their strength or expertise or experience. Verses 1 and 2 say, "May the Lord answer you in the day of trouble; may the name of the God of Jacob defend you; may He send you help from the sanctuary, and strengthen you out of Zion." The Christian trusts in the Lord, and he exemplifies this trust by praying.

When we are in trouble, what we do to solve our problems and turn our trouble into triumph is evidence of what or whom we're trusting. When the day of trouble arrives, some people reach for their checkbooks. They think money will solve their problems. Others reach for the telephone. They look to friends to solve their problems. While "some trust in chariots, and some in horses," Christians remember the name of the Lord (v. 7). Our faith is in Jesus Christ, and we should not be afraid to let people know about it. "We will rejoice in your salvation, and in the name of our God we will set up our banners!" (v. 5). In other words, we do not hesitate to wave the banner of faith because He will not fail us.

God's name is good. "The name of the God of Jacob defend you" (v. 1). Take time to trust the Lord. Roll your burden on Him. Get your strength from Him. Wave your banner in the name of the Lord, and He will turn your burden into a blessing.

◆   ◆   ◆

Where do you place your trust? Whereas wealth and others fail you, Jesus never fails. Take whatever burden you are carrying today and give it to the Lord. Trust Him, and He will work on your behalf.

FROM TROUBLE
TO THANKSGIVING

D. L. Moody did not want soloist Ira Sanky to sing the hymn "Onward Christian Soldiers" because he felt the Church was anything but a victorious army marching off to war. Yet the Bible pictures God's people as soldiers in His army. As soldiers, we must be familiar with Psalms 20 and 21. The first deals with prayer and winning the victory, and the second deals with praise and holding the victory. If we trust the Lord, we will move from trouble to thanksgiving.

Several factors lead us to triumph in battle. The first is *prayer*. This is an essential element in fighting the battles of the Lord because it releases His power. There are no battles like those of the Christian life. We struggle against the enemies of the Lord: the world (I John 2:15), the flesh and the devil (Eph. 6). We must pray according to the will of God. The Word of God and prayer go together (Heb. 4:12; Eph. 6:17,18).

Next, we need to *surrender*. Before David and his army fought, they worshiped God. That affected his battle plan and his victory. David's "burnt offering" indicated total surrender to God. If we're not walking with the Lord today, we'll not be ready when the battle comes.

Another factor is *unity*. David and his army had one goal—God's victory. And they had one joy—to serve Him and do His will. The tribes of Israel were a picture of unity. They had one army assembled from 12 tribes.

The fourth factor is *faith*. Verse 6 says the Lord "saves" His anointed. The Hebrew word used here means He "has saved." That is, God already has given David the victory (I John 5:4). The Church today often trusts in all kinds of horses and chariots but not in the Lord.

The final factor is *obedience*. David and his army obeyed God's will. The day of trouble can become a day of triumph and thanksgiving if we have trust, which is expressed by prayer, surrender, unity, faith and obedience.

◆　　◆　　◆

Although you cannot avoid battles, you can be ready for them and, with God's help, be victorious. Are you prepared to do battle? If not, trust the Lord to help you.

WHAT DO KINGS NEED?

Kings have everything. If you were a king, what would you rejoice in the most? In what did David rejoice? Psalm 21 tells us what it means to be a king—not just for a day but for a lifetime.

We are kings because we are God's children. Jesus Christ has made us kings and priests because He loves us and washed away our sins in His blood. Today, God wants us to reign in life. We are on the throne with the Lord Jesus. "The king shall have joy in Your strength, O Lord" (v. 1). David is rejoicing in the *strength* that God gave him—strength to walk and strength to war; strength to build and strength to battle; strength to carry the burdens of life. Are you rejoicing today as God's king because He gives you strength?

David continues, "And in Your salvation how greatly shall he rejoice!" (v. 1). He rejoices in God's *salvation*. We need to do the same. One day Jesus told His disciples, "Don't rejoice because the demons are subject to you. Rejoice because your names are written down in heaven" (Luke 10:20).

David also rejoices in *satisfaction*. "You have given him his heart's desire, and have not withheld the request of his lips. For You meet him with the blessings of goodness" (vv. 2,3). If we look back, we will find goodness and mercy following us (23:6), and if we look ahead, God is meeting us with His goodness (v. 3). Don't be afraid of today, and don't be afraid of the future. God will meet you with His goodness.

In verse 7 David rejoices in *stability*: "For the king trusts in the Lord, and through the mercy of the Most High he shall not be moved." I like these blessings we can rejoice in—God's strength, salvation, satisfaction and stability. All of this is for God's glory. "His glory is great in Your salvation" (v. 5).

✦ ✦ ✦

Many Christians fail to see themselves as kings. But God wants us to reign in life and has provided several blessings that enable us to live as kings. Are you enjoying the blessings of kingship? If not, claim His blessings and start living a life of victory.

DEALING
WITH ENEMIES

We don't like them or want them, but sometimes we can't help having enemies. A person is not only known by the friends he makes; sometimes he's better known by the enemies he makes. No, we can't help having enemies, but we can help how we deal with them. This is what David is talking about in this passage. How do you deal with your enemies? Paul said, "All who desire to live godly in Christ Jesus will suffer persecution" (II Tim. 3:12). Some people are enemies of the cross of Christ. So if we take our stand at the cross, they will take their stand against us.

David gives us insight for dealing with life's enemies. First, *let God's hand work*. Keep your hands off. "Your hand will find all Your enemies; Your right hand will find those who hate You" (v. 8). Then, let God's anger burn instead of yours. "You shall make them as a fiery oven in the time of Your anger" (v. 9). There is a righteous anger, a righteous indignation. Paul wrote, "Be angry, and do not sin" (Eph. 4:26). Our Lord was angry when He cleansed the temple on two occasions. Let God's anger blaze, not yours.

Second, *let God shoot His arrows*. "You will make ready Your arrows on Your string toward their [the enemies'] faces" (v. 12). God's hand will work for you. His anger will blaze for you. His arrows will be shot for you. And He will use all of this for His glory. "Be exalted, O Lord, in Your own strength! We will sing and praise Your power" (v. 13). We can't praise our power, our scheming or our vengeance. But we can praise God's glory and power. When we try to take care of our enemies in our way, we only make things worse. But when we turn the situation over to the Lord, He makes things better. Let God take care of your enemies today, because then He will be glorified, you will be satisfied, and Jesus Christ will have His way.

✦　　✦　　✦

Are you facing an enemy today? Take your hands off the problem and let God deal with those involved. He will remedy the problem in the best possible way, and Jesus Christ will be glorified.

WHAT GOD WON'T DO

"My God, My God, why have You forsaken Me?" (v. 1). Those are familiar words. Jesus spoke them from the cross (Matt. 27:46), but they were first spoken by David when he was going through a severe trial.

Jesus Christ was forsaken that we might not be forsaken. God the Father forsook His Son on the cross when He was made sin for us (II Cor. 5:21).

But David says in this psalm, "Our fathers trusted You, and You took care of them; now I'm trusting You, and nothing seems to happen" (vv. 4-6). We can envision David saying, "I am a worm, and no man; a reproach of men, and despised of the people" (v. 6). He did go through that. But our Lord went through it to an even greater degree. Can you imagine the Lord Jesus, who said, "I am the Good Shepherd," saying, "I am a worm"? But He became a worm for us so that we might become the children of God.

We cannot be forsaken because the Savior was forsaken *in our place*. We can't be forsaken because of His *promise* to never leave or forsake us (Heb. 13:5). We cannot be forsaken because of His abiding and eternal *presence* with us (Matt. 28:20). We cannot be forsaken because of His *purpose* to work all things together for good to those who love Him (Rom. 8:28). And what is His purpose? That we might be conformed to the image of His Son (Rom. 8:29). David became a beautiful picture of the Lord Jesus Christ. And he had to suffer to do it. In spite of your circumstances and feelings, remember: *God will not forsake you.*

♦   ♦   ♦

When you go through trials, your circumstances and feelings can deceive you into thinking God has forsaken you. But the Bible promises us that He will never forsake you. Next time you feel forsaken, remember that God is always true to His Word and will accomplish His purpose of conforming you to the image of His Son.

THE DEVIL'S
ZOO

Are you an animal lover? I must confess that, apart from a certain sympathy with cats and a liking for friendly dogs, I don't really care much for animals. My wife enjoys going to the zoo, and I dutifully go along, but I would much rather be in the library.

Do you know that God uses animals to teach us about sin? Today's passage talks about the Devil's entire zoo. "Many bulls have surrounded Me; strong bulls of Bashan have encircled Me" (v. 12). Our Lord was on the cross, and people were acting like animals. That's what is wrong with the world. When we leave God out of our lives, we descend to the level of animals. Here was Jesus on the cross, and the bulls had surrounded Him. Then the lions showed up. "They gape at Me with their mouths, as a raging and roaring lion" (v. 13). "Dogs have surrounded Me" (v. 16). "Save Me from the lion's mouth and from the horns of the wild oxen!" (v. 21). That is quite a zoo! When men put Jesus on the cross, they acted like animals. And He replied, "I am a worm" (Ps. 22:6). Can you imagine bulls and lions and dogs and oxen chasing a worm? Oh, how our Lord humbled Himself for us!

Don't act like a wild animal. You were made in the image of God. Let the Holy Spirit turn you into one of His gentle sheep. The Lord, our Shepherd, is glorified and honored when we don't act like vicious animals but rather like the children of God.

✦　✦　✦

God made you in His image and has placed His Holy Spirit within you. You were made to glorify Him. Are you harboring sin in any area of your life? Keep clean of sin so God can work in you and through you.

RESURRECTION GROUND

The last half of Psalm 22 is an expression of praise. In verse 22 we see a change: The psalmist goes from prayer to praise, from suffering to glory. "I will declare Your name to My brethren; in the midst of the congregation I will praise You."

In this passage we find the Lord singing in the midst of the congregation. Have you ever thought of Jesus singing? We think of Him preaching and doing miracles and teaching and counseling, but singing? "My praise shall be of You in the great congregation" (v. 25). The meek shall praise the Lord (v. 26). All this praise is starting to spread. Praising the Lord is contagious, and if Christians praise him, other people will praise Him, too.

We also find fellowship with other believers. "I will declare Your name to My brethren" (v. 22). And we find a witness to the whole world. "All the ends of the world shall remember and turn to the Lord" (v. 27). I hope you're not living between Good Friday and Easter Sunday. That's a miserable place to live. I hope you're living from Easter Sunday on. How can you tell if you're on Resurrection ground? Are you worshiping and praising the Lord? Are you fellowshipping with God's people? Are you witnessing to others? Are you serving others? "A posterity shall serve Him" (v. 30). We are on Resurrection ground. Let's live like it.

✦   ✦   ✦

Praise is a natural expression for the believer, especially when considering the implications of our Lord's Resurrection. Are you praising and worshiping our Lord for the redemption He has provided you? Do you fellowship with other believers? Are you reaching out to others who don't know the Lord? Take time to praise God for His great salvation.

EXPECT CHANGES

"**T**he Lord is my shepherd; I shall not want" (v. 1). That must be one of the most familiar quotations from the Old Testament. Everybody has some kind of shepherd. Jeremiah said, "It is not in man who walks to direct his own steps" (Jer. 10:23). We are like lost sheep, not able to guide our own lives. We need a shepherd. Who is your shepherd?

When the Lord is your Shepherd, what will happen in your life? First, *you will live a day at a time.* "Surely goodness and mercy shall follow me all the days of my life" (v. 6). Psalm 23 talks about all the days of our lives, and they are lived one day at a time when the Lord is our Shepherd. Someone has said that the average person is being crucified between two thieves—the regrets of yesterday and the worries of tomorrow. Consequently, he can't enjoy today.

Second, when the Lord is your Shepherd, *you listen for His voice.* In John 10:27 the Lord Jesus said, "My sheep hear My voice." The Shepherd does not drive his sheep from behind. Rather, He calls them from ahead. How do we listen to the Lord's voice? Through the Word of God.

Third, when the Lord is your Shepherd, *you must expect changes.* You may have green pastures and still waters. Then you go through the valley of the shadow of death. You have a table in the presence of your enemies. Then you live in the house of the Lord (heaven) forever. You will experience changes in life. Expect them; don't be afraid of them.

When you follow the Shepherd, the future is your friend, because the Lord is going before you. Live one day at a time, following the Shepherd, and you won't have to be afraid.

✦　　✦　　✦

Some people fail to adapt to life's inevitable changes. As a believer, you need never fear the future. Trust the Shepherd, who goes before you, and listen to His Word. Commit this day to the Lord and thank Him for His guidance.

THE SHEPHERD PROVIDES

Psalm 23 depicts Jesus Christ as the Great Shepherd living for His sheep. It also gives us two assurances. First, *Jesus shepherds us throughout each day*. Dr. Harry Ironside used to say that goodness and mercy are the two sheepdogs that help keep the sheep where they belong. We live our lives one day at a time, because God built the universe to run one day at a time. There must be a time for labor and a time for rest. When we try to live two or three days at a time, we cannot enjoy today. Eventually, this catches up with us physically, emotionally and spiritually. We need to remember that "as thy days, so shall thy strength be" (Deut. 33:25).

As His sheep, we can begin each day with confidence. John 10 tells us that Jesus goes before His sheep. We cannot walk into any experience where Jesus has not first been. Though we may not know or understand what is taking place around us, we will fear no evil because we are close to the Shepherd. His rod takes care of the enemies; His staff takes care of the sheep (discipline and guidance). We can stay close to the Shepherd through His Word.

Our second assurance is that *Jesus shepherds us all the days of our lives*. This psalm is a summary of the Christian life. Verses 1 and 2 speak of childhood. Children need protection and provision. God loves and watches over them. Verse 3 speaks of youth. Teenagers need direction and discipline. The Great Shepherd finds these wandering youth and brings them back. Verses 4 and 5 talk about the middle years. These are not easy years, when the children are growing up and there are bills to pay. Verse 6 speaks of the mature years.

We don't understand why some things happen. But one day we'll realize that everything is under God's goodness and mercy. Then we'll look ahead and see His house.

✦ ✦ ✦

What are your needs today? Stay close to the Shepherd by reading the Word. Resolve to follow His leading.

NO BRAGGING RIGHTS

It can make a real difference in your life if you'll remember Psalm 24:1: "The earth is the Lord's, and all its fullness, the world and those who dwell therein." Because the earth is the Lord's, we can turn it over to Him. What difference will that make?

First, *it will remind us that we are stewards and not owners.* No matter what we have, we are only stewards of it. God owns everything. He doesn't own just the cattle on a thousand hills; He owns the Cadillacs in a thousand garages! God owns what you possess, and if He doesn't want you to have it, you'd better get rid of it. That brings humility, not pride. You can't brag about what you have if God gave it to you. John the Baptist said, "A man can receive nothing unless it has been given to him from heaven" (John 3:27).

Second, *it makes us victors and not victims.* The world doesn't belong to the Devil. God has given him a certain amount of authority and freedom, but the earth is the Lord's. Jesus, not Satan, is on the throne of heaven.

Third, *it causes us to praise and not to complain.* I like the repetition at the end of this psalm: "Lift up your heads, O you gates! And be lifted up, you everlasting doors!" (v. 7). "Lift up your heads, O you gates! And lift them up, you everlasting doors! And the King of glory shall come in" (v. 9). Nothing will lift up one's head like realizing that God is in control. He's the King of glory. Wherever He rules, there will be grace and glory. If you want that kind of blessing, just remember that the earth and all its fullness is the Lord's. It doesn't belong to you; it belongs to Him, and He is in control.

✦　✦　✦

Good stewardship is one of the great responsibilities of the Christian. You need to maintain a humble attitude toward what God has given you. Make sure you submit to His control. His generosity and grace are great blessings that make you a victor.

DON'T BE ASHAMED

Have you ever been so ashamed that you wanted to go somewhere and hide forever? Did you want to dig a hole, crawl into it and then pull the hole in after you? Read verses 1-3: "To You, O Lord, I lift up my soul. O my God, I trust in You; let me not be ashamed; let not my enemies triumph over me. Indeed, let no one who waits on You be ashamed; let those be ashamed who deal treacherously without cause." David was concerned that he would bring disgrace upon the name of the Lord.

When we are anxious not to be ashamed, we want to live a life that is true to the Lord. We don't want anyone to use us as an excuse for sin or to single us out as "one of those Christians." So one of our first considerations must be *the glory of God*. This is what David talks about in verses 1-3. He is saying, "God, I don't want anybody to do anything that will rob You of glory." Why don't we do certain things? Because God won't be glorified. Some things might not hurt us, and some places might not defile us, but they might hurt the glory of God. They might harm an immature believer. When my wife and I started to have a family, we discovered we couldn't leave certain things on the table. When she and I were the only ones in the apartment, I could leave a knife on the table or a pair a scissors on the floor—but not when the children came along.

Our second consideration must be *the will of God*. "Show me Your ways, O Lord; teach me Your paths. Lead me in Your truth and teach me" (vv. 4,5). To bring glory to God and obey His will, we must depend *on the grace of God*. "Remember, O Lord, Your tender mercies and Your lovingkindnesses" (v. 6). When these three elements are in your life, you will never be ashamed or bring disgrace to the name of the Lord. Instead, you will live a life that pleases Him.

✦　　✦　　✦

Being true to the Lord involves consideration of His glory, will and grace. Do your actions and words bring glory to God? Are you living in His will? Are you depending on His grace? Take care to honor God with your life.

FOLLOW
YOUR LEADER

I have little sense of direction. Fortunately, my wife has built-in radar. If she didn't travel with me, I'm afraid I often would be lost. David talks about the guidance of God in these verses. So much has been said about God's guidance. Does He still guide us? Does He have a specific plan for each of our lives? How does He guide us? David gives us some simple advice on receiving God's guidance.

We must start with *meekness*. "The humble He guides in justice, and the humble He teaches His way" (v. 9). Meekness means that we are not telling God what to do; we are not counseling Him. Who could possibly be His counselor? The meek person receives the Word of God and is submissive to His will. "All the paths of the Lord are mercy and truth, to such as keep His covenant and His testimonies" (v. 10). God does not reveal His will to those who are curious. He reveals His will to those who are *obedient*.

God guides those who are concerned about *His glory*. "For Your name's sake, O Lord, pardon my iniquity, for it is great" (v. 11). Surely goodness and mercy follow us, but they won't unless we are walking in the will of God for His glory, for His name's sake. "He restores my soul; He leads me in the paths of righteousness for His name's sake" (Ps. 23:3). That leads us to the *fear of the Lord*. "Who is the man that fears the Lord? Him shall He teach in the way He chooses" (v. 12). "The fear of the Lord is the beginning of wisdom" (Ps. 111:10). Finally, we must be alert to God's guidance. "My eyes are ever toward the Lord" (v. 15). We must watch and pray. We must keep our eyes open if we want our Shepherd to lead us.

✦   ✦   ✦

God desires to lead His sheep and use them for His glory. Is your life characterized by meekness, obedience, a desire for God's glory and the fear of the Lord? As you remain alert to His leading, you may be assured of His guidance in the decisions and steps of your life.

I WANT OUT!

"**T**he troubles of my heart have enlarged; bring me out of my distresses!" (v. 17). Have you ever prayed like that? David did. What kind of answer did God give him? Ultimately, David was brought out of his distresses and put on the throne, and his enemies were defeated. But he had to go through some difficult years before God finally brought him to that place of glory and victory.

If you have ever prayed this way, stop and ask yourself, *Is this the most important prayer I can pray?* Our first inclination in times of difficulty is to pray, "Bring me out!" But we should be praying, "Build me up." God enlarges us by enlarging our troubles. And when He sees that we are growing, He is able to give us larger places of service and ministry. It's sort of a weaning process. When a child is being weaned from his mother, he's fretful and unhappy. He thinks, *Mother doesn't love me anymore.* But why is she weaning him? Because she wants him to grow up and mature. He cannot go through life depending on his mother. That's what David discovered.

When we are in times of difficulty and distress, the important thing is not *that* we get out of it but *what* we get out of it. "Count it all joy when you fall into various trials, knowing that the testing of your faith produces patience. But let patience have its perfect work" (James 1:2-4). If you find yourself going through a time of trouble today, if the troubles of your heart are enlarged, remember that God wants to enlarge you and give you a larger place of ministry.

◆   ◆   ◆

Growth is often a painful process. It is through difficulty and distress that God enlarges us. Are your troubles enlarged? It is important that you not waste your trials by simply enduring them or wanting to be delivered from them. Allow trials to have their "perfect work" of enlarging you for a greater ministry.

THE GUIDANCE OF GOD

In Psalm 25 David points out that we can experience God's guidance if we meet certain spiritual conditions. The first is *confidence*. We give evidence of our confidence in God through worship. We need to pray so that we might have our hearts right with Him. Waiting is another evidence (vv. 3, 5, 21). Every time I've rushed ahead, I've gotten into trouble. In verses 4 and 5 David talks about his willingness to follow. God won't show us His will unless we're willing to do it. Another evidence of our confidence is the witness of the Word (v. 5). When we have big decisions to make, we must spend time in the Scriptures.

Penitence also is a condition for receiving God's guidance. David is sorry for his sins. He wants God to remember His tender mercies, not David's transgressions. When God remembers someone, He goes to work for that person. He never forgets His children. David asks God for mercy (vv. 10,16) because he is concerned about his past sins, and he doesn't want those sins to get him off target.

Obedience is another condition. We are all sinners. We don't have to be perfect for God to guide us, just obedient. The word *humble* means "yielded to God." If we obey what God already has told us, then He will show us the next step. His guidance is not a spotlight; it's a lamp that illumines each step.

We also must exhibit *reverence*. God will guide us in our choices if we fear Him. The word *secret* (v. 14) means "friendship." Godly fear doesn't mean we are slaves; it means we have loving reverence and respect for a gracious and kind God.

Finally, we must show *perseverance*. It's not always easy to know and do the will of God. Sometimes when we're seeking the Lord, circumstances get worse, and we become lonely. David was lonely and afflicted, but he remembered that God was with him. Because of that, he maintained his integrity and obedience.

◆　　◆　　◆

Do you need God's guidance today? Make verses 1-5 your prayer for His guidance in your life. Place your confidence in Him and yield to Him in spite of circumstances. You will please God and help accomplish His purposes in your life and in the lives of others.

ON THE LEVEL

ntegrity means that your life is whole, that your heart is not divided. Jesus said, "No one can serve two masters" (Matt. 6:24). That's integrity. *Duplicity* means trying to serve two masters. Our Lord also said that nobody can look in two directions at the same time. If your eye is single, then your body is full of light. But if your eye is double, watch out. The darkness is coming in (Matt. 6:22,23). If you look at the darkness and the light simultaneously, the darkness crowds out the light.

In Psalm 25:21 David prayed: "Let integrity and uprightness preserve me, for I wait for You"; and in verse one of today's passage, "Vindicate me, O Lord, for I have walked in my integrity." When we do business with or are ministering to someone, we want that person to have integrity.

When we have integrity, David tells us, we don't have to be afraid of sliding. "I have walked in my integrity. I have also trusted in the Lord; I shall not slip" (v. 1). He also says, "My foot stands in an even place" (v. 12). The word *even* means "a level place." David says, "I'm on the level because I have integrity. I have nothing in my heart against the Lord. I am not disobeying Him."

We also need not be afraid of testing. David writes, "Examine me, O Lord, and prove me; try my mind and my heart" (v. 2). He says, in other words, "Lord, I can go through the furnace. I can go through the X ray. Go ahead and test me. I'm not afraid." When your life is whole before God and others, when you're practicing integrity, when you have a good conscience, you don't have to be afraid of the battle or the furnace or the X ray or the testing. God will see you through.

✦ ✦ ✦

When you walk with integrity, you walk on solid ground. Never try to serve two masters. Always keep your heart undivided before the Lord.

A CHRISTIAN'S DEFENSE

Have you ever been blamed for something you didn't do? Leaders often are blamed falsely. The Israelites blamed Moses for lack of water, bitter water, enemies' attacks and lack of food. In this psalm, David is falsely accused, so he takes four steps to deal with his slanderers.

Step 1: *An honest examination* (vv. 1-3). Human nature does not want to admit it's wrong, but we need to examine ourselves. David walked in integrity. *Integrity* means "wholeness of character." He also walked in faith, without wavering. We find David open before God, walking in the light and letting God examine him. We would save ourselves a lot of trouble if we would let Him examine us. He wants to teach us what we are really like. If we are right before God, it makes no difference what people say.

Step 2: *A holy separation* (vv. 4,5). People accused David of being a hypocrite, even though he did not worship false gods. We must obey the biblical doctrine of holy separation (II Cor. 6:14-18).

Step 3: *A happy celebration* (vv. 6-8). David washed his hands in innocence. He was cleansed by water and blood. He was concerned about praising , loving and glorifying God. Just as Jesus sang before His crucifixion, David sang songs of praise around the altar, the place of sacrifice. Do we sing songs of praise when we have to make sacrifices?

Step 4: *A humble determination* (vv. 9-12). David said, "As for me, I will walk in my integrity." When a person has integrity, he has a great defense, a great shield. Character is a marvelous shield against the accusations of men. A good conscience gives us courage in times of difficulty.

The Christian's defense is the grace of God, His Word and His truth. Because of this, we're able to walk. David's foot stood in an even place. He was not standing alone—he was in the congregation. Let's take the same steps David took the next time someone slanders us.

◆   ◆   ◆

People can hurt you with false accusations, but you need not let slanderers defeat you. If you walk with integrity, your character will shield you. Keep yourself pure and avoid compromising situations. When someone slanders you, God's grace, His Word and His truth will protect you.

I'M
NOT SCARED

"The Lord is my light and my salvation; whom shall I fear? The Lord is the strength of my life; of whom shall I be afraid?" (v. 1). Those are good questions. Why should we be afraid? What does God do to us and for us when we face an enemy? This psalm tells us that when we fear Him, we need not fear anyone else.

David talks about an enemy coming in. "When the wicked came against me to eat up my flesh, my enemies and foes, they stumbled and fell" (v. 2). Here we have a sudden coming of the enemy. But sometimes it's not a sudden invasion. In verse 3 we read, "Though an army should encamp against me." Here the enemy has settled in. I don't know which of these two is the more difficult. I think I'd prefer to have my enemies suddenly show up than to have them camped on my doorstep. You may have an enemy camped in your home or your office or your church. Somewhere in your life an enemy has probably settled.

But David says, "My heart shall not fear; though war should rise against me" (v. 3). This is not a sudden invasion or a settled battle. It's a sustained war, day after day. "Though war should rise against me, in this I will be confident" (v. 3). We can be confident in the Lord, because He is our Light; we don't have to be afraid of the darkness. And because He is our Salvation, we don't have to be afraid of danger. "

How can we have the protection the Lord offers? By abiding in Christ. Verse 4 tells us, "One thing I have desired of the Lord, that will I seek: that I may dwell in the house of the Lord all the days of my life, to behold the beauty of the Lord, and to inquire in His temple." Don't be afraid of your disabilities and your deficiencies. God is your Light, your Salvation and your Strength. He is all you need.

◆　　◆　　◆

The grip of fear can debilitate one's heart, mind and will. But Christians have a Strength greater than any fear we can face. Are you struggling with fear? Whatever battle you may be fighting, rest confidently in God's protection. He is your Strength, and He will deliver you.

BELIEVING OR SEEING?

Have you ever fainted? The psalmist discovered a way to keep from fainting. "I would have lost heart [fainted], unless I had believed that I would see the goodness of the Lord in the land of the living" (v. 13). David felt somewhat forsaken. His enemies were attacking him, and the circumstances were unbearable.

We have to walk by faith just as David did. "I would have lost heart, unless I had believed." Jesus taught in Luke 18 that men ought always to pray and not to faint. When you pray, it's an evidence of faith. The world says that seeing is believing. If the world had written verse 13 of this passage, it would read: "I would have fainted unless I had seen, and then I believed." That was Martha's problem. Lazarus, her brother, had been dead and in the grave for four days. But Jesus said to her, "Didn't I tell you that if you would believe, you would see?" (John 11:40). Thomas said, "Seeing is believing," but Jesus says, "Believing is seeing" (see Ps. 20:24-29).

The evidences of faith are rather obvious. First, *we seek the Lord.* "When You said, 'Seek My face,' my heart said to You, 'Your face, Lord, I will seek'" (v. 8). Do you want to build your faith and be able to walk by faith and war by faith? Then seek the Lord. Second, *call on the Lord.* "Teach me Your way, O Lord, and lead me in a smooth path, because of my enemies" (v. 11). That's prayer. Third, do the hardest thing of all—*wait on the Lord.* "Wait on the Lord; be of good courage, and He shall strengthen your heart" (v. 14). Believing is seeing. Trust the Lord today.

✦ ✦ ✦

One of the most difficult aspects of the Christian life is waiting on God. It is especially difficult in the midst of trials. But that is when He builds your faith. Don't faint under your circumstances. Wait on the Lord, and He will strengthen you.

CHECKING HANDS

When I was in grade school, each day the teacher would walk up and down the aisles and make us hold out our hands: first, with the palms up to make sure our hands were clean and then with the palms down to make sure our finger-nails were clean. Of course, none of us liked this, because little kids would much rather have dirty hands.

Psalm 28 talks a great deal about hands. The psalmist lifted up his hands. The enemies were doing evil work with their hands. But God had His hand at work as well. "Give to them [the enemies] according to their deeds, and according to the wickedness of their endeavors; give to them according to the work of their hands" (v. 4). There are wicked people in this world, and they have dirty hands. Some people defile everything they touch. This grieves us, especially when they want to touch our lives and defile us.

What did David do? He saw his enemies' evil hands, and he lifted up his hands. "Hear the voice of my supplications when I cry to You, when I lift up my hands toward Your holy sanctuary" (v. 2). When an Old Testament Jew prayed, he didn't fold his hands. He lifted them up to God in praise and in expectancy that He was going to do some-thing. When you see the evil hands of Satan's crowd doing their de-filing work, don't put your hands on their hands. You'll be defiled. Instead, lift your holy hands to the Lord and trust Him to work. "Be-cause they [the enemies] do not regard the works of the Lord, nor the operation of His hands, He shall destroy them and not build them up" (v. 5).

God's hand is at work today, and the result of this is praise (v. 7). Do you need help today? Lift up your hands to the Lord in suppli-cation and in expectation, and soon you will lift up your hands in jubilation and celebration.

✦ ✦ ✦

Unfortunately, many people fail to keep their hands clean. Their evil hands sometimes do dirty work that hurts you. When that happens, you can trust God to take care of evil hands. Keep your hands clean. Look to God, lift your hands to Him and let His hand work for you.

THE VOICE
IN THE STORM

I don't know how my psychologist friends will analyze this, but for some reason I enjoy a rainy day. I especially enjoy it during a day off at home. I find it soothing to stand at the window and see the clouds and the rain and even hear the thunder.

Psalm 29 is a description of a storm. I suppose David was out in the fields or in a cave when this storm came. He saw the power of God in the turbulence. Before it started, he said, "Give unto the Lord, O you mighty ones, give unto the Lord glory and strength. Give unto the Lord the glory due to His name; worship the Lord in the beauty of holiness" (vv. 1,2). He was concerned about God's glory. Perhaps he saw the clouds gathering. When you see clouds gathering and know that a storm is about to come into your life, do you think about the glory of God? David did. So often we don't. We think of escape rather than the glory of God.

In verses 3-9 David describe the storm. "The voice of the Lord is over the waters; the God of glory thunders; . . . the voice of the Lord is powerful" (vv. 3,4). He saw the lightning and heard the thunder. A sequence here is rather interesting. "The voice of the Lord breaks the cedars, . . . the voice of the Lord shakes the wilderness; . . . the voice of the Lord makes the deer give birth" (vv. 5,8,9). God's voice can *break* and *shake* and *make*. David ends the psalm by acknowledging God's sovereignty. He is King forever. "The Lord sat enthroned at the Flood, and the Lord sits as King forever" (v. 10). God is sovereign today. Don't be afraid of the storm. Just look for His glory and His power.

◆　　◆　　◆

God often speaks to you in the storm. The next time you find yourself in a storm, listen for His voice. Look for His glory and power and be reminded that He is in control.

NEVER BE MOVED?

T wo words are repeated seven times in Psalm 30—"you have." David is praising God for what He had done for him. Are you doing that today? Perhaps you've seen the plaque that says, "Prayer changes things," and that's true. I've also seen a plaque that says, "Praise changes things," and that also is true. It's amazing how our whole attitude and whole outlook can be transformed by praising God.

In verse 6 David gives a testimony: "Now in my prosperity I said, 'I shall never be moved.'" When we have *prosperity* without *humility*, it leads to *adversity*. Why? Because we start to be more concerned with things than we are with God. David said in his prosperity, "I shall never be moved." But then he found out that he could be moved. He found out that his prosperity did not guarantee security. So instead of saying "I shall" or "I shall not," he began saying "You have." He submitted his will to God's will. "You have" defeated the enemy. "For You have lifted me up, and have not let my foes rejoice over me" (v. 1). "You have" given me victory. "You have" answered prayer. "You have healed me" (v. 2). "You have brought my soul up from the grave; You have kept me alive" (v. 3).

God did some marvelous things for David. He defeated his enemy, answered his prayer, saved his life and established him (v. 7). And then He gave him joy. "You have turned for me my mourning into dancing; You have put off my sackcloth and clothed me with gladness" (v. 11). Do you want your life to be transformed today? Move from "I shall" to "You have" and, in humility, praise God for what He has done.

◆　　◆　　◆

Submitting to God is an exercise in humility. Until you humble yourself before Him and concern yourself with the things of God, you will not become established. For God to work in your life, your will must be aligned with His. Are you submitted to Him? If not, humble yourself before Him and allow Him to transform your life.

WHOSE HANDS?

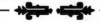

Psalm 31 is one of David's exile psalms. He wrote it when Saul was chasing him through the rough hill country of Judah. David was going from cave to cave and from hill to hill.

During his exile, David discovered that *God's hand was adequate for every need of every day.* Have you noticed in the Psalms how often David talked about hands? As a shepherd he knew the importance of his hands. He had to carry the shepherd's crook, the staff. He also used a slingshot and later exchanged it for a sword. Occasionally he would exchange his sword for a harp. The hands that had been in battle produced beautiful music for the glory of God.

David also talked about the hand of the enemy. "And [You] have not shut me up into the hand of the enemy" (v. 8). "My times are in Your hand; deliver me from the hand of my enemies" (v. 15). We do have enemies. "Be sober, be vigilant; because your adversary the devil walks about like a roaring lion, seeking whom he may devour" (I Pet. 5:8). Our enemies would like to destroy us, but God's hand protects us.

"Into Your hand I commit my spirit; You have redeemed me, O Lord God of truth" (v. 5). This is the prayer of Jewish boys and girls in the Old Testament times. Whenever he went to bed, the little child would say, "Into Your hand I commit my spirit." When our Lord Jesus Christ gave His life for us on the cross, He said, "It is finished! Into Your hands I commend My spirit" (John 19:30; Luke 23:46). When you commit your life into God's hand, you don't have to worry about any other hand, because His hand protects you, provides for you and guides you.

✦　　✦　　✦

It is good for us to depend on God's hand, the hand of provision, protection and guidance. What are your needs today? Have you asked God to provide for them? Depend on the hand of God; you will find Him faithful.

LIKE A LEPER

We can't help what others do and say. We can help only what we do. When others start talking about us or fighting against us, we may not be able to control that. It's difficult when people start to slander the righteous. But this is what David had to endure. In verse 11 we read, "I am a reproach among all my enemies." We expect that. "But especially among my neighbors." Now that hurts. "And am repulsive to my acquaintances." That hurts even more. "Those who see me outside flee from me." Can you imagine your neighbors and your acquaintances running away from you as if you were a leper?

What was causing all of this for David? Saul was lying about him. He was telling his assistants and officers, "David said this. David did that." And this gossip, this awful slander, was spreading through the nation, and David was suffering. "I am forgotten like a dead man, out of mind; I am like a broken vessel" (v. 12). David wanted to be a vessel filled to overflowing, but now he was broken.

What should you do when people start slandering you? First, *be sure your life is right.* "For my life is spent with grief, and my years with sighing; my strength fails because of my iniquity, and my bones waste away" (v. 10). David is saying, "Lord, if I've sinned, I'll confess it." Second, *trust in the Lord.* "But as for me, I trust in You, O Lord; I say, 'You are my God.' " (v. 14). Third, *remember that others have gone through this.* You're not experiencing something unique. Everyone who has done anything for the Lord has been slandered, ridiculed, criticized—including the perfect Son of God. Don't listen to the slander of the enemy; listen to the Word of God. Get close to His *heart*, and you'll have His *help* when you suffer misunderstanding.

✦　　✦　　✦

When someone falsely accuses you, take comfort in knowing that others have gone through the difficulty of slander. Then look to the Lord, for He is your Strength and Salvation. Use this difficult experience to examine your own heart and draw closer to Him.

AVAILABLE TIME

David often talked about God's hand and the hand of the enemy. "My times are in Your hand; deliver me from the hand of my enemies, and from those who persecute me" (v. 15). That's a marvelous declaration of faith. And David didn't write it from a hotel suite somewhere. He was out in the Judean wilderness, where it was dark and dirty and dry. And he was being chased by Saul.

In writing "my times are in Your hand," David teaches us several lessons. First, *time* is important. If you waste time, you're wasting *eternity*. If you waste time, you're wasting *opportunity*. All I can give to God is my body, my ability and my time. And if I don't give Him my time, He can't use my body or my ability. Time is valuable—don't waste it. Invest it.

Second, David reminds us how important *surrender* is. Who controls the available time we have when we're not working or doing the things that must be done to maintain life—that unregistered, undirected time? If we surrender to the Lord, He can control that time. I learned many years ago to turn my entire day over to Him at the beginning of every day. If I have interruptions, He's in control. If my plans are changed, He's in control.

Third, this leads to God's *blessings* for us. When our times are in His hand, we can trust Him; He has blessings especially prepared for us. "Oh, how great is Your goodness, which You have laid up for those who fear You" (v. 19). God has some wonderful blessings prepared for you today. But you are not going to enjoy them unless you truly say, "Lord, my times are in Your hand."

♦   ♦   ♦

Time is perhaps your most basic resource. How you use God's gift of time has a profound effect not only on your life but on the lives of others. It's important that you surrender your time to His care. When you give God your time, you surrender it to His control. He will bless you for it.

CONFESSING SIN

Psalm 32 is the record of David's experience after he sinned with Bathsheba and then confessed his sin to the Lord. He feels *the heavy hand of God's discipline.* "For day and night Your hand was heavy upon me; my vitality was turned into the drought of summer" (v. 4). In other words, David says, "God, Your hand was so heavy on me that it was like squeezing a sponge. You have just squeezed all of the energy out of me." It's difficult to have the heavy hand of God's discipline on us, but it shows that God loves us. "Whom the Lord loves He chastens, and scourges every son whom He receives" (Heb. 12:6).

Discipline leads to *the forgiving hand of God's mercy.* "Blessed is he whose transgression is forgiven, whose sin is covered. Blessed is the man to whom the Lord does not impute iniquity, and in whose spirit there is no guile" (vv. 1,2). While David was silent and would not confess his sin, he felt God's hand of discipline draining him. But when he confessed his sin, that heavy hand was lifted. Then God went to the record book and graciously wiped the record clean. That's the meaning of that word *impute.* It means "to put on the account." First John 1:9 tells us that "if we confess our sins, He is faithful and just to forgive us our sins and to cleanse us from all unrighteousness."

Confession leads to *the protecting hand of God's grace.* "You are my hiding place; You shall preserve me from trouble; You shall surround me with songs of deliverance" (v. 7). David went from silence to confession to singing. When your soul is clean, you have a song in your heart.

It's good to know that God forgives sin. Let's confess our sin and sing His praises.

♦   ♦   ♦

Unconfessed sin is a terrible burden. God loves His children too much to allow unconfessed sin in their lives. The hand that disciplines is the same hand that forgives and protects. Are you harboring unconfessed sin? Confess it now and thank God for His forgiveness and protecting hand of grace.

THREE LEVELS

Did you know there are three levels on which God can deal with you? You must decide whether you want Him to treat you as a thing, an animal or one of His own children. God had to treat David as a thing (a sponge), and His hand was heavy on him (vv. 3,4). David was rebelling. He was not acting like God's child. Instead of *confessing* his sin, he was *covering* it. But the Bible says, "He who covers his sins will not prosper" (Prov. 28:13). So God had to treat David like a thing. He put His hand on David and began to squeeze all the life out of him. David finally woke up and confessed his sin.

God also had to treat David like an animal. He warns us, "Do not be like the horse or like the mule, which have no understanding, which must be harnessed with bit and bridle, else they will not come near you" (v. 9). David had acted like a horse—impulsively, he rushed ahead and sinned. And then he became stubborn like a mule and would not confess his sin. So God dealt with him as He would an animal.

But God wants to deal with us as children. "I will instruct you and teach you in the way you should go; I will guide you with My eye [on you]" (v. 8). He doesn't want to control us with bits and bridles, although sometimes He has to do that. Sometimes He has to send us sickness or a handicap or an accident to break our wills. He says, "I'd much rather guide you with My eye on you. I'd much rather instruct you." You can instruct a horse or a mule to a certain extent—but not the way you can a child. Decide today: Is God going to treat you as a thing because you are rebelling or as an animal because you are stubborn? Or will you let Him guide you as His own child? Oh, how much He loves you! He wants to work *in* you and *through* you and *for* you to bring about His best in your life.

♦ ♦ ♦

God loves you and wants to guide you as His child. The way you live decides whether or not He can. Rebellion and unconfessed sin in your life will change the way He works in you. Are you living as a child of God? Decide now on which level He will treat you.

A NEW
SONG

"**S**ing to Him a new song; play skillfully with a shout of joy" (v. 3). Have you sung a new song to the Lord lately? Where do you find this new song, and how can you best express it? The psalmist is talking about worshiping the Lord. Worship should have a freshness to it. Sometimes in our worship we sing the old songs in the old way, and we lose some of our skill. David was a harpist. He said, "Praise the Lord with the harp; make melody to Him with an instrument of ten strings [a psaltery]. Sing to Him a new song" (vv. 2,3).

We get a new song from several sources. First, we get a new song from *God's Word*. "For the word of the Lord is right" (v. 4). When I read my Bible, I ask God to show me new things. Psalm 119:18 is a good prayer: "Open my eyes, that I may see wondrous things from Your law." He gives me new insights from His Word, and that gives me a new song.

Next, we get a new song from *God's works*. "For the word of the Lord is right, and all His work is done in truth. He loves righteousness and justice; the earth is full of the goodness of the Lord" (vv. 4,5). When we look around, we may see sadness, but the psalmist saw goodness. We may see unrighteousness and injustice, but the psalmist saw God's righteousness and justice. Open your eyes and look around you. See the wonderful new things God is doing.

Finally, we get a new song from *our walk with the Lord*. When we go through new experiences and new challenges, God gives us new victories. Then we have a new song to sing. I want to have freshness in my worship. I want fervor and freshness in my witness for the Lord. I want Him to do something new in my life. I want to sing a new song. Do you?

✦　　✦　　✦

God wants you to walk closely with Him so He may lead you into new experiences and challenges. If you're singing an old song, it could mean that you need to renew your walk with the Lord. Feed on the Word of God and look at what He is doing in your life. Ask Him to give you a new song.

No Carbon Copy

Are you depending on the counsel of the Lord? The Word of God, His counsel, runs this whole universe. How did God create it? "And God said, 'Let there be . . .'" (Gen. 1). He spoke, and it was done, which shows the power of His Word. Did you know that the same Word that created the universe holds the universe together and is guiding the universe and human history for you? When we are in tune with the Word of God, we're in tune with the whole universe and with what He is doing in this world.

Let no one rob you of the beautiful truth that God has His counsel for you. He has an individual plan for your life, just as He did for Moses, Joshua, David, the apostles and the great men and women of Church history.

Notice that the Lord's counsel comes from His heart. "The counsel of the Lord stands forever, the plans of His heart to all generations" (v. 11). The will of God doesn't come from a machine. He doesn't photocopy one plan for everyone's life and fax it to all believers. No, God's will comes from His heart, completely tailor-made for your life. And His will lasts forever, unlike human plans.

The will of God is His expression of love for you. Don't be afraid of it. Build your life on the counsel of the Lord.

♦　　♦　　♦

Because God's tailor-made plans for you come from His heart, they are an expression of His love. Stay in tune with the Word of God, and He will guide you according to His will.

THE
BEST CITIZEN

So often the psalmist says, "Blessed is the man" or "Blessed is the family." But in verse 12 he says, "Blessed is the nation." Does God bless nations? Yes. He blessed the nation of Israel. He endowed the Israelites with some special blessings and gave them special tasks. They failed, however, in some of the things He gave them to do. But eventually God brought His Word and His Son through the people of Israel. Christ was born of the tribe of Judah in the family of David.

Are you the kind of person God can use to be a blessing to your nation? Believers were chosen by God, in Christ, before the foundation of the world. We are His own inheritance. God looks down on us with favor and grace. And the Bible tells us that God wants us to be the right kind of citizens.

God is watching us. "The Lord looks from heaven; He sees all the sons of men" (v. 13). And He made us. "He fashions their hearts individually; He considers all their works" (v. 15). Here we are, the people of God in a wicked and dark nation. What should we do? Remember, He is watching us. He made us and He's protecting us. "Behold, the eye of the Lord is on those who fear Him" (v. 18). We don't have to be afraid.

Be the best citizen you can be. Do so by obeying the Lord, by letting your light shine for Him, by praying for your nation, by sharing His Word with others and by exercising the privileges you have as a citizen of your nation.

✦　　✦　　✦

God uses people to bless nations. Christians are to be good citizens, the kind of people He can use to strengthen a nation. Pray for your country and its leaders. Do your part to exercise the freedom you have to share the Word of God and be a witness for Him.

CAN YOU WAIT?

Waiting is one of the hardest things for me to do. I would rather work than wait. Somehow I always end up in the wrong lane or the wrong line, and I'm forced to wait. My impatience is probably why the Lord reminds me of verse 20: "Our soul waits for the Lord; He is our help and our shield." Why does God delay in answering prayer? He wants to give us a better blessing. Why does God delay in bringing deliverance or healing? He has something better in store for us. Our times are in His hands.

We must remember that when we wait on the Lord, we are not being idle or careless. Waiting prepares us. God works *in* us so that He can work *for* us. He knows what He is doing and has His own schedule. "The Lord is not slack concerning His promise, as some [people] count slackness, but is longsuffering toward us, not willing that any should perish" (II Pet. 3:9).

"Our heart shall rejoice in Him" (v. 21). Waiting ultimately leads to worship. The day will come when you will rejoice in the Lord because you have trusted in His holy name. "Let Your mercy, O Lord, be upon us, just as we hope in You" (v. 22). We have hope and faith in waiting on the Lord. If you find it hard to wait, remember that God's delays are not His denials. He has a greater blessing in store for you. You can be sure that one day the waiting will end, and you will start worshiping and praising Him.

◆　　◆　　◆

Are you waiting for God to answer a specific prayer? Keep trusting Him to work on your behalf. Your waiting will turn into worship and praise.

CONTINUAL PRAISE

"I will bless the Lord at all times; His praise shall continually be in my mouth" (v. 1). That verse is much easier to read than it is to practice. How can we praise the Lord at all times? Sometimes it's difficult to praise Him. Sometimes we are weak, and our bodies hurt or circumstances are difficult. Sometimes we must helplessly watch people we love go through hard times.

If we are to praise the Lord at all times, then praise must be important. Notice the results that come when we truly praise the Lord continually. Praise *sanctifies our lives* at all times. It sanctifies us when we're in the dentist's chair or when we are standing by an open grave. The Lord Jesus sang before He went to Calvary. "And when they [Jesus and His disciples] had sung a hymn, they went out" (Matt. 26:30). Paul and Silas praised the Lord in prison when their bodies hurt (Acts 16:25).

Praise also *unifies God's people.* One thing we can all do together is praise the Lord. We may not always agree on the sermon, but we can agree on the hymnbook. That's why there will be so much singing and praising in heaven.

Finally, praise *magnifies the Lord.* That's why we should do it at all times. Anybody can praise the Lord when things are going well. But it's during the "furnace experiences" that praise really magnifies the Lord.

Let praise sanctify your life, unify your fellowship and magnify the Lord.

◆　　◆　　◆

Is praising God part of your Christian experience? Praise Him always, for praise is a necessary part of the life of faith.

A BIBLICAL TESTIMONY

When I was a young Christian, the church I attended held testimony meetings. I would hear people say, "I thank the Lord that He saves, keeps and satisfies." So I asked myself, *That sounds good, but is it in the Bible?*

Yes, it is. We find it in Psalm 34:6-8. "This poor man cried out, and the Lord heard him, and saved him out of all his troubles" (v. 6). The Lord *saves*. It's interesting to notice that we aren't saved *from* trouble. Sometimes when we trust the Lord and pray He saves us from troubles. But here David says, "He saved me *out* of troubles."

He also *keeps*. "The angel of the Lord encamps all around those who fear Him, and delivers them" (v. 7). The word *angel* conveys the idea of many angels, not just one. David is talking about an encampment of angels surrounding us for protection. So the Lord does save and keep. I'm glad for His keeping power. He's able to save and keep us because of His work on the cross and His present ministry in heaven.

Verse 8 says that the Lord also *satisfies*: "Oh, taste and see that the Lord is good; blessed is the man who trusts in Him!" Some of the experiences of life taste sour. Sometimes the cup that is handed to us is not one of sweetness but of bitterness. Our Lord had to drink a bitter cup. Do you know what makes the bitter cup satisfying and sweet? It's "tasting" the Lord in it. When you taste the Lord in the experiences of life, they become sweet in Him. Therefore, that testimony is biblical: He saves, He keeps, He satisfies.

◆　　◆　　◆

What problem are you facing today? Perhaps you are struggling with physical or financial difficulties. Whatever your problems, God promises to help you through them. Are you trusting Jesus to save you and keep you? Have you "tasted" the Lord and found that He satisfies?

HOW TO HAVE A GOOD DAY

How often has someone said to you, "Have a good day"? That's a nice statement, but what does it mean? When you review the day's activities before you go to bed, how do you know whether the day was good or bad? When Joseph's brothers sold him into slavery, that was a bad day. But God turned it into good for him. When Potiphar's wife lied about Joseph and had him put into prison, it was a bad day. But God turned that into good for him also. You see, we don't always know what a good day is. However, we can make our days good if we follow the instructions given in today's passage.

First, *control your tongue.* David asks, "Who is the man who desires life, and loves many days, that he may see good?" (v. 12). Of course, everybody wants long life and good days. So you must "keep your tongue from evil, and your lips from speaking deceit" (v. 13). When you say the wrong thing, you will have a bad day. So keep your tongue under control.

Second, *"depart from evil and do good"* (v. 14). If you want to have a good day, do good. If you sow the seeds of goodness, you'll reap the harvest of goodness.

Third, *"seek peace and pursue it"* (v. 14). Don't go around with a revolver in your hand. Don't be bothered by every little slight or by everything that people say. If somebody cuts in front of you in a line, don't let it bother you. Be a peacemaker, not a troublemaker.

Finally, *trust the Lord because He's watching you.* "The eyes of the Lord are on the righteous, and His ears are open to their cry" (v. 15). The word *open* means "attentive to." You don't have to worry about what other people do. God is watching you, and He's listening to you. You can have a good day if you'll just follow these instructions. So, have a good day!

♦   ♦   ♦

"Have a good day!" may be a trite expression, but you can have a good day if you follow certain instructions from Scripture. Try following the guidelines of this psalm. Not only will you have a good day, but those with whom you come in contact will be blessed.

SMASHED RAINBOWS

A little girl and her mother were walking down a sidewalk after a rainstorm. Someone had spilled some automobile oil on the pavement. Seeing that, the little girl said, "Mommy, look at all of the smashed rainbows!"

Maybe your rainbows have been smashed, and you have a broken heart. Perhaps you don't feel close to God because of your heartache. What can you do to be near to Him? First, *keep in mind that nearness is likeness.* "The Lord is near to those who have a broken heart" (v. 18). The more we are *like* God, the nearer we are to Him. How close can you get to God? You can get as close to Him as *you* want. Draw near to Him, and He will draw near to you. Remember that God knows the meaning of a broken heart. Jesus Christ literally experienced one. He was "a man of sorrows and acquainted with grief" (Isa. 53:3). Let your experiences make you more like Jesus, and He will draw near to you.

Second, *remember that God gives grace to the humble.* "God resists the proud, but gives grace to the humble" (James 4:6). David also said, "A broken and a contrite heart—these, O God, You will not despise" (Ps. 51:17).

Our Lord came "to heal the brokenhearted" (Luke 4:18). Do you have a broken heart that needs healed? Here's the simple secret: Give the Lord all the pieces, and He will heal you.

✦　　✦　　✦

Everyone has experienced dashed hopes and smashed plans. Take comfort in knowing that your Lord heals the broken heart. Are you getting over a crushing experience? The Lord understands what you are going through. Draw near to Him with a humble spirit and give Him the broken pieces of your heart.

GOD'S
TOOLS

"**M**any are the afflictions of the righteous, but the Lord delivers him out of them all" (v. 19). The psalmist does not say, "I thought the Lord kept us *out of* afflictions. I thought that if I read my Bible every day and prayed and tried to obey His will, I would never have any afflictions." Instead, he says that we will face *many* afflictions.

Why do we have afflictions in our lives? We have some afflictions simply *because we are human*. They are just a part of human life. We get older, and our bodies begin to run down. Not every sickness, every accident or every problem we face comes because God is angry at us or is disciplining us. They may just be a part of life.

We also have afflictions *because Satan is against us*. He'd love to destroy us. Or, afflictions may come because we have disobeyed the Lord. I'm glad for those; I'm glad that God loves me enough to "spank" me when I've disobeyed Him.

But often, *afflictions are God's tools for helping us grow*. We don't really grow until we've been through the furnace, through the storm or through the battle. God is not raising hothouse plants that shrivel when the hot wind blows on them. No, He wants to raise mature sons and daughters, and that's why we have afflictions. "Many are the afflictions of the righteous, but the Lord delivers him out of them all" (v. 19). He doesn't keep us *out of* them. He delivers us *from* them. Sometimes He changes the circumstances. Sometimes He changes us. The real secret of deliverance is not the *circumstance around you* but the *faith within you*. Expect affliction, but trust God for deliverance.

◆　　◆　　◆

Perhaps God's greatest use of affliction is as a tool for helping you grow into a mature Christian. The good news is that you may trust Him to deliver you from your afflictions. The next time you face affliction, trust the Lord for your deliverance.

TRUSTING THE LORD

Christians must entrust five burdens to the Lord to receive blessings from Him. First, *trust the Lord with your frustrations* (v. 17). The word *trouble* means "to be in a bind" or "frustrated." Sometimes we bring trouble on ourselves, as did David. The only safe place is in the will of God. Sometimes other people cause our troubles, as Saul often did for David. And sometimes we have troubles because God knows we need them. When we have troubles, we need to pray for His help. Trust the Lord with your frustrations.

Second, *trust the Lord with your feelings* (v. 18). David was repenting because of his sin, and his heart was broken. God respects that attitude; He is always near those who have a broken heart.

Third, *trust the Lord with your future* (v. 20). The word *guard* means "to exercise great care over, to protect." When Jesus was on the cross, the Devil was doing his worst, yet he could do only what God permitted. God was guarding His own Son, and He will guard us, for He is concerned with our future.

Fourth, *trust the Lord with your foes* (v. 21). Their own sin will slay them. "Evil shall slay the wicked." Give your enemies to the Lord. Let Him be the Judge (Rom. 12:17-21).

Finally, *trust the Lord with your failures* (v. 22). The word *condemned* means "to be held guilty." David sinned against the Lord (the cause of his broken heart), but God rescued and forgave him.

If you want to have a good day, trust the Lord with these five burdens.

◆　　◆　　◆

When you became a Christian, you trusted Jesus as your Savior, and He saved you from the penalty of your sin. But don't stop there. You need to entrust your life to God daily. Entrust these burdens to Him and receive the blessings He has for you.

WHAT TO
DO FIRST

"**A**nd my soul shall be joyful in the Lord; it shall rejoice in His salvation" (v. 9). This is David's glad response to God's gracious deliverance from his enemies. David was in trouble; his enemies were accusing him and lying about him. What did he do? He prayed.

Our first reaction to false accusations is to fight. We want to fight back and defend our name and protect our reputation. But David was far more concerned about his character than his reputation. He knew that if he was right with God, it made no difference what people did to him or said about him. So he started with prayer. "Plead my cause, O Lord, with those who strive with me; fight against those who fight against me" (v. 1). When the Enemy fights against you, he's really fighting against the Lord. That's a good principle to remember. When the child of God is in the will of God, he can claim the help and the protection of the Father.

David started with prayer, and he admitted his own helplessness. "All my bones shall say, 'Lord, who is like You, delivering the poor from him who is too strong for him?'" (v. 10). Our enemies are too strong for us. We have to turn them over to the Lord. David trusted God to work on his behalf, and He did.

God will work for you today, too. In His time and in His way, He will accomplish what needs to be done. And when that day comes to an end, or whenever the opportunity might arise, you will say, "And my soul shall be joyful in the Lord; it shall rejoice in His salvation." It's not *your* salvation—it's not based on what you have done for yourself but on what God has done for you. I trust that today you'll have the joy of His victory in your life.

✦   ✦   ✦

When dealing with your enemies, your first response might be to react instead of to act positively. Your best response is to pray. As God's child, you can turn your enemies over to Him and claim His help and protection. Is the Enemy attacking you? Give your burden to the Lord, and He will work on your behalf.

THE
DIVINE LEVEL

On which level of life are you living—on the human level, the demonic level or the divine level? On the *human level* we return good for good and evil for evil. That's the way most people live. But when we live on this level, we really don't grow. In fact, we become like other people. The human level turns life into a war, into a selfish competition. And that's not the Christian way to live. Only God knows when something is truly evil. What someone does to you today might ultimately turn out to be the best thing that's ever happened to you. On the surface it may look like evil, but God can turn it into good.

Nor do we want to live on the *demonic level*. In Psalm 35 we read about those who return evil for good. David says, "They reward me evil for good, to the sorrow of my soul" (v. 12). That's the level the Devil lives on. He always returns evil for good.

But David lived on the *divine level*. He returned good for evil (vv. 13,14). He expressed love toward his enemies. He didn't simply return good for good and evil for evil. And he certainly didn't return evil for good. No, David returned good for evil. He anticipated the words of our Lord Jesus Christ: "Love your enemies, bless those who curse you, do good to those who hate you, and pray for those who spitefully use you and persecute you" (Matt. 5:44).

Let's live on the divine level—that dynamic level of love where we live like the Lord Jesus Christ.

✦   ✦   ✦

It's often difficult to do good toward those who have wronged you. But God wants you to live on the divine level and return good for evil. How do you treat others? The next time you are wronged by someone, choose to treat that person with kindness. God will use your actions to bring glory to Himself.

BEING
A LENS

Each of us is a lens that magnifies what we live for. People can look at and through our lives and see what is really important to us. The athlete magnifies his sport, his team and his winning record. The musician magnifies the instrument he plays. The scholar magnifies his discipline. As God's people, we should magnify the Lord.

The sinner, however, wants to magnify only himself. David said, "Let them be ashamed and brought to mutual confusion who rejoice at my hurt; let them be clothed with shame and dishonor who magnify themselves against me" (v. 26). Notice the phrase "who magnify themselves against me." Whenever you live to magnify yourself, you are always against someone else. This means competition. And God doesn't want us to live competitively.

Our great desire should be to magnify the Lord, not ourselves. David said, "Let them shout for joy and be glad, who favor my righteous cause; and let them say continually, 'Let the Lord be magnified'" (v. 27). The Apostle Paul said, "Christ will be magnified in my body, whether by life or by death" (Phil. 1:20). Are you magnifying the Lord today? Can people listen to your words, look at your life, measure your actions and say, "She belongs to the Lord. He belongs to the Lord"? It's important that people see the Lord, not us.

The most important quality of a lens is cleanliness. When the lenses of my glasses get dirty, I see the dirt. So I have to clean them. When we are dirty, people see us rather than the Lord. Let's keep our lives clean today. Let's magnify the Lord together; He is worthy of all praise.

◆　　◆　　◆

Christians are on display before the world. What an opportunity and responsibility you have to impact others for Christ! If you love the Lord, you will want to magnify Him. Watch your words and actions. Are you living for Jesus? Keep the lens of your life clean so that He may be magnified through you.

PROTECTED
BY A SHADOW

When we trust Jesus Christ and live in fellowship with Him, we have all we need for life and for service. When you were saved, you were born again, complete in Christ. When the Holy Spirit came into your life, He came to give you fullness of life in Jesus Christ.

Psalm 36 indicates that when we walk in the Lord and seek to serve Him, we have His *protection*. "How precious is Your lovingkindness, O God! Therefore the children of men put their trust under the shadow of Your wings" (v. 7). David is talking about the tabernacle, about the wings of the cherubim in the Holy of Holies. How strange that the safest place in the world is under a shadow! When we live in the Holy of Holies, in fellowship with God and under His wings, we have His protection.

In verse 8 David changes the picture. He says we have God's *satisfaction*: "They are abundantly satisfied with the fullness of Your house, and You give them drink from the river of Your pleasures." Our Lord not only protects us but also provides for and satisfies us. A river constantly flows, yet it's always the same. God is always the same, yet He constantly wants to bring new blessings to us. A river is known for its power and abundance. So is God. "For with You is the fountain of life" (v. 9). We don't drink at the river and get thirsty again. We always have that Fountain of Living Water within us.

We also have His *guidance*. "In Your light we see light" (v. 9). What more can you want? In Jesus Christ you have all that you need. Be sure to live under the shadow of His wings.

♦   ♦   ♦

God's lovingkindness addresses your human weaknesses. Where they might betray you or leave you vulnerable, He divinely provides. You have the promise of His care. He protects, satisfies and guides. Is your life holy and acceptable before Him? Trust yourself to God's care and rest under the shadow of His wing. "The Lord takes pleasure in those who fear him, in those who put their hope in his mercy" (Ps. 147:11).

BLESSEDNESS OF BELIEVERS

In this psalm David ponders the fourfold blessedness of believers. First, *we are under God's wings* (v. 7). His mercy is possible because of the blood of Jesus Christ. David refers to the Holy of Holies in the tabernacle, where the Ark of the Covenant held the tables of the Law, with a golden mercy seat over the box. Because he has trusted God, David is in the Holy of Holies and protected by Him (Ps. 61:4; 90:1). Christians today are living in the presence of God at the mercy seat.

Second, *we are at His table* (v. 8). When the Jews brought their sacrifices, they ate a sacrificial meal. As believers, we share all that God has for us in His house. Are you satisfied with the things of God (Ps. 63:1-5)? In the tabernacle were 12 loaves of bread representing the 12 tribes. Today believers are God's priests in His tabernacle and the only ones allowed to eat the bread.

Third, *we are by His river* (v. 8). God wants us to live in paradise and drink from His pleasures. Why would the people of God want to imitate the world and try to get their delight from it? Jerusalem was one of the few ancient cities not built beside a river. But God is the River of His people (v. 4; John 4:13,14). We shall always have satisfaction for our spiritual thirst.

Fourth, *we are in His light* (v. 9). God's light is different from what the world has to offer. If we want to see the lights in this world, we need the Light of the World, the Lord Jesus (John 8:12; Ps. 119:105). We who have eternal life need not be afraid of the wicked. The wicked keep affirming that they don't fear God and keep flattering themselves. They will fall because of their own sin. Are you living in the wickedness of sinners or in the blessedness of believers?

♦   ♦   ♦

The believer never should settle for what the world has to offer. Are you living in the presence of God and enjoying His blessings? Remember, His mercy is always available to you.

MEASURE YOURSELF

Psalm 37 begins with a personal and practical admonition: Do not fret. How do we calm a fretful spirit and bring peace to a troubled heart? "Do not fret because of evildoers, nor be envious of the workers of iniquity" (v. 1). Why do we envy the wicked? They seem to be prospering; they seem to be so happy. But what do they have that we need? In God we have everything we need. Whenever we find ourselves fretting, it's probably because we are measuring ourselves against others. That's the wrong thing to do. Instead, measure yourself against yourself. You're not competing with others; you're competing with yourself. Also measure yourself against the Lord Jesus Christ, because He is the One you are to be like: "The measure of the stature of the fullness of Christ" (Eph. 4:13).

David reminds us: "For they [the wicked] shall soon be cut down like the grass, and wither as the green herb. Trust in the Lord, and do good" (vv. 2,3). When you fix your eyes on the Lord and trust and obey Him, that fretful spirit quiets down, and peace comes to your heart. Whenever I stop trusting the Lord for my needs and for His help, my heart becomes heavy and burdened, and then I become fretful and worried. So "trust in the Lord, and do good; dwell in the land, and feed on His faithfulness" (v. 3). God takes care of His own.

We find a third admonition. "Delight yourself also in the Lord, and He shall give you the desires of your heart" (v. 4). When we delight in the Lord, we learn to appreciate the delights of the Lord. Our desires become His desires, and we pray and live in His will.

Don't fret today. Look to the Lord in faith, trust in Him and delight in Him.

✦　　✦　　✦

Competing with others and comparing yourself to them can lead to fretting. Measure yourself only against yourself and against Jesus Christ. Consider your needs. Are there any the Lord cannot provide? Place your trust in His provision. He is faithful.

HE WILL
DO IT

"**C**ommit your way to the Lord, trust also in Him, and He shall bring it to pass" (v. 5). Bring what to pass? God will bring to pass the thing that does you the most good and that brings Him the most glory. This is a good verse to memorize. No doubt there is something in your life you would like God to do. You've been thinking about it, dreaming about it and praying about it. If God is going to accomplish things *for* us and *in* us and *through* us, we must follow certain instructions.

First, *we must commit our way to the Lord.* This is a definite act of our will. We don't commit it to the Lord and then take it back, anymore than a farmer plants his seed and then keeps digging it up to see if it's growing! Committing our way to the Lord is an act of the will, an act of faith. We make our way His way, and we make His way our way.

Second, *we must trust God.* What does it mean to trust God? It means to believe His promises and to know that He is such a wonderful God that He always can be trusted. We trust people because of their good character or performance. God's character is perfect, and His record is perfect.

Third, *we must wait on the Lord.* When will He act? When He wants to. This is why David adds, "Rest in the Lord, and wait patiently for Him" (v. 7). Martin Luther translated this, "Be silent to God, and let Him hold thee." I like that. Just rest in the Lord. Wait for Him. He's working in you and on you while He's working for you. Commit, trust and wait, and He will bring it to pass.

✦ ✦ ✦

What would you like to see God do in your life? Start by aligning your will with His. Commit your way to Him, trust Him and wait on Him. God is working for you. In His time He will accomplish His work.

ARE YOU MEEK?

"**B**ut the meek shall inherit the earth, and shall delight themselves in the abundance of peace" (v. 11). Our Lord echoed this same idea when He said, "Blessed are the meek, for they shall inherit the earth" (Matt. 5:5). Meekness is not weakness. Moses was called the meekest man on the face of the earth, yet he boldly stood before Pharaoh and led the children of Israel. At times he had to execute judgment. In the same way, our Lord Jesus said, "I am gentle [meek] and lowly in heart" (Matt. 11:29). And Jesus certainly was not weak! One day He took a whip and went through the temple and cleaned house. He was not weak, but He was meek.

Meekness means "power under control." Moses had the power and authority to crush people, but he didn't. He used that power only as God guided him and worked in him. The meek are those who know they have authority and power but keep that power under control. In the New Testament the word translated "meek" also was used in that day to describe a colt that had been broken, its power brought under control.

God can afford to give an inheritance to those who are under control. It's not the proud or arrogant who inherit but the meek—those who say, "Oh, Lord, we want Your will." Too often our fists are clenched. When your fist is clenched, your hand is not open to receive what God wants to give you. What do the meek inherit? The delightful things of the Lord. All God is and has made belongs to the meek.

♦　　♦　　♦

Meekness indicates strength of character, not weakness. God uses people who exhibit power under control. Are you able to claim the inheritance He promises to those who are meek? Submit to His will and enjoy the spiritual riches you have in Christ Jesus.

HE
KNOWS

When you look at the wicked and see their prosperity, don't fret or do anything foolish. The Lord is on your side, and "if God is for us, who can be against us?" (Rom. 8:31). In this passage God gives us all the assurance we need to have peace in our hearts. "A little that a righteous man has is better than the riches of many wicked" (v. 16). Here is your first assurance: *God knows how much we need*, and all of His wealth is available to us. What good is it to have a million-dollar house if it's not a home? What good is it to have a huge bank account if our values are not right? David is telling us that it's better to have a little and have God (because then we have everything) than to have much and not have God.

Our second assurance is that *God knows how much we can take*. "For the arms of the wicked shall be broken, but the Lord upholds the righteous" (v. 17). He knows how great a burden we can bear, how fierce a battle we can fight. When God puts us in the furnace, He always keeps His eye on the clock and His hand on the thermostat.

Third, *God knows the days that we will live*. "The Lord knows the days of the upright, and their inheritance shall be forever" (v. 18). He has a plan for your life. That sounds like a Christian cliche, but it's true. Whenever we've gone on trips, I am assured to know that the tour guide knows where he's going and what he's doing. I can just sit back and let him do the driving and the worrying. That's how God wants us to live. He wants us to leave everything with Him, because He knows how much we need, how much we can take and what will happen each day. Don't worry; live a day at a time. God's Word is clear, "As your days, so shall your strength be" (Deut. 33:25).

♦　　♦　　♦

Take comfort in knowing that God is intimately aware of your needs. He knows what you need and what your limits are. Do you have pressing needs? Leave them with Him. Trust Him to provide them and resist the urge to look ahead and worry. Concentrate on what God is doing for you today.

BORROWING OR INHERITING?

Someone has said that when your outgo exceeds your income, then your upkeep is your downfall. David may have had that idea in mind when he wrote this passage. He is talking about two different attitudes toward life: *How much can I give?* and *How much can I get?*

Nothing is wrong with an honest debt or a loan. In fact, the Lord Jesus, in the parable of the pounds and the parable of the talents, talks about putting money in the bank and investing money and receiving interest. These verses say, however, that the wicked go through life depending on others by borrowing from them. They borrow their joy and their strength. But believers go through life inheriting. "For those blessed by Him shall inherit the earth" (v. 22). Because we are children of God, we are in His will. He's written our names into His last will and testament. Jesus Christ died on the cross to probate His own will. Now we are living on that inheritance.

Are you going through life borrowing? Do you have to borrow happiness, wisdom and joy? Or are you going through life inheriting—drawing from that marvelous spiritual account in the Lord Jesus Christ? The wicked go through life thinking only of getting, but God's people go through life thinking of giving, of sharing with others and of showing mercy.

God has blessed us. We have inherited everything through His Son. No matter what you're facing today, don't be afraid or alarmed. He has everything you need to live a happy, holy and victorious life. Don't go through life borrowing. Draw on His inheritance.

◆　　◆　　◆

In Christ Jesus you have everything you need. God has given you a spiritual inheritance you can draw from. You need not depend on others for your spiritual resources. Instead, confidently depend on God for your strength and resources.

STEPS
AND STOPS

I like these verses because they give us three exciting assurances as we go through each day with the Lord. First, *God directs us in the best way.* The steps of a good man or a good woman are ordered by the Lord. David isn't talking about fate or chance. He isn't saying that life is a rigid machine. But he does say, "Your Father in heaven is watching you. He has planned a wonderful day for you. You may not understand all that He has planned, but everything is in His hands." Romans 8:28 tells us that "all things work together for good to those who love God."

Second, *God delights in us as we obey Him.* Just as human fathers experience delight when their children obey them, so our Father in heaven enjoys delight when we obey Him. "This is My beloved Son, in whom I am well pleased" (Matt. 3:17). That's what God the Father said about God the Son, and I want Him to say the same about me. At the close of the day, I want to be able to come to my Father and hear Him say, "Today you've been a good son. You have delighted My heart."

Third, *God delivers us when we stumble.* "He restores my soul" (Ps. 23:3). He upholds and lifts us up, so we don't have to be afraid of stumbling. Sometimes we do stumble on the path of life, but our steps are ordered by the Lord, and He observes our stops. He knows when you've stumbled, and He's right there to pick you up and get you started again. Stay close to Him, for He guides and guards your path.

◆　　◆　　◆

God promises to guide you through life, and He gives assurances that you may depend on daily. Be encouraged that your life is not left to chance. Does God delight in you as an obedient son or daughter? Remember, your Father is ready to guide and protect you.

CAN YOU BELIEVE IT?

We see and hear all kinds of testimonials from famous people in advertising today. Quite frankly, I don't put much faith in what these celebrities say. What do football players really know about automobile tires? What do actors or actresses know about computers? We know they are used in ads to lend the authority of their name to the product. When we hear a testimonial, we'd better find out who said it, what was said and if we can really believe it.

We find a testimonial in verse 25: "I have been young, and now am old; yet I have not seen the righteous forsaken, nor his descendants begging bread." Let's ask three questions. First, *who said it?* David did. Think of him as a young shepherd taking care of his sheep. God gave him strength to overcome the lion, strength to defeat the bear and strength to overcome the giant, Goliath. As a shepherd, David saw God take care of His own. Think of David the soldier, David the king or even David the sweet singer of Israel. Oh, David knew what he was talking about. God took care of him at each stage in his life. Even David the sinner saw God provide for him.

Second, *what did David say?* "I have been young, and now I'm old; but I've never seen God forsake His own." He didn't say, "I've never seen the righteous go through trouble. I've never seen God's people suffer sorrow or affliction." David knew a great deal about sorrow, affliction, tears and trials. What he did say was this: "I have never seen one of God's children left alone." God has been faithful through the years. We don't have to be afraid of being young or getting old, because He remains with us.

Third, *can we claim this for ourselves?* Yes, we can. Jesus said, "I will never leave you nor forsake you" (Heb. 13:5). He also said, "Lo, I am with you always, even to the end of the age" (Matt. 28:20). You can trust His Word.

◆　　◆　　◆

God always is faithful to His people. The history of Israel confirms His faithfulness. That He will never leave you nor forsake you is a great promise. And you can expect Him to keep His promises. Have you claimed the promises of God's Word and experienced His faithfulness?

SAY "AH"

Visiting the doctor for an annual checkup is necessary. God, too, is concerned about us and wants to give us a spiritual checkup once in a while. My doctor says, "Open your mouth. Stick out your tongue." Then he wants to listen to my heart. He even looks at my feet. David refers to a similar examination in these verses.

God is concerned about your *mouth*. "The mouth of the righteous speaks wisdom, and his tongue talks of justice" (v. 30). What do you talk about? If God were to say to you, "Open your mouth and stick out your tongue," what would He find out about you? I hope He wouldn't discover that you are being deceitful or are speaking defiling words. It's amazing what a doctor can discover by examining the tongue. It's also amazing what God can discover about us—and what we can discover about ourselves! The Word of God needs to be on our lips.

God also is concerned about your *heart*. "The law of his God is in his heart" (v. 31). When God listens to your heart, does He hear His Word? When God's Law is in your heart, He can do something through you and in you and for you. "But his delight is in the law of the Lord, and in His law he meditates day and night" (Ps. 1:2). What's in your heart will determine what's on your lips. If the truth of God is in your heart, then the Word of God will be on your lips.

God also is concerned about your *feet*. "None of his steps shall slide" (v. 31). The righteous person doesn't backslide; his feet are walking on the right path because his heart is filled with God's truth. He's also not ashamed to tell that truth through his lips. He has a testimony and a witness for the Lord.

Taking care of the heart is the most important thing we can do. "Keep your heart with all diligence, for out of it spring the issues of life" (Prov. 4:23). If our heart is right with God, our lips and our feet will be what He wants them to be.

✦　✦　✦

Have you had a spiritual checkup lately? You can remain healthy by keeping the Word of God in your heart. That truth will spread to the other parts of your body. Do you glorify God with your mouth, feet and heart?

YOUR ROOTS

As David finished Psalm 37, he described two different kinds of people and what would happen to them. First, he described the *powerful*. "I have seen the wicked in great power, and spreading himself like a native green tree. Yet he passed away, and behold, he was no more; indeed I sought him, but he could not be found" (vv. 35, 36). The powerful are rooted in this world. They are like a tree that looks strong and stable. One day a storm comes and blows the tree over. It is then cut up for kindling and is gone. The most important part of a tree is its root system.

If you are rooted in this world, you have no security, for everything here is temporary. But if you are rooted in the Lord Jesus Christ, you have the permanence of eternity upon your life. Don't envy the powerful or those whose names are blazoned abroad. Don't worry about what happens to this crowd. God tells us what happens: They could not be found; they're gone. But "he who does the will of God abides forever" (I John 2:17). That's why it's important to live for the Lord today.

Second, David described the *perfect man* or *woman*. "Mark the blameless man, and observe the upright; for the future of that man is peace" (Ps. 37:37). The future of the powerful person is destruction; the future of the perfect person is peace. The word *perfect* doesn't mean "sinless." Nobody is sinless. Instead, David meant the sincere person, the wholehearted person, the person who practices Matthew 6:33: "But seek first the kingdom of God and His righteousness, and all these things shall be added to you."

When we are perfect in Christ, accepted in the Beloved One, we have peace, we have strength, and we have God's salvation. "And the Lord shall help them and deliver them; He shall deliver them from the wicked, and save them, because they trust in Him" (Ps. 37:40). Today, don't walk by sight, looking at the native green tree. Walk by faith. Be perfect in the Lord, and He'll bless you.

✦ ✦ ✦

Our spiritual root system is important to our spiritual well-being. Where we send our roots will determine which resources we will draw from. Are you rooted in the world or in Jesus Christ? Are you living by faith or sight? Trust in the resources you have in Christ and grow in His grace.

SAYING NO

❧❧❧❧❧❧ ❧❧❧❧

Nobody can deny there is pleasure in sin. If there were no pleasure in sin, nobody would fall into temptation. The Bible speaks about the pleasures of sin for a season. What season? The season of sowing. The pleasure of sin comes when we sow, but the pain comes when we reap. This is why David gave such a vivid description in Psalm 38 of what we suffer when we sin. "O Lord, do not rebuke me in Your wrath, nor chasten me in Your hot displeasure!" (v. 1). He went on to say that God's arrows were piercing him and His hand was pressing down on him. All of his bones hurt. His iniquities had gone over his head as if he were drowning in a sea of sin. "My wounds are foul and festering," David said. "I am troubled, I am bowed down greatly; I go mourning all the day long" (vv. 5, 6).

Why did God put this description in the Bible? Why does David compare the consequences of sin to being pierced by arrows, being pressed by His hand, sickness, a heavy burden, drowning, smothering and no peace? Because God wants us to hate sin. If for no other reason, the consequences of sin ought to warn us against sinning. The next time you're tempted, look past the pleasure to the pain and learn to say no. Remember what David says in this Psalm. You say, "I'm a Christian. I can sin." No, you can't, because you'll reap the same consequences. God chastens His own, for He wants us to walk in holiness.

Let's encourage other people to say no. Let's live in such a way that we don't encourage other people to sin. Also, let's have sympathy for those who have fallen. It's sad to reap the consequences of sin—even forgiven sin. David knew that. So let's encourage others and try to restore them. Let's also love the Lord more. Why? Because He went through all of these consequences on the cross for us. He felt the burden. He felt the arrows. And He did it so that we could be forgiven.

◆　　◆　　◆

David greatly suffered for his sin. Those who sin reap its consequences. God wants us to hate sin for what it can do to us and for what it did to His Son. If you are harboring unconfessed sin in your life, confess it and ask for God's forgiveness. Next time you're tempted to sin, remember David's description of the consequences.

DON'T
GIVE UP

Christians are not supposed to sin. But if we do sin, we are not to give up. David had sinned, and now he was paying for his sin! He had sown the seeds of sin, and now he was reaping the terrible harvest. But he didn't give up.

Let's remember that though our friends may forsake us, and though the Enemy may attack us, God never gives up on His children. David said, "My loved ones and my friends stand aloof from my plague, and my relatives stand afar off" (v. 11). Sometimes when we've disobeyed the Lord, even our closest friends and our nearest and dearest relatives are of no help to us. Sometimes we're ashamed to tell them what's happened. But even when they do know, they often avoid us.

And when we sin, the Enemy wants to fight us. He is always waiting for an opportunity. "Those also who seek my life lay snares for me" (v. 12). You would think that after we've succumbed to temptation, the Devil would leave us alone. No, he knows that we're weak and discouraged, so he lays even more snares for us.

But God sees the heart. "Lord, all my desire is before You; and my sighing is not hidden from You" (v. 9). He also hears your cry. "For in You, O Lord, I hope; You will hear, O Lord my God" (v. 15). What will God hear? He will hear our prayer of confession and repentance. "If we confess our sins, He is faithful and just to forgive us our sins and to cleanse us from all unrighteousness" (I John 1:9). God in His government must allow us to reap what we sow. But in His grace He forgives us and cleanses us. Reaping the consequences of sin is one thing; experiencing His judgment for sin is quite something else. Don't give up if you've stumbled and fallen. God sees your heart and hears your cry. He will forgive and restore you.

◆　　◆　　◆

Although God requires that we reap the consequences of our sin, He loves us and wants to restore us to fellowship. Don't allow Satan to rob you of God's grace. He forgives, cleanses and restores. Have you stumbled? Confess your sin and repent. He is faithful to forgive.

PLAYING INTO SATAN'S HANDS

"**F**or I am ready to fall, and my sorrow is continually before me" (v. 17). David was ready to quit. David, the great conqueror and disciplined soldier, the one who killed Goliath, was ready to quit. He had sinned against the Lord, and he was suffering for it. Even his friends were against him. Let's learn some lessons from David to avoid his experience.

Don't give up. Satan is so subtle and mean. When he's tempting you, he whispers in your ear, "You can get away with this." Then after you've sinned, he sneers, "You'll never get away with this. You're done for." Satan wants us to give up, but if we do, we're playing right into his hands. We're denying that God can help us and forgetting that we belong to Him. What earthly father would forsake his child when he stumbles? Instead, that father reaches down in love, picks up his child, comforts him, cleanses his wounds and helps him walk again. If you sin, don't give in to your feelings, don't watch people around you and don't listen to the Devil.

Confess your sin. "For I will declare my iniquity; I will be in anguish over my sin" (v. 18). David didn't say, "I will be sorry that I'm suffering for my sin" or, "I will be sorry for the consequences." He said, "I'm sorry I have sinned."

Trust in the Lord. "Do not forsake me, O Lord; O my God, be not far from me! Make haste to help me, O Lord, my salvation!" (vv. 21, 22). God is not going to forsake you. He cannot forsake you—He owns you, He purchased you, He made you, and He lives in you. Let Him draw near and restore you again.

♦   ♦   ♦

After you've stumbled into sin, you are vulnerable—both to your feelings and to the Devil. You must claim the truth of God's Word and not give in to your feelings or listen to the Devil. Instead, confess your sin to a loving Father and trust Him to restore you to fellowship.

No
Excuses

"**I** was mute with silence, I held my peace" (v. 2). Usually David was singing a song or giving an order or rejoicing in the Lord, but now he is silent. Why? Because God had rebuked him for a sin he had committed, and he knew better than to argue with God. Sometimes when we sin, we want to argue. We make excuses instead of confessions. We give reasons for not escaping the temptation. But David didn't do that. He was silent.

But as he meditated, something stirred within his heart. "My heart was hot within me; while I was musing, the fire burned. Then I spoke with my tongue: 'Lord, make me to know my end, and what is the measure of my days, that I may know how frail I am. Indeed, You have made my days as handbreadths, and my age is as nothing before You; certainly every man at his best state is but vapor'" (vv. 3-5). As David mused and meditated, he learned two lessons.

First, he learned about the *brevity of life*. Verse 6 reads, "Surely every man walks about like a shadow; surely they busy themselves in vain." This means that they are disquieted in vain; they're merely walking in a performance. David says, "I don't know how long this performance is going to last. My life is a handbreadth." Life's brevity ought to warn us not to waste our lives sinning.

Second, David learned about the *frailty of man*. "Help me to know how frail I am" (v. 4). He is telling us, "It's not the length of life that counts—it's the depth of life." It's not important how strong we are in ourselves but how strong we are in God. What counts is that we are investing our lives in eternal things.

Don't argue with God. Don't come with excuses. Rather, come and say, "Lord, make my life count."

◆   ◆   ◆

Life is short, so why devote precious time to sin and its destructive power? Invest your life in the eternal things of God. Draw your daily strength from Him. When you sin, confess it right away and get back to investing your life for God's glory.

A LIVING
HOPE

David asked, "And now, Lord, what do I wait for? My hope is in You" (v. 7). That's a good question. What are you waiting for? And how can you be sure that what you're waiting for is going to come?

David said his hope was in the Lord. Biblical *hope* means confidence in the future. It's a confidence born of faith. Faith, hope and love go together (I Cor. 13). When we have faith in God, we claim His promises, and they give us hope for the future. Hope for the Christian is not a feeling of "I hope it's going to happen." It's exciting expectancy because God controls the future. When Jesus Christ is your Savior and your Lord, the future is your friend. You don't have to worry.

Why is this hope so important? When we lose hope, we lose joy in the present because we have no confidence for the future. I have been in hospital rooms when the surgeon has walked in and said to a patient's loved ones, "I'm sorry. We did the best we could. There is no hope." The faces of the loved ones fall. Sadness fills the room. We live on hope; it springs eternal in the human breast. But it's more than a feeling down inside; it's a confidence that God is in control, and we have nothing to fear.

What is the basis for our hope? It is the character of God. We've been born again unto a living hope (I Pet. 1:3). It's not a dead hope that rots and falls apart but a living hope whose roots go deeper and whose fruits grow more wonderful. You can have joy, confidence, encouragement and excitement today if you will remember that you have a living hope.

✦　　✦　　✦

Your hope for the future is founded in the promises of God's Word. Do you have confidence in the future? Make a mental list of His provision on your behalf during the past year—answered prayers, met needs and other blessings. God's faithfulness in keeping His promises in the past gives you confident hope for the future.

FROM MIRE TO CHOIR

When we wait *for* the Lord and wait *on* Him, we aren't being idle. In this psalm David cries out to the Lord and asks for help. "He also brought me up out of a horrible pit, out of the miry clay, and set my feet upon a rock, and established my steps" (v. 2). Waiting on the Lord is worthwhile because of what He is going to do for us. It is not idleness, nor is it carelessness. And it certainly isn't complacency. Instead, waiting is that divine activity of expecting God to work. And He never disappoints us.

Figuratively, David had been down in a horrible pit. He was sinking in the mire. But he waited on the Lord. And God not only pulled him out of the pit, but He put him on a rock and established his footing. He said, "David, I'm going to take you out of the mire and put you in the choir." "He has put a new song in my mouth—praise to our God" (v. 3).

Are you waiting on the Lord? Are you praying about something and asking, "O God, when are You going to do this? When are You going to work?" Remember, one of these days your praying will turn to singing. Your sinking will turn to standing. Your fear will turn to security as He puts you on the rock. Just wait on the Lord. He's patient with you. Why not be patient with Him and let Him work in His time?

◆   ◆   ◆

Waiting for the Lord's help sometimes forces you to your limits. But take comfort in knowing that while you wait on Him, God is working out His purposes in your life. Are you in a difficult situation, waiting for God to do something? Leave your burden with the Lord and trust Him to act. He never disappoints you when you wait on Him.

A NEW PERSPECTIVE

What are the blessings that come to us when we make the Lord our trust? First, we start seeing life through His eyes. Look at verse 4: "Blessed is that man who . . . does not respect the proud, nor such as turn aside to lies." When we walk by faith, we have God's discernment. We see the world more clearly. But that's not all.

We also start appreciating God's works. "Many, O Lord my God, are Your wonderful works which You have done" (v. 5). He is always at work for us. Romans 8:28 is true: "All things work together for good to those who love God, to those who are the called according to His purpose."

Verse 5 continues, "And Your thoughts toward us cannot be recounted to You in order; if I would declare and speak of them, they are more than can be numbered." Not only do we start seeing and admiring God's works, but also we start enjoying His Word and contemplating His thoughts. When we trust the Lord, His Word becomes precious to us, because "faith comes by hearing, and hearing by the word of God" (Rom. 10:17).

◆　　◆　　◆

Don't trust yourself or your circumstances; trust the Lord. When you roll all your burdens onto Him, you gain a new perspective. You see life through His eyes, you appreciate His works, and you enjoy His Word. Is the Lord your Trust today?

THE HEART
OF THE MATTER

"I delight to do Your will, O my God, and Your law is within my heart" (v. 8). Ponder that statement. The will of God is not something we *do*; it's something we *enjoy and delight in*. His will is the expression of His love. He doesn't declare things and do things because He hates us but because He loves us. We may not always understand His ways. Sometimes we may even think that God has forsaken us. But we should love His will. If our hearts are delighting in His will, then we are close to His heart.

God's Word reveals His will. When the Word of God is in our hearts, then the will of God is in our hearts, and we obey Him wholeheartedly. Paul wrote about this in Ephesians 6:6: "Doing the will of God from the heart." It's possible to follow God from the will only: we can be drudges or obedient slaves, performing a duty. Or we can be children who obey out of love for our Father.

The result is that we delight in God's will. Indeed, the heart of the matter *is* our heart.

✦   ✦   ✦

Because God's will originates in His heart, we can respond to it emotionally—we can love it. Are you in touch with His will? Do you delight in it? Place the Law in your heart so you may know the will of God and obey it.

WHO'S THINKING ABOUT YOU?

Alittle boy asked his father, "Dad, what does God think about?" Now that is a profound question. After all, if God knows everything—past, present and future—what does He have to think about? According to verse 17, He thinks about you and me. "But I am poor and needy," David said, "yet the Lord thinks upon me."

God thinks about us *personally*. He doesn't have to be told about us. He doesn't have to send a committee of angels to investigate our feelings, problems, frustrations or needs. God knows us personally, and He knows our names. It always encourages me to read in the Bible that God calls His people by name. He knows us better than our closest friends or loved ones do. He knows our needs and what's bothering us today.

God thinks about us *lovingly*. He doesn't think thoughts of evil about us. He is not a policeman looking to arrest us. No, our Father in heaven thinks about us lovingly, the way a father and a mother think about their children.

God thinks about us *wisely*. He has a perfect plan for our lives. David said, "The Lord will perfect that which concerns me" (Ps. 138:8). He'll do that today. We don't see all the pieces and how they fit together, but our Father does, and that's all that matters.

Nothing is hidden from the eyes of God. Being out of His will can be a great source of conviction and fear. He knows where your sin will lead you. So walk with the Lord. Say, "Thank You, Father, for thinking about me. I'm going to think about You."

◆　　◆　　◆

God knows you intimately. He knows not only your name but your every need. He knows what is best for you and always does what is right. You are always on God's mind. Is He on your mind? Determine to know Him more intimately.

How Is Your Character?

When was the last time you heard a preacher or Sunday school teacher talk about integrity? I hope it's been recently, because integrity is an important part of the Christian life. To have integrity means to have character. Integrity is the opposite of duplicity. A person who practices duplicity is a hypocrite, a pretender. Integrity means to have one heart and one mind and to serve one master. It means not being divided, not always changing.

David wrote, "As for me, You uphold me in my integrity, and set me before Your face forever" (v. 12). God knows us by our character, whereas people judge us by our conduct. When we become more worried about conduct than about character, our conduct starts to go down the wrong road. Conduct and reputation are closely related, but neither one guarantees good character. For example, the Pharisees had a great reputation, but their character was evil. God sees us. He knows all about us, and He says, "Put Me first in your life."

Not only does God see us, we also see Him. "Set me before Your face forever" (v. 12). That is what gives us integrity: knowing that we're walking, living, thinking and speaking before the face of God. When we fear Him, we don't have to fear anything else. And when we walk in integrity and honesty, when we flee duplicity and hypocrisy, we can face anything. David was able to face all his foes because he had integrity. He prayed, "Unite my heart to fear Your name" (Ps. 86:11). Integrity unites, so it helps us put our lives together.

Today, let's walk in integrity before the face of God.

◆　◆　◆

Don't be so concerned with your reputation and conduct that you fail to look after your character, because you cannot hide that from God. How is your character? Are you unified—do you have one heart and one mind to serve one Master?

ARE YOU DOWN?

Twice in Psalm 42 the writer asks: "Why are you cast down, O my soul? And why are you disquieted within me?" (vv. 5, 11). Perhaps you have asked the same thing. Why do we have hours, sometimes days, perhaps weeks of depression and discouragement? There may be times when we are not at our best physically. I think of Elijah, who had that difficult experience on Mount Carmel when he battled the prophets of Baal and God sent fire from heaven. When it was over, he was tired. His nerves had been stretched to the breaking point, and he got discouraged and ran away. He needed food and sleep, so God sent an angel to feed him and give him rest.

Sometimes our depression is satanic. The Enemy is throwing darts at us. And instead of holding up the shield of faith, we fail to trust God. Those darts then start fires of depression and discouragement in our lives. Sometimes our depression comes from guilt because of unconfessed sin. Sometimes it's just sorrow because of circumstances. We may have lost a loved one or a friend. Sometimes we feel that we have failed and that everything has come to an end.

What's the cure for all of this? "Hope in God, for I shall yet praise Him for the help of His countenance" (v. 5). You have a secure future in Jesus Christ. The best is yet to come. Hope in God and start praising Him. The psalmist said, "I shall yet praise Him." But don't wait! Start praising Him now. I've discovered that when I get discouraged, the best thing to do is praise the Lord immediately. Praise is the greatest medicine for a broken heart. The psalmist praised God for "the help of His countenance." No matter how you feel or whatever your circumstances, if you'll look to the face of God, you'll discover that He's smiling on you.

♦   ♦   ♦

How do you cope with discouragement? Certainly, if it is caused by guilt from unconfessed sin, you need to repent and ask forgiveness. Generally, the cure for being down is to hope in God and praise Him. Your hope in Him is well founded, for He is ever faithful to His Word. Are you discouraged? You may not be able to change your circumstances, but you can praise God.

GUIDE AND GUARD

We all have days when we feel as though God has forsaken us, when it seems as if the Enemy is winning and we are losing. On such a day the psalmist prayed, "Oh, send out Your light and Your truth!" (v. 3). These words represent the deep desire of the psalmist to know and do the will of God. He was not having an easy time.

I like the words *light* and *truth*. We live in a world smothered in moral and spiritual darkness. "Everyone practicing evil hates the light and does not come to the light" (John 3:20). Not only is our world dark, but it's also deceived. People love and believe lies. Mark Twain used to say that a lie runs around the world while truth is putting on her boots! But we have God's light and truth to guide and guard us. We must pray, "Oh, send out Your light and Your truth!"

Where do we find God's light and truth? In His Word. "Your word is a lamp to my feet and a light to my path" (Ps. 119:105). God's Word is truth. "Sanctify them by Your truth. Your word is truth," Jesus said (John 17:17). The Word of God guides His children on the path He has chosen. And that path ultimately leads to Him. "Let them [light and truth] bring me to Your holy hill and to Your tabernacle" (v. 3). The psalmist is talking about the location of the tabernacle, the house of God. When we are in the will of God, it's as though we are dwelling in His house.

✦   ✦   ✦

You live in a dark and deceived world. But God has promised to guide and guard you through His Word. The Bible is a spiritual treasure, and without it, you soon lose your way and become vulnerable. Do you feed daily on the truth of His Word? If not, begin a program of daily meditation in Scripture.

OUT FROM
THE DEPTHS

The next time you feel like quitting, read these chapters. The psalmist presents contrasts that depict the ups and downs of life. First, he contrasts *the desert and the temple* (42:1-4). He is thirsting for God. In fact, he is so thirsty he is using his tears as food. We, too, have spiritual senses: taste, hearing and sight. When your soul is thirsting for the living God, you won't be satisfied with substitutes. Don't feed on your feelings, because you will poison yourself.

The psalmist then reminisces about the temple. There's nothing wrong with memories as long as you don't live in the past. They can either encourage or discourage. Let them be a rudder to guide you and not an anchor to hold you back. We find the answer to the psalmist's grief in 42:5. So often we mourn because we want to, but this verse tells us to hope in God.

Second, he contrasts *the heights and the depths* (42:6,7). The psalmist goes through a range of emotions—from the mountaintop to the valley. And then the waves roll over him. Have you ever felt as if you were drowning? Jesus went through a similar experience (Matt. 20:22). When you pray, be honest with God and tell Him how you really feel. Remember that Jesus knows exactly how you feel, and He understands every experience of life.

Third, the psalmist contrasts *day and night* (42:8). This is the central verse of Psalms 42 and 43. Sometimes we're in the darkness because of sin, but this psalmist is in darkness because he's going through a difficult time. We all have those times. God commands the daytime and nighttime (Job 35:10) and gives songs in the night (Acts 16:25). Remember to look not at yourself but to God. Hope in Him, and He will help you.

♦   ♦   ♦

The contrasts of this passage show that life has its range of experiences. You can expect to have dark days and, at times, to find yourself in the depths. Be encouraged that Jesus understands how you feel. Are you going through a dark time? Remember God's help in the past. He will be just as faithful in helping you now. Tune your spiritual senses to Him and hope in Him.

WHAT A HISTORY!

The older we get, the more we are inclined to start talking about "the good old days." The writer of this psalm must have been listening to such a discussion, because he writes, "We have heard with our ears, O God, our fathers have told us, the deeds You did in their days, in days of old" (v. 1).

Then he describes how God had driven out other nations and planted the nation of Israel. When Jewish people reviewed their history, they reviewed one miracle after another: the deliverance from Egypt, the opening of the Red Sea, the path through the wilderness, victories over great armies, the opening of the Jordan River and the conquering of the Holy Land. What a history!

Good days are not only *old*. We can have good *new* days as well. Yes, God did do some great things for Israel. We must always remember His mighty works. That includes the great things He has done for His Church, such as in the Book of Acts. And He is still doing great things for His people today. When you have a discouraging day and everything seems to be going wrong, just sit and meditate on what God has already done for you. It will lift your heart in praise and adoration.

The psalmist said, "You are my King, O God" (v. 4). When God is our King, the same power to perform miracles that was available to Moses and Joshua and David is available to us. "You are my King, O God; command victories for Jacob. Through You we will push down our enemies; . . . You have saved us from our enemies" (vv. 4,5,7). Don't live only on the memories of the good old days. God's promises are still valid. Trust Him today and make Him your King.

✦   ✦   ✦

Israel's history is a track record of God's faithfulness. The same God who worked miracles for Israel is still doing great things for His people today. Are you longing for the good old days? Don't live on nostalgia; trust God to do new works in your life.

WHERE'S THE VICTORY?

Israel in its early days recorded one victory after another. God delivered Israel from Egypt. He then took the Israelites through the terrible wilderness and brought them victoriously into the Promised Land. And there they defeated nation after nation.

But the writer of this psalm is concerned that the people of God are no longer experiencing victories. "But You have cast us off and put us to shame, and You do not go out with our armies. You make us turn back from the enemy, and those who hate us have taken spoil for themselves" (vv. 9,10). The psalmist is confused. Why isn't God doing for them now what He had done for His people centuries ago? The author describes the people as sheep being slaughtered, and those that aren't slaughtered are scattered. The people are being sold like commodities on the market. "You make us a reproach to our neighbors, a scorn and a derision to those all around us" (v. 13).

Why did this happen? Because God's people had rebelled against Him. They would not listen to His Word nor heed the message of the prophets. For 40 years Jeremiah had pleaded with the people to repent. Oh, they had religion. The temple was filled with activity: more people were attending services, and more sacrifices were being offered. It was tremendously successful, but it was not genuine worship. The Israelites turned the house of God into a den of thieves when it should have been a temple of prayer. And because they rebelled, God had to chasten them. But He also restored them.

When we rebel against God, He will forgive, but He must chasten us. We must reap what we sow. "You have cast us off" (v. 9)—but not forever. "You make us a byword among the nations" (v. 14)—but not forever. God restored His people, and He can restore us.

♦　　♦　　♦

When you fail to listen to God's Word, the Enemy tries to entice you with lies. Soon you find yourself in sin and rebelling against God, and then He must chasten you. Stay victorious in life. Feed on the truth of God's Word and stay in close fellowship with Him.

IS GOD ASLEEP?

Have you ever thought that God is asleep? Maybe it seems He isn't concerned about your problems and difficulties. Or perhaps you feel He isn't listening to your prayers. The writer of Psalm 44 had a similar feeling in his difficult situation. He writes: "Awake! Why do You sleep, O Lord? Arise! Do not cast us off forever. Why do You hide Your face, and forget our affliction and our oppression? . . . Arise for our help" (vv. 23,24,26).

God does not sleep! How we feel doesn't necessarily reflect what is true. Psalm 121:4 says that He who keeps Israel does not slumber or sleep. God is eternally vigilant and eternally alert. Our mothers learned how to sleep with one ear open. When we cried out, they were right there to help us. But God doesn't sleep at all, so both of His ears are open. "The eyes of the Lord are on the righteous, and His ears are open to their cry" (Ps. 34:15).

God is awake, and He is mindful of our needs. Then why doesn't He do something? He always waits to do His will at a time when it will do us the most good and bring Him the most glory. The delays of God are not denials.

Because His timing is perfect, we must wait, trust and not complain. It's easy to complain, but we need to wait in silence before the Lord. And praise Him, because one day you will look back and understand why you had to wait.

♦   ♦   ♦

God is ever mindful of your needs, and He will act when it will do the most good. His delays are preparation. Are you waiting for Him to answer your cry? Trust in Him and wait patiently. He will answer you.

RIDING IN MAJESTY

We often think of Jesus as gentle, meek and mild. He was that, of course. "I am gentle and lowly in heart" (Matt. 11:29) is what He said in His invitation to us. But the Lord is also a conqueror. The psalmist said about Him: "Gird Your sword upon Your thigh, O Mighty One, with Your glory and Your majesty. And in Your majesty ride prosperously because of truth, humility and righteousness" (vv. 3,4). That doesn't sound like the meek and gentle carpenter of Nazareth!

Have you ever considered Christ as Conqueror? So often we view Jesus only through the four Gospels, where we find Him a Servant. We see Him as a humble man, the Servant of God, ministering to people. But here we read about a Conqueror with a sword who is riding in majesty. On the cross, Jesus completely defeated Satan. He also overcame the world. He said to His disciples, "Be of good cheer, I have overcome the world" (John 16:33). And He certainly overcame the flesh. Christians are identified with His victory. We have crucified the flesh (Gal. 2:20). We have been raised to walk in newness of life (Rom. 6:4). And Christ wants to give us victory today.

But first, *we must want victory*. Some people would rather walk on the margin of the battlefield and be a walking victim instead of a marching victor. So examine your heart and say, "Lord, I want victory today."

Second, *we must yield ourselves to Christ*. We don't fight *for* victory; we fight *from* victory. The simple secret of winning in the Christian life is to identify ourselves with Christ, trust Him and follow Him. We'll have battles to fight, to be sure, and sometimes we might stumble and fall. But keep in mind that Christ is riding in majesty. Why don't you ride right along with Him by faith?

◆　　◆　　◆

Jesus has conquered life, and we may stand with Him in victory. Before we can, though, we must want victory, and we must yield ourselves to Him. Are you a conqueror? By faith identify with Christ and share His victory.

A RIGHTEOUS THRONE

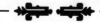

Whenever things are shaky around you, whenever you are afraid, just remember that God is on His righteous throne, which He deserves. It was not given to Him. He didn't purchase it. He didn't have to conquer kingdoms to get it. Our eternal God is on His eternal throne. "Your throne, O God, is forever and ever."

Many rulers in history thought their thrones would endure forever. But those thrones were toppled. In fact, we have to search through history books just to find the names of long-forgotten kings and queens. Not so with Jesus Christ. His throne is not ruined by the ravages of time. It is eternal and righteous, and it can never be overthrown by the attacks of men. Whatever our Lord does is right. He never rules unjustly, and He never causes evil. His scepter is righteous.

To fight against the throne of God is foolish, because that is fighting against something eternal, righteous and holy. God wants to rule in our lives. That's why it's important for us to bow before Him and say, "I crown You King of my life. You shall receive the glory." Let the eternal throne of God rule in your life today.

✦   ✦   ✦

Have you recognized God's authority and rule in your life? One day, every knee shall bow before Him (Phil. 2:10). Do you know Jesus as your Lord of lords and King of kings? If not, bow before Him now and allow Him to rule in your life.

BEAUTY WITHIN

Psalm 45 is a wedding psalm. It says this about the bride: "The king's daughter is all glorious within: her clothing is of wrought gold" (v. 13, KJV). Often after a wedding someone will ask, "What did the bride wear?" Her gown draws everyone's attention. But notice what the bride wore at this wedding. "The king's daughter is all glorious within: her clothing is of wrought gold." It's not important what we wear on the outside, but it is important what we wear on the inside. Jesus Christ wants His Bride, His people, to be beautiful within.

We are married to Jesus Christ—not because we loved Him, but because He loved us. Before we ever thought about Him, He thought about us. In His love He purchased us and came to us. When I perform a marriage ceremony, I don't ask the bride and groom, "Do you know each other?" or "Do you think about each other?" The question is, "Will you commit your lives to each other?" In the same way, trusting Christ for salvation is an act of the will. It's not enough to think about Jesus Christ or know Him intellectually. We must say, "I will trust Him." In the Book of Revelation we read, "Whosoever desires, let him take the water of life freely" (22:17).

Yes, you belong to Jesus Christ, and your true beauty ought to be within. And, if it is within, it's going to come out through your life. The Christian life is a wedding, not a funeral. Don't wear the sorrowful clothes of a mourner, for Christ has clothed you with beauty—the gold of His righteousness. Enjoy the wedding today!

◆ ◆ ◆

Christians are the Bride of Jesus Christ. He purchased you with His love and clothed you with righteousness. Are you committed and yielded to Jesus Christ? Do you love Him and trust Him? Renew your commitment to Him daily, so you may grow and enjoy Him.

HELP IN
TIGHT PLACES

"**G**od is our refuge and strength, a very present help in trouble" (v. 1). This assurance from the Lord ought to take care of all of our fears and problems. God is our refuge—He hides us. God is our strength—He helps us. These two go together. At times in our lives we need a refuge. The storm is blowing and the battle is raging, and we have to run somewhere to hide. It's not a sin to hide, but it *is* a sin to stay hidden. God hides us so that He can help us. Then we can return to the battle and face the storm. This is not escape but rejuvenation.

The Old Testament contains 21 different Hebrew words for trouble. Here the word *trouble* means "in tight places." If you are in a tight place today, let me suggest that you run by faith to Jesus. But don't go to Him to escape. Go there and tell Him, "Lord, I want to go back to the battle. I want to go back to my work. I want to carry the burdens of life, but you have to give me the strength." Then you can claim this marvelous promise of verse 1.

Notice the conclusion: "Therefore we will not fear" (v. 2). When God is available as your refuge and your strength, you have nothing to fear. Take time to run to the Lord.

✦   ✦   ✦

Are circumstances overwhelming you? Take refuge in the Lord. He will enable you to continue with renewed strength and confidence.

DRINK—
DON'T FAINT

God is our Refuge, so we need not fear. But He is also our River, so we need not faint. "There is a river whose streams shall make glad the city of God, the holy place of the tabernacle of the Most High" (v. 4).

Until I visited the Holy Land, I had no idea how *critical* water is there. Without water almost nothing can exist there. Jerusalem is one of the great ancient cities that was *not* founded on a river. It wasn't until Hezekiah dug his famous tunnel that Jerusalem had a water source within the city walls. The psalmist says here that though Jerusalem is not situated beside a river, it has a River. And it comes from the Holy Place, from the throne of God. "God is in the midst of her, she shall not be moved; God shall help her, just at the break of dawn" (v. 5).

Our Lord said, "If anyone thirsts, let him come to Me and drink" (John 7:37). The rivers of Living Water, the rivers of joy, flow out from His throne. In the Bible, water for washing is a picture of the Word of God. But water for drinking is a picture of the Spirit of God. We may drink from this hidden River. And because we drink at this River, we have the joy, the refreshment and the empowerment of the Lord.

The psalmist continues, "The Lord of hosts is with us; the God of Jacob is our refuge" (v. 7). He is the Lord of the armies. All the armies of heaven and earth belong to the Lord Jesus Christ because He has all authority. He is *with* us, not *against* us. He is Immanuel, "God with us."

Take time to drink at the River. Let God refresh you and restore you and strengthen you for the day.

♦   ♦   ♦

Hidden resources are as critical to spiritual well-being as they are to physical well-being. If you want to work and not faint, you must depend on God's provisions. His people have the Holy Spirit within them to refresh and strengthen them. When you drink from the rivers of water He provides, you find strength and the joy of the Lord.

TAKE YOUR
HANDS OFF

"**B**e still, and know that I am God; I will be exalted among the nations, I will be exalted in the earth!" (v. 10). The Hebrew word translated "be still" actually means "take your hands off." God is saying to us, "Take your hands off, and let Me be God in your life." So often we want to manipulate and control. We talk about those who are "hands on" people. In the Christian life, God uses our hands. He used Noah's hands to build the ark. He used David's hands to kill a giant. He used the apostles' hands to feed 5000 people. But sometimes only God's hand can do the job. Sometimes our hands get in the way because we are manipulating, plotting or scheming.

A friend of mine used to remind me, "Faith is living without scheming." Whenever I discover myself pushing and prodding, God says to me, "Take your hands off. Be still, and know that I am God." The difference is simply this. If we play God in our lives, everything is going to fall apart. But if we let Him truly be God in our lives, He will be exalted, He will be with us, and He will get the job done.

Are you facing a problem or a challenge today? Are you wondering what you will do? Give it to the Lord. A time will come when He will say, "All right, I will use your hands." But until then, keep your hands off. Know that He is God. He does not expect us to do what only He can do. We can roll the stone away from the tomb of Lazarus, but only He can raise the dead. We can hand out the bread, but only He can multiply it. Let Him be God in your life.

✦ ✦ ✦

To remain still seems to go against human nature. You want control. But as a believer, you need to remain yielded to God's will and give your burdens to Him. What problem are you facing? Are you keeping your hands off and allowing Him to work in your life?

HIDDEN RESOURCES

Agnostic writer H. G. Wells said, "God is an ever absentee help in times of trouble." He was wrong. Psalms 46–48 grew out of a marvelous miracle in Israel's history. Hezekiah was king of Judah when the Assyrians invaded the land. The king took this crisis to the Lord, and He protected Israel. One morning 185,000 Assyrians died by the hand of the Lord's angel. We, too, can stand strong because of the divine resources God gives us.

God is our refuge; we need not fear (vv. 1-3). He is available, accessible and sufficient—an abundantly available help in trouble. God's people go through trouble. Sometimes it's because we've been disobedient; sometimes it's because we've been obedient; and sometimes He knows we need to be strengthened and helped. Have you fled to your refuge? Hide in Him to gain the strength and grace you need to go back and face your responsibilities.

God is our strength; we need not faint (vv. 4-7). We go from the turbulent sea in verse 2 to a quiet river in verse 4. Jerusalem was not established beside a river. To compensate, Hezekiah built an underground water system that brought water into the city. Similarly, we must live on hidden resources. We can't depend on the world around us or other people. When you trust Jesus as Savior, God puts an artesian well of Living Water within you. While the world has only broken cisterns, the Fountain of Living Water becomes a River. It is from Jesus that we get the spiritual resources we need. Are you drinking today at that River? Get your eyes off the sinking world and remember that God is your Strength.

God is an ever-present help; we need not fret (vv. 8-11). "Be still" means "to take your hands off and let God be God." So often we fret about His timing and methods. Fretting leaves us vulnerable to the Devil's attacks. We should be still, stand still and sit still.

♦   ♦   ♦

Your life depends on hidden resources God gives you. You need not faint nor live with worry and fear. Perhaps you are feeling the attacks of the Enemy or are going through a trial today. Be sure to take your strength and nourishment from God's spiritual resources. He is your Refuge and Strength.

OUR SONG
OF PRAISE

"**F**or God is the King of all the earth; sing praises with understanding" (v. 7). If anything should turn our hearts to joy and praise, it is that God is the King of all the earth. "God reigns over the nations" (v. 8). Circumstances may not always reflect this. What we read in the newspapers or see on the news may not give evidence that God is reigning, but He is! The Lord Jesus is enthroned in heaven today, and everything is under His sovereign control.

Someone may say, "But if He's running the whole world, He can't take much time for me." That isn't true. God sees your needs. He knows your name. He has numbered the hairs on your head. The King of all the universe *is* concerned about *you*.

Because God is King, we should sing. This psalm starts, "Oh, clap your hands, all you peoples! Shout to God with the voice of triumph. For the Lord Most High is awesome; He is a great King over all the earth" (vv. 1,2). God is sovereign, gracious and loving and therefore deserves our adoration. The psalmist implores in verse 6, "Sing praises to God, sing praises! Sing praises to our King, sing praises!" The best way to prove you believe that God is King is to sing praises. When we complain, we are saying that God doesn't know what He is doing, that He is not in control. But when we sing praises to the Lord, we acknowledge that He is King over all the earth.

✦ ✦ ✦

The world refuses to acknowledge God as King and rebels against His authority. But God's people know He reigns over all the earth. You can sing His praises, for you know that He is also a gracious and loving God. You can praise Him because, as your personal Lord, He meets your needs. Praise Him today for who He is and what He has done in your life.

TIMELESS PRAISE

Our praise of God is a timeless act of worship. We can look at this psalm from three different points in time. First, we can view it from the *historic past*. This is one of three psalms that highlight Hezekiah's great victory over Sennacherib (Ps. 46–48). What did the Lord do for the people of Judah? He came down (vv. 1-4), went up (v. 5) and sat down (vv. 8,9). This is a picture of what the Lord did for us: He came to earth to die for our sins, was resurrected and is now seated in heaven.

We also can view this psalm from the *prophetic future*. Israel has yet to go through the time of Jacob's trouble. But Jesus will come down and win the victory (Rev. 19), and Israel will enter into the glorious praises of the Lord. Today all the nations rage, but in the future they will praise Him. Jesus will come and establish His kingdom and keep His promise to Abraham to multiply his descendants so that they are innumerable.

Or we can view this psalm from the *practical present*. To worship God means to render to Him all the praise and adoration of our heart—a total response of all we are for all that He is. This psalm gives us hints about worship. First, the center of our worship is God (v. 1). We worship a victorious God. Second, the purpose of our worship is to exalt Him (v. 9). We are to magnify His greatness. Praise is a witness as well as an experience of worship. Let's exalt the Lord, for He is worthy of our praise.

♦ ♦ ♦

Praising God knows no time boundaries. His people always have and always will praise Him. We praise God to exalt Him and to magnify His greatness. Do you worship Him with praise?

CITIZENS OF ZION

The people of Israel always have been proud of Jerusalem. Psalm 48 describes the city this way: "Beautiful in elevation, the joy of the whole earth, is Mount Zion" (v. 2). Not everyone would agree with that description today, especially in light of the serious political and racial problems connected with Jerusalem. But I think the psalmist is referring here to the heavenly Mount Zion as well. Hebrews 12 tells us that Christians are citizens of the heavenly Zion.

God dwelt in Jerusalem. The psalmist describes how armies came to capture Zion. But when they saw this great city, they went away in fear. "For behold, the kings assembled, they passed by together. They saw it, and so they marveled; they were troubled, they hastened away. Fear and pain took hold of them (vv. 4-6). What did the armies discover when they looked at Jerusalem? First, they discovered the *greatness of God.* "Great is the Lord, and greatly to be praised in the city of our God" (v. 1).

Second, they realized God is a *Refuge to His people.* "God is in her palaces; He is known as her refuge" (v. 3). God is not only a King; He's One to whom we can come with all of our problems and needs. As God established Mount Zion, so He will establish us. As God built this city, He is building our lives. You may wonder why you experience sorrow, disappointment, heartache, perhaps even tragedy. God is building you and protecting you. So you don't have to be afraid.

◆　　◆　　◆

God established the city of Jerusalem, and His greatness in and around the city was evident. Likewise, you are a citizen of the heavenly Zion, and He dwells within. As your Refuge, God protects and looks after your needs. Let Him care for you and establish you.

EVEN UNTO DEATH

No one has more civic pride than the Jewish people who live in Jerusalem. While talking to a tour guide in Israel, my wife asked, "Where were you born?" The guide stood tall, his face brightened, and he said, "I was born in Jerusalem." The Jews love their city, and for good reason.

The psalmist says, "Walk about Zion, and go all around her. Count her towers; mark well her bulwarks; consider her palaces; that you may tell it to the generation following" (vv. 12,13). But he isn't referring to a city.

He means God, the One in whom you trust: "For this is God, our God forever and ever; He will be our guide even to death." That is a marvelous statement! *He is our God.* He owns us. He purchased us. He made us. He lives in us. He is our God forever and ever. The thought overwhelms me!

But He is more than just our God—*He is also our Guide.* He will be our guide even unto death. He guides us in this life, so we don't have to be afraid. He has a path for each of us to follow today. He wants to keep us off detours and help us reach the goal He has planned for us. Verse 14 applies to you and me today. He is our God and our Guide, so we don't have to be afraid. Whatever He starts, He finishes.

✦　　✦　　✦

God is your God not only for this present life but for eternity. As you meditate on the Word of God, His Spirit uses its truth to guide you along the path of His will. You never have to fear death, for your Lord is with you in death and beyond it. Is Jesus Christ your Savior? If so, let Him also be your Guide throughout life.

PILGRIMAGE
TO ZION

Many Jews made a pilgrimage to Jerusalem to celebrate when they heard about Hezekiah's great victory over Sennacherib (II Kings 18,19). Christians today are citizens of the heavenly Zion and are also making a pilgrimage (Heb. 12:18-24).

As pilgrims, *we talk about Zion* (vv. 1-3). We talk about the God who has made Zion great and about His protection. We talk about Zion's beauty. Spiritually, Zion is the joy of the whole earth (Gen. 12:1-3).

As pilgrims, *we see Zion* (vv. 4-8). We look to Jerusalem and are encouraged in our faith. Hezekiah had no way to fight the Assyrians, but he had the Lord. He spread a blasphemous letter from the Assyrians before the Lord and turned everything over to Him. God acted. The Assyrian army was outside, waiting to plunder the city, but they were gone as suddenly as a woman who is taken by child-birth (v. 5). When we're in the will of God, we have His protection.

As pilgrims, *we enter Zion* (vv. 9-11). The Jews went to the temple first. It's good to ponder history. I trust that when you are at church you think about God's lovingkindness and about taking His praise to the ends of the earth (v. 10). We have a greater victory to share with the earth: our Lord Jesus died for us and has risen again.

As pilgrims, *we walk about Zion* (vv. 12-14). This is a triumphant procession of praise. When Nehemiah rededicated the wall, two choirs walked around the wall and met (Neh. 12:27-47). Appreciate what you have and what God has done for you, that you may tell the following generation. Unfortunately, the people of Israel did not stay faithful (Lam. 2:15). Let's be careful that we don't take our blessings for granted.

✦   ✦   ✦

You are making a pilgrimage to the heavenly Zion. Be encouraged, for you have God's protection. That you are on a pilgrimage should be evident in your daily living. Praise Him for what He has done for you.

DON'T TRUST
IN WEALTH

The writer of this psalm certainly had the right attitude toward wealth. He warns, "Those who trust in their wealth and boast in the multitude of their riches, none of them can by any means redeem his brother, nor give to God a ransom for him" (vv. 6,7). *Money cannot take us to heaven,* "for the redemption of their souls is costly" (v. 8). It cost the precious blood of the Lord Jesus Christ! In fact, Jesus warned that money keeps some people out of heaven. "It is hard for a rich man to enter the kingdom of heaven" (Matt. 19:23).

Not only can money not take us to heaven, but *money cannot rescue us from death.* "Their inner thought [the thoughts of these wealthy people] is that their houses will continue forever, and their dwelling places to all generations; they call their lands after their own names" (v. 11). But, the psalmist says, these wealthy people will die just as animals die.

Money cannot conquer death, and *money cannot go with us,* but we can use it wisely while we have it. "For he sees that wise men die; likewise the fool and the senseless person perish, and leave their wealth to others" (v. 10).

The psalmist advises us not to trust in wealth but to trust in the Lord. It is not a sin to have the things that money *can* buy as long as you don't lose the things that money *can't* buy (eternal life). Don't have any false confidence that simply because the bank account looks good you're going to live. You can't take your money with you, but you can use it today for God's glory. When you do that, you are investing it in eternity. Make your wealth eternal by letting God direct your use of it.

◆　　◆　　◆

Wealth can't be trusted. Although a powerful resource, its power is limited to this temporal world. It cannot get you into heaven or conquer death. Do you trust in the world's resources when you should be trusting in God?

TWO
WARNINGS

"**D**o not be afraid when one becomes rich, when the glory of his house is increased; for when he dies he shall carry nothing away" (vv. 16,17). Wealth is temporary. We can't take it with us, so we must use it for the glory of God while we have it. God gives us riches because of His goodness. First Timothy 6:17 says He gives to us "richly all things to enjoy." But we are stewards of wealth, not owners. That comes as a shock to some people. A person may think he owns his house and all of the possessions he has purchased. Yet when he dies, he is separated from them forever.

The psalmist gives two warnings regarding material possessions. First, *beware of having a false security*. People buy houses and put their names on them, but one day those houses will be torn down. Or, if the house isn't torn down, someone will come by and say, "That name on that house. Who was that fellow?" And the reply will be, "I don't know. Never heard of him." People try to perpetuate their fame through their wealth, but eventually they fail.

Second, *beware of wasted opportunity*. We can invest what God has entrusted to us in His work. We can help other people. The wealth that God gives to us—if we are faithful stewards—can be transformed into ministry that brings everlasting glory to Him. Don't waste your opportunity to serve Him this way.

◆　　◆　　◆

To many, wealth often is their security. But it is a false security because riches are temporary. God alone gives wealth, and He expects it to be shared and used for His glory. Are you a faithful steward of what God has given you?

COURT
SUMMONS

The psalmist is describing God's arrival at the court He is convening. "From the rising of the sun [the east] to its going down [the west]" (v. 1), God calls everyone together and says, "I am going to have a judgment." We don't usually think of God as the Judge, but He is. "He shall call to the heavens from above, and to the earth, that He may judge His people" (v. 4).

Why does God judge His people? Shouldn't the wicked be judged instead? Peter tells us that judgment begins at the house of the Lord (I Pet. 4:17). Our *sins* were judged at Calvary. "There is therefore now no condemnation to those who are in Christ Jesus" (Rom. 8:1). But our *works* will be judged at the Judgment Seat of Christ.

God does this because *He's concerned about His glory*. "Out of Zion . . . God will shine" (v. 2). He wants us to glorify Him. He wants us to do His will. Also, *God wants to reward His faithful servants*. If you need a motivation for faithful service, remember that God will judge and will reward those who are faithful. If you are obeying Him today, you won't have to fear your court summons.

✦　　✦　　✦

God will one day judge all His saints. Have you been faithful to the Lord? Have you glorified Him with your life? Make your "court appearance" a time that will glorify Him.

WHAT
GOD WANTS

"**O**ffer to God thanksgiving, and pay your vows to the Most High. Call upon Me in the day of trouble; I will deliver you, and you shall glorify Me" (vv. 14,15). The people had come to God's court and said, "You can't judge us. We have been offering You sacrifices." And God replied, "I will not rebuke you for your sacrifices or your burnt offerings, which are continually before Me. I will not take a bull from your house, nor goats out of your folds" (vv. 8,9). He also said, "If I were hungry, I would not tell you; for the world is Mine, and all its fullness" (v. 12). He was saying, "When you bring Me these sacrifices, you are only giving to Me what I have already given to you."

Think about that. When you put your offering in the plate, are you giving God something that isn't already His? Who gives you the strength to work? God. Who protects you to and from work? God. Who gives you the skills to work? God. Therefore, when we bring material offerings to Him (and He wants us to do this), we are only bringing what He already has given us. God wants us to give Him what He has *not* given us: "Offer to God thanksgiving, and pay your vows to the Most High" (v. 14).

The sacrifices God wants most from us originate in our hearts—calling upon Him, thanking Him and obeying Him. Bring to Him *thanksgiving* and *praise*. God does not give us thanksgiving and then say, "Give it back to Me." No, He waits for us to praise Him. Bring to Him *obedience*: "Pay your vows to the Most High" (v. 14). Bring to Him *prayer*: "Call upon Me in the day of trouble" (v. 15). When we bring these sacrifices, we glorify the Lord.

◆ ◆ ◆

God wants your sacrifices to be from the heart. So often we receive from Him without returning thanks and praise. Do you want to bring glory to God this day? Thank Him for what He is doing for you. Obey His Word. Bring your problems to Him. These are all opportunities He can use to bring glory to Himself.

IS GOD SELFISH?

"**W**hoever offers praise glorifies Me" (v. 23). Today we don't sacrifice bulls and goats and lambs. We don't have a literal altar to which we bring literal sacrifices. The sacrifices God wants from us come from our hearts. Even when we bring money—which is a literal and real sacrifice—it must be given from a heart of love, sincerity and faith. Our purpose for living is to glorify God and enjoy Him forever.

The more you glorify God, the more you delight in Him. The more you delight in Him, the more you enjoy Him. Your life becomes enriched as you glorify God.

Is God selfish when He wants us to glorify Him? If I walked up to you and said, "I want you to glorify me by praising me," it would sound terribly proud. But God is the greatest Being in the universe. None is greater. None is higher. God is sovereign. So when He asks us to praise Him, He wants us to experience the highest thing possible—the praise and worship of God.

One way we praise God is by doing good works. "Let your light so shine before men, that they may see your good works and glorify your Father in heaven" (Matt. 5:16). We praise Him through worship. We praise Him through an orderly, godly lifestyle. "And to him who orders his conduct aright I will show the salvation of God" (v. 23). We have something to *offer*, and we have something to *order*. We offer praise by faith. We order our lives by obedience. Verse 23 is simply saying what the well-known hymn "Trust and Obey" says:

> Trust and obey,
> For there's no other way
> To be happy in Jesus,
> But to trust and obey.

♦   ♦   ♦

God deserves to be glorified. And He gives us the privilege of worshiping Him. Do you delight in the Lord? Live in obedience to His Word and start enjoying Him.

A REPRIEVE FOR THE GUILTY

This psalm describes God's courtroom and the judgment of His people, who made a covenant with Him by sacrifice. There are three stages to this trial. First, *God convenes the court* (vv. 1-6). God calls the earth and then comes. He comes shining and will not keep silent (v. 3; Heb. 12:29). He calls heaven and earth to witness (vv. 5,6).

Second, *God presents the charges* (vv. 7-21). He starts with those who bring sacrifices to Him. He doesn't rebuke their sacrifices, but He is concerned about the way they bring them. God wants spiritual sacrifices from the heart: praise, obedience and prayers (v. 15).

Then he speaks to the wicked. They declare God's statutes, yet they aren't obeying them (Matt. 7:21). They think His silence is His approval.

Third, *God declares the conclusion* (vv. 22,23). He could declare everyone guilty. Instead, He offers a reprieve. "Whoever offers praise glorifies Me; and to him who orders his conduct aright I will show the salvation of God."

One day our lives will be judged. Let's do what God asks us to do and walk out of the courtroom free.

◆ ◆ ◆

Someday you will be on trial at the Judgment Seat of Christ, where your works will be judged by God. Are you prepared for trial in His courtroom? Do your sacrifices come from your heart?

RESTORED FELLOWSHIP

All of us struggle with sin. Human nature pulls us down as gravity does, yet God has made us and saved us to lift us up (I John 1:5–2:6). There are three ways we may deal with our sins.

C*over them.* We cover our sins with our words. This is lying— deceiving others and ourselves and lying to God. Lies are darkness, whereas God's truth is light. When we lie, our character erodes (Prov. 28:13). When we cover sin, we lose God's light, fellowship and character.

C*onfess them.* Admit and judge them—agree with God about your sin. This involves the heart and the will. Some people have died be- cause they repeatedly, willfully, proudly and arrogantly defied the will of God. Admit you are a sinner, say what is wrong and then come to Him and name it. Confess your sin only in the circle of those influenced by it—individuals or family. (Don't become an exhibitionist with the public.) Confession brings release, freedom, forgiveness and a new beginning.

C*onquer them.* Jesus is in heaven today as our Advocate—as a Lawyer before the Father. Abide in Him, love Him, walk with Him in the light of His Word. Keep His commandments. Fellowship is a by-product of our walk with God. To love Him is to serve Him and obey His commandments.

♦   ♦   ♦

Are you covering sin or conquering sin in your life? Confess any known sin and ask God to clean your heart. He wants to forgive you so He can restore fellowship with you.

THE HIGH COST
OF COMMITTING SIN

The most priceless thing in the universe is the human soul. We see its value at Calvary, because the most costly thing in the world—our sin—required the payment of Jesus' blood to redeem us.

We also see sin's toll on our lives. Before David sinned he was a friend of God, straight, meeting His goals. After he sinned he was a crooked rebel, missing the mark. Psalms 32 and 51 relate the spiritual change that took place when David confessed his sin of adultery and murder.

We don't have to rehearse David's sin. The story of how he committed adultery, murdered a man and tried to cover up his sin for a year is well known. The effects were disasterous. If we really understood what sin is and what sin does, it would keep us from deliberately sinning against God. But we don't see sin the way He does.

Sin is a process. David uses three different words for what he did. *Transgressions* refers to rebellion against God. *Iniquity* conveys the crookedness of the sinner. *Sin* means to miss the mark. David also uses three verbs to ask for forgiveness. *Blot out* refers to paying a debt. *Wash* indicates that sin defiles the entire person. *Cleanse* means the sinner is like a leper, in need of total healing.

Before you yield to temptation, remember how it damaged David. Count the high cost of committing sin, and you will be less inclined to do it.

✦　　✦　　✦

The human soul was purchased at the highest cost possible—the death of God's Son. Do you entertain temptations? The cost of committing sin is greater than you can afford. When you find yourself beginning the process of sin, claim the promises of God's Word. God will strengthen and protect you and enable you to overcome temptation. Also, rejoice that He forgives you when you do sin.

DIRTY WINDOWS

Sin is much more than a word in the dictionary. It is a powerful evil that damages our lives and our world. David describes a guilty conscience: "For I acknowledge my transgressions, and my sin is ever before me" (v. 3). Conscience is a marvelous gift from God, the window that lets in the light of His truth. If we sin against Him deliberately, that window becomes dirty, and not as much truth can filter through. Eventually, the window becomes so dirty that it no longer lets in the light. The Bible calls this a defiled, seared conscience.

David covered his sin for about a year. He refused to be broken. He refused to humble himself before God. And what was his life like? "He who covers his sins will not prosper" (Prov. 28:13). Did David prosper? No. Wherever he looked he saw his sin.

Before he sinned, David saw *God* wherever he looked. His heart was pure. "Blessed are the pure in heart, for they shall see God" (Matt. 5:8). Your heart affects your eyes; what you love in your heart, your eyes will seek.

God wants truth in our inner being. "Behold, You desire truth in the inward parts, and in the hidden part You will make me to know wisdom" (v. 6). David confessed because he wanted to see God again—in nature, in His Word and in the temple.

✦   ✦   ✦

Do you keep a clean conscience? It is a part of your inner being that responds to God's truth. When you sin, the window of your conscience becomes dirty and filters out truth. Avoid sin in your life and live with a clean conscience. Every day feed yourself truth from the Word of God.

WHAT DO YOU HEAR?

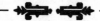

When we sin, it does terrible damage to our spiritual life. David's sin affected his eyes, but it also affected his ears. "Make me hear joy and gladness" (v. 8). Keep in mind that David was not only a soldier but also a singer. He would come back from the battlefield, put down his sword and pick up his harp. He played it and sang praises to God. He listened to the choirs in God's house as they sang praises to Him. David's ears were open to the music of heaven—but not in this psalm.

David heard sorrow and sadness. The choir was off-key. Everything he heard was wrong. We, too, have days like that. When we are not right on the inside, nothing is going to be right on the outside. The good news will be bad news, and the bad news will be worse news. No wonder David prays, "Wash me, and I shall be whiter than snow" (v. 7). He also asks to be purged with hyssop, the little shrub the Jews used to put blood on the doorposts at Passover. "The blood of Jesus Christ His Son cleanses us from all sin" (I John 1:7), if we confess our sins.

If your ears have not been hearing joy and gladness, perhaps the problem is not *around* you but *within* you. Perhaps your heart needs to be cleansed. When your heart is tuned to the music of God and the harmony of heaven, then everything around you will remind you of the Lord.

✦　　✦　　✦

Unconfessed sin leaves you with a dirty heart. When your heart is not right, you don't hear joy and gladness—the music of God. Confess your sin to the Lord, and He will forgive you and restore you.

GOOD FAUCET, BAD WATER

This verse was David's prayer as he confessed his sins to the Lord. *Sin defiles the heart.* You may say, "Well, no one can see that. David didn't look any different after he sinned." But when your heart is defiled, everything is defiled. Solomon wrote, "Keep your heart with all diligence, for out of it spring the issues of life" (Prov. 4:23).

Suppose you turn on a faucet at home, and out comes dirty water. You go to the hardware store, buy a brand-new faucet (a more expensive one), install it and turn it on. Out comes dirty water. Obviously, the problem is not the faucet but the water source. So it is with us. Jesus said, "Out of the abundance of the heart the mouth speaks" (Matt. 12:34). The heart is the center of our lives, and sin defiles it. This is why David said that everything around him was defiled: his eyes (Ps. 51:3), his ears (v. 8), his heart (v. 10) and his spirit.

Sin also weakens the spirit. All of us want an enthusiastic, steadfast spirit. But David was vacillating. Every time he saw someone, he wondered, *What does he know about me?* Whenever people were talking together in a corner, David wondered, *Are they talking about me?* He had a dirty conscience, a vacillating spirit.

God can create a new heart and give a steadfast spirit. How? Not by our excuses but by our confession. We are so prone to excuse our sin. Instead, David confessed his sin, and God forgave him. Yes, David had to pay dearly for his sin. He suffered the discipline of God. But God cleansed his heart, strengthened his spirit and created something new within.

✦   ✦   ✦

What is your heart condition? Is it clean or dirty? Unconfessed sin in the heart defiles the whole body. Never hold onto a sin or cover it; confess it immediately. When you do, God can cleanse and restore you.

THE
GREATEST LOSS

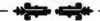

Many sad consequences occur when a believer sins, but the worst is the loss of close fellowship with the Lord. No wonder David prayed, "Do not cast me away from Your presence, and do not take Your Holy Spirit from me" (v. 11). David was remembering what had happened to his predecessor, King Saul. Saul turned against the Lord and became rebellious. So God took His Spirit from him and gave the power of His Spirit to David.

God does not remove His Holy Spirit from us today. Jesus told His disciples that the Spirit of God would abide with them forever. When the Holy Spirit comes into your life at conversion, He seals your salvation. He is the witness that you are a child of God and assures you that you belong to Christ.

But when we sin against the Lord, we lose that closeness of the Holy Spirit, the source of our blessing. Everything in the Christian life depends on our fellowship with the Lord. David constantly depended on God's presence, whether he was writing a psalm or leading an army. Therefore, he was anguished about losing the powerful presence of the Holy Spirit.

Fellowship is the New Testament word for the presence of the Lord. Sonship and fellowship are two different things. Sonship comes from our faith in Jesus Christ—we are born into the family of God. Fellowship is the result of our faithfulness to Him. We keep our lives clean. We obey Him. We talk to Him in prayer. And He talks to us in His Word. Don't lose this by sinning.

◆　　◆　　◆

Fellowship with God is conditional. If we have sin in our lives, we cannot have fellowship with Him. Do you take care to walk with the Lord daily? If you're not careful, the Enemy will gain a foothold in your life. Avoid sin, obey the Word of God and maintain a prayer time with Him. Make walking with the Lord a priority.

LOST JOY

David did not lose his salvation when he sinned, but he did lose the joy of his salvation. It's interesting to see how much David said about joy in the Psalms. Joy is essential in the Christian life. It is the evidence that we are truly born again. Jesus said, "Do not rejoice in this, that the spirits are subject to you, but rather rejoice because your names are written in heaven" (Luke 10:20). Whatever your circumstances today, you can rejoice in the salvation of the Lord.

Nehemiah 8:10 says that the joy of the Lord is our strength. When you enjoy doing something, the enjoyment gives you sufficient strength to do the task. On the other hand, all of us have tasks to perform that we don't enjoy. We do them out of duty and because it's the right thing to do, but they don't provide the strength that comes from joy.

We need the joy of the Lord to witness for Him. Joy shows unsaved people that it is worthwhile to know Jesus. He is the Power for our service.

David lost that joy, so he prayed, "Restore to me the joy of Your salvation, and uphold me with Your generous Spirit" (v. 12). Joy and willing obedience go together. When you enjoy doing something or when you enjoy the person for whom you are doing it, you serve willingly. David is saying, "I have been in bondage because I have not confessed my sin. Therefore, I lost my joy and my willing spirit. I lost that real delight that comes from obeying God."

How can you restore joy? Confess your sin. Then look to Jesus Christ, not yourself. If you look at yourself, you won't rejoice. But if you look to Him, you will rediscover the joy of His salvation.

✦   ✦   ✦

God intends that you rejoice in your salvation. Have you lost the joy of your salvation? Do you miss the delight that comes from obeying the Lord? Make sure your life is free from sin, and then ask Him to restore your joy.

SILENCED WITNESS

The sins we commit not only affect us, but they affect others—even the unsaved. David discovered this when he tried to witness for the Lord. No wonder he wrote, "Deliver me from blood-guiltiness, O God, the God of my salvation, and my tongue shall sing aloud of Your righteousness" (v. 14). *His hands were bloody.* Why? He had killed Uriah, the husband of the woman with whom he had committed adultery. God saw him do it, and Joab, the general of David's army, knew what he had done.

Sin *also silenced his tongue.* He had no song and no witness. "O Lord, open my lips, and my mouth shall show forth Your praise" (v. 15). David was accustomed to praising the Lord, but now he is silent. When we lose our song and our praise and our testimony, we affect others. David was not able to talk to people about the Lord. But when God forgave him and his sin was washed away, he was able to say, "Then I will teach transgressors Your ways, and sinners shall be converted to You" (v. 13).

If you are ever tempted to say, "I can sin and get away with it," just remember David. He sinned, but he didn't get away with it. Sin affected his whole being, his family and the people to whom he should have brought the witness of the Lord.

God has called each of us to be His witness. Our task is to teach transgressors His ways. Our privilege is to lead sinners to the Lord. "You shall receive power; . . . and you shall be witnesses to Me" (Acts 1:8). Our sin affects our witness. Let's ask God to cleanse us and open our lips so we can share the good news of the Gospel with others.

✦   ✦   ✦

Sin spreads like a disease. It not only robs your joy, but it affects your witness to others. As long as you give sin room in your life, your spiritual life will be ineffective. Don't let sin steal your witness for the Lord. Keep your heart clean before Him.

BROKEN THINGS

Have you ever studied the broken things in the Bible? A woman broke a vessel at the feet of Jesus and anointed Him. Jesus took bread and broke it as a picture of His body given for us. God uses broken things, and He starts with broken hearts. This is what repentance is all about. God doesn't listen to the lips. He doesn't measure a material sacrifice. He looks at the heart and says, "If your heart is broken, then I can cleanse it."

When David sinned, he could have brought all kinds of sacrifices. But they would not have pleased the Lord. God was waiting for the sacrifice of a broken heart. That's why David said, "The sacrifices of God are a broken spirit, a broken and a contrite heart—these, O God, You will not despise" (v. 17). David's sins should have brought him condemnation and death. He committed adultery, and he murdered a man. No sacrifice could be found in God's sacrificial system for this kind of flagrant, rebellious, deliberate sin. But David did not die. Even though no sacrifice was available for his sin at the time, God looked down the corridors of time and saw a cross where Jesus Christ would die for David's sin.

God looks at the heart, not the hand. He wants sincerity from the heart, not religious routine.

✦   ✦   ✦

A broken heart is not remorse, nor is it regret. It is repentance, a turning away from sin. It's telling God you hate sin, are judging it and claiming his forgiveness. Bring to Him the sacrifice of a contrite heart.

WHAT PLEASES GOD?

We can live to please ourselves. We can live to please others. But above all we should live to please the Lord. David closes his prayer of confession, "Then You shall be pleased with the sacrifices of righteousness" (v. 19). Everything we do should please the Lord.

A. W. Tozer used to say, "God is not hard to get along with." And this is true. One day David said, "Let [me] fall into the hand of the Lord, for His mercies are great, but do not let me fall into the hand of man" (II Sam. 24:14). God knows us, loves us and is patient with us. Everything He plans for us is for our good, our enjoyment and His glory. So what pleases Him the most? An obedient walk, not sacrifices. David says, "If I brought sacrifices without repentance, You wouldn't accept them. But if I repent and bring you a broken and a contrite heart, then you will accept my sacrifice and my service."

It's interesting how David ends this psalm. "Do good in Your good pleasure to Zion; build the walls of Jerusalem" (v. 18). David in his sin had been tearing down, not building up. He had given opportunity to the enemies of Israel to blaspheme God. The word got out. Soon everyone knew what David had done. So he says, "O God, when I was sinning, I was tearing down. I was not pleasing You. Now I want to please You. And because I'm pleasing You, I will be building up. And the walls of Jerusalem, walls of protection, will be strong." Are you tearing down or building up?

◆   ◆   ◆

God plans everything for your good, your enjoyment and His glory. As His child, strive to please and honor Him in all you do. Is your walk with God one of obedience? Make your life the kind that pleases Him.

THE HIGH COST OF CONFESSION

What does it mean to confess sin? It does not mean to admit our sins, for we can hide nothing from God. The word *confess* means "to say the same thing." We are to see sin as God sees it. This is repentance, not penance. Jesus' blood is the only thing that can pay the cost of sin.

True repentance involves the *mind*, the *emotions* and the *will*. David had to change his mind about his affair with Bathsheba, with Nathan's help (v. 4). The prophet confronted David about his sin (II Sam. 12). He wisely told him a story about the ewe lamb to illustrate his sin. David replied, "I have sinned." Pharaoh also said this, but he didn't mean it. King Saul also said this when he got caught doing wrong. Saul had regret; Pharaoh had remorse. *Regret* involves only the mind—we are upset that we got into a mess or got caught. *Remorse* involves only the mind and emotions—we feel terrible.

Confessing sin means that we have David's attitude and recognize that we are sinners by nature: each of us is capable of committing *any* sin.

The high cost of confessing sin is a broken heart. When we see ourselves as God does, we will have broken hearts. He does not have to discipline us to break our hearts. Jesus only had to look at Peter, and Peter's heart was broken (Luke 22:61). If you come to God with a broken heart and confess your sin, He will forgive and restore you.

◆　　◆　　◆

Confession of sin is not a light matter. It involves the whole inner person. When you see sin as God does, it breaks your heart. Bring your broken heart to God, and He will heal it.

THE HIGH COST OF CLEANSING

Cleansing sin is not cheap. Keep in mind what God has to do. Sin creates debt, defilement and disease, which can be rooted out and forgiven only through the shed blood of Jesus Christ. Every one of us deserves eternal death, but He died in our place. Mercy is God not giving us what we deserve; grace is God giving us what we don't deserve.

When we confess sin, Jesus represents us before God (I John 2). He is our Advocate. When you are tempted to sin, remember that your sin put Jesus on the cross. And when you sin, you don't simply sin against family and friends; you sin against the Savior, who died for you. He is standing in heaven, wounded, representing you before the throne. The high cost of cleansing sin is that Somebody had to die. This is a great motivation not to sin.

If you are saved, you are forgiven—your debt to sin is eliminated. Remember, God is not keeping a record of your sins, but He is keeping a record of your works, and sin hinders your ability to serve Him.

✦　　✦　　✦

Never take for granted God's act of cleansing sin. Forgiveness was purchased at a great price—the blood of Christ. Next time you are tempted to sin, remember that it cost Jesus His life to provide redemption for you.

THE HIGH COST
OF CONQUERING

 One element of spiritual maturity is realizing the horror of sin. It brings great tragedy. Bishop William Culbertson used to speak of the tragic consequences of forgiven sin. For example, David was forgiven, but his baby died, and Absalom and Amnon were slain. God will forgive our sins. In His grace He forgives; in His government we face the consequences. God requires that we reap what we sow.

Temptation is not sin, but it is a sin to cultivate temptation and yield to it. Sin is usually a process, and David went through several stages that led to his sin.

First, *David laid down his armor* (II Sam. 11). Do you put on the spiritual armor? (Eph. 6). We put it on through prayer. We need to come to the Lord each morning and put on the armor. Second, *David was not looking to God*. He was looking at Bathsheba. We need to make sure our bodies belong to God. After you put on your armor, turn yourself completely over to Him (Rom. 12:1). Third, *David did not watch and pray*. The flesh is weak. As we mature in the Christian life, sin becomes more subtle. We must guard against this. Fourth, *David was alone*. He was not fellowshipping with the saints. When people try to rely solely on themselves, they usually fail. Fifth, *David ignored God's Word*. The Word keeps us clean. Finally, *David did not depend upon the Spirit*. We need to yield to Him. If you do, you will conquer sin.

♦   ♦   ♦

Commit these six stages to memory and read Ephesians 6. Don't make the same mistakes David made. Never cultivate a temptation with a view to yielding to sin. Meditate on the Word of God, obey it and guard your heart with its truth. Stay in fellowship with the Lord.

WHEN PEOPLE HATE YOU

Ahimelech was a priest who assisted David. Because of that, he was considered a traitor, and Saul ordered Ahimelech and his family killed. When David heard about it, he was saddened and wrote this psalm.

Psalm 52 gives a threefold description that puts man's evil into perspective. First, *David describes the treacherous man* (vv. 1-4). Doeg was a descendant of Esau, who represents the worldly person (Heb. 12:16). Esau's descendants were enemies of the Jews. Doeg was probably a proselyte. Although he was a mighty and wealthy man, he didn't get his strength from God. Doeg boasted of, reveled in and loved evil. It's dangerous to love a lie (II Thess. 2:11; Rev. 22:15). As in Doeg's case, lying can be telling the truth with a wrong motive.

Second, *David describes the righteous Judge* (vv. 2-7). God will break down this evil man and uproot him from the land of the living. Those who depend on themselves will one day be uprooted and destroyed.

Third, *David describes the victorious servant* (vv. 8,9). He had seen the olive trees by the house of God. He knew God would take care of him, just as He did the trees, and he depended on Him for his strength. David was planted, productive and praising God.

When people are treacherous to us, we must focus on God's goodness, not on man's badness. Leave all judgment to the Lord. Continue to bear fruit for God, and praise Him in the midst of trouble.

✦　　✦　　✦

You can be victorious when others target you with their hatred. The next time someone treats you with hate, focus on God; leave the matter in His hands and praise His name.

LIKE A
RAZOR

The tongue is one of the smallest parts of the body, yet it can do the most damage. In these verses David writes about an experience he had with Doeg, who had a wicked, boastful tongue. David cautions us about two kinds of damaging tongues.

First, beware of a *boastful tongue*. Doeg was a proud man. In his boastful pride, he told Saul about David, and it cost people's lives. We like to boast because it inflates our ego. But those who boast should boast in the Lord. If we boast in the Lord, we glorify Him.

Second, beware of a *sharp tongue*. David says of Doeg, "Your tongue devises destruction, like a sharp razor, working deceitfully" (v. 2). He had a lying, sharp tongue. "You love evil more than good, and lying rather than speaking righteousness. You love all devouring words, you deceitful tongue" (vv. 3,4). Have you ever been cut by someone's sharp tongue? Or worse, have you ever cut someone with your words? What really hurts is when we cut someone with lies. Lying is a terrible sin. Satan is a liar and a murderer. He wants to use our tongues to spread deceit, not righteousness.

In verse 1 David magnifies the goodness of God: "The goodness of God endures continually." When we boast of the goodness of God, our tongues are medicine that heals, not sharp razors that cut. Our tongues are used to speak righteousness, not to spread lies. They will boast about the Lord, not about ourselves. Let's yield our hearts to God so that our tongues might be used for blessing.

♦   ♦   ♦

We need to keep our tongues under control. They are capable of causing great damage. Beware of having a boastful or sharp tongue. Be careful that your tongue does not spread lies. And when others slander you, don't reciprocate with your own tongue. Instead, use your tongue to glorify God and to speak of His goodness.

THE
LAST LAUGH

One of the problems with humanistic philosophy is that it causes people to think they are self-sufficient. They think they don't need any outside help, that in and of themselves they have all they need for life and for death. David describes this kind of person: "Here is the man who did not make God his strength, but trusted in the abundance of his riches, and strengthened himself in his wickedness" (v. 7). That's a description of the self-sufficient person who doesn't know how dangerous his situation really is. Notice that *God was not his strength*. He trusted in his own wickedness. He was strengthened in his sin.

When life is built on sin, it has no foundation. Remember the parable Jesus told about the two men who built houses (Matt. 7:24-27). The foolish man built his house on the sand; he didn't obey God. The wise man built his house on the rock; he obeyed God. And when the storm came, the house that was built on the rock remained strong and firm, whereas the house built on the sand collapsed.

God was not this self-sufficient person's strength, and *God was not his confidence*. He depended on his wealth. Most people today think that money can solve every problem. This person "trusted in the abundance of his riches," David said (v. 7). And what happened to him? "God shall likewise destroy you forever; He shall take you away, and pluck you out of your dwelling place, and uproot you from the land of the living" (v. 5).

We can see this person in his home, surrounded by his wealth. But God reaches in and plucks him out—the way you would reach into a den and pull out a rabbit. This person is like a beautiful tree. But God says, "I'm going to uproot you." The righteous get the last laugh. "The righteous also shall see and fear, and shall laugh at him" (v. 6). Are you going to be a part of the last laugh, or is someone going to be laughing at you?

✦　✦　✦

God is your strength and confidence. Don't be like the self-sufficient person, who trusts in the world's substitutes for strength and confidence. Let the Word of God permeate your mind and hide its truth in your heart. Place yourself in God's care and let Him establish you.

BE AN
OLIVE BRANCH

I f you compared yourself to something in nature, what would you choose? Would you say you are like a mountain, or a hill or perhaps a lake? David wrote, "But I am like a green olive tree in the house of God; I trust in the mercy of God forever and ever" (v. 8). David compared himself to something *permanent,* in contrast to the wicked, who will be uprooted from the land of the living (v. 5).

David's permanent position was also a *privileged* position because he was planted in the house of the Lord. The most important part of a tree is the root system, for it absorbs nourishment. In addition, it provides stability and strength in the storm. We can discern what kind of root system people have when the winds of life blow harder. Some people are like tumbleweeds; they just rootlessly blow from one place to another.

David was also *productive.* He was like a green olive tree in the house of God, bearing fruit for His glory. Fruitfulness is one of the great joys in the Christian life. Jesus used the image of a vine to tell believers that we should produce a lot of fruit (John 15:1-8).

Look at these symbols. A green tree symbolizes freshness and power. Olives contain oil, which is a symbol of the Holy Spirit. No wonder David ended this psalm by praising the Lord! "I will praise You forever, because You have done it; and in the presence of Your saints I will wait on Your name, for it is good" (Ps. 52:9).

✦   ✦   ✦

An olive tree in the house of God is an accurate picture of the believer's position. You are permanent, privileged and productive. You bear fruit for God's glory only when you are yielded to Him and allow the Holy Spirit to work in your life. Can you describe yourself as an olive tree in the house of God?

PRACTICAL ATHEISM

"**T**he fool has said in his heart, 'There is no God'" (v. 1). He doesn't say this outwardly with his lips. He simply says it in his heart. This is a description of practical atheism. Most people would not say, "I don't believe God exists." But most people *live* as though He doesn't exist. David reminds us that what we believe about God in our hearts determines how we live.

Most of the people in this world do not know God. Perhaps that's the fault of Christians. Perhaps we should be praying more, giving more and witnessing more. But the fact is that most people live as if God doesn't exist. They rarely think about Him unless they're facing sickness or tragedy or death, and even then they forget about Him soon after. But David tells us that *what you believe about God affects your will*. "They are corrupt, and have done abominable iniquity; there is none who does good" (v. 1). To say there is no God is to say there is no good.

Verse 2 tells us that *what you believe about God also affects your mind*. God looked down from heaven upon humanity to see if there were any who understood, who sought Him. Not one was found. They do not understand, and they don't want to understand. They want to live their lives without God.

Verse 5 says that *what you believe about God affects your heart*. "There they are in great fear where no fear was." The fear of God comes upon people even though they don't believe in Him.

Do we live our lives as though God were not watching? Do we speak as though He were not listening? Do we think and ponder in our hearts as though He were not aware? Let's live as those who say, "Yes, we know God, and we want to glorify Him."

✦   ✦   ✦

It has been said that everybody believes in someone or something. Trust involves the whole inner being; what you believe affects your heart, mind and will. God responds to your inner man and fellowships with you. He wants you to trust Him and glorify Him with your life. Are you a witness to those around you? Do you live to glorify God?

THE
FOOL'S FOLLY

This psalm describes the atheist and gives eight reasons why he is a fool. First, *he does not acknowledge God* (v. 1). He lives as if there is no God. *He does not obey God* (v. 1). Some people think that human nature is basically kind and good. Not so. We are abominably corrupt by nature (Rom. 3:9). *He does not understand God* (v. 2). If you don't have the Spirit of God, you can't understand the things of God. Atheists say they won't accept anything they can't understand. Actually, there is little in the world they *do* understand!

The fool does not seek God (v. 2). No one by himself seeks God and comes to know Him. God invites us to seek Him, and He has mercy on us. *He does not follow God's way* (v. 3). God has ordained the right path for us. Being a Christian is not easy, and many people do not want to pay the price. The narrow road leads to life and is tough; the broad road is the easy way until the end (Matt. 7:13,14).

The fool does not call on God (v. 4). Such people are mercenary and do not treat others right. *He does not fear God* (v. 5). The day will come when the fool will be afraid. He lives with a false confidence and one day will face judgment. *He does not hope in God* (v. 6). The person who leaves God out of his life has no future.

God's people have a future of eternal life. However, anyone who professes to be a Christian but lives like an atheist also is a fool. May Jesus help us to acknowledge the goodness, greatness and majesty of Almighty God.

✦   ✦   ✦

The atheist lives as if there is no God. You, as God's child, eagerly await eternal life. However, if you fail to walk with the Lord, you behave as a fool. Lay hold of your spiritual resources in Christ and hope in Him.

WHO'S YOUR MAINSTAY?

"**B**ehold, God is my helper; the Lord is with those who uphold my life" (v. 4). David wrote those words when he was hiding from King Saul. We can translate this verse, "The Lord is the mainstay of my life." Is God the mainstay, the main support, of your life today?

David went through several stages waiting for God to help him. He began with *prayer*. "Save me, O God, by Your name, and vindicate me by Your strength. Hear my prayer, O God; give ear to the words of my mouth" (vv. 1, 2). That's a great way to pray. David was being attacked by the enemy, by those who did not believe in God. He needed help, so he cried out to Him.

We see a turning point at verse 4, where David's *faith* goes to work. "Behold, God is my helper; the Lord is with those who uphold my life [the Lord is the mainstay of my life]. He will repay my enemies for their evil. Cut them off in Your truth" (vv. 4,5). David now is trusting the Lord. It's one thing to cry out to God, but it's something else to believe that He is going to hear and answer.

David ends his psalm with *praise*. "I will freely sacrifice to You; I will praise Your name, O Lord, for it is good" (v. 6). Why? "For He has delivered me out of all trouble; and my eye has seen its desire upon my enemies" (v. 7). This is an interesting sequence of experiences: David had *trouble*. This led him to *trust* God, which resulted in *triumph*. He had a *problem*, so he turned to *prayer*, which brought about *praise* to the Lord.

♦   ♦   ♦

When you're in trouble and forced to wait for help, where you place your faith is all-important. Is your sequence of experiences similar to David's? (Problem to prayer to praise? Trouble to trust to triumph?) Next time you must wait for help, let your faith go to work. God will hear you and answer your prayer.

SOAR ABOVE
THE STORM

David wrote this psalm during the early stages of Absalom's conspiracy. He tells us that in times of trial we can take one of three approaches. One is that *we can flee* (vv. 1-8). David talks about his emotions. He was in a difficult situation and wanted to fly away. But these troubles were part of God's discipline for him.

Second, *we can fight* (vv. 9-15). Absalom's conspiracy had gone so far that David could not overcome his enemies. He could only try to save his own life. He saw a sinful city and his friends turn against him, but God was able to overcome them. Absalom and his followers were rebels who had to be disciplined.

Third, *we can fly above our trials* (v. 16-23). The wind that blows down everything lifts up the eagle. We get that kind of power when we wait on the Lord in prayer and worship. David looked at his feelings and foes, but then he focused on his faith in the Lord.

David triumphed because he sought God: *I will call* (v. 16); *I will cast* (v. 22); and *I will trust* (v. 23). God gives us burdens, and we are to give them back to Him. Don't ask for wings like a dove to fly away. Instead, let God give you wings like an eagle so you can soar above the storm.

✦   ✦   ✦

Trials force you to respond. You can flee, fight or fly above them. Are you facing a trial today? God has a purpose in your trial and wants you to learn how to fly above it. Cast your burden upon Him and trust Him for the strength to fly above your difficulty.

WANT TO FLY AWAY?

Have you ever felt like flying away just to get away from it all? Has life ever been such a burden that all you can think about is escaping? David felt like that one day. That's why he wrote, "And I said, 'Oh, that I had wings like a dove! For then I would fly away and be at rest. Indeed, I would wander far off, and remain in the wilderness. I would hasten my escape from the windy storm and tempest'" (vv. 6-8).

Now let's be honest. This is a natural feeling. All of us have felt like getting away, just packing our bags and saying, "I've had enough! I can't take anymore! I've got to get away." It's a normal, natural reaction. But it is *not* a good solution to any problem. We usually take our problems with us. We can go on vacation and enjoy a short respite. But when we return, the battles and burdens are still there. In fact, sometimes when we try to run away, we only make the problems worse.

Why does the Lord allow us to go through windy storms and tempests? They help us grow and mature. If we keep running away, we are like children who never grow up. No, we don't need the wings of a dove to fly away. We need the wings of an eagle. Isaiah 40:31 says, "Those who wait on the Lord shall renew their strength; they shall mount up with wings like eagles." The eagle faces the storm, spreads his great wings and allows the wind to lift him above the storm.

Don't run away. Run *to* the Lord, and let Him lift you high above the storm.

♦   ♦   ♦

God allows trials to make you grow and mature and become like His Son. The next time you go through a storm, resist the pressure to run from it. Let God use the storm to accomplish His purposes.

NOT MY FRIEND

Perhaps the greatest trial is when someone you really love—a friend, a family member—betrays you. David wrote: "For it is not an enemy who reproaches me; then I could bear it. Nor is it one who hates me who has exalted himself against me; then I could hide from him. But it was you, a man my equal, my companion and my acquaintance" (vv. 12,13). It takes a diamond to cut a diamond, and sometimes our friends can hurt us deeply. And we can deeply hurt them. David said about his friend, "The words of his mouth were smoother than butter, but war was in his heart; his words were softer than oil, yet they were drawn swords" (v. 21).

Jesus could have applied these words to Judas. He could have said, "Yes, my own familiar friend, the one who walked with me, the one who ate with me—he is the one who betrayed me."

"We took sweet counsel together, and walked to the house of God in the throng" (v. 14). How sad it is when church members, people we fellowship with in the house of God, turn against us and hurt us. But we must do what David did. He simply said, "Lord, you are the only One who can take care of this. I don't understand it. I'm not going to return evil for evil. I'm just going to leave it with You." God met David's needs. He magnified him and healed his wounds.

We find two lessons here. First, *all of us are human*. Others will hurt you sometimes. But leave your hurt with the Lord and don't fight back. Second, be careful *not to hurt others*. Be a friend who blesses, not betrays.

◆　　◆　　◆

Betrayed trust is one of life's most difficult pills to swallow. How you respond to those who hurt you is a true test of your faith. When someone hurts you, do you live on the divine level and return good for evil? When others do their worst, leave it with God. He will meet your needs and use you to glorify Himself.

LEARNING FROM CHANGE

David was going through intense difficulty. Some of his friends, including his most familiar friend, were turning against him, and it was painful.

How did David solve this problem? First, *he called upon the Lord.* "As for me [no matter what they may do], I will call upon God, and the Lord shall save me. Evening and morning and at noon I will pray, and cry aloud, and He shall hear my voice" (vv. 16,17). Apparently, David had a systematic prayer life. He called upon God and told Him his troubles.

Second, *he let God do the judging.* "God will hear, and afflict them, even He who abides from of old" (v. 19). David believed God would resolve the problem. We should do the same. Let God give you the friends you need to help you in your ministry, and let Him take care of your enemies. Don't treat others the way they treat you. Instead, treat them the way you would want to be treated. Don't return evil for evil.

Third, *David was determined to learn from this experience.* "Because they do not change, therefore they do not fear God" (v. 19). David was going through a change of friends, and this was helping him to fear God more. We usually don't like changes. But whenever God brings change to our lives, we can learn from it. Let's not get so comfortable, so settled, that God can't do anything new in our lives.

◆　　　◆　　　◆

Determine to learn from difficult experiences. God has a purpose for allowing every difficulty and problem. Let Him teach you new truths and work in your life in new ways.

GIVE IT BACK

"Cast your burden on the Lord, and He shall sustain you; He shall never permit the righteous to be moved" (v. 22). This promise tells us that *Christians do have burdens*. David is not talking about concern for others, although it's good to bear one another's burdens. Instead, he means the burdens that the Lord allows each one of us to bear. One translation reads, "Cast what he has given thee upon the Lord."

Burdens are not accidents but appointments. The burdens you have in your life today are what God has ordained for you—unless they are the result of your own rebellious sin against Him. Burdens help us grow; they help us exercise the muscles of our faith. They teach us how to trust God and live a day at a time.

This promise also tells us that *we can cast these burdens on the Lord.* Peter said, "Casting all your care upon Him, for He cares for you" (I Pet. 5:7). The Lord gives us the burden, and then He says, "Now give that burden back to Me. But don't stop there; give Me yourself as well." If we try to give Him our burdens without giving Him ourselves, He really can't help us. It's like stepping onto an elevator with many heavy packages and failing to put them down on the floor until you reach your destination. Let the elevator carry both you and your packages.

Notice that the verse doesn't say He'll *keep* you from problems all the time. He's going to use problems to build your character. But he'll make sure the righteous will not be moved. Cast your burden on the Lord. Let Him sustain you today.

✦ ✦ ✦

Giving your burden to God is an act of faith. But giving yourself to Him and letting Him use that burden to help you grow is taking an extra step of faith. He will invest that burden in building your character. Give your burdens to the Lord today.

BOTTLES AND BOOKS

Are you the kind of person who keeps a daily record of what you do? When I was in the pastorate, I carried a special diary with me. I wrote down where I visited and who I saw. When I got back to the office, I told my staff, "Here is what I did, and here are the needs we have to pray about."

Did you know that God is keeping a journal about you? His journal is composed of bottles and books. David said, "You number my wanderings; put my tears into Your bottle; are they not in Your book?" (v. 8). God watches our traveling and notices our weeping. He has His eyes on our feet, and He has His eyes on our eyes.

God sees where we walk. He knows the paths we've been on. Some of these paths are rather bumpy. But that can be for our good, for as a little boy once said, "The bumps are what you climb on." God sees our wanderings, and He's marked it all in His record.

God sees when we weep. He sees and records our tears and files them for future reference. Among the Semitic peoples, mourners often catch their tears in a little bottle, a symbol of their sorrow. Then they place the bottle in a tomb or casket. One day God will show you the book and the bottle. He's going to say, "I knew when your heart was broken. I knew what you were going through. I've kept a record of it. Now, that sorrow shall be turned into joy." And every one of your tears will become a jewel of beauty to the glory of God.

♦   ♦   ♦

God knows your difficulties and sorrows. The day is coming when your sorrow will be turned to joy, and your tears will glorify Him.

DAVID'S PATTERN

Many of David's psalms contain a pattern. He starts with a problem, then he prays, and finally he praises God for solving the problem. At the end of this psalm David praises the Lord. "In God I have put my trust; I will not be afraid. What can man do to me? Vows made to You are binding upon me, O God; I will render praises to You, for You have delivered my soul from death. Have You not delivered my feet from falling, that I may walk before God in the light of the living?" (vv. 11-13).

First, *he praises God for His Word.* David didn't have as much of the Bible as we have. In fact, he was writing some of it for us! But he had the Word of God, and he depended on it rather than on his feelings or his circumstances. When we love the Word and depend on it daily, ultimately we will praise God for it.

David praises God for being trustworthy. Where did this faith come from? The Word of God. "Faith comes by hearing, and hearing by the word of God" (Rom. 10:17). David is saying, "I'm so grateful for the Word of God because it has taught me to trust the God of the Word. And where there is faith, there will not be fear.

David praises God for all the help He has given him. God delivered his soul from death. I wonder how many times that happened in David's life. God's past deliverance was the assurance of His future care and concern. "Have You not kept my feet from falling, that I may walk before God in the light of the living?" (v. 13). God delivers us so He can delight in us and direct us that we might bring glory to His name.

♦ ♦ ♦

Is David's pattern evident in your life? Are you able to praise God in the midst of difficult situations? Praise Him even before He answers your prayers. Praise Him for His Word, His trustworthiness and His previous help.

HANDLING FEAR

Fear can grip us when we feel life is out of control, and that's what happened to David when he was hiding from King Saul. But instead of running from his fears, with God's help he faced them. By understanding how David handled his fears, we can better handle ours.

First, David honestly admitted his fears (vv. 1-7). He admitted the enemy was against him (v. 2). We won't win the victory if we pretend the Enemy is not there or if we try to suppress our fears. David's enemies were chasing him like ferocious animals, and they oppressed him all day long. They were slandering him and hunting him. It was a matter of life and death. What did he do? He admitted his fears and trusted in God.

A lady once came to D. L. Moody and said, "I've found a verse to help me conquer my fear—Psalm 56:3." Moody replied, "I'll give you a better verse—Isaiah 12:2." Psalm 56:3 tells us that when we're afraid, we'll trust. Isaiah 12:2 says that we'll "trust and not be afraid." Faith overcomes everything (Ps. 103:5). Let's face our fears honestly.

Second, David humbly confessed his faith (vv. 8-13). He spoke about God, not his enemies. He clung to the Word of God and did not back out of his commitment to Him just because he was going through trouble. What was the result of David's ordeal? God's protection and provision brought forth David's prayer and praise (vv. 12,13).

Although everything may seem stacked against you, God is on your side. He knows who you are, where you are and what you're up against. He will protect you and deliver you.

◆　　◆　　◆

If you are facing enemies and are gripped by fear, admit your fear and then turn to the Word of God. Trust in His promises to protect and provide. God knows what you are going through, and He will deliver you. Your faith will overcome your fear and lead to praise.

CONCERT IN
A CAVE

I have attended concerts at concert halls, parks and churches, but I have never attended a concert in a cave. David wrote this song when he fled from Saul into a cave. It's difficult to sing even in the midst of the blessings of life, so how could David possibly turn his situation into a song? How could he turn a cave into a concert hall?

He had God's protection. "My soul trusts in You; and in the shadow of Your wings I will make my refuge, until these calamities have passed by" (v. 1). This means David is in the Holy of Holies, protected by the presence of God. Our protection does not come from circumstances. It comes from the presence of the Lord.

He knew that God would perform all things for him. "I will cry out to God Most High, to God who performs all things for me" (v. 2). While he was in the cave, David couldn't do very much. But God could— and did—intervene for him.

He was concerned only about God's glory. "Be exalted, O God, above the heavens; let Your glory be above all the earth" (v. 5). No matter where you are—even in a cave—if you're concerned about the glory of God, that's all that really matters.

David had a joyful tongue because he had a fixed heart. "My heart is steadfast, O God, my heart is steadfast; I will sing and give praise" (v. 7). I don't know what kind of cave you might be in today. Perhaps it's one of your own making. I can assure you of these two truths: you have God's protection, and He is working for you. So be concerned only about His glory.

✦　　✦　　✦

Do your circumstances have you under siege? Do you find yourself in a "cave"? Be encouraged that God will protect you and intervene for you. Be concerned about His glory, not your own. Take time today to praise Him for His care.

HOW TO BEGIN AND END EACH DAY

David wrote this psalm when he fled from Saul into a cave. He records one day's experience and gives advice on how to live our lives. First, *close each day in prayer* (vv. 1-4). Take all your concerns to God. When you start trusting Him, He changes you, and you see your surroundings in a new way. By faith you enter into His presence. Storms don't last forever, but when they come, God will take care of your problems. He performs and perfects all things for you.

Second, *open each day with praise* (vv. 5-8). While David was sleeping, God was working for him. When he awoke, David wanted God to have all the glory and wanted to tell the world what He had done for him. God answers prayer, and whatever He does is for your good and His glory. Calamities pass, so praise God for seeing you through them.

Lock up each day with prayer and unlock each day with praise. Praise is great medicine and will take all bitterness, envy, jealousy and unrest out of your life.

♦   ♦   ♦

When you are in a tight place, your great concern should not be how you can get out of it but how God will be glorified because of it. Do you find yourself simply enduring difficulties instead of using them to help yourself grow? Try closing each day in prayer and opening each day with praise. Give God an opportunity to accomplish His purposes in your life.

RIGHTEOUS INDIGNATION

Today there is a need for God's people to display righteous indignation. May we never complacently accept babies being aborted, the poor being exploited and politicians breaking the law. God does not want people in authority to use their authority for themselves. A true statesman uses his authority to build people and his country. David was righteously indignant when he wrote this psalm. He was not angry but anguished.

David denounces the leaders' sin (vv. 1-5). Their speech was unrighteous, and they did not judge uprightly (Job 31:6). Their hands were tipping the scales the wrong way because their hearts were evil. David compares these leaders to snakes (v. 4).

David pronounces the leaders' judgment (vv. 6-9). He presents six pictures of coming judgment for the leaders: (1) a lion without teeth (v. 6)—God one day will pull their teeth and they will be defenseless; (2) water soaking into the ground (v. 7)—after the dry season, rain disappears and is soaked into the soil; (3) broken arrows (v. 7)—God will take away all their defense; (4) a snail melting away (v. 8)—the wicked will gradually destroy themselves the further they go; (5) a stillborn child (v. 8)—they will experience a lot of pain and then death; and (6) a meal being cooked that is destroyed by a whirlwind (v. 9)—their schemes won't last, and they will be destroyed by God's living, burning wrath.

David announces his praise of God (vv. 10,11). We do not avenge our ourselves, but we can rejoice at God's righteous judgment of the wicked (Rev. 18,19). He will stand on His enemies (Ps. 68:23).

The righteous will one day enjoy the victory of God. He is patiently waiting to judge the world. When that happens, God will be vindicated, and Jesus will be glorified.

✦　　✦　　✦

The misuse of authority is an age-old problem. The Bible tells us what will become of those who abuse their positions of authority. God's people may confidently express their righteous indignation, for we know that He will one day judge corrupt leaders. Praise Him for His coming victory and vindication.

THE BEST IS
YET TO COME

Does it ever trouble you that the righteous seem to suffer, while the wicked seem to escape suffering? Have you ever gotten the bad end of a deal while somebody else—perhaps even a professing Christian—came out on top after doing something he shouldn't have done? If so, this passage will encourage you: "The righteous shall rejoice when he sees the vengeance . . . so that men will say, 'Surely there is a reward for the righteous; surely He is God who judges in the earth.'"

When someone else hurts us, when we get the bad end of a deal, we must first *accept the burden and realize there is no real justice in the world today.* Oh, there's some justice, of course. We are grateful for what the law is doing. But fundamentally, it seems that those who are doing good are being persecuted, while those who are doing evil are being promoted. Accept the burden of this seeming inequality. That's the way things are in this world.

Second, *leave the situation with the Lord.* When someone does something that shouldn't be done, we immediately want to right the wrong and punish the wrongdoer. But we must leave it with God. He says, "Vengeance is Mine, I will repay" (Rom. 12:19).

That leads to a third word of counsel: *Wait on the Lord.* Your reward is yet to come. This world is heaven for the unsaved. They never will experience the joys and blessings in the glory of eternity with the Lord. But a believer's heaven is yet to come. Heaven is a place of unmixed joy; hell is a place of undiluted sorrow. In this world we have a mixture of sorrow and joy. Wait, for your reward is yet to come.

♦   ♦   ♦

At times this world appears to lack justice. You need not fret over this. When you are faced with inequality, leave your burden with the Lord and wait patiently for Him to resolve the issue. For God's people, the best is yet to come.

WHO'S WATCHING YOU?

Have you ever been in a public place and noticed that someone was watching you? I've been in restaurants when my wife has said, "Those people at that table keep watching us. I wonder if we know them." It usually turns out that we don't know them, and they don't know us, but maybe we look like someone they know.

In this psalm David records his experience when Saul's men were watching his house. They wanted to arrest and kill him. But David was rejoicing in the Lord. He was singing in a time of danger. And he was crying out to the Lord for mercy.

What God is to you determines what He does for you. "I will sing of Your power" (v. 16). David knew that God is a God of power. Saul could not overthrow Him. "I will sing aloud of Your mercy" (v. 16). That's what David needed more than anything else. We need to pray all day long that the mercy of God will sustain us. David discovered mercy in the morning (v. 16). Start your day by singing to the Lord and drawing upon His mercy.

"To You, O my Strength, . . . God is my defense" (v. 17). Those are words of security and dependability. When God is your Power, when God gives you mercy, when God is your Strength and Defense, then you can face any enemy. You can face any circumstance, because God is going to see you through.

✦　　✦　　✦

God responds according to your faith and surrounds you with His mercy. Is yours the kind of faith that can sing to Him in times of danger? The next time you face threatening circumstances, trust the Lord. He will protect you and deliver you from your enemies.

DEFENSE AND DELIVERANCE

Have you ever had to escape danger by going out a window? Paul escaped from Damascus that way (Acts 9), and David through a window as well (I Sam. 19). One day David went home and discovered that he was being spied on. His wife let him down through a window, and he escaped from his enemies. As we read this psalm, we notice four assurances that kept David going.

First, *David knows that God sees, so he prays* (vv. 1-5). David needed to be defended and delivered. His enemies were lying about him. Suffering is hard to take when you haven't sinned. But God is on the throne and is watching us. He knows our difficulties. The next time you're in trouble, remember that God sees you. Pray to Him—He's listening.

Second, *David is sure that God hears, so he waits* (vv. 6-9). While we wait, God accomplishes many things, and we regain our strength (v. 9; Isa. 40:31).

Third, *David is sure that God rules, so he trusts* (vv. 10-13). God meets David with mercy and the enemy with judgment. David prays that God will scatter his enemies, stop them and consume them.

Fourth, *David is sure that God delivers, so he sings* (vv. 14-17). We cannot always stop people's actions. David's wife warned him that he had to leave or he would be dead by morning (I Sam. 19:11), yet he was able to sing about God's mercy in the morning (v. 16). Always thank God after He answers prayer.

♦   ♦   ♦

How do you exercise your faith when the enemy is pursuing? Respond by praying, waiting, trusting and singing.

AFTER THE VICTORY

"**T**hrough God we will do valiantly, for it is He who shall tread down our enemies" (v. 12). Psalm 60 is unusual because David didn't write it in the midst of trouble. So many of his psalms were written from a cave or a battlefield. But this psalm was written after a great victory. The army had achieved a tremendous victory in Edom for the people of God.

What do we learn from this psalm? First, *we must be cautious after a victory*. "O God, You have cast us off; You have broken us down; You have been displeased; oh, restore us again!" (v. 1). David was crying out to God and saying, "O God, we have just won a great victory. But there are battles yet to fight." Some of God's great people had their biggest defeats after their victories. Elijah won a great victory on Mount Carmel, and then he became discouraged and suffered a great defeat. We must be careful to win the victory after we have won the battle.

Second, *we are always carrying God's banner*. Even after the victory has ended, we are still His ambassadors. "You have given a banner to those who fear You, that it may be displayed because of the truth" (v. 4). We carry a banner of truth because we are standing for the Word of God. After we've won the victory, let's not put down the banner. Let's continue to carry it to the glory of God.

Third, *we must give God the glory*. David gave Him all of the glory for what He had done. It's so easy to claim the victory for yourself. It's so easy after the victory to say, "This is what I have done." Pride moves in, and that can lead to defeat.

◆　　◆　　◆

One of your most vulnerable times comes after God has given you a victory, for you may let down your guard. And the Devil stands poised to attack again. How do you seal the victory? Always carry the banner of God and be sure to give Him the glory. The next time God gives you a victory, stay grounded in the truth of His Word and avoid entertaining any prideful thoughts. God deserves all the glory.

FIGHTING BATTLES

About the time one problem is solved, another one begins. That's the situation David found himself in when he wrote this psalm. He was leading one battle and praying about another. In your own battles, seek to imitate David's four responses in this psalm.

First, *he surveys the situation* (vv. 1-3). David always looked at situations through the eyes of a poet. He pictures this predicament as a sudden flood, an earthquake and staggering, drunken people. David thinks God will prevent the Moabites from invading the land, but He allows them to come in. David then asks the Lord to forgive and re-store the people and stop the flood. The Jews think the mountains and the earth are sure and steadfast, but David feels everything trembling and breaking open. He sees the people staggering as though drunk. The cup of wrath, of judgment, has come. David looks at the situation and says, "Can things get any worse?"

Second, *he lifts the banner of God's truth* (vv. 4,5). David fought these wars because he was God's king and the Israelites were God's people. We need to realize that even though there are problems, struggles and battles in life, God still loves us (Rom 8:35). His love cannot change and will not fail, *no matter how we feel*. David lifts the banner of God's truth. That is one of God's names: "The-Lord-Is-My-Banner" (Ex. 17:15). David was capable, but he was depending on God's right hand. The Lord rallies His troops around His banner.

Third, *he listens to the Commander* (vv. 6-8). David knew he was sec-ond in command, for God was the Leader of the armies of Israel. God says, "Wherever you go in Israel, it all belongs to me; I own the land. So stop worrying." When David heard the Commander talk like that, he knew he didn't have to be afraid. He rested in the victory of the Lord (I Cor. 15:58).

Finally, *he launches out by faith* (vv. 9-12). David says, "I don't have any confidence in myself. God has to lead me to victory." Almighty God always goes before us. He gives us help and the victory (Ps. 118:8).

♦ ♦ ♦

On whose strength you draw, the Lord's or your own, will determine victory or defeat. If you let Him lead, He will take you to victory.

FEEL LIKE GIVING UP?

When his son Absalom rebelled against him, David had to flee from Jerusalem to save his life. Out of that experience he wrote this psalm. "Hear my cry, O God; attend to my prayer. From the end of the earth I will cry to You, when my heart is overwhelmed; lead me to the rock that is higher than I. For You have been a shelter for me, and a strong tower from the enemy" (vv. 1-3).

David was asking for God's help and strength. He may have been in a cave when he wrote these words or hiding in a shelter in the wilderness. We don't know. But his true Rock was God. His true Shelter and his true Strong Tower was God. It's good to know that when we are away from the safety of home and city, we still have the safety of the Lord.

David was abiding. "I will abide in Your tabernacle forever; I will trust in the shelter of Your wings" (v. 4). This means the Holy of Holies, where the wings of the cherubim overshadowed the Ark of the Covenant. We might ask, "How can you abide in the tabernacle, David, when you're out there in the wilderness? You're running away." He would say, "My God is always with me. As long as I abide in Him, I am abiding in His tabernacle." David realized he didn't need city walls for protection. God was his Rock. He didn't need the tabernacle for his worship. God was his Tabernacle.

David was rejoicing. "So I will sing praise to Your name forever, that I may daily perform my vows" (v. 8). When you bring your requests to the Lord and rely on Him, you discover you can rejoice in Him. "For You, O God, have heard my vows. . . . You will prolong the king's life" (v. 5). God answered David's prayer.

What is God to you? Is He your Rock, your Shelter, your Strong Tower, your Tabernacle? Are you trusting Him to meet your specific needs today?

♦   ♦   ♦

God never intended that His people "throw in the towel." Remember these truths. He is always listening to your cry. He is always with you and will never forsake you, whatever your circumstances. You can always rejoice in God's protection. Apply the truths of this psalm to your situation today.

THE ACCOMPLISHMENTS OF PRAYER

Whenever David found himself in a tight spot, he instinctively turned to God in prayer. Prayer is the natural breath of the believer. It enables you to accomplish what you cannot accomplish by yourself.

First, *prayer enables you to reach farther* (v. 2). David was homesick. Although he was away from Jerusalem, he was not away from God. No matter where you are, you can reach out through prayer and touch the lives of family, friends and missionaries.

Second, *prayer enables you to go higher* (v. 2). David was overwhelmed and wrapped in gloom. When he prayed, God lifted him up and put him on a high rock, in a tower that He built for him (v. 3). Prayer puts you on the mountaintop and enables you to get a clear perspective of your situation.

Third, *prayer enables you to come closer* (v. 4). "The shelter of your wings" is not referring to a mother hen gathering her chicks before a storm breaks; it is talking about getting under the wings of the cherubim in the Holy of Holies. Through Jesus you can enter into the presence of God and dwell under His wings.

Fourth, *prayer enables you to grow richer* (v. 5). In prayer you draw upon the heritage you have in Jesus Christ (Eph. 1:3).

Fifth, *prayer enables you to live fuller* (vv. 6,7). It's not the length of life that counts but the depth. Prayer puts depth into your life. I pity people who depend upon worldly entertainment instead of the fullness of life in Christ.

Finally, *prayer enables you to be happier* (v. 8). Prayer and praise always go together. David starts out crying and ends up praising. He starts out praying and ends up rejoicing. Spend time with the Lord in prayer. It will change your life.

♦   ♦   ♦

Evaluate your praying. Is it accomplishing in your life what it accomplished in David's? If not, spend more time in prayer and determine to experience its accomplishment in your life.

TRIPLE ASSURANCE

Verses 2, 5 and 12 contain three assurances that help us wait: God is our Salvation. God is our Expectation. God is our Vindication. Let's look closer at these three assurances.

God is our Salvation. David refers to salvation not from sin but from danger. "He only is my rock and my salvation; He is my defense; I shall not be greatly moved" (v. 2). David's enemies were pursuing him as usual. Saul was trying to kill him as usual. And yet David says, "I'm going to wait on the Lord. I'm not going to run around and lose control of myself. I'm going to wait on the Lord because from Him comes my salvation." That's true today also. We live in a dangerous world. We never know what may be just around the corner, but we have the assurance that God is our Rock and our Defense.

God is our Expectation. Where do you look for your expectation? To yourself, your wallet, your bankbook, your friends? Where do you look when the future seems bleak and dark? David looked to God. "My soul, wait silently for God alone, for my expectation is from Him" (v. 5).

God is our Vindication. It relieves us of a great deal of pressure and burden to know that we are not judges but witnesses. We are not here to vindicate ourselves. Our vindication comes from God, "who will render to each one according to his deeds" (Rom. 2:6). Today, as you face difficulties with people or things or circumstances, wait on the Lord. From Him come your salvation, your expectation and your vindication.

✦   ✦   ✦

In troubled times, how often do you first look to yourself or others for answers before looking to God? If you look to God and wait for Him, He will see you through. Put God first and wait for Him to act on your behalf.

ARE YOU THIRSTY?

King David wrote this psalm when he was in the wilderness of Judah. I never really appreciated what he wrote until my wife and I visited the same spot. What a dry and barren place it is! Look at what David wrote, "O God, You are my God; early will I seek You; my soul thirsts for You; my flesh longs for You in a dry and thirsty land where there is no water" (v. 1). In other words, David says, "Here I am in this dry, hot, dangerous wilderness, and I really would love to have some water. However, what I really want is God."

When you find yourself in a dry wilderness situation in life, what do you do? Follow the stages in David's experience. First, *he seeks God*. He wanted to see God's power and glory as he had seen it in the sanctuary. He wanted to see that wilderness turned into a sanctuary. David had been in the tabernacle. He had seen the glory of God, but he wasn't satisfied with that. We are satisfied to hear about God and sing about Him in church. Then we come to the wilderness. We should be like David and say, "I want to see God's glory through this wilderness experience just as though I were worshiping God in the church service."

Next, he *blesses God*. "Thus I will bless You while I live" (v. 4). David also *is satisfied with God*. Satisfaction doesn't come from circumstances on the outside. It comes from blessing on the inside. "When I remember You on my bed, I meditate on You in the night watches" (v. 6). Finally, he *rejoices in God*. "But the king shall rejoice in God" (v. 11). That's what God wants from us, even in the wilderness.

♦ ♦ ♦

Wilderness experiences are good for you, for they teach you an important truth: You draw satisfaction from blessing on the inside, not from circumstances on the outside. When you face a wilderness experience, follow David's response. God will meet your needs.

FREE FROM FEAR

Most of us live relatively safe and secure lives, but David was in exile. He was being hounded by King Saul, who wanted to kill him. Here David prays for protection, and he closes the psalm by saying, "The righteous shall be glad in the Lord, and trust in Him. And all the upright in heart shall glory" (v. 10). We find three key concepts in this verse that encourage us: joy, faith and glory.

Are you glad in the Lord today? So many times we are not glad because of circumstances. David prayed, "Hear my voice, O God, in my meditation; preserve my life from fear of the enemy" (v. 1). I would have said, "Preserve my life from the enemy." But David said, "Preserve me from fear of the enemy." In other words, instead of fear he had faith. Instead of fear he had joy. Instead of fear he wanted to bring glory to God.

Most of our problems are not on the outside but on the inside. When the disciples were in the boat in the middle of the Sea of Galilee on a stormy night, Jesus came to them and rebuked them for their unbelief. Their problem wasn't the storm on the outside—it was the storm on the inside. Likewise, your problem today may not be the circumstances around you or the people against you. It may be the fear that's inside you.

"All men shall fear, and shall declare the work of God" (v. 9). David sang praises to the Lord. He was glad in the Lord. He trusted in and gave glory to Him. "All the upright in heart shall glory" (v. 10). It's easy to read this verse but much more difficult to practice it. Take your eyes off the circumstances and put them on the Lord. Trust in His promises, not your own power. And most of all, seek to bring Him all the glory.

♦ ♦ ♦

Fear can rob you of your joy and trust in God. Don't allow fear or circumstances to take your eyes off the Lord. Let the truth of the Word of God control your mind and heart.

THE
THREE PS

"**P**raise is awaiting You, O God, in Zion; and to You the vow shall be performed" (v. 1). David was a great soldier. But he also was a great singer and a great saint. In spite of difficulties and problems and even dangers, he was able to praise the Lord.

He continues, "O You who hear prayer, to You all flesh will come" (v. 2). Some people only pray. They don't really praise. And yet praise and prayer belong together. Prayer means coming to God and telling Him your needs. David says, "All flesh will come." Anyone who knows the Lord can pray anywhere in the world anytime. All the world can come to God, and all the world can pray.

The more we pray, the more answers we have to praise the Lord for. But sometimes we can't pray because sin is in the way. This is why David says, "Iniquities prevail against me; as for our transgressions, You will provide atonement for them" (v. 3). The more we praise the Lord, the more we see how needy and dirty we are. And so we come for purging, confessing our sin to God.

"**B**lessed is the man whom You choose, and cause to approach You, that he may dwell in Your courts. We shall be satisfied with the goodness of Your house, of Your holy temple" (v. 4). That's the experience God wants us to have—to approach Him, to dwell with Him, to be satisfied with Him. How do we do this? By prayer, praise and purging of sins. Then we will draw near to Him as He draws near to us.

◆　◆　◆

Do you have a close relationship with God? You can draw nearer to Him. Confess any sins you may be harboring. Then praise Him and come to Him in prayer.

An
Invitation

Psalm 66 contains several invitations that are tied to the word *come*: "come and sing"; "come and see"; and "come and hear." Let's look at the first two invitations.

The first invitation is *come and sing,* or praise the Lord. "Sing out the honor of His name; make His praise glorious" (v. 2). Sometimes we act as if praise is tedious. Sometimes we praise Him in a tired fashion. But the psalmist asks for glorious praise. Why? "Through the greatness of Your power Your enemies shall submit themselves to You. All the earth shall worship You and sing praises to You" (vv. 3,4). This is missionary zeal. We aren't to praise the Lord by ourselves. We come and sing, and we invite the whole world to join us.

The second invitation is *come and see* the works of God. Today people call the works of God natural law or scientific law. We try to explain everything, but we can't. Come and see the works of God—what happens in the heavens, what happens in your body and what happened in history. This is the work of God. I like verse 7: "He rules by His power forever." Satan is not ruling this world system—God is. He is allowing Satan to do some things, but He's going to use even that to glorify Himself. God is ruling by His power, and He will rule forever.

If you want to enjoy today, come and sing. If you've lost your song, come and see the works of the Lord. You'll be singing before long.

✦   ✦   ✦

Have you lost your song of praise? Come and see the works of God; it will restore your song. His works reveal His greatness and His love. If you are walking with the Lord, praise Him and tell others what He is doing in your life.

WHY THE TRIALS?

This psalm is for the discouraged. "Oh, bless our God, you peoples! And make the voice of His praise to be heard" (v. 8). Why? "Who keeps our soul among the living, and does not allow our feet to be moved" (v. 9). God holds our life in His hand. "In Him we live and move and have our being" (Acts 17:28). So let's praise Him.

"For You, O God, have tested us; You have refined us as silver is refined" (v. 10). The reason God tries us and tests us is to prove us. He's proving nothing to Himself. He knows us from top to bottom. Instead, He's proving something to *us*. God considers us as valuable as silver, and He puts us into situations that test and strengthen us.

Notice the images in these next two verses. "You brought us *into the net*; You laid affliction *on our backs*. You have caused men to ride *over our heads*; we went through fire and through water; but You brought us out to rich fulfillment" (vv. 11,12, italics mine). This indicates total defeat. We go through fire and water, but we are brought out into a wealthy place. That word *wealthy* means "an abundant place, a moist place, a place of running water and fruitfulness." The wilderness of Judea, where David so often found himself, was dry and barren.

The psalmist does not say, "Well, here I am in trouble again." No, he says, "God brought me *in*, and God's going to bring me *through*. And when He brings me *out*, I'm going to be in a wealthy place." God always enriches us when we go through difficulty. He proves us and tries us to make us more like Jesus.

◆   ◆   ◆

The trials of God have a refining and strengthening effect. The result is they make us more like Jesus. Are you discouraged today by trials? Be encouraged that God will see you through and that He will use your trials to build you.

WILL YOU SHARE?

The author of this psalm is unknown, but it was someone who had a vision of the whole world. God had blessed him, and he wanted to share that blessing with everyone. He writes, "God be merciful to us and bless us, and cause His face to shine upon us" (v. 1). That sounds like a priestly benediction, doesn't it? "The Lord bless you and keep you; the Lord make His face shine upon you, and be gracious unto you" (Num. 6:24,25).

Three times in verse 1 the psalmist uses the word *us*. He refers to the Jewish people, but he doesn't stop there. "That Your way may be known on earth, Your salvation among all nations" (v. 2). So many Old Testament Jews wanted to keep what they had for themselves. They did not want to share it. How unlike God's plan! After all, why did He call Abraham? That he might be a blessing to the whole world. Why did Jesus die? That the Gospel message might go out to the whole world.

Why has the Lord blessed us? That we might share the Gospel with others. We have no problem praying verse 1: "Oh, be merciful to us and bless us and make Your face shine upon us." But what about verse 2? Do we want to be blessed so that we might be a blessing? That's the reason God blesses us in the first place. Likewise, He answers our prayers so that we might become an answer to someone else's prayer.

The result of making God's salvation known among all the nations is praise. "Let the peoples praise You, O God; let all the peoples praise You" (v. 3). This doesn't mean just the Israelites. Even the Gentiles are included. "Oh, let the nations be glad and sing for joy!" (v. 4). "Let all the peoples praise You" (v. 5).

Notice how the psalm ends: "Then the earth shall yield her increase; God, our own God, shall bless us. God shall bless us, and all the ends of the earth shall fear Him" (vv. 6, 7). The sequence in this psalm is significant. The psalmist begins by saying, "Lord, bless me so that I may bless others." He does become a blessing to others, so God blesses him again. What a marvelous experience of God's grace.

◆　　◆　　◆

Are you part of God's sequence of blessing? If you will share, He will bless you so that you may be a blessing. Experience the fullness of His grace by telling others about Him.

LIKE SMOKE AND WAX

Someone has said that a person is known not only by the friends he keeps but also by the enemies he makes. The Lord Jesus had enemies. David had enemies. Anyone who stands up for what is right will have enemies. But notice what these enemies are like— "as smoke is driven away" (v. 2). Who's afraid of smoke? It can smother us, but if we keep fresh air coming in—the fresh wind of the Holy Spirit—it can't bother us. David also compares his enemies to melting wax (v. 2). A burning candle is a picture of what will happen to God's enemies. The smoke is quickly blown away, and the wax quietly melts. God gets the victory.

"So let the wicked perish at the presence of God. But let the righteous be glad; let them rejoice before God" (vv. 2,3). Why? Because of what God does for us. "Sing to God, sing praises to His name; extol Him who rides on the clouds" (v. 4). I like that picture. God is the Great Conqueror, riding upon the heavens.

He also is "a father of the fatherless" (v. 5). He comes right where we are to comfort and heal our broken hearts. Furthermore, God is Judge and Redeemer. He frees those who are bound with chains.

♦ ♦ ♦

Are you feeling oppressed by your enemies? Leave the burden with your Father, and let Him be your Conqueror.

SHARING
THE WEALTH

Here David describes the victories of God. "You have ascended on high, You have led captivity captive; You have received gifts among men" (v. 18). This is a picture of our Lord's ascension. We find this verse quoted in the New Testament, referring to Jesus Christ (Eph. 4:8).

Look at what Jesus has performed for us. First, *He went before us.* "O God, when You went out before Your people" (v. 7). Wherever you are today, if you're in the will of God, He has already gone before you. The picture here is of the nation of Israel going through the wilderness. God didn't expect the Israelites to figure out the logistics for themselves. By night He led them by a pillar of fire and by day by a cloud. The Ark of the Covenant—the presence of the Lord—went before them. He also went before us and bore our sins on the cross.

Second, *He has gone above us.* "You have ascended on high" (v. 18). The Lord Jesus has ascended to glory, and He is seated there at the right hand of the Father in majesty. He who went before us to win the victory has now gone above us to share the victory.

Now *He dwells among us.* Notice the end of verse 18: "That the Lord God might dwell there." And what is He doing? He is giving gifts to His people. It's a picture of the Conqueror distributing the spoil. How wealthy we are! How much we have to thank Him for. Will you trust the Victor today?

♦   ♦   ♦

Because of Christ's death and Resurrection, you are wealthy. God freely shares with you the spoils of His victory at the cross. You need never be defeated in this life.

BURDENS AND BENEFITS

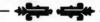

"**B**lessed be the Lord, who daily loads us with benefits, the God of our salvation!" (v. 19). We can translate that verse, "Blessed be the Lord, who daily bears our burdens." Let's think about benefits and burdens. God is the One who gives us the burdens of life. Sometimes we bring burdens upon ourselves by our disobedience, rebellion, sin, unbelief, lack of love and unkindness. But if we are walking in the will of God on the path of His choosing, and if we have burdens to bear, He is the One who has given them to us. Let's view the burdens of life as benefits.

Perhaps the greatest example of this is the Apostle Paul. How he was burdened with his thorn in the flesh! He prayed three times that God would take it away. Instead, God turned that burden into a benefit. He told Paul, "I'm going to give you the grace that you need" (see II Cor. 12:7-9). Sometimes God answers prayer by taking things away. Sometimes He answers prayer by adding things to us. That's what he did for Paul, and the burden became a benefit.

"But," you say, "I have some heavy burdens. I don't see much benefit to them." Notice the word *daily* in verse 19: "Blessed be the Lord, who daily loads us with benefits." We live a day at a time. To think of all of life's burdens coming at once can be crushing. Remember what you have been through in your life. You've been through circumstances you never thought you would get through. But God brought you through. "Give us this day our daily bread" (Matt. 6:11). "And, Lord, give us this day our daily burdens and benefits."

♦　　♦　　♦

God knows how much we can bear, and His grace is sufficient for each day. But there is another dimension to our burdens. God can turn them into benefits. Has He given you a heavy burden? Perhaps He wants to turn it into a benefit and do something special for you.

How Strong
Is God?

We don't go far on our own strength. Here, David instructs us how to understand and appropriate the strength of God. He tells us to *ascribe strength to God*. Realize that He is a God of strength. "His excellence is over Israel, and His strength is in the clouds" (v. 34). That means His strength is high up. God can get strength even from the clouds (nothing but rolling vapor). We think of God as loving, gracious and merciful. But let's also think of Him as strong.

We also need to *ask for strength from God*. "Strengthen, O God, what You have done for us" (v. 28). We have every privilege to come and ask God for the strength we need today. "But those who wait on the Lord shall renew their strength; they shall mount up with wings like eagles, they shall run and not be weary, they shall walk and not faint" (Isa. 40:31). God has already determined what He wants to do. He'll do it when we request it. "You do not have because you do not ask" (James 4:2).

Next, we need to *acknowledge our strength is from God*. "The God of Israel is He who gives strength and power to His people. Blessed be God" (v. 35). If you need strength today, don't look to yourself or to anyone else. Look up, because God is the God of strength, and He wants to command strength for you if you'll ask Him.

✦   ✦   ✦

Often Satan will tempt you to draw your strength from the world's substitutes. When that happens, remember the truths of this psalm. When you need strength to continue the battle, spend time in prayer with God. Ascribe strength to Him, ask Him for strength and acknowledge that your strength is from Him.

THE
WORST DEATH

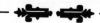

I was chatting about death with a neighbor once, using it as an opportunity to witness to him. We were discussing what the most difficult way to die would be. I finally said, "Perhaps the most difficult way to die would be to be smothered—to be sinking in quicksand and be smothered."

David had that kind of experience spiritually. "Save me, O God! For the waters have come up to my neck. I sink in deep mire, where there is no standing; I have come into deep waters, where the floods overflow me" (vv. 1, 2). It's bad enough to be sinking in quicksand, but David also had the floods coming over him. What did he do? He did what every Christian should do. First, *he waited*. "My throat is dry; my eyes fail while I wait for my God" (v. 3). "Let not those who wait for You, O Lord God of hosts, be ashamed" (v. 6). David knew the situation was in God's control. Yes, he did cry out to God for rescue. Nothing is wrong with that. But he also waited.

Second, *he wept*. "When I wept and chastened my soul with fasting, that became my reproach" (v. 10). *Reproach* is used again and again in Psalm 69. (This is a messianic psalm that talks about the reproach Jesus endured for us.) Nothing is wrong with weeping. Pain hurts, and some situations can break your heart. David waited and wept, and he knew that God was going to see him through.

Third, *he watched*. "Let not those who wait for You, O Lord God of hosts, be ashamed because of me; let not those who seek You be confounded because of me, O God of Israel" (v. 6). In other words David says, "It's not important what happens to me. But I don't want to create any problems for anybody else." Throughout this psalm David becomes more and more like the Lord. When you find yourself sinking, wait, weep, watch and let God work.

◆　　◆　　◆

When you find yourself sinking in the quicksand, there is little else you can do but cry to the Lord. Sometimes He allows the "quicksand" experiences to turn you to Him. Wait for God. Acknowledge that He is in control. Give Him the pieces of your broken heart and watch Him work for you. You can depend on His faithfulness.

No Comforters

"**R**eproach has broken my heart, and I am full of heaviness; I looked for someone to take pity, but there was none; and for comforters, but I found none" (v. 20). When we read Psalm 69, we meet Jesus Christ, for many verses from this psalm are quoted in the New Testament, relating to Him. For example, "I have become a stranger to my brothers, an alien to my mother's children; because zeal for Your house has eaten me up, and the reproaches of those who reproach You have fallen on me" (vv. 8,9; John 2:17). David is going through difficulty, and it is making him more like Jesus. Therefore, it enabled him to reveal the Lord to us.

What breaks your heart? Is it broken when you can't have your way? Is it broken when something is taken away from you? Jesus and David both said, "Reproach has broken my heart" (v. 20). What can you do about a broken heart? David prayed, "Deliver me. Hear me. Draw near to my soul. Redeem me" (vv. 14, 16, 18). And God answered him.

Sometimes you bear reproach because of others. You feel heavy, brokenhearted and alone. But Jesus went through all of this for us. Be thankful that you can share in the fellowship of His sufferings (Phil. 3:10). Also, while others are going through this experience, be an encouragement to them. If you've known what it's like to have a broken heart, and if you've looked for someone to take pity, then you know how much it means to have a friend. Today, find someone with a broken heart and start to bring healing to him.

◆　◆　◆

When your heart is broken, be encouraged that Jesus knows what you are going through and that you are becoming like Him. But there's another purpose: You can help others whose hearts are broken. God will use you to help bring healing to them. Don't waste your experiences; they have great value.

RECIPE FOR REJOICING

"I will praise the name of God with a song and will magnify Him with thanksgiving." This verse seems out of place here, because this psalm has an atmosphere of trial and sorrow. Six times we find the word *reproach* in Psalm 69. David cries out to God for help, so it's strange to find him saying, "I will praise the name of God with a song, and will magnify Him with thanksgiving." When you are sinking, when you think that everything has gone wrong, when others are persecuting you and smiting you, *praise the name of God with a song.*

Paul and Silas must have thought of verse 30 when they were suffering in jail in Philippi (see Acts 16:16-34). They were in the stocks. They had been humiliated and arrested. Their rights were taken from them. They had been beaten with rods, and their bodies ached. But they began to sing and praise God. The concert brought down the house, and the jailer was saved. When you find yourself sinking, start singing.

Magnify the Lord. When I hurt, I have a tendency to magnify myself. I think, *Nobody ever felt the way I feel. Nobody's ever been through what I've been through.* But David said, "I'm not going to do that. I'm going to magnify the Lord."

Thank the Lord. Anyone can thank Him when things are going well. Anyone can thank Him in the sunshine. But when you are sinking in the deep mire, it's difficult to give thanks to God. But we need to do so.

Here you have a threefold recipe for rejoicing when you are sinking: Praise the name of the Lord, seek to magnify Him and bring your thanksgiving from your heart.

◆　◆　◆

Are you overwhelmed by your circumstances? Trust the Lord and follow this recipe. He will cause you to rejoice.

Hurry Up, God!

Has God ever been slow in your life? He was in David's. This undoubtedly was one of the psalms written when David was being harassed by King Saul. So he cries out, "Lord, why don't You do something? You're being awfully slow."

Have you ever pondered the delays of God? He is never in a hurry, but once He starts to work, watch out! He patiently accomplishes His work. David pleads, "Make haste, make haste" (v. 1). He repeats his plea in verse 5: "I am poor and needy; make haste to me, O God! You are my help and my deliverer; O Lord, do not delay." If right now it seems as though God is tarrying instead of working, if it seems as though He is delaying instead of acting, what should you do? Seek Him and wait on Him and love Him. Verse 4 says it beautifully: "Let all those who seek You rejoice and be glad in You; and let those who love Your salvation say continually, 'Let God be magnified!'" We've seen that phrase before. David, when he was sinking, said, "I . . . will magnify Him with thanksgiving" (Ps. 69:30).

Here's a good lesson for us. When God is not moving as rapidly as we think He should, when our timetables do not coincide, what should we do? Rejoice in Him, love Him and magnify Him. Let Him worry about the timetable. God is always working, and we know that all things are working together for good (Rom. 8:28). But He waits for the right time to reveal His victories. Let Him watch the clock.

✦   ✦   ✦

God's delays are a part of your character-building process. The next time God gives you a delay, encourage yourself by remembering that He never stops working for you, and He knows when and how to help you. Submit to His timetable and His care.

WHEN I AM OLD

The older I become, the more I appreciate this psalm. It focuses on God's special blessings for those who are getting older. "Do not cast me off in the time of old age; do not forsake me when my strength fails" (v. 9).

What does God do for us as we get older? He helps us meet and solve some of the problems that we encounter in our later years. Take the problem of *weakness,* for example. That's what David talks about in verse 9: "Do not forsake me when my strength fails." The outward man is failing, but the inward man can be renewed day by day. God will provide you with the spiritual strength that you need."

Another problem we face as we get older is *confusion.* "In You, O Lord, I put my trust; let me never be put to shame [confusion]" (v. 1). We can't always keep up with so many rapid changes in this world. As we get older, we might say, "I don't quite know what's going on." But God says, "Look, don't worry about it. You trust Me, and I'll never allow you to be confused."

A third problem we experience is that of *living in the past.* Too often we say, "Back in the good old days. . . ." I've concluded that perhaps the good old days were not that good. David acknowledges, "For You are my hope, O Lord God" (v. 5). He was living in the future. We don't know what the future holds, but we do know that God holds our future.

Finally, we may face the problem of *complaining.* How easy it is to complain as we grow older. But David said, "Let my mouth be filled with Your praise and with Your glory all the day" (v. 8). When we're walking with the Lord, He takes care of weakness and confusion. He takes care of our fear of the future. He also substitutes praise for complaining, and therefore, we grow old graciously.

♦　♦　♦

Each phase of life has unique advantages and problems. And God stays with you through each phase. Are you facing the problems of old age? Are you struggling with weakness, confusion, living in the past and complaining? Bring your fears to God. He delights in caring for His people.

FOR THOSE WHO FOLLOW

As we get older, things change. We must drop some things, and we must start others. Not much goes on continually—except in Psalm 71. David uses the word *continually* three times. First, he tells us that we can continually resort to the Lord in prayer: "Be my strong refuge, to which I may resort continually" (v. 3). No matter how old we get, we can pray, because the Lord never fails. We also can have continual praise. "My praise shall be continually of You" (v. 6). If prayer is without ceasing, then praise will be without ceasing. David also tells us, "I will hope continually" (v. 14).

"**N**ow also when I am old and grayheaded, O God, do not forsake me, until I declare Your strength to this generation, Your power to everyone who is to come" (v. 18). Notice that David's focus is not simply on his needs. He wants to have his needs met so he can share the Lord with others. "You shall increase my greatness and comfort me on every side. . . . I will praise You" (vv. 21,22).

If we are resorting to the Lord continually in prayer, if we are rejoicing in Him continually in praise, if we are hoping in Him continually and laying hold of His promises, if we are saying that the best is yet to come and praise Him more and more, then we can grow old and grayheaded without fear. We'll be able to glorify the Lord, and we'll be able to share Him with others in the next generation. What kind of heritage are you leaving for future generations? What are you teaching them by word and example about God's strength and power? Will others put their faith in the Lord on the basis of your life and testimony?

♦   ♦   ♦

You can always live to bring glory to God no matter what your age is. Those of us who are older can do that in a special way; we can teach the younger generation about His faithfulness. Preserve your Christian heritage for future generations. Let your life be a continual testimony for God.

GREATER THAN SOLOMON

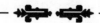

Psalm 72 was written for Solomon, probably when he became king. But looking beyond this psalm, we will see someone who is greater than Solomon—Jesus Christ. Notice what the writer says, "Give the king Your judgments, O God, and Your righteousness to the king's Son" (v. 1). In fact, he mentions *righteousness* several times in this psalm. "He will judge Your people with righteousness" (v. 2). "The mountains will bring peace to the people, and the little hills, by righteousness" (v. 3). "In His days the righteous shall flourish" (v. 7). Jesus is to us the righteousness of God. The psalmist wants Solomon to be a righteous man, to have the kind of integrity and honesty that it takes to exercise kingly judgment. Jesus Christ has never made a mistake. He is our righteousness, and He does what is righteous.

Next, the writer talks about *peace*. "The mountains will bring peace to the people" (v. 3). "In His days the righteous shall flourish, and abundance of peace, until the moon is no more" (v. 7). We can have righteousness without peace. We can turn soldiers loose and let them execute people who are breaking the law. But we can't have peace without righteousness. We must first have righteousness with God before we can have peace with Him.

The righteousness and peace of our Lord are emphasized in the Book of Hebrews, in the person of Melchizedek. Jesus is the King of righteousness and peace. He also brings refreshment. "He shall come down like rain upon the mown grass, like showers that water the earth" (v. 6). We have days when our hearts are dry like a desert. But the Lord showers blessings upon us and produces fruitfulness in us, and all of this leads to victory. "All kings shall fall down before Him; all nations shall serve Him" (v. 11). We worship and obey Him who is infinitely greater than Solomon.

♦　　♦　　♦

One day Christ will establish His kingdom on the earth. Through His righteous rule He will bring peace. Today, He establishes His kingdom in the hearts and lives of believers. Because of His righteousness, you may have the peace of God in your heart. Do you have this peace?

WHAT A NAME!

"**H**is name shall endure forever; His name shall continue as long as the sun. And men shall be blessed in Him; all nations shall call Him blessed" (v. 17). Originally, that was written about Solomon. But as we read this verse, we see that it also refers to Jesus.

It speaks of His name. "You shall call His name Jesus, for He will save His people from their sins" (Matt. 1:21). That's what His name means—Savior. What kind of a name is it? It is enduring: "His name shall endure forever" (v. 17). I'm a student of biography. When I go to used-book sales, I buy books about old people—old preachers, missionaries and statesmen—folks who have been forgotten. Have you ever read an old edition of an encyclopedia and thought, *Who are these people? I've never heard of them.* Their names did not endure. In fact, some of the names in the headlines today will be forgotten a few months from now. But not so with Jesus. He has the *enduring name,* a name that "is above every name" (Phil. 2:9).

Jesus also has an *enriching name.* "Men shall be blessed in Him." The names of some people don't bring blessing—they bring cursing. You certainly wouldn't call your son "Judas" or your daughter "Jezebel." But Jesus has an enriching name. It brings blessing. We have been blessed in Him "with every spiritual blessing" (Eph. 1:3).

His name also is an *enabling name.* "Blessed be the Lord God, the God of Israel, who only does wondrous things!" (v. 18). God enables us, through the name of Jesus, to do wonderful things. In the Book of Acts we find the name of Jesus on the lips of the apostles. "In the name of Jesus Christ of Nazareth rise up and walk" (3:6). What a privilege it is to know His name. What a privilege it is to have the authority of His name as we pray and serve Him.

♦   ♦   ♦

There is no other name like Jesus. It is full of power and authority. It is enduring and brings blessing and enablement to those who know His name. Do you know Jesus as your Savior? "Whoever calls on the name of the Lord shall be saved" (Rom. 10:13).

THANKSGIVING MESSAGE

Asaph begins by standing true in what he believes about God, but he slips because he starts to look at neighbors and becomes envious. He wonders why the wicked prosper. When he loses his praise, he starts stumbling and suffering. He should have sought answers by looking up, not by looking around or within.

Asaph understands the end of the evil ones. The key question is not "Where are you?" but "Where are you going?" Are you taking the broad road that leads to destruction or the narrow road that leads to life (v. 20)? The psalmist looks to God and makes several discoveries. First, he discovers that we can be thankful for *the guarantee of His presence*. His name is Immanuel, which means "God with us" (Matt. 1:23; Isa. 41:10; 43:2; Ps. 23:4).

Second, we have *the grasp of His hand*. We see God's powerful hand in creation. We see His gentle hand lead us beside the still waters. And we see His pierced hands on the cross as He dies for us.

Third, we have *the guidance of His counsel*. God's commands and commissions are for everyone, but He knows each of us personally. He knew us in the womb and has arranged for us the lives He wants us to live. Live one day at a time and walk one step at a time (Prov. 4:18). That counsel comes from the Word of God and through prayer.

Finally, we will have *the glory of His heaven*. As Christians, we know we are going to heaven because of the price Jesus paid on the cross (I Thess. 5:10), the promise He made (John 14:2,3) and the prayer He prayed (John 17:24). We may not understand completely today, but we have a future glory (I Pet. 1:3; II Pet. 1:11; Phil 4:4).

◆　　◆　　◆

As a Christian, you have much for which to be thankful. God is with you. When you find yourself becoming frustrated by the world's inequalities, stop, look up and give thanks to God for His blessings.

DISTORTED
VISION

When we are burdened and bothered by what we see in this world, we need to read this psalm. It starts with a wonderful affirmation of faith. "Truly God is good to Israel, to such as are pure in heart" (v. 1). Asaph believes in the God of Israel, and he believes that God honors and rewards those who keep their lives clean. But in verse 2 he turns his eyes off of God, and he starts looking around at other people. "But as for me, my feet had almost stumbled; my steps had nearly slipped. For I was envious of the boastful, when I saw the prosperity of the wicked" (vv. 2,3).

Let's look at his two major problems. First, *something is wrong with his vision.* He is not looking to God. He is looking at the wicked people around him. Who are these people? He describes them in verses 4-9. "For there are no pangs in their death, but their strength is firm" (v. 4). They don't get sick; they don't have the bills others have. They're not troubled. They are proud and violent. "Their eyes bulge with abundance; they have more than heart could wish" (v. 7), yet they are corrupt. They set their mouth against God. In verse 10 he says, "Waters of a full cup are drained by them." Asaph was drinking a bitter cup. His vision was distorted. This is what happens when we walk by sight instead of by faith.

Second, *something is wrong with his values.* "I was envious . . . when I saw the prosperity of the wicked" (v. 3). Does he think that people without God are prosperous? Has his values suddenly changed? The psalmist is living by the values of the world, not the values of the world to come. "They increase in riches" (v. 12)—but what kind of riches? When your feet start to slip and you start questioning God's goodness and His government in the world, check your vision and your values.

♦   ♦   ♦

To live the life of faith, you need to understand God's perspective on the world. You must walk by faith, not sight. Keep your eyes on the Lord and don't conform to the values of this world. God is faithful to provide. "Seek first the kingdom of God and His righteousness, and all these things shall be added to you" (Matt. 6:33).

GOD'S PERSPECTIVE

Is it really worth it to be a dedicated Christian? Is it worth it to obey the Lord when those who disobey Him seem to be more prosperous than we are? That's what Asaph wondered when he wrote Psalm 73. In the first 12 verses he thought he had really missed the good life: "I have cleansed my heart in vain, and washed my hands in innocence. For all day long I have been plagued, and chastened every morning. If I had said, 'I will speak thus,' behold, I would have been untrue to the generation of Your children" (vv. 13-15). How does it all end? "It was too painful for me—until I went into the sanctuary of God; then I understood their end" (vv. 16,17). Asaph's perspective was wrong, and that made him question his life until he sought God.

If you look at a distant mountain from one vantage point, you see one thing. But if you move closer or farther back, you see something else. The same thing is true with pictures, such as a beautiful painting or a photograph in a gallery. Your perspective doesn't change the painting or the facts, but it does change your *reaction* to the facts. So we need to go into the sanctuary of God. We need to know from His point of view what it means to live for the Lord.

Have you cleansed your heart in vain? Of course not. We all want a clean heart. Have you washed your hands in innocence? We all want clean hands. Is your tongue speaking something it shouldn't speak? According to verse 15, don't be afraid. Tell God exactly how you feel. Is your mind perplexed? Is your heart pained? Then you need to go to the sanctuary of God. That means getting God's point of view by spending time with Him in the Word, in prayer and in meditation.

Check your values with God's values and your vision with His point of view. Make sure your perspective is the perspective of heaven. That will keep your feet from slipping, and you'll walk with God in victory.

♦   ♦   ♦

In times of need, your point of view can make a big difference. God wants us to gain His perspective. To do that, you must enter His sanctuary. Meditate on the Word, and fill your heart and mind with it. Then bring your burden to the Lord. He will help you gain His point of view.

SEEING BEYOND

"You will guide me with Your counsel, and afterward receive me to glory" (v. 24). Asaph wrote this verse after he had gone through a period of doubt, and it was a wonderful conclusion to his severe depression. He came out of his experience with several certainties.

First, *God holds us.* "Nevertheless I am continually with You; You hold me by my right hand" (v. 23). The wicked may have violence, bounty, prosperity and a full cup of apparent blessing. But we have God, and He holds us.

Second, *God guides us.* "You will guide me with Your counsel, and afterward receive me to glory" (v. 24). That's the important thing— the afterward. What is going to happen afterward? We can be sure that we will be with Him forever. It makes little difference what happens to us materially and physically in this life as long as we have riches in the next life. Some who are rich in this world will be poor in the next world. But many who are poor in this world will be rich in the next world.

Third, *God strengthens us.* "My flesh and my heart fail; but God is the strength of my heart and my portion forever" (v. 26). Fourth, *God helps us in every stage of life.* "But it is good for me to draw near to God" (v. 28). Wherever we are, whatever we're going through, we must draw near to God. "I have put my trust in the Lord God, that I may declare all Your works" (v. 28).

◆　　◆　　◆

The promise of an eternal home in heaven with the Lord encourages you in this life. God purchased you with a great price, and He keeps and protects you through everything. What assurances you have!

A NEW
TEMPLE

It must have been difficult for the Jewish people to watch the Babylonians destroy their city and temple. No wonder Asaph wrote, "O God, why have You cast us off forever? Why does Your anger smoke against the sheep of Your pasture?" (v. 1). Keep in mind that this happened because the people had sinned. They had their great city. They had their beautiful temple. The problem was they trusted the city and the temple, but they did not obey the Lord. In their sin, they had defiled the temple. Jeremiah said they had turned it into a den of thieves (Jer. 7:11). God would not permit this, so He allowed the Babylonians to destroy the city and the temple. Psalm 74 reveals the heartbreak of Asaph.

Even today the Enemy is destroying God's work. "They seem like men who lift up axes among the thick trees" (v. 5). What can God's people do? Notice what Asaph said about God's people. We are the sheep of His pasture (v. 1). He's the Good Shepherd, and He has given His life for the sheep. What defense do sheep have against a Babylonian army? Jesus, the Shepherd.

We are also God's congregation. "Remember Your congregation, which You have purchased of old, the tribe of Your inheritance, which You have redeemed" (v. 2). We are a purchased and redeemed people. "Remember . . . this Mount Zion where You have dwelt"(v. 2). God lives with us. Jerusalem and the temple were destroyed, but He had even greater things in store. Jesus came to earth and revealed the glory of God. Now He's building a new temple, His Church, and it can never be destroyed.

◆   ◆   ◆

God is your trust. If you trust Him, you will want to obey Him. Be careful that you don't misplace your trust in the world's substitutes. The Enemy will do all he can to divert your trust in God. Keep trusting in the Lord and rejoice that He never fails.

A Night Season

"**F**or God is my King from of old, working salvation in the midst of the earth" (v. 12). Asaph wrote those words after surveying the damage the Babylonians wrought in Jerusalem and the temple. In verses 1-11 he looked around and saw perpetual desolations. He saw the enemy had wrecked the sanctuary of God. The Babylonians had removed God's banners and set up their own. All the beauty, all the splendor of Jerusalem had gone up in smoke. When you look around and see the Enemy's destructive influence, remember: "God is my King from of old, working salvation in the midst of the earth" (v. 12).

In verse 12 Asaph stopped looking around and looked up. He realized that *God was on the throne*. At times we cry, "How long, O Lord? How long? Why are these things happening? Why don't You do something?" We know why He permitted the Babylonians to destroy Jerusalem and the temple: The spiritual leaders of the people had led the nation into idolatry and blasphemy, so God disciplined them. Asaph looked up and said, "God is King. He has never failed, and *He is working salvation*. The Enemy may be working destruction; but my God is King, and He is working salvation in the midst of the earth."

Asaph had a third encouragement. He remembered *what God had done in the past* (vv. 13-23). God divided the Red Sea. He broke the armies that attacked His people. He led His people through the wilderness. He opened the rock and provided water. He dried up the rivers. I like verse 16: "The day is Yours, the night also is Yours." We like the day but not the night. Remember, God controls the night as well as the day. Asaph was going through a night season in his soul as he saw everything around him falling apart. What was his solution? Trust. "For God is my King from of old, working salvation in the midst of the earth" (v. 12).

♦   ♦   ♦

Has the Enemy been doing his destructive work in your life? Lay hold of the encouragements of this psalm: God is on the throne; He is helping to deliver you; and He is faithful to act as He has in the past. Start by acknowledging His control in your life. Ask Him to help you and courageously place your trust in Him.

WHO PUT THEM THERE?

In this day when people promote themselves and take care of "number one," it's good to read verse 7: "But God is the Judge: He puts down one, and exalts another." This *rebukes our pride.* Who is the One who allows people to be where they are? God. John the Baptist said, "A man can receive nothing unless it has been given to him from heaven" (John 3:27). Peter wrote: "Therefore humble yourselves under the mighty hand of God, that He may exalt you in due time" (I Pet. 5:6). Who is the One who exalts people to places of leadership? God. Who is the One who removes people from certain positions? God. Who is wise enough to know when to do all of this? God. No one in any position should think that he is there because God *needs* him.

Let's realize that we are where we are because God put us there. But verse 7 not only rebukes our pride—it also *encourages our patience.* Think of Joseph, waiting for God to put down his enemies and set him up where he was supposed to be. Consider Moses or Nehemiah. Oh, how we need patience! Sometimes God allowed His people to be under the tyranny of bad leaders or foreign dictators. Just as He did in the Old Testament, God allows us to go through difficult situations to break our wills and make us more like Him.

Third, this *relieves the pressure in our lives.* Are you in a place of leadership? God put you there. And because He put you there, He will keep you there for as long as He wants. He will use you the way He chooses. Be careful of pride. When we become proud and haughty and think we have all the answers, God says, "It's time to put you down." But if we put ourselves down, He will exalt us. If we humble ourselves under His hand, that hand will turn over and lift us up. "God resists the proud, but gives grace to the humble" (I Pet. 5:5).

◆　　◆　　◆

Have you been struggling because you are under bad leaders at your workplace or in your church? Did poor decisions by others put them there? Bring your burden to God and talk to Him about it. Ask for His strength to continue and remember that He is the Judge.

DUE
RESPECT

We read and hear so much about the love of God that we sometimes forget the fear of God. "You, Yourself, are to be feared; and who may stand in Your presence when once You are angry?" (v. 7). What is this fear Asaph mentions? It's the fear of the Lord, that reverent respect and awe that we show to Him because of His greatness and power. We are God's children, and the Holy Spirit in our hearts says, "Abba, Father." We can pray, "Our Father, who art in heaven." We can draw close to God, and He will draw close to us. But remember that God is God and we are human beings. He is in heaven, and we are on earth. He is eternal, and someday we will be with Him in heaven. Meanwhile, our earthly existence is temporal.

The fear of God is not like the dread of a prisoner before a judge. It's not the cringing of a servant before a master. It's the reverent respect and awe of a child realizing the greatness and the glory of God. We fear Him because He is so *great*. "In Judah God is known; His name is great in Israel" (v. 1). Oh, what a great name He has! How sad that the people of the world take His great name in vain. We also fear Him because He is *glorious*. "You are more glorious and excellent than the mountains of prey" (v. 4).

We also fear God because of *who He is* and *what He has done*. "At Your rebuke, O God of Jacob, both the chariot and horse were cast into a dead sleep" (v. 6). What is the result of fearing Him? God fights our battles. He goes before those who fear Him. We can stand before Him because Jesus intercedes for us. God will not be angry because of our sins. Jesus has taken care of that. Let's fear the Lord, and He will fight our battles for us.

✦   ✦   ✦

God deserves your reverent respect. And you have many reasons for giving it to Him. Do you give God His due respect? Take time to meditate on who He is and what He has done for you. Come into His presence and worship Him. "The fear of the Lord is the beginning of wisdom" (Prov. 9:1).

CONVERSATIONS IN THE NIGHT

It doesn't have to be dark outside for us to be in the middle of the night. Sometimes the darkness is in us. Discouragement moves in, and we are like Asaph, who said, "My hand was stretched out in the night without ceasing; my soul refused to be comforted" (v. 2). Some translations read, "My sore was running in the night." What do you do when your soul refuses to be comforted?

Asaph tells us what we should do. First, *talk to God*. "I cried out to God with my voice—to God with my voice; and He gave ear to me" (v. 1). Someone has suggested that when you can't sleep at night, instead of counting sheep, talk to the Shepherd. That's what Asaph did. Sometimes approaching the Lord is painful. "I remembered God, and was troubled" (v. 3). What did he remember about God that troubled him? Perhaps he disobeyed a commandment or doubted a promise. Or perhaps he realized how holy God is and how sinful he is.

But talking to the Lord also brings reassurance. "I have considered the days of old, the years of ancient times" (v. 5). In other words, God can be trusted. He has cared for you in the past, and He will care for you in the future.

Second, *talk to yourself*. "I meditate within my heart, and my spirit makes diligent search" (v. 6). Talk to yourself about the Lord. Examine your life and your Christian walk. Your discouragement will be replaced by a song. "I call to remembrance my song in the night" (v. 6).

♦ ♦ ♦

When you feel discouraged, get your eyes off your circumstances and onto the Lord. Also, examine your life. Have you disobeyed the Lord? Talk to Him and let Him encourage you. Then talk to yourself and encourage yourself with the things of God. He will give you a song in the night.

UNANSWERED QUESTIONS

Asking questions is much easier than answering them. If you have children or grandchildren, you know how true that is. These verses contain a series of questions from a discouraged man. "Will the Lord cast off forever? And will He be favorable no more? Has His mercy ceased forever? Has His promise failed forevermore? Has God forgotten to be gracious? Has He in anger shut up His tender mercies?" (vv. 7-9). Then he concludes by saying, "This is my anguish; but I will remember the years of the right hand of the Most High" (v. 10).

It's normal to ask questions when we are going through difficulty and pain. David prayed, "My God, my God, why have You forsaken Me?" (Ps. 22:1). Jesus also quoted those words on the cross (Matt. 27:46). When we are going through difficulty, we expect God to move in, help us and deliver us. And when we are waiting for that deliverance, we get impatient. That's when the questions come.

Don't be afraid to be open and honest with God. Tell Him how you feel and what you're thinking. He would rather you be honest about your feelings than hypocritical. But remember this: As Christians, we do not live on explanations; we live on promises. Suppose God started to answer these questions. Will the Lord cast off forever? No. Will He be favorable no more? Of course, He's going to be favorable. Is His mercy completely gone forever? No. If God answered all of these questions, would it make any difference? It might ease your mind a little bit, but it wouldn't really change your situation. Live by faith, not by sight. Trust the promises of the Lord. He will not change.

◆   ◆   ◆

God does not always provide explanations for your difficulties, but He does provide the promises of His Word. The next time you find yourself in the midst of discouragement, bring your questions and concerns to Him in prayer. Then rely on the promises of His Word. God knows your needs and will meet them.

HOLY AND HIDDEN

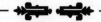

Asaph refused to be comforted. He asked a lot of questions of the Lord. At the close of his discouragement, he came to two wonderful conclusions. First, "Your way, O God, is in the sanctuary; who is so great a God as our God?" (v. 13). And second, "Your way was in the sea, your path in the great waters, and your footsteps were not known" (v. 19).

What an unusual way to express faith! First, Asaph tells us that *God's way is in the sanctuary*. His way is a way of sanctification and holiness. God leads us in grace and from grace to glory. He makes no mistakes—His way is the best way and always has been. If we are living in the Holy of Holies, we will be able to discover God's way. If we are in the Holy Word of God, we can have a holy walk with Him.

Second, *God's way is in the sea*. His way is hidden. We may not understand all of God's leading, but this we can know: God *is* leading. Asaph said, "You led Your people like a flock by the hand of Moses and Aaron" (v. 20). His way is in the sea, and if He has to, He will open up the sea for you. If necessary, He will help you walk on the water. But the psalmist came to the right conclusion. God's way is holy, so obey Him. His way is hidden, so trust Him.

◆   ◆   ◆

Perhaps you're going through a difficulty today and asking the Lord a lot of questions—why, how, when, how long—the questions Asaph asked. Let God bring you closer to Himself by following His guidance.

SERVANTS OF
TOMORROW

We have a responsibility to the next generation. The psalmist wrote, "We will not hide them from their children, telling to the generation to come the praises of the Lord, and His strength and His wonderful works that He has done" (v. 4).

Why should we share the *Word of the Lord* with the generation to come? "That they may set their hope in God, and not forget the works of God, but keep His commandments" (v. 7). That's preparing them for the future, because hope looks to the future. Christians are born again unto a living hope by the Resurrection of Jesus Christ. We know that our Lord is going to return and take us home to heaven. Too many people in the younger generation are setting their hope in money, in government or in their abilities. So we share the blessing of the Lord with the next generation to help them set their hope in Him.

Second, we want the next generation to remember the *works of God*. How easy it is to forget what He has done for us! Yet if we keep reminding the next generation, they will remember, too. The past must not be forgotten. Those who forget the past are condemned to repeat its mistakes.

Finally, we must share the *things of the Lord* with the younger generation so they will keep His commandments. The psalmist wasn't talking about a legalistic life. He was talking about a loving obedience to the Lord. Yes, we do have a responsibility to the new generation, and we fulfill that responsibility by being a good example, by teaching, sharing and encouraging.

✦　✦　✦

You are entrusted with your Christian heritage. When you share with the next generation the Word and works of God, you teach them valuable lessons about how He still works in the lives of His people. Strive to be an example that encourages the next generation to obey the Lord.

ALWAYS FAITHFUL

The children of Ephraim mentioned in Psalm 78 failed the Lord, and they failed their fellow Israelites when their help was badly needed. "The children of Ephraim, being armed and carrying bows, turned back in the day of battle. They did not keep the covenant of God; they refused to walk in His law, and forgot His works and His wonders that He had shown them" (vv. 9-11).

What a tragedy it is when people fail in their warfare. Jesus warned us about those who look back and do not fulfill the will of God (Luke 9:62). If we are looking back, we cannot plow ahead. And if we look back, we cannot fight as we ought. Yes, there is a spiritual battle going on, and we need every soldier. But something was wrong with these warriors. They were *unfaithful*. Even though they were armed, they turned back in the day of battle.

Something was wrong with their walk. "They did not keep the covenant of God; they refused to walk in His law" (v. 10). That's where failure always starts. God wanted them to walk in His law that He might help them win the battle, but they would not obey Him.

Finally, they *forgot what God had done for them.* "And forgot His works and His wonders that He had shown them" (v. 11). Can you imagine forgetting a miracle? If a miracle took place in your life today, you would talk about it until the day the Lord called you home. You'd call a press conference! Think of the miracles God did for His people. But they forgot them. The Ephraimites were undependable on the battlefield because they forgot what He had done for them. They turned against the law of God, and they turned from the works of the Lord. Consequently, they were unable to help in His work.

✦ ✦ ✦

Unfaithfulness is common in people. But not so with God. Faithfulness is part of His character. This truth ought to encourage you if you know the Lord. Be faithful in your walk with Him. Remember His works and be a faithful soldier in your battle for Him.

FUTILITY AND FEAR

The history of Israel in the Old Testament is really the history of all Christians. Like Israel, we have been redeemed through the blood of the Lamb. And like the people of Israel, we are heading for the Promised Land.

What is the one thing you need most on the journey from earth to heaven? Love? Yes, that's important. Hope? That's important, too. But I think faith is needed most. The one thing you must do is trust God. That's what the psalmist talks about in this passage. The people would not believe in God and continued to sin. We see the consequence in verse 33: "Therefore their days He consumed in futility, and their years in fear." When the Israelites got to the edge of the Promised Land, they refused to go in. They were at Kadesh-Barnea and would not trust God to lead them. So they had to wander around for some 40 years in vanity and emptiness, struggling with problem after problem.

Unfortunately, many of God's people are betweeners—they are living between Egypt and Canaan. They have been delivered from bondage by the blood of the Lamb, but they have never entered into their inheritance. They are living between Good Friday and Easter Sunday. They believe that Jesus died on the cross, but they are not living in the power of His Resurrection.

Don't be a betweener today. Consider how God blessed the people of Israel. He sent them manna and fowl to feed them. He provided them with water. But also consider how God disciplined them because of their unbelief. In His patience, however, He finally brought them through. We are like the people of Israel. Our greatest need is to believe God. We don't live by explanations; we live by promises. Today, while you hear His voice, don't harden your heart.

◆　　◆　　◆

Unbelief leads to futility and fear. Perhaps you are a "betweener" today—refusing to trust God's leading. When Israel believed the promises of God, He blessed them. Trust Him, obey Him and believe Him, and His blessing will come!

FLATTERY GETS YOU NOWHERE

Flattery is not communication; it is manipulation. We flatter people because we want something from them. It's bad enough to flatter people, but it's even worse to flatter God. "Nevertheless they flattered Him with their mouth, and they lied to Him with their tongue; for their heart was not steadfast with Him, nor were they faithful in His covenant" (vv. 36,37).

How do we flatter God? First, *when we praise Him but don't mean it.* It is so easy to stand in church and sing songs of praise with our minds somewhere else and our hearts not in our singing. We are simply going through an empty ritual. We also flatter God *when we make promises to Him that we don't intend to keep.* We do this sometimes in our praying.

We flatter God a third way *when we pray to Him but don't really seek His will.* It's easy for us to go through routine prayers and make promises. "Dear Lord, today I'm going to witness," or, "Dear Lord, today I'm going to read my Bible," or, "Dear Lord, today I am not going to yield to that temptation." But in our hearts we have no intention of following through. We lie to God. So often the Israelites lied to Him. They brought sacrifices, hoping to buy God's blessing. They went through the ritual and the routine of worship, hoping that He would somehow deliver them. They were flattering Him—their hearts were not right with God.

What does it mean to have a heart right with God? It means we are honest and open with Him. We are sincere, not lying. We tell Him just how we feel and exactly what we're going through. That's what God wants. He wants us to walk in the light as He is in the light (I John 1:7), not trying to cover up or excuse our sins, but confessing them. To have our hearts right with the Lord, we must stop flattering God and always deal with Him in truth.

◆　　◆　　◆

God wants you to be open and honest with Him. Never flatter Him with dishonesty, insincerity or deception. One way to be honest in your relationship with God is to keep your heart clean. Confess your sins instead of trying to cover them. He knows your heart, so be truthful in your praying.

FLAWED MEMORY

T he older we get, the more we forget. This is especially true when it comes to our relationship with God.

The people of Israel often remembered what they should have forgotten and forgot what they should have remembered! "They did not remember His power: the day when He redeemed them from the enemy, when He worked His signs in Egypt, and His wonders in the field of Zoan" (vv. 42,43). How amazing. The Jews had seen God perform ten miracles on their behalf in Egypt. Moses even pointed out that this was the hand of the Lord, yet they forgot all about it. After they were delivered from Egypt and living in the desert, the first time they were thirsty, they complained. The first time they were hungry, they complained.

Their constant cry was, "Let's go back." What did they remember about Egypt? The bondage? The taskmasters? Being beaten and whipped? Carrying the heavy burdens? They didn't remember those things. They remembered the leeks and the onions and the garlic and the cucumbers. They remembered the things that satisfied their stomachs. They did not remember the spiritual victories that God had given, His deliverance or His guidance. He had fed and led them, protected and provided for them; and they forgot about it. The same is often true of us. We forget what God has done for us, and when we forget, we start to go backward.

Forgetfulness has consequences. "Yes, again and again they tempted God, and limited the Holy One of Israel" (v. 41). Imagine—feeble, unbelieving man limiting Almighty God! But that's what happens when we forget Him. Don't limit God in your life today. He has unlimited wisdom and unlimited power, and your life has unlimited potential in His hands. Don't turn back. Look ahead. Don't test Him. Trust Him and remember his mercies.

♦ ♦ ♦

The same God who worked miracle after miracle for Israel is the One who is working for you today. Don't live with a flawed memory. Meditate on God's faithfulness and goodness.

TEMPTING GOD

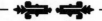

There is only one direction for Christians to travel—forward. We must not think back or look back or turn back. We must move ahead, out of the old life and into the new.

That's the picture of the Israelites. God delivered them from Egypt. He brought them into the Promised Land, yet when they got there, they failed Him. "Yet they tested and provoked the Most High God, and did not keep His testimonies, but turned back and acted unfaithfully like their fathers; they were turned aside like a deceitful bow. For they provoked Him to anger with their high places, and moved Him to jealousy with their carved images" (vv. 56-58). They ignored all of God's greatness. He defeated the other nations. He gave the Jews houses they did not build. They drank from wells they did not dig. They ate from trees they never cultivated. They ignored God's goodness, and then they deliberately tempted Him.

How do you tempt God? When you deliberately disobey Him and dare Him to do something. You are not walking in ignorance—you know what you are doing. To tempt God means to sin with your eyes wide open. This provokes Him.

The people of Israel even adopted the idolatrous worship of the people they had defeated! We do this today, too. How easy it is for us to accept the idols of this world, to trust in money and position, to trust in the words of men instead of the words of God. And the result? "He forsook the tabernacle" (v. 60). God moved out. He said, "If you don't want me, I'm leaving." As a consequence, the people of Israel went into captivity.

What a tragedy to enter into the blessing God has for us and get so confident and selfish we forget the One who gave us the blessing.

◆　　◆　　◆

Be careful never to place your trust in God's blessings rather than in God. Enjoy the Blesser—the God who gives and guides you—rather than the blessing.

FROM SERVANT TO RULER

We know that David committed adultery and that he made a man drunk and had him murdered. In addition, he once took a census of the Israelites out of disobedience to God—70,000 people died as a result. But David is still a great man. God forgave him and used him in a wonderful way.

David was a man of humility. "He also chose David His servant, and took him from the sheepfolds; from following the ewes that had young He brought him, to shepherd Jacob His people, and Israel His inheritance" (vv. 70,71). David began as a servant, and God made him a ruler. That's always God's pattern. There are those who make themselves leaders, but God's blessing is not upon them. David had God's blessing because he was faithful in his job. That's what Jesus said in one of His parables. "Well done, good and faithful servant; you were faithful over a few things, I will make you ruler over many things. Enter into the joy of your lord" (Matt. 25:21). If you want to be a leader, learn how to be a follower. If you want to be a ruler, learn how to be a servant, faithfully doing what God has called you to do.

David was a man of integrity. "So he shepherded them according to the integrity of his heart" (v. 72). *Integrity* means having one heart, whereas a double-minded man is unstable in all his ways (James 1:8). David's sole purpose was to serve the Lord.

David was a man of ability. He "guided them by the skillfulness of his hands" (v. 72). Integrity ties your heart and your hands together. Your heart serves the Lord, and your hands are busy for Him. We need people like that today. No amount of dedication can compensate for a lack of skill, but no amount of skill can compensate for a lack of dedication. We need both.

◆　　◆　　◆

David exhibited the traits of a true ruler—humility, integrity and ability. They also are required of you for faithful service. Where has God placed you for service? Are you a faithful leader or follower? He rewards His faithful servants. Dedicate yourself to the Lord today and serve Him faithfully.

WHEN ALL SEEMS LOST

There are days when we look around and it seems as though the Enemy has won. That's the way Asaph felt when he wrote Psalm 79.

He looked around and saw *defilement*. "Oh God, the nations have come into Your inheritance; Your holy temple they have defiled; they have laid Jerusalem in heaps" (v. 1). Asaph refers to the destruction of the temple and the city of Jerusalem. We, too, can look around today and see defilement in people's minds and hearts.

Then Asaph saw *death*. "The dead bodies of Your servants they have given as food for the birds of the heavens. . . . Their blood they have shed like water all around Jerusalem" (vv. 2,3). Our world is basically a cemetery. The wages of sin is death. We see it wherever we look.

Asaph also saw *derision*. "We have become a reproach to our neighbors, a scorn and derision to those who are around us" (v. 4). People today don't magnify the Lord; they laugh at Him. They laugh at the Church, at God's people. We are a derided people because so often it looks as though we are losing and they have won the battle.

Finally, Asaph saw the enemy *devouring*. "For they have devoured Jacob, and laid waste his dwelling place" (v. 7). Yes, the devouring, destroying hand of Satan was at work. But Asaph says, "Help us, O God of our salvation." Why? "For the glory of Your name; and deliver us" (v. 9). How? "And provide atonement for our sins, for Your name's sake!" Asaph isn't concerned so much about his own comfort as he is about God's glory. So he prays, "Help us."

God helps by purging us from our sins. In addition, verses 11 and 12 tell us that He will come and save us. How wonderful that day will be when Jesus Christ comes to deliver us! Meanwhile, in the world we see defilement, death, derision, destruction and devouring. Now is the time to cry and say, "O God, for the glory of Your name, help us do Your will."

◆　　◆　　◆

Satan is at work in the world, but one day God will be glorified, and He will deliver His people from this world. God promises to be with you and to be your Salvation. Rest on that promise.

RESTORATION

"**R**estore us, O God; cause Your face to shine, and we shall be saved" (v. 3). We find this prayer three times in Psalm 80. Christians ought to pray this every day.

We certainly ought to pray this in times of *affliction*. The people of Israel were going through the affliction of God. He was angry with them and had to chasten them. The psalmist says, "You are feeding us with the bread of tears. We are drinking our tears. We are a strife to our neighbors. Our enemies are laughing at us" (vv. 5,6). Asaph doesn't pray for the Lord to change his circumstances. Rather, he says, "Lord, restore us. We have wandered away. We are not what we ought to be. Turn us right again."

We also ought to pray Asaph's prayer in times of *rebellion*. God's people were rebelling against Him, and that's why He was chastening them. But in spite of their failures, in spite of their unbelief, God never changes. The psalmist prays, "O Lord God of hosts, how long will You be angry against the prayer of Your people?" (v. 4).

What was wrong with their prayers? They were praying selfishly for their own comfort and deliverance. They weren't thinking about the glory of God. But Asaph is different. He prays for their restoration. When you look at your failure, immediately look for God's favor and His salvation.

✦　　✦　　✦

There are times when you need God's restoration. Sometimes He afflicts you and chastens you because His glory is at stake—He wants you to glorify Him. Have you failed God? Do you need His restoration? Pray Asaph's prayer today from your heart.

BLOOM WHERE YOU'RE PLANTED

One of the greatest tragedies in life is wasted opportunity—not making the most of what God has given us. We came into this world with certain abilities, and when God saved us, He gave us gifts and the grace to exercise those gifts to help others, to build our own lives and to glorify His name.

This is why God puts us through certain experiences. Asaph said, "You have brought a vine out of Egypt; you have cast out the nations, and planted it. You prepared room for it, and caused it to take deep root, and it filled the land" (vv. 8,9). That vine, of course, was the nation of Israel. God delivered Israel from Egypt and planted her like a luxurious vine in the land of Canaan. But soon He had to break that vine. He had to discipline His people. The vine was not producing the fruit God wanted it to produce.

God blesses us to make us a blessing. He planted the people of Israel in the land that they might, by their life and testimony, bear spiritual fruit, letting the Gentile nations know about the true and living God. He gave them an opportunity to show the other nations what He could do for those who would trust and obey Him. Instead, the vine became like all the other vines. The Israelites compromised and sinned. So God had to cut down His vine and discipline His people.

Remember, God has planted you where you are that you might be a blessing. He wants you to take deep root. He wants you to bear rich fruit. And if you will draw upon His spiritual power, He will enable you to be a blessing. Bloom where you are planted and bear fruit to the glory of God and the enrichment of others.

♦   ♦   ♦

God has blessed you with certain abilities so you may invest them in others and bring glory to Him. As you use your God-given talents, you glorify Him and bless others. Draw from God's spiritual resources and let Him use you to enrich others.

REVIVE
US AGAIN

L ook at two important words in Psalm 80. One is *return.* "Return, we beseech You, O God of hosts; look down from heaven and see, and visit this vine" (v. 14). The other word is *revive.* "Then we will not turn back from You; revive us, and we will call upon Your name" (v. 18).

God had departed from His people. He had planted this vine, the nation of Israel, in the land of Canaan. He had cast out the other nations to make room for Israel. The vine took root and began to bear fruit. But the people of Israel began to sin against the Lord. Instead of being distinctively separate, they began to imitate the other nations and visit their altars and participate in their sacrifices. So God said, "If that's the way you want it, you can have it." God left His people. The word *Ichabod* means "the glory has departed" (I Sam. 4:21).

Jesus said, "I will never leave you nor forsake you" (Heb. 13:5). God will never take away His presence, but He will take away His power and His blessing. If necessary, He will withhold that extra anointing He wants to give us. Verses 18 and19 are a prayer for revival: "Revive us, and we will call upon Your name. Restore us, O Lord God of hosts; cause your face to shine, and we shall be saved!"

✦　　✦　　✦

God will never leave you, but there are times when He may need to with-hold His power and blessing because of sin in your life. Are you in need of God's restoration? He hears the prayer of revival. Ask Him to clean your heart and then pray Asaph's prayer.

WHAT MIGHT HAVE BEEN

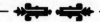

Life is made up of things that were, things that are and things that might have been. We find all three in Psalm 81.

First, we find *the things that were* (vv. 1-10). The psalmist talks about the God of Jacob and says, "Let's get our orchestra together. Let's get our trumpets and let's sing to the Lord. He gave us a statute. He delivered us from Egypt." He reflects on and rejoices in the past. But the things that *were* did not last long, because the people rebelled against the Lord.

Next, we see *the things that are.* "But My people would not heed My voice, and Israel would have none of Me. So I gave them over to their own stubborn heart, to walk in their own counsels" (vv. 11,12). The things that *were* brought rejoicing. The things that *are* spoke of rebellion. The people of God rebelled against Him. They wouldn't listen to Him, call upon Him or obey His Word. So they lost all that He had for them.

Finally, we see *the things that might have been* (vv. 13-16). "Oh, that My people would listen to Me, that Israel would walk in My ways! I would soon subdue their enemies, and turn my hand against their adversaries. The haters of the Lord would pretend submission to Him, but their fate would endure forever. He would have fed them also with the finest of wheat; and with honey from the rock I would have satisfied you." What might have been? Victory, satisfaction, joy, the finest wheat and honey out of the rock.

Don't rebel against God and thus miss the blessings He wants to give you.

◆　　◆　　◆

Dwelling on past failures only turns life into regret. If you have failed the Lord, come back to Him and pray for forgiveness. Dedicate yourself to Him and start experiencing those things that might have been. God has the best plan for you.

THE ULTIMATE JUDGE

✦➤◆ ◆➤◆

When we watch the news on television or read it in a magazine or newspaper, we may think that the unjust are winning and the just are losing. We get the same idea when we read Psalm 82. But this psalm also says that God is part of the judicial system.

God attends court. "God stands in the congregation of the mighty; He judges among the gods" (v. 1). The word gods means "the judges." When the judges get together in court, God is there whether they recognize Him or not.

God admonishes the judges. "How long will you judge unjustly, and show partiality to the wicked?" (v. 2). He tells them what to do: "Defend the poor and fatherless; do justice to the afflicted and needy. Deliver the poor and needy; free them from the hand of the wicked" (vv. 3,4).

God judges the judges. The judges think they are trying others, but God is trying them. "They do not know, nor do they understand; they walk about in darkness; all the foundations of the earth are unstable" (v. 5). When the law is not being upheld, all the nations fall apart. "I said, 'You are gods, and all of you are children of the Most High. But you shall die like men, and fall like one of the princes'" (vv. 6,7). The psalmist believes that God will one day make everything right. "Arise, O God, judge the earth; for You shall inherit all nations" (v. 8).

Yes, there is going to be injustice in this world until Jesus comes. But when the King of kings is reigning and the Lord of lords is supremely in control, we finally will have justice in this world.

◆ ◆ ◆

In spite of the world's injustice, God is in control, and He sees all that happens. Until Jesus comes to reign, we must live here. In the meantime, trust Him, obey Him and do His will.

ENEMIES OF THE KING

Christians are strangers living in enemy territory. Our enemies are those who do not love Jesus Christ, His Church or His Word. What shall we do about our enemies, who also are God's enemies? Follow the example of the psalmist and turn them over to the Lord. "For behold, Your enemies make a tumult; and those who hate You have lifted up their head" (v. 2). He refers to Israel's enemies—the Edomites, the Ishmaelites, the Moabites and other heathen nations around her. Through the centuries Israel has had many enemies, and God has defeated them. But He has blessed those nations that have blessed Israel.

What is God going to do about our enemies? The psalmist says He will judge them, though we don't know where or when. He paints some vivid pictures. "O my God, make them like the whirling dust" (v. 13). One translation says "like a wheel of whirling dust." When a wheel goes down a dusty road, it stirs up dust. The enemies are nothing but dirt, like whirling dust that blows away, "like the chaff before the wind! As the fire burns the woods, and as the flame sets the mountains on fire" (vv. 13,14). One day God's fire of judgment is going to sweep through them, and they will be destroyed. Verse 15 compares this to a storm: "So pursue them with Your tempest, and frighten them with Your storm."

Why does God judge His enemies? "That men may know that You, whose name alone is the Lord, are the Most High over all the earth" (v. 18). God is the King. Turn your enemies over to Him. He knows how to take care of them.

✦   ✦   ✦

For centuries God has dealt with the enemies of Israel. He takes an active part in dealing with your enemies, too. When they surround you, turn them over to the Lord and rest in His care.

DESIRING GOD

Psalm 84 expresses the thoughts of a man who wants to go to Jerusalem for a feast but cannot. We do not know why. Perhaps he is ill, or there is some problem at home. He writes, "How lovely is Your tabernacle, O Lord of hosts! My soul longs, yes, even faints for the courts of the Lord; my heart and my flesh cry out for the living God" (vv. 1,2).

His great desire was not to go to Jerusalem solely to observe a holy day. Instead, he wanted to go to the temple and meet God. "Even the sparrow has found a home, and the swallow a nest for herself, where she may lay her young" (v. 3). In other words, God's house is to his soul what a nest is to a swallow—a place of rest and security and satisfaction. The psalmist even envies the priests. "Blessed are those who dwell in Your house; they will still be praising You" (v. 4). Outsiders were not allowed to live there, and they were limited in where they could go inside. Only the priests could enter the Holy of Holies.

We have the privilege of fellowshiping with God without going through a priest. Do you have a great desire to worship Him today? Or are you happy for an excuse to stay home from God's house?

◆　　◆　　◆

If you have been saved by God's grace, you ought to have a strong desire to worship Him and fellowship with Him. You have the privilege of attending God's house and worshiping with His people. Do you desire to be with them? Does your heart cry out for the living God?

THE ROAD TO ZION

At the time this psalm was written, every Jewish man was required to go to Jerusalem to celebrate the feast three times a year. Whole villages would make their pilgrimage together, singing along the way. "Blessed is the man whose strength is in You, whose heart is set on pilgrimage. As they pass through the Valley of Baca, they make it a spring; the rain also covers it with pools. They go from strength to strength; every one of them appears before God in Zion" (vv. 5-7).

As they traveled down the road, the men looked in three different directions. First, *they looked within* (v. 5). "Blessed is the man whose strength is in You, whose heart is set on pilgrimage," or, "in whose heart are the highways to Zion." Everyone has a road map in his heart that takes him where he really wants to go. Look within yourself today. What kind of road map do you have? Where does it lead? Have you limited yourself, or are you entering into all the fullness of walking with the Lord?

They looked back (v. 6). They passed through a valley, Baca, which means "weeping." As they passed through Baca, they left behind a blessing for someone else. Sometimes on our pilgrimage we go through the valley of weeping. When you go through it, do you leave behind a blessing for somebody else? Or do you expect others to give you a blessing?

Then they looked ahead. "They go from strength to strength; every one of them appears before God in Zion" (v. 7). They were looking forward to meeting with the living God as they went to celebrate the feast. We, too, go from strength to strength. You may look ahead and say, "I'll never make it." But you will. He gives you the strength to keep going as you make your pilgrimage.

◆　◆　◆

You, too, look in three directions in your pilgrimage. It is often a difficult journey, but God will give you the strength to continue and progress. In your heart you have a road map to Zion. Follow it, and one day you will meet the living God face to face.

GRACE AND GLORY

The psalmist yearns to go to the courts of the Lord. But as he meditates on Him, he realizes he can have God's blessing right where he is. He does not have to go to the temple. "The Lord God is a sun and shield; the Lord will give grace and glory; no good thing will He withhold from those who walk uprightly" (v. 11).

Grace—that's how the spiritual journey begins. We are saved by God's grace. We trust Jesus, and in grace God saves us. *Glory*—that's how it ends. One day we will be in heaven and share the glory of the Lord forever.

But between grace and glory, life can be rather difficult. We read in I Peter 5:10 that the "God of all grace, who called us to His eternal glory by Christ Jesus, after you have suffered a while, [will] perfect, establish, strengthen, and settle you." Whatever begins with grace leads to glory, but how do we make the journey between grace and glory? "For the Lord God is a sun and shield" (v. 11). He is a *sun*. That's provision and sufficiency. He is a *shield*. That's protection and security. We start the journey with grace; we continue the journey trusting God's provision and protection; and we end the journey by entering into the glory of the Lord.

What does it mean to walk uprightly? It means walking in the light, obeying His word, loving Him and trusting Him.

♦   ♦   ♦

Psalm 84:11 is a great verse to claim for your pilgrim journey. Begin with God's grace and end in His glory. Along the way you have the promise of His provision and protection. Do you qualify for God's provisions for the journey? Determine always to walk uprightly by obeying the Word of God and trusting its promises.

THE REVIVAL PEOPLE

"**W**ill You not revive us again, that Your people may rejoice in You?" (v. 6). This prayer has been set to music in the song "Revive Us Again," and it's a prayer we need to pray.

Who needs revival? Unsaved people can't be revived because they never had life to begin with. The unsaved person is dead in trespasses and sins. But Christians, through faith in Jesus Christ, have been raised from the dead. We've been given eternal, abundant life. Unfortunately, sometimes we turn away from the Lord and lose that spiritual vibrancy. We don't lose our salvation, but we lose the joy of our salvation, its power and the overflowing blessings we give each other.

God's people are *the revival people*. We desperately need to be revived. The psalmist cries out to God for new life. Someone has said that our church services start at eleven o'clock sharp and end at twelve o'clock dull. How we need the breath of God to blow upon us! How we need His life to touch us!

What is *the revival purpose*? A. W. Tozer used to say, "It's difficult to get Christians to attend any meeting where God is the only center of attraction." We have to have entertainment, food and all sorts of distractions. But the psalmist wants God's people to rejoice in Him alone.

◆　◆　◆

God's people should live with a vibrancy that comes from the joy of their salvation. Does your life still sparkle as it did when you came to know the Lord? Pray that He will revive the Church. And pray that your testimony will bless others and glorify the Lord.

ENCOURAGEMENTS TO PRAY

"**F**or You, Lord, are good, and ready to forgive, and abundant in mercy to all those who call upon You" (v. 5). What a promise to claim today! Just two verses later the psalmist says, "In the day of my trouble I will call upon You, for You will answer me" (v. 7).

The psalmist gives a number of encouragements to pray. First, *remember who God is.* Never forget His attributes. The better we know Him, the better we are able to pray. What kind of God are we praying to? One who is good, merciful and ready to forgive. You may say, "I can't pray to God. My hands are dirty. My heart is dirty. I'm not what I ought to be." Then come to Him and say, "I know You are ready to forgive; You are abundant in mercy." And God will forgive you. He hears all who cry out to Him.

Second, *remember what God does.* "For You are great, and do wondrous things; You alone are God" (v. 10). "Call to Me, and I will answer you, and show you great and mighty things, which you do not know" (Jer. 33:3).

Third, *remember what God promises.* He promises to answer us. Jesus said, "Ask, and it will be given to you" (Matt. 7:7). "You do not have because you do not ask" (James 4:2).

Remember who God is, the kind of God to whom you are praying. Remember the great and wonderful things He does. He can do the impossible for you today. And remember, He promises to answer.

✦   ✦   ✦

These are wonderful encouragements to pray. When you pray, keep them before you. Contemplate God's character. Remember what He has done in your life. Recount His faithfulness to you. And be sure to claim the promises of the Bible.

MIND, HEART AND WILL

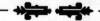

Here is a good prayer for you today. "Teach me Your way, O Lord; I will walk in Your truth; unite my heart to fear Your name" (v. 11). The whole person is wrapped up in this prayer.

First, we see *an open mind*. "Teach me Your way; . . . I will walk in Your truth." Is your mind open to God's truth? Do you really want Him to teach you His way? He revealed His ways to Moses and to the Israelites. He will do the same for you also. We need people today who will say, "Lord, I have an open mind. I want you to show me Your way and truth."

But that's not enough. We need to have *an obedient will*. The psalmist makes a promise in verse 11: "Lord, if you show me your way, I will obey it." Jesus said, "If anyone wants to do His will, he shall know concerning the doctrine, whether it is from God or whether I speak on My own authority" (John 7:17).

Finally, we see *a united heart*. "Unite my heart to fear your name." A united heart is wholly fixed upon the Lord. A divided heart is dangerous. Jesus said, "No one can serve two masters; for either he will hate the one and love the other, or else he will be loyal to the one and despise the other. You cannot serve God and mammon" (Matt. 6:24). James 1:8 says a double-minded man is unstable in all of his ways.

If you want God to guide and bless you today, follow the example of this prayer. Give to Him an open mind and say, "Teach me." Give to Him an obedient will and say, "I will do what you want me to do." And give to Him a united heart. Fear His name, and you'll end up praising Him, glorifying Him and enjoying His blessings.

✦ ✦ ✦

Is your mind open to the truth of God's Word? Does your will respond to truth and obey it? Is your heart undivided, fixed upon the Lord? Today, dedicate your mind, heart and will to God.

CITY
OF GOD

Most of us have places in this world we love in special ways. It might be an old home or perhaps a school. It might even be a church or a place in that church building where God met you in a significant way. God also has a place He loves especially. "The Lord loves the gates of Zion more than all the dwellings of Jacob" (v. 2). The psalmist refers to the city of God.

Zion is important to Christians also. Of course, our citizenship is in the heavenly Zion (Phil. 3:20), where one day we shall walk the golden streets. But we can give thanks for Jerusalem, the earthly city of God.

First, *our foundations are in Zion*. This means the foundations of our spiritual life. The Word of God, the Bible, originated from the Jewish nation. The knowledge of the true God came from the Jewish nation. And the Son of God, the Savior of the world, came from the Jewish nation.

Second, *our family is in Zion*. The psalmist speaks about one who was born there. People born in Jerusalem are proud of their birthplace, just as we are proud of our birthplace. But Christians have been born from above. We have been born again spiritually because we trust Christ as our Savior.

Third, *our fountains are in Zion*. "All my springs are in you" (v. 7). The word *springs* means "fountains"—our refreshment, our strength, our spiritual power. They all come from our heavenly Zion.

◆　　◆　　◆

Believers in Christ are citizens of heavenly Zion. Are you a citizen of the city of God? If not, why not trust Him as your Savior and begin your pilgrimage to Zion?

HOLDING ON

There are days when it's difficult to rejoice. Oh, we talk about having the joy of the Lord and walking in the sunshine of His countenance. We are grateful for days like that, but there are also difficult days. The author of Psalm 88 penned these words when he was having one of those difficult days. He tells us about his problems.

First, he is struggling with unanswered prayer. "O Lord, God of my salvation, I have cried out day and night before You. Let my prayer come before You; incline Your ear to my cry." (v. 1). This is not an unsaved man crying out to a God he doesn't worship. This is a true believer pleading with God for help. And so far, He hasn't done anything.

He also is coping with *trouble* and *sickness*. "For my soul is full of troubles, and my life draws near to the grave. I am counted with those who go down to the pit; I am like a man who has no strength. . . . You have put away my acquaintances far from me; You have made me an abomination to them; I am shut up, and I cannot get out" (vv. 3,4,8). Some scholars think that the psalmist had leprosy, since he was segregated from everyone else.

The foundations of his life seem to be slipping away, and the possibility of death looms before him. In his desolation, what does he do? He holds on to God's power, loving-kindness and faithfulness.

What do you do on difficult days? Hold on to all that God is and all that He does. God is still working for you. All things are still working together for good (Rom. 8:28). Don't turn away from Him. Wait. He will bring you out of your affliction.

♦　　♦　　♦

Whenever you experience a difficult day, encourage yourself by focusing on God's character and His attributes—power, loving-kindness and faithfulness. Remember what He has done for you in the past. In spite of what you see around you, trust the Lord. He will see you through your affliction.

LIGHT IN THE DARKNESS

When nothing seems to go right, when people are neglecting you and God seems to have forgotten you, *don't stop praying*. This troubled psalmist did not cease to pray. "Lord, I have called daily upon You; I have stretched out my hands to You" (v. 9). Even though the light is not shining, don't stop praying, because God will answer.

Start each day with the Lord. "But to You I have cried out, O Lord, and in the morning my prayer comes before You" (v. 13). Always begin your day with the Lord, and He will give you the strength to finish it.

Look to God alone. We have a tendency to trust circumstances, ourselves and other people. Not the psalmist. He said, "I'm going to look to God alone. I'm going to trust the Lord of my salvation."

Yes, there are those dark, dismal, disappointing days. But God is still on the throne. Trust Him to see you through.

◆　◆　◆

How well do you fare when the days are dark? Follow the example of the psalmist. Start your day with God in prayer and draw strength from His Word. Keep your eyes on the Lord, not on your circumstances, and He will deliver you.

GREAT IS HIS FAITHFULNESS

Have you thought lately about the faithfulness of God? Too often we are prone to focus on our own faithfulness and our own faith. Our living a victorious Christian life indicates that we are trusting a faithful God who cannot fail, not that we are faithful to Him.

How should we respond to the faithfulness of God? First, *sing of His faithfulness.* "I will sing of the mercies of the Lord forever; with my mouth will I make known Your faithfulness to all generations" (v. 1). Are you praising God today for His faithfulness? When you find yourself unfaithful to the Lord, consider His faithfulness. After all, "He is faithful and just to forgive us our sins and to cleanse us from all unrighteousness" (I John 1:9).

Second, *share God's faithfulness with others.* "With my mouth will I make known Your faithfulness to all generations." In giving our testimonies, we sometimes brag about ourselves. I was in a meeting once where the leader said, "Let's give praise to the Lord, and let's be careful not to give praise to ourselves." The psalmist said, "I'm going to share the faithfulness of God—not what I have done, but what He has done; not what I am, but what He is."

Third, *submit to His faithfulness.* "God is greatly to be feared in the assembly of the saints, and to be held in reverence by all those who are around Him" (v. 7). Our God is faithful.

Can we trust Him today? Yes, we can. Is His Word going to fail? No, not one word of all His promises has failed. Is His grace going to run out? No, He has vast riches of His grace. God is faithful in everything.

◆ ◆ ◆

Have you learned to respond to God's faithfulness? Praise Him for His faithfulness, share it with others and submit to it. He can be trusted.

THE JOYFUL SOUND

"**B**lessed are the people who know the joyful sound! They walk, O Lord, in the light of Your countenance. In Your name they rejoice all day long, and in Your righteousness they are exalted" (vv. 15,16). That describes how God's people ought to be.

We should walk in joy. Throughout the year the people of Israel heard joyful sounds. The trumpets would call them to a feast or remind them of the faithfulness and goodness of God. The psalmist is talking here about that festal blowing of the trumpet. Today we might hear a joyful sound—the sound of the trumpet, the voice of the archangel—and meet the Lord. God's people should be walking in joy. Every day should be a joyful experience of anticipation, excitement and enrichment.

We should walk in the light. "But if we walk in the light as He is in the light, we have fellowship with one another, and the blood of Jesus Christ His Son cleanses us from all sin" (I John 1:7). When you walk in the light, you see things as they really are. You don't stumble or cause someone else to stumble.

We should walk in faith. "In Your name they rejoice all day long" (v. 16). Why? His name can be trusted. Those who know God's name know victory and blessing.

We should walk in the heights. "In Your righteousness they are exalted" (v. 16). There's not only excitement and enrichment in our life with God, we are also exalted, lifted high. This doesn't mean that we are glorified instead of God. It means that He lifts us up.

Keep your ears tuned. You might hear that joyful sound today.

♦   ♦   ♦

Do others know you are a Christian by your life? If you walk with joy and in the light, you will bless others and glorify God. Do you find your walk with God enriching? Enjoy Him to the fullest. Let Him exalt you.

UNBREAKABLE COVENANTS

There is one thing that God cannot do—He cannot lie. When He makes a covenant, He keeps it, and we can hold on to His Word forever. This is what God said concerning David and his family: "If his sons forsake My law and do not walk in My judgments, if they break My statutes and do not keep My commandments, then I will visit their transgression with the rod, and their iniquity with stripes. Nevertheless My lovingkindness I will not utterly take from him, nor allow My faithfulness to fail. My covenant I will not break, nor alter the word that has gone out of My lips" (vv. 30-34).

God is faithful to His Word. He's not going to alter what He has said. "Forever, O Lord, Your word is settled in heaven" (Ps. 119:89). "Heaven and earth will pass away, but My words will by no means pass away" (Matt. 24:35). God's Word is not going to change, but it should change us.

God is faithful to chasten. He said, "If David's descendants don't live as they ought to live, I'll chasten them. My promise won't fail even though they fail." Even if we are not faithful, God is still faithful. He will not deny His Word. He is faithful to discipline us when we need it.

God is faithful to forgive. When we ask Him for His forgiveness, He forgives our sins and cleanses us from all our unrighteousness (I John 1:9). I'm glad I don't have to figure out every day what God's attitude is toward me. He doesn't change; He is faithful.

◆　　◆　　◆

Have you experienced God's faithfulness in your life lately? Trust His Word, submit to His chastening and ask His forgiveness.

DOWN, DOWN, DOWN

God did wonderful things for the people of Israel, and He gave them wonderful promises. We would expect the Israelites to be loyal followers of God, but they were not. They turned their back on Him and sinned, so God had to discipline them. This passages depicts His chastening.

What really happens when God disciplines His people? "You have renounced the covenant of Your servant; you have profaned his crown by casting it to the ground" (v. 39). God wants us to reign in life. Jesus Christ has made us kings and priests. But when God chastens us, He takes our crowns from us. Our authority is gone; the glory is gone; and the honor is gone. Instead of acting like kings, we live like slaves. When God chastened the Israelites, their crowns were cast down.

In verse 40 the walls were broken down. "You have broken down all his hedges; you have brought his strongholds to ruin." There is no security in what we build. God casts it down.

In verse 43 the soldiers were smitten down. "You have also turned back the edge of his sword, and have not sustained him in the battle." When we disobey the Lord, everything falls apart.

In verse 44 the glory ceased, and God cast down the king's throne.

Yet God will forgive. Don't lose your joy in the Lord. Let's live today with authority and security because we are walking with Him. If you find yourself down, look up. Ask Him to raise you up and restore you to victory again.

◆   ◆   ◆

Sometimes God's discipline can be hard. Have you lost your joy in life because of His chastening? Regain the reign in your life. Look to God for forgiveness and restoration.

A FEW REMINDERS

"**H**ow long, Lord? Will You hide Yourself forever? Will Your wrath burn like fire?" (v. 46). These questions come from the broken heart of a man who wondered why God's people were going through so much trouble. Several times we see the word *remember* in these verses. "Remember how short my time is; for what futility have You created all the children of men?" (v. 47). What could the psalmist possibly remind God about?

He reminds Him that *life is short*. God did not make us in vain. Sometimes we receive His grace in vain. Sometimes what He does for us is in vain. But that's our fault, not His. Life is short. That's good to remember the next time you are tempted to sin. Why waste time disobeying God?

Then *he reminds God of His promises*. "Lord, where are Your former lovingkindnesses, which You swore to David in Your truth?" (v. 49). This refers to the covenant God had made with David. It looked as though God had broken His promise. He doesn't break His promises, but He likes to have us remind Him of them.

Next, *he reminds God of their reproach*. "Remember, Lord, the reproach of Your servants—how I bear in my bosom the reproach of all the many peoples, with which Your enemies have reproached, O Lord" (vv. 50,51). Remember our reproach. Why? Because it detracts from the glory of God.

Let's remind ourselves that we are here to bring glory to His name. The psalmist ends on the mountains: "Blessed be the Lord forevermore! Amen and Amen" (v. 52). He starts with burdens and ends with blessing. He starts with sighing and ends with singing, because he lifts his broken heart to the Lord in prayer.

♦   ♦   ♦

When you go through troubled times, remember God's promises and remind Him of them. He is faithful to His Word.

TIME AND ETERNITY

First there were sundials. Then came water clocks, hourglasses and mechanical clocks. Now we have digital clocks and watches that split time into hundredths of a second. Our culture certainly is concerned with time. That's why it's good to read what Moses says: "Lord, You have been our dwelling place in all generations. Before the mountains were brought forth, or ever You had formed the earth and the world, even from everlasting to everlasting, You are God. . . . For a thousand years in Your sight are like yesterday when it is past, and as a watch in the night" (vv. 1,2,4).

It's good to contemplate God's eternity in the light of man's frailty. We are creatures of time, but God is eternal. He is our dwelling place from generation to generation. The eternity we face is in His hands.

The psalmist also tells us that God is faithful. From generation to generation, from everlasting to everlasting, He has been faithful, and He will continue to be faithful. He's the God of Abraham, Isaac and Jacob. He's the God of individuals, the God of different personalities. He's the One we can trust.

Let Him be God in your life today. When you abide in Him and live for His glory, you are partaking of the eternal. The Bible says, "He who does the will of God abides forever" (I John 2:17).

✦   ✦   ✦

When you compare time with eternity, you gain a bit of God's perspective. You can incorporate eternal values into this life. You can partake of the eternal by allowing God into your life. Is He your dwelling place? Have you partaken of His faithfulness?

DEATH:
A REASON FOR LIFE

Life expectancy in the United States is up to 75 years. That's good news; 25 years ago it was only 70 years. Perhaps it will keep going up, but in comparison to eternity, the human life span is short. That's why we read, "The days of our lives are seventy years; and if by reason of strength they are eighty years, yet their boast is only labor and sorrow; for it is soon cut off, and we fly away" (v. 10).

That sounds like a rather doleful statement, but it's true. The setting of Psalm 90 is found in the events recorded in Numbers 14. God had brought the Jews directly to Kadesh-Barnea. He said, "Now go in and possess the land." And they would not do it. They doubted God's promise and questioned His wisdom. They did not believe He would enable them to conquer the land. As a consequence, God said, "All right, everybody 20 years and older is going to die within the next 40 years." And that's what happened—the world's longest funeral march. For the next 40 years the nation wandered in the wilderness, while that older generation died. Then God took the younger generation on a whole new crusade, and they conquered the Promised Land.

The older people knew they were going to die before they got to the Promised Land. But Christians today know that when we die we'll go to the place Jesus is preparing for us. It's important to make our lives count while we are on earth. Yes, our lives have their difficulties, and if the Lord doesn't return soon, our lives will end in death. But death will lead to eternity. And we can live a life of the eternal today. The Bible says, "He who does the will of God abides forever" (I John 2:17). Let's touch the eternal today by abiding in the Almighty and doing His will.

◆　　◆　　◆

You need not die to bring eternity to the present. You do so by abiding in God and doing His will. Determine to make your life count. Invest it in eternity.

A HEART OF WISDOM

"**S**o teach us to number our days, that we may gain a heart of wisdom" (v. 12). Moses' words summarize what we need to know if we want to make our lives count.

We live a day at a time. Usually, we don't number our days; we number our years. When you have a birthday and someone asks how old you are, you tell them your age in the number of years. But we'd better number our days, because we live a day at a time. "Give us this day our daily bread" (Matt. 6:11). God has ordained that the entire universe functions a day at a time.

We live from the heart. "So teach us to number our days, that we may gain a heart of wisdom." We need to take care of the heart. That's why Solomon wrote in Proverbs 4:23, "Keep your heart with all diligence; for out of it spring the issues of life." What is in your heart will direct your life.

We also live by God's wisdom. Wisdom is knowing and having discernment, so that we can apply the truth of the Word of God at the right time, in the right way, with the right motive. Wisdom comes from the Word of God and from getting to know Him and ourselves better.

♦   ♦   ♦

Moses gives the secret of making life count—live it a day at a time. You need God's help to apply His Word to your life. Live as though this may be your last day. Ask God for the wisdom you need and apply it by faith.

SAFETY IN THE SHADOW

I wonder what the safest place in the world is. A bomb shelter? A bank vault? Perhaps a prison surrounded by an army? According to Psalm 91, the safest place in the world is a shadow. "He who dwells in the secret place of the Most High shall abide under the shadow of the Almighty" (v. 1). "He shall cover you with His feathers, and under His wings you shall take refuge; His truth shall be your shield and buckler" (v. 4).

What does this mean? The psalmist refers to the Holy of Holies in the tabernacle and the temple. In the Holy of Holies, two cherubim were over the mercy seat, and their wings touched each other. "Under his wings" means at the mercy seat, where the blood was sprinkled, there in the presence of the glory of God. The Holy of Holies was God's throne. It was the place of God's glory. In other words, the safest place in the world is in fellowship with God—not just visiting the Holy Place, as the high priest did once a year, but *dwelling* in the Holy Place. The psalmist is urging, "Live in the Holy of Holies."

According to Hebrews 10, we have an open invitation to come right into the presence of God and dwell in the secret place—under His wings, at the mercy seat. This is where God meets with us, where His glory is revealed, where He gives us His guidance and shows us His will. My shadow is not much protection for anyone. But when it belongs to the Almighty, a shadow is a strong protection. Live in the Holy of Holies, under the shadow of the Almighty.

♦   ♦   ♦

God invites you to fellowship with Him—to live in the Holy of Holies. What an invitation! You may come into the safety of His presence and receive His mercy, guidance and protection. Do you live under God's shadow?

GUARDIAN ANGELS

"**F**or He shall give His angels charge over you, to keep you in all your ways" (v. 11). This is the promise Satan quoted to Jesus when he tempted Him in the wilderness.

This promise speaks about our *security*. We can't see the angels. But they are God's messengers, servants sent to help us. If we are in the will of God, we have the protection of His army. He is called the "Lord of Hosts" (the Lord of the armies). The hosts of the heavens are under His control—the stars and planets and all the universe. But so is the great host of angels—thousands and thousands of angels, God's creation, His army sent for our ministry.

When the child of God is in His will, then he is immortal until his work is done. This suggests that we have a *responsibility*—"to keep you in all your ways"—to be in the will of God. "Because you have made the Lord, who is my refuge, even the Most High, your dwelling place" (v. 9). When you are dwelling with God, abiding in Him, then He says, "No evil shall befall you" (v. 10). It doesn't say we won't be hurt; it says we won't be harmed. We may have to go through the valley, go through the battle or go through difficulty. But it will not bring evil to us.

Our security and our responsibility lead to our *victory*. What kind of victory does God give us? "You shall tread upon the lion and cobra; the young lion and the serpent you shall trample underfoot" (v. 13). Satan is the lion and the serpent. The psalmist tells us that because we are abiding in the Lord, because His truth is our shield and our buckler, we have victory. We can call upon Him, and He will answer. It's wonderful to know that God gives us security as we fulfill our responsibility.

✦ ✦ ✦

Angels are God's messengers sent to help and protect you. As you think about angels and their ministry, keep in mind your responsibility to stay in the will of God and abide with Him. Thank God for the "invisible" ministry of His angels and for the part they have in your victory over Satan.

AN IDEAL DAY

As we begin each day, we trust we'll still be around at the end of the day. What happens in between depends on how we start in the morning and how we end in the evening. Verses 1 and 2 describe an ideal day: "It is good to give thanks to the Lord, and to sing praises to Your name, O Most High; to declare Your lovingkindness in the morning, and Your faithfulness every night."

That's how we ought to live each day. When you wake up in the morning, *remember His lovingkindness.* Don't wake up grouchy, saying, "Oh my, another day." Wake up saying, "Today the Lord loves me, and His lovingkindness endures forever. God has my life in His hands. There's nothing to be afraid of."

During the day offer *praise* and *thanksgiving.* "It is good to give thanks to the Lord, and to sing praises to Your name, O Most High." Find every reason you can to praise Him—even for little things like parking places, phone calls that bring a blessing to you or perhaps news of a friend.

At the close of the day, *remember God's faithfulness.* In the morning we look forward to lovingkindness. During the day we experience that lovingkindness. And at the end of the day, we can look back and say, "God has been faithful." No matter how difficult this day may be for you, when you get to the end, you're going to be able to look back and say, "Great is Thy faithfulness."

◆　　◆　　◆

Each day has its own set of burdens, blessings and challenges. How you begin and end a day determines what kind of day you will have. Begin your day with lovingkindness. Praise God and thank Him during the day. In the evening, remember His faithfulness during the day. What a great recipe for living a day at a time!

FRESH AND FLOURISHING

Someone has said that there are three stages in life: childhood, adolescence and "My, you're looking good." We can't stop aging. But no matter how old we grow, we ought to continue growing in the Lord. "The righteous shall flourish like the palm tree; he shall grow like a cedar in Lebanon. Those who are planted in the house of the Lord shall flourish in the courts of our God. They shall still bear fruit in old age; they shall be fresh and flourishing" (vv. 12-14). I am greatly encouraged by those words, because as I get older, I want my life to count more and more for Jesus.

God tells us to be like palm trees. That means we should be *planted*—"planted in the house of the Lord." We must abide in Christ, whose roots are in the spiritual. What a tragedy it is to get older and move into the world and into sin, abandoning what you were taught from the Word of God.

We should also be *productive*. "They shall be fresh and flourishing"—fruitful trees to the glory of God. Palm trees stand a lot of abuse, storms and wind. The wind that breaks other trees bends the palm tree, but then it comes back up. Palm trees have roots that go down deep to draw up the water in the desert area. They can survive when other trees are dying. And palm trees just keep on producing fruit. The fruit doesn't diminish; it gets better and sweeter.

Finally, we should be *flourishing* "in the courts of our God." When some people get old, they get grouchy, mean and critical. Let's not be like that. Allow the Lord to make you fresh and flourishing. Have roots that go deep. You can stand the storms and still be fruitful, feeding others from the blessing of the Lord.

✦ ✦ ✦

God wants you to grow like strong, productive trees that bear much fruit. He wants your roots to grow deep to draw nourishment from His hidden spiritual resources. Are you planted and feeding on the Word of God daily? Are you producing fruit and bringing glory to Him? Are you flourishing and feeding others?

LOOKING ABOVE THE FLOOD

While I was ministering at a Bible conference in the Pacific Northwest, I watched the ocean as it moved in. The last day of the conference was rainy and stormy. The ocean waves looked as though they were right at our back door. The scene reminded me of verse 3 in today's passage: "The floods have lifted up, O Lord, the floods have lifted up their voice; the floods lift up their waves."

What do you do when you find yourself threatened by the floods of wickedness? Do what the psalmist did. He looked at God's throne. "The Lord reigns, He is clothed with majesty. The Lord is clothed, He has girded Himself with strength. Surely the world is established, so that it cannot be moved. Your throne is established from of old; You are from everlasting" (v. 1). No waves or floods can disturb the throne of God. But often we don't look high enough. We see the floods, but we don't see God. We see the waves getting higher and higher, and we don't lift up our eyes by faith and see the eternal, established, secure, strong throne of God.

The psalmist also heard God's testimonies. He didn't listen to the sound of the waves. Today, you might hear a lot of threatening sounds. Don't pay any attention to them. "Your testimonies are very sure" (v. 5). The psalmist heard God's testimonies and said, "I can trust the Word of God."

This psalm also reminds me of Peter when he walked on the water (see Matt. 14:28-31). He took his eyes off the Lord and forgot His promise. Jesus said to him, "Come." That's all Peter needed. He should have said to himself, "If Jesus says, 'Come,' I can come"— because His commandments are always His empowerments.

◆　　◆　　◆

God's throne is established, and His testimony is sure. When you see the flood approaching, lift your eyes higher to see the throne of God and open your ears to hear His Word. Put your faith to work and trust His promises of strength and power.

TRUST GOD'S TIMING

"**L**ord, how long will the wicked . . . triumph?" (v. 3). I'm sure you also have asked that question. This sentiment is expressed many times in Scripture. The great saints of God cried out, "O Lord, how long?" When David was being chased by King Saul, many times he said, "How long, O Lord, before I get my throne? You've promised it to me."

The psalmist tells us that God has His plan. He hears our prayers and sees our need. He knows exactly what is going on. The wicked think that they have everything under control. "Yet they say, 'The Lord does not see, nor does the God of Jacob understand'" (v. 7). "God can't see what we're doing; God's not going to do anything." That's the false confidence of the wicked. But the psalmist answers that with inspired logic. "He who planted the ear, shall He not hear? He who formed the eye, shall He not see? He who instructs the nations, shall not He correct, He who teaches man knowledge?" (vv. 9,10). In other words, is God dumber than we are? He sees what's going on in this world. He hears the cries of His own people and disciplines those who need discipline.

Our tendency, of course, is to take things into our own hands. Moses tried that approach, and it sent him to the wilderness for 40 years to learn how to trust God's timing and method. When you find yourself crying out, "How long, O Lord, how long," focus on God and remember that He knows as much about the situation as you do—probably more. Then wait on Him. Watch and pray. You can be sure that He will keep His promises.

♦　　♦　　♦

Learning to trust God's methods and timing is a lifelong course. When you need to wait patiently for God to act, first look to Him and lay hold of His promises in Scripture. Then rest in His care. He knows your situation, and He keeps His word. He will act at the right time.

PRAY, WAIT OR ACT?

"**W**ho will rise up for me against the evildoers? Who will stand up for me against the workers of iniquity?" (v. 16). I wonder what kind of an answer we would give to these questions.

There are times when we only *pray* about a problem. There are times when we *wait*. There are times when God says, "Not now—I'll take care of it later." But there are times when we must *act*, as when Moses had to stand up and lead the people out of Egypt, or when David had to perform the judgment of God. There are times when we who are the light of the world must stand up and shine, when we who are the salt of the earth must apply that salt to the decay in the world today.

How easy it is to be a spectator and say, "Well, I'll pray about it." Good—be sure you do. But God says, "Who's going to stand up for Me against the workers of iniquity?" The answer: those who know that God is their Help. "Unless the Lord had been my help, my soul would soon have settled in silence" (v. 17). "But the Lord has been my defense, and my God the rock of my refuge" (v. 22). When God is your Help, when you have the strength of God that comes from His Word, you can stand up against the sin in this world.

Those who are separated from sin are also called to action. "Shall the throne of iniquity, which devises evil by law, have fellowship with You?" (v. 20). We have laws today that provide defense from a lot of sin. Yet those who are separated from sin must stand up with God against iniquity—those who believe that He will give us the ultimate victory. We may lose a few battles, but thank God we're going to win the war!

✦   ✦   ✦

Christians are never to become complacent about evildoers. We deal with them by praying, waiting and acting. God wants you to be an influence for Him. Be an active witness where He has placed you. Ask for His leading in knowing when to pray, wait or take a stand.

RESPONDING TO GREATNESS

"**F**or the Lord is the great God, and a great King above all gods" (v. 3). That's a great affirmation of faith the psalmist wrote as he looked at the heathen gods of other nations.

In his book *Your God Is Too Small*, J. B. Phillips affirms the greatness of God. If you have a small God, you'll have small faith; if you have a great God, you'll have great faith—not great faith in your faith but great faith in a great God. If God truly is a great God, then how should we respond to His greatness?

First, *thank Him.* "Let us come before His presence with thanksgiving; let us shout joyfully to Him with psalms" (v. 2). Be thankful that He is a great God. Note that His greatness extends to creation. "In His hand are the deep places of the earth; the heights of the hills are His also" (v. 4). Isn't it good to know that God is a God of the depths as well as a God of the heights? When we're living on the mountaintop, He is there. When we're down in the valley, He is there. "The sea is His, for He made it; and His hands formed the dry land" (v. 5). I'm glad that my God is God of the changing places, such as the sea, and of the stable places, such as the dry land. No matter where we are, we can experience His greatness.

Second, *sing to Him.* "Oh, come, let us sing to the Lord! Let us shout joyfully to the Rock of our salvation" (v. 1). And *worship Him.* "Oh, come, let us worship and bow down; let us kneel before the Lord our Maker" (v. 6).

◆　　◆　　◆

The greatness of God is the answer to the smallness of man. When you see great sin and great disappointment or when you have a great burden to carry, remember that you are worshiping a great God. As you kneel before Him, He becomes even greater.

HARDENED HEARTS

We find a warning in today's passage. "Today, if you will hear His voice: Do not harden your hearts" (vv. 7,8). The context is the nation of Israel in the wilderness. From Egypt to Canaan, they saw God at work. He led them out of Egypt, through the wilderness and into the Promised Land. And what did they do in return? They hardened their hearts.

How do we harden our hearts? It's a process that occurs gradually as we complain about God's work and ignore His Word. The Israelites complained about the way He led them and the way He fed them. They heard God's Word and deliberately disobeyed. This is called tempting God. "When your fathers tested Me; they tried Me, though they saw My work. For forty years I was grieved with that generation" (v. 9).

When you see God at work and you complain instead of rejoice, when you hear His Word and deliberately disobey it—you're tempting Him. It's like a little child just daring mom or dad to discipline him. When you harden your heart, you miss God's best for your life. The people of Israel saw the miracles. They heard the messages. They were fed day after day. But in a period of 40 years, that whole older generation died. They did not enter into the fullness of their inheritance.

What should you do to prevent a hard heart? Repent. Listen to God's Word and respond to it tenderly. Watch God's work and respond to it thankfully. Stop complaining and disobeying. Worship the Lord and keep a tender heart before Him.

♦   ♦   ♦

When you take God and His provisions for granted, you become less thankful and less responsive to Him. Heed the warning of these verses: Keep your heart open to God's Word and obey Him.

STRENGTH AND BEAUTY

Early one spring morning I walked out the front door of my home and saw a spiderweb. It was beautiful, but it wasn't strong. Before the day was over, the web was gone.

Some things are beautiful but not strong. And other things are strong but not beautiful. A concrete slab is strong, but you're not likely to want one in your living room. Similarly, a steel girder exists to support, not to be seen. There was a beauty about the tabernacle and temple. "Honor and majesty are before Him; strength and beauty are in His sanctuary" (v. 6). The tabernacle was a tent—it had beauty but not a great deal of strength. The temple had both strength and beauty.

Our God is practical, but not so practical that He leaves out the beautiful. He gave both strength and beauty to His creation, such as trees, mountains and rivers.

God also wants us to have beauty. He wants us to have the kind of strength that is beautiful and the kind of beauty that is strong. We can "worship the Lord in the beauty of holiness" because "strength and beauty are in His sanctuary."

♦ ♦ ♦

God's works have both beauty and strength. If you are walking in fellowship with Him, your life will have a beauty that is strong and a strength that is beautiful. You'll become more and more like Jesus.

TRUE HOLINESS

"**O**h, worship the Lord in the beauty of holiness!" (v. 9). God desires holiness for His people. "Be holy, for I am holy" is repeated several times in the Old Testament. And the apostle Peter used it in one of his letters (I Pet. 1:16). It means to be separated, unique and distinct.

God the Father, God the Son and God the Holy Spirit work together to lead us into a life of holiness. The cross of Jesus indicates that God wants us to be holy. On the cross Jesus died for our sins to make us holy, to bring us to God. The Holy Spirit within us urges us to a holy life by His power. The Word of God helps us grow in holiness. Jesus said to His Father, "Sanctify them by Your truth; Your word is truth" (John 17:17).

True holiness is beautiful; false holiness is not. The Pharisees had a false holiness—an artificial, manufactured piety. Jesus had true holiness, and He attracted people. The Pharisees repelled them. The fruit of the Spirit—love, joy, peace, patience and the rest—make for a beautiful life.

True holiness is beautiful, and this beauty comes from worship. Did you know that you become like what you worship? If your god is selfish, you become selfish. If your god is ugly, you become ugly. The person who worships money becomes hard. The person who worships pleasure becomes soft. But the person who worships the true and living God becomes beautiful—more and more like Christ.

✦　　✦　　✦

God has given you the necessary resources to live a holy life. Allow His Word to teach you and the Holy Spirit to guide you. Live so that you may become more like Christ.

BALANCING
LOVE AND HATE

Afriend of mine likes to quote a beatitude that he has either invented or borrowed: "Blessed are the balanced." It's a good point. We can't easily walk unless we're balanced. When I was learning how to ride a bicycle, my parents put me on one and gave me a push, but I could not keep balanced. To roller skate, ice skate or ski, you've got to maintain balance.

This is also true of the Christian life. That's why the psalmist says, "You who love the Lord, hate evil!" (v. 10). There's a balance for you. Christians are not supposed to hate one another, but they are supposed to hate evil.

We can have one of several attitudes toward the evil in the world today. First, we can defend it. I don't see how Christians can do that, but there are those who do. There are even those who promote it. They're playing right into the hands of Satan. Or, we can close our eyes and ignore it, like the priest and the Levite in the parable of the Good Samaritan, who passed by on the other side. Or we can endure it and say, "Well, it's here, and I'll just grit my teeth and clench my fists and put up with it." But the Word of God says we should *hate it* and *oppose it*.

We hate evil because we love the Lord. If we love Him, we love the things He loves and hate the things He hates. This is also true in human relationships. When you love someone, you love the things he or she loves, and you want to share those things. When God judges evil, we want to be on His side. We don't want to be like Lot, who, though it grieved his soul, tolerated the evil in Sodom. Everything Lot lived for was burned up when Sodom went up in smoke (Gen. 19). "He preserves the souls of His saints; He delivers them out of the hand of the wicked." God is on our side. And if God is for us, who can be against us?

✦   ✦   ✦

What is your attitude toward evil in the world? If you love the Lord, you cannot remain neutral. You must hate evil and oppose it, for it is dangerous to tolerate it. Ask God for the strength to take a stand against evil and be a witness to those who practice it.

A SINGING FAITH

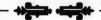

One of my seminary professors was a missionary in Africa for many years. When he first arrived on the field by riverboat, from the banks of the river he could hear screaming and wailing and the beating of drums. But 25 years later, when he went down to the river to leave the field, people lined the banks and were singing, "All hail the power of Jesus' name, let angels prostrate fall." What a difference!

The Christian faith is a singing faith. Christians ought to be singing people. We are admonished in the Word of God to sing to the Lord. "Oh, sing to the Lord a new song! For He has done marvelous things; His right hand and His holy arm have gained Him the victory" (v. 1).

Sing about God's victories. If you think you have no victory in your life, start singing about the victory of the Lord, and you'll be surprised what He'll do for you.

Sing about His salvation. "The Lord has made known His salvation; His righteousness He has revealed in the sight of the nations" (v. 2). We should proclaim the message of salvation to people today.

Sing about His mercy and faithfulness. "He has remembered His mercy and his faithfulness" (v. 3). The Lord has been merciful to us, and His faithfulness endures to all generations.

Sing about His coming. Verse 9 tells us that the hills are rejoicing before the Lord, "for He is coming to judge the earth. With righteousness He shall judge the world, and the peoples with equity." Sing about His coming, for Jesus may come back today!

♦　　♦　　♦

Are you singing the praises of God in your life? If you've lost your song, it may mean that you've lost something else—your vision of God, faith in His Word—or perhaps sin has come into your life. Follow the instructions of this psalm and "sing to the Lord a new song."

PREREQUISITES OF ANSWERED PRAYER

One of the greatest joys in the Christian life is the joy of answered prayer—to be able to say to someone, "God answered my prayer today," or to hear someone say, "Thank you for praying—let me tell you what God did." The psalmist writes about this: "Moses and Aaron were among his priests, and Samuel was among those who called upon His name. They called upon the Lord, and He answered them" (v. 6). Moses called upon the Lord many times when he had the burdens of the people on his shoulders. Aaron, as the high priest, also called upon the Lord. Samuel had some disappointments in his life. His family was not all it ought to have been, and Israel was not all it ought to have been. So he cried out to the Lord as well.

If we call upon the Lord, will He answer us? Yes, if we have met the conditions that Moses, Aaron and Samuel met. First, *they listened to God's Word*. "He spoke to them in the cloudy pillar" (v. 7). "If you abide in Me, and My words abide in you, you will ask what you desire, and it shall be done for you" (John 15:7). We want to talk to God and tell Him about all of our problems. He wants to talk to us and tell us about all of His promises. We should listen to Him first, and then He will listen to us.

Second, *they obeyed Him*. They kept His testimonies and the ordinances. Obedience is important to answered prayer. If we're abiding in Christ, we will obey His Word, and then we will be able to call upon Him.

Third, *they confessed their sin*. God forgave their sins, and He enabled them to do what He wanted them to do. As a result, they wanted to exalt the Lord. The purpose of prayer is to glorify God. "Exalt the Lord our God, and worship at His holy hill; for the Lord our God is holy" (v. 9).

How glad I am to know that my High Priest in heaven is interceding for me. I can come to Him any time for the grace that I need.

♦ ♦ ♦

Do you enjoy answered prayer? Do you listen to God's Word and obey it? Is your heart clean of unconfessed sin? Meet God's conditions for answered prayer and let Him bless you.

THE HIGHEST OCCUPATION

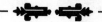

The next time you sing the doxology in a worship service, remember that you are singing Scripture, a version of Psalm 100. This psalm is a digest of instructions on how to worship the Lord.

Who should worship the Lord? "Make a joyful shout to the Lord, all you lands!" (v. 1). God wants the whole world to worship and give thanks to Him. Why are we to go into all the world and preach the Gospel? So that all the world will one day be able to make a joyful shout to the Lord.

How should we worship the Lord? First, *by serving.* "Serve the Lord with gladness; come before His presence with singing" (v. 2). We are to serve the Lord with gladness because there's joy in our hearts and because the joy of the Lord gives strength.

Second, we worship Him *by singing.* "Come before His presence with singing." I fear that too often in our services, singing becomes routine. We hold the hymnal and sing the songs that we know so well, but our minds and hearts are a million miles away. Think about and rejoice in the words you sing.

We also worship the Lord *by submitting to Him.* "Know that the Lord, He is God; it is He who has made us, and not we ourselves; we are His people and the sheep of His pasture" (v. 3). Submit to Him. Follow Him. Obey Him.

Finally, we worship the Lord *by sacrificing.* "Enter into His gates with thanksgiving, and into His courts with praise" (v. 4). You don't need to sacrifice animals on an altar, but you can give your time, money and skills.

Why should we worship the Lord? "For the Lord is good; His mercy is everlasting, and His truth endures to all generations" (v. 5).

◆   ◆   ◆

The highest occupation of the Christian life is worshiping the Lord. Never allow your worship to become routine or artificial. Worship Him with a joyful and thankful heart by serving, singing, submitting and sacrificing.

PRAISE THROUGH SERVICE

Joyful noise leads to joyful service. If we are to serve the Lord joyfully, our words must become deeds. Jesus warns against hypocritical worship (Matt. 15:8). How are we to serve the Lord genuinely?

First, *we serve willingly*. We are redeemed to do what God wants us to do. This verse was meaningful to Old Testament Jews, because they knew about servitude. God delivered them from slavery in Egypt so they might serve Him.

Second, *we serve exclusively*. We cannot serve the Lord and some-one else at the same time (Matt. 6:24; Ex. 20:2,3). But we can serve others for Jesus' sake. Our goal is to please Him alone. Our power, wisdom and the plans for our lives come from Him alone.

Third, *we serve joyfully*. Sometimes we are like the elder brother in the parable of the Prodigal Son; we may do the Father's will and work, but we are far from His heart. God doesn't want our service to be drudgery or to be done grudgingly. That tears us down. When we serve Him joyfully, we enjoy growth, development and excitement. Are you happy serving the Lord?

◆　　◆　　◆

We praise God most effectively through our service to Him. Are you en-gaged in service to the Lord in your church or community? When you offer your service to the Lord willingly and joyfully, you glorify His name. Let your words of praise lead to acts of praise!

Praise Through Submission

Psalm 100 is God's instruction sheet for praise. Praise is both an action and an attitude of the heart, and one way we praise God is to submit to Him. This passage suggests three acts of submission that bring praise to God.

First, *we submit as creatures to the Creator* (v. 3). Satan wants us to think he is God. Some people behave as though they are God. But only Jehovah is God (Isa. 46:9; Ps. 46:10; I Chron. 16:25). A man once said to his girlfriend, "I'm a self-made man." She replied, "It's nice of you to take the blame." We are not self-made. God, in His wisdom, power and patience, has made us. In man is a mingling of dust and deity, for God made us in His image.

Second, *we submit as children to the Father*. We are chosen by grace (Ex. 19:5,6). He died for us and saved us because He loves us. When we believe on the Lord Jesus Christ as Savior, we enter into a spiritual family, with God as our loving Father. As we develop in our relationship with Him, we submit to His authority.

Third, *we submit as sheep to the Shepherd*. We need a shepherd. Jesus is the Good Shepherd (John 10:11) and the Great Shepherd (Heb. 13:20), and we are the sheep of His pasture (Ps. 73:13). It's important to feed on the green pastures of the Word of God.

◆　　◆　　◆

When you submit to God the Creator, God the Father and Christ the Shepherd, you are praising God. Submitting to Him is aligning your will to His will and obeying His Word. Submit to God—He will love and guide you.

PRAISE THROUGH SACRIFICE

I n Old Testament days, God's people brought animal sacrifices to the altar. Today, instead of bringing the Lord dead sacrifices, we present living sacrifices to Him. The Bible speaks of several sacrifices that praise God.

We have the *sacrifice of praise* (Heb. 13:15). When our lips thank God for what He has done and for who He is, our praise pleases Him. We have the *sacrifice of a broken heart* (Ps. 51:17). We are to present our bodies as a *living sacrifice* to Him (Rom. 12:1,2). There is the *sacrifice of good works* (Matt. 5:16; Heb. 13:16). And there is the *sacrifice of finances* (Phil 4:18). When we share our money, time, possessions and energy with others, we bring a sacrifice to God.

Examine your life to see if you are making sacrifices for His glory. Many jobs are waiting to be done, and you might be the person for a specific job.

♦ ♦ ♦

Have you found that place of ministry God has for you? Are you using the gifts He has given you? Offer your sacrifices of praise to God, that you may bring glory to Him and minister to others.

WHY WE SHOULD PRAISE THE LORD

Praise is the highest use of man's faculties. When we contemplate the attributes of God, we can't help but thank and praise Him. This verse speaks of three of God's attributes that make Him worthy of our praise.

First, we see *His goodness*. It's part of God's nature to be kind and benevolent. He is not frowning upon us; He's smiling on us through Jesus. We see His goodness in creation (Gen. 1:31; Ps. 33:5), even though man has wrecked it (Rom. 8:19-23). God even shows His goodness to the unsaved nations of the world (Acts 14:17). His goodness ought to lead to man's gladness.

His goodness keeps us from fainting (Ps. 27:13). He gives us courage (v. 14). God wants to guide us (25:8,9) and protect us (31:19,20). We should respond to His goodness in three ways: (1) We should be repentant; (2) we should want to enjoy Him; and (3) we should draw near to Him.

Next, we see *His mercy*. (Ps. 23:6). When God is merciful, He does not give us what we deserve, which is eternal death for our sins. Mercy is forever a part of His nature (Heb. 4:16; I Pet. 1:3; Ps. 107).

Last, we see *His faithfulness*. This attribute speaks of God's reliability and stability. He is faithful to chasten us (Ps. 119:75). He is faithful to confirm us (I Cor. 1:9). He is faithful to care for us and give us victory over temptation (I Cor. 10:13). He is faithful to forgive us (I John 1:9). God is not going to change (Heb. 13:8). He is faithful in all He does. Share with your children and your grandchildren that God is good, merciful and faithful.

◆　　◆　　◆

God's goodness, mercy and faithfulness reveal much about Him. The more you contemplate His attributes, the more you can praise Him.

HEART AND HOME

Apleasant elderly couple who attended the first church I pastored came to me one day and said, "Pastor, we have moved into a new house, and we'd like you to come and dedicate it." So my wife and I went to the house, read Scripture, prayed and dedicated that house to the glory of the Lord.

What is the most important part of a house? At first you might say the foundation, the heating system or the plumbing. But the most important part of a house is the home. And the most important part of that home is the hearts of the people who live there.

That's what David said when He was dedicating his house to the Lord. "I will behave wisely in a perfect way. Oh, when will You come to me? I will walk within my house with a perfect heart" (v. 2). If you want to wreck your house, start wrecking your home. And if you want to wreck your home, start wrecking your heart. But if you want your house and your home to be all that God wants them to be, then make your heart perfect.

What is a perfect heart? It's one that has integrity, wholeness and oneness—a heart that is not divided. Nobody can serve two masters. No one can plow and look back. You need to have a heart that is integrated and united. "Unite my heart to fear Your name," David said (Ps. 86:11). He walked around his new house and said, "I want my heart to be perfect, to be wholly fixed upon the Lord. I want Him to reign supremely in my home, because He reigns supremely in my heart."

Can you say the same?

✦　　✦　　✦

Your heart affects your home. Both need to be dedicated to the Lord. Are you fixed upon the Lord? Does He reign in your home? Determine to walk with integrity always and to make yours a united heart that serves God.

DAYS OF
TROUBLE

O ne day I phoned a friend of mine who is in the ministry and asked, "How's it going?" His quiet reply was, "Well, I'm having one of those days." The next time you're having one of those days when everything seems to be going wrong—your plans are falling apart, you don't feel well, there are problems and burdens, and it seems as if all of the forces of the enemy are against you—read this psalm. "Hear my prayer, O Lord, and let my cry come to You. Do not hide Your face from me in the day of my trouble" (vv. 1,2). What kind of a day was the psalmist having? A day of trouble. In fact, he compares himself to a lonely bird. "I am like a pelican of the wilderness; I am like an owl of the desert. . . . I am like a sparrow alone upon the housetop" (vv. 6,7). That's the way he feels—like a bird alone on a housetop. He wants to go into the house and enjoy some fellowship, but he's alone.

The psalmist's enemies were reproaching him (v. 8). But in a day of trouble and reproach, he says, "I'm going to change this by the grace of God." And it becomes a *day of prayer.* He tells God how he feels and what he sees. He cries out, "God, You are the only one who can change things." God can change things for you also. He may not change the circumstances on the outside, but He does change your feelings on the inside. Then the day of trouble becomes a day of triumph.

✦ ✦ ✦

Everyone has days of trouble. When circumstances entrap you and trouble closes around you, pray to the Lord. He knows how to turn your trouble into triumph. Although He may not answer your prayers the way you expect, He will do what is best for you and for His glory.

MORE SURE
THAN THE WORLD

Have you heard the phrase, "It's as sure as the world"? In fact, nothing is more *unsure* than the world. "Of old You laid the foundation of the earth, and the heavens are the work of Your hands. They will perish, but You will endure" (vv. 25,26). The "sure" world will perish. Jesus said, "Heaven and earth will pass away, but My words will by no means pass away" (Matt. 24:35). What is the surest thing in your life? On what are you building your life? You'd better be building it on the Lord; He's the only One who is sure.

Jesus always is the same. "But You are the same, and Your years will have no end" (v. 27). Jesus Christ is the same yesterday, today and forever. God has made this universe, and everything around us looks so certain. We are so sure of the way things work. We can send people from the earth to the moon. God's universe is precisely crafted, but He says that all of this will perish.

What should you do, knowing that you live in a temporary world? Trust God, who is sure. Pray to Him. "He shall regard the prayer of the destitute, and shall not despise their prayer" (v. 17). Trust His Word and praise Him. Prayer and praise go together. "This will be written for the generation to come, that a people yet to be created may praise the Lord" (v. 18).

◆   ◆   ◆

Many people foolishly build their entire lives on the cracked foundations of this world and will one day perish with it. But God is changeless and eternal. He wants you to build your life on Him. When you pray, praise Him for His creation and for His work in your life.

DON'T STOP PRAISING

I wonder how long we could talk to the Lord without asking for something. "Bless the Lord, O my soul; and all that is within me, bless His holy name! Bless the Lord, O my soul, and forget not all His benefits" (vv. 1,2). Psalm 103 has no requests. It is nothing but praise; David is blessing the Lord.

What are some of these benefits David sings about? They are ones we may have forgotten or that we may be taking for granted. First, *the Lord saves.* "Who forgives all your iniquities, who heals all your diseases" (v. 3). The last part of that statement is an illustration of the first part. He forgives all our iniquities in the same way He heals the human body. Often in the Bible, sin is compared to sickness, and salvation is compared to health. God brings saving health to our souls.

Second, *He keeps.* "Who redeems your life from destruction, who crowns you with lovingkindness and tender mercies" (v. 4). He keeps us and protects us from the destruction around us. He puts a crown on our heads and makes us kings.

Third, *He satisfies.* "Who satisfies your mouth with good things" (v. 5). In fact, David says God so satisfies us that our youth is renewed like the eagle's. The eagle molts, loses its old feathers, gets a new coat and soars again.

◆　　◆　　◆

Do you pray to God for the sole purpose of praising Him? You have much for which to praise Him, for His love and care never cease. He saves, keeps and satisfies you. Never take God for granted; always take time to praise Him.

GREAT THINGS HE HAS *NOT* DONE

We usually praise the Lord for something He has done for us. Today, let's thank the Lord for something He has *not* done. "He has not dealt with us according to our sins, nor punished us according to our iniquities" (v. 10).

Everyone knows the plague of his heart—not only the occasional sins but those that try to get us into bondage. What's more, God knows all about it, too. In fact, He knows our sins better than we do. God sees the origin and the outcome of our sins. One reason He hates sin so much is that He is holy, and He sees where sin leads. James tells us that lust, when it conceives, produces sin. And then sin, when it's full-grown, produces death (1:15). Sin is pictured as an evil pregnancy.

But the psalmist says that God "has not dealt with us according to our sins." On what basis does He deal with us? On the basis of the cross, the grace of God. Jesus Christ died for our sins, and God forgives them through the blood of His Son. We can come to Him and ask Him to forgive any sin.

But the knowledge that God does not deal with you the way you deserve to be dealt with should not tempt you to tempt Him. Do not be fast and loose with sin. Hate sin, and rejoice today that you're walking with the Father on the basis of the cross of Jesus Christ.

✦   ✦   ✦

Rejoice today that God does not deal with you according to your sin but according to the cross of Jesus Christ. Your forgiveness comes at a great cost. The next time you're tempted to sin, consider its wages and cost. You are greatly indebted to Christ, so live to please Him.

DUST AND DESTINY

Our God remembers what we often forget. Sometimes we forget the things He wants us to remember, and that gets us into trouble. Have you remembered lately what you are made of? "As a father pities his children, so the Lord pities those who fear Him. For He knows our frame; He remembers that we are dust" (vv. 13,14). God took the dust of the ground and made Adam. Then He breathed into Adam the breath of life, and he became a living soul. Physically, we are made from the dust. But we have the mark of deity upon us, for we are made in the image of God.

When we think of dust, we think of something common and ordinary. You can walk out the back door and find dust. Perhaps you don't even have to go that far. You might just want to look on top of the radio or the dining room table. Dust speaks of *weakness* and *frailty*. But it also speaks of tremendous *potential*. God made us from dust that we might be weak in ourselves but strong in Him. God took the dust and made clay, and then He took the clay and made a man. Where there is dust, there is potential. He is the Potter; we are the clay.

You have to say, "Lord, You made me out of dust but full of potential. And you made me this way that I might be weak in myself but strong in You. 'Mold me and make me after Your will, while I am waiting, yielded and still.'" Paul said, "I can do all things through Christ, who strengthens me" (Phil. 4:13). He also said, "We have this treasure in earthen vessels, that the excellence of the power may be of God and not of us" (II Cor. 4:7).

♦   ♦   ♦

Where there is dust, there is potential. Where there is dust, there is opportunity for growth. Continue to yield to Him and His creative process in your life. Ask Him to mold you after His will.

AT HIS
COMMAND

No matter how difficult your situation may be today, no matter how discouraging the news, you can still lean on this: "The Lord has established His throne in heaven, and His kingdom rules over all" (v. 19).

God is enthroned in heaven and in control of everything that happens. Sometimes it may not look like it. If you're walking by sight, you may wonder if there is a God at all. Or if there is a God, does He care? Or if He cares, can He do anything? The psalmist tells us, "Don't walk by sight; walk by faith."

God has an army. "Bless the Lord, you His angels, who excel in strength, who do His word, heeding the voice of His word" (v. 20). The angels act at His command. If we read and study the Word of God and obey it, everything in the universe will work with us. If we disobey the Word of God, everything will work against us—just as it did against Jonah, who was running in the wrong direction, going on the wrong ship, with the wrong motive, for the wrong purpose. God finally brought him to a place of obedience.

Don't be like Jonah. Have faith that God is in control and working on you in every situation.

♦ ♦ ♦

No matter how difficult your day or how discouraging the news might be, lean on the wonderful assurance that God is on His throne. He is ruling, and His servants are at work accomplishing His Word. Obey God's Word today and keep walking by faith.

Engraved Blessings

Someone has said that memory is a sepulcher of broken bones. Someone else has said that memory is a nursery in which children who have grown old play with their broken toys. Memory is the library and the treasury of the mind. Psychiatrist Rollo Mays says, "Memory is not just the imprint of the past upon us; it is the keeper of what is meaningful for our deepest hopes and fears."

Memory is selective. Often we forget what God has done for us. Charles Spurgeon said, "We write our blessings in the sand, and we engrave our complaints in the marble." Memory becomes impressed with burdens. The word *remember* is used 14 times in Deuteronomy, and 9 of those warn of forgetting.

True praise ought to come from the heart, not the memory (Matt. 15:8). Worship is the believer's adoring response to all that God says and does.

Engrave God's blessings in your heart, and you'll never grow weary of praising Him.

◆　　◆　　◆

Never forget God's blessings. Praise Him for all He has done. Don't load your mind with past burdens but enrich it with a memory of His blessings.

ILLUSTRATED BLESSINGS

This psalm has no petitions, only praise. Verses 3 through 5 are Hebrew poetry with parallel construction. Each verse has two statements. The idea that is presented in the first statement is repeated, illustrated or amplified in the second statement of the verse. The second statements in verses 3 through 5 are illustrations of three blessings: forgiveness, redemption and satisfaction.

The first blessing is *forgiveness* (v. 3). The psalmist illustrates forgiveness with the concept of spiritual healing. God doesn't have to heal us, but He does, and every blessing He gives is an atonement. What healing is to the body, salvation (forgiveness) is to the soul. Jesus is our Great Physician (Eph. 1:7).

The second blessing is *redemption* (v. 4). *Redeem* refers to a "kinsman redeemer." The Book of Ruth illustrates redemption, with Boaz as a kinsman redeemer. God protects and provides, and He keeps us safe and saved. He has lifted us from slavery to sovereignty.

The third blessing is *satisfaction* (v. 5). One translation reads, "[He] satisfies thy old age with good things." This verse applies to every stage in life. God restores and renews us. He keeps us young spiritually, for we find satisfaction in His Word.

✦   ✦   ✦

Do you have God's blessings of forgiveness and redemption? If so, do you enjoy the satisfaction that comes from knowing Him and obeying His Word? God restores, renews and blesses you that you might bless others.

UNIVERSAL PRAISE

"**B**less the Lord, O my soul" (v. 1). The psalmist opens by addressing God on a personal level. He is praising God for what He does and for who He is. As we read this psalm, we discover why God is so wonderful.

He is the merciful Savior (vv. 8-12). God in His grace gives us what we don't deserve and in His mercy doesn't give us what we do deserve. But He does have a holy temper, and we must not provoke Him by deliberately sinning.

He is the tender Father (vv. 13-18). Why does God show mercy? Because it is His nature to exercise compassion and love. He is tender because He knows we are made of dust. We are frail. We're temporary, like a flower that soon fades and dies. Our response to God's tenderness should be praise and obedience.

He deserves universal praise (vv. 19-22). We see in the Book of Revelation that praise for God increases and spreads over all the universe. We will be part of that someday.

Why do we praise Him? Because His throne is secure. We praise Him because we can keep His commandments, serve Him and please Him. We praise Him because His works are so wonderful, and He's allowed us to be part of them.

◆　◆　◆

The psalm ends the way it begins—on a personal level. "Bless the Lord, O my soul." Follow the psalmist's lead and praise God for His wonderful attributes and deeds.

GOD'S
SECRET AGENTS

Have you thought lately about angels? We usually don't think about them because we don't see or hear them. But God's Word tells us they are His special messengers. "Who makes His angels spirits, His ministers a flame of fire" (v. 4). We have a fire of God at work—His angels, accomplishing His will.

The angels have always served God. They sang at creation. They visited Abraham. They came to Hezekiah when Jerusalem was under attack, and one angel destroyed 185,000 soldiers. They announced the coming of the Messiah. They sang at Jesus' birth. They were with Him in the wilderness when He was tempted. They were with Him when He was in the Garden of Gethsemane. And now that Jesus has ascended to heaven, the angels worship and glorify Him there.

Angels also serve us. Hebrews 1:14 says, "Are they not all ministering spirits sent forth to minister for those who will inherit salvation?" Angels are God's invisible army, His servants, working for us.

I have a feeling that when we get to heaven we'll find out that there were many times when angels protected us from harm and strengthened us. Let's rejoice today that we are not alone. Greater are those who are with us than those who are against us.

♦ ♦ ♦

God sends angels to minister to you. It should encourage you to know that they are working on your behalf. Today, thank Him for His angels and for their ministry.

QUENCHING THE THIRST

People who live in the city sometimes forget that God is the God of creation and nature. In the United States alone, more than 2700 acres of pavement are laid each day. Before long, God's creation might be completely covered by concrete and asphalt. We need to pause and get reacquainted with the God of creation. "You who laid the foundations of the earth, so that it should not be moved forever, You covered it with the deep as with a garment; the waters stood above the mountains. At Your rebuke they fled; at the voice of Your thunder they hastened away. . . . You have set a boundary that they may not pass over, that they may not return to cover the earth" (vv. 5-7,9). The psalmist refers to the Flood in Noah's day. It was God's judgment. But the next judgment He sends will be by fire, not water.

Water also is a blessing. "He sends the springs into the valleys; they flow among the hills" (v. 10). This is a beautiful picture of the rivers and springs and hills, all of which enable animals to have food and drink. "They give drink to every beast of the field; the wild donkeys quench their thirst" (v. 11). The birds of the heavens nest in the trees by these rivers. I like the phrase in verse 12—"they sing among the branches." God waters the earth. The crops grow, and man and beast are able to live. And as an extra blessing, He puts the birds in the branches to sing. All of creation is satisfied. "The earth is satisfied with the fruit of Your works" (v. 13).

The God of creation also is the God of salvation, and He can satisfy your thirsty soul today.

◆　　◆　　◆

As you observe nature, you are reminded of God's physical provision. He also provides for the spiritual needs of His people. Do you have a need today? Ask God to flood your soul with His blessing!

A BALANCED DIET

The psalmists were captivated by the God of creation. Of course, the world they lived in was a little cleaner, a little purer, maybe a little more beautiful, because man had not yet exploited it. They recognized their dependence on Him for their sustenance: "He causes the grass to grow for the cattle, and vegeta-tion for the service of man, that he may bring forth food from the earth, and wine that makes glad the heart of man, oil to make his face shine, and bread which strengthens man's heart" (vv. 14,15).

Food, wine, oil, bread—these were staples for Jewish people in that day. Do not think that because the psalmist mentions wine he's talk-ing about drunkenness. The Bible certainly warns against being drunk. Rather, he says that God supplies our every physical need and even above and beyond those needs. "God . . . gives us richly all things to enjoy" (I Tim. 6:17).

In the Bible wine is a picture of the Holy Spirit. At Pentecost, when the people of God were rejoicing and worshiping and praising the Lord, the crowd said, "They are full of new wine" (Acts 2:13). Do you have the joy of the Spirit today? "Be not drunk with wine," Paul said, "but be filled with the Spirit" (Eph. 5:18).

Oil also is a picture of the Holy Spirit, who makes the face to shine. Moses had a shining face because he fellowshipped with God. Stephen had a shining face because he gave his life for God. Jesus had a shin-ing face on the Mount of Transfiguration.

Bread is a picture of the Word of God. It strengthens the heart. "Man shall not live by bread alone, but by every word of God" (Luke 4:4).

God wants to give us gladness; He wants to give us radiance; and He wants to give us strength. The Holy Spirit uses the Word of God to make the child of God more like Jesus.

♦   ♦   ♦

Do you maintain a balanced spiritual diet with the staples God provides? Food, wine, oil and bread are symbols of how He nurtures and nourishes you. Feed on His Word and allow the Spirit to control your life.

CONSIDERING
CREATION

After surveying God's work in creation, the psalmist wrote: "O Lord, how manifold are Your works! In wisdom You have made them all; the earth is full of Your possessions" (v. 24). This verse shows us important traits of God.

First, *creation reveals God's wisdom.* We ought to take time to admire His wisdom in creation. I've read that if the proportion of gases in the air were changed ever so slightly, all of us would die. The way God tilted the earth, the way He arranged the seasons, the way He put creation together is a revelation of His great wisdom. It's logical that the God who is wise enough to run creation is wise enough to run our lives. If He can keep the stars and the planets and the seasons and all these things going as they should, can He not put our lives together and make them what they ought to be?

Second, *creation contains God's wealth.* "The earth is full of Your possessions" (v. 24). Without His wealth, we could not exist. Not only are gold and silver and other precious stones measures of His wealth, but so are ore and rock, fruit and grain.

Third, *creation makes possible man's work.* "Man goes out to his work and to his labor until the evening" (v. 23). Even Adam had work to do in the Garden of Eden. Work is a blessing, not a burden, if we're doing it for the Lord.

Fourth, *creation motivates us to worship the Lord.* "O Lord, how manifold are Your works!" We don't worship creation—that's idolatry. We worship the God of creation. We recognize that He gives every good and perfect gift (James 1:17). O let us adore Him, our great Creator, our great Savior.

◆　　◆　　◆

Creation shows God's wisdom, so rejoice! Creation contains His wealth, so use it for His glory. Creation provides work for man, so view work as a blessing. But greatest of all, creation should move you to worship the Lord.

SPRING RENEWAL

Scientists tell us that our world is governed by what they call "natural law." Most of them forget that behind the law is the Lawgiver. Behind creation is a Creator, who cares for His creation and His people. Who unifies the universe? The God who made it. All of creation waits upon Him and trusts Him to supply what is needed. As the psalmist wrote, "These all wait for You, that You may give them their food in due season. What You give them they gather in; You open Your hand, they are filled with good" (vv. 27,28).

God gives and we gather. He provides and we take. He is dependable; He takes care of His own. "I have been young, and now am old," David said. "Yet I have not seen the righteous forsaken, nor his descendants begging bread" (Ps. 37:25). God is also generous. He does not give carelessly or selfishly. He opens His hand, and all of creation is filled with good.

God controls life and death and the changing seasons. "You hide Your face, they are troubled; You take away their breath, they die and return to their dust. You send forth Your Spirit, they are created; and You renew the face of the earth" (vv. 29,30). Spring is so beautiful, summer so delightful and autumn so fruitful. Then winter comes, and it seems so dismal. But the same God of spring and summer and autumn is the God of winter. He brings the refreshing, renewing springtime again.

✦ ✦ ✦

God can renew your life today. He can bring you seasons of fruitfulness and seasons of sunshine. Don't worry about the seasons of life. The God who runs this universe can manage the changing seasons of your life. If you are in a winter season, wait; when He is ready, God will send you a springtime.

A NEW WORLD

When Jesus Christ is your Savior and God is your Father, when the Holy Spirit is within you and the Word of God is teaching you, all of creation takes on new beauty and new blessing. The sky is a deeper blue, and the earth is a richer green. You don't see just creation; you see the Creator. And you don't simply see a Creator; you see the Heavenly Father, who cares for you.

"I will sing to the Lord as long as I live; I will sing praise to my God while I have my being. May my meditation be sweet to Him; I will be glad in the Lord" (vv. 33,34). The psalmist wrote these words after considering all of God's creation. He looked at the waters, the mountains springs and the rushing rivers. He heard the birds singing in the branches. He saw the cattle eating grass. He saw man baking bread and making oil. He watched the sun rise and set. "See all this?" he said. "I'm going to rejoice in this Creator, who is my God."

All creation is travailing in pain because of sin (Rom. 8:22). But our Creator is still in charge, and His creation, in spite of sin, still has great beauty and great wealth. Did you know that God rejoices in His creation? "The glory of the Lord shall endure forever; the Lord shall rejoice in His works" (v. 31). He rejoices to hear the birds sing. He rejoices to see the rivers flow.

Let's rejoice in His works also. And let's rejoice that God is glorified as we obey Him today.

◆　　◆　　◆

God is glorified by His works, for they reflect His greatness. When you look at creation, do you see His greatness? Rejoice with Him as He rejoices in His creative works. "Rejoice in the Lord always. Again I will say, rejoice!" (Phil. 4:4).

SPIRITUAL HEALTH

Nutritionists remind us that we must have the minimum daily requirements of vitamins and minerals if we are to be physically healthy. Similarly, David gives God's minimum daily requirements we need if we are to be spiritually healthy.

The first requirement is *praise*. "Oh, give thanks to the Lord! . . . Sing to Him, sing psalms to Him" (vv. 1,2). Praise means giving thanks for all that God is, all that He does and all that He shares with us. Praise is rejoicing in the presence of the Lord because of who He is and because we are His children.

Prayer also is essential. "Call upon His name" (v. 1). We call upon the Lord when we need strength and grace and help in a time of need. And He always hears us.

Witnessing is another element. "Make known His deeds among the peoples. . . . Talk of all His wondrous works. Glory in His holy name" (vv. 1-3). If we only praise and pray but don't present the Lord to other people, our lives will become narrow, shallow and selfish. We need to tell others that He is the only Savior.

The final requirement is *seeking His face*. "Seek the Lord and His strength; seek His face evermore!" (v. 4). In other words, live in the light of God's countenance. Live with the smile of God upon your life and seek to please Him alone.

◆　　◆　　◆

Just as your physical health requires care, so does your spiritual health. Are you taking proper care of your soul? God's minimum daily requirements help you maintain a healthy spiritual life. Make sure you meet your daily minimum. It will please Him and bring glory to Him.

SPIRITUAL MEMORY

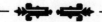

Your spiritual memory is vital to your spiritual health. Do you remember what God wants you to remember? Are you grateful for what He remembers? "Remember His marvelous works which He has done, His wonders, and the judgments of His mouth. . . . He has remembered His covenant forever, the word which He commanded, for a thousand generations" (vv. 5,8).

We should remember God's words, His wonders and His works, but we often forget. How easy it was for the Israelites to forget what God had done for them. Each year they celebrated the Passover, and one reason for that celebration was to remind them that God had delivered them out of slavery in Egypt. Some things we ought to forget, such as "those things which are behind" (Phil. 3:13). But the psalmist tells us to "remember His marvelous works" (v. 5). Are you remembering God's blessings? The next time you are tempted to criticize or get angry with God, just remember His marvelous works.

God also remembers: "He has remembered His covenant forever" (v. 8). He deals with us on the basis of His covenant promises, not on the basis of the Law, and He has sealed that covenant with the blood of His Son.

Finally, don't forget that His promises never fail. Not one word of all of God's promises has failed. Even when we forget, He remembers. Even when we neglect God's Word, He remembers it. God keeps His promises. He is faithful and will never lie.

✦   ✦   ✦

Claim a promise from God's Word that especially encourages you today. As you remember that promise, remember also that God is ever faithful to keep His promises.

PREPARED TO BE AN ANSWER

How wonderful it is to receive an answer to prayer. But there is something even more wonderful—to be an answer to prayer. Have you been an answer to prayer lately? Joseph was. In verse 17 we read, "He sent a man before them—Joseph—who was sold as a slave." At the time, Joseph could not see what God was doing. But God was preparing him to be an answer to prayer. He was going to use Joseph to protect the people of Israel. If Joseph had not done this, the nation might have perished. If the nation had perished, we wouldn't have a Bible, and we wouldn't have a Savior.

God plans His work. We never have to worry about what is going on, because God knows. He is never caught off guard, and He is never surprised. God never says, "How did that happen?" He chose Abraham and Isaac and Jacob and Jacob's sons to accomplish some great purposes in this world—to bear witness of the true and living God, to give us the Bible and the Savior.

God also works His plan. He uses people to accomplish His purposes. We don't always know what God is doing. He didn't send an angel down to prison to explain to Joseph all of His plans. Joseph worked and walked by faith. He went through trials and dishonor, but he ultimately triumphed. From trial to triumph, from bondage to blessing, Joseph was an answer to prayer.

You may be wondering today, *Why am I going through this experience? Why doesn't God make life easier for me?* Remember Joseph. God chose him, prepared him and used him as an answer to prayer.

◆　　◆　　◆

God doesn't waste your trials. He designs them for your good and His glory. Perhaps you are going through difficulties and trials today. Let God prepare you for what He has prepared for you. He might be planning to use you as an answer to prayer.

SALT AND LIGHT IN "EGYPT"

Suppose you were an Egyptian during the time of Moses and Aaron. You lived through the plagues that came on your land because of the stubbornness of Pharaoh. What would be your response when you saw the Jews leave Egypt? The psalmist wrote, "Egypt was glad when they departed, for the fear of them had fallen upon them" (v. 38). I have no problem believing that at all. Furthermore, I suspect that when God's people depart from this world, when our Lord comes again, the world will be glad.

Egypt is a picture of the world. To the people of God (Israel), it was a place of slavery and monotonous toil. It also is flat and barren in many areas. But Canaan is a land of hills and valleys, a land of rain and fruitfulness, milk and honey. When you were saved, God removed you from Egypt, spiritually speaking. He put you into Canaan and said, "Enjoy all of these blessings."

Why was Egypt glad when Israel left? One thing is sure—the Egyptians were afraid. Israel was worshiping the true God, and their true God was showing His power through the plagues. Israel was an irritant to Egypt—like salt in a wound, like light that exposes evil. God used Israel to witness to Egypt, but it did not receive that witness.

Christians are salt and light. Sometimes we irritate people. Sometimes by our conduct we expose what is wrong. One of these days we are going to be gone. It could be today. Jesus Christ might return today and take His people home to glory. No more salt. No more light. But what then? Judgment. Let's remember that we have a job to do while we are waiting for our Lord to come.

◆　　◆　　◆

One of the Church's responsibilities is to be light and salt in the world. Sometimes you affect others without being aware of it. Other times you have obvious opportunities to impact others for Christ. Can you think of opportunities to be salt and light in your daily routine? Ask God to use you to make a difference in someone's life today.

WHO CAN PRAISE THE LORD?

"**W**ho can utter the mighty acts of the Lord? Or can declare all His praise?" (v. 2).

Who can truly praise the Lord? *Those who know God through faith in Jesus Christ.* "His mercy endures forever" (v. 1). Only when we've experienced the mercy and the grace of God can we utter His mighty acts. We've been saved by His grace. This was God's greatest act—greater than bringing Israel out of Egypt and even greater than the creation of the universe.

Who else can praise the Lord? *Those who obey Him.* "Blessed are those who keep justice, and he who does righteousness at all times!" (v. 3). If we are walking with the Lord and obeying Him, then we can praise Him and speak of His wondrous acts.

Also, *those who call upon the Lord* can praise Him. "Remember me, O Lord, with the favor You have toward Your people. Oh, visit me with Your salvation" (v. 4). People who pray are people who praise. People who pray for God's will in their lives are those who rejoice in His work.

Finally, *those who trust His promises* can praise the Lord. "That I may see the benefit of Your chosen ones, that I may rejoice in the gladness of Your nation, that I may glory with Your inheritance" (v. 5). God promised His people an inheritance in Canaan, and He gave it to them. We now have our inheritance in Jesus Christ. We are rich! We are richer than kings, and we can draw upon that inheritance. We are sharing in His goodness and His gladness, and one day we will share in His glory. Let's praise Him today.

✦   ✦   ✦

Those who obey, trust and call upon the Lord know of the acts of God. They have claimed their inheritance in Jesus Christ. Are you among those who can praise the Lord? Have you claimed your inheritance?

THANKS FOR NOTHING

Sometimes an unanswered prayer is the best thing for us. The psalmist says, "And He gave them their request, but sent leanness into their soul" (v. 15). The Israelites had prayed selfishly. God was feeding them with manna from heaven, angel's food, but they wanted meat. All they had to do every morning was step out of their tents, stoop down and pick up the precious, clean, sweet, life-giving manna. But after a while their old appetites came back. They said, "Oh, if somebody would give us some meat to eat." So God sent them meat, but while they were eating it, many of them died (Num. 11:31-33).

We can learn from this experience. First, *selfish prayers are dangerous.* How dangerous it is to say, "Oh, God, I simply have to have this." Such prayers are never beneficial. "You ask and do not receive, because you ask amiss, that you may spend it on your pleasures" (James 4:3).

Second, *prayer must change our character.* The Israelites got their request, but it didn't help their character. In fact, they were in worse shape spiritually after they got what they wanted. The prodigal son said, "Father, give me." He got what he asked for, and it almost ruined him. Then he came home and said, "Father, make me"—and his character changed. He began to be a real son (Luke 15:19). Selfish praying erodes our character, but praying in the will of God builds our character.

Third, *we must always pray for God's will.* The purpose of prayer, it has well been said, is not to get man's will done in heaven but to get God's will done on earth. Never be afraid to say, "Thy will be done."

◆　◆　◆

God knows best how to answer your prayers—even whether or not to answer them! The psalmist has given three valuable guidelines for effective prayer. Do you apply these to your prayers? Let God use your prayer time to align you to His will and His point of view. Let Him prepare you for His answer.

STAND IN THE GAP

We often think of Moses as a great leader and a great legislator, and indeed he was one of the greatest. But have you ever thought of Moses as a great intercessor, a man of prayer? I was amazed to discover how many instances of prayer are recorded in the life of Moses. For instance, when the Israelites turned against God, made a golden calf and began to worship like the heathen, God was prepared to judge them. But Moses went up on the mountain and interceded, or "stood in the gap." "Therefore He said that He would destroy them, had not Moses His chosen one stood before Him in the breach, to turn away His wrath, lest He destroy them" (v. 23).

The people of Israel had been delivered from Egypt and were standing at Mount Sinai, where God was giving Moses the Law. But they built an idol. How soon we forget what God has done for us; how soon we forget what He has said to us. We turn away and start living on substitutes.

Moses could have profited personally from their sin. God said, "Moses, I'll start with you and make a whole new nation, and no longer will the Jewish nation be the people of Abraham. It will be the people of Moses." But Moses replied, "No, Lord, you love these people. They are your people. Don't judge them." God did judge their sin, but He did not destroy the nation. Of course, the people did not appre-ciate what Moses had done for them, and they began to criticize him as well.

I thank God that today in heaven we have an Intercessor, the Lord Jesus Christ, who ever lives to make intercession for us at the Father's throne (Heb. 7:25). He and the Father love us and together are guiding and building our lives.

♦   ♦   ♦

Intercession is one of the believer's most important ministries. Are you an intercessor? Others need your prayer support. Follow the example of Moses and stand in the gap.

A LEADER
SINS

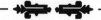

Moses wanted one thing that God would not give him: the privilege of entering the Promised Land. You'll remember that Moses had sinned against the Lord and therefore was not permitted to go into Canaan (Num. 20). He brought the nation right up to the border and then had to go up on the mountain and die.

The Israelites were partly to blame for Moses' sin. "They angered Him also at the waters of strife, so that it went ill with Moses on account of them; because they rebelled against His Spirit, so that he spoke rashly with his lips" (vv. 32,33). Moses and Aaron asked God for water for the thirsty people, and He said, "Speak to the rock, and the water will come out." But Moses lost his temper—the people provoked him—and he struck the rock. God gave them the water, but He said to Moses, "You have not sanctified me before the people in what you said or in what you did."

Leaders sin, and sometimes God's people encourage them to sin. If only the Israelites had gone to Moses and said, "Moses, we are praying for you," "Moses, we love you," or, "Thank you, Moses, for interceding for us. Thank you for all that you've done for us." But instead they complained and criticized. My heart goes out to pastors and Christian workers who are surrounded by people who cannot say thank you but constantly criticize and complain.

Many people don't realize the costs of being a spiritual leader. The higher we are in leadership, the greater our discipline. If Moses had been an ordinary citizen of Israel, God might not have stopped him from going into the Promised Land. But Moses was a leader. When leaders sin, they pay dearly for it. Let's not cause anyone else to sin today. Be an encouragement to the people of God.

♦ ♦ ♦

Are you a leader in your church or group? You have an awesome responsibility to God and to those under your direction. The sin of a leader can cause widespread damage. Take special measures to avoid compromising situations and don't let others cause you to take your eyes off the Lord. Also, always pray for, encourage and support your leaders.

THE COST
OF MINGLING

It has been well said that the one thing we learn from history is that we don't learn from history. Anyone who has raised children or is trying to help raise grandchildren knows this. Somehow the new generation doesn't believe that the older generation knows anything.

Psalm 106 certainly bears this out. It is a record of how the people of Israel were blessed and then sinned. God helped them repeatedly, and they repeatedly sinned. We see one cause of their sin in verse 35: "But they mingled with the Gentiles." There's step one—they started mingling and breaking down the walls of separation. God had warned Israel not to mingle among the nations. They were not to get involved with them, but as verse 35 says, they "learned their works." First we mingle with the world, and then we start learning the world's way of doing things. And before long, Israel "served their idols, which became a snare to them" (v. 36). They mingled, they learned, and they served.

The tragedy is that the families suffered the most. "They even sacrificed their sons and their daughters to demons" (v. 37). Thus, they lost the next generation.

Many Christians today have broken down the walls of separation. They are mingling with and serving the world and are figuratively sacrificing their own children to demons. "Thus they were defiled by their own works, and played the harlot" (v. 39). Israel was married to Jehovah God, but she was unfaithful to her marriage vows.

Don't be defiled by the world. Keep your walk with the Lord holy.

◆　　◆　　◆

Sin contaminates. That's why you need "walls of separation." Don't mingle with the world, for one step of compromise will lead to another. Keep your heart clean of sin and do not entertain temptations. Let nothing come between you and your relationship with God.

FROM WANDERER TO PILGRIM

One phrase is repeated four times in Psalm 107: "Oh, that men would give thanks to the Lord for His goodness, and for His wonderful works to the children of men!" (v. 8). The psalmist gives us five vivid illustrations of what God has done for us and why we should praise His name. He talks about wanderers, prisoners, hospital patients, mariners and people seeking to build the city and sow the seed.

About wanderers the psalmist writes, "They wandered in the wilderness in a desolate way. They found no city to dwell in. Hungry and thirsty, their soul fainted in them. Then they cried out to the Lord in their trouble, and he delivered them out of their distresses. And He led them forth by the right way, that they might go to a city for habitation" (vv. 4-7). God rescued them. Then there's that refrain. "Oh, that men would give thanks to the Lord for His goodness, and for His wonderful works to the children of men!" God has done this for you, so thank Him.

I was a wanderer before the Lord saved me—lonely, solitary, hungry, thirsty, aimless and wondering where to go next. Then someone told me about Jesus Christ—that He died on the cross for my sins, was buried, rose again on the third day and today is a living Savior for all who will call upon Him. So I cried unto the Lord in my trouble, and He delivered me out of my distresses. Now I'm delivered and guided and part of His family, no longer lonely, no longer hungry and thirsty, for Christ is the Bread of Life; He is the Living Water. I am a pilgrim on my way to a heavenly home.

♦ ♦ ♦

Consider God's goodness to you and the guidance He gives. He deserves your praise. He saved you and delivered you from the penalty of your sins. Give thanks to God for changing you from a wanderer to a pilgrim.

CONSEQUENCES OF REBELLION

It is dangerous to rebel against the will and the Word of God and to turn away from His path. Psalm 107 describes the fate of people who did. "Those who sat in darkness and in the shadow of death, bound in affliction and irons . . . therefore He brought down their heart with labor; they fell down, and there was none to help" (vv. 10,12). Verse 11 tells us why this happened: "Because they rebelled against the words of God, and despised the counsel of the Most High."

This is the terrible and painful plight of all who rebel against God's will and Word—darkness, death and despair. Instead of being on that wonderful road that leads to glory, they are down in the dungeon in darkness and in bondage, under the shadow of death. People say, "I want to do my own thing. I want to do it my way." They shouldn't. The greatest judgment God might bring to our lives is to let us have our own way. Paul wrote that God gave mankind over to uncleanness, vile passions and a debased mind (Rom. 1:18-32). God says to those who rebel against Him, "Do you want to go in that direction? All right, I won't stop you, but neither will I change the consequences."

The people described in Psalm 107 who rebelled against God's Word ended up in darkness and death, in the dungeon of defeat and despair. But they cried out to God, and He delivered them. It's never too late for God's mercy. You can cry out to Him just as these people did. "Then they cried out to the Lord in their trouble, and He saved them out of their distresses. He brought them out of darkness and the shadow of death, and broke their chains in pieces" (vv. 13,14). They received light and life and liberty because they called upon the Lord.

◆　◆　◆

Some people need to realize that they have rebelled against God's will. If that is true in your case, call upon Him. He'll deliver you. Then you can praise the Lord "for His goodness and for His wonderful works to the children of men" (v. 15).

GOOD
MEDICINE

Psalm 107 contains four vivid pictures of sin and salvation. In today's passage, the psalmist likens sin to a disease and God's Word to medicine: "Fools, because of their transgression, and because of their iniquities, were afflicted. . . . He sent His word and healed them" (vv. 17,20).

Disease starts secretly. It enters your body secretly and grows secretly. Then it begins to sap your strength, rob your appetite and weaken you. Unless something is done, it will kill you.

So it is with sin. People play with sin without realizing its danger. That's like treating cancer or AIDS lightly. Sin brings death. To be healed, we need the medicine of God's Word.

Scripture can heal the brokenhearted. It can heal those who have been ravaged by sin, who have rebelled against the Lord. But the sick have to reach out by faith and admit their need (Matt. 9:12). We have to admit that we can't help ourselves and that no one else can help us.

Medicine can be expensive and even hard to obtain sometimes. But the Word of God is free and available. It can cure every malady of the soul.

✦　　✦　　✦

Perhaps your life has been ravaged by sin and you have yet to admit your need and reach out to the Lord for help. Never delay treatment for your soul. Read the Word of God and ask the Holy Spirit to apply its truths to your heart.

THE GREAT PHYSICIAN

Yesterday we learned that the Bible is the only medicine that can cure the disease of sin. Now let's consider the Great Physician, who administers the medicine.

Jesus Christ came to call sinners to repent, and only He can save them. There are false physicians in this world today. What they offer does not solve the problems of the soul. The false prophets of Jeremiah's day were guilty of applying salves when they sould have performed surgery (Jer. 8:11,22). How would you like your doctor to lie to you about your health—to gloss over your physical ailments? That's what these "prophets" did to the Israelites regarding their spiritual condition.

Doctors are busy people and often cannot be there right when you need them. But Jesus comes when you call Him. His diagnosis is always accurate. He can cleanse every wound and heal every sickness. He won't force His medicine on you; He waits for you to admit your needs first. And the amazing thing is the He already paid the bill for your care on Calvary's cross.

Lost sinners deserve to die, but "whoever calls on the name of the Lord shall be saved" (Acts 2:21). If you've never trusted Him for your salvation, do so now.

♦   ♦   ♦

The Great Physician administers the medicine of His Word to your ailing soul. He can save the unbeliever, heal a broken heart and restore a fractured relationship. Whatever your need, ask Jesus for His healing touch.

WEATHERING THE STORM

Quite frankly, I don't like large bodies of water. I don't like to be on them, and I don't like to be in them. I don't mind being by them; to sit by the ocean and watch the waves is fine.

When I read these verses I almost get seasick. They describe a storm at sea. "For He commands and raises the stormy wind, which lifts up the waves of the sea. They mount up to the heavens, they go down again to the depths; their soul melts because of trouble. They reel to and fro, and stagger like a drunken man, and are at their wits' end" (vv. 25-27).

Storms do come to our lives. What causes them? Sometimes other people cause them. In Acts 27 Paul got into a storm because the people in charge of the ship would not listen to the Word of God. Sometimes God causes the storm to test us and build us. In Matthew 14 Jesus sent His disciples directly into a storm to teach them an important lesson of faith. Sometimes we cause the storm by disobedience— we are like Jonah running away from God, and the only way He can bring us back is to send a storm.

But the greatest storm that ever occurred was at Calvary. When the sun was blackened for three hours and God the Son was made sin for us, all of the waves and the billows of God's judgment came upon Jesus on the cross. Because He weathered that storm, you and I can cry out to God. He can deliver us from the storms of life or take us through them, giving us the strength and courage we need. The psalmist promises, "He calms the storm, so that its waves are still. . . . So He guides them to their desired haven" (vv. 29,30).

♦　　♦　　♦

Do you find yourself in a storm today? Ask God for the strength and courage to weather it and for the wisdom to understand it, not waste it.

REMEMBER THE GIVER

I t is dangerous for Christians to depend on comfortable circumstances. When God sees that we are depending on our circumstances and not on Him, He will change those circumstances in a hurry. "He turns rivers into a wilderness, and the watersprings into dry ground; a fruitful land into barrenness, for the wickedness of those who dwell in it. He turns a wilderness into pools of water, and dry land into watersprings. There He makes the hungry dwell, that they may establish a city for a dwelling place" (vv. 33-36).

You can picture people saying, "My, we are blessed. We have these wonderful rivers and springs. We have all of this fruitful land. Let's just eat, drink and be merry." But God says, "Wait a minute. Are you enjoying the gifts and forgetting the Giver? Are you looking at My hand and forgetting My heart? Are you enjoying my wealth but neglecting My will?"

That's what often happens—we turn to idolatry. We start living on substitutes. The rivers and springs and fruitful land become our god. So God stops the rivers. He shuts off the water springs. He makes the fruitful land barren. Then we cry out and say, "Oh, God, what shall we do?" His answer is, "Start worshiping Me instead of your blessings. Start looking to the Blesser instead of the blessing. Don't be idolaters, who live on substitutes. Give thanks to Me for all the good things I have given you." In other words, get smart. "Whoever is wise will observe these things, and they will understand the lovingkindness of the Lord" (v. 43).

♦ ♦ ♦

Satan will do his best to get you to depend on the world's substitutes. When he succeeds, you forget God and trust in your resources and wealth— you become an idolater. Perhaps you enjoy comfortable circumstances. Thank God for them, but continue to draw your strength from the spiritual resources He has provided. If God has shut off His watersprings of blessings to you, start worshiping Him.

WHAT IS YOUR HEART CONDITION?

"**O** God, my heart is steadfast; I will sing and give praise." David begins this psalm by reminding us of the importance of a steadfast or "fixed" heart in the Christian life.

What is a fixed heart? First, it *trusts* in the Lord for salvation. Jesus died for us on the cross. If we have trusted Him, we have fixed our hearts upon Him, and we have experienced His mercy. "For Your mercy is great above the heavens, and Your truth reaches to the clouds" (v. 4).

A fixed heart is also *devoted*. Jesus said that we can't serve two masters. We're going to love one and hate the other or be loyal to the one and despise the other. We can't serve God and money—or, for that matter, God and anything else (Matt. 6:24). So a fixed heart is devoted and loving—a heart that is devoted solely to the Lord.

Marriage is one of the many pictures of the Christian life found in the Bible. Those who trust Jesus Christ as Savior are married to Him. We are waiting for that day when the Bridegroom will come and claim His Bride, and we'll enter our heavenly home. Meanwhile, we want to be faithful to Him. We do not want to be guilty of spiritual adultery, being unfaithful to our Savior.

A fixed heart is *serving*. If your heart is fixed, you will be busy serving others. A person fixed upon the Lord in faith and love reaches out to serve others—to put others ahead of himself.

Finally, a fixed heart is *hopeful*. We anticipate the return of our Lord. When you love and trust someone, you look forward to being with that person. We wait and hope for the day when we will be in the Lord's presence.

◆　　◆　　◆

The condition of a person's heart reveals much about the condition of his soul. A fixed heart is in tune with the Lord—trusting, devoted, serving and hopeful. What is your heart condition?

WHY IS GOD SILENT?

What do you do when heaven is silent? What do you do when you cry out to God and there is no answer, or at least you can't hear it? This happened to David. He kept crying out to God, "Do not keep silent, O God of my praise!" (v. 1). David was being attacked by the wicked—a frequent occurrence in his life. You must remember that when he prayed these prayers of judgment (v. 13), he was not seeking personal revenge. No, he was praying as God's king over Israel. David wanted to see the wicked judged because they were attacking the people of God, the ones from whom God's Word and His Son would come.

Why is God silent at times? It may be because *we aren't listening* or *we don't want to listen.* Evangelist Billy Sunday used to say that a sinner can't find God for the same reason a criminal can't find a policeman—he's not looking. Sin makes us turn a deaf ear to God. When Adam and Eve heard the voice of God in the Garden of Eden, they ran and hid. Children often do that when they disobey.

Sometimes God is silent because *we aren't ready for the message.* He wants to talk to us about something, but we aren't ready. We have to go through refining trials to make us ready to listen.

God is sometimes silent because *He knows we aren't willing to obey.* He is always ready to show us His will, but He shows His will only to those who really want to do it. Jesus said in John 7:17, "If anyone wants to do His will, he shall know concerning the doctrine." Obedient people always hear the voice of God.

Finally, sometimes God is silent that He might test us—*to teach us the importance of silence,* the importance of waiting on Him. Waiting helps remind us of God's sovereignty.

◆   ◆   ◆

The silence of God is one of the difficult tests of faith. What should you do when He is silent? Remember His faithfulness and past blessings. Live today on what He has already told you. Trust Him and wait. You will hear the voice of God again.

CAREFUL
CULTIVATING

What we love determines how we live. What delights us also directs us. David wrote about his enemies, "As he loved cursing, so let it come to him; as he did not delight in blessing, so let it be far from him."

What do you love? What do you delight in? You reap exactly what you sow. David's enemies were sowing curses, and he knew they were going to reap a harvest of misery. They were running away from the blessing of God, and David knew that in missing the blessing of God, they were going to miss the joys and purposes of life.

Let's be careful how we cultivate the appetites of our inner person. What we love we may get, and after we get it we may regret it. There may be some fun in sowing sin, but there's no joy in the reaping. Christians' tears and toil are in the sowing; our joy is in the reaping. But for those who live for the flesh and for the world, the joy is in the sowing, and the trial and the tears are in the reaping. If you take what you want from life, you pay for it.

How important it is to cultivate spiritual appetites—to have an appetite for the Word of God, for prayer, to be with His people and to delight in the worship and service of God!

♦   ♦   ♦

Cultivate those appetites of your inner person that lead to spiritual growth. Keep them in check by feeding on God's Word and by walking with the Lord. He will use your appetites to bring blessing to your life and others.

PRAISE IN PERSECUTION

When David wrote this psalm he was being sorely persecuted by his enemies. He was praying for them; they were preying on him. Yet throughout this psalm he expresses some rather vehement thoughts. He calls upon God to bring judgment upon them because of the way they lived. Again, keep in mind that David was not seeking personal revenge. He was above that. Instead, he was praying as God's anointed king, concerned about the needs of his people.

I like the way Psalm 109 ends: "I will greatly praise the Lord with my mouth; yes, I will praise Him among the multitude. For He shall stand at the right hand of the poor, to save him from those who condemn him" (vv. 30,31). Even though he sees all these enemies around him, even though they are persecuting the poor and needy, even though they love cursing, David says, "I'm going to praise God. I'm not going to look at them and walk by sight. I'm going to walk by faith and praise God." Praise can change a negative situation. It helps us see more clearly and lifts our hearts to the Lord when the world around us seems so difficult.

David not only praises God, he also witnesses. "I will praise Him among the multitude" (v. 30). In other words, "I'm going to tell others about what God has done for me. Instead of focusing on the enemy, I'm going to go out and share the Word of God with others." That's a good way to get victory. Instead of thinking constantly about the problems in life, let's go out and tell others about the One who solves them.

Then he makes a third resolution. He says, "I'm going to trust my Advocate in heaven." God is standing at our right hand (v. 31). At the right hand of God is Jesus Christ, our heavenly High Priest, our Advocate. So let's not be afraid. Let's not be bitter. Let's praise the Lord and realize that He is at our right hand, and we dare not trust anyone or anything but Him.

♦   ♦   ♦

To trust God when you are surrounded by enemies requires that you walk by faith, not sight. Perhaps you are in a similar situation today. By a courageous act of your will, get your eyes off your enemies and begin praising God. It can change your situation.

EAVESDROPPING ON ETERNITY

I t is not usually polite to listen in on other people's conversations, but in Psalm 110 we can do that. We hear God the Father speaking to God the Son. "The Lord said to my Lord, 'Sit at My right hand, till I make Your enemies Your footstool'" (v. 1). This is quoted often in the New Testament. It talks about when our Lord Jesus Christ returned to heaven and was enthroned at the right hand of the Majesty.

What does this Father-Son conversation say to us? First, it speaks of our Lord's *majesty*. He has returned to heaven in glory. He had prayed, "Father, glorify me together with Yourself, with the glory I had with You before the world was" (John 17:5), and God did that. God the Father gave God the Son His majesty, and now He is the King-Priest in heaven. "You are a priest forever according to the order of Melchizedek" (v. 4). Nowhere in the Old Testament do we find a priest on a throne, but Jesus in His majesty is both our King and our Priest. As our King, He tells us what to do. As our Priest, He gives us the strength to do it.

Psalm 110 also speaks of *victory*—He has won the battle. "Sit at My right hand, till I make your enemies Your footstool" (v. 1). That's about as low as you can get. Our Savior is victorious. He has won every battle. He is the Conqueror, the King of kings and Lord of lords. There is nothing for us to fear.

This psalm also speaks about His *ministry*. Most people on thrones have others serve them. Not so with Jesus. He serves us.

Finally, the psalmist speaks of our *security*. "He ever lives to make intercession" for us (Heb. 7:25). As long as He lives, we live—and that's forever.

◆　　◆　　◆

Because Christ is the King of kings, He has won the victory. He has conquered sin and death. Because He is our High Priest, we have security, for He is interceding for us. Do you know Jesus as your Savior? Is He your King and High Priest?

REAL WISDOM

We live in a world with a great deal of knowledge but not a great deal of wisdom. So-called smart people do stupid things. David tells us the secret of wisdom and understanding in Psalm 111. "The fear of the Lord is the beginning of wisdom; a good understanding have all those who do His command-ments. His praise endures forever" (v. 10). Here we have three secrets of wisdom, and a person doesn't have to go through a university to learn them.

Fear God. "The fear of the Lord is the beginning of wisdom." This is not the fear of a slave before an angry master. This is the reverence and respect of a loving child for a loving Father—showing respect for God, His Word, His presence and His will for our lives.

Obey Him. "A good understanding have all those that do His commandments." The Word of God is given to us not just to read and study but to obey. We are to be doers of the Word, not just auditors who sit in class and take notes. When we obey God, we begin to understand what He is doing. Obedience is the organ of spiritual understanding.

Praise Him. "His praise endures forever." Praise takes the selfishness out of our lives. It takes us away from idolatry, from living on substitutes.

The more we fear Him, the more we obey Him. The more we obey Him, the more we praise Him. These are the ingredients of a happy and successful life.

♦　♦　♦

The world's wisdom is based on faulty foundations. Genuine wisdom begins by fearing God. You increase your wisdom as you obey His Word and praise Him. As you walk with the Lord today, do so with the wisdom that comes from fearing Him.

ONE LEGITIMATE FEAR

Psychiatrists call the fear of certain things phobias. There are people who fear heights (acrophobia) and people who fear closed-in places (claustrophobia). There are people afraid of water, dogs and even other people. But there is one fear that drives out all other fears, and we find it in Psalm 112. "Praise the Lord! Blessed is the man who fears the Lord, who delights greatly in His commandments" (v. 1).

All kinds of fears are taken care of if we fear the Lord. One is *family fears*. "His descendants will be mighty on earth; the generation of the upright will be blessed" (v. 2). Commit your children to Him and you won't have to worry about their lives.

Fear of the Lord also drives out *financial fears*. "Wealth and riches will be in his house" (v. 3). This doesn't mean we will all be millionaires. It means we'll always have what we need. If we fear the Lord, we can let go of our financial fears.

Some *fear the dark*. "Unto the upright there arises light in the darkness" (v. 4). Fear God and you'll always have light when you need it. You will have His guidance and direction.

Some *fear the future and change*. "Surely he will never be shaken; the righteous will be in everlasting remembrance" (v. 6). God says, "Don't be afraid of the changes that are going on around you or in you. I am the God of the universe. Fear Me, and I'll take care of the changes."

Finally, some people have a fear of *bad news*. But verse 7 reads, "He will not be afraid of evil tidings; his heart is steadfast, trusting in the Lord." No news is bad if you're walking in the will of God.

♦   ♦   ♦

When you fear the Lord, every other fear is conquered. Walk today in the fear of the Lord, trusting Him with your future. He will give you peace.

THE RESPONSIBILITY OF PRAISE

"**B**lessed be the name of the Lord from this time forth and forevermore! From the rising of the sun to its going down the Lord's name is to be praised" (vv. 2,3).

These verses tell us that we have some responsibilities. First, *we are to praise God.* It's tragic when we forget to praise the Lord. Someone has said that he feels sorry for atheists and agnostics because when they want to be thankful, they have no one to talk to. How can a person really enjoy a beautiful sunrise or a sunset, a beautiful spring day or even a beautiful winter day, if he can't thank the One who creates these things? God deserves our praise, for He does so much for us.

The psalmist also tells us to *praise God all day long,* "from the rising of the sun to its going down" (v. 3). Praise Him when you have to get up in the morning. Praise Him when you're tired at the end of the day. Praise Him during the day for the good things that happen and for the difficult things. Give Him thanks for seeing you through every situation.

We also should *praise Him all over the world*—as suggested by the psalmist's reference to the daily journey of the sun from the east to the west. What are we doing about those who do not know the Lord, the many who have never heard about Jesus Christ and His salvation? Let's begin by witnessing right where we are. Let's pray and give. Missionaries need our support. Perhaps God wants you to go and carry the Gospel message overseas.

◆ ◆ ◆

God has attached responsibility to your privilege of praising Him. You never run out of reasons to praise the Lord. Your praise to Him should encompass the whole day and the whole world. Is praise part of your daily walk with the Lord?

OBSTACLES ON THE JOURNEY

Have you ever seen the sea flee? Have you ever seen the mountains skip like rams or the hills run like lambs? That's the vivid description the psalmist gives of the Exodus of Israel from Egypt. "The sea saw it and fled; Jordan turned back. The mountains skipped like rams, the little hills like lambs. . . . Tremble, O earth, at the presence of the Lord, at the presence of the God of Jacob, who turned the rock into a pool of water, the flint into a fountain of waters" (vv. 3,4,7,8).

The psalmist mentions the time God opened the Red Sea and the Israelites walked across on dry land. He talks about when the nation entered the Promised Land over the dry bed of the Jordan River. Then he refers to their experience in the wilderness, when they were thirsty and God turned the rock into a pool of water.

What are we to learn from all of these experiences? God helps us in the obstacles of life. When you turn your obstacles over to the Lord, He acts. What will He do? Sometimes He *overcomes the obstacles*. God is with us in the hopeless places. How hopeless the Israelites were at the Red Sea! The enemy soldiers were behind them; the wilderness was around them; the sea was in front of them. But God opened a way to escape.

Sometimes God *removes the obstacles*—the "hills" and the "mountains." He just makes them skip and run away like animals.

He also can *turn the obstacles into blessings*. He "turned the rock into a pool of water, the flint into a fountain of waters" (v. 8). If God doesn't overcome or remove your obstacle, let Him turn it into a blessing.

◆　　◆　　◆

Trust God with your obstacles. He can help you in the hopeless places, the high places and the hard places.

POINTLESS WORSHIP

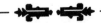

Psalm 115 tells us about the blessings we have because our God is the living God. He's not one of the "idols of the nations." "Their idols are silver and gold, the work of men's hands" (v. 4). How true that is today also. Many people worship silver and gold as their god. They think money can do anything. We do need money for some of the practical things in life. But what good are the things that money can buy if you don't have the things that money *can't* buy?

The psalmist describes the idols and the pointlessness of worshiping them. "They have mouths, but they do not speak [no promises]; eyes they have, but they do not see [no protection]; they have ears, but they do not hear [no prayer]; noses they have, but they do not smell [no praise]; they have hands, but they do not handle [no power]; feet they have, but they do not walk [no presence]; nor do they mutter through their throat. Those who make them are like them; so is everyone who trusts in them" (vv. 5-8). How unlike God. Christians have *promises*—our God talks to us. We have *protection* because He sees all that happens. We have *prayer* because His ears are open to us. We can *praise* Him. (In the Bible, the smelling of a fragrant offering is a picture of God's acceptance of our praise to Him.) We have *power* because He has an omnipotent hand.

We become like the god we worship. Those who worship silver and gold become like that—dead, lifeless and hard. Many people are making a god in their own image. But God made us in His image, and He wants us to have an active faith in Him.

✦   ✦   ✦

Christians have a living faith and serve a living God. The more you read His Word, fellowship with Him and praise Him, the more you become like Him. You have His promises, protection, prayer and power.

DEAD FAITH

Years ago there was a "God is dead" movement in theology. Of course, He is very much alive, as Psalm 115 tells us: "But our God is in heaven. He does whatever He pleases" (v. 3). The problem with people is not that God is dead but that their faith is dead. They do not have living faith in the living God.

The psalmist addresses three groups of people in this passage. First, he speaks to the nation. "O Israel, trust in the Lord; He is their help and their shield" (v. 9). Then he talks to the priests. "O house of Aaron, trust in the Lord; He is their help and their shield" (v. 10). Then He talks to all believers. "You who fear the Lord, trust in the Lord; He is their help and their shield" (v. 11).

If we are going to have the kind of relationship with God that we ought to have, if He is going to be to us the living God with living power and blessing, first of all we must *trust Him*. That means to rely on Him, to believe that what He says is right and true, that He does not lie. It means to believe that what God is doing is the best thing for us. He is our Help. He is our Shield. He is our Provision. He is our Protection and our Security. He also is our Sufficiency.

Second, we must *fear Him*. "He will bless those who fear the Lord, both small and great" (v. 13). The blessing that He gives is the best blessing. To fear God means to show reverence to Him, to respect Him when He speaks and acts, to have a heart that does not tempt or test Him.

Third, we must *bless Him*. "But we will bless the Lord from this time forth and forevermore. Praise the Lord!" (v. 18). We are always asking God to bless us, but the psalmist says, "We bless God."

✦　　✦　　✦

When you fear the Lord, trust Him and experience the blessings He has for you, you cannot help but bless Him. If your relationship with Him is what it ought to be, then you will be praising Him "from this time forth and forevermore."

DELIVERED!

Whoever wrote Psalm 116 went through some difficult experiences to give us these verses. In fact, he almost died. But the Lord heard his cry and delivered him, and that's why he wrote, "I love the Lord, because He has heard my voice and my supplications. Because He has inclined His ear to me" (vv. 1,2).

Picture God leaning down to His little child, getting close enough to hear. Sometimes I have to get close to people who are speaking because my hearing is not as good as it used to be. God can hear as well as He always has, but He gets close to us—not to hear us better but to help us. The psalmist tells us, "I was brought low, and He saved me" (v. 6). God comes down where we are to deliver us and make us all that He wants us to be. "For You have delivered my soul from death, my eyes from tears, and my feet from falling" (v. 8).

The psalmist discovered the grace of God. "Gracious is the Lord, and righteous; yes, our God is merciful. The Lord preserves the simple; I was brought low, and He saved me" (vv. 5,6). God delivered him from death and stopped his tears. He strengthened and guided his feet so that he did not stumble.

We, too, have all this help through Jesus Christ. He is the source of grace and mercy. The psalmist said, "The pains of death surrounded me" (v. 3), but he did not die spiritually. Jesus died in his place.

◆　　◆　　◆

Do you need God's deliverance today? Rejoice that He hears and helps you. All you need comes from His bountiful hand. He is gracious and merciful. Call upon His name; He will deliver you.

PRECIOUS DEATH

Few people really want to talk about death. Yet verse 15 says, "Precious in the sight of the Lord is the death of His saints." This statement is often misunderstood, so let's examine it and see what it means to our lives today.

Death is the penalty of sin; God is the Author of life. When God made His original creation, there was no death. But when man sinned, death came on the scene. It now reigns as a king. "It is appointed for men to die once, but after this the judgment" (Heb. 9:27). Certainly God doesn't enjoy it when unsaved people die, because He knows they go to a Christless, dark eternity (Ezek. 18:23). Nor does He enjoy it when His own people die. Jesus stood at the grave of Lazarus and wept (John 11:35).

The death of God's children is so precious to Him that it will not be an accident. The psalmist was brought low and almost died. "The pains of death encompassed me, and the pangs of Sheol laid hold of me; I found trouble and sorrow" (Ps. 116:3). He was going to die, and then he cried out to God, who replied, "Your death is so precious to me, I will not allow you to die just by accident." The death of everyone who goes home to be with the Lord is not an accident—it is an appointment. We are immortal until our work is done. That, to me, is a real encouragement. There's a lot of danger that can come to us in this world. But God says, "Your death is too precious for me to permit it to just happen." Death for the believer is precious because Jesus bore our sins on the cross to give us eternal life.

♦   ♦   ♦

Neither your life nor your death is an accident. Take comfort in the fact that God knew every detail about your life before you were born. You have work to do for Him, and only when that is finished will He take you to be with Himself.

SHORT BUT DEEP

Psalm 117 is the shortest of the psalms—only two verses. "Praise the Lord, all you Gentiles! Laud Him, all you peoples! For His merciful kindness is great toward us, and the truth of the Lord endures forever. Praise the Lord!" What a tremendous psalm of praise this is; it's short but deep.

We don't find too much difficulty in thanking people for what they have done for us. Even when we pay someone to work for us, we still say thank you. But sometimes we take advantage of the Lord and take for granted the things He has done for us—especially the "little" things. Do we thank Him for eyes to see, for ears to hear? Recognize and thank God for His numerous blessings.

The psalmist says, "Laud Him, all you peoples." But billions of people in this world don't praise the Lord because they don't know Him. They've never been told that Jesus Christ is the Savior of the world. Unfortunately, many Christians for some reason are not concerned about this. How can all the nations praise Him until all the nations trust Him?

Praise the Lord for His merciful kindness and enduring truth. And make every effort to tell others about the One you praise.

✦　　✦　　✦

Think of some of the blessings you can praise God for. It's easy to take His blessings for granted and overlook some of His greatest provisions. But though you praise the Lord, there are many who don't. Ask Him to use you today to reach someone who does not know Christ as Savior.

ASSURED, CONFIDENT, DEFIANT

"The Lord is on my side; I will not fear. What can man do to me?" (v. 6). This is a *word of assurance.* "If God is for us, who can be against us?" (Rom. 8:31). The God of the universe is on our side—Father, Son and Holy Spirit. No matter who may be against us, He is on our side.

It's also a *word of confidence.* "I will not fear." As I look at the past, I see that God has cared for me every step of the way. As I look at the present, I know He is with me. As I look to the future, I know He is ahead of me. He surrounds me. He promises, "I will never leave you nor forsake you" (Heb. 13:5). I respond, "I will not fear. What can man do to me?" (v. 6).

Finally, it is a *word of defiance.* "What can man do unto me?" In other words, fear God, not humans. Jesus taught this to His disciples. "And do not fear those who kill the body but cannot kill the soul. But rather fear Him who is able to destroy both soul and body in hell" (Matt. 10:28).

When you fear God, you need not fear anyone else. To fear God means to love Him, revere Him and respect Him.

✦　　✦　　✦

No matter how difficult your experiences are, the Lord is on your side. You need not fear the past, present or future or what anybody can do to you, because you fear God. You have His words of assurance, confidence and defiance.

MEETING LIFE'S DEMANDS

"**T**he Lord is my strength and song, and He has become my salvation" (v. 14). This also is found in Exodus 15:2 and Isaiah 12:2. The Israelites sang these words when they were delivered from Egypt, as they saw their enemy drowned in the sea. And Isaiah 12 promises that Israel will sing this song in the future when God restores her and establishes His kingdom. We, too, can rejoice for what these words mean for us today.

God is our Strength. That takes care of the demands of life. Where do you look to find strength? Your experience? Your health? Your money? Your job? All these things could vanish. Only the strength of the Lord can meet the demands of life. "Those who wait on the Lord shall renew their strength" (Is. 40:31).

He is our Song. That takes care of the dullness of life. Many people have to go through boring, tedious experiences. Perhaps your job is not as exciting as you'd like it to be. Perhaps you are a shut-in, and you can't get out and do and see what others have the privilege of doing and seeing. The Lord will give you joy.

He is our Salvation. That takes care of the dangers of life. He delivers us and is always at our side. "The right hand of the Lord is exalted; the right hand of the Lord does valiantly" (v. 16). That right hand is available to us today.

◆   ◆   ◆

Believers may sing this song of praise, for God takes care of the demands, the dullness and the dangers of life. He is your Strength, your Song and your Salvation. Remember that God is ever available to deliver you from the difficult experiences of life.

REJOICING IN
EACH DAY

"**T**his is the day which the Lord has made; we will rejoice and be glad in it" (v. 24). When you are having one of those difficult days—a day when the storm is blowing and the battle is raging, when the burdens are heavy, when your heart is broken and your tears are flowing, when it feels like everybody is turned against you, including your Heavenly Father—that's the time to heed this verse by faith.

The psalmist was going through battles and difficulties, yet he was able to say, "If God put this day together, I'm going to rejoice and be glad in it. Even though I may not see the blessing now, eventually by faith I'll be able to say, 'It all worked together for good.' So I'll say it now."

Jews sing this psalm at Passover. Jesus also sang this song before He was crucified. Can you imagine saying on your way to Calvary, "This is the day which the Lord has made; I will rejoice and be glad in it"? That's another way of saying, "Not my will, but Your will be done." If Jesus sang this song, we should sing it also.

♦　　♦　　♦

Perhaps your day is full of overwhelming burdens or sorrows. Jesus also suffered days like that. Accept the day God has given you and acknowledge that He is in charge. Anticipate what God is going to do for you today; rejoice and be glad in it. You may not understand His purposes now, but one day you will.

THE BIBLE'S ABCS

What would your Christian life be like if you had no Bible? Would that make any difference? After all, what is the Bible supposed to do for our lives?

God gives us some answers to those questions in this Psalm. Almost every verse in this long psalm in some way refers to the Word of God. The psalm is arranged according to the Hebrew alphabet. The first eight verses all begin with the Hebrew letter *aleph*; the next eight verses start with *beth*; the next eight, *gimel*; and so on. It's as though God were saying, "Here are the ABCs of how to use the Word of God in your life."

"Blessed are the undefiled in the way, who walk in the law of the Lord!" (v. 1). *Undefiled* means "people who are blameless, those who have integrity." *Integrity* is the opposite of duplicity and hypocrisy, which is the pretense to be something we are not. If we have integrity, our whole lives are built around the Word of God.

The psalmist says, "Blessed are those who keep His testimonies, who seek Him with the whole heart!" (v. 2). Are you wholeheartedly into the Word of God? In the Bible, *heart* refers to the inner person, and that includes the mind. "I will praise You with uprightness of heart, when I learn Your righteous judgments" (v. 7). It also includes the will. "I will keep Your statutes!" (v. 8). In other words, when you give your whole heart, mind and will to the Word of God, it starts to put your life together. Is your life or your home "falling apart" today? Turn to the Word of God.

The Bible has one author—God. It has one theme—Jesus Christ. It has one message—the salvation of your soul. And it has one blessing to bring—a life of integrity.

◆ ◆ ◆

The Word of God is a powerful spiritual resource. Its truth feeds your soul. As you walk in the life of faith, the Holy Spirit uses the Bible to minister to you. Get into the Word and allow it to make you whole and build integrity into your life.

KEEPING CLEAN

How does a person keep clean in this dirty world? The psalmist asks this question in verse 9: "How can a young man cleanse his way?" The answer: "By taking heed according to Your word." Of course this doesn't apply only to a young man. The same is true for a young woman, a child or an older person. We are living in a dirty world, and because of the pollution around us, we have to walk in the Word of God. The psalmist gives us several instructions to follow to keep us spiritually clean.

First, *heed the Word*. We first have to read and study the Word so we know it. And if we know it, we should obey it.

Second, *hide the Word*. "Your word I have hidden in my heart, that I might not sin against You" (v. 11). G. Campbell Morgan used to say of this verse, "It tells us about the best book— 'Thy Word'—in the best place— 'my heart'—for the best purpose— 'that I might not sin' against God." Are you obeying the Word of God? Are you treasuring it in your heart?

Third, *herald the Word* by sharing it with others. "With my lips I have declared all the judgments of Your mouth" (v. 13). If we have Scripture in our hearts, it has to come out through our lips, because "out of the abundance of the heart the mouth speaks" (Matt. 12:34).

Finally, *honor the Word*. "I will meditate on Your precepts, and contemplate Your ways" (v. 15). In other words, "I will honor God's Word. I will respect what He wants me to do. My Father is telling me what to do, and I am going to obey Him."

◆　　◆　　◆

God's Word has a cleansing effect. But you must get into the Word before it can become effective in your life. Obey God's Word, and He will keep you clean in this dirty world.

HANDLING THE CRITICS

What do you do when people criticize you? What goes through your mind when you are in the presence of people who are unkind, especially people who don't believe the Word of God? The psalmist gives one answer: "Princes also sit and speak against me, but Your servant meditates on Your statutes. Your testimonies also are my delight and my counselors" (vv. 23,24).

Meditate on the Word of God. Get your mind fixed upon what God says. If we ponder and think about the things other people say, we will be agitated and anxious and uptight. But if we meditate on what God says, those things that are true and right and holy and beautiful, His peace will fill us.

Delight in the Word of God. "Your testimonies also are my delight" (v. 24). Some people delight in gossip. They enjoy listening to rumors about people. But the psalmist says, "While they were gossiping and telling lies, I was meditating on the Word of God, because I delight in it."

Obey the Word of God. "Your testimonies also are my delight and my counselors" (v. 24). The Hebrew text means, "the men of my counsel." Authorities, friends and even enemies may want to give you counsel. But get your counsel from the Word of God.

♦   ♦   ♦

Whatever your difficulty today, turn to the Bible and let it counsel you. Let it saturate your mind, heart and will.

OPEN, OBEDIENT, OCCUPIED

An enlarged heart, in the physical sense, is dangerous. But spiritually speaking, an enlarged heart can be a blessing. "I will run in the way of Your commandments, for You shall enlarge my heart" (v. 32). If you have an enlarged heart physically, you don't do much running. But if you have an enlarged heart spiritually, you are ready to walk and run with the Lord and accomplish His purposes. When an athlete is running, he is on a path and has a goal in mind, which gives him the energy to continue. That's what God wants for us today. He has a goal for us to reach and a path for us to follow. And He gives us His strength through His Word.

What does it mean to have an enlarged heart? First, *an enlarged heart is open to God's truth.* It's a heart that's honest and says, "Lord, I want Your truth even if it hurts."

Second, *an enlarged heart is obedient to God's will.* It's a humble heart that says, "O God, what You have said, I will do. I am the servant. You are the master."

Third, *an enlarged heart is occupied with God's glory.* It's a happy heart. Some people's hearts are small and narrow. They live in their own little world and have their own narrow view. What a wonderful thing it is to grow in grace and the knowledge of truth (II Pet. 3:18)! Our horizons are expanded. We can see what we haven't seen before. We can hear what we haven't heard before. God gives us an enlarged life because we have an enlarged heart.

◆　　◆　　◆

Open your heart to God's truth and be obedient to His will. Every step of obedience expands your horizon of blessing and ministry. Most of all, be occupied with God's glory.

YOU BECOME
WHAT YOU SEE

Outlook determines outcome. What you are seeing helps to determine what you are becoming. So you'd better be careful what you look at. It's no wonder that the psalmist prays, "Turn away my eyes from looking at worthless things, and revive me in Your way" (v. 37). *Worthless things* here literally means "vanity." Much of what we see every day in the media, for example, is worthless and false. It doesn't come from God, who is Truth; it comes from Satan and the world. And it doesn't last; it's all vanity. The word for *vanity* means "emptiness"—what is left after you break a soap bubble.

Look at the Word of God. It is truth. It is God's treasure. It will endure forever. "Forever, O Lord, Your word is settled in heaven" (Ps. 119:89). When we fill our lives with the Word of God, we fight vanity. When we turn our eyes upon the pages of the Bible, we grow in truth and value and are in touch with eternity. It's an interesting coincidence that we find the letters "T" and "V" in verse 37 (in the words *turn* and *vanity*). I think a lot of people need to put this verse on their television sets. You may say, "TV is just harmless entertainment." But so much of what you see goes right into your mind and heart, making you cheap, false, worthless and temporary. The Bible tells us that "he who does the will of God abides forever" (I John 2:17).

✦   ✦   ✦

So much of what the world offers is trivial, false and worthless. Don't build your life on the world's foundations. Build your life instead on the Word of God, for it endures forever.

REAL FREEDOM

Many people have the strange idea that God's Law and man's liberty are enemies. They say, "I want freedom. I want to do my own thing." How wrong they are. God's Law and your liberty go hand-in-hand, and verse 45 makes this clear. "And I will walk at liberty, for I seek Your precepts." Now, the world would write that verse like this: "And I will walk at liberty, for I reject and break Thy precepts. I'm going to do my own thing, my own way."

Let's get down to basics. What is freedom? Some may say freedom means the privilege of doing what you want to do. But that is not freedom. In fact, that's the worst kind of slavery in the world—to be controlled only by your impulses and inclinations. Real freedom is a life controlled by God's truth and motivated by His love.

This is true in every area of life. If we obey the traffic laws, we have the freedom to drive on the streets and highways. If we obey the laws of truth, we have the freedom to speak, and people will believe us. If we obey the laws of science, we won't blow up the laboratory. If the airplane pilot obeys the laws of aerodynamics, he will be able to fly his plane. You see, we have the freedom to enjoy the power of the Law when we have yielded to the commandment of the Law. So when I submit myself to the will of God, I am taking my first step toward freedom. As Charles Wesley wrote, God "breaks the power of canceled sin; He sets the prisoner free." He says, "If you submit to me, together we will enjoy truth and love."

◆ ◆ ◆

Are you enjoying real freedom in your Christian life? If not, you may have real freedom by submitting to the will of God. He gives us His Word so that we may know His will. Submit to Him and take your first step toward freedom.

SING
THE LAW

I enjoy classical music. I often tune my radio to classical music while I'm studying. I also enjoy going to concerts. Before a concert begins, I browse through the concert program to see what will be played. I might read that the orchestra is going to play Tchaikovsky's "Pathetique." Or perhaps I will hear a Bordin string quartet. But what if, right in the middle of the program, I read that the choir is going to sing the local housing code? I'd ask, "What is going on? Choirs don't sing the law. What musician would waste time putting the housing code to music?" Look at verse 54: "Your statutes have been my songs in the house of my pilgrimage." The psalmist says, "I sing the Law."

This verse presents three different attitudes toward life. To a *child*, life is like a prison, with nothing but rules. "Don't do this. Don't do that. Don't go there." We have to protect children so they can grow up and live their own lives. To *adolescents*, life is a party. They don't want statutes. "Don't tell me what to do," they say. They just want the songs. But when we become *mature adults*, we realize that life is not a prison or a party. It's a pilgrimage. We make this pilgrimage in obedience to God's Word. I don't know where I would have been during all these years of my life without the guidance of the Bible. God's Word is not a burden; it's a blessing. Duty becomes delight when you are yielded to the will of God.

I hope you are not trying to run away from the will of God and turn life into one continual party. Realize that your life is a pilgrimage and that, as a pilgrim and a stranger in this world, you need the guidance of Scripture.

◆　　◆　　◆

Are you having difficulty today on the pilgrim road? Take the mature view—yield to God's will and seek guidance in His Word. Without it, you will lose your way.

CHOOSING YOUR FRIENDS

All of us enjoy having friends. We need them. The psalmist says that the Word of God pertains to our friendships. "I am a companion of all who fear You, and of those who keep Your precepts" (v. 63). He let the Word of God guide him in his choice of friends and associates. We have many acquaintances but few real friends. A friend is someone you don't have to talk to all the time. You can be together for long periods without saying a word, yet your hearts are united. At the other extreme, a friend is someone you aren't afraid to talk to. You can unburden your heart, and you are a better person for having been with him.

God is our best friend. Abraham was called the friend of God, and we can be His friends also. Jesus said to His disciples, "I'm not going to call you slaves. I'm going to call you friends" (John 15:15). Friends talk to each other. And if we talk to God and let Him speak to us through His Word, we will be a companion of those who fear Him and keep His commandments.

One of the most important tests of friendship is what my friend's attitude is toward the Bible. Does he accept it? Does he receive the Word of God as truth? Does he fear God with a reverential awe and love for Him?

If I am in a right relationship to God through His Word, I will be in a right relationship with people. My friends will be God's friends. The Bible calls this separation—not isolation, but separation. It's the blessed by-product of a life lived in Scriptures.

✦ ✦ ✦

Choose your friends carefully. Do they fear God? Do they receive the Word of God in their hearts? Use your friends' attitudes toward the Bible as an important test of friendship. Relationships are investments of our time and other resources. Make them count for eternity.

TRUE RICHES

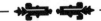

"The law of Your mouth is better to me than thousands of coins of gold and silver" (v. 72). Can we honestly say that we would rather have God's Word than money?

Many people in the Bible had that testimony. For example, Abraham led his army to a great victory. He brought back all of the captives and all the spoil. The King of Sodom showed up and said, "Abraham, you can have all this spoil. Just give me the people." But Abraham said, "Before this battle started, I lifted my hand to the Lord and said, 'When I win this battle, I'm not taking one thing from these people.' I would rather have the Word of God than have thousands of shekels of gold and silver" (see Gen. 14). Abraham kept his testimony clean.

But I also think of Achan in Joshua 7. God had commanded that no spoil be taken from Jericho. But Achan stole some silver and gold and clothing and buried them under his tent. He thought no one knew, but God knew. Achan wanted riches rather than God. Judas made the same mistake. He sold Jesus Christ, the greatest Treasure in the universe, for 30 pieces of silver.

If we love the Word of God, we'll read it, meditate on it and seek to obey it. If the Bible does not change our values, it will not change our lives. Jesus was the poorest of the poor. He made Himself poor to make us rich. We, in turn, should make ourselves poor to make other people rich, for we have the riches of the Word of God.

◆　　◆　　◆

You have a choice to make today: you can seek the kingdom of God and His righteousness, or you can bow down to the kingdom of man and seek riches. Would you rather have the temporal possessions of this world or the spiritual riches of God's Word?

CONSULT THE MANUAL

Whenever my wife and I purchase a new appliance, we add another instruction manual to our collection. We have instruction manuals for the various appliances in our home, for the automobile and for office equipment, such as tape recorders, computers and copying machines.

Someone may say, "I wish we had a manual of instruction for life." We do. It's called the Bible, the Word of God. "Your hands have made me and fashioned me; give me understanding, that I may learn Your commandments" (v. 73). God made and fashioned us in His image. According to Psalm 139, He had plans for each of our lives before we were born. He gave each of us a unique mind and genetic structure. He wrote into His book the days that He assigned to us, and He planned the best for us. He also wrote a manual to help us live the way we ought.

He gives us the Bible and says, "I want to give you understanding. The better you understand this Book, the better you will understand yourself. You are made in My image. I want to reveal to you from My Word how to use your hands, your feet, your eyes, your ears and your tongue. I want to tell you how My Word can make your heart work the way it is supposed to work." The psalmist says, "Your hands have made me and fashioned me"—that's our origin. "Give me understanding, that I may learn Your commandments"—that's our operation. The Bible is the operation manual for life.

How strange it is that people try to live their lives without an instruction book. They wonder why their marriages fall apart, why their bodies are in trouble and why they've gotten themselves into a jam. *Before* all else fails, read the Word of God, the instruction manual for everyday living.

◆　　◆　　◆

The Word of God covers the spectrum of life and provides guidelines for living in faith. When life presents new challenges and problems, refer to God's operation manual for life. It will help you align with His plans for your life.

REVIVING POWER

Some days everything seems to go wrong. Every phone call brings bad news. The mail is nothing but bills. The children come home from school with some kind of injury or a bad report. Work is frustrating. What do you do when you have one of these days?

"**M**y soul faints for Your salvation, but I hope in Your word. My eyes fail from searching Your word, saying, 'When will You comfort me?' For I have become like a wineskin in smoke, yet I do not forget Your statutes. . . . The proud have dug pits for me, which is not according to Your law" (vv. 81-83,85). Here's a man who was fainting and failing. He was like a wineskin in the smoke. Wherever he walked there was a pit for him to drop into. What did he do? He turned to God. His source of hope was His Word.

If you hope in circumstances, you will be disappointed, because they change. The psalmist hoped in the Word and trusted in God's faithfulness, and God comforted him.

People will fail you, but God never will. "All Your commandments are faithful" (v. 86). The psalmist clung to the comfort, hope and faithfulness of God, and as a result he experienced revival. "Revive me according to Your lovingkindness" (v. 88). God came with a Breath of fresh, heavenly air—the Holy Spirit—and revived him.

◆　　◆　　◆

Thank God for His faithfulness. If you are having a rough day, remember that you can depend on Him. He is your Hope and your Comfort, and He's always faithful. He'll give you the reviving power you need to rise above your circumstances and continue.

SETTLED QUESTIONS

Have you ever noticed that very little gets settled in this world? Few things are resolved politically. We sign treaties and contracts, and then they're broken or reinterpreted. Nothing seems final. Your life may be unsettled because of a situation or person. If that's the case, consider verse 89: "Forever, O Lord, Your word is settled in heaven."

My word—or anyone's, for that matter—is not settled. I've changed my opinions and my beliefs on certain things. I hope that when I give my word it is trustworthy. But God's Word is always *true*. We can trust it. We don't have to worry about Him lying to us. He can't.

God's Word is *eternal*. I often go to used bookstores and find best-sellers from years ago being sold for 25 cents each. Not so with God's Word. Jesus said, "Heaven and earth will pass away, but My words will by no means pass away" (Matt. 24:35).

God's Word also is *changeless*. God is not a diplomat who argues endlessly. He simply says, "This is the way it is going to be." If you want to find out how He has settled things, read His Word.

I'm glad that when I open my Bible, I find that things are settled. God tells us how to stop wars, how to solve problems, how to take care of sin. Best of all, He tells us how we can go to heaven. That's all settled. The Lord Jesus Christ died for us on the cross, rose again and will save all who will come to Him by faith.

✦ ✦ ✦

The strength and stability of God's Word stand out as a beacon in the instability and unsettledness of life. Because it is true, eternal and changeless, we may trust it and live by its truths. God has settled the questions of sin, death, salvation and eternal life. Do you need to settle these questions for yourself? Read and study His Word.

SWEETER THAN HONEY

How well I remember the day my doctor looked at me and said, "Reverend, you will not eat any more sweets." I've learned to do without desserts, but there's one sweet I cannot do without—God's Word: "How sweet are Your words to my taste, sweeter than honey to my mouth!" (v. 103).

Is the Word of God like honey or medicine to you? The way some people treat it, you'd think it is castor oil. True, there are times when we need the healing medicine of the Scripture. But the Bible is much more than medicine. It also is honey. Having an appetite for God's Word is one sign that a person is truly born again, for the Bible is food for the soul. Job said, "I have treasured the words of His mouth more than my necessary food" (Job 23:12). Jeremiah said, "Your words were found, and I ate them, and Your word was to me the joy and rejoicing of my heart" (Jer. 15:16). Jesus said, "Man shall not live by bread alone, but by every word that proceeds from the mouth of God" (Matt. 4:4). And Peter urges us to "desire the pure milk of the word" (I Pet. 2:2).

When people are sick, their appetites change—in fact, they often lose their appetites completely. Likewise, sin in our lives robs our spiritual appetite, and we lose our desire for the Word. May we always have an appetite for the sweetness of the Word of God, even when we have to read things that convict us. That first bite of Scripture may taste sour sometimes, but it will turn sweet.

♦ ♦ ♦

It's important to feed your soul a proper diet. Do you feed and nourish on God's Word? The Bible is sweet to those who love it, learn it and live it.

A LIGHT IN THE DARKNESS

You probably know the following verse well, but read it aloud as though you were hearing it for the first time. "Your word is a lamp to my feet and a light to my path" (v. 105). What lessons can we learn from that statement?

The world is dark. It is in a constant state of moral and intellectual darkness. We have more education today and less wisdom. People make foolish decisions. The world is also dark spiritually. Satan has numbed people's minds. They don't want to see the light of the glory of God in Jesus Christ.

The way is definite. How do we make it through this dark world? God has marked out a definite path for each one of us, and we don't have to be afraid of where it leads. It is a path of life, blessing and righteousness.

Our walk is deliberate. As we take each step, we see more of what God has for us. Sometimes I would like to have a spotlight that shines for miles down the road. But God says, "You're going to learn to walk by faith. You're going to learn to walk by patience, by My promise."

The Word is dependable. That lamp of the Word will not go out, and it will not lead us astray. When you read your Bible and let its truth shine on your path, God will show you what He wants you to do.

◆　　◆　　◆

Because your walk is by faith, you can see ahead only a step at a time. Be encouraged that the way is definite and deliberate and that God's Word is dependable. Let it be the light of life that guides you as you walk through this dark world today.

HOW THE LIGHT WORKS

What does it mean to have the Word of God as light? Verse 105 gives us four statements that answer that question. First, *the Word is a light that shines from above*. It is revelation. We know that God is Light (I John 1:5). He gave us the Word, just as He gave us the sun. The sun is at the center of our solar system; if it ever burned out, we would die. Likewise, God is the center of our universe through His Word. The Word is a necessity, not a luxury. Like a ray of light going into a prism, the Word of God gives us a multicolored exhibition of His grace. It provides whatever kind of light we need. But if you turn your back on the Word, you'll walk in darkness.

Second, *the Word is a light that shines within* (II Cor. 4:3-6). Paul uses the Old Testament story of creation to illustrate the new creation (Gen. 1:1-3). God formed that which was formless and filled that which was empty. That's a picture of salvation. The light shines in our hearts, and then God begins to form and fill our lives. He works on us through His Word and the power of His Spirit (Ps. 119:130). He has given the Holy Spirit and the gift of teaching to help us understand His Word. The devil tries to confuse us. How tragic it is that some people radiate darkness! Everything they touch is made dark. It's so important to study and read the Word, because the unfolding of the Word brings light and understanding to the simple.

Third, *the Word is a light that shines around* (v. 105). The life of the believer is dangerous. Satan is a roaring lion and a deceiving serpent. He, the world, the flesh and other pitfalls surround us. We need God's Word (Ps. 43:3), for it guides us (Prov. 6:23; Eph. 5:8). Don't walk in this world without a lamp. And remember that human teachers are fallible. Depend ultimately on the Spirit of God (John 16:13; I John 2:20). The Author of the Bible lives inside you!

Finally, *the light shines ahead* (II Pet. 1:19). We can see what is coming: Jesus will return for His Church. Only in the Bible do we have assurance about the future, so walk in the light of His Word.

♦   ♦   ♦

The Word of God is indispensable to the believer. It shines from above, within, around and ahead of you. Avoid the hidden snares and pitfalls of the world. Improve your vision—use the Word as a lamp to your feet and a light to your path.

INVENTORY
TIME

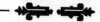

Let's take time for a spiritual inventory and ask three simple questions: What do you hate? Where are you hiding? In what do you hope? The best answers to those questions are found in verses 113 and 114. "I hate the double-minded, but I love Your law. You are my hiding place and my shield; I hope in Your word."

What do you hate? The psalmist hated vain thoughts (Ps. 119:37). *Vanity* means that which is empty, false and temporary. Thoughts are important, because what you think is what you become. "As he thinks in his heart, so is he" (Prov. 23:7). Thinking leads to doing, and doing leads to being. Sow a thought and you reap an action. Sow an action and you reap a habit. Sow a habit and you reap a character. Sow a character and you reap a destiny. If we love God's Law, we will hate the things that are contrary to His will.

Where are you hiding? "You are my hiding place and my shield." Are you hiding in the Lord? Is He your Shield? Christians have enemies who want to rob us of the blessing of God. Maybe you are hurting today. Run and hide in Jesus Christ.

In what do you hope? "I hope in Your word." If your hope is anywhere other than in God, your future is hopeless. But if you are hoping in the Word of God, the future is secure, because God is preparing the way for you. What a glory it is to be able to hope in the Word of God.

♦   ♦   ♦

Spiritual inventories force you to see if you are aligning with God's will and Word. Today, ponder the three questions found in these verses. Stay aligned to God's Word.

A PERFECT BOOK

I have a large library, and I've written a few books myself, but I cannot point to the books I've written or collected and say that everything in them is absolutely right. In fact, I've been embarrassed to find typographical, factual or other kinds of errors in the ones I've written. Only one book can carry an unqualified endorsement, and that is the Word of God. That's why the psalmist writes, "Therefore all our precepts concerning all things I consider to be right; I hate every false way" (v. 128). All of the Bible is *inspired*. That means it is God-breathed. "All Scripture is given by inspiration of God, and is profitable" (II Tim. 3:16). Inspiration is a miracle. The Spirit of God spoke through Moses, Isaiah, Matthew, Mark, Paul and others, and each put his own fingerprints on what he wrote. Yet this is God's Word.

Remember also that all of God's Word is *inerrant*. It is absolute truth. What the Bible says about history is correct. What the Bible says about prophecy is correct. Even what it says about science is correct, although it's not a science book. We don't test the Bible by the wisdom of men. We test the wisdom of men by the Bible. This means that we should live by all of Scripture. Jesus said we must live "by every word that proceeds from the mouth of God" (Matt. 4:4). Every word. Oh, what you might be missing if you are not reading the whole Word of God! Because the Bible is inspired and true, we can go to it and say, "Lord, what should I do?" He has an answer for us.

◆　　◆　　◆

The Bible is a miracle, for it is inspired by God. Live by its wisdom and truth. It leads to a miraculous life when you accept and obey it.

THE ANSWER BOOK

Have you ever faced the problems of dullness, darkness and dryness? Certain days come to us that are simply dull. There may be sameness and tameness about them. And sometimes we have to go through periods of darkness, and we wonder what in the world God is doing. Or we experience dryness—we are so spiritually dry, hungry and thirsty.

What is the answer to *dullness*? The Word of God. "Your testimonies are wonderful; therefore my soul keeps them" (v. 129). Life cannot be dull when we read and obey the Bible. It has a way of taking the ordinary things of life and making them wonderful. When our minds and hearts are filled with Scripture, everything we see appears different.

What is the answer to *darkness*? "The entrance of Your words gives light; it gives understanding to the simple" (v. 130). *Entrance* means the opening up, the expounding, the unfolding of God's Word. As Scripture is explained to us, it illuminates us. If you find yourself in darkness today, read your Bible, and it will give you light.

What is the answer to *dryness*? Sometimes we feel so dry and needy. "I opened my mouth and panted, for I longed for Your commandments" (v. 131). The Word of God is like fresh air when we feel smothered, like water when we are parched, like food when we are famished.

◆   ◆   ◆

If you are having a dull, dark or dry day, turn to the Word of God. Its truths will brighten your soul, and its promises will encourage you. God designed the Bible to meet your needs. So when the discouraging days come, feed your mind and heart with the Word.

TRIED
AND TRUE

Whenever we buy appliances, we want a guarantee that they're going to work efficiently. So we look for those special seals of approval that indicate the product has been tested. Similarly, when we buy food at the store, we want to be sure that the ingredients are safe for consumption.

God's Word has been tested and found true. It is guaranteed. "Your word is very pure [refined]; therefore Your servant loves it" (v. 140). It has gone through the furnace. Gold ore is put into a furnace to be tested. The assayer wants to know if it's really gold; likewise with silver. As we read through the Bible and through Church history, we find that the Word of God also has been through the fire. Abraham tested it and found that it was true. He left his home without knowing where he was going, but he had the Word of God, and God saw him through. Moses also tested the Word of God during those 40 years in the wilderness. Furthermore, when we read the Psalms, we see the furnaces that David went through. What was he doing? Testing the Word of God.

The Bible has been tested and has passed the test. Therefore, it can be trusted. It's pure, void of falsehoods. All the people who have trusted the Lord throughout history can say, "You can lean upon the Word of God."

◆　　◆　　◆

Have you tested the Word of God in your own life? You may be going through the furnace right now. If so, remember that one reason you endure such difficulties is so you will discover that the Word of God is pure, refined and trustworthy. Test the Word for yourself and find that it is true.

SACRIFICING SLEEP

Would you rather have the Word of God than sleep? Don't misunderstand me. We need sleep. In fact, the Bible makes it clear that God expects us to take care of our bodies, and sleep is part of that care. But the psalmist says that he would rather have the Word of God than sleep. "I rise before the dawning of the morning, and cry for help; I hope in Your word. My eyes are awake through the night watches, that I may meditate on Your word" (vv. 147,148).

Imagine being married to a person who gets up early in the morning to cry out to God and hope in His Word. Then late at night he's still awake, reading and meditating on the Scriptures.

Jesus also was up early in the morning, praying and meditating on the Word. And on the Mount of Transfiguration, Jesus, Moses and Elijah were discussing Christ's plan to die in Jerusalem. Peter, James and John were there, but they were asleep (Luke 9:32). They slept through perhaps the greatest Bible conference ever held on earth!

I'm afraid some of us have done the same thing. We've slept through the blessing. For God to bless us through His Word, we have to start each day with it. Do you set your alarm clock early enough in the morning to read the Bible? Sure, that extra half hour in bed would be pleasant. But like the psalmist, we need to say, "I'm going to anticipate the dawning of the morning. I want to spend time with God and meditate in His Word."

◆　　◆　　◆

Sacrificing sleep to meditate in the Word of God is not a loss; it's an investment in your spiritual life. The Bible contains blessings you can use the rest of the day. Let it be the key that opens and locks your day.

"PLEAD MY CASE"

Nobody enjoys going to court. I once was a character witness in a court case, and it wasn't fun. How much worse it must be for the accused. But if you must stand trial, it's good to know that somebody is there to plead your case. This is what the psalmist talks about when he says to the Lord, "Plead my cause and redeem me; revive me according to Your word" (v. 154).

The greatest Advocate we have is God. "If God is for us, who can be against us?" (Rom. 8:31). During the week we may go through difficulties. People may lie about us, and uncomfortable situations may arise because people don't like us. Sometimes we are misunderstood and criticized. You may be going through such an experience today. But God is with you in the trials of life. When you and I are on trial, He pleads and defends our case.

He can handle the dispute. When we pray to God and say, "Plead my case," He goes to work. He also can accomplish our redemption, our deliverance. We are not going to be found guilty, and we are not going to be put in jail. God sets His people free in the difficulties of life.

God can overcome your discouragement. When you've been through a tough experience, you feel discouraged and let down. But God lifts you above discouragement with His reviving power.

Today, Jesus is pleading your case in heaven. He is your Heavenly Advocate and your High Priest. He gives you the grace to stay away from temptation and sin. But if you sin, you can go to your Advocate. He will forgive you, cleanse you and plead your case.

◆　　◆　　◆

When others create difficulties for you, let God handle your dispute. He will deliver you and lift you above your discouragement. Likewise, Jesus will plead your case before the Father and forgive you.

A TREASURE TO WIN

"**I** rejoice at Your word as one who finds great treasure" (v. 162). When do we find great treasure or spoil? Usually after a battle. Thus, this verse indicates that Bible study involves a battle or conflict that starts with our own flesh.

The flesh and the natural mind don't want to be disciplined enough to read and study the Word of God. Of course, the world doesn't want this either. The world wants us to ignore Scripture and believe its own lies and vain thoughts. And Satan hates the Bible. He will do anything he can to keep us from reading, studying, meditating on and obeying the Word of God.

So the Bible can become an arena for conflict. Sometimes I'll be reading it and think of something that needs to be done, or I'll see a book out of place on my shelf and want to get up and fix it. The Devil puts distractions all around me to keep me from winning the battle of studying the Word of God.

Scripture is indeed a treasure to win. And sometimes there is a battle that must be fought first to win it. But there is also a joy to experience. "I rejoice at Your word as one who finds great treasure." It's beautiful to think your way through a portion of Scripture, to meditate, study and pray and then see the treasure that is revealed. Bible study enriches our lives. It not only helps you understand the Word but also enables you to become more like the Author.

◆　　◆　　◆

The Devil rages a battle against believers who read and study the Bible. Why? Because when you study the Word, you become more like Jesus. If you win the battle, you will gain the spoils. Let the Word enrich your life. Win the treasure and experience the joy of Bible study.

A CHAIN REACTION

Let me tell you about a spiritual chain reaction that has the power to transform our lives. It begins in verse 169: "Let my cry come before You, O Lord; give me understanding according to Your word." *Prayer leads to understanding.* This is the first part of the chain reaction. Do you pray for understanding as you read your Bible? Do you pray, "Open my eyes, that I may see wondrous things from Your law" (119:18)?

Next, *understanding leads to freedom.* "Let my supplication come before You; deliver me according to Your word" (v. 170). The psalmist asks for the freedom that comes from the truth of God. Jesus said, "You shall know the truth, and the truth shall make you free" (John 8:32). The greatest bondage in the world is the bondage to lies. If you believe a lie, you are in slavery; but if you believe God's truth, you live in freedom.

The third stage in this spiritual chain reaction is found in verse 171: "My lips shall utter praise, for You teach me Your statutes." *Freedom leads to praise.* When we understand the statutes of God, we can sing. Knowing His Word makes us want to praise Him.

Finally, *praise leads to witnessing.* "My tongue shall speak of Your word, for all Your commandments are righteousness" (v. 172). As a result of our witness, people may come to know Jesus Christ as their Savior.

✦   ✦   ✦

Read the Word of God and pray, and let the Spirit begin this life-transforming chain reaction in your life.

PEACEMAKERS

Jesus said, "Blessed are the peacemakers" (Matt. 5:9). But not everybody in this world is a peacemaker. Some people are troublemakers. They enjoy making trouble, and sometimes we have to live or work with them. That's the kind of situation the psalmist found himself in when he wrote Psalm 120. "In my distress I cried to the Lord, and He heard me. Deliver my soul, O Lord, from lying lips and from a deceitful tongue" (vv. 1,2). He continues, "My soul has dwelt too long with one who hates peace. I am for peace; but when I speak, they are for war" (vv. 6,7). That sounds like a description of Jesus when He was on earth. He was the Prince of Peace and came to bring peace to the hearts and lives of people, yet people did not want to follow or trust Him.

Ever since Cain killed Abel, we've had conflict in this world. Nations war against one another; families fall apart; and even Christians don't get along with each other. David went through conflict. Jesus went through it. And we experience it also.

Still, we are to be peacemakers—not peace breakers. After all, we have the peace of God in our hearts, and we have peace with Him— we are not at war with Him the way unsaved people are. So wherever we are, we will experience conflict but also the opportunity to bring peace.

"I am for peace," the psalmist says. Literally, the Hebrew text means, "I am peace. They are war." Each of us is either a battlefield or a blessing. Each of us is either declaring war or declaring peace. Some people enter a situation, and peace comes in with them. Other people walk in, and war follows. Let's ask God to help us in this wicked, conflicting world to be people who promote peace, not war.

✦   ✦   ✦

God's people are to be peacemakers. This world of never-ending conflict affords many opportunities for you to make peace. However, peacemaking often is not easy. Are you quick to promote peace when you confront conflict? Strive to be a blessing to others—be a peacemaker.

OUR HELPER AND KEEPER

This psalm is special to my family. When our children were young and we were all in the car ready to leave on a trip or a vacation, we often read Psalm 121 and then prayed. The children became accustomed to hearing the words, "I will lift up my eyes to the hills—from whence comes my help? My help comes from the Lord, who made heaven and earth" (vv. 1,2). God is our *Helper*. You don't have to go on a vacation or drive on a busy highway to know that.

Where does your help come from? The psalmist lifted his eyes to the hills. The most stable, secure thing the Jews knew were the mountains around Jerusalem. Then the psalmist lifted his eyes higher and said, "No, I don't get my help from the hills. I get my help from the heavens. God is my Helper." Whatever your need or task is today, your help will come from the Lord, the Creator of the heavens and the earth. A God big enough to make this world and keep it going is big enough to help you with your problems today.

God is also our *Keeper*. "He will not allow your foot to be moved; He who keeps you will not slumber. Behold, He who keeps Israel shall neither slumber nor sleep" (vv. 3,4). This is a dangerous world we live in. Enemies would like to attack and destroy us. But as we walk in the will of God and depend on His power, He is there as our Keeper and Preserver. "The Lord shall preserve you from all evil" (v. 7). This verse doesn't say we won't have pain. It doesn't say we will never suffer or sorrow. Though we may be hurt, we won't be harmed. "He shall preserve your soul. The Lord shall preserve your going out and your coming in from this time forth, and even forevermore" (vv. 7,8).

◆　　◆　　◆

God is your Helper and Keeper. No matter where your path in life leads, if you walk in His will, He will preserve you. Walk with confidence today. You have a Helper, a Keeper and a Preserver, who will see you through.

A PLACE OF PRAYER AND PRAISE

Are you glad when it's time to go to the house of God to worship? Are you really happy when, on the Lord's Day or any other day, you can go to church? The psalmist was. "I was glad when they said to me, 'Let us go into the house of the Lord'" (v. 1). We worship the Lord privately as well. I trust that every day you read His Word and pray and worship Him. But Christians belong to each other. We are the sheep of God's flock. We're the children in His family, and we should want to worship Him together.

The house of God is a *place for praise*. Verse 4 talks about the tribes of Israel going up to give thanks to the name of the Lord. We also go into the house of God to praise Him, and how much we have to praise Him for! Charles Spurgeon used to say that Christians are prone to write their complaints in marble and their blessings in the sand. How soon we forget what God has done for us. The next time you go to church, praise Him for all He has done.

God's house is also a *place for prayer*. In verse 6 the psalmist says to pray for the peace of Jerusalem. I hope you are praying for God's people, Israel, and for peace in Jerusalem. I hope you also are praying for peace in your congregation, in your community and for those who are in authority. We are also to pray for prosperity—the riches of grace and spiritual blessing. "May they prosper who love you" (v. 6). The psalmist also prays for God's people. "For the sake of my brethren and companions, I will now say, 'Peace be within you'" (v. 8). We should be praying for God's people and seeking good for them. "Because of the house of the Lord our God I will seek your good" (v. 9).

◆　　◆　　◆

Do not take your privilege of worship for granted. God's people should gather to praise Him and to pray to Him. When you do this, you become a vehicle through which God can give His peace to others.

LIFT YOUR EYES

If the outlook in your life is disturbing, try the uplook. That's what the psalmist did. "Unto You I lift up my eyes, O You who dwell in the heavens" (v. 1).

What does it mean to lift your eyes to the Lord? First, it means to *acknowledge His sovereignty*. We lift our eyes because He is higher than we are. Isaiah focused his eyes on the throne of God and saw Him "high and lifted up" in the temple (Isa. 6:1). He is sovereign. He is the Master; we are the servants. He is the Creator; we are the creatures. He is the Heavenly Father; we are the children.

Second, we *admit His sufficiency*. "Behold, as the eyes of servants look to the hand of their masters, as the eyes of a maid to the hand of her mistress, so our eyes look to the Lord our God, until He has mercy on us" (v. 2). We look to Him because of His sufficiency. Whatever we need, He is able to provide. "My God shall supply all your need according to His riches in glory by Christ Jesus" (Phil. 4:19).

Third, when we lift up our eyes to the Lord, we can *accept His generosity*. "Have mercy on us, O Lord, have mercy on us!" the psalmist prays in verse 3. God is generous, the Giver of every good and perfect gift. "If you then, being evil, know how to give good gifts to your children, how much more will your Father who is in heaven give good things to those who ask Him!" (Matt. 7:11).

◆ ◆ ◆

Acknowledge the sovereignty of God today. He is in control. Recognize His sufficiency. He can give you what you need for this day. Then accept His generosity. He enjoys giving to those who trust Him and glorify Him in all that they do.

HE BREAKS
THE SNARE

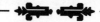

"If God is for us, who can be against us?" Paul asked in Romans 8:31, and we know the answer. No one can be against us if God is for us. That's the theme of Psalm 124. "If it had not been the Lord who was on our side, when men rose up against us, then they would have swallowed us alive, when their wrath was kindled against us" (vv. 2,3).

Because God is on our side, men cannot devour us. The psalmist compares his enemies to ferocious lions or bears who might come down upon him and eat him. There are people who would like to "eat us up" also. When men are determined to devour you, remember that God will stop them.

But it may not be that men are devouring you. Perhaps circumstances are drowning you. "Then the waters would have overwhelmed us, the stream would have gone over our soul; then the swollen waters would have gone over our soul" (vv. 4,5). Life seems to drown us and sink us as the waters rush over our souls. But because God is for us, circumstances cannot drown us.

The psalmist changes the picture from swallowing and drowning to escaping from a trap. "Our soul has escaped as a bird from the snare of the fowlers; the snare is broken, and we have escaped" (v. 7). God not only keeps us from drowning and being devoured, He keeps us from being deceived and trapped by the Devil. He doesn't just set us free; He breaks the snare. In other words, the Devil can't trap us again as long as we are following the Lord.

Don't let life devour you. Don't let life drown you. Don't let the Devil deceive you. If God is for you, who can be against you?

♦   ♦   ♦

On those days when you feel overwhelmed by people or circumstances, you must never forget the truth that God is on your side. You have the promises of His Word. Look past your circumstances and place your confidence in God alone. He will protect you.

LIKE A
MOUNTAIN

"**A**s the mountains surround Jerusalem, so the Lord surrounds His people from this time forth and forever" (v. 2). We don't have to know much about geography to understand what the psalmist is saying. It's a declaration we can believe and put to work in our own lives today. God is compared to many things in the Bible. For example, "our God is a consuming fire" (Heb. 12:29). Or, "God is our refuge and strength, a very present help in trouble" (Ps. 46:1). Here the psalmist says God is like the mountains surrounding Jerusalem. That was the most special city to God and the Jewish people, and it still is. And when the psalmist looked at the mountains surrounding the city, he said, "That's the way God is."

How is God like a mountain? First, a mountain has *stability*. When the psalmist was a little boy, he saw the mountains surrounding Jerusalem. When he became a young man, those mountains were still there. When he grew older, the mountains were there, and the mountains are still there today. Likewise with God. He is stable, dependable. He doesn't change. God is the same yesterday, today and forever (Heb. 13:8).

Second, a mountain offers *security*. God surrounds and guards us. He is like Mount Zion to us. Verse 1 says, "Those who trust in the Lord are like Mount Zion." In other words, God can make you to be like a mountain also—stable and secure because He is your Refuge and Strength.

Therefore, we should trust Him. Those who trust in the Lord have stability and security. They have all they ever will need. "Do good, O Lord, to those who are good, and to those who are upright in their hearts" (v. 4).

♦   ♦   ♦

The next time you need a refuge, remember that God has a special way of caring for His people. The strength and security God gives His people is solid and unchanging. Trust Him.

REAP IN JOY

Did you know that each one of us is a sower? Each of us today is sowing seed that will produce a harvest. Some people are sowing to the flesh. Paul tells us in Galatians 6:8 that those who sow to the flesh will reap corruption. Some are sowing discord among the brethren. Some are sowing lies. Psalm 126 tells us to be careful what and how we sow, because we're the ones who will reap the harvest.

Notice what the psalmist says: "Those who sow in tears shall reap in joy. He who continually goes forth weeping, bearing seed for sowing, shall doubtless come again with rejoicing, bringing his sheaves with him" (vv. 5,6). God's people weep as they sow, but they will reap in joy. As a Christian, you are to sow the seed of the Word of God by sowing good deeds, truth and His love. You plant the seed that produces the fruit of the Spirit—love, joy, peace, long-suffering, kindness, goodness, faithfulness, gentleness and self-control.

Life is often serious and difficult. That may cause us to sow with tears, but we will reap in joy. Non-Christians are not like that. The Devil's crowd goes out and sows with laughter. Oh, they have a good time. But when the harvest comes, they will reap in sorrow.

Each of us has a decision to make: Are we going to get pleasures now or wait until the harvest of the Holy Spirit? "Do not be deceived, God is not mocked; for whatever a man sows, that he will also reap" (Gal. 6:7). In fact, we will reap more than what we've sown, because seed multiplies.

◆　◆　◆

If today you are living for the pleasures of sin, the harvest will bring weeping. But if you're living for the will of God, the harvest will bring joy. What kind of harvest will you have? Ask God to help you sow the seeds that will bring His fruit in your life and in the lives of others.

HAPPY HARVESTERS

The context of this psalm is II Kings 19 and Isaiah 37, when Hezekiah, king of Judah, was attacked by Sennacharib and the Assyrian forces. The enemy forces surrounded Jerusalem, so the Jews had to protect their food supply. They already had lost an entire season of sowing and reaping. Grain was precious. When the people went back to their farms after being delivered, they had to make a decision. Should they use the grain to feed the children, or should they sow it? The farmer wept because his sustenance had to go into the ground (v. 6).

All of us are sowers and reapers. What must we sow to be happy harvesters? First, *sow the seed of the Gospel.* The Bible contains many pictures of witnessing (II Cor. 5:20; Zech. 3:2; Matt. 4:19; 5:14). Reaching people with the Gospel is like farming. It requires cooperation, because one sows and another reaps. Are you a part of the harvest? We need to pray for the harvesters. You may be weeping today over unsaved loved ones, but one day you will rejoice (Gal. 6:9). Those who sow the Gospel will be happy harvesters.

Second, *sow your wealth to the glory of God.* The way we use our money is like sowing seed. We reap in the measure that we sow (II Cor. 9:6-11). Many people are wasting money on foolish things, while missionaries are waiting for support, and churches are waiting to be built or expanded. Paul says we can be a happy harvester if we sow the seed bountifully.

Third, *sow to the Holy Spirit of God* (Gal. 6:6-8; 5:16-23). How do we do this? We take the things of the Spirit and put them into our hearts. When we memorize and meditate on the Word of God (Ps. 119:11), we cultivate a spiritual harvest. The heart is like a garden, so we must weed it. That's repentance. Take time to be holy, to pray, to meditate on the Word and to plant the seed in your heart.

♦   ♦   ♦

You are sowing today in all you do; be sure you sow the right seed.

INHERITANCE FROM GOD

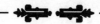

feel like weeping when I think about the tragedy of more than 1.5 million babies murdered in their mothers' wombs in the United States every year. Abortion has turned the womb into a tomb.

I wonder what those presiding doctors and nurses would think if they read Psalm 127. "Behold, children are a heritage from the Lord, the fruit of the womb is His reward. Like arrows in the hand of a warrior, so are the children of one's youth. Happy is the man who has his quiver full of them; they shall not be ashamed, but shall speak with their enemies in the gate" (vv. 3-5). The psalmist tells us that children are wealth—a heritage and inheritance from the Lord.

What are we to do with wealth? First, we *accept it*. When our children come to us, we accept them. They are God's gift to us, a treasure. We protect our wealth, and we ought to protect our children. It's so wrong that many are not protected before they are born.

Then we are to *invest it*. We train our children, teaching them to live righteously. Their lives become as invested money, and the dividends start to return. One of the great delights of getting older is seeing those godly dividends. Children enrich our lives.

But children are also weapons—"like arrows in the hand of a warrior" (v. 4). Who's going to fight God's battles if Christians don't bring children into this world and raise them to know the Lord? Whenever God wanted to do something great, he brought a baby into the world—Moses, Samuel, David, John the Baptist and our Lord Jesus Christ. In this world of sin, when truth is being attacked on every side, we need to raise our children to be able to stand with authority and say, "Thus says the Lord."

♦ ♦ ♦

Children are God's blessing but also a great responsibility. Ask God for wisdom as you invest in and train your children or other's children. Prepare them for the ministries He has for them and rejoice at the inheritance He has given you.

THE BLESSINGS OF FEAR

We don't hear much these days about the fear of the Lord. All too often the Lord is looked upon only as a heavenly friend, someone who walks with us and smiles on us constantly. But verse 1 says, "Blessed is every one who fears the Lord."

What does it mean to fear the Lord? It means to be in reverential awe of Him. It means we don't tempt Him. We don't jest with Him. We don't try to make Him do things He will not do. The Israelites did not fear the Lord. They tempted Him. They played with His Law and tried to see how close they could get to the world. So God had to discipline them.

God blesses us in three areas of our life when we truly fear Him. First, He will bless us in *our walk*. "Blessed is every one who fears the Lord, who walks in His ways" (v. 1). This means that our conduct and our character become holy.

Second, God blesses us in *our work*. "When you eat the labor of your hands, you shall be happy, and it shall be well with you" (v. 2) Some people are unhappy in their work. But if we are obedient to God, we are doing His work no matter what our occupation is and therefore can rejoice in it. When we fear the Lord, we can go to work and be happy.

Third, God blesses us in *our homes*. "Your wife shall be like a fruitful vine in the very heart of your house, your children like olive plants all around your table" (v. 3). This does not mean that everybody is going to have a family, let alone a big family. It does mean that you'll be a blessing to your family. "Behold, thus shall the man be blessed who fears the Lord" (v. 4).

♦   ♦   ♦

Never become so "familiar" with God that you lose your reverence for Him. He is your personal God, but He deserves your awe and respect. The fear of the Lord is the key to His blessings. Fear Him. Walk in His ways and receive His blessings.

PLOWS OF PAIN

Verse 3 is a vivid description of personal suffering: "The plowers plowed on my back; they made their furrows long." Many other pictures of personal suffering are found in the Word of God: going through the storm, going through the furnace, going through a battle and carrying a burden. Why would the psalmist use plowing as a picture of personal suffering?

For one thing, he felt as if people were treating him like dirt. They were saying, "You're just like a dirty field, and we're going to plow right up this field, and we don't care how you feel." If we live for Jesus, we can expect people to treat us the way they treated Him. They treated Him like dirt.

The central truth in this picture is that plowing is preparation for a harvest. When people are treating you like dirt, when the plows of criticism and accusation dig in your back, remember: God is preparing you for a harvest. What kind of a harvest? That depends on the kind of seed you plant. If you plant seeds of revenge and hatred and malice, saying, "I'll get even with them someday," the harvest will be bitter. But if you plant the seeds of the Word of God, letting love and peace and patience reign in your heart, you can say with the psalmist that the Lord is righteous—He will resolve this problem. Then the harvest will be one of blessing, as in verse 8: "The blessing of the Lord be upon you; we bless you in the name of the Lord!"

♦ ♦ ♦

If you want a harvest in your life, you must plow, plant and water. When people treat you like dirt, when the trials of life go right through your life like a plow, get ready for the harvest. God has a harvest of blessing for you today, so remember to plant the right seed.

WAITING
AND HOPING

The next time you feel at rock bottom, read Psalm 130. "Out of the depths I have cried to You, O Lord" (v. 1). Three basic requests in this psalm echo the concerns in our hearts today.

First, the psalmist says, "Lord, hear my voice!" (v. 2). Why? "I can't swim; I am in the deep waters, and they are coming over my head. I am drowning, and I'm afraid I can't make it." No matter how far down you may go or feel, God always hears you.

Then he says, "If You, Lord, should mark iniquities, O Lord, who could stand? But there is forgiveness with You, that You may be feared" (vv. 3,4). We can't stand before God in the courtroom of His justice; we are helpless. Only Jesus Christ can stand there, because only He is perfect. But He stands with us; He's our Savior. God not only hears us when we are down, but He holds us. He says, "I forgive you. You've trusted my Son; you've confessed your sin; and now you can stand before Me." The psalmist expresses his confidence in this truth: "I wait for the Lord, my soul waits, and in His word I do hope. My soul waits for the Lord more than those who watch for the morning" (vv. 5,6).

Next he asks, "O Israel, hope in the Lord; for with the Lord there is mercy, and with Him is abundant redemption" (v. 7). We are sometimes like soldiers in the watchtower, waiting for the light. We can't see, but God can see, and there is a future hope for His people.

◆   ◆   ◆

Place your confidence in the promises of God's Word. No matter how down you may feel, God hears you, holds you and helps you. Turn to Him; He'll see you through.

A METHOD
FOR MATURITY

One day King David was walking through the palace, and he heard a child crying. What was going on? The child was being weaned. The mother was saying, "Now, my child, you are growing up, and it is time for you to be weaned." The child was saying, "You don't love me; you hate me. If you loved me, you wouldn't do this." Then David went to his desk, got his pen and wrote Psalm 131.

The problem with too many of us is that we have grown old without growing up—we still need to be weaned. The weaning process is important. God's goal for your life is maturity, and His method for maturity is weaning. He has to wean us away from things we think are important.

How do you convince a child that he doesn't want to be attached to his mother for the rest of his life? Love him? Yes! But he must grow up, step out and be a man. And so it is with us. God has to wean us away from the things of the world, from the cheap toys that we hold on to. He wants to give us the best, and His desire in weaning is our submission. The weaned child of Psalm 131 was not losing; he was gaining. He was moving out into a larger life. Likewise, God has to take things away from our lives, not because they are bad, but because they are keeping us from the best.

The next time you whimper and cry because God takes something away from you, remember: He might be weaning you. He might be saying, "Get closer to me. Step out into a life of maturity and let's go together."

◆　　◆　　◆

God wants His children to grow into mature believers and eventually to become like His Son. When He decides to wean you from something in your life, be an obedient child. Let Him prepare you and develop you for what He has in store for you.

THE NEXT BEST THING

What is the consuming ambition of your life? What is the dream that fills your mind and heart? King David's dream was to build a temple for the Lord. He tells us about it in this psalm. I wish more people had this same wonderful ambition—to be builders, not destroyers.

During much of his life, David was a soldier. He defended Israel from her enemies and brought about peace in the land. But then he wanted to turn from battling to building. He wanted to exchange the sword for a trowel. He said, "I am not going to have any sleep until I find a place for God to dwell."

But God did not allow David to fulfill this high and holy ambition. Solomon, his son, built the temple instead. David was disappointed at first but then said, "If this is the will of God, I'll accept it." Then he did the most wonderful thing: he helped the next generation build the temple. David provided the plans and millions of dollars in gold, silver, precious stones, bronze and iron.

We may not fulfill all of our plans and ambitions, but we can do the next best thing. If God doesn't let us accomplish our goals, let's help somebody else meet his goals. Let's pay the bill. Let's give our wisdom. Let's encourage. We can't do everything, but we can do something.

◆　　◆　　◆

If your dreams are not fulfilled in the will of God, help fulfill someone else's dreams by sharing your talents and resources. When you're concerned more with God's glory and not with who gets the credit, He can use you in more ways to accomplish His purposes. Let God use you in the ways He sees best.

A HOUSE
FOR DAVID

God did not permit King David to build Him a house. Instead, He did just the opposite; He built a house for David. God said, "David, I am not going to build you a physical house but a house made of people. There will always be one of your descendants on the throne of Israel."

He also said some things about David's children. "If your sons will keep My covenant and My testimony which I shall teach them, their sons also shall sit upon your throne forevermore. For the Lord has chosen Zion; He has desired it for His habitation" (vv. 12,13).

There is an application here for God's children. He chose us in Christ before the foundation of the world (Eph. 1:4). Jesus said, "You did not choose Me, but I chose you" (John 15:16). What a high and holy privilege! We were chosen to be God's children. "Beloved, now we are children of God" (I John 3:2). What a wonderful calling! Paul tells us we also reign in life (Rom. 5:17). God wants us to reign as kings, even as David's children did. We reign through obedience and holiness.

God wants us to reign in righteousness for His glory. Because we are His children through faith in Jesus Christ, we are seated with Christ in the heavenlies. Therefore, let's be clothed with salvation. Let's shout for joy!

◆　　◆　　◆

Someday believers will reign with Christ in His kingdom. But today He wants you to reign in life. Do you reign in life with Christ? As you obey the Word of God and keep your heart pure, you become a king. Don't live beneath your spiritual station in life. Be a king!

THE UNITY OF THE SPIRIT

"**B**ehold, how good and how pleasant it is for brethren to dwell together in unity!" (v. 1). This is as true today as when it was written centuries ago. We would expect brothers and sisters to dwell together in unity. After all, they share the same nature because they have the same parents. Until they move out, they live at the same address and eat at the same table.

We also would expect God's people to dwell together in unity—but not uniformity. My wife and I currently have seven grand-children. We can tell that they all belong to the same family, but each is an individual. Similarly, God does not want uniformity among His children; He wants unity.

The psalmist gives us two descriptions of spiritual unity. "It is like the precious oil upon the head, running down on the beard, the beard of Aaron, running down on the edge of his garments" (v. 2). Over his chest, his heart, Aaron wore a breastplate that had twelve stones—one for each of the tribes of Israel. The oil bathed all of those stones, and they all became one in that anointing oil. That's a picture of the Holy Spirit of God, who baptizes us into the Body of Jesus Christ and gives us spiritual unity. Unity is not something we create; it's something God gives us.

Spiritual unity also is fruitful like dew. "It is like the dew of Hermon" (v. 3). With the mountain dew comes God's blessing.

We should strive to maintain the unity of the Spirit. Ask God to help you be a part of the answer, not a part of the problem.

◆　　◆　　◆

As a believer in the Body of Christ, you must do your part to dwell in unity. The Holy Spirit helps you live in unity with your brothers and sisters in Christ. Pray for the fragrant oil and fruitful dew of spiritual unity in your life today.

NIGHT SHIFT

Years ago when I was attending seminary, I worked the night shift on occasion. It paid a little more money than the day shift, but I was a bit lonely. If you've ever had to work the night shift, you will appreciate Psalm 134.

God never slumbers or sleeps. Therefore, we can serve and praise Him any time of day. The psalmist says there were priests who prayed and praised God in His temple at night. There was a constant repetition of praise and prayer from the temple.

We can bless the Lord in the night seasons. It's not easy when we are going through the nighttime experiences of life to lift our hands and bless the Lord. But He does give us songs in the night. Paul and Silas were able to lift their hearts in praise to God while in the Philippian jail (Acts 16). They were on the night shift. They knew that God was awake, so they blessed Him, and He sent deliverance. We can get some strange blessings in the night seasons, for God speaks to us in different ways. Others may not see your praise at night, but God sees and hears.

◆　　◆　　◆

Whether you are in the sunshine or in the darkness, whether you are serving on the day shift or the night shift, remember that you are serving the Lord. Because He never slumbers or sleeps, He hears your prayer and praise at all times, and He will bless you.

GREAT GOVERNMENT

"**P**raise the Lord! Praise the name of the Lord; praise Him, O you servants of the Lord!" (v. 1). That's the way Psalm 135 begins. It's strange that the psalmist has to instruct us to shout hallelujah, but he goes on to tell us why.

First, *we should praise God because of His goodness.* "Praise the Lord, for the Lord is good; sing praises to His name, for it is pleasant" (v. 3). We sometimes take God's goodness for granted. He is good, and His goodness is unsearchable. God shows us His goodness in both material and spiritual blessings.

Second, *we should praise the Lord for His grace.* "For the Lord has chosen Jacob for Himself, Israel for His special treasure" (v. 4). Israel was not a treasure before God chose her. After He chose her, she became precious. God also chose us. Jesus said, "You did not choose me, but I chose you" (John 15:16). God showed His grace by choosing us to be His children.

Third, *we should praise Him for His greatness.* "For I know that the Lord is great, and our Lord is above all gods" (v. 5). What god is like our God?

Finally, the psalmist tells us *we should praise God for His government.* "Whatever the Lord pleases He does, in heaven and in earth, in the seas and in all deep places" (v. 6). He then describes God's sovereignty in creation and in history.

◆　　◆　　◆

Whatever your situation, you can stop and praise the Lord for His goodness, His grace, His greatness and His government. He is managing all of creation and all of history to bring about His purposes. Let God use you to do His work.

THE COST OF
IDOLATRY

Some things in the Bible are so important that God repeats them. The last verses in Psalm 135 parallel Psalm 115. These two psalms describe the dead idols of other nations. The psalmist says, "The idols of the nations are silver and gold, the work of men's hands. They have mouths, but they do not speak; eyes they have, but they do not see; they have ears, but they do not hear; nor is there any breath in their mouths. Those who make them are like them; so is everyone who trusts in them" (vv. 15-18). Here we see the folly of idolatry—worshiping silver and gold, the work of men's hands. But that's going on today, isn't it? Many people worship the works of their hands.

How do you know what you are worshiping? The thing you work for, sacrifice for and live for is your god. For some people, it's money. For others, it's possessions. With still others, it's ambition or people. The psalmist shows us how foolish this is. Idols have mouths, yet they can't make promises. But our God speaks to us, and He gives us promises in His Word. Idols have eyes, but they cannot see. They offer no protection. But "the eyes of the Lord are on the righteous" (Ps. 34:15). God's eyes are watching us every moment of the day. He never goes to sleep. He cares for His children. Idols have ears, but they cannot hear your prayers. If you talk to an idol, you are talking to yourself. But God's ears are open to our cries. He says, "Call to Me, and I will answer you" (Jer. 33:3).

The saddest thing about idolatry is that we become like the god we worship. "Those who make them are like them; so is everyone who trusts in them" (v. 18). But if we worship the true and living God, we become like Him. We are transformed into the image of Jesus Christ.

✦　　✦　　✦

Be careful what you worship. Satan wants you to substitute many idols for the Lord. Place no gods before Him; worship Him only. Today, get rid of any idols that might prevent your worship of the Lord.

ENDURING MERCY

Psalm 136 magnifies the mercy of God. Every verse ends with the refrain, "For His mercy endures forever." I would like to have heard this psalm sung in the Jewish temple. One group of priests would say, "Oh, give thanks to the Lord, for He is good!" (v. 1). Then the priests on the other side of the court would answer, "For His mercy endures forever."

Mercy and grace go together. God, in His grace, gives me what I don't deserve, and God, in His mercy, does not give me what I do deserve. His mercy endures forever, and our response should be thanksgiving and praise.

Praise the Lord for His wonders. "To Him who alone does great wonders, for His mercy endures forever" (v. 4). "His name will be called Wonderful" (Isa. 9:6). Jesus Christ said and did wonderful things. When God touches a life, it becomes filled with wonder. I think of Peter, Andrew, James and John—men who would have remained ordinary fishermen had they not met Jesus. They went to a wedding at Cana, and wonders happened. They went to funerals, and wonders happened.

Praise God for His wisdom. "To Him who by wisdom made the heavens" (v. 5). The God who created the universe has the wisdom to run it, and He has the wisdom you need for your life. "If any of you lacks wisdom, let him ask of God" (James 1:5). He'll guide you.

Praise Him for His works. "To Him who laid out the earth above the waters" (v. 6). Let's worship God today because of His wonders. Let's seek His guidance because of His wisdom. Let's enjoy all that He gives to us through His manifold creation.

◆   ◆   ◆

You would not be saved were it not for God's grace and mercy. Never take those two gifts for granted. Do you devote time to praising and thanking Him for what He does in your life?

A COMPLETE HISTORY

Israel is the only nation for which we have a complete history. We know how it started, how it grew, where it is today and where it will be for the rest of history—thanks to the Word of God.

In Psalm 136 the psalmist reviewed Israel's history. As he looked, he saw the mercy of God. He performed three marvelous ministries for the Israelites: He brought them out; He brought them through; and He brought them in. God wants to care for us in the same way today.

God brought Israel *out of the slavery* and the bondage of Egypt (vv. 10-12). That's redemption. He then brought them *through* the Red Sea and the wilderness. Finally, He brought them *into the Promised Land*. The old generation died off in their unbelief, but the new generation entered in with great glory and power and claimed their inheritance.

God wants to do this for us today. He wants to free us from sin's slavery. He wants to bring us through the deep water and wilderness experiences of life, that He might bring us into the inheritance that He has for us. Our history is already complete with God.

✦　　✦　　✦

Today you might be facing some seemingly impossible situation in your life. Trust God to open the way for you. Let Him bring you out of your bondage and through your difficulty and bring you into your inheritance.

FINDING YOUR SONG

One of test of your spiritual condition is whether or not you really have a song. Psalm 137 tells us about people who lost their song. They lost it because they lost their sanctity—they repeatedly sinned against the Lord.

Here's the record: "By the rivers of Babylon, there we sat down, yea, we wept when we remembered Zion. We hung our harps upon the willows in the midst of it. For there those who carried us away captive required of us a song, and those who plundered us required of us mirth, saying, 'Sing us one of the songs of Zion!'" (vv. 1-3). Can't you just picture the Babylonians taunting the Jews? The Jews responded, "How shall we sing the Lord's song in a foreign land?" (v. 4).

It can be done. They were there because of their disobedience, and they had lost their song. But even in a foreign land, we can have a song to the Lord. Jesus came down to earth from heaven, and He had a song. In fact, the night on which He was betrayed, He sang a song of Zion in the upper room (Matt. 26:30).

When you are not walking with the Lord, you lose your song and start living on memories. "If I forget you, O Jerusalem, let my right hand forget her skill! If I do not remember you . . . if I do not exalt Jerusalem above my chief joy" (vv. 5,6). Are you living on memories, or are you daily receiving blessings from the Lord?

In verses 7-9 we find the Jews looking for revenge. This is understandable from a human perspective, for they had seen their babies dashed against the stones. So they pray, "Lord, render to them what they deserve. You are the Judge. You remember them." But as Christians, we must think first of forgiveness.

✦   ✦   ✦

If you are without your song, living on memories and looking for revenge, you are not walking closely with the Lord. Your first task is to get that song back by confessing your sins to the Lord. God will restore the joy of your salvation.

A PERFECT PURPOSE

"**T**he Lord will perfect that which concerns me" (v. 8). God has a purpose for each of our lives. We are not numbers in a computer; He knows our names. In fact, He has numbered all the hairs on our heads (Matt 10:30). God knows our needs today. We are His personal concern, the work of His hands.

When does God perfect that which concerns us? When can we expect Him to work in our lives? First, *when we praise Him*. Verse 1 says, "I will praise You with my whole heart." Verse 2 reads, "I will worship toward Your holy temple, and praise Your name." When we take time to worship and praise God, He can perfect that which concerns us. But if we go our own way, we lose that special blessing from God.

God also perfects that which concerns us *when we pray to Him*. "In the day when I cried out, You answered me, and made me bold with strength in my soul" (v. 3). It doesn't say God changed the outside circumstances. Instead, He changed the psalmist on the inside. When we worship and cry out to the Lord, He can work on our behalf.

Finally, God perfects that which concerns us *when we glorify Him*. "All the kings of the earth shall praise You, O Lord, when they hear the words of Your mouth. Yes, they shall sing of the ways of the Lord, for great is the glory of the Lord" (vv. 4,5). Praising Him to others should be a natural part of our conversations.

◆　　◆　　◆

The God of the universe desires to work personally in your life. When you worship the Lord by praying to Him, glorifying Him, witnessing for Him and submitting to Him, He works on your behalf. If you need a reviving blessing today, turn to Him. He will give it.

RIGHT THOUGHTS

Some people never think about God. They live and die as strangers in His world. Others think wrong thoughts about Him. They live and die in the shadows of superstition and confusion. Still others think right thoughts about God, but somehow it makes no difference in their lives. They live and die disappointed and defeated. Psalm 139 was written by a man who had right thoughts about God that made a difference. He lived with confidence, security and fulfillment. He submitted to God. Let's look at the four discoveries David made as he thought about God and the difference He made in his life.

God *knows everything* (vv. 1-6). Theologians call this God's *omniscience*. God knows you personally. We find nearly 50 personal pronouns throughout the psalm. He knows your name, nature, needs and even the number of hairs on your head. He knows you intimately, including your actions and your thoughts. He knows you sovereignly.

God *is everywhere* (vv. 7-12). You cannot flee from Him. This is a beautiful description of His *omnipresence*. "Where shall I go to get away from God?" Jonah asked this and never got an answer. You cannot hide even in darkness. God is in all places at all times (v. 11).

God *can do anything* (vv. 13-18). He is *omnipotent*. David says the greatest marvel of all is human birth. God can make life. He gives each baby the genetic structure He wants him or her to have. If you leave God out of your life, you will never fulfill what you were born for.

God *can guide your life* (vv. 19-24). You dare not fight against Him. David said he was going to serve God—a decision that led to dedication (vv. 23,24). When we put the whole psalm together, we discover a man who knows God. You, too, can know God through Jesus Christ (John 14:9; 17:3).

✦ ✦ ✦

God knows everything about you. Be open and honest with Him, and He can lead and bless you. Strive to do His will. God made you and wants to fulfill in your life that for which He made you.

INTIMATE KNOWLEDGE

Psalm 139 is a short course in theology, the science of God. In the first six verses the psalmist says, "God knows everything; don't try to fool Him."

"O Lord, You have searched me and known me" (v. 1). In these first six verses we find 13 personal pronouns. God knows us *personally*. Few people can recognize us in a crowd, but God does. With Him there are no crowds, only individuals. At times you may feel lonely and say, "Nobody knows me. Nobody cares about me." But God knows you intimately. He knows your every action and thought. "You know my sitting down and my rising up; You understand my thought afar off" (v. 2). He also knows your words. "For there is not a word on my tongue, but behold, O Lord, you know it altogether" (v. 4). The psalmist is saying, "He's behind me. He's before me. He's laid His hand upon me. He is sovereign."

What should be our response to this? Simple. "Praise the Lord!" I am glad that my Father in heaven understands me personally and intimately and that His hand is upon me. This doesn't make me afraid; it gives me confidence. What an encouragement to know that our Father in heaven knows all about us—where we are and what we're doing. Of course, we don't want to be in the wrong place, doing the wrong thing. But if the child of God is walking in the will of God, he has the confidence that His Father in heaven is caring for Him and knows his every need.

✦   ✦   ✦

God has a thorough knowledge of you. That gives you all the more reason to pray honestly to the Lord and walk uprightly before Him. His knowledge of you ought to encourage you and make you confident. Thank Him that His intimate knowledge of you leads to His complete care for you.

HERE, THERE, EVERYWHERE

Have you ever tried to run away from God? Don't try; it can't be done. "Where can I go from Your Spirit? Or where can I flee from Your presence? If I ascend into heaven, You are there. If I make my bed in hell, behold, You are there. If I take the wings of the morning, and dwell in the uttermost parts of the sea, even there Your hand shall lead me, and Your right hand shall hold me" (vv. 7-10).

No matter where we go in the will of God, He is there. Why should we flee from Him? Why should we try to find height or depth, east or west, darkness or light? "If I say, 'Surely the darkness shall fall on me,' even the night shall be light about me; indeed, the darkness shall not hide from You, but the night shines as the day; the darkness and the light are both alike to You" (vv. 11,12). Sometimes I've found myself in dark places and have wondered, "Does God know?" He indeed knows. If we sin, we go out into the darkness, but God sees us. And sometimes when we are walking with the Lord, we still find ourselves in darkness. But that darkness is as light to God.

God is everywhere and sees everything. Rather than flee *from* Him, we should flee *to* Him. "God is our refuge and strength, a very present help in trouble" (Ps. 46:1). Nothing can separate us from the love of God—neither height nor depth, east nor west, darkness nor light (Rom. 8:38,39).

✦　　✦　　✦

God promises to "never leave you nor forsake you" (Heb. 13:5). The next time you go through dark days, remember that God knows your problems and needs. You may take refuge in Him; He will see you through.

FLEE
TO GOD

Years ago, A. W. Tozer wrote, "The essence of idolatry is the entertainment of thoughts about God that are unworthy of Him." God is much greater than we are, and our thoughts of Him must be great thoughts. David's thoughts of God in this psalm center on His omnipresence. As we read his words, we can answer three simple questions.

Can we flee from God? The psalmist says no. Height and depth will not enable us to run away from God. Life has its ups and downs. God is there when we're up, and He's there when we're down. In essence, David says in verse 9, "If at sunrise, I could jump on one of the sunbeams, if I could fly across the sky from east to west at 186,000 miles per second, when I got there, You'd be there already, Lord." The word *dwell* means "to arrest." Even if we try to run away, God's hand is going to catch us and lead us.

Who would flee from God? Those who are afraid of Him. Among those in the Bible who tried to flee Him are Adam and Eve, Jonah and Judas Iscariot. No true believer would ever try to run away from God. As believers, we have fled *to* God, and we are hiding *in* Him.

What are the blessings of fleeing to God? If you have problems, difficulties and sin, run to God. The Lord's presence kept Paul going during difficult times. Like the apostle, we need to discover that no matter how difficult a situation is, the Lord is with us. When we hide in the Lord, we receive courage, encouragement, comfort and strength for the battle. Respond to God's invitation: "Come to Me, and I will give you rest" (Matt. 11:28). Hide in the Lord. He's the only place of safety and satisfaction.

◆   ◆   ◆

God's omnipresence is a blessing to those who hide in Him. Perhaps you have tried to run from the Lord. Return to Him; He is always ready to receive you when you've gone astray. Whatever difficulty you may be facing, don't hide from life—hide in the Lord. He will give you strength to fight the battle.

WONDERFULLY MADE

"**I** will praise You, for I am fearfully and wonderfully made" (v. 14). The psalmist is talking about the miracle of conception and birth. It's an amazing story. "For You have formed my inward parts; You have covered me in my mother's womb. . . . Marvelous are Your works, and that my soul knows very well" (vv. 13,14).

Someone defined a baby as something that gets you up at night and gets you down during the day. That may be true, but so are the words of poet Carl Sandburg: "A baby is God's opinion that the world should go on." When we contemplate human birth, our first response ought to be *reverence*. The God of the galaxies is the God who is concerned about the color of a baby's hair and the genetic structure of a yet unborn child. We ought to bow in reverence before God and worship Him, because each individual child is a part of His handiwork. We don't understand why some children are born handicapped or exceptional in some areas. But God knows.

Our next response should be *confidence*. We can trust God because He made us as we are. Instead of complaining about what we're not, we can gratefully accept from God what we are. He knew all about each of us before we were born.

Finally, we should respond with *obedience*. We can take what God has given us and use it for His glory. Instead of searching for something you can't have, invest what you do have to serve Him.

♦　　♦　　♦

When you contemplate the miracle of birth, praise God. As you respond in reverence, confidence and obedience, determine to be a good steward with the personal resources and talents He gave you. Good stewardship honors God.

THE MARVEL OF LIFE

The greatest evidence of God's power is human birth. When a baby is born, there is promise, potential and excitement. David considered babies to be miracles from the hand of God. Eugene Peterson has said, "In the presence of birth we don't calculate, we marvel." As we ponder these truths, what should be our response?

W*e worship God.* The word *fearfully* means "I am shuddering with astonishment; I am trembling with awe" (v. 14). I fear that today people have taken sex, conception, birth and babies and turned the process into something functional instead of miraculous. Some people think of sex as animal excitement, but David thought of spiritual enrichment. No wonder we are aborting babies today; we don't see anything holy about sex, conception and birth.

W*e show confidence in God.* What we are is God's gift to us. What we do with our lives is our gift to Him. He accepts us as we are. He's not going to judge us on the basis of what He has given someone else, but on the basis of what we have done with what He has given us. Never be discouraged by what you don't have. Having confidence in God about your life brings eager expectation.

W*e obey God.* The more we glorify God, the more we enjoy Him. We can take the miracle of life He gave us and wreck it, or we can present our bodies to the Lord as a living sacrifice.

◆　　◆　　◆

To leave God out of your life is simply to exist, not really to live. Jesus died that you might be saved from your sins and one day go to heaven. But while you're here on earth, God wants you to fulfill all that He has built into you. Are you responding to His power for your life? Worship Him, place your confidence in Him and obey Him.

INTERRUPTING
A MIRACLE

Since the 1973 Supreme Court decision *Roe v. Wade*, more than 21 million babies have been killed. These verses are an amazing statement about conception, growth and birth. When a baby is aborted, what really happens?

First, *a miracle is interrupted* (v. 14). *Fearfully* means "I am trembling with astonishment." By thinking about birth, David also was contemplating God's attributes. The world has cheapened sex, conception and birth to the point that it treats pregnancy as a nuisance, not a miracle. God made us and has covered (protected) us. The baby in the womb is covered by God. Let's not turn the womb into a tomb!

Second, *a real person is murdered.* Today, medical science calls the fetus a P.O.C. (a product of conception)—a mass of tissues or a collection of cells. But God calls it a human being, and we had better be careful how we treat the child.

Third, *a divine law is broken* (Ex. 20:13). Dr. Gleason Archer, commenting on Exodus 21:22-25, says that if a fight occurred and it resulted in a baby being born dead, then the assailant had to pay with his life. God protected the unborn by His Law. But today it is legal to kill them.

God gives and takes life—not man. An even greater tragedy awaits us in this country. Abortion leads to infanticide, which leads to mercy killing. In some parts of the world, voluntary euthanasia is legal.

God's people need to take a strong stand to protect the miracle of human life.

✦   ✦   ✦

God loves children and wants to protect them. Rejoice in the miracle of birth and protect the sanctity of the womb and the lives of unborn babies. What can you do in your community to take a stand against abortion?

GOD'S THOUGHTS
PART 1

A.W. Tozer used to say, "The only real world is the Bible world." Nothing is more unsure than the world, for it is passing away. But the will and Word of God will abide forever (see Mark 13:31). As we consider the character of God's thoughts, we will want to do His will.

God's thoughts are *personal* (v. 17). They concern you and me. He makes the individual and then plans for him. He knows all about us. Paradoxically, the sovereignty of God is the basis for our freedom. If He were not on the throne, this world would be run by chance. But the psalmist tells us that life is not a gamble. God put your substance together and ordained your genetic structure (vv. 13,14). We must use what He has given us for His glory. And our obedience to His will reaches beyond this life, for our future is wrapped up in God's plan for us (Jer. 29:11).

God's thoughts are *precious* (v. 17). *Precious* means "weighty, valuable." His thoughts toward us are unique, tailor-made, and that makes them valuable. When we accept God's plan for us and exercise believing faith, then He can work out His perfect will in our lives. Remember, His thoughts are deep (Ps. 92:5); they are higher than ours (Isa. 55:8).

◆　　◆　　◆

God's thoughts about you are more than mere "thoughts." They include His purposes and His care. As you meditate on His thoughts, renew your commitment to know and do His will for your life.

GOD'S THOUGHTS
PART 2

Yesterday, we learned that God's thoughts are personal and precious. They are full of His purpose and care. Let's consider three additional characteristics of God's thoughts.

God's thoughts are *practical*. Paul said, "none of these things [tribulations] move me; nor do I count my life dear to myself, so that I may finish my race with joy, and the ministry which I received from the Lord Jesus, to testify to the gospel of the grace of God" (Acts 20:24). Paul was living to do one thing—finish his course. As we run the race of life, following God's thoughts leads to fulfillment, courage and the strength to continue.

God's thoughts are *vast* and *inexhaustible* (v. 17). How great is the "sum of them." The Hebrew word for *sum* is plural. Thus, His thoughts just keep growing. People who don't want to do the will of God live their lives in a little bucket of water. But when we accept His will for our lives, we launch out on an ocean of possibility. God said to Abraham, "You walk before Me and do My will, and I am going to give you horizons like you've never seen before" (see Gen. 15:5). If you want to be a stagnant Christian, reject the will of God. You will not grow, and you will miss what He has for you. He wants to do great things in your life.

God's thoughts are *unfailing* (v. 18). He works out His plans even while we sleep. Adam went to sleep, and God gave him a wife. Abraham went to sleep, and God worked out His covenant to him. God already has revealed things about our daily living to us by His Spirit in the Scriptures.

♦   ♦   ♦

Are you discouraged by events in your life or weary of the day's routine? Think God's thoughts by reading His Word and obey His thoughts by doing His will. He will work in your life. He will open horizons of blessing and help you along your pilgrimage.

A PENETRATING PRAYER

There is no higher occupation than the contemplation and the worship of God. David says, "My God knows everything; I can't fool Him. My God is everywhere; I can't flee from Him. My God can do anything; I can't fight Him. What should I do?" We find his answer in verses 23 and 24. "Search me, O God, and know my heart; try me, and know my anxieties; and see if there is any wicked way in me, and lead me in the way everlasting." That's one of the most penetrating prayers found in the Bible.

If we can't fool God, flee from Him or fight Him, the only thing for us to do is surrender to Him—in awe, reverence and worship. Notice the psalmist's request: "Search me, O God, and know my heart." God knows our hearts. He knows us from top to bottom, inside out. But we don't know our own hearts. Jeremiah said, "The heart is deceitful above all things, and desperately wicked; who can know it?" (Jer. 17:9). Only God can know it. The Hebrew word for *search* used in verse 23 means to dig in a mine and find ore. "Search me, O God; I am like a mine. I am deep, but dig out the potential that is in me. Dig out all the treasure you have put into me, even before I was born." It also means to explore a land. How broad and wide are the horizons of possibility in life. "Search me, O God; bring out of me all that is there for your glory."

Then David says, "Try me, and know my anxieties." *Try* means to test metal in a furnace. That's why we suffer sometimes. "See if there is any wicked way in me, and lead me in the way everlasting" (v. 24).

Here, then, are three penetrating requests: search me, try me and lead me. Are you asking God to lead you in His will today? If you do, He will bring out of the mine of your life treasures that will glorify His name.

♦ ♦ ♦

Can you echo David's prayer? If not, perhaps you need to surrender to God's will or ask Him to forgive some sin in your life. Remember, He knows you intimately. Ask Him for the grace to stand up to His scrutiny.

CONFRONTING EVIL

Many people are bothered by the problem of evil. They say, "If God is a loving and good God, why does He allow evil?" David did not ignore this problem, nor did he give in to it. Instead, he made a decision and took his stand with God. Only our God can permit evil and be able to overrule it to accomplish His purposes. As David confronted the problem of evil in the world, he did so in stages.

Stage one: He evaluated (v. 22). David looked at the wicked, violent, blasphemous, deceitful and rebellious crowd. He showed courage and honesty in taking his stand against them. When we start asking ourselves, *Is it safe?* or, *Is it popular?* we have moved away from biblical ethics and integrity.

Stage two: He grieved (v. 21). God the Father grieves (Gen. 6:6); God the Son grieves (Mark 3:5); and God the Holy Spirit grieves (Eph. 4:30) over sin. We also ought to grieve over sin. When Nehemiah heard that the walls of Jerusalem were destroyed, he sat and wept (Neh. 1:4). Today, we need people who will sit down long enough to weep over sin.

Stage three: He hated (vv. 21,22). We could use a little more holy anger today. Christians sometimes are too bland, too complacent and too comfortable. Edmund Burke said, "All that is required for evil to triumph is for good men to do nothing." Love and hate are not contradictory when dealing with sin. Jesus showed both compassion toward sinners and hatred of sin.

Stage four: He decided (v. 19). David decided to separate himself from evil (Ps. 119:115). We need to stand among sinners as the salt of the earth and the light of the world, but we need to have contact without contamination.

Stage five: He trusted (v. 19). We must leave vengeance with God; He will punish the wicked (Rom. 12:19). Our job is to give ourselves to Him and do the work He wants us to do.

♦　　♦　　♦

If you fail to make a decision, the world will make it for you. Take your stand with God and use David's experience as a guide for confronting the problem of evil. Determine to live a holy life that honors the Lord.

NOTHING TO HIDE

The most important knowledge in the world is the knowledge of God. The second most important is the knowledge of yourself. To know God, we must know Jesus Christ as our Savior (John 17:3). In his prayer, David makes two basic requests that should also be our prayer.

Our prayer should be that *we want God to know us*. This doesn't mean we want God to get information about us; it means that we have nothing to hide from Him. We hide from God with our words. When we lie to other people, we're lying to ourselves, and we are lying to God.

God has purposes for us to fulfill. He wants us to explore new territory and expand the horizons of our lives. Let God put you through the furnace (if He needs to) to remove the dross from your life. Let Him prepare you for what He has planned for you.

Our prayer also should be that *we want God to guide us*. We can't flee from God or fight Him, so we might as well follow Him. Jeremiah said, "O Lord, I know the way of man is not in himself; it is not in man who walks to direct his steps" (Jer. 10:23).

When we are willing to obey, God is more than willing to reveal His way to us. He guides us through *His Word* and through *prayer*. Don't be stingy with God, giving Him only a minute or two of your time every day. He also guides us through the *prompting of the Holy Spirit*, through *circumstances* and through His *people*. How glorious it is to have Christian friends with whom you can pray and to have a pastor who prays for you and ministers to you.

♦   ♦   ♦

If you want God to know you and guide you, He will. You'll know yourself better and know Him better. And then He will guide you and lead you in an everlasting way.

OUR
DELIVERER

King David was going through another battle. He needed deliverance from an attacking enemy. "Deliver me, O Lord, from evil men; preserve me from violent men, who plan evil things in their hearts; they continually gather together for war. They sharpen their tongues like a serpent; the poison of asps is under their lips. Keep me, O Lord, from the hands of the wicked; preserve me from violent men" (vv. 1-4). David's enemies had hidden snares to trap him.

What do you do when you face this situation—when evil, violent, lying people are busy setting traps for you? Remember that *God hears you.* "I said to the Lord: 'You are my God; hear the voice of my supplications, O Lord'" (v. 6). *God also strengthens you.* "O God the Lord, the strength of my salvation, You have covered my head in the day of battle" (v. 7). If you have to do battle against the Enemy today, let God outfit you in the armor you need. Finally, *God vindicates you.* David prayed that God would vindicate him and that his enemies' own sins would destroy them.

David concluded by giving thanks to the Lord. "I know that the Lord will maintain the cause of the afflicted, and justice for the poor. Surely the righteous shall give thanks to Your name; the upright shall dwell in Your presence" (vv. 12,13). The battle over, he said, "One day I am going to dwell in Your presence, where there will be no more lying, slandering, battling, fighting or sinning." We will enjoy the peace of God forever.

♦   ♦   ♦

If you are a believer, God has already delivered you from the penalty of sin. Today He works to deliver you from sin's effects. Perhaps enemies are slandering your reputation. Call upon the Lord for help. He will hear you, strengthen you and vindicate you. Let Him give you the victory today.

MIXED PRAYERS

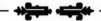

One of the greatest privileges we have as children of God is prayer, yet so often we take it for granted. As the gospel song goes, "O what peace we often forfeit, O what needless pain we bear, all because we do not carry everything to God in prayer!"

In Psalm 141 David pictures prayer in a beautiful way that will help us appreciate it more. "Lord, I cry out to You; make haste to me! Give ear to my voice when I cry out to You. Let my prayer be set before You as incense, the lifting up of my hands as the evening sacrifice" (vv. 1,2). The Jewish priest would go to the altar of incense in the holy place and offer a special incense that no one was allowed to duplicate. As the smoke of the incense rose from the altar, it was as though prayer were going up to God. David was not in the temple; he was a king, not a priest. He may well have been out somewhere in the battlefield when he wrote this. But he says, "I am going to lift up my hands to you as the evening sacrifice. My prayer is going to come to you as incense."

The incense at the altar was mixed together carefully; it was well prepared. Likewise, let's mix our prayers carefully. Our prayers should contain adoration and confession to the Lord, petition, thanksgiving and submission to Him. Let's allow the Holy Spirit to ignite the altar of our souls. Do not pray from a cold heart. David goes on to say, "Set a guard, O Lord, over my mouth; keep watch over the door of my lips. Do not incline my heart to any evil thing" (vv. 3,4). After we pray to the Lord, let's make sure that our lips and hearts do not sin.

✦　　✦　　✦

Are your prayers a good mix rather than a series of petitions? When you pray from the heart, you can't help but praise God and thank Him for His grace and generosity. Make your prayers like fragrant incense that brings joy to the heart of God.

LOOK
AHEAD

I do not like caves. When I visited Mammoth Cave in Kentucky, I could hardly wait to get out. Thus, I somewhat understand David's distress as he wrote this psalm while hiding from Saul in a cave. In his distress, he looked in four directions.

First, *David looked within.* "I cry out to the Lord with my voice; with my voice to the Lord I make my supplication. I pour out my complaint before Him; I declare before Him my trouble. When my spirit was overwhelmed within me, then you knew my path" (vv. 1-3). He looked within and said, "Look, I'm in trouble; I'm complaining; I'm overwhelmed." Introspection sometimes can be good for you, but don't spend too much time looking within, or you will get discouraged.

Then *David looked around,* hoping to find help. "Look on my right hand and see, for there is no one who acknowledges me; refuge has failed me; no one cares for my soul" (v. 4). Do you ever feel like that? Do you look around and say, "Nobody even cares—everyone is bearing his own burdens, and nobody wants to share mine"? Perhaps in those situations you should take time to bear other people's burdens—then they might be interested in your concerns.

After looking within and around and finding only discouragement, *David looked up.* "I cried out to You, O Lord: I said, 'You are my refuge, my portion in the land of the living'" (v. 5). In other words, "God, you're going to hear my cry. You're going to deliver me from my persecutors; they are stronger than I am."

Finally, *David looked ahead.* "Bring my soul out of prison, that I may praise Your name; the righteous shall surround me, for You shall deal bountifully with me" (v. 7). After you have seen the glory and the blessing of the Lord, you can look ahead with confidence.

♦   ♦   ♦

Perhaps you are in a cave of discouragement today. Your hope lies not within yourself or with your circumstances. Look to the Lord and obey His Word. Then look ahead with confidence, for God's promises are sure and His Word is true.

WILLING TO LEAD

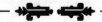

How should we pray when we are going through trouble? We find several requests in David's prayer, and if we follow his example, God will lead us through our difficulties into blessing.

First, he says, "Hear my prayer" (v. 1) and "answer me speedily, O Lord; my spirit fails!" (v. 7). We don't have to shout to God; we don't have to argue with Him. We simply can come to Him and say, "Lord, hear me." When a child comes to his father or mother, the parent has his ears open. "The eyes of the Lord are on the righteous, and His ears are open to their cry" (Ps. 34:15). Have you prayed to God about what worries you today?

David's second request is, "Cause me to hear Your lovingkindness in the morning, for in You do I trust" (v. 8). In other words, "Speak to me, Lord." Each morning David meditated on the Word of God, and God guided him. Have you taken time to read the Bible and let its Author speak to you? He'll show you the way you ought to go.

David's next request is, "Deliver me, O Lord, from my enemies" (v. 9). God can do that if we are walking in the way He wants us to walk. In verse 10 David asks for instruction and guidance. "Teach me to do Your will, for you are my God; Your Spirit is good. Lead me in the land of uprightness." Oh, how willing He is to do this!

Finally, David says, "Revive me, O Lord, for Your name's sake!" (v. 11). Why do we want God to bring us out of times of difficulty? Sure, we want relief, but we also should want Him to be glorified. We want Him to deliver us for His name's sake, that He might receive all the glory.

◆ ◆ ◆

Your spirit can begin to fail when you go through extended trials. Ask the Lord for help, and He will lead you through difficult times. Always stay open to the guidance and instruction of God's Word. God will speak to you through Scripture as He leads you through your trial. Keep trusting Him, and He will accomplish what is best for you and what glorifies Him.

JEHOVAH'S COVENANT

Why should Almighty God pay attention to us? Who are we that we should receive His mercy? David asks these questions in verse 3. "Lord, what is man, that You take knowledge of him? Or the son of man, that You are mindful of him?"

What are we that God should pay any attention to us? Are we smart? I don't think so. Are we strong? Some animals are much stronger than we are. Are we righteous? No, we have sinned against God. Are we faithful? Too often we disobey Him. From the human point of view, there is no reason why God should pay any attention to us. "Man is like a breath; his days are like a passing shadow" (v. 4). Compared to eternity, our lives are just a puff of smoke. They appear, and then they are gone.

Why should God pay any attention to us? Because God, in all of His mercy and grace, loves us. The word David uses for God in this psalm means Jehovah God, the God of the gracious covenant. He has made promises to us, and we can trust Him. David describes Him as "my lovingkindness and my fortress, my high tower and my deliverer, my shield and the One in whom I take refuge" (v. 2).

This is a mystery too deep for us to explain, but it's not too deep for us to experience. We may not understand why God should pay any attention to us, but we know that His Son came to be a servant for us. He died on the cross, a sacrifice for us, and now He lives in heaven, interceding for us.

◆ ◆ ◆

God pays attention to you because He loves you and wants to be glorified through your life. Walk with Him and glorify Him with your life.

THE JOYS OF GOD'S PEOPLE

"**H**appy are the people whose God is the Lord!" (v. 15). That's the way David concludes Psalm 144. In the first half of this psalm, he cries out to God for help. In the last half, he sings praises to the Lord because of the help He gave him.

"**I** will sing a new song to You, O God; on a harp of ten strings I will sing praises to You, the One who gives salvation to kings, who delivers David His servant from the deadly sword" (vv. 9,10). This shows David's *personal joy* in the Lord. We can picture him laying down his sword, picking up his harp and composing a new song to praise and glorify God. We ought to have personal joy in our hearts also. We have many reasons for praising God, but too often we remember only the sorrows of life and forget the blessings.

Then there is *national joy*—"the One who gives salvation to kings" (v. 10). David was the king, and when God delivered him, it was for the good of the nation. How we need national righteousness and national repentance to have national joy!

Finally, there is *family joy*. David talks in verse 12 about his sons being like plants and his daughters like cornerstones that are polished for a palace. What a joy it is in the home to praise the Lord and see family members growing in Him.

✦　　✦　　✦

God's people ought to be joyful—expressing personal, national and family joy. Our joy is founded on what God does and who He is. Rejoice in the Lord today for all of His goodness, grace and mercy toward you in Christ Jesus.

GREATLY TO BE PRAISED

This psalm has special meaning for me. Several years ago a drunken driver hit me going 80 or 90 miles an hour. When I woke up in the intensive care ward of a hospital with broken bones and lacerations, this is the verse that went through my mind: "Great is the Lord, and greatly to be praised; and His greatness is unsearchable" (v. 3).

Let's praise God for His *greatness*. The psalmist says His greatness is eternal. "I will extol You, my God, O King; and I will bless Your name forever and ever. Every day I will bless You, and I will praise Your name forever and ever" (vv. 1,2). We will spend all eternity praising the greatness of God. His greatness also is unsearchable. We can't begin to measure it. We can't know its depth, its height or its breadth. And the greatness of God is memorable. "One generation shall praise Your works to another, . . . I will meditate on the glorious splendor of Your majesty" (vv. 4,5). We must tell the next generation of the greatness of God.

Then the psalmist praises the *goodness* of God. Verse 7 says, "They shall utter the memory of Your great goodness, and shall sing of Your righteousness. . . . The Lord is good to all, and His tender mercies are over all His works" (vv. 7,9). Verse 8 expounds the *grace* of the Lord: "The Lord is gracious and full of compassion." Aren't you grateful that He is slow to anger?

All of this leads to the *glory* of the Lord. "They shall speak of the glory of Your kingdom, and talk of Your power" (v. 11).

♦ ♦ ♦

As finite beings, we can scarcely comprehend God's attributes. But we can certainly praise Him for who He is and what He has done in our lives. Thank God for saving you. Praise Him for His greatness, His goodness, His grace and His glory.

GOD IS NEAR

"**T**he Lord is near to all who call upon Him, to all who call upon Him in truth" (v. 18). Isn't that a great promise? It's one you can put to work today. Let's look at it more closely.

First, *God is near to those who are stumbling*. "The Lord upholds all who fall, and raises up all those who are bowed down" (v. 14). You may have stumbled and fallen. Perhaps you just didn't do what you should have. Maybe you stumbled in your job, and you are embarrassed and worried about it. Perhaps you have stumbled into sin.

Second, *God is near to those who carry burdens*. Those who are bowed down with the weight of care can find rest if they will call upon Him.

Third, *God is near to those who are hungry*. "The eyes of all look expectantly to You, and You give them their food in due season" (v. 15). Verse 16 shows how simple it is for God to answer prayer: "You open Your hand and satisfy the desire of every living thing." All God has to do is open His hand to meet our needs today. The problem is, we often don't open our hearts and cry out to Him.

Fourth, *God is near to those who call upon Him*. We have this great promise: He will fulfill the desire of those who fear Him; He also will hear their cry and will save them" (v. 19).

Finally, *God is near to those who love Him*. "The Lord preserves all who love Him, but all the wicked He will destroy" (v. 20). Follow the advice of James: "Draw near to God and He will draw near to you" (James 4:8).

✦   ✦   ✦

God is not far from you. He's waiting for you to take that first step, to cry out to Him and say, "Lord, I want to draw close to You. Here I am." Have you stumbled? Are you carrying a burden, or are you needy? He promises to be near to all those who call upon Him.

THE GOD OF JACOB

✦✦✦

"**H**appy is he who has the God of Jacob for his help, whose hope is in the Lord his God" (v. 5). This tells us that God is all we need for today—and for tomorrow. When you know God, you have happiness, help and hope: happiness in walking with Him, help for the burdens of the day and hope for the concerns of the future. What more could you want?

Who is the God of Jacob? First, *He is the creator*. Verse 6 says He is the One "who made heaven and earth, the sea, and all that is in them; who keeps truth forever." Any God great enough, wise enough and strong enough to create and sustain and run this universe can take care of our problems today.

Second, *He is the Judge* "who executes justice for the oppressed" (v. 7). God knows when you have been wrongly criticized. He knows when others have tried to make life difficult for you. Leave the judgment with Him. Don't waste your time and energy trying to fight battles that only God can fight for you. He's with all of His people, and He does what is right.

Third, *He is the Father*. Verse 7 offers a picture of the Father feeding the hungry. God's Word always assures us of His provision. "My God shall supply all your need according to His riches in glory by Christ Jesus" (Phil. 4:19).

Fourth, *He is the Redeemer*. "The Lord gives freedom to the prisoners. The Lord opens the eyes of the blind; . . . The Lord loves the righteous" (vv. 7,8).

Finally, *He is the King*. "The Lord shall reign forever" (v. 10). Sometimes you may feel like saying, "I don't deserve to have a God like this." That's true, but He's the God of Jacob. Jacob stumbled and made mistakes, but God remained his God. The eternal God is our Refuge.

◆　　◆　　◆

God is your greatest Refuge. But He doesn't simply shelter you; He provides for you and strengthens you. Is the God of Jacob your God? If so, call upon Him, and He will be your help, hope and happiness.

THE GOD OF YOUR HEART

The God of the galaxies is also the God of the brokenhearted. That's what David tells us in verses 3 and 4: "He heals the brokenhearted and binds up their wounds. He counts the number of the stars; He calls them all by name."

The contrast we see in these two verses—between the heavens and the broken heart—ought to encourage us. God made the heavens. He spoke and it was done. His creation stood steadfast. The God who made the heavens is concerned about your broken heart. Others may not be concerned, but God is. He's not so far away that He doesn't know your heart is hurting. He's not so great that He can't stoop down to you when you are pained, weeping and looking for help.

Yes, the God of the heavens is the God of your heart. The God who numbers and names the stars knows your needs. He knows all about you, and thus He is able to meet your every need. The God who controls the planets in their orbits is able to take the pieces of your broken heart and put them together again. He will heal your broken heart, provided you give Him all the pieces and yield to His tender love.

"Great is our Lord, and mighty in power; His understanding is infinite" (v. 5). His love and understanding are limitless. His power is great. He can do what needs to be done.

✦   ✦   ✦

The One who set the galaxies in motion is the same One who addresses your needs. There is no limit to God's love, His understanding or His power. Perhaps you have a broken heart today. Give Him the pieces and let Him heal your heart.

PRECIOUS TREASURE

I wonder if the Old Testament people of Israel realized how privileged they were. This is what the psalmist addresses in today's passage. He's telling the Jewish people to praise the Lord because of all He had done for them. "For He has strengthened the bars of your gates; He has blessed your children within you" (v. 13). He gave peace in their borders. He fed them. He gave them His Word and His Law. He gave them land. "He has not dealt thus with any nation; and as for His judgments, they have not known them" (v. 20). God deposited with Israel the precious treasure of His Word.

Notice what the psalmist says about the Word of God. Verse 15 tells us that *God's Word runs*: "He sends out His command to the earth; His word runs very swiftly." When God speaks, that Word goes out like a rapidly running messenger and accomplishes His purposes. God runs the universe by His Word. He decrees things, and they happen.

God's Word also melts obstacles. "He sends out His word and melts them" (v. 18). God's Word can melt the cold, hard heart. Are you facing an impossible situation? The Word of God can melt any bars or walls and open the way for you.

Finally, *God's Word blesses*. "He declares His word to Jacob, His statutes and His judgments to Israel. . . . Praise the Lord!" (vv. 19,20). Read the Word of God. It's a great treasure that, when invested in your life, bears fruit.

◆　◆　◆

God's Word runs and accomplishes His will. It melts and opens the way. And it blesses all who will receive it, obey it and trust it. God desires that you spend time daily appropriating the riches of His Word. Do you invest God's Word in your life?

RUN BY
DECREE

When I was a young pastor in my first church, we had to build a new sanctuary. My friends know that I don't know the first thing about construction. I can't read blueprints. I can't even make a birdhouse. But we began the project. Construction went slowly, and it was difficult. Then winter came.

I recall standing by that piece of property, looking at those snow-covered arches and wondering, "Lord, why is it taking so long?" Then the Lord led me to Psalm 148 and showed me that when we complain about the weather, we should remember that He is in control. He gave me a great word of assurance from verse 8: "Fire and hail, snow and clouds; stormy wind, fulfilling His word."

All of Psalm 148 tells us that the Word of God is in control. When He speaks in heaven, things happen on earth. In verses 1-6 the heavens praise the Lord. In verses 7-10 the earth praises the Lord. And in verses 11-14, all people, young and old, praise the Lord, including kings, princes, judges and ordinary people. Why? Because His Word is creative. Verse 5 tells us He commanded, and they were created. He also has "established them forever" (v. 6).

God does not run this world by consensus but by decree. His Word is sufficient to guide our lives.

✦   ✦   ✦

God's Word creates, establishes and fulfills His will. The next time you find yourself in a storm, don't complain; instead, surrender. Remember, the stormy wind as well as the calm wind fulfills the Word of God. Submit to God's control and to His creative Word in your life.

SINGING IN STRANGE PLACES

"**P**raise the Lord! Sing to the Lord a new song" (v. 1). We have a tendency to want to sing the same songs in church, and there's nothing wrong with that. The psalmist isn't telling us to buy a new hymnbook. He means we should have a new experience with the Lord so that we will have a new song of praise to give to Him.

Every new valley that we go through, every new mountaintop we climb, every experience of life ought to be writing on our hearts a new song of praise. When we face a difficulty, we have an opportunity to have renewed faith and see God do new things.

In verse 1 the psalmist tells us to sing in the congregation. I can understand that command. I enjoy congregational singing when people sing to the Lord. "Let Israel rejoice in their Maker; let the children of Zion be joyful in their King" (v. 2). I am glad when God's people gather in a congregation of celebration, rejoicing in the goodness and the glory of the Lord.

But he also tells us we should be joyful on our beds. "Let them sing aloud on their beds" (v. 5). This could be while we're resting or recuperating from an illness. Perhaps you're lying in bed right now, and you don't feel well. Sing praises to the Lord upon your bed and worship Him. Then the psalmist says, "Let the high praises of God be in their mouth, and a two-edged sword in their hand, to execute vengeance on the nations" (vv. 6,7). This is a picture of warriors on the battlefield, singing in the midst of the battle.

It is easy to sing in the congregation, not quite so easy to sing on our beds and difficult to sing on the battlefield. But if we sing, we'll glorify the Lord, and we'll grow. "He will beautify the humble with salvation" (v. 4). We'll be happier and holier and more beautiful if we sing to the Lord.

◆   ◆   ◆

God brings you through different experiences so you may learn new dimensions of His love and grace. What difficulty are you facing today? Don't simply endure or waste it. Use it as an opportunity to find a new song of praise to God.

AN ORCHESTRA
OF PRAISE

The hymnbook of the Bible is the Book of Psalms, and the last psalm summarizes what God wants us to know about praise and worship. The Christian faith is a singing and praising faith. No other religion has praise and singing such as we have, because we have the song of the Lord in our hearts. The psalmist answers some important questions about praise in this psalm.

Who *is it that we praise?* "Praise the Lord" (v. 1)—not the church, not the preacher, but the Lord. Our problem is that we often don't see the Lord. We look at gifts or lack of gifts from God. We say, "Why didn't the Lord do this, or why wasn't it done differently?" We don't really see Him. Let's get beyond the gift to the Giver. Let's get beyond the blessing to the Blesser. Let's praise the Lord. "Rejoice in the Lord," Paul said. "Again I will say, rejoice!" (Phil. 4:4).

Where *do we praise Him?* "Praise God in His sanctuary; praise Him in His mighty firmament" (v. 1). What an interesting combination. When we praise God in church, it's just like the praise of the angels in heaven. In the sanctuary or wherever we are, let's praise Him.

Why *do we praise Him?* "Praise Him for His mighty acts; praise Him according to His excellent greatness!" (v. 2). We praise Him for what He is and for what He does.

How *do we praise Him?* With the sound of the trumpet, with the psaltery, the harp, the timbrel, the dance, the stringed instruments, the flute and the loud cymbals. The psalmist is saying, "Get the whole orchestra together. Find every instrument you can, and let's praise the Lord." Some people don't like that kind of praise, but we are commanded here to praise Him and to make a loud song to His glory.

◆   ◆   ◆

All of nature is praising God today, but His people are prone to forget to praise Him. Ask yourself these praise questions of Psalm 150 and then meditate on the psalmist's answers. You have much for which to give praise. Bring joy to God's heart by praising Him.

NOTES

NOTES